LK
KD

The Charles Dickens Library

A Tale of Two Cities

Great Expectations

Master Humphrey's Clock

The Charles Dickens Library

A TALE OF TWO CITIES

GREAT EXPECTATIONS

MASTER HUMPHREY'S CLOCK

Complete and Unabridged

GRAMERCY BOOKS
New York • Avenel

Copyright © 1996 by Random House Value Publishing, Inc.
All rights reserved.

This edition is published by Gramercy Books,
distributed by Random House Value Publishing, Inc.,
40 Engelhard Avenue, Avenel, New Jersey 07001.

Random House
New York • Toronto • London • Sydney • Auckland

Printed and bound in the United States of America

A CIP catalog record for this book is available from the Library of Congress.

The Charles Dickens Library: A Tale of Two Cities / Great Expectations /
Master Humphrey's Clock / by Charles Dickens: ISBN 0-517-14967-2

8 7 6 5 4 3 2 1

CONTENTS

FOREWORD

IF, AS SOME SUGGEST, OURS IS THE CENTURY OF FILM, THEN
the nineteenth century was, arguably, the century of the novel. Across the
continents, throughout Europe and the Americas, novelists were propelling
the art forward. In France, Flaubert, Dumas, Hugo, and Zola labored; in
Russia, Turgenev, Dostoevski, and Tolstoy were hard at work. In the United
States, Hawthorne, Melville, Stephen Crane, and Henry James were changing the shape of American literature; while in England, writers like Walter
Scott, Thackeray, and the Brontës pursued to perfection their literary craft.

Yet, there remains one writer who perhaps best reflects this extraordinary
period in the history of the novel. For the life and work of Charles Dickens
come close to defining not only the century in which they flourished, but
defining, also, that century's vision of what a novel was and of what a novelist could do.

Considered by many to be the master of English fiction, Charles Dickens himself may be the quintessential Dickensian character. Much like his

remarkable novels (where the panoply of life in Victorian England is unfurled with consummate wit, grace, and skill), Dickens himself was a large, sprawling, complex, and contradictory creation, bursting with vigor. Both a critic and a prophet where social issues were concerned, Dickens, nonetheless, dressed his message in some of the world's most entertaining and delightful prose. One of the most popular and, along with Shakespeare and Dr. Johnson, most quoted of English authors, Dickens endures as perhaps the most purely pleasurable of the great writers. Reading Dickens is, nearly always, an unequivocal joy.

Charles Dickens was born on February 7, 1812, in Portsea, England, the second of seven children. His father, John, the son of domestic servants, had worked his way up the social ladder to the post of clerk in the Naval Pay Office; but his improvident ways left his family in a state of uncertain—and chronic—near-poverty. His mother, the former Elizabeth Barrow, was of a more genteel background. Intelligent and well-educated, as well as possessing a delicious sense of the comic and the absurd, it was she who taught young Charles the rudiments of English and Latin. But, as with most children of the lower economic classes, Dickens's formal education was left largely to chance. Work, of course, came first. When a relative offered to employ Charles at his shoe-blacking business, the twelve-year-old found himself laboring long hours in a London factory with little hope of returning to school.

Soon afterwards, early in 1824, John Dickens was arrested for debt and jailed in the Marshalsea Prison. While Mrs. Dickens and her younger children went to live near John in his confinement, Charles, in order to continue earning money to help the family, took lodgings in London. Alone and frightened, condemned to a life of drudgery and despair, the boy was forced to function as an adult. "I have been," Dickens would say sadly, many years later, "abroad in the world from a mere child."

Yet Dickens, "a lively boy of a good, genial, open disposition," was also extremely lucky. After a period of several months, a sudden, if small, inheritance freed John Dickens from prison, liberating his son from the hated factory as well. By March of 1825, Charles was back in school at Wellington House Academy.

At fifteen Dickens went to work as an office boy for an attorney. Ambitious, talented, and undeniably driven, he taught himself shorthand; soon afterwards, he became a freelance reporter, at which he quickly made a name for himself. Dickens then made the transition from reporter to writer swiftly and with apparent ease. His first professional writings were published pseudonymously as *Sketches by Boz,* which appeared in the *Monthly Magazine* of December 1833. Other sketches soon appeared in a variety of magazines, including the *Morning Chronicle, Evening Chronicle,* and *Bell's Life in London.* A mix of descriptive journalism pieces, Dickens's early work reflects beautifully—and with the comic flair and wit of the Dickens yet-to-come— the manners, mores, and social conditions of their time.

Of Dickens as a young man, his friend and biographer John Forster wrote:

A look of youthfulness first attracted you, and then a candour and openness of expression which made you sure of the qualities within. . . . There
was that in the face as I first recollect it which no time could change, and
which remained implanted on it unalterably to the last. This was the
quickness, keenness, and practical power, the eager, restless, energetic
outlook on each feature, and so much a man of action and business in
the world. . . . "What a face is his to meet in a drawing room!" wrote
Leigh Hunt to me the morning after I made them known to each other.
"It has the life and soul in it of fifty human beings."

Indeed, Charles Dickens was a man of astounding energy and activity.
With the publication of the *Pickwick Papers,* written when its author was
only twenty-four, Dickens found overnight celebrity and success. He would
labor, with demonic intensity, to maintain this lofty position for the rest of
his life.

While writing (between 1836 and 1870) fourteen major novels, all of
which were published serially—some simultaneously—Charles Dickens
fathered ten children (he had married Catherine Hogarth in 1836), wrote and
edited his own magazine, wrote, acted, and produced amateur theatricals,
and embarked on long reading tours throughout America and the Continent.
Penning voluminous letters to newspapers and articles for magazines, Dickens matched his novelist's goal of describing human suffering with a clear-
eyed social activist's determination to effect social change. And, despite a
frenetic social schedule, he wrote copious personal letters, which when published ran to three volumes—more than twenty-five hundred pages, and over
one million words. Driving himself ever harder, Charles Dickens was to die,
on June 9, 1870, midway through his fifteenth novel (the unfinished *Mystery
of Edwin Drood*), of a brain aneurysm. He was mourned, universally, as the
most popular literary figure of his day.

In this collection of three of Dickens's most fascinating and moving
works can be found much of what makes their author so memorable today:
his gloriously vivid characters; the visualization of the vanished London in
which those characters moved; his penetrating analyses of the social conditions and climate of Victorian England; the twists and turns of his complicated plots; his sometimes dark but always delightful humor; and, above all,
his richly textured vision of the world in which he lived. Good and evil, light
and dark, false and true, honor and shamelessness—all of these are abundantly found in Dickens's world and the people who inhabit it. And, if Good
is not always triumphant, in reading Dickens one often is struck, amidst the
most appalling circumstances and horrors, by the strength of his women, by
the tenderness of his men.

Master Humphrey's Clock, first published in 1840 as a threepenny weekly,
was an ingenious device developed by Dickens: a periodical that would both

reintroduce some of his best-loved characters and acquaint his readers with a variety of newer ones. This work introduced the poignant figure of Master Humphrey, "a miss-shapen, deformed old man," who gathers a choice circle of friends around him to form a highly unusual reading club. Each club member is required to place a manuscript in the case of Master Humphrey's beloved old grandfather clock. The tales told in those manuscripts—"a pile of dusty old papers"—contain some of Dickens's most enduring creations. A dizzying wealth of characters and tales abound: the wonderful Wellers—Sam, the embodiment of Cockney wit and charm, his tiny son, Tony, and his father, "old Tony," "a rayther stout gen'l'm'n of eight-and-fifty" with a propensity for contracting and regretting marriage; Gog and Magog, two huge and frightful statues that adorn London's ancient Guildhall; and the renowned Samuel Pickwick himself, who relates the ironic tale of John Podgers's feckless perse-cution of the local "witch." This series, which ran in weekly parts from April 4, 1840, to November 27 of the following year, astonished even its author. For three weeks into the series, the first chapter of what was to become *The Old Curiosity Shop* was "found" in the case of Master Humphrey's clock. What was to have been a series of stories, of humorous essays and comments on con-temporary issues, satiric views on government administration, and tales of the Old London that Dickens loved to tell soon mushroomed into a full-blown novel, serialized within the context of *Master Humphrey's Clock*. At the con-clusion of this first, unexpected novel, *Barnaby Rudge* soon surfaced, again overwhelming the purpose of Master Humphrey's club. At the conclusion of this serialized novel, *Master Humphrey's Clock* was forever stopped. Included in this book are the stories of the Master Humphrey series, minus the two novels that today stand independently.

As the years passed, Dickens sharpened his talents even further. Moving far beyond his earlier vision of the comedy of life, where social injustice exists but can be conquered by goodwill and sound common sense, his later work presented a darker, more complex view of the sins of the age. And if he still found humor in the blackest of situations, he no longer promised solutions born of the innate goodness of humanity.

In 1859 he published his twelfth novel, *A Tale of Two Cities,* a romantic and stirring story of the French Revolution, yet one superbly calculated to caution Britain as to the danger social conditions might yet bring to English shores. This book—which may contain both the most famous beginning and ending of any novel ever written—was developed during a time of great political and social turmoil. Abroad, revolutions deposed the rulers of Parma, Modena, Romagna, and Tuscany; there were insurrections in the Papal States; in France, a serious attempt had been made to assassinate Napoleon III. In the United States, men and women were debating the structure and very existence of the Union. In Britain, the Industrial Revolution had dis-placed hundreds of thousands of workers and forever altered the social fabric of that nation; throughout the country there was a rising tide of anger, frustration, and grief. "Take my knowledge for what it may be worth a dozen years hence," Dickens prophesied. "The people will not bear for any length of time what they bear now."

The fates, therefore, of Dr. Manette and his daughter, Lucie, of her husband, Charles Darnay—and of Sydney Carton, the Englishman whose stunning sacrifice makes their future possible—reflect, against the backdrop of the terrible excesses of the French Revolution, both the inevitable retribution of the common people for past evils and the futility of vengeance. Ultimately, this magnificent novel reminds us that the people must look not to terror but to the healing force of human love.

Dickens's thirteenth, and, many critics believe, his finest novel, *Great Expectations*, was published in serial form in 1860, first appearing in book form in 1861. The story of Philip (Pip) Pirrip, it traces the boy's growth from a youth of selfish and shallow worldly goals to a man of substance and compassion. "I have conceived," Dickens wrote at the time, "a very fine, new, and grotesque idea" for a novel, "the whole of a serial revolving on it, in a most singular and comic manner." Indeed, in much of this work, despite the tragic unfolding of its often sinister plot, Dickens's humor gleams wickedly. It is as though the famous author were making sport of his young hero's pretensions. The folly of sham gentility, the hopelessness of making over another's character, the corruption of easy wealth and social status—Pip's sad trajectory from poor boy to young man of "great expectations" to a debt-ridden protégé of an unexpected benefactor illuminates these delusions beautifully.

It is possible, however, that Dickens is more nearly satirizing himself, and who he was in his own miserable and wonderful past. Surely, there are many similarities between Pip and the young Charles Dickens. Perhaps Pip's fall and eventual rise, through sheer hard work, to self- and worldly respect, may best express how Dickens viewed the achievement of his own "great expectations." Certainly, the legendary novelist worked—literally—until his dying day "like the dickens," as if all he had achieved might still be taken away.

One of the most celebrated artists of his time—an international success before the concept of globalization had been dreamt of—he continually fought back feelings of failure. A man of tremendous humor and vitality, he was haunted, also, by the ghosts of an impoverished and socially unstable youth. Yet, blessed with the true novelist's depth of feeling and imagination, Dickens knew, quite simply, how to make a story soar.

Indeed, throughout his career, Charles Dickens displayed his prodigious talents as a storyteller, amply proving, as the formidable critic G. K. Chesterton once said, that "whatever 'great' means, Dickens was it."

KATHRYN KNOX SOMAN

New York City
1996

A TALE OF TWO CITIES

RECALLED
TO LIFE

One

THE PERIOD

IT WAS THE BEST OF TIMES, IT WAS THE WORST OF TIMES, IT was the age of wisdom, it was the age of foolishness, it was the epoch of belief, it was the epoch of incredulity, it was the season of Light, it was the season of Darkness, it was the spring of hope, it was the winter of despair, we had everything before us, we had nothing before us, we were all going direct to Heaven, we were all going direct the other way—in short, the period was so far like the present period, that some of its noisiest authorities insisted on its being received, for good or for evil, in the superlative degree of comparison only.

There were a king with a large jaw, and a queen with a plain face, on the throne of England; there were a king with a large jaw and a queen with a fair face, on the throne of France. In both countries it was clearer than crystal to the Lords of the State preserves of loaves and fishes, that things in general were settled forever.

It was the year of Our Lord one thousand seven hundred and seventy-five. Spiritual revelations were conceded to England at that favored period, as at this. Mrs. Southcott had recently attained her five-and-twentieth blessed birthday, of whom a prophetic private in the Life Guards had heralded the sublime appearance by announcing that arrangements were made for the swallowing up of London and Westminster. Even the Cock-lane ghost had been laid only a round dozen of years, after rapping out its messages, as the spirits of this very year last past (supernaturally deficient in originality) rapped out theirs. Mere messages in the earthly order of events had lately come to the English Crown and People, from a congress of British subjects in America; which, strange to relate, have proved more important to the human race than any communications yet received through any of the chickens of the Cock-lane brood.

France, less favored on the whole as to matters spiritual than her sister of the shield and trident, rolled with exceeding smoothness downhill, making paper-money and spending it. Under the guidance of her Christian pastors, she entertained herself, besides, with such humane achievements as sentencing a youth to have his hands cut off, his tongue torn out with pincers, and his body burned alive, because he had not kneeled down in the rain to do honor to a dirty procession of monks which passed within his view, at a distance of some fifty or sixty yards. It is likely enough that, rooted in the woods of France and Norway, there were growing trees, when that sufferer was put to death, already marked by the Woodman, Fate, to come down and be sawn into boards, to make a certain movable framework with a sack and a knife in it, terrible in history. It is likely enough that in the rough outhouses of some tillers of the heavy lands adjacent to Paris, there were sheltered from the weather that very day, rude carts, bespattered with rustic mire, snuffed about by pigs, and roosted in by poultry, which the Farmer, Death, had already set apart to be his tumbrils of the Revolution. But, that Woodman and that Farmer, though they work unceasingly, work silently, and no one heard them as they went about with muffled tread: the rather, forasmuch as to entertain any suspicion that they were awake, was to be atheistical and traitorous.

In England, there was scarcely an amount of order and protection to justify much national boasting. Daring burglaries by armed men, and highway robberies, took place in the capital itself every night; families were publicly cautioned not to go out of town without removing their furniture to upholsterers' warehouses for security; the highwayman in the dark was a City tradesman in the light, and, being recognized and challenged by his fellow-tradesman whom he stopped in his character of "the Captain," gallantly shot him through the head and rode away; the mail was waylaid by seven robbers, and the guard shot three dead, and then got shot dead himself by the other four, "in consequence of the failure of his ammunition"; after which the mail was robbed in peace; that magnificent potentate, the Lord Mayor of London, was made to stand and deliver on Turnham Green by one highwayman, who despoiled the illustrious creature in sight of all his retinue; prisoners in London gaols fought battles with their turnkeys, and the majesty of the law fired blunderbusses in among them, loaded with rounds of shot and ball; thieves snipped off diamond crosses from the necks of noble lords at Court drawing-rooms; musketeers went into St. Giles's to search for contraband goods, and the mob fired on the musketeers, and the musketeers fired on the mob, and nobody thought any of these occurrences much out of the common way. In the midst of them, the hangman, ever busy and ever worse than useless, was in constant requisition; now, stringing up long rows of miscellaneous criminals; now, hanging a housebreaker on Saturday who had been taken on Tuesday; now, burning people in the hand at Newgate by the dozen, and now burning pamphlets at the door of Westminster Hall; today, taking the life of an atrocious murderer, and tomorrow of a wretched pilferer who had robbed a farmer's boy of sixpence.

All these things, and a thousand like them, came to pass in and close upon the dear old year one thousand seven hundred and seventy-five. Environed by them, while the Woodman and the Farmer worked unheeded, those two of the large jaws, and those other two of the plain and the fair faces, trod with stir enough, and carried their divine rights with a high hand. Thus did the year one thousand seven hundred and seventy-five conduct their Greatness, and myriads of small creatures—the creatures of this chronicle among the rest—along the roads that lay before them.

T w o

THE MAIL

I T WAS THE DOVER ROAD THAT LAY, ON A FRIDAY NIGHT LATE in November, before the first of the persons with whom this history has business. The Dover road lay, as to him, beyond the Dover mail, as it lumbered up Shooter's Hill. He walked uphill in the mire by the side of the mail, as the rest of the passengers did; not because they had the least relish for walking exercise, under the circumstances, but because the hill, and the harness, and the mud, and the mail, were all so heavy, that the horses had three times already come to a stop, besides once drawing the coach across the road, with the mutinous intent of taking it back to Blackheath. Reins and whip and coachman and guard, however, in combination, had read that article of war which forbade a purpose otherwise strongly in favor of the argument, that some brute animals are endued with reason; and the team had capitulated and returned to their duty.

With drooping heads and tremulous tails, they mashed their way through the thick mud, floundering and stumbling between whiles, as if they were falling to pieces at the larger joints. As often as the driver rested them and brought them to a stand, with a wary "Wo-ho! so-ho then!" the near leader violently shook his head and everything upon it—like an unusually emphatic horse, denying that the coach could be got up the hill. Whenever the leader made this rattle, the passenger started, as a nervous passenger might, and was disturbed in mind.

There was a steaming mist in all the hollows, and it had roamed in its forlornness up the hill, like an evil spirit, seeking rest and finding none. A clammy and intensely cold mist, it made its slow way through the air in ripples that visibly followed and overspread one another, as the waves of an unwholesome sea might do. It was dense enough to shut out everything from the light of the coach-lamps but these its own workings, and a few yards of road; and the reek of the laboring horses steamed into it, as if they had made it all.

Two other passengers, besides the one, were plodding up the hill by the side of the mail. All three were wrapped to the cheekbones and over the ears, and wore jack-boots. Not one of the three could have said, from anything he saw, what either of the other two was like; and each was hidden under almost as many wrappers from the eyes of the mind, as from the eyes of the body, of his two companions. In those days, travelers were very shy of being confidential on a short notice, for anybody on the road might be a robber or in league with robbers. As to the latter, when every posting-house and ale-house could produce somebody in "the Captain's" pay, ranging from the landlord to the lowest stable nondescript, it was the likeliest thing upon the cards. So the guard of the Dover mail thought to himself, that Friday night in November, one thousand seven hundred and seventy-five, lumbering up Shooter's Hill, as he stood on his own particular perch behind the mail, beating his feet, and keeping an eye and a hand on the arm-chest before him, where a loaded blunderbuss lay at the top of six or eight loaded horse-pistols, deposited on a substratum of cutlass.

The Dover mail was in its usual genial position that the guard suspected the passengers, the passengers suspected one another and the guard, they all suspected everybody else, and the coachman was sure of nothing but the horses; as to which cattle he could with a clear conscience have taken his oath on the two Testaments that they were not fit for the journey.

"Wo-ho!" said the coachman. "So then! One more pull and you're at the top and be damned to you, for I have had trouble enough to get you to it!—Joe!"

"Halloa!" the guard replied.

"What o'clock do you make it, Joe?"

"Ten minutes good, past eleven."

"My blood!" ejaculated the vexed coachman, "and not atop of Shooter's yet! Tst! Yah! Get on with you!"

The emphatic horse, cut short by the whip in a most decided negative, made a scramble for it, and the three other horses followed suit. Once more, the Dover mail struggled on, with the jack-boots of its passengers squashing along by its side. They had stopped when the coach stopped, and they kept close company with it. If anyone of the three had had the hardihood to propose to another to walk on a little ahead into the mist and darkness, he would have put himself in a fair way of getting shot instantly as a highwayman.

The last burst carried the mail to the summit of the hill. The horses stopped to breathe again, and the guard got down to skid the wheel for the descent, and open the coach door to let the passengers in.

"Tst! Joe!" cried the coachman in a warning voice, looking down from his box.

"What do you say, Tom?"

They both listened.

"I say a horse at a canter coming up, Joe."

"*I* say a horse at a gallop, Tom," returned the guard, leaving his hold of the door, and mounting nimbly to his place. "Gentlemen! In the king's name, all of you!"

With this hurried adjuration, he cocked his blunderbuss, and stood on the offensive.

The passenger booked by this history was on the coach-step, getting in; the two other passengers were close behind him, and about to follow. He remained on the step, half in the coach and half out of it; they remained in the road below him. They all looked from the coachman to the guard, and from the guard to the coachman, and listened. The coachman looked back and the guard looked back, and even the emphatic leader pricked up his ears and looked back, without contradicting.

The stillness consequent on the cessation of the rumbling and laboring of the coach, added to the stillness of the night, made it very quiet indeed. The panting of the horses communicated a tremulous motion to the coach, as if it were in a state of agitation. The hearts of the passengers beat loud enough perhaps to be heard; but at any rate, the quiet pause was audibly expressive of people out of breath, and holding the breath, and having the pulses quickened by expectation.

The sound of a horse at a gallop came fast and furiously up the hill.

"So-ho!" the guard sang out, as loud as he could roar. "Yo there! Stand! I shall fire!"

The pace was suddenly checked, and, with much splashing and floundering, a man's voice called from the mist, "Is that the Dover mail?"

"Never you mind what it is!" the guard retorted. "What are you?"

"*Is* that the Dover mail?"

"Why do you want to know?"

"I want a passenger, if it is."

"What passenger?"

"Mr. Jarvis Lorry."

Our booked passenger showed in a moment that it was his name. The guard, the coachman, and the two other passengers eyed him distrustfully.

"Keep where you are," the guard called to the voice in the mist, "because, if I should make a mistake, it could never be set right in your lifetime. Gentleman of the name of Lorry answer straight."

"What is the matter?" asked the passenger, then, with mildly quavering speech. "Who wants me? Is it Jerry?"

("I don't like Jerry's voice, if it is Jerry," growled the guard to himself. "He's hoarser than suits me, is Jerry.")

"Yes, Mr. Lorry."

"What is the matter?"

"A dispatch sent after you from over yonder. T. and Co."

"I know this messenger, guard," said Mr. Lorry, getting down into the road—assisted from behind more swiftly than politely by the other two passengers, who immediately scrambled into the coach, shut the door, and pulled up the window.

"He may come close; there's nothing wrong."

"I hope there ain't, but I can't make so 'nation sure of that," said the guard, in gruff soliloquy. "Hallo you!"

"Well! And hallo you!" said Jerry, more hoarsely than before.

"Come on at a footpace; d'ye mind me? And if you've got holsters to that saddle o' yourn, don't let me see your hand go nigh 'em. For I'm a devil at a quick mistake, and when I make one it takes the form of Lead. So now let's look at you."

The figures of a horse and rider came slowly through the eddying mist, and came to the side of the mail, where the passenger stood. The rider stooped, and, casting up his eyes at the guard, handed the passenger a small folded paper. The rider's horse was blown, and both horse and rider were covered with mud, from the hoofs of the horse to the hat of the man.

"Guard!" said the passenger, in a tone of quiet business confidence.

The watchful guard, with his right hand at the stock of his raised blunderbuss, his left at the barrel, and his eye on the horseman, answered curtly, "Sir."

"There is nothing to apprehend. I belong to Tellson's Bank. You must know Tellson's Bank in London. I am going to Paris on business. A crown to drink. I may read this?"

"If so be as you're quick, sir."

He opened it in the light of the coach-lamp on that side, and read—first to himself and then aloud: " 'Wait at Dover for Ma'amselle.' It's not long, you see, guard. Jerry, say that my answer was, RECALLED TO LIFE."

Jerry started in his saddle. "That's a blazing strange answer, too," said he, at his hoarsest.

"Take that message back, and they will know that I received this, as well as if I wrote. Make the best of your way. Good night."

With those words the passenger opened the coach door and got in; not at all assisted by his fellow-passengers, who had expeditiously secreted their watches and purses in their boots, and were now making a general pretense of being asleep, with no more definite purpose than to escape the hazard of originating any other kind of action.

The coach lumbered on again, with heavier wreaths of mist closing round it as it began the descent. The guard soon replaced his blunderbuss in his arm-chest, and having looked to the rest of its contents, and having looked to the supplementary pistols that he wore in his belt, looked to a smaller chest beneath his seat, in which there were a few smith's tools, a couple of torches, and a tinder-box. For he was furnished with that completeness, that if the coach-lamps had been blown and stormed out, which did occasionally happen, he had only to shut himself up inside, keep the flint and steel sparks well off the straw, and get a light with tolerable safety and ease (if he were lucky) in five minutes.

"Tom!" softly over the coach-roof.

"Hallo, Joe."

"Did you hear the message?"

"I did, Joe."

"What did you make of it, Tom?"

"Nothing at all, Joe."

"That's coincidence, too," the guard mused, "for I made the same of it myself."

Jerry, left alone in the mist and darkness, dismounted meanwhile, not only to ease his spent horse, but to wipe the mud from his face, and shake the wet out of his hat-brim, which might be capable of holding about half a gallon. After standing with the bridle over his heavily-splashed arm, until the wheels of the mail were no longer within hearing, and the night was quite still again, he turned to walk down the hill.

"After that there gallop from Temple-bar, old lady, I won't trust your forelegs till I get you on the level," said this hoarse messenger, glancing at his mare. " 'Recalled to life.' That's a blazing strange message. Much of that wouldn't do for you, Jerry! I say, Jerry! You'd be in a blazing bad way if recalling to life was to come into fashion, Jerry!"

Three

THE NIGHT SHADOWS

A WONDERFUL FACT TO REFLECT UPON, THAT EVERY HUMAN creature is constituted to be that profound secret and mystery to every other. A solemn consideration, when I enter a great city by night, that every one of those darkly clustered houses encloses its own secret; that every room in every one of them encloses its own secret; that every beating heart in the hundreds of thousands of breasts there, is, in some of its imaginings, a secret to the heart nearest it! Something of the awfulness, even of Death itself, is referable to this. No more can I turn the leaves of this dear book that I loved, and vainly hope in time to read it all. No more can I look into the depths of this unfathomable water, wherein, as momentary lights glanced into it, I have had glimpses of buried treasure and other things submerged. It was appointed that the book should shut with a spring, forever and forever, when I had read but a page. It was appointed that the water should be locked in an eternal frost, when the light was playing on its surface, and I stood in ignorance on the shore. My friend is dead, my neighbor is dead, my love, the darling of my soul, is dead; it is the inexorable consolidation and perpetuation of the secret that was always in that individuality, and which I shall carry in mine to my life's end. In any of the burial-places of this city through which I pass, is there a sleeper more inscrutable than its busy inhabitants are, in their innermost personality, to me, or than I am to them?

As to this, his natural and not to be alienated inheritance, the messenger on horseback had exactly the same possessions as the King, the first Minister of State, or the richest merchant in London. So with the three passengers shut up in the narrow compass of one lumbering old mail coach; they were mysteries to one another, as complete as if each had been in his own coach and six, or his own coach and sixty, with the breadth of a county between him and the next.

The messenger rode back at an easy trot, stopping pretty often at ale-houses by the way to drink, but evincing a tendency to keep his own counsel, and to keep his hat cocked over his eyes. He had eyes that assorted very well with that decoration, being of a surface black, with no depth in the color or form, and much too near together—as if they were afraid of being found out in something, singly, if they kept too far apart. They had a sinister expression, under an old cocked-hat like a three-cornered spittoon, and over a great muffler for the chin and throat, which descended nearly to the wearer's knees. When he stopped for drink, he moved this muffler with his left hand, only while he poured his liquor in with his right; as soon as that was done, he muffled again.

"No, Jerry, no!" said the messenger, harping on one theme as he rode. "It wouldn't do for you, Jerry. Jerry, you honest tradesman, it wouldn't suit *your* line of business! Recalled—! Bust me, if I don't think he'd been a drinking!"

His message perplexed his mind to that degree that he was fain, several times, to take off his hat to scratch his head. Except on the crown, which was raggedly bald, he had stiff, black hair standing jaggedly all over it, and growing downhill almost to his broad, blunt nose. It was so like smith's work, so much more like the top of a strongly spiked wall than a head of hair, that the best of players at leapfrog might have declined him, as the most dangerous man in the world to go over.

While he trotted back with the message he was to deliver to the night watchman in his box at the door of Tellson's Bank, by Temple-bar, who was to deliver it to greater authorities within, the shadows of the night took such shapes to him as arose out of the message, and took such shapes to the mare as arose out of *her* private topics of uneasiness. They seemed to be numerous, for she shied at every shadow on the road.

What time, the mail-coach lumbered, jolted, rattled, and bumped upon its tedious way, with its three fellow inscrutables inside. To whom, likewise, the shadows of the night revealed themselves, in the forms their dozing eyes and wandering thoughts suggested.

Tellson's Bank had a run upon it in the mail. As the bank passenger— with an arm drawn through the leathern strap, which did what lay in it to keep him from pounding against the next passenger, and driving him into his corner, whenever the coach got a special jolt—nodded in his place, with half-shut eyes, the little coach windows, and the coach-lamp dimly gleaming through them, and the bulky bundle of opposite passenger, became the bank, and did a great stroke of business. The rattle of the harness was the chink of money, and more drafts were honored in five minutes than even Tellson's, with all its foreign and home connection, ever paid in thrice the time. Then, the strong-rooms underground, at Tellson's, with such of their valuable stores and secrets as were known to the passenger (and it was not a little that he knew about them), opened before him, and he went in among them with the great keys and the feebly-burning candle, and found them safe, and strong, and sound, and still, just as he had last seen them.

But, though the bank was almost always with him, and though the coach (in a confused way, like the presence of pain under an opiate), was always with him, there was another current of impression that never ceased to run, all through the night. He was on his way to dig someone out of a grave.

Now, which of the multitude of faces that showed themselves before him was the true face of the buried person, the shadows of the night did not indicate; but they were all the faces of a man of five-and-forty by years, and they differed principally in the passions they expressed, and in the ghastliness of their worn and wasted state. Pride, contempt, defiance, stubbornness, submission, lamentation, succeeded one another; so did varieties of sunken cheek, cadaverous color, emaciated hands and figures. But the face was, in the main, one face, and every head was prematurely white. A hundred times the dozing passenger inquired of this spectre:

"Buried how long?"

The answer was always the same; "Almost eighteen years."

"You had abandoned all hope of being dug out?"

"Long ago."

"You know that you are recalled to life?"

"They tell me so."

"I hope you care to live?"

"I can't say."

"Shall I show her to you? Will you come and see her?"

The answers to this question were various and contradictory. Sometimes the broken reply was, "Wait! It would kill me if I saw her too soon." Sometimes, it was given in a tender rain of tears, and then it was, "Take me to her." Sometimes, it was staring and bewildered, and then it was, "I don't know her. I don't understand."

After such imaginary discourse, the passenger in his fancy would dig, dig, dig—now, with a spade, now with a great key, now with his hands—to dig this wretched creature out. Got out at last, with earth hanging about his face and hair, he would suddenly fall away to dust. The passenger would then start to himself, and lower the window, to get the reality of mist and rain on his cheek.

Yet even when his eyes were opened on the mist and rain, on the moving patch of light from the lamps, and the hedge at the roadside retreating by jerks, the night-shadows outside the coach would fall into the train of the night shadows within. The real Banking-house by Temple-bar, the real business of the past day, the real strong-rooms, the real express sent after him, and the real message returned, would all be there. Out of the midst of them, the ghostly face would rise, and he would accost it again.

"Buried how long?"

"Almost eighteen years."

"I hope you care to live?"

"I can't say."

Dig—dig—dig—until an impatient movement from one of the two passengers would admonish him to pull up the window, draw his arm securely through the leathern strap, and speculate upon the two slumbering forms, until his mind lost its hold of them, and then again slid away into the bank and the grave.

"Buried how long?"

"Almost eighteen years."

"You had abandoned all hope of being dug out?"

"Long ago."

The words were still in his hearing as just spoken—distinctly in his hearing as ever words had been in his life—when the weary passenger started to the consciousness of daylight, and found that the shadows of the night were gone.

He lowered the window, and looked out at the rising sun. There was a ridge of plowed land, with a plow upon it where it had been left last night when the horses were unyoked; beyond, a quiet coppice-wood, in which many leaves of burning red and golden yellow still remained upon the trees. Though the earth was cold and wet, the sky was clear, and the sun rose bright, placid, and beautiful.

"Eighteen years!" said the passenger, looking at the sun. "Gracious Creator of Day! To be buried alive for eighteen years!"

Four

THE PREPARATION

WHEN THE MAIL GOT SUCCESSFULLY TO DOVER, IN THE course of the forenoon, the head-drawer at the Royal George Hotel opened the coach-door, as his custom was. He did it with some flourish of ceremony, for a mail journey from London in winter, was an achievement to congratulate an adventurous traveler upon.

By that time, there was only one adventurous traveler left to be congratulated; for, the two others had been set down at their respective roadside destinations. The mildewy inside of the coach, with its damp and dirty straw, its disagreeable smell, and its obscurity, was rather like a larger dog-kennel. Mr. Lorry, the passenger, shaking himself out of it, in chains of straw, a tangle of shaggy wrapper, flapping hat, and muddy legs, was rather like a larger sort of dog.

"There will be a packet to Calais tomorrow, drawer?"

"Yes, sir, if the weather holds and the wind sets tolerable fair. The tide will serve pretty nicely at about two in the afternoon, sir. Bed, sir?"

"I shall not go to bed till night; but I want a bedroom and a barber."

"And then breakfast, sir? Yes, sir. That way, sir, if you please. Show Concord! Gentleman's valise and hot water to Concord. Pull off gentleman's boots in Concord. (You will find a fine sea-coal fire, sir.) Fetch barber to Concord. Stir about there, now, for Concord!"

The Concord bedchamber being always assigned to a passenger by the mail, and passengers by the mail being always heavily wrapped up from head to foot, the room had the odd interest for the establishment of the Royal George, that although but one kind of man was seen to go into it, all kinds and varieties of men came out of it. Consequently another drawer, and two porters, and several maids, and the landlady, were all loitering by accident at various points of the road between the Concord and the coffee-room, when a gentleman of sixty, formally dressed in a brown suit of clothes, pretty well worn, but very well kept, with large square cuffs, and large flaps to the pockets, passed along on his way to his breakfast.

The coffee-room had no other occupant, that forenoon, than the gentleman in brown. His breakfast-table was drawn before the fire, and as he sat, with the light shining on him, waiting for the meal, he sat so still, that he might have been sitting for his portrait.

Very orderly and methodical he looked, with a hand on each knee, and a loud watch ticking a sonorous sermon under his flapped waistcoat, as though it pitted its gravity and longevity against the levity and evanescence of the brisk fire. He had a good leg, and was a little vain of it, for his brown stockings fitted sleek and close, and were of a fine texture; his shoes and buckles, too, though plain, were trim. He wore an odd little sleek crisp flaxen wig, setting very close to his head: which wig, it is to be presumed, was made of hair, but which looked far more as though it were spun from filaments of silk or glass. His linen, though not of a fineness in accordance with his stockings, was as white as the tops of the waves that broke upon the neighboring beach, or the specks of sail that glinted in the sunlight far at sea. A face, habitually suppressed and quieted, was still lighted up under the quaint wig by a pair of moist bright eyes that must have cost their owner, in years gone by, some pains to drill to the composed and reserved expression of Tellson's Bank. He had a healthy color in his cheeks, and his face, though lined, bore few traces of anxiety. But, perhaps the confidential bachelor clerks in Tellson's Bank were principally occupied with the cares of other people; and perhaps secondhand cares, like secondhand clothes, come easily off and on.

Completing his resemblance to a man who was sitting for his portrait, Mr. Lorry dropped off asleep. The arrival of his breakfast roused him, and he said to the drawer, as he moved his chair to it:

"I wish accommodation prepared for a young lady who may come here at any time today. She may ask for Mr. Jarvis Lorry, or she may only ask for a gentleman from Tellson's Bank. Please to let me know."

"Yes, sir. Tellson's Bank in London, sir?"

"Yes."

"Yes, sir. We have oftentimes the honor to entertain your gentlemen in their traveling backward and forward betwixt London and Paris, sir. A vast deal of traveling, sir, in Tellson and Company's house."

"Yes, we are quite a French house, as well as an English one."

"Yes, sir. Not much in the habit of such traveling yourself, I think, sir?"

"Not of late years. It is fifteen years since we—since I—came last from France."

"Indeed, sir? That was before my time here, sir. Before our people's time here, sir. The George was in other hands at that time, sir."

"I believe so."

"But I would hold a pretty wager, sir, that a house like Tellson and Company was flourishing, a matter of fifty, not to speak of fifteen years ago?"

"You might treble that, and say a hundred and fifty, yet not be far from the truth."

"Indeed, sir!"

Rounding his mouth and both his eyes, as he stepped backward from the table, the waiter shifted his napkin from his right arm to his left, dropped into a comfortable attitude, and stood surveying the guest while he ate and drank, as from an observatory or watchtower. According to the immemorial usage of waiters in all ages.

When Mr. Lorry had finished his breakfast, he went out for a stroll on the beach. The little, narrow, crooked town of Dover hid itself away from the beach, and ran its head into the chalk-cliffs, like a marine ostrich. The beach was a desert of heaps of sea and stones tumbling wildly about, and the sea did what it liked, and what it liked was destruction. It thundered at the town, and thundered at the cliffs, and brought the coast down, madly. The air among the houses was of so strong a piscatory flavor that one might have supposed sick fish went up to be dipped in it, as sick people went down to be dipped in the sea. A little fishing was done in the port, and a quantity of strolling about by night and looking seaward: particularly at those times when the tide made and was near flood. Small tradesmen, who did no business whatever, sometimes unaccountably realized large fortunes, and it was remarkable that nobody in the neighborhood could endure a lamplighter.

As the day declined into the afternoon, and the air, which had been at intervals clear enough to allow the French coast to be seen, became again charged with mist and vapor, Mr. Lorry's thoughts seemed to cloud too. When it was dark, and he sat before the coffee-room fire, awaiting his dinner as he had awaited his breakfast, his mind was busily digging, digging, digging, in the live red coals.

A bottle of good claret after dinner does a digger in the red coals no harm, otherwise than as it has a tendency to throw him out of work. Mr. Lorry had been idle a long time, and had just poured out his last glassful of wine with as complete an appearance of satisfaction as is ever to be found in an elderly gentleman of a fresh complexion who has got to the end of a bottle, when a rattling of wheels came up the narrow street, and rumbled into the inn-yard.

He set down his glass untouched. "This is Mam'selle!" said he.

In a very few minutes the waiter came in, to announce that Miss Manette had arrived from London, and would be happy to see the gentleman from Tellson's.

"So soon?"

Miss Manette had taken some refreshment on the road, and required none then, and was extremely anxious to see the gentleman from Tellson's immediately, if it suited his pleasure and convenience.

The gentleman from Tellson's had nothing left for it but to empty his glass with an air of stolid desperation, settle his odd, little flaxen wig at the ears, and follow the waiter to Miss Manette's apartment. It was a large, dark room, furnished in a funereal manner with black horsehair, and loaded with heavy dark tables. These had been oiled and oiled, until the two tall candles on the table in the middle of the room were gloomily reflected on every leaf; as if *they* were buried in deep graves of black mahogany, and no light to speak of could be expected from them until they were dug out.

The obscurity was so difficult to penetrate that Mr. Lorry, picking his way over the well-worn Turkey carpet, supposed Miss Manette to be, for the moment, in some adjacent room, until, having got past the two tall candles, he saw standing to receive him by the table between them and the fire, a young lady of not more than seventeen, in a riding-cloak, and still holding her straw traveling-hat by its ribbon, in her hand. As his eyes rested on a short, slight-pretty figure, a quantity of golden hair, a pair of blue eyes that met his own with an inquiring look, and a forehead with a singular capacity (remembering how young and smooth it was), of lifting and knitting itself into an expression that was not quite one of perplexity, or wonder, or alarm, or merely of a bright fixed attention, though it included all the four expressions—as his eyes rested on these things, a sudden vivid likeness passed before him, of a child whom he had held in his arms on the passage across that very Channel, one cold time, when the hail drifted heavily and the sea ran high. The likeness passed away, say, like a breath along the surface of the gaunt pier-glass behind her, on the frame of which, a hospital procession of negro cupids, several headless and all cripples, were offering black baskets of Dead Sea fruit to black divinities of the feminine gender—and he made his formal bow to Miss Manette.

"Pray take a seat, sir." In a very clear and pleasant young voice: a little foreign in its accent, but a very little indeed.

"I kiss your hand, Miss," said Mr. Lorry, with the manners of an earlier date, as he made his formal bow again, and took his seat.

"I received a letter from the Bank, sir, yesterday, informing me that some new intelligence—or discovery—"

"The word is not material, Miss; either word will do."

"—respecting the small property of my poor father whom I never saw—so long dead—"

Mr. Lorry moved in his chair, and cast a troubled look toward the hospital procession of negro cupids. As if *they* had any help for anybody in their absurd baskets!

"—rendered it necessary that I should go to Paris, there to communicate with a gentleman of the Bank, so good as to be dispatched to Paris for the purpose."

"Myself."

"As I was prepared to hear, sir."

She courtesied to him (young ladies made courtesies in those days), with a pretty desire to convey to him that she felt how much older and wiser he was than she. He made her another bow.

"I replied to the Bank, sir, that as it was considered necessary, by those who know, and who are so kind as to advise me, that I should go to France, and that as I am an orphan and have no friend who could go with me, I should esteem it highly if I might be permitted to place myself, during the journey, under that worthy gentleman's protection. This gentleman had left London, but I think a messenger was sent after him to beg the favor of his waiting for me here."

"I was happy," said Mr. Lorry, "to be entrusted with the charge. I shall be more happy to execute it."

"Sir, I thank you indeed. I thank you very gratefully. It was told me by the Bank that the gentleman would explain to me the details of the business, and that I must prepare myself to find them of a surprising nature. I have done my best to prepare myself, and I naturally have a strong and eager interest to know what they are."

"Naturally," said Mr. Lorry. "Yes—I—"

After a pause, he added, again settling the crisp, flaxen wig at the ears:

"It is very difficult to begin."

He did not begin, but, in his indecision, met her glance. The young forehead lifted itself into that singular expression—but it was pretty and characteristic, besides being singular—and she raised her hand, as if with an involuntary action she caught at, or stayed some passing shadow.

"Are you quite a stranger to me, sir?"

"Am I not?" Mr. Lorry opened his hands, and extended them outward with an argumentative smile.

Between the eyebrows and just over the little feminine nose, the line of which was as delicate and fine as it was possible to be, the expression deepened itself as she took her seat thoughtfully in the chair by which she had hitherto remained standing. He watched her as she mused, and, the moment she raised her eyes again, went on:

"In your adopted country, I presume, I cannot do better than address you as a young English lady, Miss Manette?"

"If you please, sir."

"Miss Manette, I am a man of business. I have a business charge to acquit myself of. In your reception of it, don't heed me anymore than if I was a speaking machine—truly, I am not much else. I will, with your leave, relate to you, Miss, the story of one of our customers."

"Story!"

He seemed willfully to mistake the word she had repeated, when he added, in a hurry, "Yes, customers; in the banking business we usually call our connection our customers. He was a French gentleman; a scientific gentleman; a man of great acquirements—a Doctor."

"Not of Beauvais?"

"Why, yes, of Beauvais. Like Monsieur Manette, your father, the gentleman was of Beauvais. Like Monsieur Manette, your father, the gentleman was of repute in Paris. I had the honor of knowing him there. Our relations were business relations, but confidential. I was at that time in our French House, and, had been—oh! twenty years."

"At that time—I may ask, at what time, sir?"

"I speak, Miss, of twenty years ago. He married—an English lady—and I was one of the trustees. His affairs, like the affairs of many other French gentlemen and French families, were entirely in Tellson's hands. In a similar way, I am, or I have been, trustee of one kind or other for scores of our customers. These are mere business relations, Miss; there is no friendship in them, no particular interest, nothing like sentiment. I have passed from one to another, in the course of my business life, just as I pass from one of our customers to another, in the course of my business day; in short, I have no feelings; I am a mere machine. To go on—"

"But this is my father's story, sir; and I begin to think"—the curiously roughened forehead was very intent upon him—"that when I was left an orphan, through my mother's surviving my father only two years, it was you who brought me to England. I am almost sure it was you."

Mr. Lorry took the hesitating little hand that confidingly advanced to take his, and he put it with some ceremony to his lips. He then conducted the young lady straightway to her chair again, and, holding the chair-back with his left hand, and using his right by turns to rub his chin, pull his wig at the ears, or point what he said, stood looking down into her face while she sat looking up into his.

"Miss Manette, it *was* I. And you will see how truly I spoke of myself just now, in saying I had no feelings, and that all the relations I hold with my fellow-creatures are mere business relations, when you reflect that I have never seen you since. No; you have been the ward of Tellson's House since, and I have been busy with the other business of Tellson's House since. Feelings! I have no time for them, no chance of them. I pass my whole life, Miss, in turning an immense pecuniary Mangle."

After this odd description of his daily routine of employment, Mr. Lorry flattened his flaxen wig upon his head with both hands (which was most unnecessary, for nothing could be flatter than its shining surface was before), and resumed his former attitude.

"So far, Miss (as you have remarked), this is the story of your regretted father. Now comes the difference. If your father had not died when he did— Don't be frightened! How you start!"

She did indeed, start. And she caught his wrist with both her hands.

"Pray," said Mr. Lorry, in a soothing tone, bringing his left hand from the back of the chair to lay it on the supplicatory fingers that clasped him in so violent a tremble: "pray control your agitation—a matter of business. As I was saying—"

Her look so discomposed him that he stopped, wandered, and began anew:

"As I was saying: if Monsieur Manette had not died; if he had suddenly and silently disappeared; if he had been spirited away; if it had not been difficult to guess to what dreadful place, though no art could trace him; if he had an enemy in some compatriot who could exercise a privilege that I in my own time have known the boldest people afraid to speak of in a whisper, across the water, there; for instance, the privilege of filling up blank forms for the consignment of anyone to the oblivion of a prison for any length of time; if his wife had implored the king, the queen, the court, the clergy, for any tidings of him, and all quite in vain;—then the history of your father would have been the history of this unfortunate gentleman, the Doctor of Beauvais."

"I entreat you to tell me more, sir."

"I will. I am going to. You can bear it?"

"I can bear anything but the uncertainty you leave me in at this moment."

"You speak collectedly, and you—*are* collected. That's good!" (Though his manner was less satisfied than his words.) "A matter of business. Regard it as a matter of business—business that must be done. Now, if this Doctor's wife, though a lady of great courage and spirit, had suffered so intensely from this cause before her little child was born—"

"The little child was a daughter, sir?"

"A daughter. A—a—matter of business—don't be distressed. Miss, if the poor lady had suffered so intensely before her little child was born, that she came to the determination of sparing the poor child the inheritance of any part of the agony she had known the pains of, by rearing her in the belief, that her father was dead— No, don't kneel! In Heaven's name why should you kneel to me!"

"For the truth. O dear, good, compassionate sir, for the truth!"

"A—a matter of business. You confuse me, and how can I transact business if I am confused? Let us be clearheaded. If you could kindly mention now, for instance, what nine times ninepence are, or how many shillings in twenty guineas, it would be so encouraging. I should be so much more at my ease about your state of mind."

Without directly answering to this appeal, she sat so still when he had very gently raised her, and the hands that had not ceased to clasp his wrists were so much more steady than they had been, that she communicated some reassurance to Mr. Jarvis Lorry.

"That's right, that's right. Courage! Business! You have business before you; useful business. Miss Manette, your mother took this course with you. And when she died—I believe broken-hearted—having never slackened her unavailing search for your father, she left you, at two years old, to grow to be blooming, beautiful, and happy, without the dark cloud upon you of living in uncertainty whether your father soon wore his heart out in prison, or wasted there through many lingering years."

As he said the words, he looked down, with admiring pity, on the flowing golden hair; as if he pictured to himself that it might have been already tinged with gray.

"You know that your parents had no great possession, and that what they had was secured to your mother and to you. There has been no new discovery of money, or of any other property; but—"

He felt his wrist held closer, and he stopped. The expression of the forehead, which had so particularly attracted his notice, and which was now immovable, had deepened into one of pain and horror.

"But he has been—been found. He is alive. Greatly changed, it is too probable; almost a wreck, it is possible; though we will hope the best. Still, alive. Your father has been taken to the house of an old servant in Paris, and we are going there: I, to identify him if I can: you, to restore him to life, love, duty, rest, comfort."

A shiver ran through her frame, and from it through his. She said, in a low distinct, awe-stricken voice, as if she were saying it in a dream, "I am going to see his Ghost! It will be his Ghost—not him!"

Mr. Lorry quietly chafed the hands that held his arm. "There, there, there! See now, see now! The best and the worst are known to you now. You are well on your way to the poor wronged gentleman, and, with a fair sea voyage, and a fair land journey, you will be soon at his dear side."

She repeated in the same tone, sunk to a whisper, "I have been free, I have been happy, yet his Ghost has never haunted me!"

"Only one thing more," said Mr. Lorry, laying stress upon it as a wholesome means of enforcing her attention: "he has been found under another name; his own, long forgotten or long concealed. It would be worse than useless now to inquire which; worse than useless to seek to know whether he has been for years overlooked, or always designedly held prisoner. It would be worse than useless now to make any inquiries, because it would be dangerous. Better not to mention the subject, anywhere or in any way, and to remove him—for a while at all events—out of France. Even I, safe as an Englishman, and even Tellson's, important as they are to French credit, avoid all naming of the matter. I carry about me, not a scrap of writing openly referring to it. This is a secret service altogether. My credentials, entries, and memoranda, are all comprehended in the one line, 'Recalled to Life'; which may mean anything. But what is the matter! She doesn't notice a word! Miss Manette!"

Perfectly still and silent, and not even fallen back in her chair, she sat under his hand, utterly insensible, with her eyes open and fixed upon him, and with that last expression looking as if it were carved or branded into her forehead. So close was her hold upon his arm, that he feared to detach himself lest he should hurt her; therefore he called out loudly for assistance without moving.

A wild-looking woman, whom, even in his agitation, Mr. Lorry observed to be all of a red color, and to have red hair, and to be dressed in some extraordinary tight-fitting fashion, and to have on her head a most wonderful bonnet like a Grenadier wooden measure, and good measure too, or a great Stilton cheese, came running into the room in advance of the inn servants, and soon settled the question of his detachment from the poor young lady, by laying a brawny hand upon his chest, and sending him flying back against the nearest wall.

("I really think this must be a man!" was Mr. Lorry's breathless reflection, simultaneously with his coming against the wall.)

"Why look at you all!" bawled this figure, addressing the inn servants. "Why don't you go and fetch things, instead of standing there staring at me? I am not so much to look at, am I? Why don't you go and fetch things? I'll let you know, if you don't bring smelling salts, cold water, and vinegar, quick, I will."

There was an immediate dispersal for these restoratives, and she softly laid the patient on a sofa, and tended her with great skill and gentleness: calling her "my precious!" and "my bird!" and spreading her golden hair aside over her shoulders with great pride and care.

"And you in brown!" she said, indignantly turning on Mr. Lorry; "couldn't you tell her what you had to tell her, without frightening her to death? Look at her, with her pretty pale face and her cold hands. Do you call *that* being a banker?"

Mr. Lorry was so exceedingly disconcerted by a question so hard to answer, that he could only look on, at a distance, with much feebler sympathy and humility, while the strong woman, having banished the inn servants under the mysterious penalty of "letting them know" something not mentioned if they stayed there, staring, recovered her charge by a regular series of gradations, and coaxed her to lay her drooping head upon her shoulder.

"I hope she will do well now," said Mr. Lorry.

"No thanks to you in brown, if she does. My darling pretty!"

"I hope," said Mr. Lorry, after another pause of feeble sympathy and humility, "that you accompany Miss Manette to France?"

"A likely thing, too!" replied the strong woman. "If it was ever intended that I should go across salt water, do you suppose Providence would have cast my lot in an island?"

This being another question hard to answer, Mr. Jarvis Lorry withdrew to consider it.

Five

THE WINE-SHOP

A LARGE CASK OF WINE HAD BEEN DROPPED AND BROKEN, IN the street. The accident had happened in getting it out of a cart; the cask had tumbled out with a run, the hoops had burst, and it lay on the stones just outside the door of the wine-shop, shattered like a walnut-shell.

All the people within reach had suspended their business, or their idleness, to run to the spot and drink the wine. The rough, irregular stones of the street, pointing every way, and designed, one might have thought, expressly to lame all living creatures that approached them, had dammed it into little pools; these were surrounded, each by its own jostling group or crowd, according to its size. Some men kneeled down, made scoops of their two hands joined, and sipped, or tried to help women, who bent over their shoulders, to sip, before the wine had all run out between their fingers. Others, men and women, dipped in the puddles with little mugs of mutilated earthenware, or even with handkerchiefs from women's heads, which were squeezed dry into infants' mouths; others made small mud-embankments, to stem the wine as it ran; others, directed by lookers-on at high windows, darted here and there, to cut off little streams of wine that started away in new directions; others, devoted themselves to the sodden and lee-dyed pieces of the cask, licking, and even champing the moister wine-rotted fragments with eager relish. There was no drainage to carry off the wine, and not only did it all get taken up, but so much mud got taken up along with it, that there might have been a scavenger in the street, if anybody acquainted with it could have believed in such a miraculous presence.

A shrill sound of laughter and of amused voices—voices of men, women, and children—resounded in the street while this wine-game lasted. There was little roughness in the sport, and much playfulness. There was a special companionship in it, an observable inclination on the part of every one to join some other one, which led, especially among the luckier or lighter-hearted, to frolicsome embraces, drinking of healths, shaking of hands, and even joining of hands and dancing, a dozen together. When the wine was gone, and the places where it had been most abundant were raked into a grid-iron-pattern by fingers, these demonstrations ceased, as suddenly as they had broken out. The man who had left his saw sticking in the firewood he was cutting, set it in motion again; the woman who had left on a doorstep the lit-tle pot of hot ashes, at which she had been trying to soften the pain in her own starved fingers and toes, or in those of her child, returned to it; men with bare arms, matted locks, and cadaverous faces, who had emerged into the winter light from cellars, moved away to descend again; and a gloom gath-ered on the scene that appeared more natural to it than sunshine.

The wine was red wine, and had stained the ground of the narrow street in the suburb of Saint Antoine, in Paris, where it was spilled. It had stained many hands, too, and many faces, and many naked feet, and many wooden shoes. The hands of the man who sawed the wood, left red marks on the bil-lets; and the forehead of the woman who nursed her baby was stained with the stain of the old rag she wound about her head again. Those who had been greedy with the staves of the cask, had acquired a tigerish smear about the mouth; and one tall joker so besmirched, his head more out of a long squalid bag of a nightcap than in it, scrawled upon a wall with his finger dipped in muddy wine lees—BLOOD.

The time was to come, when that wine too would be spilled on the street-stones, and when the stain of it would be red upon many there.

And now that the cloud settled on Saint Antoine, which a momentary gleam had driven from his sacred countenance, the darkness of it was heavy—cold, dirt, sickness, ignorance, and want, were the lords in waiting on the saintly presence—nobles of great power all of them; but, most espe-cially the last. Samples of a people that had undergone a terrible grinding and regrinding in the mill, and certainly not in the fabulous mill which ground old people young, shivered at every corner, passed in and out at every door-way, looked from every window, fluttered in every vestige of a garment that the wind shook. The mill which had worked them down, was the mill that grinds young people old; the children had ancient faces and grave voices; and upon them, and upon the grown faces, and plowed into every furrow of age and coming up afresh, was the sign, Hunger. It was prevalent everywhere. Hunger was pushed out of the tall houses, in the wretched clothing that hung upon poles and lines; Hunger was patched into them with straw and rag and wood and paper; Hunger was repeated in every fragment of the small mod-icum of firewood that the man sawed off; Hunger stared down from the smokeless chimneys, and started up from the filthy street that had no offal, among its refuse, of anything to eat. Hunger was the inscription on the baker's shelves, written in every small loaf of his scanty stock of bad bread; at the sausage-shop, in every dead-dog preparation that was offered for sale.

Hunger rattled its dry bones among the roasting chestnuts in the turned cylinder: Hunger was shred into atomies in every farthing porringer of husky chips of potato, fried with some reluctant drops of oil.

Its abiding-place was in all things fitted to it. A narrow winding street, full of offense and stench, with other narrow winding streets diverging, all peopled by rags and nightcaps, and all smelling of rags and nightcaps, and all visible things with a brooding look upon them that looked ill. In the hunted air of the people there was yet some wild-beast thought of the possibility of turning at bay. Depressed and slinking though they were, eyes of fire were not wanting among them; nor compressed lips, white with what they suppressed; nor foreheads knitted into the likeness of the gallows-rope they mused about enduring, or inflicting. The trade signs (and they were almost as many as the shops) were, all, grim illustrations of Want. The butcher and the porkman painted up, only the leanest scrags of meat; the baker, the coarsest of meager loaves. The people rudely pictured as drinking in the wine-shops, croaked over their scanty measures of thin wine and beer, and were gloweringly confidential together. Nothing was represented in a flourishing condition, save tools aud weapons; but the cutler's knives and axes were sharp and bright, the smith's hammers were heavy, and the gunmaker's stock was murderous. The crippling stones of the pavement, with their many little reservoirs of mud and water, had not footways, but broke off abruptly at the doors. The kennel, to make amends, ran down the middle of the street—when it ran at all: which was only after heavy rains, and then it ran, by many eccentric fits, into the houses. Across the streets, at wide intervals, one clumsy lamp was slung by a rope and pulley; at night, when the lamplighter had let these down, and lighted, and hoisted them again, a feeble grove of dim wicks swung in a sickly manner overhead, as if they were at sea. Indeed they were at sea, and the ship and crew were in peril of tempest.

For, the time was to come, when the gaunt scarecrows of that region should have watched the lamplighter, in their idleness and hunger, so long, as to conceive the idea of improving on his method, and hauling up men by those ropes and pulleys, to flare upon the darkness of their condition. But, the time was not come yet; and every wind that blew over France shook the rags of the scarecrows in vain, for the birds, fine of song and feather, took no warning.

The wine-shop was a corner-shop, better than most others in its appearance and degree, and the master of the wine-shop had stood outside it, in a yellow waistcoat and green breeches, looking on at the struggle for the lost wine. "It's not my affair," said he, with a final shrug of his shoulders. "The people from the market did it. Let them bring another."

There, his eyes happening to catch the tall joker writing up his joke, he called to him across the way:

"Say then, my Gaspard, what do you do there?"

The fellow pointed to his joke with immense significance, as is often the way with his tribe. It missed its mark, and completely failed, as is often the way with his tribe too.

"What now? Are you a subject for the mad-hospital?" said the wine-shop keeper, crossing the road, and obliterating the jest with a handful of mud, picked up for the purpose, and smeared over it. "Why do you write in the public streets? Is there—tell me thou—is there no other place to write such words in?"

In his expostulation he dropped his cleaner hand (perhaps accidentally, perhaps not), upon the joker's heart. The joker rapped it with his own, took a nimble spring upward, and came down in a fantastic dancing attitude, with one of his stained shoes jerked off his foot into his hand, and held out. A joker of an extremely, not to say wolfishly, practical character, he looked, under those circumstances.

"Put it on, put it on," said the other. "Call wine, wine; and finish there." With that advice, he wiped his soiled hand upon the joker's dress, such as it was—quite deliberately, as having dirtied the hand on his account; and then recrossed the road and entered the wine-shop.

This wine-shop keeper was a bull-necked, martial-looking man of thirty, and he should have been of a hot temperament, for, although it was a bitter day, he wore no coat, but carried one slung over his shoulder. His shirtsleeves were rolled up, too, and his brown arms were bare to the elbows. Neither did he wear anything more on his head than his own crisply-curling, short, dark hair. He was a dark man altogether, with good eyes and a good bold breadth between them. Good-humored-looking on the whole, but implacable-looking, too; evidently a man of a strong resolution and a set purpose; a man not desirable to be met, rushing down a narrow pass with a gulf on either side, for nothing would turn the man.

Madame Defarge, his wife, sat in the shop behind the counter as he came in. Madame Defarge was a stout woman of about his own age, with a watchful eye that seldom seemed to look at anything, a large hand heavily ringed, a steady face, strong features, and great composure of manner. There was a character about Madame Defarge, from which one might have predicated that she did not often make mistakes against herself in any of the reckonings over which she presided. Madame Defarge being sensitive to cold, was wrapped in fur, and had a quantity of bright shawl twined about her head, though not to the concealment of her large earrings. Her knitting was before her, but she had laid it down to pick her teeth with a toothpick. Thus engaged, with her right elbow supported by her left hand, Madame Defarge said nothing when her lord came in, but coughed just one grain of cough. This, in combination with the lifting of her dark, defined eyebrows over her toothpick by the breadth of a line, suggested to her husband that he would do well to look round the shop among the customers, for any new customer who had dropped in while he stepped over the way.

The wine-shop keeper accordingly rolled his eyes about, until they rested upon an elderly gentleman and a young lady, who were seated in a corner. Other company were there: two playing cards, two playing dominoes, three standing by the counter lengthening out a short supply of wine. As he passed behind the counter, he took notice that the elderly gentleman said in a look to the young lady, "This is our man."

"What the devil do *you* do in that galley there!" said Monsieur Defarge to himself; "I don't know you."

But he feigned not to notice the two strangers, and fell into discourse with the triumvirate of customers who were drinking at the counter.

"How goes it, Jacques?" said one of these three to Monsieur Defarge. "Is all the spilt wine swallowed?"

"Every drop, Jacques," answered Monsieur Defarge.

When this interchange of Christian name was effected, Madame Defarge, picking her teeth with her toothpick, coughed another grain of cough, and raised her eyebrows by the breadth of another line.

"It is not often," said the second of the three, addressing Monsieur Defarge, "that many of these miserable beasts know the taste of wine, or of anything but black bread and death. Is it not so, Jacques?"

"It is so, Jacques," Monsieur Defarge returned.

At this second interchange of the Christian name, Madame Defarge, still using her toothpick with profound composure, coughed another grain of cough, and raised her eyebrows by the breadth of another line.

The last of the three now said his say, as he put down his empty drinking vessel and smacked his lips.

"Ah! So much the worse! A bitter taste it is that such poor cattle always have in their mouths, and hard lives they live, Jacques. Am I right, Jacques?"

"You are right, Jacques," was the response of Monsieur Defarge.

This third interchange of the Christian name was completed at the moment when Madame Defarge put her toothpick by, kept her eyebrows up, and slightly rustled in her seat.

"Hold then! True!" muttered her husband. "Gentlemen—my wife!"

The three customers pulled off their hats to Madame Defarge, with three flourishes. She acknowledged their homage by bending her head, and giving them a quick look. Then she glanced in a casual manner round the wine-shop, took up her knitting with great apparent calmness and repose of spirit, and became absorbed in it.

"Gentlemen," said her husband, who had kept his bright eye observantly upon her, "good day. The chamber, furnished bachelor-fashion, that you wished to see, and were inquiring for when I stepped out, is on the fifth floor. The doorway of the staircase gives on the little courtyard close to the left here," pointing with his hand, "near to the window of my establishment. But, now that I remember, one of you has already been there, and can show the way. Gentlemen, adieu!"

They paid for their wine, and left the place. The eyes of Monsieur Defarge were studying his wife at her knitting, when the elderly gentleman advanced from his corner, and begged the favor of a word.

"Willingly, sir," said Monsieur Defarge, and quietly stepped with him to the door.

Their conference was very short, but very decided. Almost at the first word, Monsieur Defarge started and became deeply attentive. It had not lasted a minute, when he nodded and went out. The gentleman then beckoned to the young lady, and they, too, went out. Madame Defarge knitted with nimble fingers and steady eyebrows, and saw nothing.

Mr. Jarvis Lorry and Miss Manette, emerging from the wine-shop thus, joined Monsieur Defarge in the doorway to which he had directed his other company just before. It opened from a stinking little black courtyard, and was the general public entrance to a great pile of houses, inhabited by a great number of people. In the gloomy, tile-paved entry to the gloomy, tile-paved staircase, Monsieur Defarge bent down on one knee to the child of his old master, and put her hand to his lips. It was a gentle action, but not at all gently done; a very remarkable transformation had come over him in a few seconds. He had no good humor in his face, nor any openness of aspect left, but had become a secret, angry, dangerous man.

"It is very high; it is a little difficult. Better to begin slowly." Thus Monsieur Defarge, in a stern voice, to Mr. Lorry, as they began ascending the stairs.

"Is he alone?" the latter whispered.

"Alone! God help him, who should be with him!" said the other in the same voice.

"Is he always alone, then?"

"Yes."

"Of his own desire?"

"Of his own necessity. As he was, when I first saw him after they found me and demanded to know if I would take him, and, at my peril, be discreet—as he was then, so he is now."

"He is greatly changed?"

"Changed!"

The keeper of the wine-shop stopped to strike the wall with his hand, and muttered a tremendous curse. No direct answer could be half so forcible. Mr. Lorry's spirits grew heavier and heavier, as he and his two companions ascended higher and higher.

Such a staircase, with its accessories, in the older and more crowded parts of Paris, would be bad enough now; but, at that time, it was vile indeed to unaccustomed and unhardened senses. Every little habitation within the great foul nest of one high building—that is to say, the room or rooms within every door that opened on the general staircase—left its own heap of refuse on its own landing, besides flinging other refuse from its own windows. The uncontrollable and hopeless mass of decomposition so engendered would have polluted the air, even if poverty and deprivation had not loaded it with their intangible impurities; the two bad sources combined made it almost insupportable. Through such an atmosphere, by a steep dark shaft of dirt and poison, the way lay. Yielding to his own disturbance of mind, and to his young companion's agitation, which became greater every instant, Mr. Jarvis Lorry twice stopped to rest. Each of these stoppages was made at a doleful grating by which any languishing good airs that were left uncorrupted, seemed to escape, and spoilt and sickly vapors seemed to crawl in. Through the rusted bars, tastes, rather than glimpses, were caught of the jumbled neighborhood; and nothing within range, nearer or lower than the summits of the two great towers of Notre Dame, had any promise on it of healthy life or wholesome aspirations.

At last, the top of the staircase was gained, and they stopped for the third time. There was yet an upper staircase, of a steeper inclination and of contracted dimensions, to be ascended, before the garret story was reached. The keeper of the wine-shop, always going a little in advance, and always going on the side which Mr. Lorry took, as though he dreaded to be asked any questions by the young lady, turned himself about here, and, carefully feeling in the pockets of the coat he carried over his shoulder, took out a key.

"The door is locked then, my friend?" said Mr. Lorry, surprised.

"Ay. Yes," was the grim reply of Monsieur Defarge.

"You think it necessary to keep the unfortunate gentleman so retired?"

"I think it necessary to turn the key." Monsieur Defarge whispered it closer in his ear, and frowned heavily.

"Why?"

"Why! Because he has lived so long, locked up, that he would be frightened—rave—tear himself to pieces—die—come to I know not what harm—if his door was left open."

"Is it possible!" exclaimed Mr. Lorry.

"Is it possible?" repeated Defarge, bitterly. "Yes. And a beautiful world we live in, when it *is* possible, and when many other such things are possible, and not only possible, but done—done, see you!—under that sky there, every day. Long live the Devil. Let us go on."

This dialogue had been held in so very low a whisper, that not a word of it had reached the young lady's ears. But, by this time, she trembled under such strong emotion, and her face expressed such deep anxiety, and, above all, such dread and terror, that Mr. Lorry felt it incumbent on him to speak a word or two of reassurance.

"Courage, dear Miss! Courage! Business! The worst will be over in a moment; it is but passing the room door, and the worst is over. Then, all the good you bring to him, all the relief, all the happiness you bring to him, begin. Let our good friend here assist you on that side. That's well, friend Defarge. Come, now. Business, business!"

They went up slowly and softly. The staircase was short, and they were soon at the top. There, as it had an abrupt turn in it, they came all at once in sight of three men, whose heads were bent down close together at the side of a door, and who were intently looking into the room to which the door belonged, through some chinks or holes in the wall. On hearing footsteps close at hand, these three turned, and rose, and showed themselves to be the three of one name who had been drinking in the wine-shop.

"I forgot them in the surprise of your visit," exclaimed Monsieur Defarge. "Leave us, good boys; we have business here."

The three glided by, and went silently down.

There appearing to be no other door on that floor, and the keeper of the wine-shop going straight to this one when they were left alone, Mr. Lorry asked him in a whisper, with a little anger:

"Do you make a show of Monsieur Manette?"

"I show him in the way you have seen, to a chosen few."

"Is that well?"

"*I* think it is well."

"Who are the few? How do you choose them?"

"I choose them as real men, of my name—Jacques is my name—to whom the sight is likely to do good. Enough; you are English; that is another thing. Stay there, if you please, a little moment."

With an admonitory gesture to keep them back, he stooped and looked in through the crevice in the wall. Soon raising his head again, he struck twice or thrice upon the door—evidently with no other object than to make a noise there. With the same intention, he drew the key across it, three or four times, before he put it clumsily into the lock, and turned it as heavily as he could.

The door slowly opened inward under his hand, and he looked into the room and said something. A faint voice answered something. Little more than a single syllable could have been spoken on either side.

He looked back over his shoulder and beckoned them to enter. Mr. Lorry got his arm securely round the daughter's waist and held her; for he felt that she was sinking.

"A—a—a—business, business!" he urged, with a moisture that was not of business shining on his cheek. "Come in, come in!"

"I am afraid of it," she answered, shuddering.

"Of it? What?"

"I mean of him. Of my father."

Rendered in a manner desperate, by her state and by the beckoning of their conductor, he drew over his neck the arm that shook upon his shoulder, lifted her a little, and hurried her into the room. He set her down just within the door, and held her, clinging to him.

Defarge drew out the key, closed the door, locked it on the inside, took out the key again, and held it in his hand. All this he did methodically, and with as loud and harsh an accompaniment of noise as he could make. Finally, he walked across the room with a measured tread to where the window was. He stopped there, and faced around.

The garret, built to be a dry depository for firewood and the like, was dim and dark: for, the window of a dormer shape was in truth a door in the roof, with a little crane over it for the hoisting up of stores from the street: unglazed, and closing up the middle in two pieces, like any other door of French construction. To exclude the cold, one half of this door was fast closed, and the other was opened but a very little way. Such a scanty portion of light was admitted through the seams, that it was difficult, on first coming in, to see anything; and long habit alone could have slowly formed in anyone, the ability to do any work requiring nicety in such obscurity. Yet, work of that kind was being done in the garret; for, with his back toward the door, and his face toward the window where the keeper of the wine-shop stood looking at him, a white-haired man sat on a low bench, stooping forward and very busy, making shoes.

Six

THE SHOEMAKER

"Good day!" said Monsieur Defarge, looking down at the white head that bent low over the shoemaking.

It was raised for a moment, and a very faint voice responded to the salutation, as if it were at a distance:

"Good day!"

"You are still hard at work, I see?"

After a long silence, the head was lifted for another moment, and the voice replied, "Yes—I am working." This time, a pair of haggard eyes had looked at the questioner, before the face had dropped again.

The faintness of the voice was pitiable and dreadful. It was not the faintness of physical weakness, though confinement and hard fare no doubt had their part in it. Its deplorable peculiarity was, that it was the faintness of solitude and disuse. It was like the last feeble echo of a sound made long and long ago. So entirely had it lost the life and resonance of the human voice, that it affected the senses like a once beautiful color faded away into a poor weak stain. So sunken and suppressed it was, that it was like a voice underground. So expressive it was, of a hopeless and lost creature, that a famished traveler, wearied out by lonely wandering in a wilderness, would have remembered home and friends in such a tone before lying down to die.

Some minutes of silent work had passed, and the haggard eyes had looked up again: not with any interest or curiosity, but with a dull, mechanical perception, beforehand, that the spot where the only visitor they were aware of had stood, was not yet empty.

"I want," said Defarge, who had not removed his gaze from the shoe-maker, "to let in a little more light here. You can bear a little more?"

The shoemaker stopped his work; looked, with a vacant air of listening, at the floor on one side of him; then, similarly, at the floor on the other side of him; then, upward at the speaker.

"What did you say?"

"You can bear a little more light?"

"I must bear it, if you let it in." (Laying the palest shadow of a stress upon the second word.)

The opened half-door was opened a little further, and secured at that angle for the time. A broad ray of light fell into the garret, and showed the workman, with an unfinished shoe upon his lap, pausing in his labor. His few common tools and various scraps of leather were at his feet and on his bench. He had a white beard, raggedly cut, but not very long, a hollow face, and exceedingly bright eyes. The hollowness and thinness of his face would have caused them to look large, under his yet dark eyebrows and his con-fused white hair, though they had been really otherwise; but they were nat-urally large, and looked unnaturally so. His yellow rags of shirt lay open at the throat, and showed his body to be withered and worn. He, and his old canvas frock, and his loose stockings, and all his poor tatters of clothes, had, in a long seclusion from direct light and air, faded down to such a dull uni-formity of parchment-yellow, that it would have been hard to say which was which.

He had put up a hand between his eyes and the light, and the very bones of it seemed transparent. So he sat, with a steadfastly vacant gaze, pausing in his work. He never looked at the figure before him, without first looking down on this side of himself, then on that, as if he had lost the habit of asso-ciating place with sound; he never spoke without first wandering in this man-ner, and forgetting to speak.

"Are you going to finish that pair of shoes today?" asked Defarge, motioning to Mr. Lorry to come forward.

"What did you say?"

"Do you mean to finish that pair of shoes today?"

"I can't say that I mean to. I suppose so. I don't know."

But the question reminded him of his work, and he bent over it again.

Mr. Lorry came silently forward, leaving the daughter by the door. When he had stood, for a minute or two, by the side of Defarge, the shoemaker looked up. He showed no surprise at seeing another figure, but the unsteady fingers of one of his hands strayed to his lips as he looked at it (his lips and his nails were of the same pale lead color), and then the hand dropped to his work, and he once more bent over the shoe. The look and the action had occupied but an instant.

"You have a visitor, you see," said Monsieur Defarge.

"What did you say?"

"Here is a visitor."

The shoemaker looked up as before, but without removing a hand from his work.

"Come!" said Defarge. "Here is monsieur, who knows a well-made shoe when he sees one. Show him that shoe you are working at. Take it, monsieur."

Mr. Lorry took it in his hand.

"Tell monsieur what kind of shoe it is, and the maker's name."

There was a longer pause than usual, before the shoemaker replied.

"I forget what it was you asked me. What did you say?"

"I said, couldn't you describe the kind of shoe, for monsieur's information?"

"It is a lady's shoe. It is a young lady's walking shoe. It is in the present mode. I never saw the mode. I have had a pattern in my hand." He glanced at the shoe, with some little passing touch of pride.

"And the maker's name?" said Defarge.

Now that he had no work to hold, he laid the knuckles of the right hand in the hollow of the left, and then the knuckles of the left hand in the hollow of the right, and then passed a hand across his bearded chin, and so on in regular changes, without a moment's intermission. The task of recalling him from the vacancy into which he always sank when he had spoken, was like recalling some very weak person from a swoon, or endeavoring, in the hope of some disclosure, to stay the spirit of a fast dying man.

"Did you ask me for my name?"

"Assuredly I did."

"One Hundred and Five, North Tower."

"Is that all?"

"One Hundred and Five, North Tower."

With a weary sound that was not a sigh, nor a groan, he went to work again, until the silence was again broken.

"You are not a shoemaker by trade?" said Mr. Lorry, looking steadfastly at him.

His haggard eyes turned to Defarge as if he would have transferred the question to him; but as no help came from that quarter, they turned back on the questioner when they had sought the ground.

"I am not a shoemaker by trade? No, I was not a shoemaker by trade. I— I learnt it here. I taught myself. I asked leave to—"

He lapsed away, even for minutes, ringing those measured changes on his hands the whole time. His eyes came slowly back, at last, to the face from which they had wandered; when they rested on it, he started, and resumed, in the manner of a sleeper that moment awake, reverting to a subject of last night.

"I asked leave to teach myself, and I got it with much difficulty after a long while, and I have made shoes ever since."

As he held out his hand for the shoe that had been taken from him, Mr. Lorry said, still looking steadfastly in his face:

"Monsieur Manette, do you remember nothing of me?"

The shoe dropped to the ground, and he sat looking fixedly at the questioner.

"Monsieur Manette"; Mr. Lorry laid his hand upon Defarge's arm; "do you remember nothing of this man? Look at him. Look at me. Is there no old banker, no old business, no old servant, no old time, rising in your mind, Monsieur Manette?"

As the captive of many years sat looking fixedly by turns at Mr. Lorry and Defarge, some long-obliterated marks of an actively intent intelligence in the middle of the forehead, gradually forced themselves through the black mist that had fallen on him. They were overclouded again, they were fainter, they were gone; but, they had been there. And so exactly was the expression repeated on the fair young face of her who had crept along the wall to a point where she could see him, and where she now stood looking at him, with hands which at first had been only raised in frightened compassion, if not even to keep him off and shut out the sight of him, but which were now extending toward him, trembling with eagerness to lay the spectral face upon her warm young breast, and love it back to life and hope—so exactly was the expression repeated (though in stronger characters) on her fair young face, that it looked as though it had passed, like a moving light, from him to her.

Darkness had fallen on him in its place. He looked at the two, less and less attentively, and his eyes in gloomy abstraction sought the ground and looked about him in the old way. Finally, with a deep, long sigh, he took the shoe up, and resumed his work.

"Have you recognized him, monsieur?" asked Defarge, in a whisper.

"Yes; for a moment. At first I thought it quite hopeless, but I have unquestionably seen, for a single moment, the face that I once knew well. Hush! Let us draw further back. Hush!"

She had moved from the wall of the garret, very near to the bench on which he sat. There was something awful in his unconsciousness of the figure that could have put out its hand and touched him as he stooped over his labor.

Not a word was spoken, not a sound was made. She stood, like a spirit, beside him, and he bent over his work.

It happened, at length, that he had occasion to change the instrument in his hand, for his shoemaker's knife. It lay on that side of him which was not the side on which she stood. He had taken it up, and was stooping to work again, when his eyes caught the skirt of her dress. He raised them, and saw her face. The two spectators started forward, but she stayed them with a motion of her hand. She had no fear of his striking at her with the knife, though they had.

He stared at her with a fearful look, and after a while his lips began to form some words, though no sound proceeded from them. By degrees, in the pauses of his quick and labored breathing, he was heard to say:

"What is this!"

With the tears streaming down her face, she put her two hands to her lips, and kissed them to him; then clasped them on her breast, as if she laid his ruined head there.

"You are not the gaoler's daughter?"

She signed "No."

"Who are you?"

Not yet trusting the tones of her voice, she sat down on the bench beside him. He recoiled, but she laid her hand upon his arm. A strange thrill struck him when she did so, and visibly passed over his frame; he laid the knife down softly, as he sat staring at her.

Her golden hair, which she wore in long curls, had been hurriedly pushed aside, and fell down over her neck. Advancing his hand by little and little, he took it up and looked at it. In the midst of the action he went astray, and, with another deep sigh, fell to work at his shoemaking.

But, not for long. Releasing his arm, she laid her hand upon his shoulder. After looking doubtfully at it, two or three times, as if to be sure that it was really there, he laid down his work, put his hand to his neck, and took off a blackened string with a scrap of folded rag attached to it. He opened this, carefully, on his knee, and it contained a very little quantity of hair: not more than one or two long, golden hairs, which he had, in some old day, wound off upon his finger.

He took her hair into his hand again, and looked closely at it. "It is the same. How can it be! When was it! How was it!"

As the concentrating expression returned to his forehead, he seemed to become conscious that it was in hers too. He turned her full to the light, and looked at her.

"She laid her head upon my shoulder, that night when I was summoned out—she had a fear of my going, though I had none—and when I was brought to the North Tower they found these upon my sleeve. 'You will leave me them? They can never help me to escape in the body, though they may in the spirit.' Those were the words I said. I remember them very well."

He formed this speech with his lips many times before he could utter it. But when he did find spoken words for it, they came to him coherently, though slowly.

"How was this— *Was it you?*"

Once more, the two spectators started, as he turned upon her with a frightful suddenness. But, she sat perfectly still in his grasp, and only said, in a low voice, "I entreat you, good gentlemen, do not come near us, do not speak, do not move!"

"Hark!" he exclaimed. "Whose voice was that?"

His hands released her as he uttered this cry, and went up to his white hair, which they tore in a frenzy. It died out, as everything but his shoemaking did die out of him, and he refolded his little packet and tried to secure it in his breast; but, he still looked at her, and gloomily shook his head.

"No, no, no; you are too young, too blooming. It can't be. See what the prisoner is. These are not the hands she knew, this is not the face she knew, this is not a voice she ever heard. No, no. She was—and he was—before the slow years of the North Tower—ages ago. What is your name, my gentle angel?"

Hailing his softened tone and manner, his daughter fell upon her knees before him, with her appealing hands upon his breast.

"Oh, sir, at another time you shall know my name, and who my mother was, and who my father, and how I never knew their hard, hard history. But I cannot tell you at this time, and I cannot tell you here. All that I may tell you, here and now, is, that I pray to you to touch me and to bless me. Kiss me, kiss me! O my dear, my dear!"

His cold white head mingled with her radiant hair, which warmed and lighted it as though it were the light of Freedom shining on him.

"If you hear in my voice—I don't know that it is so, but I hope it is—if you hear in my voice any resemblance to a voice that once was sweet music in your ears, weep for it, weep for it! If you touch, in touching my hair, anything that recalls a beloved head that lay in your breast when you were young and free, weep for it, weep for it! If, when I hint to you of a home there is before us, where I will be true to you with all my duty and with all my faithful service, I bring back the remembrance of a home long desolate, while your poor heart pined away, weep for it, weep for it!"

She held him closer round the neck, and rocked him on her breast like a child.

"If, when I tell you, dearest dear, that your agony is over, and that I have come here to take you from it, and that we go to England to be at peace and at rest, I cause you to think of your useful life laid waste, and of our native France so wicked to you, weep for it, weep for it! And if, when I shall tell you of my name, and of my father who is living, and of my mother who is dead, you learn that I have to kneel to my honored father, and implore his pardon for having never for his sake striven all day, and lain awake and wept all night, because the love of my poor mother hid his torture from me, weep for it, weep for it! Weep for her then, and for me! Good gentlemen, thank God! I feel his sacred tears upon my face, and his sobs strike against my heart. O, see! Thank God for us, thank God!"

He had sunk in her arms, with his face dropped on her breast: a sight so touching, yet so terrible in the tremendous wrong and suffering which had gone before it, that the two beholders covered their faces.

When the quiet of the garret had been long undisturbed, and his heaving breast and shaken form had long yielded to the calm that must follow all storms—emblem to humanity, of the rest and silence into which the storm called Life must hush at last—they came forward to raise the father and daughter from the ground. He had gradually dropped to the floor, and lay there in a lethargy, worn out. She had nestled down with him, that his head might lie upon her arm; and her hair drooping over him curtained him from the light.

"If, without disturbing him," she said, raising her hand to Mr. Lorry as he stooped over them, after repeated blowings of his nose, "all could be arranged for our leaving Paris at once, so that, from the very door, he could be taken away—"

"But, consider. Is he fit for the journey?" asked Mr. Lorry.

"More fit for that, I think, than to remain in this city, so dreadful to him."

"It is true," said Defarge, who was kneeling to look on and hear. "More than that; Monsieur Manette is, for all reasons, best out of France. Say, shall I hire a carriage and post-horses?"

"That's business," said Mr. Lorry, resuming on the shortest notice his methodical manners; "and if business is to be done, I had better do it."

"Then be so kind," urged Miss Manette, "as to leave us here. You see how composed he has become, and you cannot be afraid to leave him with me now. Why should you be? If you will lock the door, to secure us from interruption, I do not doubt that you will find him, when you come back, as quiet as you leave him. In any case, I will take care of him until you return, and then we will remove him straight."

Both Mr. Lorry and Defarge were rather disinclined to this course, and in favor of one of them remaining. But, as there were not only carriages and horses to be seen to, but traveling papers; and as time pressed, for the day was drawing to an end, it came at last to their hastily dividing the business that was necessary to be done, and hurrying away to do it.

Then, as the darkness closed in, the daughter laid her head down on the hard ground close at the father's side, and watched him. The darkness deepened and deepened, and they both lay quiet, until a light gleamed through the chinks in the wall.

Mr. Lorry and Monsieur Defarge had made all ready for the journey, and brought with them, besides traveling cloaks and wrappers, bread and meat, wine, and hot coffee. Monsieur Defarge put this provender, and the lamp he carried, on the shoemaker's bench (there was nothing else in the garret but a pallet bed), and he and Mr. Lorry roused the captive, and assisted him to his feet.

No human intelligence could have read the mysteries of his mind, in the scared blank wonder of his face. Whether he knew what had happened, whether he recollected what they had said to him, whether he knew that he was free, were questions which no sagacity could have solved. They tried speaking to him; but he was so confused, and so very slow to answer, that they took fright at his bewilderment, and agreed for the time to tamper with him no more. He had a wild, lost manner of occasionally clasping his head in his hands, that had not been seen in him before; yet, he had some pleasure in the mere sound of his daughter's voice, and invariably turned to it when she spoke.

In the submissive way of one long accustomed to obey under coercion, he ate and drank what they gave him to eat and drink, and put on the cloak and other wrappings that they gave him to wear. He readily responded to his daughter's drawing her arm through his, and took—and kept—her hand in both his own.

They began to descend; Monsieur Defarge going first with the lamp, Mr. Lorry closing the little procession. They had not traversed many steps of the long main staircase when he stopped, and stared at the roof and round at the walls.

"You remember the place, my father? You remember coming up here?"

"What did you say?"

But, before she could repeat the question, he murmured an answer as if she had repeated it.

"Remember? No, I don't remember. It was so very long ago."

That he had no recollection whatever of his having been brought from his prison to that house, was apparent to them. They heard him mutter, "One Hundred and Five, North Tower"; and when he looked about him, it evidently was for the strong fortress-walls which had long encompassed him. On their reaching the courtyard, he instinctively altered his tread, as being in expectation of a drawbridge; and when there was no drawbridge, and he saw the carriage waiting in the open street, he dropped his daughter's hand, and clasped his head again.

No crowd was about the door; no people were discernible at any of the many windows; not even a chance passer-by was in the street. An unnatural silence and desertion reigned there. Only one soul was to be seen, and that was Madame Defarge—who leaned against the door-post, knitting, and saw nothing.

The prisoner had got into the coach, and his daughter had followed him, when Mr. Lorry's feet were arrested on the step by his asking, miserably, for his shoemaking tools and the unfinished shoes. Madame Defarge immediately called to her husband that she would get them, and went, knitting, out of the lamplight, through the courtyard. She quickly brought them down and handed them in; and immediately afterward leaned against the door-post, knitting, and saw nothing.

Defarge got upon the box, and gave the word "To the Barrier!" The postilion cracked his whip, and they clattered away under the feeble over-swinging lamps.

Under the over-swinging lamps—swinging ever brighter in the better streets, and ever dimmer in the worse—and by lighted shops, gay crowds, illuminated coffeehouses, and theater doors, to one of the city gates. Soldiers with lanterns, at the guardhouse there. "Your papers, travelers!" "See here then, Monsieur the Officer," said Defarge, getting down, and taking him gravely apart, "these are the papers of monsieur inside, with the white head. They were consigned to me, with him, at the—." He dropped his voice, there was a flutter among the military lanterns, and one of them being handed into the coach by an arm in uniform, the eyes connected with the arm looked, not an every-day or an every-night look, at monsieur with the white head. "It is well. Forward!" from the uniform. "Adieu!" from Defarge. And so, under a short grove of feebler and feebler over-swinging lamps, out under the great grove of stars.

Beneath that arch of unmoved and eternal lights; some, so remote from this little earth, that the learned tell us it is doubtful whether their rays have even yet discovered it, as a point in space where anything is suffered or done: the shadows of the night were broad and black. All through the cold and restless interval until dawn, they once more whispered in the ears of Mr. Jarvis Lorry—sitting opposite the buried man who had been dug out, and wondering what subtle powers were forever lost to him, and what were capable of restoration—the old inquiry:

"I hope you care to be recalled to life?"

And the old answer:

"I can't say."

THE GOLDEN THREAD

One

FIVE YEARS LATER

Tellson's Bank by Temple-bar was an old-fashioned place, even in the year one thousand seven hundred and eighty. It was very small, very dark, very ugly, very incommodious. It was an old-fashioned place, moreover, in the moral attribute that the partners in the House were proud of its smallness, proud of its darkness, proud of its ugliness, proud of its incommodiousness. They were even boastful of its eminence in those particulars, and were fired by an express conviction that, if it were less objectionable, it would be less respectable. This was no passive belief, but an active weapon which they flashed at more convenient places of business. Tellson's (they said) wanted no elbow-room, Tellson's wanted no light, Tellson's wanted no embellishment. Noakes and Co.'s might, or Snooks Brothers' might; but Tellson's, thank Heaven!—

Any one of these partners would have disinherited his son on the question of rebuilding Tellson's. In this respect the house was much on a par with the country; which did very often disinherit its sons for suggesting improvements in laws and customs that had long been highly objectionable, but were only the more respectable.

Thus it had come to pass, that Tellson's was the triumphant perfection of inconvenience. After bursting open a door of idiotic obstinacy with a weak rattle in its throat, you fell into Tellson's down two steps, and came to your senses in a miserable little shop, with two little counters, where the oldest of men made your check shake as if the wind rustled it, while they examined the signature by the dingiest of windows, which were always under a shower-bath of mud from Fleet Street, and which were made the dingier by their own iron bars proper, and the heavy shadow of Temple-bar. If your business necessitated your seeing "the House," you were put into a species of Condemned Hold at the Back, where you meditated on a misspent life, until the House came with its hands in its pockets, and you could hardly blink at it in the dismal twilight.

Your money came out of, or went into, wormy old wooden drawers, particles of which flew up your nose and down your throat when they were opened and shut. Your bank-notes had a musty odor, as if they were fast decomposing into rags again. Your plate was stowed away among the neighboring cesspools, and evil communications corrupted its good polish in a day or two. Your deeds got into extemporised strong-rooms made of kitchen and sculleries, and fretted all the fat out of their parchments into the banking-house air. Your lighter boxes of family papers went upstairs into a Barmecide room, that had always a great dining-table in it and never had a dinner, and where, even in the year one thousand seven hundred and eighty, the first letters written to you by your old love, or by your little children, were but newly released from the horror of being ogled through the windows by the heads exposed on Temple-bar with an insensate brutality and ferocity worthy of Abyssinia or Ashantee.

But, indeed, at that time, putting to Death was a recipe much in vogue with all trades and professions, and not least of all with Tellson's. Death is Nature's remedy for all things, and why not Legislation's? Accordingly the forger was put to Death; the utterer of a bad note was put to Death; the unlawful opener of a letter was put to Death; the purloiner of forty shillings and sixpence was put to Death; the holder of a horse at Tellson's door, who made off with it, was put to Death; the coiner of a bad shilling was put to Death; the sounders of three-fourths of the notes in the whole gamut of Crime, were put to Death. Not that it did the least good in the way of prevention—it might almost have been worth remarking that the fact was exactly the reverse—but, it cleared off (as to this world) the trouble of each particular case, and left nothing else connected with it to be looked after. Thus, Tellson's, in its day, like greater places of business, its contemporaries, had taken so many lives, that, if the heads laid low before it had been ranged on Temple-bar instead of being privately disposed of, they would probably have excluded what little light the ground floor had, in a rather significant manner.

Cramped in all kinds of dim cupboards and hutches at Tellson's the oldest of men carried on the business gravely. When they took a young man into Tellson's London house, they hid him somewhere till he was old. They kept him in a dark place, like a cheese, until he had the full Tellson flavor and blue-mold upon him. Then only was he permitted to be seen, spectacularly poring over large books, and casting his breeches and gaiters into the general weight of the establishment.

Outside Tellson's—never by any means in it, unless called in—was an odd-job-man, an occasional porter and messenger, who served as the live sign of the house. He was never absent during business hours, unless upon an errand, and then he was represented by his son; a grisly urchin of twelve, who was his express image. People understood that Tellson's, in a stately way, tolerated the odd-job-man. The house had always tolerated some person in that capacity, and time and tide had drifted this person to the post. His surname was Cruncher, and on the youthful occasion of his renouncing by proxy the works of darkness, in the easterly parish church of Hounsditch, he had received the added appellation of Jerry.

The scene was Mr. Cruncher's private lodging in Hangingsword Alley, Whitefriars; the time, half-past seven of the clock on a windy March morning, Anno Domini, seventeen hundred and eighty. (Mr. Cruncher himself always spoke of the year of our Lord as Anna Dominoes; apparently under the impression that the Christian era dated from the invention of a popular game, by a lady who had bestowed her name upon it.)

Mr. Cruncher's apartments were not in a savory neighborhood, and were but two in number, even if a closet with a single pane of glass in it might be accounted as one. But, they were very decently kept. Early as it was, on the windy March morning, the room in which he lay a-bed was already scrubbed throughout; and between the cups and saucers arranged for breakfast, and the lumbering deal table, a very clean, white cloth was spread.

Mr. Cruncher reposed under a patchwork counterpane, like a Harlequin at home. At first, he slept heavily, but by degrees, began to roll and surge in bed, until he rose above the surface, with his spiky hair looking as if it must tear the sheets to ribbons. At which juncture, he exclaimed, in a voice of dire exasperation:

"Bust me, if she ain't at it agin!"

A woman of orderly and industrious appearance rose from her knees in a corner, with sufficient haste and trepidation to show that she was the person referred to.

"What!" said Mr. Cruncher, looking out of bed for a boot. "You're at it agin, are you?"

After hailing the morn with this second salutation, he threw a boot at the woman as a third. It was a very muddy boot, and may introduce the odd circumstance connected with Mr. Cruncher's domestic economy, that, whereas he often came home after banking hours with clean boots, he often got up next morning to find the same boots covered with clay.

"What," said Mr. Cruncher, varying his apostrophe after missing his mark— "what are you up to Aggerawayter?"

"I was only saying my prayers."

"Saying your prayers! You're a nice woman! What do you mean by flopping yourself down and praying agin me?"

"I was not praying against you; I was praying for you."

"You weren't. And if you were, I won't be took the liberty with. Here! your mother's a nice woman, young Jerry, going a praying agin your father's prosperity. You've got a dutiful mother, you have, my son. You've got a religious mother, you have, my boy: going and flopping herself down, and praying that the bread-and-butter may be snatched out of the mouth of her only child!"

Master Cruncher (who was in his shirt) took this very ill, and, turning to his mother, strongly deprecated any praying away of his personal board.

"And what do you suppose, you conceited female," said Mr. Cruncher, with unconscious inconsistency, "that the worth of *your* prayers may be? Name the price that you put *your* prayers at!"

"They only come from the heart, Jerry. They are worth no more than that."

"Worth no more than that," repeated Mr. Cruncher. "They ain't worth much, then. Whether or no, I won't be prayed agin, I tell you. I can't afford it. I'm not a going to be made unlucky by *your* sneaking. If you must go flopping yourself down, flop in favor of your husband and child, and not in opposition to 'em. If I had had any but a unnat'ral wife, and this poor boy had had any but a unnat'ral mother, I might have made some money last week, instead of being counterprayed and countermined and being religiously circumwented into the worst of luck. Bu-u-ust me!" said Mr. Cruncher, who all this time had been putting on his clothes, "if I ain't, what with piety and one blowed thing and another, been choused this last week into as bad luck as ever a poor devil of a honest tradesman met with! Young Jerry, dress yourself, my boy, and while I clean my boots keep a eye upon your mother now and then, and if you see any signs of more flopping, give me a call. For, I tell you," here he addressed his wife once more, "I won't be gone agin in this manner. I am as rickety as a hackney-coach. I'm as sleepy as laudanum, my lines is strained to that degree that I shouldn't know, if it wasn't for the pain in 'em, which was me and which somebody else, yet I'm none the better for it in pocket; and it's my suspicion that you've been at it from morning to night to prevent me from being the better for it in pocket; and I won't put up with it, Aggerawayter, and what do you say now!"

Growling, in addition, such phrases as "Ah! yes! You're religious, too. You wouldn't put yourself in opposition to the interests of your husband and child, would you? Not you!" and throwing off other sarcastic sparks from the whirling grindstone of his indignation, Mr. Cruncher betook himself to his boot-cleaning and his general preparations for business. In the meantime, his son, whose head was garnished with tenderer spikes, and whose young eyes stood close by one another, as his father's did, kept the required watch upon his mother. He greatly disturbed that poor woman at intervals, by darting out of his sleeping-closet, where he made his toilet, with a suppressed cry of "You are going to flop, mother. Halloa, father!" and, after raising this fictitious alarm, darting in again with an undutiful grin.

Mr. Cruncher's temper was not at all improved when he came to his breakfast. He resented Mrs. Cruncher's saying grace with particular animosity.

"Now, Aggerawayter! What are you up to? At it agin?"

His wife explained that she had merely "asked a blessing."

"Don't do it!" said Mr. Cruncher, looking about, as if he rather expected to see the loaf disappear under the efficacy of his wife's petitions. "I ain't a going to be blest out of house and home. I won't have my wittles blest off my table. Keep still!"

Exceedingly red-eyed and grim, as if he had been up all night at a party which had taken anything but a convivial turn, Jerry Cruncher worried his breakfast rather than ate it, growling over it like any four-footed inmate of a menagerie. Toward nine o'clock he smoothed his ruffled aspect, and, presenting as respectful and businesslike an exterior as he could overlay his natural self with, issued forth to the occupation of the day.

It could scarcely be called a trade, in spite of his favorite description of himself as "a honest tradesman." His stock consisted of a wooden stool, made out of a broken-backed chair cut down, which stool Young Jerry, walking at his father's side, carried every morning to beneath the banking-house window that was nearest Temple-bar: where, with the addition of the first handful of straw that could be gleaned from any passing vehicle to keep the cold and wet from the odd-job-man's feet, it formed the encampment for the day. On this post of his, Mr. Cruncher was as well known to Fleet Street and the Temple, as the Bar itself—and was almost as ill-looking.

Encamped at a quarter before nine, in good time to touch his three-cornered hat to the oldest of men as they passed in to Tellson's, Jerry took up his station on this windy March morning, with young Jerry standing by him, when not engaged in making forays through the Bar, to inflict bodily and mental injuries of an acute description on passing boys who were small enough for his amiable purpose. Father and son, extremely like each other, looking silently on at the morning traffic in Fleet Street, with their two heads as near to one another as the two eyes of each were, bore a considerable resemblance to a pair of monkeys. The resemblance was not lessened by the accidental circumstance, that the mature Jerry bit and spat out straw, while the twinkling eyes of the youthful Jerry were as restlessly watchful of him as of everything else in Fleet Street.

The head of one of the regular indoor messengers attached to Tellson's establishment was put through the door, and the word was given:

"Porter wanted!"

"Hooray, father! Here's an early job to begin with!"

Having thus given his parent Godspeed, Young Jerry seated himself on the stool, entered on his reversionary interest in the straw his father had been chewing, and cogitated.

"Al-ways rusty! His fingers is al-ways rusty!" muttered Young Jerry. "Where does my father get all that iron rust from? He don't get no iron rust here!"

T w o

A SIGHT

"Y OU KNOW THE OLD BAILEY WELL, NO DOUBT?" SAID ONE OF the oldest of clerks to Jerry the messenger.

"Ye-es, sir," returned Jerry, in something of a dogged manner. "I *do* know the Bailey."

"Just so. And you know Mr. Lorry."

"I know Mr. Lorry, sir, much better than I know the Bailey. Much better," said Jerry, not unlike a reluctant witness at the establishment in question, "than I, as a honest tradesman, wish to know the Bailey."

"Very well. Find the door where the witnesses go in, and show the door-keeper this note for Mr. Lorry. He will then let you in."

"Into the court, sir?"

"Into the court."

Mr. Cruncher's eyes seemed to get a little closer to one another, and to interchange the inquiry, "What do you think of this?"

"Am I to wait in the court, sir?" he asked, as the result of that conference.

"I am going to tell you. The doorkeeper will pass the note to Mr. Lorry, and do you make any gesture that will attract Mr. Lorry's attention, and show him where you stand. Then what you have to do, is, to remain there until he wants you."

"Is that all, sir?"

"That's all. He wishes to have a messenger at hand. This is to tell him you are there."

As the ancient clerk deliberately folded and superscribed the note, Mr. Cruncher, after surveying him in silence until he came to the blotting-paper stage, remarked:

"I suppose they'll be trying forgeries this morning?"

"Treason!"

"That's quartering," said Jerry. "Barbarous!"

"It is the law," remarked the ancient clerk, turning his surprised spectacles upon him. "It is the law!"

"It's hard in the law to spile a man, I think. It's hard enough to kill him,
but it's very hard to spile him, sir."

"Not at all," returned the ancient clerk. "Speak well of the law. Take care
of your chest and voice, my good friend, and leave the law to take care of
itself. I give you that advice."

"It's the damp, sir, what settles on my chest and voice," said Jerry. "I leave
you to judge what a damp way of earning a living mine is."

"Well, well," said the old clerk; "We all have our various ways of gaining
a livelihood. Some of us have damp ways, and some of us have dry ways. Here
is the letter. Go along."

Jerry took the letter, and, remarking to himself with less internal deference than he made an outward show of, "You are a lean old one, too," made
his bow, informed his son in passing of his destination, and went his way.

They hanged at Tyburn, in those days, so the street outside Newgate had
not obtained one infamous notoriety that has since attached to it. But the
gaol was a vile place, in which most kinds of debauchery and villainy were
practiced, and where dire diseases were bred, that came into court with the
prisoners, and sometimes rushed straight from the dock at my Lord Chief
Justice himself, and pulled him off the bench. It had more than once happened, that the Judge in the black cap pronounced his own doom as certainly
as the prisoner's, and even died before him. For the rest, the Old Bailey was
famous as a kind of deadly inn-yard, from which pale travelers set out continually, in carts and coaches, on a violent passage into the other world:
traversing some two miles and a half of public street and road, and shaming
few good citizens, if any. So powerful is use, and so desirable to be good use
in the beginning. It was famous, too, for the pillory, a wise old institution,
that inflicted a punishment of which no one could foresee the extent; also, for
the whipping-post, another dear old institution, very humanizing and softening to behold in action; also, for extensive transactions in blood-money,
another fragment of ancestral wisdom, systematically leading to the most
frightful mercenary crimes that could be committed under Heaven. Altogether, the Old Bailey, at that date, was a choice illustration of the precept
that "Whatever is is right"; an aphorism that would be as final as it is lazy, did
it not include the troublesome consequence, that nothing that ever was, was
wrong.

Making his way through the tainted crowd, dispersed up and down this
hideous scene of action, with the skill of a man accustomed to make his way
quietly, the messenger found out the door he sought, and handed in his letter through a trap in it. For people then paid to see the play at the Old Bai-

ley, just as they paid to see the play in Bedlam—only the former entertainment was much the dearer. Therefore, all the Old Bailey doors were well guarded—except, indeed, the social doors by which the criminals got there, and they were always left wide open.

After some delay and demur, the door grudgingly turned on its hinges a very little way, and allowed Mr. Jerry Cruncher so to squeeze himself into court.

"What's on?" he asked, in a whisper, of the man he found himself next to.

"Nothing yet."

"What's coming on?"

"The Treason case."

"The quartering one, eh?"

"Ah!" returned the man, with a relish; "he'll be drawn on a hurdle to be half-hanged, and then he'll be taken down and sliced before his own face, and then his inside will be taken out and burnt while he looks on, and then his head will be chopped off, and he'll be cut into quarters. That's the sentence."

"If he's found Guilty, you mean to say?" Jerry added, by way of proviso.

"Oh! they'll find him Guilty," said the other. "Don't you be afraid of that."

Mr. Cruncher's attention was here diverted to the doorkeeper, whom he saw making his way to Mr. Lorry, with the note in his hand. Mr. Lorry sat at a table, among the gentlemen in wigs: not far from a wigged gentleman, the prisoner's counsel, who had a great bundle of papers before him: and nearly opposite another wigged gentleman with his hands in his pockets, whose whole attention, when Mr. Cruncher looked at him then or afterward, seemed to be concentrated on the ceiling of the court. After some gruff coughing and rubbing of his chin and signing with his hand, Jerry attracted the notice of Mr. Lorry, who had stood up to look for him, and who quietly nodded, and sat down again.

"What's *he* got to do with this case?" asked the man he had spoken with.

"Blest if I know," said Jerry.

"What have *you* to do with it, then, if a person may inquire?"

"Blest if I know that either," said Jerry.

The entrance of the Judge, and a consequent great stir and settling-down in the court, stopped the dialogue. Presently, the dock became the central point of interest. Two gaolers, who had been standing there, went out, and the prisoner was brought in, and put to the bar.

Everybody present, except the one wigged gentleman who looked at the ceiling, stared at him. All the human breath in the place rolled at him, like a sea, or a wind, or a fire. Eager faces strained round pillars and corners, to get a sight of him; spectators in back rows stood up, not to miss a hair of him; people on the floor of the court, laid their hands on the shoulders of the people before them, to help themselves, at anybody's cost, to a view of him—stood a-tiptoe, got upon ledges, stood upon next to nothing, to see every inch of him. Conspicuous among these latter, like an animated bit of the spiked wall of Newgate, Jerry stood; aiming at the prisoner the beery breath of a whet he had taken as he came along, and discharging it to mingle with the waves of other beer, and gin, and tea, and coffee, and what not, that flowed at him, and already broke upon the great windows behind him in an impure mist and rain.

The object of all this staring and blaring, was a young man of about five-and-twenty, well-grown and well-looking, with a sunburnt cheek and a dark eye. His condition was that of a young gentleman. He was plainly dressed in black, or very dark gray, and his hair, which was long and dark, was gathered in a ribbon at the back of his neck: more to be out of his way than for orna-ment. As an emotion of the mind will express itself through any covering of the body, so the paleness which his situation engendered came through the brown upon his cheek, showing the soul to be stronger than the sun. He was otherwise quite self-possessed, bowed to the judge, and stood quiet.

The sort of interest with which this man was stared and breathed at, was not a sort that elevated humanity. Had he stood in peril of a less horrible sen-tence—had there been a chance of any one of its savage details being spared—by just so much would he have lost in his fascination. The form that was to be doomed to be so shamefully mangled, was the sight; the immortal creature that was to be so butchered and torn asunder, yielded the sensation. Whatever gloss the various spectators put upon the interest, according to their several arts and powers of self-deceit, the interest was, at the root of it, ogreish.

Silence in the court! Charles Darnay had yesterday pleaded Not Guilty to an indictment denouncing him (with infinite jingle and jangle) for that he was a false traitor to our serene, illustrious, excellent and so forth, prince, our Lord the King, by reason of his having, on divers occasions, and by divers means and ways, assisted Lewis, the French king, in his wars against our said serene, illustrious, excellent, and so forth; that was to say, by coming and going between the dominions of our said serene, illustrious, excellent, and so forth, and those of the said French Lewis, and wickedly, falsely, traitorously, and otherwise evil-adverbiously, revealing to the said French Lewis what forces our said serene, illustrious, excellent, and so forth, had in preparation to send to Canada and North America. This much, Jerry, with his head becoming more and more spiky as the law terms bristled it, made out with huge satisfaction, and so arrived circuitously at the understanding that the aforesaid, and over and over again aforesaid Charles Darnay, stood there before him upon his trial; that the jury were swearing in; and that Mr. Attorney-General was making ready to speak.

The accused, who was, (and who knew he was) being mentally hanged, beheaded, and quartered, by everybody there, neither flinched from the situ-ation, nor assumed any theatrical air in it. He was quiet and attentive; watched the opening proceedings with a grave interest; and stood with his hands resting on the slab of wood before him, so composedly, that they had not displaced a leaf of the herbs with which it was strewn. The court was all bestrewn with herbs and sprinkled with vinegar, as a precaution against gaol air and gaol fever.

Over the prisoner's head, there was a mirror, to throw the light down upon him. Crowds of the wicked and the wretched had been reflected in it, and had passed from its surface and from the earth's together. Haunted in a most ghastly manner that abominable place would have been, if the glass could ever have rendered back its reflections, as the ocean is one day to give up its dead. Some passing thought of the infamy and disgrace for which it had been reserved, may have struck the prisoner's mind. Be that as it may, a change in his position, making him conscious of a bar of light across his face, he looked up; and when he saw the glass his face flushed, and his right hand pushed the herbs away.

It happened, that the action turned his face to that side of the court which was on his left. About on a level with his eyes, there sat, in that corner of the Judge's bench, two persons upon whom his look immediately rested; so immediately, and so much to the changing of his aspect, that all the eyes that were turned upon him, turned to them.

The spectators saw in the two figures, a young lady of little more than twenty, and a gentleman who was evidently her father; a man of a very remarkable appearance in respect of the absolute whiteness of his hair, and a certain indescribable intensity of face: not of an active kind, but pondering and self-communing. When this expression was upon him, he looked as if he were old; but, when it was stirred and broken up—as it was now, in a moment, on his speaking to his daughter—he became a handsome man, not past the prime of life.

His daughter had one of her hands drawn through his arm, as she sat by him, and the other pressed upon it. She had drawn close to him, in her dread of the scene, and in her pity for the prisoner. Her forehead had been strikingly expressive of an engrossing terror and compassion that saw nothing but the peril of the accused. This had been so very noticeable, so very powerfully and naturally shown, that starers who had had no pity for him were touched by her; and the whisper went about, "Who are they?"

Jerry, the messenger, who had made his own observations in his own manner, and who had been sucking the rust off his fingers in his absorption, stretched his neck to hear who they were. The crowd about him had pressed and passed the inquiry on to the nearest attendant, and from him it had been more slowly pressed and passed back; at last it got to Jerry.

"Witnesses."

"For which side?"

"Against."

"Against what side?"

"The prisoner's."

The Judge, whose eyes had gone in the general direction, recalled them, leaned back in his seat, and looked steadily at the man whose life was in his hand, as Mr. Attorney-General rose to spin the rope, grind the axe, and hammer the nails into the scaffold.

Three

A DISAPPOINTMENT

M R. ATTORNEY-GENERAL HAD TO INFORM THE JURY, THAT the prisoner before them, though young in years, was old in the treasonable practices which claimed the forfeit of his life. That this correspondence with the public enemy was not a correspondence of today, or of yesterday, or even of last year, or of the year before. That it was certain the prisoner had, for longer than that, been in the habit of passing and repassing between France and England, on secret business of which he could give no honest account. That, if it were in the nature of traitorous ways to thrive (which, happily, it never was), the real wickedness and guilt of his business might have remained undiscovered. That, Providence, however, had put it into the heart of a person who was beyond fear and beyond reproach, to ferret out the nature of the prisoner's schemes, and, struck with horror, to disclose them to his Majesty's Chief Secretary of State and most honorable Privy Council. That this patriot would be produced before them. That, his position and attitude were, on the whole, sublime. That, he had been the prisoner's friend, but, at once in an auspicious and an evil hour detecting his infamy, had resolved to immolate the traitor he could no longer cherish in his bosom, on the sacred altar of his country. That, if statues were decreed in Britain, as in ancient Greece and Rome, to public benefactors, this shining citizen would assuredly have had one. That, as they were not so decreed, he probably would not have one. That, Virtue, as had been observed by the poets (in many passages which he well knew the jury would have, word for word, at the tips of their tongues; whereat the jury's countenances displayed a guilty consciousness that they knew nothing about the passages), was in a manner contagious; more especially the bright virtue known as patriotism, or love of country. That, the lofty example of this immaculate and unimpeachable witness for the Crown, to refer to whom, however unworthily, was an honor, had communicated itself to the prisoner's servant, and had engendered in him a holy determination to examine his master's table-drawers and pockets, and secrete his papers. That, he (Mr. Attorney-General) was prepared to hear some disparagement attempted of this admirable servant; but that, in a general way, he preferred him to his (Mr. Attorney-General's) brothers and sisters, and honored him more than his (Mr. Attorney-General's) father and mother. That, he called with confidence on the jury to come and do likewise. That, the evidence of these two witnesses, coupled with the documents of their discovering that would be produced, would show the prisoner to have been furnished with lists of his Majesty's forces, and of their disposition and preparation, both by sea and land, and would leave no doubt that he had habitually conveyed such information to a hostile power. That, these lists could not be proved to be in the prisoner's handwriting; but that it was all the same; that, indeed, it was rather the better for the prosecution, as showing the prisoner to be artful in his precautions. That, the proof would go back five years, and would show the prisoner already engaged in these pernicious missions, within a few weeks before the date of the very first action fought between the British troops and the Americans. That, for these reasons, the jury, being a loyal jury (as he knew they were), and being a responsible jury (as *they* knew they were), must positively find the prisoner guilty, and make an end of him, whether they liked it or not. That, they never could lay their heads upon their pillows; that, they never could tolerate the idea of their wives laying their heads upon their pillows; that, they never could endure the notion of their children laying their heads upon their pillows; in short, that there never more could be, for them or theirs, any laying of heads upon pillows at all, unless the prisoner's head was taken off. That head Mr. Attorney-General concluded by demanding of them, in the name of everything he could think of with a round turn in it, and on the faith of his solemn asseveration that he already considered the prisoner as good as dead and gone.

When the Attorney-General ceased, a buzz arose in the court as if a cloud of great blue-flies were swarming about the prisoner, in anticipation of what he was soon to become. When toned down again, the unimpeachable patriot appeared in the witness-box.

Mr. Solicitor-General then, following his leader's lead, examined the patriot: John Barsad, gentleman, by name. The story of his pure soul was exactly what Mr. Attorney-General had described it to be—perhaps, if it had a fault, a little too exactly. Having released his noble bosom of its burden, he would have modestly withdrawn himself, but that the wigged gentleman with the papers before him, sitting not far from Mr. Lorry, begged to ask him a few questions. The wigged gentleman sitting opposite, still looked at the ceiling of the court.

Had he ever been a spy himself? No, he scorned the base insinuation. What did he live upon? His property. Where was his property? He didn't precisely remember where it was. What was it? No business of anybody's. Had he inherited it? Yes, he had. From whom? Distant relation? Very distant? Rather. Ever been in prison? Certainly not. Never in a debtors' prison?

Didn't see what that had to do with it. Never in a debtors' prison? Come, once again. Never? Yes. How many times? Two or three times. Not five or six? Perhaps. Of what profession? Gentleman. Ever been kicked? Might have been. Frequently? No. Ever kicked down stairs? Decidedly not; once received a kick on the top of a staircase, and fell down stairs of his own accord. Kicked on that occasion for cheating at dice? Something to that effect was said by the intoxicated liar who committed the assault, but it was not true. Swear it was not true? Positively. Ever live by cheating at play? Never. Ever live by play? Not more than other gentlemen do. Ever borrow money of the prisoner? Yes. Ever pay him? No. Was not this intimacy with the prisoner, in reality a very slight one, forced upon the prisoner in coaches, inns, and packets? No. Sure he saw the prisoner with these lists? Certain. Knew no more about the lists? No. Had not procured them himself, for instance? No. Expect to get anything by this evidence? No. Not in regular government pay and employment, to lay traps? Oh dear, no. Or to do anything? Oh dear, no. Swear that? Over and over again. No motives but motives of sheer patriotism? None whatever.

The virtuous servant, Roger Cly, swore his way through the case at a great rate. He had taken service with the prisoner, in good faith and simplicity, four years ago. He had asked the prisoner, aboard the Calais packet, if he wanted a handy fellow, and the prisoner had engaged him. He had not asked the prisoner to take the handy fellow as an act of charity—never thought of such a thing. He began to have suspicions of the prisoner, and to keep an eye upon him soon afterward. In arranging his clothes, while traveling, he had seen similar lists to these in the prisoner's pockets, over and over again. He had taken these lists from the drawer of the prisoner's desk. He had not put them there first. He had seen the prisoner show these identical lists to French gentlemen at Calais, and similar lists to French gentlemen, both at Calais and Boulogne. He loved his country, and couldn't bear it, and had given information. He had never been suspected of stealing a silver teapot; he had been maligned respecting a mustard-pot, but it turned out to be only a plated one. He had known the last witness seven or eight years; that was merely a coincidence. He didn't call it a particularly curious coincidence; most coincidences were curious. Neither did he call it a curious coincidence that true patriotism was *his* only motive too. He was a true Briton, and hoped there were many like him.

The blue-flies buzzed again, and Mr. Attorney-General called Mr. Jarvis Lorry.

"Mr. Jarvis Lorry, are you a clerk in Tellson's Bank?"

"I am."

"On a certain Friday night in November one thousand seven hundred and seventy-five, did business occasion you to travel between London and Dover by the mail?"

"It did."

"Were there any other passengers in the mail?"

"Two."

"Did they alight on the road in the course of the night?"

"They did."

"Mr. Lorry, look upon the prisoner. Was he one of those two passengers?"

"I cannot undertake to say that he was."

"Does he resemble either of these two passengers?"

"Both were so wrapped up, and the night was so dark, and we were all so reserved, that I cannot undertake to say even that."

"Mr. Lorry, look again upon the prisoner. Supposing him wrapped up as those two passengers were, is there anything in his bulk and stature to render it unlikely that he was one of them?"

"No."

"You will not swear, Mr. Lorry, that he was not one of them?"

"No."

"So at least you say he may have been one of them?"

"Yes. Except that I remember them both to have been—like myself—timorous of highwaymen, and the prisoner has not a timorous air."

"Did you ever see a counterfeit of timidity, Mr. Lorry?"

"I certainly have seen that."

"Mr. Lorry, look once more upon the prisoner. Have you seen him, to your certain knowledge, before?"

"I have."

"When?"

"I was returning from France a few days afterward, and, at Calais, the prisoner came on board the packet-ship in which I returned, and made the voyage with me."

"At what hour did he come on board?"

"At a little after midnight."

"In the dead of the night. Was he the only passenger who came on board at that untimely hour?"

"He happened to be the only one."

"Never mind about 'happening,' Mr. Lorry. He was the only passenger who came on board in the dead of the night?"

"He was."

"Were you traveling alone, Mr. Lorry, or with any companion?"

"With two companions. A gentleman and lady. They are here."

"They are here. Had you any conversation with the prisoner?"

"Hardly any. The weather was stormy, and the passage long and rough, and I lay on a sofa, almost from shore to shore."

"Miss Manette!"

The young lady, to whom all eyes had been turned before, and were now turned again, stood up where she had sat. Her father rose with her, and kept her hand drawn through his arm.

"Miss Manette, look upon the prisoner."

To be confronted with such pity, and such earnest youth and beauty, was far more trying to the accused than to be confronted with all the crowd. Standing, as it were, apart with her on the edge of his grave, not all the staring curiosity that looked on, could, for the moment, nerve him to remain quite still. His hurried right hand parceled out the herbs before him into imaginary beds of flowers in a garden; and his efforts to control and steady his breathing, shook the lips from which the color rushed to his heart. The buzz of the great flies was loud again.

"Miss Manette, have you seen the prisoner before?"

"Yes, sir."

"Where?"

"On board of the packet-ship just now referred to, sir, and on the same occasion."

"You are the young lady just now referred to?"

"O! most unhappily, I am!"

The plaintive tone of her compassion merged into the less musical voice of the Judge, as he said, something fiercely: "Answer the questions put to you, and make no remark upon them."

"Miss Manette, had you any conversation with the prisoner on that passage across the Channel?"

"Yes, sir."

"Recall it."

In the midst of a profound stillness, she faintly began.

"When the gentleman came on board—"

"Do you mean the prisoner?" inquired the Judge, knitting his brows.

"Yes, my Lord."

"Then say the prisoner."

"When the prisoner came on board, he noticed that my father," turning her eyes lovingly to him as he stood beside her, "was much fatigued and in a very weak state of health. My father was so reduced, that I was afraid to take him out of the air, and I had made a bed for him on the deck near the cabin steps, and I sat on the deck at his side to take care of him. There were no other passengers that night, but we four. The prisoner was so good as to beg permission to advise me how I could shelter my father from the wind and weather, better than I had done. I had not known how to do it well, not understanding how the wind would set when we were out of the harbor. He did it for me. He expressed great gentleness and kindness for my father's state, and I am sure he felt it. That was the manner of our beginning to speak together."

"Let me interrupt you for a moment. Had he come on board alone?"

"No."

"How many were with him?"

"Two French gentlemen."

"Had they conferred together?"

"They had conferred together until the last moment, when it was necessary for the French gentlemen to be landed in their boat."

"Had any papers been handed about among them, similar to these lists?"

"Some papers had been handed about among them, but I don't know what papers."

"Like these in shape and size?"

"Possibly, but indeed I don't know, although they stood whispering very near to me: because they stood at the top of the cabin steps to have the light of the lamp that was hanging there; it was a dull lamp, and they spoke very low, and I did not hear what they said, and saw only that they looked at papers."

"Now, to the prisoner's conversation, Miss Manette."

"The prisoner was as open in his confidence with me—which arose out of my helpless situation—as he was kind, and good, and useful to my father. I hope," bursting into tears, "I may not repay him by doing him harm today."

Buzzing from the blue-flies.

"Miss Manette, if the prisoner does not perfectly understand that you give the evidence which it is your duty to give—which you must give—and which you cannot escape from giving—with great unwillingness, he is the only person present in that condition. Please to go on."

"He told me that he was traveling on business of a delicate and difficult nature, which might get people into trouble, and that he was therefore traveling under an assumed name. He said, that this business had, within a few days, taken him to France, and might, at intervals, take him backward and forward between France and England, for a long time to come."

"Did he say anything about America, Miss Manette? Be particular."

"He tried to explain to me how that quarrel had arisen, and he said that, so far as he could judge, it was a wrong and foolish one on England's part. He added, in a jesting way, that perhaps George Washington might gain almost as great a name in history as George the Third. But there was no harm in his way of saying this: it was said laughingly, and to beguile the time."

Any strongly marked expression of face on the part of a chief actor in a scene of great interest to whom many eyes are directed, will be unconsciously imitated by the spectators. Her forehead was painfully anxious and intent as she gave this evidence, and, in the pauses when she stopped for the Judge to write it down, watched its effect upon the counsel for and against. Among the lookers-on there was the same expression in all quarters of the court; insomuch, that a great majority of the foreheads there, might have been mirrors reflecting the witness, when the Judge looked up from his notes to glare at that tremendous heresy about George Washington.

Mr. Attorney-General now signified to my Lord, that he deemed it necessary, as a matter of precaution and form, to call the young lady's father, Doctor Manette. Who was called accordingly.

"Doctor Manette, look upon the prisoner. Have you ever seen him before?"

"Once. When he called at my lodgings in London. Some three years, or three years and a half, ago."

"Can you identify him as your fellow-passenger on board the packet, or speak to his conversation with your daughter?"

"Sir, I can do neither."

"Is there any particular and special reason for your being unable to do either?"

He answered, in a low voice, "There is."

"Has it been your misfortune to undergo a long imprisonment without trial, or even accusation, in your native country, Dr. Manette?"

He answered, in a tone that went to every heart, "A long imprisonment."

"Were you newly released on the occasion in question?"

"They tell me so."

"Have you no remembrance of the occasion?"

"None. My mind is a blank, from some time—I cannot even say what time—when I employed myself in my captivity, in making shoes, to the time when I found myself living in London with my dear daughter here. She had become familiar to me, when a gracious God restored my faculties; but I am quite unable even to say how she had become familiar. I have no remembrance of the process."

Mr. Attorney-General sat down, and the father and daughter sat down together.

A singular circumstance then arose in the case. The object in hand, being, to show that the prisoner went down, with some fellow-plotter untracked, in the Dover mail on that Friday night in November five years ago, and got out of the mail in the night, as a blind, at a place where he did not remain, but from which he traveled back some dozen miles or more, to a garrison and dockyard, and there collected information; a witness was called to identify him as having been at the precise time required, in the coffee-room of an hotel in that garrison-and-dockyard town, waiting for another person. The prisoner's counsel was cross-examining this witness with no result, except that he had never seen the prisoner on any other occasion, when the wigged gentleman who had all this time been looking at the ceiling of the court, wrote a word or two on a little piece of paper, screwed it up, and tossed it to him. Opening this piece of paper in the next pause, the counsel looked with great attention and curiosity at the prisoner.

"You say again, you are quite sure that it *was* the prisoner?"

The witness was quite sure.

"Did you ever see anybody very like the prisoner?"

Not so like (the witness said), as that he could be mistaken.

"Look well upon that gentleman, my learned friend there," pointing to him who had tossed the paper over, "and then look well upon the prisoner. How say you? Are they very like each other?"

Allowing for my learned friend's appearance being careless and slovenly, if not debauched, they were sufficiently like each other to surprise, not only the witness, but everybody present, when they were thus brought into comparison. My Lord being prayed to bid my learned friend lay aside his wig, and giving no very gracious consent, the likeness became much more remarkable. My Lord inquired of Mr. Stryver, (the prisoner's counsel), whether they were next to try Mr. Carton (name of my learned friend) for treason? But, Mr. Stryver replied to my Lord, no; but he would ask the witness to tell him whether what happened once, might happen twice; whether he would have been so confident if he had seen this illustration of his rashness sooner; whether he would be so confident, having seen it; and more. The upshot of which, was, to smash this witness like a crockery vessel, and shiver his part of the case to useless lumber.

Mr. Cruncher had by this time taken quite a lunch of rust off his fingers, in his following of the evidence. He had now to attend while Mr. Stryver fitted the prisoner's case on the jury, like a compact suit of clothes; showing them how the patriot, Barsad, was a hired spy and traitor, an unblushing trafficker in blood, and one of the greatest scoundrels upon earth since accursed Judas—which he certainly did look rather like. How the virtuous servant, Cly, was his friend and partner, and was worthy to be; how the watchful eyes of those forgers and false swearers had rested on the prisoner as a victim, because some family affairs in France, he being of French extraction, did require his making those passages across the Channel—though what those affairs were, a consideration for others who were near and dear to him, forbade him, even for his life, to disclose. How the evidence that had been warped and wrested from the young lady, whose anguish in giving it they had witnessed, came to nothing, involving the mere little innocent gallantries and politenesses likely to pass between any young gentleman and young lady so thrown together:—with the exception of that reference to George Washington, which was altogether too extravagant and impossible, to be regarded in any other light than as a monstrous joke. How it would be a weakness in the government to break down in this attempt to practice for popularity on the lowest national antipathies and fears, and therefore Mr. Attorney-General had made the most of it; how, nevertheless, it rested upon nothing, save that vile and infamous character of evidence too often disfiguring such cases, and of which the State Trials of this country were full. But, there my Lord interposed (with as grave a face as if it had not been true), saying that he could not sit upon that Bench and suffer those allusions.

Mr. Stryver then called his few witnesses, and Mr. Cruncher had next to attend while Mr. Attorney-General turned the whole suit of clothes Mr.

Stryver had fitted on the jury, inside out; showing how Barsad and Cly were even a hundred times better than he had thought them, and the prisoner a hundred times worse. Lastly, came My Lord himself, turning the suit of clothes, now inside out, now outside in, but on the whole decidedly trimming and shaping them into grave-clothes for the prisoner.

And now, the jury turned to consider, and the great flies swarmed again.

Mr. Carton, who had so long sat looking at the ceiling of the court, changed neither his place nor his attitude, even in this excitement. While his learned friend, Mr. Stryver, massing his papers before him, whispered with those who sat near, and from time to time glanced anxiously at the jury; while all the spectators moved more or less, and grouped themselves anew; while even My Lord himself arose from his seat, and slowly paced up and down his platform, not unattended by a suspicion in the minds of the audience that his state was feverish; this one man sat leaning back, with his torn gown half off him, his untidy wig put on just as it had happened to light on his head after its removal, his hands in his pockets, and his eyes on the ceiling as they had been all day. Something especially reckless in his demeanor, not only gave him a disreputable look, but so diminished the strong resemblance he undoubtedly bore to the prisoner (which his momentary earnestness, when they were compared together, had strengthened), that many of the lookers-on, taking note of him now, said to one another they would hardly have thought the two were so alike. Mr. Cruncher made the observation to his next neighbor, and added, "I'd hold half a guinea that *he* don't get no law-work to do. Don't look like the sort of one to get any, do he?"

Yet, this Mr. Carton took in more of the details of the scene than he appeared to take in; for now, when Miss Manette's head dropped upon her father's breast, he was the first to see it, and to say audibly: "Officer! look to that young lady. Help the gentleman to take her out. Don't you see she will fall!"

There was much commiseration for her as she was removed and much sympathy with her father. It had evidently been a great distress to him, to have the days of his imprisonment recalled. He had shown strong internal agitation when he was questioned, and that pondering or brooding look which made him old, had been upon him like a heavy cloud, ever since. As he passed out, the jury, who had turned back and paused a moment, spoke, through their foreman.

They were not agreed, and wished to retire. My Lord (perhaps with George Washington on his mind) showed some surprise that they were not agreed, but signified his pleasure that they should retire under watch and ward, and retired himself. The trial had lasted all day, and the lamps in the court were now being lighted. It began to be rumored that the jury would be out a long while. The spectators dropped off to get refreshment, and the prisoner withdrew to the back of the dock, and sat down.

Mr. Lorry, who had gone out when the young lady and her father went out, now reappeared, and beckoned to Jerry: who, in the slackened interest, could easily get near him.

"Jerry, if you wish to take something to eat, you can. But, keep in the way. You will be sure to hear when the jury come in. Don't be a moment behind them, for I want you to take the verdict back to the bank. You are the quickest messenger I know, and will get to Temple-bar long before I can."

Jerry had just enough forehead to knuckle, and he knuckled it in acknowledgment of this communication and a shilling. Mr. Carton came up at the moment, and touched Mr. Lorry on the arm.

"How is the young lady?"

"She is greatly distressed; but her father is comforting her, and she feels the better for being out of court."

"I'll tell the prisoner so. It won't do for a respectable bank-gentleman like you, to be seen speaking to him publicly, you know."

Mr. Lorry reddened, as if he were conscious of having debated the point in his mind, and Mr. Carton made his way to the outside of the bar. The way out of court lay in that direction, and Jerry followed him, all eyes, ears, and spikes.

"Mr. Darnay!"

The prisoner came forward directly.

"You will naturally be anxious to hear of the witness, Miss Manette. She will do very well. You have seen the worst of her agitation."

"I am deeply sorry to have been the cause of it. Could you tell her so for me, with my fervent acknowledgments?"

"Yes, I could. I will, if you ask it."

Mr. Carton's manner was so careless as to be almost insolent. He stood, half turned from the prisoner, lounging with his elbow against the bar.

"I do ask it. Accept my cordial thanks."

"What," said Carton, still only half turned toward him, "do you expect, Mr. Darnay?"

"The worst."

"It's the wisest thing to expect, and the likeliest. But I think their withdrawing is in your favor."

Loitering on the way out of court not being allowed, Jerry heard no more; but left them—so like each other in feature, so unlike each other in manner—standing side by side, both reflected in the glass above them.

An hour and a half limped heavily away in the thief-and-rascal-crowded passages below, even though assisted off with mutton pies and ale. The hoarse messenger, uncomfortably seated on a form, after taking that refection, had dropped into a doze, when a loud murmur and a rapid tide of people setting up the stairs that led to the court, carried him along with them.

"Jerry! Jerry!" Mr. Lorry was already calling at the door when he got there.

"Here, sir! It's a fight to get back again. Here I am, sir!"

Mr. Lorry handed him a paper through the throng. "Quick! Have you got it?"

"Yes, sir."

Hastily written on the paper was the word "ACQUITTED."

"If you had sent the message, 'Recalled to Life,' again," muttered Jerry, as he turned, "I should have known what you meant, this time."

He had no opportunity of saying, or so much as thinking, anything else, until he was clear of the Old Bailey; for, the crowd came pouring out with a vehemence that nearly took him off his legs, and a loud buzz swept into the street as if the baffled blue-flies were dispersing in search of other carrion.

F o u r

CONGRATULATORY

FROM THE DIMLY-LIGHTED PASSAGES OF THE COURT, THE last sediment of the human stew that had been boiling there all day, was straining off, when Doctor Manette, Lucie Manette his daughter, Mr. Lorry, the solicitor for the defense, and its counsel, Mr. Stryver, stood gathered around Mr. Charles Darnay—just released—congratulating him on his escape from death.

It would have been difficult by a far brighter light, to recognize in Doctor Manette, intellectual of face and upright of bearing, the shoemaker of the garret in Paris. Yet, no one could have looked at him twice, without looking again: even though the opportunity of observation had not extended to the mournful cadence of his low, grave voice, and to the abstraction that overclouded him fitfully, without any apparent reason. While one external cause, and that a reference to his long, lingering agony, would always—as on the trial—evoke this condition from the depths of his soul, it was also in its nature to arise of itself, and to draw a gloom over him, as incomprehensible to those unacquainted with his story as if they had seen the shadow of the actual Bastille thrown upon him by a summer sun, when the substance was three hundred miles away.

Only his daughter had the power of charming this black brooding from his mind. She was the golden thread that united him to a Past beyond his misery, and to a Present beyond his misery: and the sound of her voice, the light of her face, the touch of her hand, had a strong beneficial influence with him almost always. Not absolutely always, for she could recall some occasions on which her power had failed; but, they were few and slight, and she believed them over.

Mr. Darnay had kissed her hand fervently and gratefully, and had turned to Mr. Stryver, whom he warmly thanked. Mr. Stryver was of little more than thirty, but looking twenty years older than he was, stout, loud, red, bluff, and free from any drawback of delicacy, had a pushing way of shouldering himself (morally and physically) into companies and conversations, that argued well for his shouldering his way up in life.

He still had his wig and gown on, and he said, squaring himself at his late client to that degree that he squeezed the innocent Mr. Lorry clean out of the group: "I am glad to have brought you off with honor, Mr. Darnay. It was an infamous prosecution, grossly infamous; but not the less likely to succeed, on that account."

"You have laid me under an obligation to you for life—in two senses," said his late client, taking his hand.

"I have done my best for you, Mr. Darnay; and my best is as good as another man's, I believe."

It clearly being incumbent on someone to say, "Much better," Mr. Lorry said it; perhaps not quite disinterestedly, but with the interested object of squeezing himself back again.

"You think so?" said Mr. Stryver. "Well! you have been present all day, and you ought to know. You are a man of business, too."

"And as such," quoth Mr. Lorry, whom the counsel learned in the law had now shouldered back into the group, just as he had previously shouldered him out of it—"as such, I will appeal to Doctor Manette, to break up this conference and order us all to our homes. Miss Lucie looks ill, Mr. Darnay has had a terrible day; we are worn out."

"Speak for yourself, Mr. Lorry," said Stryver; "I have a night's work to do yet. Speak for yourself."

"I speak for myself," answered Mr. Lorry, "and for Mr. Darnay, and for Miss Lucie, and—Miss Lucie, do you not think I may speak for us all?" He asked her the question pointedly, and with a glance at her father.

His face had become frozen, as it were, in a very curious look at Darnay: an intent look, deepening into a frown of dislike and distrust, not even unmixed with fear. With this strange expression on him, his thoughts had wandered away.

"My father," said Lucie, softly laying her hand on his.

He slowly shook the shadow off and turned to her.

"Shall we go home, my father?"

With a long breath, he answered, "Yes."

The friends of the acquitted prisoner had dispersed, under the impression—which he himself had originated—that he would not be released that night. The lights were nearly all extinguished in the passages, the iron gates were being closed with a jar and a rattle, and the dismal place was deserted until tomorrow morning's interest of gallows, pillory, whipping-post, and branding-iron, should repeople it. Walking between her father and Mr. Darnay, Lucie Manette passed into the open air. A hackney-coach was called, and the father and daughter departed in it.

Mr. Stryver had left them in the passages, to shoulder his way back to the robing-room. Another person who had not joined the group, or interchanged a word with any one of them, but who had been leaning against the wall where its shadow was darkest, had silently strolled out after the rest, and had looked on until the coach drove away. He now stepped up to where Mr. Lorry and Mr. Darnay stood upon the pavement.

"So, Mr. Lorry! Men of business may speak to Mr. Darnay now?"

Nobody had made any acknowledgment of Mr. Carton's part in the day's proceedings; nobody had known of it. He was unrobed, and was none the better for it in appearance.

"If you knew what a conflict goes on in the business mind, when the business mind is divided between good-natured impulse and business appearances, you would be amused, Mr. Darnay."

Mr. Lorry reddened, and said, warmly, "You have mentioned that before, sir. We men of business who serve a House, are not our own masters. We have to think of the House, more than ourselves."

"*I* know, *I* know," rejoined Mr. Carton, carelessly. "Don't be nettled, Mr. Lorry. You are as good as another, I have no doubt; better, I dare say."

"And indeed, sir," pursued Mr. Lorry, not minding him, "I really don't know what you have to do with the matter. If you'll excuse me, as very much your elder, for saying so, I really don't know that it is your business."

"Business! Bless you, *I* have no business," said Mr. Carton.

"It is a pity you have not, sir."

"I think so too."

"If you had," pursued Mr. Lorry, "perhaps you would attend to it."

"Lord love you, no!—I shouldn't," said Mr. Carton.

"Well, sir," cried Mr. Lorry, thoroughly heated by his indifference, "business is a very good thing, and a very respectable thing. And, sir, if business imposes its restraints and its silences and impediments, Mr. Darnay, as a young gentleman of generosity, knows how to make allowance for that circumstance. Mr. Darnay, good night, God bless you, sir! I hope you have been this day preserved for a prosperous and happy life. Chair there!"

Perhaps a little angry with himself, as well as with the barrister, Mr. Lorry bustled into the chair, and was carried off to Tellson's. Carton, who smelt of port wine, and did not appear to be quite sober, laughed then, and turned to Darnay:

"This is a strange chance that throws you and me together. This must be a strange night to you, standing alone here with your counterpart on these street-stones?"

"I hardly seem yet," returned Charles Darnay, "to belong to this world again."

"I don't wonder at it; it's not so long since you were pretty far advanced on your way to another. You speak faintly."

"I begin to think I *am* faint."

"Then why the devil don't you dine? I dined myself, while those numskulls were deliberating which world you should belong to—this, or some other. Let me show you the nearest tavern to dine well at."

Drawing his arm through his own, he took him down Ludgate-hill to Fleet Street, and so, up a covered way, into a tavern. Here, they were shown into a little room, where Charles Darnay was soon recruiting his strength with a good, plain dinner and good wine: while Carton sat opposite to him at the same table, with his separate bottle of port before him, and his fully half-insolent manner upon him.

"Do you feel, yet, that you belong to this terrestrial scheme again, Mr. Darnay?"

"I am frightfully confused regarding time and place; but I am so far mended as to feel that."

"It must be an immense satisfaction!"

He said it bitterly, and filled up his glass again: which was a large one.

"As to me, the greatest desire I have, is to forget that I belong to it. It has no good in it for me—except wine like this—nor I for it. So we were not much alike in that particular. Indeed, I begin to think we are not much alike in any particular, you and I."

Confused by the emotion of the day, and feeling his being there with this Double of coarse deportment, to be like a dream, Charles Darnay was at a loss how to answer; finally, answered not at all.

"Now your dinner is done," Carton presently said, "why don't you call a health, Mr. Darnay? why don't you give your toast?"

"What health? What toast?"

"Why, it's on the tip of your tongue. It ought to be, it must be, I'll swear it's there."

"Miss Manette, then!"

"Miss Manette, then!"

Looking his companion full in the face while he drank the toast, Carton flung his glass over his shoulder against the wall, where it shivered to pieces; then, rang the bell, and ordered in another.

"That's a fair young lady to hand to a coach in the dark, Mr. Darnay!" he said, filling his new goblet.

A light frown and a laconic "Yes," were the answer.

"That's a fair young lady to be pitied by and wept for by! How does it feel? Is it worth being tried for one's life, to be the object of such sympathy and compassion, Mr. Darnay?"

Again Darnay answered not a word.

"She was mightily pleased to have your message, when I gave it her. Not that she showed she was pleased, but I suppose she was."

The allusion served as a timely reminder to Darnay that this disagreeable companion had, of his own free will, assisted him in the strait of the day. He turned the dialogue to that point, and thanked him for it.

"I neither want any thanks, nor merit any," was the careless rejoinder. "It was nothing to do, in the first place; and I don't know why I did it, in the second. Mr. Darnay, let me ask you a question."

"Willingly, and a small return for your good offices."

"Do you think I particularly like you?"

"Really, Mr. Carton," returned the other, oddly disconcerted, "I have not asked myself the question."

"But ask yourself the question now."

"You have acted as if you do; but I don't think you do."

"*I* don't think I do," said Carton. "I begin to have a very good opinion of your understanding."

"Nevertheless," pursued Darnay, rising to ring the bell, "there is nothing in that, I hope, to prevent my calling the reckoning, and our parting without ill-blood on either side."

Carton rejoining, "Nothing in life!" Darnay rang. "Do you call the whole reckoning?" said Carton. On his answering in the affirmative, "Then bring me another pint of this same wine, drawer, and come and wake me at ten."

The bill being paid, Charles Darnay rose and wished him good night. Without returning the wish, Carton rose too, with something of a threat or defiance in his manner, and said, "A last word, Mr. Darnay: you think I am drunk!"

"I think you have been drinking, Mr. Carton."

"Think? You know I have been drinking."

"Since I must say so, I know it."

"Then you shall likewise know why. I am a disappointed drudge, sir. I care for no man on earth, and no man on earth cares for me."

"Much to be regretted. You might have used your talents better."

"May be so, Mr. Darnay; may be not. Don't let your sober face elate you, however; you don't know what it may come to. Good night!"

When he was left alone, this strange being took up a candle, went to a glass that hung against the wall, and surveyed himself minutely in it.

"Do you particularly like the man?" he muttered, at his own image; "why should you particularly like a man who resembles you? There is nothing in you to like; you know that. Ah, confound you! What a change you have made in yourself! A good reason for taking to a man, that he shows you what you have fallen away from and what you might have been! Change places with him, and would you have been looked at by those blue eyes as he was, and commiserated by that agitated face as he was? Come on, and have it out in plain words! You hate the fellow."

He resorted to his pint of wine for consolation, drank it all in a few minutes, and fell asleep on his arms, with his hair straggling over the table, and a long winding-sheet in the candle dripping down upon him.

F i v e

THE JACKAL

THOSE WERE DRINKING DAYS, AND MOST MEN DRANK hard. So very great is the improvement Time has brought about in such habits, that a moderate statement of the quantity of wine and punch which one man would swallow in the course of a night, without any detriment to his reputation as a perfect gentleman, would seem, in these days, a ridiculous exaggeration. The learned profession of the Law was certainly not behind any other learned profession in its Bacchanalian propensities; neither was Mr. Stryver, already fast shouldering his way to a large and lucrative practice, behind his compeers in this particular, any more than in the drier parts of the legal race.

A favorite at the Old Bailey, and eke at the Sessions, Mr. Stryver had begun cautiously to hew away the lower staves of the ladder on which he mounted. Sessions and Old Bailey had now to summon their favorite, specially, to their longing arms; and shouldering itself toward the visage of the Lord Chief Justice in the Court of King's Bench, the florid countenance of Mr. Stryver might be daily seen, bursting out of the bed of wigs, like a great sunflower pushing its way at the sun from among a rank garden full of flaring companions.

It had once been noted at the Bar, that while Mr. Stryver was a glib man, and an unscrupulous, and a ready, and a bold, he had not that faculty of extracting the essence from a heap of statements, which is among the most striking and necessary of the advocate's accomplishments. But, a remarkable improvement came upon him as to this. The more business he got, the greater his power seemed to grow of getting at its pith and marrow; and however late at night he sat carousing with Sydney Carton, he always had his points at his fingers' ends in the morning.

Sydney Carton, idlest and most unpromising of men, was Stryver's great ally. What the two drank together, between Hilary Term and Michaelmas, might have floated a king's ship. Stryver never had a case in hand, anywhere, but Carton was there, with his hands in his pockets, staring at the ceiling of the court; they went the same Circuit, and even there they prolonged their usual orgies late into the night, and Carton was rumored to be seen at broad day, going home stealthily and unsteadily to his lodging, like a dissipated cat. At last, it began to get about, among such as were interested in the matter, that although Sydney Carton would never be a lion, he was an amazingly good jackal, and that he rendered suit and service to Stryver in that humble capacity.

"Ten o'clock, sir," said the man at the tavern, whom he had charged to wake him—"ten o'clock, sir."

"*What's* the matter?"

"Ten o'clock, sir."

"What do you mean? Ten o'clock at night?"

"Yes, sir. Your honor told me to call you."

"Oh! I remember. Very well, very well."

After a few dull efforts to get to sleep again, which the man dexterously combated by stirring the fire continuously for five minutes, he got up, tossed his hat on, and walked out. He turned into the Temple, and, having revived himself by twice pacing the pavements of King's Benchwalk and Paper-buildings, turned into the Stryver's chambers.

The Stryver clerk, who never assisted at these conferences, had gone home, and the Stryver principal opened the door. He had his slippers on, and a loose bedgown, and his throat was bare for his greater ease. He had that rather wild, strained, seared marking about the eyes, which may be observed in all free livers of his class, from the portrait of Jeffries downward, and which can be traced, under various disguises of Art, through the portraits of every Drinking Age.

"You are a little late, Memory," said Stryver.

"About the usual time; it may be a quarter of an hour later."

They went into a dingy room lined with books and littered with papers, where there was a blazing fire. A kettle steamed upon the hob, and in the midst of the wreck of papers a table shone, with plenty of wine upon it, and brandy, and rum, and sugar, and lemons.

"You have had your bottle, I perceive, Sydney."

"Two tonight, I think. I have been dining with the day's client; or seeing him dine—it's all one!"

"That was a rare point, Sydney, that you brought to bear upon the identification. How did you come by it? When did it strike you?"

"I thought he was rather a handsome fellow, and I thought I should have been much the same sort of fellow, if I had had any luck."

Mr. Stryver laughed, till he shook his precocious paunch.

"You and your luck, Sydney! Get to work, get to work."

Sullenly enough, the jackal loosened his dress, went into an adjoining room, and came back with a large jug of cold water, a basin, and a towel or two. Steeping the towels in the water, and partially wringing them out, he folded them on his head in a manner hideous to behold, sat down at the table, and said, "Now I am ready!"

"Not much boiling down to be done tonight, Memory," said Mr. Stryver, gaily, as he looked among his papers.

"How much?"

"Only two sets of them."

"Give me the worst first."

"There they are, Sydney. Fire away!"

The lion then composed himself on his back on a sofa on one side of the drinking-table, while the jackal sat at his own paper-bestrewn table proper, on the other side of it, with the bottles and glasses ready to his hand. Both resorted to the drinking-table without stint, but each in a different way; the lion for the most part reclining with his hands in his waistband, looking at the fire, or occasionally flirting with some lighter document; the jackal, with knitted brows and intent face, so deep in his task, that his eyes did not even follow the hand he stretched out for his glass—which often groped about, for a minute or more, before it found the glass for his lips. Two or three times, the matter in hand became so knotty, that the jackal found it imperative on him to get up, and steep his towels anew. From these pilgrimages to the jug and basin, he returned with such eccentricities of damp headgear as no words can describe; which were made the more ludicrous by his anxious gravity.

At length the jackal had got together a compact repast for the lion, and proceeded to offer it to him. The lion took it with care and caution, made his selections from it, and his remarks upon it, and the jackal assisted both. When the repast was fully discussed, the lion put his hands in his waistband again, and lay down to meditate. The jackal then invigorated himself with a bumper for his throttle, and a fresh application for his head, and applied himself to the collection of a second meal; this was administered to the lion in the same manner, and was not disposed of until the clocks struck three in the morning.

"And now we have done, Sydney, fill a bumper of punch," said Mr. Stryver.

The jackal removed the towels from his head, which had been steaming again, shook himself, yawned, shivered, and complied.

"You were very sound, Sydney, in the matter of those crown witnesses today. Every question told."

"I always am sound; am I not?"

"I don't gainsay it. What has roughened your temper? Put some punch to it and smooth it again."

With a deprecatory grunt, the jackal again complied.

"The old Sydney Carton of old Shrewsbury School," said Stryver, nodding his head over him as he reviewed him in the present and the past, "the old seesaw Sydney. Up one minute and down the next; now in spirits and now in despondency!"

"Ah!" returned the other, sighing: "yes! The same Sydney, with the same luck. Even then, I did exercises for other boys, and seldom did my own."

"And why not?"

"God knows. It was my way, I suppose."

He sat, with his hands in his pockets and his legs stretched out before him, looking at the fire.

"Carton," said his friend, squaring himself at him with a bullying air, as if the fire-grate had been the furnace in which sustained endeavor was forged, and the one delicate thing to be done for the old Sydney Carton of old Shrewsbury School was to shoulder him into it, "your way is, and always was, a lame way. You summon no energy and purpose. Look at me."

"Oh, botheration!" returned Sydney, with a lighter and more good-humored laugh, "don't *you* be moral!"

"How have I done what I have done?" said Stryver; "how do I do what I do?"

"Partly through paying me to help you, I suppose. But it's not worth your while to apostrophize me, or the air, about it; what you want to do, you do. You were always in the front rank, and I was always behind."

"I had to get into the front rank; I was not born there, was I?"

"I was not present at the ceremony; but my opinion is you were," said Carton. At this, he laughed again, and they both laughed.

"Before Shrewsbury, and at Shrewsbury, and ever since Shrewsbury," pursued Carton, "you have fallen into your rank, and I have fallen into mine. Even when we were fellow-students in the Quartier Latin, picking up French, and French law, and other French crumbs that we didn't get much good of, you were always somewhere, and I was always—nowhere."

"And whose fault was that?"

"Upon my soul, I am not sure that it was not yours. You were always driving and riving and shouldering and pressing, to that restless degree that I had no chance for my life but in rust and repose. It's a gloomy thing, however, to talk about one's own past, with the day breaking. Turn me in some other direction before I go."

"Well then! Pledge me to the pretty witness," said Stryver, holding up his glass. "Are you turned in a pleasant direction?"

Apparently not, for he became gloomy again.

"Pretty witness," he muttered, looking down into his glass. "I have had enough of witnesses today and tonight; who's your pretty witness?"

"The picturesque doctor's daughter, Miss Manette."

"*She* pretty?"

"Is she not?"

"No."

"Why, man alive, she was the admiration of the whole Court."

"Rot the admiration of the whole Court! Who made the Old Bailey a judge of beauty? She was a golden-haired doll?"

"Do you know, Sydney," said Mr. Stryver, looking at him with sharp eyes, and slowly drawing a hand across his florid face: "do you know, I rather thought, at the time, that you sympathized with the golden-haired doll, and were quick to see what happened to the golden-haired doll?"

"Quick to see what happened! If a girl, doll or no doll, swoons within a yard or two of a man's nose, he can see it without a perspective-glass. I pledge you, but I deny the beauty. And now I'll have no more drink; I'll get to bed."

When his host followed him out on the staircase with a candle, to light him down the stairs, the day was coldly looking in through its grimy windows. When he got out of the house, the air was cold and sad, the dull sky overcast, the river dark and dim, the whole scene like a lifeless desert. And wreaths of dust were spinning round and round before the morning blast, as if the desert-sand had risen far away, and the first spray of it in its advance had begun to overwhelm the city.

Waste forces within him, and a desert all around, this man stood still on his way across a silent terrace, and saw for a moment, lying in the wilderness before him, a mirage of honorable ambition, self-denial, and perseverance. In the fair city of this vision, there were airy galleries from which the loves and graces looked upon him, gardens in which the fruits of life hung ripening, waters of Hope that sparkled in his sight. A moment, and it was gone. Climbing to a high chamber in a well of houses, he threw himself down in his clothes on a neglected bed, and its pillow was wet with wasted tears.

Sadly, sadly, the sun rose; it rose upon no sadder sight than the man of good abilities, and good emotions, incapable of their directed exercise, incapable of his own help and his own happiness, sensible of the blight on him, and resigning himself to let it eat him away.

Six

HUNDREDS OF PEOPLE

THE QUIET LODGINGS OF DOCTOR MANETTE WERE IN A quiet street-corner not far from Soho-square. On the afternoon of a certain fine Sunday when the waves of four months had rolled over the trial for treason, and carried it, as to the public interest and memory, far out to sea,

Mr. Jarvis Lorry walked along the sunny streets from Clerkenwell, where he lived, on his way to dine with the Doctor. After several relapses into business-absorption, Mr. Lorry had become the Doctor's friend, and the quiet street-corner was the sunny part of his life.

On this certain fine Sunday, Mr. Lorry walked toward Soho, early in the afternoon, for three reasons of habit. Firstly, because, on fine Sundays, he often walked out, before dinner, with the Doctor and Lucie; secondly, because, on unfavorable Sundays, he was accustomed to be with them as the family friend, talking, reading, looking out of window, and generally getting through the day; thirdly, because he happened to have his own little shrewd doubts to solve, and knew how the ways of the Doctor's household pointed to that time as a likely time for solving them.

A quainter corner than the corner where the Doctor lived, was not to be found in London. There was no way through it, and the front windows of the Doctor's lodgings commanded a pleasant little vista of street that had a con-genial air of retirement on it. There were few buildings then, north of the Oxford road, and forest-trees flourished, and wildflowers grew, and the hawthorn blossomed, in the now vanished fields. As a consequence, country airs circulated in Soho with vigorous freedom, instead of languishing into the parish like stray paupers without a settlement; and there was many a good south wall, not far off, on which the peaches ripened in their season.

The summer light struck into the corner brilliantly in the earlier part of the day; but, when the streets grew hot, the corner was in shadow, though not in shadow so remote but that you could see beyond it into a glare of bright-ness. It was a cool spot, staid but cheerful, a wonderful place for echoes, and a very harbor from the raging streets.

There ought to have been a tranquil bark in such an anchorage, and there was. The Doctor occupied two floors of a large still house, where several call-ings purported to be pursued by day, but whereof little was audible any day, and which was shunned by all of them at night. In a building at the back, attainable by a courtyard where a plane-tree rustled its green leaves, church-organs claimed to be made, and silver to be chased, and likewise gold to be beaten by some mysterious giant who had a golden arm starting out of the wall of the front hall—as if he had beaten himself precious, and menaced a similar conversion of all visitors. Very little of these trades, or of a lonely lodger rumored to live upstairs, or of a dim coach-timming maker asserted to have a countinghouse below, was ever heard or seen. Occasionally, a stray workman putting his coat on, traversed the hall, or a stranger peered about there, or a distant clink·was heard across the courtyard, or a thump from the golden giant. These, however, were only the exceptions required to prove the rule that the sparrows in the plane-tree behind the house, and the echoes in the corner before it, had their own way from Sunday morning unto Saturday night.

Doctor Manette received such patients here as his old reputation, and its revival in the floating whispers of his story, brought him. His scientific knowledge, and his vigilance and skill in conducting ingenious experiments, brought him otherwise into moderate request, and he earned as much as he wanted.

These things were within Mr. Jarvis Lorry's knowledge, thoughts, and notice, when he rang the doorbell of the tranquil house in the corner, on the fine Sunday afternoon.

"Doctor Manette at home?"

Expected home.

"Miss Lucie at home?"

Expected home.

"Miss Pross at home?"

Possibly at home, but of a certainty impossible for handmaid to anticipate intentions of Miss Pross, as to admission or denial of the fact.

"As I am at home myself," said Mr. Lorry, "I'll go upstairs."

Although the Doctor's daughter had known nothing of the country of her birth, she appeared to have innately derived from it that ability to make much of little means, which is one of its most useful and most agreeable characteristics. Simple as the furniture was, it was set off by so many little adornments, of no value but for their taste and fancy, that its effect was delightful. The disposition of everything in the rooms, from the largest object to the least; the arrangement of colors, the elegant variety and contrast obtained by thrift in trifles, by delicate hands, clear eyes, and good sense; were at once so pleasant in themselves, and so expressive of their originator, that, as Mr. Lorry stood looking about him, the very chairs and tables seemed to ask him, with something of that peculiar expression which he knew so well by this time, whether he approved?

There were three rooms on a floor, and, the doors by which they communicated being put open that the air might pass freely through them all, Mr. Lorry, smilingly observant of that fanciful resemblance which he detected all around him, walked from one to another. The first was the best room, and in it were Lucie's birds, and flowers, and books, and desk, and worktable, and box of watercolors; the second was the Doctor's consulting room, used also as the diningroom; the third, changingly speckled by the rustle of the plane-tree in the yard, was the Doctor's bedroom—and there, in a corner, stood the disused shoemaker's bench and tray of tools, much as it had stood on the fifth floor of the dismal house by the wine-shop, in the suburb of Saint Antoine in Paris.

"I wonder," said Mr. Lorry, pausing in his looking about, "that he keeps that reminder of his sufferings by him!"

"And why wonder at that?" was the abrupt inquiry that made him start.

It proceeded from Miss Pross, the wild red woman, strong of hand, whose acquaintance he had first made at the Royal George Hotel at Dover, and had since improved.

"I should have thought—" Mr. Lorry began.

"Pooh! You'd have thought!" said Miss Pross; and Mr. Lorry left off.

"How do you do?" inquired that lady then—sharply, and yet as if to express that she bore him no malice.

"I am pretty well, I thank you," answered Mr. Lorry, with meekness, "how are you?"

"Nothing to boast of," said Miss Pross.

"Indeed?"

"Ah! indeed!" said Miss Pross. "I am very much put out about my Ladybird."

"Indeed?"

"For gracious sake say something else besides 'indeed,' or you'll fidget me to death," said Miss Pross: whose character (dissociated from stature) was shortness.

"Really, then?" said Mr. Lorry, as an amendment.

"Really, is bad enough," returned Miss Pross, "but better. Yes, I am very much put out."

"May I ask the cause?"

"I don't want dozens of people who are not at all worthy of Ladybird, to come here looking after her," said Miss Pross.

"*Do* dozens come for that purpose?"

"Hundreds," said Miss Pross.

It was characteristic of this lady (as of some other people before her time and since) that whenever her original proposition was questioned, she exaggerated it.

"Dear me!" said Mr. Lorry, as the safest remark he could think of.

"I have lived with the darling—or the darling has lived with me, and paid me for it; which she certainly should never have done, you may take your affidavit, if I could have afforded to keep either myself or her for nothing—since she was ten years old. And it's really very hard," said Miss Pross.

Not seeing with precision what was very hard, Mr. Lorry shook his head; using that important part of himself as a sort of fairy cloak that would fit anything.

"All sorts of people who are not in the least degree worthy of the pet, are always turning up," said Miss Pross. "When you began it—"

"*I* began it, Miss Pross?"

"Didn't you? Who brought her father to life?"

"Oh! If *that* was beginning it—" said Mr. Lorry.

"It wasn't ending it, I suppose? I say, when you began it, it was hard enough; not that I have any fault to find with Doctor Manette, except that he is not worthy of such a daughter, which is no imputation on him, for it was not to be expected that anybody should be, under any circumstances. But it really is doubly and trebly hard to have crowds and multitudes of people turning up after him (I could have forgiven him), to take Ladybird's affections away from me."

Mr. Lorry knew Miss Pross to be very jealous, but he also knew her by this time to be, beneath the surface of her eccentricity, one of those unselfish creatures—found only among women—who will, for pure love and admiration, bind themselves willing slaves, to youth when they have lost it, to beauty that they never had, to accomplishments that they were never fortunate enough to gain, to bright hopes that never shone upon their own sombre lives. He knew enough of the world to know that there is nothing in it better than the faithful service of the heart; so rendered and so free from any mercenary taint, he had such an exalted respect for it, that in the retributive arrangements made by his own mind—we all make such arrangements, more or less—he stationed Miss Pross much nearer to the lower Angels than many ladies immeasurably better got up both by Nature and Art, who had balances at Tellson's.

"There never was, nor will be, but one man worthy of Ladybird," said Miss Pross; "and that was my brother Solomon, if he hadn't made a mistake in life."

Here again: Mr. Lorry's inquiries into Miss Pross's personal history, had established the fact that her brother Solomon was a heartless scoundrel who had stripped her of everything she possessed as a stake to speculate with, and had abandoned her in her poverty forevermore, with no touch of compunction. Miss Pross's fidelity of belief in Solomon (deducting a mere trifle for this slight mistake) was quite a serious matter with Mr. Lorry, and had its weight in his good opinion of her.

"As we happen to be alone for the moment, and are both people of business," he said, when they had got back to the drawingroom, and had sat down there in friendly relations, "let me ask you—does the Doctor, in talking with Lucie, never refer to the shoemaking time, yet?"

"Never."

"And yet keeps that bench and those tools beside him?"

"Ah!" returned Miss Pross, shaking her head. "But I don't say he don't refer to it within himself."

"Do you believe that he thinks of it much?"

"I do," said Miss Pross.

"Do you imagine—" Mr. Lorry had begun, when Miss Pross took him up short with:

"Never imagine anything. Have no imagination at all."

"I stand corrected; do you suppose—you go so far as to suppose, sometimes?"

"Now and then," said Miss Pross.

"Do you suppose," Mr. Lorry went on, with a laughing twinkle in his bright eye, as it looked kindly at her, "that Doctor Manette has any theory of his own, preserved through all those years, relative to the cause of his being so oppressed; perhaps, even to the name of his oppressor?"

"I don't suppose anything about it but what Ladybird tells me."

"And this is——?"

"That she thinks he has."

"Now don't be angry at my asking all these questions; because I am a mere dull man of business, and you are a woman of business."

"Dull?" Miss Pross inquired, with placidity.

Rather wishing his modest adjective away, Mr. Lorry replied, "No, no, no. Surely not. To return to business:—Is it not remarkable that Doctor Manette, unquestionably innocent of any crime, as we are well assured he is, should never touch upon that question? I will not say with me, though he had business relations with me many years ago, and we are now intimate; I will say with the fair daughter to whom he is so devotedly attached, and who is so devotedly attached to him? Believe me, Miss Pross, I don't approach the topic with you, out of curiosity, but out of zealous interest."

"Well! To the best of my understanding, and bad's the best you'll tell me," said Miss Pross, softened by the tone of the apology, "he is afraid of the whole subject."

"Afraid?"

"It's plain enough, I should think, why he may be. It's a dreadful remembrance. Besides that, his loss of himself grew out of it. Not knowing how he lost himself, or how he recovered himself, he may never feel certain of not losing himself again. That alone wouldn't make the subject pleasant, I should think."

It was a profounder remark than Mr. Lorry had looked for. "True," said he, "and fearful to reflect upon. Yet, a doubt lurks in my mind, Miss Pross, whether it is good for Doctor Manette to have that suppression always shut up within him. Indeed, it is this doubt and the uneasiness it sometimes causes me, that has led me to our present confidence."

"Can't be helped," said Miss Pross, shaking her head. "Touch that string, and he instantly changes for the worse. Better leave it alone. In short, must leave it alone, like or no like. Sometimes, he gets up in the dead of the night, and will be heard, by us overhead there, walking up and down, walking up and down, in his room. Ladybird has learnt to know then, that his mind is walking up and down, walking up and down, in his old prison. She hurries to him, and they go on together, walking up and down, walking up and down, until he is composed. But he never says a word of the true reason for his restlessness, to her, and she finds it best not to hint at it to him. In silence they go walking up and down together, walking up and down together, till her love and company have brought him to himself."

Notwithstanding Miss Pross's denial of her own imagination, there was a perception of the pain of being monotonously haunted by one sad idea, in her repetition of the phrase, walking up and down, which testified to her possessing such a thing.

The corner has been mentioned as a wonderful corner for echoes; it had begun to echo so resoundingly to the tread of coming feet, that it seemed as though the very mention of that weary pacing to and fro had set it a going.

"Here they are!" said Miss Pross, rising to break up the conference; "and now we shall have hundreds of people pretty soon!"

It was such a curious corner in its acoustical properties, such a peculiar ear of a place, that as Mr. Lorry stood at the open window, looking for the father and daughter whose steps he heard, he fancied they would never approach. Not only would the echoes die away, as though the steps had gone; but echoes of other steps that never came, would be heard in their stead, and would die away for good when they seemed close at hand. However, father and daughter did at last appear, and Miss Pross was ready at the street door to receive them.

Miss Pross was a pleasant sight, albeit wild, and red, and grim, taking off her darling's bonnet when she came upstairs, and touching it up with the ends of her handkerchief, and blowing the dust off it, and folding her mantle ready for laying by, and smoothing her rich hair with as much pride as she could possibly have taken in her own hair if she had been the vainest and handsomest of women. Her darling was a pleasant sight too, embracing her and thanking her, and protesting against her taking so much trouble for her—which last she only dared to do playfully, or Miss Pross, sorely hurt, would have retired to her own chamber and cried. The Doctor was a pleasant sight too, looking on at them, and telling Miss Pross how she spoilt Lucie, in accents and with eyes that had as much spoiling in them as Miss Pross had, and would have had more if it were possible. Mr. Lorry was a pleasant sight too, beaming at all this in his little wig, and thanking his bachelor stars for having lighted him in his declining years to a Home. But, no Hundreds of people came to see the sights, and Mr. Lorry looked in vain for the fulfillment of Miss Pross's prediction.

Dinner time, still no Hundreds of people. In the arrangements of the little household, Miss Pross took charge of the lower regions, and always acquitted herself marvelously. Her dinners, of a very modest quality, were so well cooked and so well served, and so neat in their contrivances, half English and half French, that nothing could be better. Miss Pross's friendship being of the thoroughly practical kind, she had ravaged Soho and the adjacent provinces, in search of impoverished French, who, tempted by shillings and half-crowns, would impart culinary mysteries to her. From these decayed sons and daughters of Gaul, she had acquired such wonderful arts, that the woman and girl who formed the staff of domestics regarded her as quite a Sorceress, or Cinderella's Godmother: who would send out for a fowl, a rabbit, a vegetable or two from the garden, and change them into anything she pleased.

On Sunday, Miss Pross dined at the Doctor's table, but on other days persisted in taking her meals, at unknown periods, either in the lower regions, or in her own room on the second floor—a blue chamber, to which no one but her Ladybird ever gained admittance. On this occasion Miss

Pross, responding to Ladybird's pleasant face and pleasant efforts to please her, unbent exceedingly; so the dinner was very pleasant too.

It was an oppressive day, and, after dinner, Lucie proposed that the wine should be carried out under the plane-tree, and they should sit there in the air. As everything turned upon her and revolved about her, they went out under the plane-tree, and she carried the wine down for the special benefit of Mr. Lorry. She had installed herself, sometime before, as Mr. Lorry's cup-bearer; and while they sat under the plane-tree, talking, she kept his glass replenished. Mysterious backs and ends of houses peeped at them as they talked, and the plane-tree whispered to them, in its own way, above their heads.

Still, the Hundreds of people did not present themselves. Mr. Darnay presented himself while they were sitting under the plane-tree, but he was only One.

Doctor Manette received him kindly, and so did Lucie. But Miss Pross suddenly became afflicted with a twitching in the head and body, and retired into the house. She was not unfrequently the victim of this disorder, and she called it, in familiar conversation, "a fit of the jerks."

The Doctor was in his best condition, and looked specially young. The resemblance between him and Lucie was very strong at such times and as they sat side by side, she leaning on his shoulder, and he resting his arm on the back of her chair, it was very agreeable to trace the likeness.

He had been talking, all day, on many subjects and with unusual vivacity. "Pray, Doctor Manette," said Mr. Darnay, as they sat under the plane-tree—and he said it in the natural pursuit of the topic in hand, which happened to be the old buildings of London—"have you seen much of the Tower?"

"Lucie and I have been there; but only casually. We have seen enough of it, to know that it teems with interest; little more."

"*I* have been there, as you remember," said Darnay, with a smile, though reddening a little angrily, "in another character, and not in a character that gives facilities for seeing much of it. They told me a curious thing when I was there."

"What was that?" Lucie asked.

"In making some alterations, the workmen came upon an old dungeon, which had been, for many years, built up and forgotten. Every stone of its inner wall was covered by inscriptions which had been carved by prisoners—dates, names, complaints, and prayers. Upon a corner stone in an angle of the wall, one prisoner, who seemed to have gone to execution, had cut, as his last work, three letters. They were done with some very poor instrument, and hurriedly, with an unsteady hand. At first, they were read as D. I. C.; but, on being more carefully examined, the last letter was found to be G. There was no record or legend of any prisoner with those initials, and many fruitless guesses were made what the name could have been. At length it was suggested that the letters were not initials, but the complete word, DIG. The floor was examined very carefully under the inscription, and, in the earth, beneath a stone, or tile, or some fragment of paving were found the ashes of a paper, mingled with the ashes of a small leathern case or bag. What the unknown prisoner had written will never be read, but he had written something, and hidden it away to keep it from the gaoler."

"My father!" exclaimed Lucie, "you are ill!"

He had suddenly started up, with his hand to his head. His manner and his look quite terrified them all.

"No, my dear, not ill. There are large drops of rain falling, and they made me start. We had better go in."

He recovered himself almost instantly. Rain was really falling in large drops, and he showed the back of his hand with raindrops on it. But he said not a single word in reference to the discovery that had been told of, and, as they went into the house, the business eye of Mr. Lorry either detected, or fancied it detected, on his face, as it turned toward Charles Darnay, the same singular look, that had been upon it when it turned toward him in the passage of the Court House.

He recovered himself so quickly, however, that Mr. Lorry had doubts of his business eye. The arm of the golden giant in the hall was not more steady than he was, when he stopped under it to remark to them that he was not yet proof against slight surprises (if he ever would be), and that the rain had startled him.

Teatime, and Miss Pross making tea, with another fit of the jerks upon her, and yet no Hundreds of people. Mr. Carton had lounged in, but he made only Two.

The night was so very sultry, that although they sat with doors and windows open, they were overpowered by heat. When the tea-table was done with, they all moved to one of the windows, and looked out into the heavy twilight. Lucie sat by her father; Darnay sat beside her; Carton leaned against a window. The curtains were long and white, and some of the thunder-gusts that whirled into the corner, caught them up to the ceiling, and waved them like spectral wings.

"The raindrops are still falling, large, heavy, and few," said Doctor Manette. "It comes slowly."

"It comes surely," said Carton.

They spoke low, as people watching and waiting mostly do; as people in a dark room, watching and waiting for Lightning, always do.

There was a great hurry in the streets, of people speeding away to get shelter before the storm broke; the wonderful corner for echoes resounded with the echoes of footsteps coming and going, yet not a footstep was there.

"A multitude of people, and yet a solitude!" said Darnay, when they had listened for a while.

"Is it not impressive, Mr. Darnay?" asked Lucie. "Sometimes, I have sat here of an evening, until I have fancied—but even the shade of a foolish fancy makes me shudder tonight, when all is so black and solemn—"

"Let us shudder, too. We may know what it is?"

"It will seem nothing to you. Such whims are only impressive as we originate them, I think; they are not to be communicated. I have sometimes sat alone here of an evening, listening, until I have made the echoes out to be the echoes of all the footsteps that are coming by-and-by into our lives."

"There is a great crowd coming one day into our lives, if that be so," Sydney Carton struck in, in his moody way.

The footsteps were incessant, and the hurry of them became more and more rapid. The corner echoed and re-echoed with the tread of feet; some, as it seemed, under the windows; some, as it seemed, in the room; some coming, some going, some breaking off, some stopping altogether; all in the distant streets, and not one within sight.

"Are all these footsteps destined to come to all of us, Miss Manette, or are we to divide them among us?"

"I don't know, Mr. Darnay; I told you it was a foolish fancy, but you asked for it. When I have yielded myself to it, I have been alone, and then I have imagined them the footsteps of the people who are to come into my life, and my father's."

"I take them into mine!" said Carton. "*I* ask no questions and make no stipulations. There is a great crowd bearing down upon us, Miss Manette, and I see them—by the lightning." He added the last words, after there had been a vivid flash which had shown him lounging in the window.

"And I hear them!" he added again, after a peal of thunder. "Here they come, fast, fierce, and furious!"

It was the rush and roar of rain that he typified, and it stopped him, for no voice could be heard in it. A memorable storm of thunder and lightning broke with that sweep of water, and there was not a moment's interval in crash, and fire, and rain until after the moon rose at midnight.

The great bell of Saint Paul's was striking One in the cleared air, when Mr. Lorry, escorted by Jerry, high-booted, and bearing a lantern, set forth on his return-passage to Clerkenwell. There were solitary patches of road on the way between Soho and Clerkenwell, and Mr. Lorry, mindful of footpads, always retained Jerry for this service: though it was usually performed a good two hours earlier.

"What a night it has been! Almost a night, Jerry," said Mr. Lorry, "to bring the dead out of their graves."

"I never see the night myself, master—nor yet I don't expect to it—what would do that," answered Jerry.

"Good night, Mr. Carton," said the man of business. "Good night, Mr. Darnay. Shall we ever see such a night again, together!"

Perhaps. Perhaps, see the great crowd of people with its rush and roar, bearing down upon them, too.

Seven

MONSIEUR THE MARQUIS IN TOWN

MONSEIGNEUR, ONE OF THE GREAT LORDS IN POWER AT THE Court, held his fortnightly reception in his grand hotel in Paris. Monseigneur was in his inner room, his sanctuary of sanctuaries, the Holiest of Holiest to the crowd of worshipers in the suite of rooms without. Monseigneur was about to take his chocolate. Monseigneur could swallow a great many things with ease, and was by some few sullen minds supposed to be rather rapidly swallowing France; but, his morning's chocolate could not so much as get into the throat of Monseigneur, without the aid of four strong men besides the cook.

Yes. It took four men, all four ablaze with gorgeous decoration. And the Chief of them, unable to exist with fewer than two gold watches in his pocket, emulative of the noble and chaste fashion set by Monseigneur, to conduct the happy chocolate to Monseigneur's lips. One lackey carried the chocolate-pot into the sacred presence; a second, milled and frothed the chocolate with the little instrument he bore for that function; a third, presented the favored napkin; a fourth, (he of the two gold watches) poured the chocolate out. It was impossible for Monseigneur to dispense with one of these attendants on the chocolate and hold his high place under the admiring Heavens. Deep would have been the blot upon his escutcheon if his chocolate had been ignobly waited on by only three men; he must have died of two.

Monseigneur had been out at a little supper last night, where the Comedy and the Grand Opera were charmingly represented. Monseigneur was out at a little supper most nights, with fascinating company. So polite and so impressible was Monseigneur, that the Comedy and the Grand Opera had far more influence with him in the tiresome articles of State affairs and State secrets, than the needs of all France. A happy circumstance for France, as the like always is for all countries similarly favored!—always was for

England (by way of example), in the regretted days of the merry Stuart who sold it.

Monseigneur had one truly noble idea of general public business, which was, to let everything go on in its own way; of particular public business, Monseigneur had the other truly noble idea that it must all go his way—tend to his own power and pocket. Of his pleasures, general and particular, Monseigneur had the other truly noble idea, that the world was made for them. The text of his order (altered from the original by only a pronoun, which is not much) ran: "The earth and the fullness thereof are mine, said Monseigneur."

Yet, Monseigeur had slowly found that vulgar embarrassments crept into his affairs, both private and public, and he had, as to both classes of affairs, allied himself perforce with a Farmer-General. As to finances public, because Monseigneur could not make anything at all of them, and must consequently let them out to somebody who could; as to finances private, because Farmer-Generals were rich, and Monseigneur, after generations of great luxury and expense, was growing poor. Hence, Monseigneur had taken his sister from a convent, while there was yet time to ward off the impending vail, the cheapest garment she could wear, and had bestowed her as a prize upon a very rich Farmer-General, poor in family. Which Farmer-General, carrying an appropriate cane with a golden apple on the top of it, was now among the company in the outer rooms, much prostrated before by mankind—always excepting superior mankind of the blood of Monseigneur, who, his own wife included, looked down upon him with the loftiest contempt.

A sumptuous man was the Farmer-General. Thirty horses stood in his stables, twenty-four male domestics sat in his halls, six body-women waited on his wife. As one who pretended to do nothing but plunder and forage where he could, the Farmer-General—howsoever his matrimonial relations conduced to social morality—was at least the greatest reality among the personages who attended at the hotel of Monseigneur that day.

For, the rooms, though a beautiful scene to look at, and adorned with every device of decoration that the taste and skill of the time could achieve, were, in truth, not a sound business; considered with any reference to the scarecrows in the rags and nightcaps elsewhere (and not so far off either, but that the watching towers of Notre Dame, almost equidistant from the two extremes, could see them both), they would have been an exceedingly uncomfortable business—if that could have been anybody's business, at the house of Monseigneur. Military officers destitute of military knowledge; naval officers with no idea of a ship; civil officers without a notion of affairs; brazen ecclesiastics, of the worst world worldly, with sensual eyes, loose tongues, and looser lives; all totally unfit for their several callings, all lying horribly in pretending to belong to them, but all nearly or remotely of the order of Monseigneur, and therefore foisted on all public employments from which anything was to be got; these were to be told off by the score and the score. People not immediately connected with Monseigneur or the State, yet equally unconnected with anything that was real, or with lives passed in traveling by any straight road to any true earthly end, were no less abundant. Doctors who made great fortunes out of dainty remedies for imaginary disorders that never existed, smiled upon their courtly patients in the antechambers of Monseigneur. Projectors who had discovered every kind of remedy for the little evils with which the State was touched, except the remedy of setting to work in earnest to root out a single sin, poured their distracting babble into any ears they could lay hold of, at the reception of Monseigneur. Unbelieving Philosophers who were remodeling the world with words, and making card-towers of Babel to scale the skies with, talked with Unbelieving Chemists who had an eye on the transmutation of metals, at this wonderful gathering accumulated by Monseigneur. Exquisite gentlemen of the finest breeding, which was at that remarkable time—and has been since—to be known by its fruits of indifference to every natural subject of human interest, were in the most exemplary state of exhaustion, at the hotel of Monseigneur. Such homes had these various notabilities left behind them in the fine world of Paris, that the Spies among the assembled devotees of Monseigneur—forming a goodly half of the polite company—would have found it hard to discover among the angels of that sphere, one solitary wife, who, in her manners and appearance, owned to being a mother. Indeed, except for the mere act of bringing a troublesome creature into this world—which does not go far toward the realization of the name of mother—there was no such thing known to the fashion. Peasant women kept the unfashionable babies close, and brought them up; and charming grandmammas of sixty dressed and supped as at twenty.

The leprosy of unreality disfigured every human creature in attendance upon Monseigneur. In the outermost room were half a dozen exceptional people who had had, for a few years, some vague misgiving in them that things in general were going rather wrong. As a promising way of setting them right, half of the half-dozen had become members of a fantastic sect of Convulsionists, and were even then considering within themselves whether they should foam, rage, roar, and turn cataleptic on the spot—thereby setting up a highly intelligible finger-post to the Future, for Monseigneur's guidance. Besides these Dervishes, were other three who had rushed into another sect, which mended matters with a jargon about "The Center of truth:" holding that Man had got out of the Center of truth—which did not need much demonstration—but had not got out of the Circumference, and that he was to be kept from flying out of the Circumference, and was even to be shoved back into the Center, by fasting and seeing of spirits. Among these, accordingly, much discoursing with spirits went on—and it did a world of good which never became manifest.

But, the comfort was, that all the company at the grand hotel of Monseigneur were perfectly dressed. If the Day of Judgment had only been ascertained to be a dress day, everybody there would have been eternally correct. Such frizzling and powdering and sticking up of hair, such delicate complexions artificially preserved and mended, such gallant swords to look at, and such delicate honor to the sense of smell, would surely keep anything going, forever and ever. The exquisite gentlemen of the finest breeding wore little pendent trinkets that chinked as they languidly moved; these golden fetters rang like precious little bells; and what with that ringing, and with the rustle of silk and brocade and fine linen, there was a flutter in the air that fanned Saint Antoine and his devouring hunger far away.

Dress was the one unfailing talisman and charm used for keeping all things in their places. Everybody was dressed for a Fancy Ball that was never to leave off. From the Palace of the Tuileries, through Monseigneur and the whole Court, through the Chambers, the Tribunals of Justice, and all society (except the scarecrows), the Fancy Ball descended to the Common Executioner; who, in pursuance of the charm, was required to officiate "frizzled, powdered, in a gold-laced coat, pumps, and white silk stockings." At the gallows and the wheel—the axe was a rarity—Monsieur Paris, as it was the episcopal mode among his brother Professors of the provinces, Monsieur Orleans, and the rest, to call him, presided in this dainty dress. And who among the company at Monseigneur's reception in that seventeen hundred and eightieth year of our Lord, could possibly doubt, that a system rooted in a frizzled hangman, powdered, gold-laced, pumped, and white-silk stockinged, would see the very stars out!

Monseigneur having eased his four men of their burdens and taken his chocolate, caused the doors of the Holiest of Holiests to be thrown open, and issued forth. Then, what submission, what cringing and fawning, what servility, what abject humiliation! As to bowing down in body and spirit, nothing in that way was left for Heaven—which may have been one among other reasons why the worshipers of Monseigneur never troubled it.

Bestowing a word of promise here and a smile there, a whisper on one happy slave and a wave of the hand on another, Monseigneur affably passed through his rooms to the remote region of the Circumference of Truth. There, Monseigneur turned, and came back again, and so in the due course of time got himself shut up in his sanctuary by the chocolate sprites, and was seen no more.

The show being over, the flutter in the air became quite a little storm, and the precious little bells went ringing downstairs. There was soon but one person left of all the crowd, and he, with his hat under his arm and his snuff-box in his hand, slowly passed among the mirrors on his way out.

"I devote you," said this person, stopping at the last door on his way, and turning in the direction of the sanctuary, "to the Devil!"

With that, he shook the snuff from his fingers as if he had shaken the dust from his feet, and quietly walked downstairs.

He was a man of about sixty, handsomely dressed, haughty in manner, and with a face like a fine mask. A face of a transparent paleness; every feature in it clearly defined; one set expression on it. The nose, beautifully formed otherwise, was very slightly pinched at the top of each nostril. In those two compressions, or dints, the only little change that the face ever showed, resided. They persisted in changing color sometimes, and they would be occasionally dilated and contracted by something like a faint pulsation; then, they gave a look of treachery, and cruelty, to the whole countenance. Examined with attention, its capacity of helping such a look was to be found in the line of the mouth, and the lines of the orbits of the eyes, being much too horizontal and thin; still, in the effect the face made, it was a handsome face, and a remarkable one.

Its owner went downstairs into the courtyard, got into his carriage, and drove away. Not many people had talked with him at the reception; he had stood in a little space apart, and Monseigneur might have been warmer in his manner. It appeared, under the circumstances, rather agreeable to him to see the common people dispersed before his horses, and often barely escaping from being run down. His man drove as if he were charging an enemy, and the furious recklessness of the man brought no check into the face, or to the lips, of the master. The complaint had sometimes made itself audible, even in that deaf city and dumb age, that, in the narrow streets without footways, the fierce patrician custom of hard driving endangered and maimed the mere vulgar in a barbarous manner. But, few cared enough for that to think of it a second time, and, in this matter, as in all others, the common wretches were left to get out of their difficulties as they could.

With a wild rattle and clatter, and an inhuman abandonment of consideration not easy to be understood in these days, the carriage dashed through streets and swept round corners, with women screaming before it, and men clutching each other and clutching children out of its way. At last, swooping at a street corner by a fountain, one of its wheels came to a sickening little jolt, and there was a loud cry from a number of voices, and the horses reared and plunged.

But for the latter inconvenience, the carriage probably would not have stopped; carriages were often known to drive on, and leave their wounded behind, and why not? But, the frightened valet had got down in a hurry, and there were twenty hands at the horses' bridles.

"What has gone wrong?" said Monsieur, calmly looking out.

A tall man in a nightcap had caught up a bundle from among the feet of the horses, and had laid it on the basement of the fountain, and was down in the mud and wet, howling over it like a wild animal.

"Pardon, Monsieur the Marquis!" said a ragged and submissive man, "it is a child."

"Why does he make that abominable noise? Is it his child?"

"Excuse me, Monsieur the Marquis—it is a pity—yes."

The fountain was a little removed; for the street opened, where it was, into a space some ten or twelve yards square. As the tall man suddenly got up from the ground, and came running at the carriage, Monsieur the Marquis clapped his hand for an instant on his sword-hilt.

"Killed!" shrieked the man, in wild desperation, extending both arms at their length above his head, and staring at him. "Dead!"

The people closed round, and looked at Monsieur the Marquis. There was nothing revealed by the many eyes that looked at him but watchfulness and eagerness; there was no visible menacing or anger. Neither did the people say anything; after the first cry, they had been silent, and they remained so. The voice of the submissive man who had spoken, was flat and tame in its extreme submission. Monsieur the Marquis ran his eyes over them all, as if they had been mere rats come out of their holes.

He took out his purse.

"It is extraordinary to me," said he, "that you people cannot take care of yourselves and your children. One or the other of you is forever in the way. How do I know what injury you have done my horses? See! Give him that."

He threw out a gold coin for the valet to pick up, and all the heads craned forward that all the eyes might look down at it as it fell. The tall man called out again with a most unearthly cry, "Dead!"

He was arrested by the quick arrival of another man, for whom the rest made way. On seeing him, the miserable creature fell upon his shoulder, sobbing and crying, and pointing to the fountain, where some women were stooping over the motionless bundle, and moving gently about it. They were as silent, however, as the men.

"I know all, I know all," said the last comer. "Be a brave man, my Gaspard! It is better for the poor little plaything to die so, than to live. It has died in a moment without pain. Could it have lived an hour as happily?"

"You are a philosopher, you there," said the Marquis, smiling. "How do they call you?"

"They call me Defarge."

"Of what trade?"

"Monsieur the Marquis, vendor of wine."

"Pick up that, philosopher and vendor of wine," said the Marquis, throwing him another gold coin, "and spend it as you will. The horses there; are they right?"

Without deigning to look at the assemblage a second time, Monsieur the Marquis leaned back in his seat, and was just being driven away with the air of a gentleman who had accidentally broken some common thing, and had paid for it, and could afford to pay for it; when his ease was suddenly disturbed by a coin flying into his carriage and ringing on its floor.

"Hold!" said Monsieur the Marquis. "Hold the horses! Who threw that?"

He looked to the spot where Defarge the vendor of wine had stood, a moment before; but the wretched father was groveling on his face on the pavement in that spot, and the figure that stood beside him was the figure of a dark stout woman, knitting.

"You dogs!" said the Marquis, but smoothly, and with an unchanged front, except as to the spots on his nose: "I would ride over any of you very willingly, and exterminate you from the earth. If I knew which rascal threw at the carriage, and if that brigand were sufficiently near it, he should be crushed under the wheels."

So cowed was their condition, and so long and so hard their experience of what such a man could do to them, within the law and beyond it, that not a voice, or a hand, or even an eye, was raised. Among the men, not one. But, the woman who stood knitting looked up steadily, and looked the Marquis in the face. It was not for his dignity to notice it; his contemptuous eyes passed over her, and over all the other rats; and he leaned back in his seat again, and gave the word "Go on!"

He was driven on, and other carriages came whirling by in quick succession; the Minister, the State-Projector, the Farmer-General, the Doctor, the Lawyer, the Ecclesiastic, the Grand Opera, the Comedy, the whole Fancy Ball in a bright continuous flow, came whirling by. The rats had crept out of their holes to look on, and they remained looking on for hours; soldiers and police often passing between them and the spectacle, and making a barrier behind which they slunk, and through which they peeped. The father had long ago taken up his bundle and hidden himself away with it, when the woman who had tended the bundle while it lay on the base of the fountain, sat there watching the running of the water and the rolling of the Fancy Ball—when the one woman who had stood conspicuous, knitting, still knitted on with the steadfastness of Fate. The water of the fountain ran, the swift river ran, the day ran into evening, so much life in the city ran into death according to rule, time and tide waited for no man, the rats were sleeping close together in their dark holes again, the Fancy Ball was lighted up at supper, all things ran their course.

E i g h t

MONSIEUR THE MARQUIS IN THE COUNTRY

A BEAUTIFUL LANDSCAPE, WITH THE CORN BRIGHT IN IT, but not abundant. Patches of poor rye where corn should have been, patches of poor peas and beans, patches of most coarse vegetable substitutes for wheat. On inanimate nature, as on the men and women who cultivated it, a prevalent tendency toward an appearance of vegetating unwillingly—a dejected disposition to give up, and wither away.

Monsieur the Marquis in his traveling carriage (which might have been lighter), conducted by four post-horses and two postilions, fagged up a steep hill. A blush on the countenance of Monsieur the Marquis was no impeachment of his high breeding; it was not from within; it was occasioned by an external circumstance beyond his control—the setting sun.

The sunset struck so brilliantly into the traveling carriage when it gained the hilltop, that its occupant was steeped in crimson. "It will die out," said Monsieur the Marquis, glancing at his hands, "directly."

In effect, the sun was so low that it dipped at the moment. When the heavy drag had been adjusted to the wheel, and the carriage slid downhill, with a cinderous smell, in a cloud of dust, the red glow departed quickly; the sun and the Marquis going down together, there was no glow left when the drag was taken off.

But, there remained a broken country, bold and open, a little village at the bottom of the hill, a broad sweep and rise beyond it, a churchtower, a windmill, a forest for the chase, and a crag with a fortress on it used as a prison. Round upon all these darkening objects as the night drew on, the Marquis looked, with the air of one who was coming near home.

The village had its one poor street, with its poor brewery, poor tannery, poor tavern, poor stable-yard for relays of post-horses, poor fountain, all usual poor appointments. It had its poor people too. All its people were poor, and many of them were sitting at their doors, shredding spare onions and the like for supper, while many were at the fountain, washing leaves, and grasses, and any such small yieldings of the earth that could be eaten. Expressive signs of what made them poor, were not wanting; the tax for the state, the tax for the church, the tax for the lord, tax local, and tax general, were to be paid here and to be paid there, according to solemn inscription in the little village, until the wonder was, that there was any village left unswallowed.

Few children were to be seen, and no dogs. As to the men and women, their choice on earth was stated in the prospect—Life on the lowest terms that could sustain it, down in the little village under the mill; or captivity and Death in the dominant prison on the crag.

Heralded by a courier in advance, and by the cracking of his postilions' whips, which twined snakelike about their heads in the evening air, as if he came attended by the Furies, Monsieur the Marquis drew up in his traveling carriage at the posting-house gate. It was hard by the fountain, and the peasants suspended their operations to look at him. He looked at them, and saw in them, without knowing it, the slow, sure filing down of misery-worn face and figure, that was to make the meagerness of Frenchmen an English superstition which should survive the truth through the best part of a hundred years.

Monsieur the Marquis cast his eyes over the submissive faces that drooped before him, as the like of himself had drooped before Monseigneur of the

Court—only the difference was, that these faces drooped merely to suffer and not to propitiate—when a grizzled mender of the roads joined the group.

"Bring me hither that fellow!" said the Marquis to the courier.

The fellow was brought, cap in hand, and the other fellows closed round to look and listen, in the manner of the people at the Paris fountain.

"I passed you on the road?"

"Monseigneur, it is true. I had the honor of being passed on the road."

"Coming up the hill, and at the top of the hill, both?"

"Monseigneur, it is true."

"What did you look at, so fixedly?"

"Monseigneur, I looked at the man."

He stooped a little, and with his tattered blue cap pointed under the carriage. All his fellows stooped to look under the carriage.

"What man, pig? And why look there?"

"Pardon, Monseigneur; he swung by the chain of the shoe—the drag."

"Who?" demanded the traveler.

"Monseigneur, the man."

"May the Devil carry away these idiots! How do you call the man? You know all the men of this part of the country. Who was he?"

"Your clemency, Monseigneur! He was not of this part of the country. Of all the days of my life, I never saw him."

"Swinging by the chain? To be suffocated?"

"With your gracious permission, that was the wonder of it, Monseigneur. His head hanging over—like this!"

He turned himself sideways to the carriage, and leaned back, with his face thrown up to the sky, and his head hanging down; then recovered himself, fumbled with his cap, and made a bow.

"What was he like?"

"Monseigneur, he was whiter than the miller. All covered with dust, white as a spectre, tall as a spectre!"

The picture produced an immense sensation in the little crowd; but all eyes, without comparing notes with other eyes, looked at Monsieur the Marquis. Perhaps, to observe whether he had any spectre on his conscience.

"Truly, you did well," said the Marquis, felicitously sensible that such vermin were not to ruffle him, "to see a thief accompanying my carriage, and not open that great mouth of yours. Bah! Put him aside, Monsieur Gabelle!"

Monsieur Gabelle was the Postmaster, and some other taxing functionary, united; he had come out with great obsequiousness to assist at this examination, and had held the examined by the drapery of his arm in an official manner.

"Bah! Go aside!" said Monsieur Gabelle.

"Lay hands on this stranger if he seeks to lodge in your village tonight, and be sure that his business is honest, Gabelle."

"Monseigneur, I am flattered to devote myself to your orders."

"Did he run away, fellow?—where is that accursed?"

The accursed was already under the carriage with some half-dozen particular friends, pointing out the chain with his blue cap. Some half-dozen other particular friends promptly hauled him out, and presented him breathless to Monsieur the Marquis.

"Did the man run away, Dolt, when we stopped for the drag?"

"Monseigneur, he precipitated himself over the hillside, head first, as a person plunges into the river."

"See to it, Gabelle. Go on!"

The half-dozen who were peering at the chain were still among the wheels, like sheep; the wheels turned so suddenly that they were lucky to save their skins and bones; they had very little else to save, or they might not have been so fortunate.

The burst with which the carriage started out of the village and up the rise beyond, was soon checked by the steepness of the hill. Gradually, it subsided to a foot-pace, swinging and lumbering upward among the many sweet scents of a summer night. The postilions, with a thousand gossamer gnats circling about them in lieu of the Furies, quietly mended the points to the lashes of their whips; the valet walked by the horses; the courier was audible, trotting on ahead into the dim distance.

At the steepest point of the hill there was a little burial-ground, with a cross, and a new, large figure of Our Savior on it; it was a poor figure in wood, done by some inexperienced rustic carver, but he had studied the figure from the life—his own life, maybe—for it was dreadfully spare and thin.

To this distressful emblem of a great distress that had long been growing worse, and was not at its worst, a woman was kneeling. She turned her head as the carriage came up to her, rose quickly, and presented herself at the carriage door.

"It is you, Monseigneur! Monseigneur, a petition!"

With an exclamation of impatience, but with his unchangeable face, the Marquis looked out.

"How, then! What is it? Always petitions!"

"Monseigneur. For the love of the great God! My husband, the forester."

"What of your husband, the forester? Always the same with you people. He cannot pay something?"

"He has paid all, Monseigneur. He is dead."

"Well! He is quiet. Can I restore him to you?"

"Alas, no, Monseigneur! But he lies yonder, under a little heap of poor grass."

"Well?"

"Monseigneur, there are so many little heaps of poor grass."

"Again, well?"

She looked an old woman, but was young. Her manner was one of passionate grief; by turns she clasped her veinous and knotted hands together with wild energy, and laid one of them on the carriage-door—tenderly, caressingly, as if it had been a human breast, and could be expected to feel the appealing touch.

"Monseigneur, hear me! Monseigneur, hear my petition! My husband died of want; so many die of want; so many more will die of want."

"Again, well? Can I feed them?"

"Monseigneur, the good God knows; but I don't ask it. My petition is, that a morsel of stone or wood, with my husband's name, may be placed over him to show where he lies. Otherwise, the place will be quickly forgotten, it will never be found when I am dead of the same malady. I shall be laid under some other heap of poor grass. Monseigneur, they are so many, they increase so fast, there is so much want. Monseigneur! Monseigneur!"

The valet had put her away from the door, the carriage had broken into a brisk trot, the postilions had quickened the pace, she was left far behind, and the Marquis, again escorted by the Furies, was rapidly diminishing the league or two of distance that remained between him and his chateau.

The sweet scents of the summer night rose all around him, and rose, as the rain falls, impartially, on the dusty, ragged, and toil-worn group at the fountain not far away; to whom the mender of roads, with the aid of the blue cap without which he was nothing, still enlarged upon his man like a spectre, as long as they could bear it. By degrees, as they could bear no more, they dropped off one by one, and the lights twinkled in little casements; which lights, as the casements darkened, and more stars came out, seemed to have shot up into the sky instead of having been extinguished.

The shadow of a large high-roofed house, and of many overhanging trees, was upon Monsieur the Marquis by that time; and the shadow was exchanged for the light of a flambeau, as his carriage stopped, and the great door of his chateau was opened to him.

"Monsieur Charles, whom I expect; is he arrived from England?"

"Monseigneur, not yet."

N i n e

THE GORGON'S HEAD

IT WAS A HEAVY MASS OF BUILDING, THAT CHATEAU OF Monsieur the Marquis, with a large stone courtyard before it, and two stone sweeps of staircase meeting in a stone terrace before the principal door.

A stony business altogether, with heavy stone balustrades, and stone urns, and stone flowers, and stone faces of men, and stone heads of lions, in all directions. As if the Gorgon's head had surveyed it, when it was finished, two centuries ago.

Up the broad flight of shallow steps, Monsieur the Marquis, flambeau preceded, went from his carriage, sufficiently disturbing the darkness to elicit loud remonstrance from an owl in the roof of the great pile of stable-building away among the trees. All else was so quiet, that the flambeau carried up the steps, and the other flambeau held at the great door, burnt as if they were in a close room of state, instead of being in the open night-air. Other sound than the Owl's voice there was none, save the falling of a fountain into its stone basin; for, it was one of those dark nights that hold their breath by the hour together, and then heave a long, low sigh, and hold their breath again.

The great door clanged behind him, and Monsieur the Marquis crossed a hall grim with certain old boar spears, swords, and knives of the chase; grimmer with certain heavy riding-rods and riding-whips, of which many a peasant, gone to his benefactor, Death, had felt the weight when his lord was angry.

Avoiding the larger rooms, which were dark and made fast for the night, Monsieur the Marquis, with his flambeau-bearer going on before, went up the staircase to a door in a corridor. This thrown open, admitted him to his own private apartment of three rooms: his bedchamber and two others. High vaulted rooms, with cool uncarpeted floors, great dogs upon the hearths for the burning of wood in wintertime, and all luxuries befitting the state of a marquis in a luxurious age and country. The fashion of the last Louis but one, of the line that was never to break—the fourteenth Louis—was conspicuous in their rich furniture; but, it was diversified by many objects that were illustrations of old pages in the history of France.

A supper-table was laid for two, in the third of the rooms; a round room, in one of the chateau's four extinguisher-topped towers; a small lofty room, with its window wide open, and the wooden jalousie-blinds closed, so that the dark night only showed in slight horizontal lines of black, alternating with their broad lines of stone color.

"My nephew," said the Marquis, glancing at the supper preparation; "they said he was not arrived."

Nor was he; but he had been expected with Monseigneur.

"Ah! It is not probable he will arrive tonight; nevertheless, leave the table as it is. I shall be ready in a quarter of an hour."

In a quarter of an hour, Monseigneur was ready, and sat down alone to his sumptuous and choice supper. His chair was opposite to the window, and he had taken his soup, and was raising his glass of Bordeaux to his lips, when he put it down.

"What is that?" he calmly asked, looking with attention at the horizontal lines of black and stone color.

"Monseigneur? That?"

"Outside the blinds. Open the blinds."

It was done.

"Well?"

"Monseigneur, it is nothing. The trees and the night are all that are here."

The servant who spoke, had thrown the blinds wide, had looked out into the vacant darkness, and stood, with that blank behind him, looking round for instructions.

"Good," said the imperturbable master. "Close them again."

That was done too, and the Marquis went on with his supper. He was halfway through it, when he again stopped with his glass in his hand, hearing the sound of wheels. It came on briskly, and came up to the front of the chateau.

"Ask who is arrived."

It was the nephew of Monseigneur. He had been some few leagues behind Monseigneur, early in the afternoon. He had diminished the distance rapidly, but not so rapidly as to come up with Monseigneur on the road. He had heard of Monseigneur, at the posting-houses, as being before him.

He was to be told (said Monseigneur) that supper awaited him then and there, and that he was prayed to come to it. In a little while, he came. He had been known in England as Charles Darnay.

Monseigneur received him in a courtly manner, but they did not shake hands.

"You left Paris yesterday, sir?" he said to Monseigneur, as he took his seat at table.

"Yesterday. And you?"

"I come direct."

"From London?"

"Yes."

"You have been a long time coming," said the Marquis, with a smile.

"On the contrary, I come direct."

"Pardon me! I mean, not a long time on the journey; a long time intending the journey."

"I have been detained by"—the nephew stopped a moment in his answer—"various business."

"Without doubt," said the polished uncle.

So long as a servant was present, no other words passed between them. When coffee had been served and they were alone together, the nephew, looking at the uncle and meeting the eyes of the face that was like a fine mask, opened a conversation.

"I have come back, sir, as you anticipate, pursuing the object that took me away. It carried me into great and unexpected peril; but it is a sacred object, and if it had carried me to death, I hope it would have sustained me."

"Not to death," said the uncle; "it is not necessary to say, to death."

"I doubt, sir," returned the nephew, "whether, if it had carried me to the utmost brink of death, you would have cared to stop me there."

The deepened marks in the nose, and the lengthening of the fine straight lines in the cruel face, looked ominous as to that; the uncle made a graceful gesture of protest, which was so clearly a slight form of good breeding that it was not reassuring.

"Indeed, sir," pursued the nephew, "for anything I know, you may have expressly worked to give a more suspicious appearance to the suspicious circumstances that surrounded me."

"No, no, no," said the uncle, pleasantly.

"But, however that may be," resumed the nephew, glancing at him with deep distrust, "I know that your diplomacy would stop me by any means, and would know no scruple as to means."

"My friend, I told you so," said the uncle, with a fine pulsation in the two marks. "Do me the favor to recall that I told you so, long ago."

"I recall it."

"Thank you," said the Marquis—very sweetly indeed.

His tone lingered in the air, almost like the tone of a musical instrument.

"In effect, sir," pursued the nephew, "I believe it to be at once your bad fortune, and my good fortune, that has kept me out of a prison in France here."

"I do not quite understand," returned the uncle, sipping his coffee. "Dare I ask you to explain?"

"I believe that if you were not in disgrace with the court, and had not been overshadowed by that cloud for years past, a letter *de cachet* would have sent me to some fortress indefinitely."

"It is possible," said the uncle, with great calmness. "For the honor of the family, I could even resolve to incommode you to that extent. Pray excuse me!"

"I perceive that, happily for me, the reception of the day before yesterday was, as usual, a cold one," observed the nephew.

"I would not say happily, my friend," returned the uncle, with refined politeness; "I would not be sure of that. A good opportunity for consideration, surrounded by the advantages of solitude, might influence your destiny to far greater advantage than you influence it for yourself. But it is useless to discuss the question. I am, as you say, at a disadvantage. These little instruments of correction, these gentle aids to the power and honor of families, these slight favors that might so incommode you, are only to be obtained now by interest and importunity. They are sought by so many, and they are granted (comparatively) to so few! It used not to be so, but France in all such things is changed for the worse. Our not remote ancestors held the right of life and death over the surrounding vulgar. From this room, many such dogs have been taken out to be hanged; in the next room (my bedroom), one fellow, to our knowledge, was poniarded on the spot for professing some insolent delicacy respecting his daughter—*his* daughter! We have lost many privileges; a new philosophy has become the mode; and the assertion of our station, in these days, might (I do not go so far as to say would, but might) cause us real inconvenience. All very bad, very bad!"

The Marquis took a gentle little pinch of snuff, and shook his head; as elegantly despondent as he could becomingly be, of a country still containing himself, that great means of regeneration.

"We have so asserted our station, both in the old time and in the modern time also," said the nephew, gloomily, "that I believe our name to be more detested than any name in France."

"Let us hope so," said the uncle. "Detestation of the high, is the involuntary homage of the low."

"There is not," pursued the nephew in his former tone, "a face I can look at, in all this country round about us, which looks at me with any deference on it but the dark deference of fear and slavery."

"A compliment," said the Marquis, "to the grandeur of the family, merited by the manner in which the family has sustained its grandeur. Hah!" And he took another gentle little pinch of snuff, and lightly crossed his legs.

But, when his nephew, leaning an elbow on the table, covered his eyes thoughtfully and dejectedly with his hand, the fine mask looked at him sideways, with a stronger concentration of keenness, closeness, and dislike, than was comportable with its wearer's assumption of indifference.

"Repression is the only lasting philosophy. The dark deference of fear and slavery, my friend," observed the Marquis, "will keep the dogs obedient to the whip, as long as this roof," looking up to it, "shuts out the sky."

That might not be so long as the Marquis supposed. If a picture of the chateau as it was to be a very few years hence, and of fifty like it as they too were to be a very few years hence, could have been shown to him that night, he might have been at a loss to claim his own from the ghastly, fire-charred, plunder-wrecked ruins. As for the roof he vaunted, he might have found *that* shutting out the sky in a new way—to wit, forever, from the eyes of the bodies into which its lead was fired, out of the barrels of a hundred thousand muskets.

"Meanwhile," said the Marquis, "I will preserve the honor and repose of the family, if you will not. But you must be fatigued. Shall we terminate our conference for the night?"

"A moment more."

"An hour, if you please."

"Sir," said the nephew, "we have done wrong, and are reaping the fruits of wrong."

"*We* have done wrong?" repeated the Marquis, with an inquiring smile, and delicately pointing, first to the nephew, then to himself.

"Our family; our honorable family, whose honor is of so much account to both of us, in such different ways. Even in my father's time, we did a world of wrong, injuring every human creature who came between us and our pleasure, whatever it was. Why need I speak of my father's time, when it is equally yours? Can I separate my father's twin brother, joint inheritor, and next successor, from himself?"

"Death has done that," said the Marquis.

"And has left me," answered the nephew, "bound to a system that is frightful to me, responsible for it, but powerless in it; seeking to execute the last request of my dear mother's lips, and obey the last look of my dear mother's eyes, which implored me to have mercy and to redress; and tortured by seeking assistance and power in vain."

"Seeking them from me, my nephew," said the Marquis, touching him on the breast with his forefinger—they were now standing by the hearth—"you will forever seek them in vain, be assured."

Every fine straight line in the clear whiteness of his face, was cruelly, craftily, and closely compressed, while he stood looking quietly at his nephew, with his snuff-box in his hand. Once again he touched him on the breast, as though his finger were the fine point of a small sword, with which, in delicate finesse, he ran him through the body, and said,

"My friend, I will die, perpetuating the system under which I have lived."

When he had said it, he took a culminating pinch of snuff, and put his box in his pocket.

"Better to be a rational creature," he added then, after ringing a small bell on the table, "and accept your natural destiny. But you are lost, Monsieur Charles, I see."

"This property and France are lost to me," said the nephew, sadly; "I renounce them."

"Are they both yours to renounce? France may be, but is the property? It is scarcely worth mentioning; but, is it yet?"

"I had no intention, in the words I used, to claim it yet. If it passed to me from you, tomorrow—"

"Which I have the vanity to hope is not probable."

"—or twenty years hence—"

"You do me too much honor," said the Marquis; "still, I prefer that supposition."

"—I would abandon it, and live otherwise and elsewhere. It is little to relinquish. What is it but a wilderness of misery and ruin!"

"Hah!" said the Marquis, glancing round the luxurious room.

"To the eye it is fair enough, here; but seen in its integrity, under the sky and by the daylight, it is a crumbling tower of waste, mismanagement, extortion, debt, mortgage, oppression, hunger, nakedness, and suffering."

"Hah!" said the Marquis again, in a well satisfied manner.

"If it ever becomes mine, it shall be put into some hands better qualified to free it slowly (if such a thing is possible) from the weight that drags it down, so that the miserable people who cannot leave it and who have been long wrung to the last point of endurance, may, in another generation, suffer less; but it is not for me. There is a curse on it, and on all this land."

"And you?" said the uncle. "Forgive my curiosity; do you, under your new philosophy, graciously intend to live?"

"I must do, to live, what others of my countrymen, even with nobility at their backs, may have to do some day—work."

"In England, for example?"

"Yes. The family honor, sir, is safe from me in this country. The family name can suffer from me in no other, for I bear it in no other."

The ringing of the bell had caused the adjoining bedchamber to be lighted. It now shone brightly, through the door of communication. The Marquis looked that way, and listened for the retreating step of his valet.

"England is very attractive to you, seeing how indifferently you have prospered there," he observed then, turning his calm face to his nephew with a smile.

"I have already said, that for my prospering there, I am sensible I may be indebted to you, sir. For the rest, it is my Refuge."

"They say, those boastful English, that it is the Refuge of many. You know a compatriot who has found a Refuge there? A Doctor?"

"Yes."

"With a daughter?"

"Yes."

"Yes," said the Marquis. "You are fatigued. Good night!"

As he bent his head in his most courtly manner, there was a secrecy in his smiling face, and he conveyed an air of mystery to those words, which struck the eyes and ears of his nephew forcibly. At the same time, the thin straight lines of the setting of the eyes, and the thin straight lips, and the markings in the nose, curved with a sarcasm that looked handsomely diabolic.

"Yes," repeated the Marquis. "A Doctor with a daughter. Yes. So commences the new philosophy! You are fatigued. Good night!"

It would have been of as much avail to interrogate any stone face outside the chateau, as to interrogate that face of his. The nephew looked at him, in vain, in passing on to the door.

"Good night!" said the uncle. "I look to the pleasure of seeing you again in the morning. Good repose! Light Monsieur my nephew to his chamber there!—And burn Monsieur my nephew in his bed, if you will," he added to himself, before he rang his little bell again, and summoned his valet to his own bedroom.

The valet come and gone, Monsieur the Marquis walked to and fro in his loose chamber-robe, to prepare himself gently for sleep, that hot, still night. Rustling about the room, his softly-slippered feet making no noise on the floor, he moved like a refined tiger:—looked like some enchanted marquis of the impenitently wicked sort, in story, whose periodical change into tiger form was either just going off, or just coming on.

He moved from end to end of his voluptuous bedroom, looking again at the scraps of the day's journey that came unbidden into his mind; the slow toil up the hill at sunset, the setting sun, the descent, the mill, the prison on the crag, the little village in the hollow, the peasants at the fountain, and the mender of roads with his blue cap pointing out the chain under the carriage. That fountain suggested the Paris fountain, the little bundle lying on the step, the women bending over it, and the tall man with his arms up, crying, "Dead!"

"I am cool now," said Monsieur the Marquis, "and may go to bed."

So, leaving only one light burning on the large hearth, he let his thin gauze curtains fall around him, and heard the night break its silence with a long sigh as he composed himself to sleep.

The stone faces on the outer walls stared blindly at the black night for three heavy hours; for three heavy hours, the horses in the stables rattled at their racks, the dogs barked, and the owl made a noise with very little resemblance in it to the noise conventionally assigned to the owl by men-poets. But, it is the obstinate custom of such creatures hardly ever to say what is set down for them.

For three heavy hours, the stone faces of the chateau, lion and human, stared blindly at the night. Dead darkness lay on all the landscape, dead darkness added its own hush to the hushing dust on all the roads. The burial-place had got to the pass that its little heaps of poor grass were undistinguishable from one another; the figure on the Cross might have come down, for anything that could be seen of it. In the village, taxers and taxed were fast asleep. Dreaming, perhaps, of banquets, as the starved usually do, and of ease and rest, as the driven slave and the yoked ox may, its lean inhabitants slept soundly, and were fed and freed.

The fountain in the village flowed unseen and unheard, and the fountain at the chateau dropped unseen and unheard—both melting away, like the minutes that were falling from the spring of Time—through three dark hours. Then, the gray water of both began to be ghostly in the light, and the eyes of the stone faces of the chateau were opened.

It grew lighter and lighter, until at last the sun touched the tops of the still trees, and poured its radiance over the hill. In the glow, the water of the chateau fountain seemed to turn to blood, and the stone faces crimsoned. The carol of the birds was loud and high, and, on the weather-beaten sill of the great window of the bedchamber of Monsieur the Marquis, one little bird sang its sweetest song with all its might. At this, the nearest stone face seemed to stare amazed, and, with open mouth and dropped under-jaw, looked awe-stricken.

Now, the sun was full up, and movement began in the village. Casement windows opened, crazy doors were unbarred, and people came forth shivering—chilled, as yet, by the new sweet air. Then began the rarely lightened toil of the day among the village population. Some, to the fountain; some, to the fields; men and women here, to dig and delve; men and women there, to see to the poor livestock, and lead the bony cows out, to such pasture as could be found by the roadside. In the church and at the Cross, a kneeling figure or two; attendant on the latter prayers, the led cow, trying for a breakfast among the weeds at the Cross-foot.

The chateau awoke later, as became its quality, but awoke gradually and surely. First, the lonely boar-spears and knives of the chase had been reddened as of old; then, had gleamed trenchant in the morning sunshine; now, doors and windows were thrown open, horses in their stables looked round over their shoulders at the light and freshness pouring in at doorways, leaves sparkled and rustled at iron-grated windows, dogs pulled hard at their chains, and reared impatient to be loosed.

All these trivial incidents belonged to the routine of life, and the return of morning. Surely, not so the ringing of the great bell of the chateau, nor the running up and down the stairs, nor the hurried figures on the terrace, nor the booting and tramping here and there and everywhere, nor the quick saddling of horses and riding away?

What winds conveyed this hurry to the grizzled mender of roads, already at work on the hilltop beyond the village, with his day's dinner (not much to carry) laying in a bundle that it was worth no crow's while to peck at, on a heap of stones? Had the birds, carrying some grains of it to a distance, dropped one over him as they sow chance seeds? Whether or no, the mender of roads ran, on the sultry morning, as if for his life, down the hill, knee-high in dust, and never stopped till he got to the fountain.

All the people of the village were at the fountain, standing about in their depressed manner, and whispering softly, but showing no other emotions than grim curiosity and surprise. The led cows, hastily brought in and tethered to anything that would hold them, were looking stupidly on, or lying down chewing the cud of nothing particularly repaying their trouble, which they had picked up in their interrupted saunter. Some of the people of the chateau, and some of those of the posting-house, and all the taxing authorities, were armed more or less, and were crowded on the other side of the little street in a purposeless way, that was highly fraught with nothing. Already, the mender of roads had penetrated into the midst of a group of fifty particular friends, and was smiting himself in the breast with his blue cap. What did all this portend, and what portended the swift hoisting-up of Monsieur Gabelle behind a servant on horseback, and the conveying away of the said Gabelle (double-laden though the horse was), at a gallop, like a new version of the German ballad of Leonora?

It portended that there was one stone face too many, up at the chateau.

The Gorgon had surveyed the building again in the night, and had added the one stone face wanting; the stone face for which it had waited through about two hundred years.

It lay back on the pillow of Monsieur the Marquis. It was like a fine mask, suddenly startled, made angry, and petrified. Driven home into the heart of the stone figure attached to it, was a knife. Round its hilt was a frill of paper, on which was scrawled:

"*Drive him fast to his tomb. This, from* JACQUES."

Ten

TWO PROMISES

MORE MONTHS, TO THE NUMBER OF TWELVE, HAD COME and gone, and Mr. Charles Darnay was established in England as a higher teacher of the French language who was conversant with French literature. In this age, he would have been a Professor; in that age, he was a Tutor. He read with young men who could find any leisure and interest for the study of a living tongue spoken all over the world, and he cultivated a taste for its stores of knowledge and fancy. He could write of them, besides, in sound English, and render them into sound English. Such masters were not at that time easily found; Princes that had been, and Kings that were to be, were not yet of the Teacher class, and no ruined nobility had dropped out of Tellson's ledgers, to turn cooks and carpenters. As a tutor, whose attainments made the student's way unusually pleasant and profitable, and as an elegant translator, who brought something to his work besides mere dictionary knowledge, young Mr. Darnay soon became known and encouraged. He was well acquainted, moreover, with the circumstances of his country, and those were of ever-growing interest. So, with great perseverance and untiring industry, he prospered.

In London, he had expected neither to walk on pavements of gold, nor lie on beds of roses; if he had had any such exalted expectation, he would not have prospered. He had expected labor, and he found it, and did it, and made the best of it. In this, his prosperity consisted.

A certain portion of his time was passed at Cambridge, where he read with undergraduates as a sort of tolerated smuggler who drove a contraband trade in European languages, instead of conveying Greek and Latin through the Custom-house. The rest of his time he passed in London.

Now, from the days when it was always summer in Eden, to these days when it is mostly winter in fallen latitudes, the world of a man has invariably gone one way—Charles Darnay's way—the way of the love of a woman.

He had loved Lucie Manette from the hour of his danger. He had never heard a sound so sweet and dear as the sound of her compassionate voice; he had never seen a face so tenderly beautiful as hers, when it was confronted with his own on the edge of the grave that had been dug for him. But, he had not yet spoken to her on the subject; the assassination at the deserted chateau far away beyond the heaving water and the long, long, dusty roads—the solid stone chateau which had itself become the mere mist of a dream—had been done a year, and he had never yet, by so much as a single spoken word, disclosed to her the state of his heart.

That he had his reasons for this, he knew full well. It was again a summer day when, lately arrived in London from his college occupation, he turned into the quiet corner in the Soho, bent on seeking an opportunity of opening his mind to Doctor Manette. It was the close of the summer day, and he knew Lucie to be out with Miss Pross.

He found the Doctor reading in his armchair at a window. The energy which had at once supported him under his old sufferings and aggravated their sharpness, had been gradually restored to him. He was now a very energetic man indeed, with great firmness of purpose, strength of resolution, and vigor of action. In his recovered energy he was sometimes a little fitful and sudden, as he had at first been in the exercise of his other recovered faculties; but this had never been frequently observable, and had grown more and more rare.

He studied much, slept little, sustained a great deal of fatigue with ease, and was equably cheerful. To him, now entered Charles Darnay, at sight of whom he laid aside his book and held out his hand.

"Charles Darnay! I rejoice to see you. We have been counting on your return these three or four days past. Mr. Stryver and Sydney Carton were both here yesterday, and both made you out to be more than due."

"I am obliged to them for their interest in the matter," he answered, a little coldly as to them, though very warmly as to the Doctor. "Miss Manette—"

"Is well," said the Doctor, as he stopped short, "and your return will delight us all. She has gone out on some household matters, but will soon be home."

"Doctor Manette, I knew she was from home. I took the opportunity of her being from home, to beg to speak to you."

There was a blank silence.

"Yes"; said the Doctor, with evident constraint. "Bring your chair here, and speak on."

He complied as to the chair, but appeared to find the speaking on less easy.

"I have had the happiness, Doctor Manette, of being so intimate here," so he at length began, "for some year and a half, that I hope the topic on which I am about to touch may not—"

He was stayed by the Doctor's putting out his hand to stop him. When he had kept it so a little while, he said, drawing it back:

"Is Lucie the topic?"

"She is."

"It is hard for me to speak of her, at any time. It is very hard for me to hear her spoken of in that tone of yours, Charles Darnay."

"It is a tone of fervent admiration, true homage and deep love, Doctor Manette!" he said, deferentially.

There was another blank silence before her father rejoined:

"I believe it. I do you justice; I believe it."

His constraint was so manifest, and it was so manifest, too, that it orig-inated in an unwillingness to approach the subject, that Charles Darnay hesitated.

"Shall I go on, sir?"

Another blank.

"Yes, go on."

"You anticipate what I would say, though you cannot know how earnestly I say it, how earnestly I feel it, without knowing my secret heart, and the hopes and fears and anxieties with which it has long been laden. Dear Doctor Manette, I love your daughter fondly, dearly, disinterestedly, devot-edly. If ever there were love in the world, I love her. You have loved yourself; let your old love speak for me!"

The Doctor sat with his face turned away, and his eyes bent on the ground. At the last words, he stretched out his hand again, hurriedly, and cried:

"Not that, sir! Let that be! I adjure you, do not recall that!"

His cry was so like a cry of actual pain, that it rang in Charles Darnay's ears long after he had ceased. He motioned with the hand he had extended, and it seemed to be an appeal to Darnay to pause. The latter so received it, and remained silent.

"I ask your pardon," said the Doctor, in a subdued tone, after some moments. "I do not doubt your loving Lucie; you may be satisfied of it."

He turned toward him in his chair, but did not look at him, or raise his eyes. His chin dropped upon his hand, and his white hair overshadowed his face:

"Have you spoken to Lucie?"

"No."

"Nor written?"

"Never."

"It would be ungenerous to affect not to know that your self-denial is to be referred to your consideration for her father. Her father thanks you."

He offered his hand; but his eyes did not go with it.

"I know," said Darnay, respectfully, "how can I fail to know, Doctor Manette, I who have seen you together from day to day, that between you and Miss Manette there is an affection so unusual, so touching, so belonging to the circumstances in which it has been nurtured, that it can have few parallels, even in the tenderness between a father and child. I know, Doctor Manette— how can I fail to know—that, mingled with the affection and duty of a daugh-ter who has become a woman, there is, in her heart toward you, all the love and reliance of infancy itself. I know that, as in her childhood she had no par-ent, so she is now devoted to you with all the constancy and fervor of her present years and character, united to the trustfulness and attachment of the early days in which you were lost to her. I know perfectly well that if you had been restored to her from the world beyond this life, you could hardly be invested, in her sight, with a more sacred character than that in which you are always with her. I know that when she is clinging to you, the hands of baby, girl, and woman, all in one, are round your neck. I know that in loving you she sees and loves her mother at her own age, sees and loves you at my age, loves her mother broken-hearted, loves you through your dreadful trial and in your blessed restoration. I have known this, night and day, since I have known you in your home."

Her father sat silent, with his face bent down. His breathing was a little quickened; but he repressed all other signs of agitation.

"Dear Doctor Manette, always knowing this, always seeing her and you with this hallowed light about you, I have forborne, and forborne, as long as it was in the nature of man to do it. I have felt, and do even now feel, that to bring my love—even mine—between you, is to touch your history with something not quite so good as itself. But I love her. Heaven is my witness that I love her!"

"I believe it," answered her father, mournfully. "I have thought so, before now. I believe it."

"But, do not believe," said Darnay, upon whose ear the mournful voice struck with a reproachful sound, "that if my fortune were so cast as that, being one day so happy as to make her my wife, I must at any time put any separation between her and you I could or would breathe a word of what I now say. Besides that I should know it to be hopeless, I should know it to be baseness. If I had any such possibility, even at a remote distance of years, har-bored in my thoughts and hidden in my heart—if it ever had been there—if it ever could be there—I could not now touch this honored hand."

He laid his own upon it as he spoke.

"No, dear Doctor Manette. Like you, a voluntary exile from France; like you, driven from it by its distractions, oppressions, and miseries; like you, striving to live away from it by my own exertions, and trusting in a happier future; I look only to sharing your fortunes, sharing your life and home, and being faithful to you to the death. Not to divide with Lucie her privilege as your child, companion, and friend; but to come in aid of it, and bind her closer to you, if such a thing can be."

His touch still lingered on her father's hand. Answering the touch for a moment, but not coldly, her father rested his hands upon the arms of his chair, and looked up for the first time since the beginning of the conference. A struggle was evidently in his face; a struggle with that occasional look which had a tendency in it to dark doubt and dread.

"You speak so feelingly and so manfully, Charles Darnay, that I thank you with all my heart, and will open all my heart—or nearly so. Have you any reason to believe that Lucie loves you?"

"None. As yet, none."

"Is it the immediate object of this confidence, that you may at once ascertain that, with my knowledge?"

"Not even so. I might not have the hopefulness to do it for weeks; I might (mistaken or not mistaken) have that hopefulness tomorrow."

"Do you seek any guidance from me?"

"I ask none, sir. But I have thought it possible that you might have it in your power, if you should deem it right, to give me some."

"Do you seek any promise from me?"

"I do seek that."

"What is it?"

"I well understand that, without you, I could have no hope. I well understand that, even if Miss Manette held me at this moment in her innocent heart—do not think I have the presumption to assume so much—I could retain no place in it against her love for her father."

"If that be so, do you see what, on the other hand, is involved in it?"

"I understand equally well, that a word from her father in any suitor's favor, would outweigh herself and all the world. For which reason, Doctor Manette," said Darnay, modestly but firmly, "I would not ask that word, to save my life."

"I am sure of it. Charles Darnay, mysteries arise out of close love, as well as out of wide division; in the former case, they are subtle and delicate, and difficult to penetrate. My daughter Lucie is, in this one respect, such a mystery to me; I can make no guess at the state of her heart."

"May I ask, sir, if you think she is—" As he hesitated, her father supplied the rest.

"Is sought by any other suitor?"

"It is what I meant to say."

Her father considered a little before he answered:

"You have seen Mr. Carton here, yourself. Mr. Stryver is here too, occasionally. If it be at all, it can only be by one of these."

"Or both," said Darnay.

"I had not thought of both; I should not think either, likely. You want a promise from me. Tell me what it is."

"It is, that if Miss Manette should bring to you at any time, on her own part, such a confidence as I have ventured to lay before you, you will bear testimony to what I have said, and to your belief in it. I hope you may be able to think so well of me, as to urge no influence against me. I say nothing more of my stake in this; this is what I ask. The condition on which I ask it, and which you have an undoubted right to require, I will observe immediately."

"I give the promise," said the Doctor, "without any condition. I believe your object to be, purely and truthfully, as you have stated it. I believe your intention is to perpetuate, and not to weaken, the ties between me and my other and far dearer self. If she should ever tell me that you are essential to her perfect happiness, I will give her to you. If there were—Charles Darnay, if there were—"

The young man had taken his hand gratefully; their hands were joined as the Doctor spoke:

"—any fancies, any reasons, any apprehensions, anything whatsoever, new or old, against the man she really loved—the direct responsibility thereof not lying on his head—they should all be obliterated for her sake. She is everything to me; more to me than suffering, more to me than wrong, more to me— Well! This is idle talk."

So strange was the way in which he faded into silence, and so strange his fixed look when he had ceased to speak, that Darnay felt his own hand turn cold in the hand that slowly released and dropped it.

"You said something to me," said Doctor Manette, breaking into a smile. "What was it you said to me?"

He was at a loss how to answer, until he remembered having spoken of a condition. Relieved as his mind reverted to that, he answered:

"Your confidence in me ought to be returned with full confidence on my part. My present name, though but slightly changed from my mother's, is not, as you will remember, my own. I wish to tell you what that is, and why I am in England."

"Stop!" said the Doctor of Beauvais.

"I wish it, that I may the better deserve your confidence, and have no secret from you."

"Stop!"

For an instant, the Doctor even had his two hands at his ears; for another instant, even had his two hands laid on Darnay's lips.

"Tell me when I ask you, not now. If your suit should prosper, if Lucie should love you, you shall tell me on your marriage morning. Do you promise?"

"Willingly."

"Give me your hand. She will be home directly, and it is better she should not see us together tonight. Go! God bless you!"

It was dark when Charles Darnay left him, and it was an hour later and darker when Lucie came home; she hurried into the room alone—for Miss Pross had gone straight upstairs—and was surprised to find his reading chair empty.

"My father!" she called to him. "Father dear!"

Nothing was said in answer, but she heard a low hammering sound in his bedroom. Passing lightly across the intermediate room, she looked in at his door and came running back frightened, crying to herself, with her blood all chilled, "What shall I do! What shall I do!"

Her uncertainty lasted but a moment; she hurried back, and tapped at his door, and softly called to him. The noise ceased at the sound of her voice, and he presently came out to her, and they walked up and down together for a long time.

She came down from her bed, to look at him in his sleep that night. He slept heavily, and his tray of shoemaking tools, and his old unfinished work, were all as usual.

Eleven

A COMPANION PICTURE

"SYDNEY," SAID MR. STRYVER, ON THAT SELF-SAME NIGHT, or morning, to his jackal; "mix another bowl of punch; I have something to say to you."

Sydney had been working double tides that night, and the night before, and the night before that, and a good many nights in succession, making a grand clearance among Mr. Stryver's papers before the setting in of the long vacation. The clearance was effected at last; the Stryver arrears were handsomely fetched up; everything was got rid of, until November should come with its fogs atmospheric and fogs legal, and bring grist to the mill again.

Sydney was none the livelier and none the soberer for so much application. It had taken a deal of extra wet-toweling to pull him through the night; a correspondingly extra quantity of wine had preceded the toweling; and he was in a very damaged condition, as he now pulled his turban off and threw it into the basin in which he had steeped it at intervals for the last six hours.

"Are you mixing that other bowl of punch?" said Stryver the portly, with his hands in his waistband, glancing round from the sofa where he lay on his back.

"I am."

"Now, look here! I am going to tell you something that will rather surprise you, and that perhaps will make you think me not quite as shrewd as you usually do think me. I intend to marry."

"*Do* you?"

"Yes. And not for money. What do you say now?"

"I don't feel disposed to say much. Who is she?"

"Guess."

"Do I know her?"

"Guess."

"I am not going to guess, at five o'clock in the morning, with my brains frying and sputtering in my head. If you want me to guess, you must ask me to dinner."

"Well, then, I'll tell you," said Stryver, coming slowly into a sitting posture. "Sydney, I rather despair of making myself intelligible to you, because you are such an insensible dog."

"And you," returned Sydney, busy concocting the punch, "are such a sensitive and poetical spirit."

"Come!" rejoined Stryver, laughing boastfully, "though I don't prefer any claim to being the soul of Romance (for I hope I know better), still I am a tenderer sort of fellow than *you*."

"You are a luckier, if you mean that."

"I don't mean that. I mean, I am a man of more—more—"

"Say gallantry, while you are about it," suggested Carton.

"Well! I'll say gallantry. My meaning is that, I am a man," said Stryver, inflating himself at his friend as he made the punch, "who cares more to be agreeable, who takes more pains to be agreeable, who knows better how to be agreeable, in a woman's society, than you do."

"Go on," said Sydney Carton.

"No; but before I go on," said Stryver, shaking his head in his bullying way, "I'll have this out with you. You have been at Doctor Manette's house as much as I have, or more than I have. Why, I have been ashamed of your moroseness there! Your manners have been of that silent and sullen and hangdog kind, that, upon my life and soul, I have been ashamed of you, Sydney!"

"It should be very beneficial to a man in your practice at the bar, to be ashamed of anything," returned Sydney; "you ought to be much obliged to me."

"You shall not get off in that way," rejoined Stryver, shouldering the rejoinder at him; "no, Sydney, it's my duty to tell you—and I tell you to your face to do you good—that you are a devilish ill-conditioned fellow in that sort of society. You are a disagreeable fellow."

Sydney drank a bumper of the punch he had made, and laughed.

"Look at me!" said Stryver, squaring himself; "I have less need to make myself agreeable than you have, being more independent in circumstances. Why do I do it?"

"I never saw you do it yet," muttered Carton.

"I do it because it's politic; I do it on principle. And look at me! I get on."

"You don't get on with your account of your matrimonial intentions," answered Carton, with a careless air, "I wish you would keep to that. As to me—will you never understand that I am incorrigible?"

He asked the question with some appearance of scorn.

"You have no business to be incorrigible," was his friend's answer, delivered in no very soothing tone.

"I have no business to be, at all, that I know of," said Sydney Carton. "Who is the lady?"

"Now, don't let my announcement of the name make you uncomfortable, Sydney," said Mr. Stryver, preparing him with ostentatious friendliness for the disclosure he was about to make, "because I know you don't mean half you say; and if you meant it all, it would be of no importance. I make this little preface, because you once mentioned the young lady to me in slighting terms."

"I did?"

"Certainly; and in these chambers."

Sydney Carton looked at his punch and looked at his complacent friend; drank his punch and looked at his complacent friend.

"You made mention of the young lady as a golden-haired doll. The young lady is Miss Manette. If you had been a fellow of any sensitiveness or delicacy of feeling in that kind of way, Sydney, I might have been a little resentful of your employing such a designation; but you are not. You want that sense altogether; therefore, I am no more annoyed when I think of the expression, than I should be annoyed by a man's opinion of a picture of mine, who had no eye for pictures; or of a piece of music of mine, who had no ear for music."

Sydney Carton drank the punch at a great rate; drank it by bumpers, looking at his friend.

"Now you know all about it, Syd," said Mr. Stryver. "I don't care about fortune: she is a charming creature, and I have made up my mind to please myself: on the whole, I think I can afford to please myself. She will have in me a man already pretty well off, and a rapidly rising man, and a man of some distinction: it is a piece of good fortune for her, but she is worthy of good fortune. Are you astonished?"

Carton, still drinking the punch, rejoined, "Why should I be astonished?"

"You approve?"

Carton, still drinking the punch, rejoined, "Why should I not approve?"

"Well!" said his friend Stryver, "you take it more easily than I fancied you would, and are less mercenary on my behalf than I thought you would be; though, to be sure, you know well enough by this time that your ancient chum is a man of a pretty strong will. Yes, Sydney, I have had enough of this style of life, with no other as a change from it; I feel that it is a pleasant thing for a man to have a home when he feels inclined to go to it (when he doesn't, he can stay away), and I feel that Miss Manette will tell well in any station, and will always do me credit. So I have made up my mind. And now, Sydney, old boy, I want to say a word to *you* about *your* prospects. You are in a bad way, you know; you really are in a bad way. You don't know the value of money, you live hard, you'll knock up one of these days, and be ill and poor; you really ought to think about a nurse."

The prosperous patronage with which he said it, made him look twice as big as he was, and four times as offensive.

"Now, let me recommend you," pursued Stryver, "to look it in the face. I have looked it in the face, in my different way; look it in the face, you, in your different way. Marry. Provide somebody to take care of you. Never mind your having no enjoyment of women's society, nor understanding of it, nor tact for it. Find out somebody. Find out some respectable woman with a little property—somebody in the landlady way, or lodging-letting way—and marry her against a rainy day. That's the kind of thing for *you*. Now, think of it, Sydney."

"I'll think of it," said Sydney.

Twelve

THE FELLOW OF DELICACY

Mr. Stryver having made up his mind to that magnanimous bestowal of good fortune on the doctor's daughter, resolved to make her happiness known to her before he left town for the Long Vacation. After some mental debating of the point, he came to the conclusion that it would be as well to get all the preliminaries done with, and they could then arrange at their leisure whether he should give her his hand a week or two before Michaelmas Term, or in the little Christmas vacation between it and Hilary.

As to the strength of his case, he had not a doubt about it, but clearly saw his way to the verdict. Argued with the jury on substantial worldly grounds—the only grounds ever worth taking into account—it was a plain case, and had not a weak spot in it. He called himself for the plaintiff, there was no getting over his evidence. The counsel for the defendant threw up his brief, and the jury did not even turn to consider. After trying it, Stryver, C. J., was satisfied that no plainer case could be.

Accordingly, Mr. Stryver inaugurated the Long Vacation with a formal proposal to take Miss Manette to Vauxhall Gardens; that failing, to Ranelagh; that unaccountably failing too, it behooved him to present himself in Soho, and there declare his noble mind.

Toward Soho, therefore, Mr. Stryver shouldered his way from the Temple, while the bloom of the Long Vacation's infancy was still upon it. Anybody who had seen him projecting himself into Soho while he was yet on Saint Dunstan's side of Temple-bar, bursting in his full-blown way along the pavement, to the jostlement of all weaker people, might have seen how safe and strong he was.

His way taking him past Tellson's, and he both banking at Tellson's and knowing Mr. Lorry as the intimate friend of the Manettes, it entered Mr. Stryver's mind to enter the bank, and reveal to Mr. Lorry the brightness of the Soho horizon. So, he pushed open the door with the weak rattle in its throat, stumbled down the two steps, got past the two ancient cashiers, and shouldered himself into the musty back closet where Mr. Lorry sat at great books ruled for figures, with perpendicular iron bars to his window, as if that were ruled for figures too, and everything under the clouds were a sum.

"Halloa!" said Mr. Stryver. "How do you do? I hope you are well!"

It was Stryver's grand peculiarity that he always seemed too big for any place, or space. He was so much too big for Tellson's that old clerks in distant corners looked up with looks of remonstrance, as though he squeezed them against the wall.

The House itself, magnificently reading the paper quite in the far-off perspective, lowered displeased, as if the Stryver head had been butted into its responsible waistcoat.

The discreet Mr. Lorry said, in a sample tone of the voice he would recommend under the circumstances, "How do you do, Mr. Stryver? How do you do, sir?" and shook hands. There was a peculiarity in his manner of shaking hands, always to be seen in any clerk at Tellson's who shook hands with a customer when the House pervaded the air. He shook in a self-abnegating way, as for one who shook for Tellson and Co.

"Can I do anything for you, Mr. Stryver?" asked Mr. Lorry, in his business character.

"Why, no thank you; this is a private visit to yourself, Mr. Lorry; I have come for a private word."

"Oh indeed!" said Mr. Lorry, bending down his ear, while his eyes strayed to the House afar off.

"I am going," said Mr. Stryver, leaning his arms confidentially on the desk: whereupon, although it was a large double one, there appeared to be not half desk enough for him: "I am going to make an offer of myself in marriage to your agreeable little friend Miss Manette, Mr. Lorry."

"Oh dear me!" cried Mr. Lorry, rubbing his chin, and looking at his visitor dubiously.

"Oh dear me, sir?" repeated Stryver, drawing back. "Oh dear you, sir? What may your meaning be, Mr. Lorry?"

"My meaning?" answered the man of business, "is, of course, friendly and appreciative, and that it does you the greatest credit, and, in short, my meaning is everything you could desire. But—really, you know, Mr. Stryver—" Mr. Lorry paused, and shook his head at him in the oddest manner, as if he were compelled against his will to add, internally, "you know there really is so much too much of you!"

"Well!" said Stryver, slapping the desk with his contentious hand, opening his eyes wider, and taking a long breath, "if I understand you, Mr. Lorry, I'll be hanged!"

Mr. Lorry adjusted his little wig at both ears as a means toward that end, and bit the feather of a pen.

"D—n it all, sir!" said Stryver, staring at him, "am I not eligible?"

"Oh dear, yes! Yes. Oh yes, you're eligible!" said Mr. Lorry. "If you say eligible, you are eligible."

"Am I not prosperous?" asked Stryver.

"Oh! if you come to prosperous, you are prosperous," said Mr. Lorry.

"And advancing?"

"If you come to advancing, you know," said Mr. Lorry, delighted to be able to make another admission, "nobody can doubt that."

"Then what on earth is your meaning, Mr. Lorry?" demanded Stryver, perceptibly crestfallen.

"Well! I—Were you going there now?" asked Mr. Lorry.

"Straight!" said Stryver, with a plump of his fist on the desk.

"Then I think I wouldn't, if I was you."

"Why?" said Stryver. "Now, I'll put you in a corner," forensically shaking a forefinger at him. "You are a man of business and bound to have a reason. State your reason. Why wouldn't you go?"

"Because," said Mr. Lorry, "I wouldn't go on such an object without having some cause to believe that I should succeed."

"D—n ME!" cried Stryver, "but this beats everything!"

Mr. Lorry glanced at the distant House, and glanced at the angry Stryver.

"Here's a man of business—a man of years—a man of experience—in a Bank," said Stryver; "and having summed up three leading reasons for complete success, he says there's no reason at all! Says it with his head on!" Mr. Stryver remarked upon the peculiarity as if it would have been infinitely less remarkable if he had said it with his head off.

"When I speak of success, I speak of success with the young lady; and when I speak of causes and reasons to make success probable, I speak of causes and reasons that will tell as such with the young lady. The young lady, my good sir," said Mr. Lorry, mildly tapping the Stryver arm, "the young lady. The young lady goes before all."

"Then you mean to tell me, Mr. Lorry," said Stryver, squaring his elbows, "that it is your deliberate opinion that the young lady at present in question is a mincing Fool?"

"Not exactly so. I mean to tell you, Mr. Stryver," said Mr. Lorry, reddening, "that I will hear no disrespectful word of that young lady from any lips; and that if I knew any man—which I hope I do not—whose taste was so coarse, and whose temper was so overbearing, that he could not restrain himself from speaking disrespectfully of that young lady at this desk, not even Tellson's should prevent my giving him a piece of my mind."

The necessity of being angry in a suppressed tone had put Mr. Stryver's blood-vessels into a dangerous state when it was his turn to be angry. Mr. Lorry's veins, methodical as their courses could usually be, were in no better state now it was his turn.

"That is what I mean to tell you, sir," said Mr. Lorry. "Pray let there be no mistake about it."

Mr. Stryver sucked the end of a ruler for a little while, and then stood hitting a tune out of his teeth with it, which probably gave him the toothache. He broke the awkward silence by saying:

"This is something new to me, Mr. Lorry. You deliberately advise me not to go up to Soho and offer myself—*my*self, Stryver of the King's Bench bar?"

"Do you ask me for my advice, Mr. Stryver?"

"Yes, I do."

"Very good. Then I give it, and you have repeated it correctly."

"And all I can say of it, is," laughed Stryver with a vexed laugh, "that this—ha, ha!—beats everything past, present, and to come."

"Now understand me," pursued Mr. Lorry. "As a man of business, I am not justified in saying anything about this matter, for, as a man of business, I know nothing of it. But, as an old fellow, who has carried Miss Manette in his arms, who is the trusted friend of Miss Manette and of her father too, and who has a great affection for them both, I have spoken. The confidence is not of my seeking, recollect. Now, you think I may not be right?"

"Not I!" said Stryver, whistling. "I can't undertake to find third parties in common sense; I can only find it for myself. I suppose sense in certain quarters; you suppose mincing bread-and-butter nonsense. It's new to me, but you are right, I dare say."

"What I suppose, Mr. Stryver, I claim to characterize for myself. And understand me, sir," said Mr. Lorry, quickly flushing again. "I will not—not even at Tellson's—have it characterized for me by any gentleman breathing."

"There! I beg your pardon!" said Stryver.

"Granted. Thank you. Well, Mr. Stryver, I was about to say:—it might be painful to you to find yourself mistaken, it might be painful to Doctor Manette to have the task of being explicit with you, it might be very painful to Miss Manette to have the task of being explicit with you. You know the terms upon which I have the honor and happiness to stand with the family. If you please, committing you in no way, representing you in no way, I will undertake to correct my advice by the exercise of a little new observation and judgment expressly brought to bear upon it. If you should then be dissatisfied with it, you can but test its soundness for yourself; if, on the other hand, you should be satisfied with it, and it should be what it now is, it may spare all sides what is best spared. What do you say?"

"How long would you keep me in town?"

"Oh! It is only a question of a few hours. I could go to Soho this evening, and come to your chambers afterward."

"Then I say yes," said Stryver: "I won't go up there now. I am not so hot upon it as that comes to; I say yes, and I shall expect you to look in tonight. Good morning."

Then Mr. Stryver turned and burst out of the Bank, causing such a concussion of air on his passage through, that to stand up against it, bowing behind the two counters, required the utmost remaining strength of the two ancient clerks. Those vulnerable and feeble persons were seen by the public in the act of bowing, and were popularly believed, when they had bowed a customer out, still to keep on bowing in the empty office until they bowed another customer in.

The barrister was keen enough to divine that the banker would not have gone so far in his expression of opinion on any less solid ground than moral certainty. Unprepared as he was for the large pill he had to swallow, he got it down. "And now," said Mr. Stryver, shaking his forensic forefinger at the Temple in general, when it was down, "my way out of this, is, to put you all in the wrong."

It was a bit of the art of an Old Bailey tactician, in which he found great relief. "You shall not put me in the wrong, young lady," said Mr. Stryver; "I'll do that for you."

Accordingly, when Mr. Lorry called that night as late as ten o'clock, Mr. Stryver, among a quantity of books and papers littered out for the purpose, seemed to have nothing less on his mind than the subject of the morning. He even showed surprise when he saw Mr. Lorry, and was altogether in an absent and preoccupied state.

"Well!" said that good-natured emissary, after a full half-hour of bootless attempts to bring him round to the question, "I have been to Soho."

"To Soho?" repeated Mr. Stryver, coldly. "Oh, to be sure! What am I thinking of!"

"And I have no doubt," said Mr. Lorry, "that I was right in the conversation we had. My opinion is confirmed, and I reiterate my advice."

"I assure you," returned Mr. Stryver, in the friendliest way, "that I am sorry for it on your account, and sorry for it on the poor father's account. I know this must always be a sore subject with the family; let us say no more about it."

"I don't understand you," said Mr. Lorry.

"I dare say not," rejoined Stryver, nodding his head in a smoothing and final way; "no matter, no matter."

"But it does matter," Mr. Lorry urged.

"No it doesn't; I assure you it doesn't. Having supposed that there was sense where there is no sense, and a laudable ambition where there is not a laudable ambition, I am well out of my mistake, and no harm is done. Young women have committed similar follies often before, and have repented them in poverty and obscurity often before. In an unselfish aspect, I am sorry that the thing has dropped, because it would have been a good thing for others in a worldly point of view; in a selfish aspect, I am glad that the thing has dropped, because it would have been a bad thing for me in a worldly point of view—it is hardly necessary to say I could have gained nothing by it. There is no harm at all done. I have not proposed to the young lady, and between ourselves, I am by no means certain, on reflection, that I ever should have committed myself to that extent. Mr. Lorry, you cannot control the mincing vanities and giddinesses of empty-headed girls; you must not expect to do it, or you will always be disappointed. Now, pray say no more about it. I tell you, I regret it on account of others, but I am satisfied on my own account. And I am really very much obliged to you for allowing me to sound you, and for giving me your advice; you know the young lady better than I do; you were right, it never would have done."

Mr. Lorry was so taken aback, that he looked quite stupidly at Mr. Stryver shouldering him toward the door, with an appearance of showering generosity, forbearance and goodwill, on his erring head. "Make the best of it, my dear sir," said Stryver; "say no more about it; thank you again for allowing me to sound you; good night!"

Mr. Lorry was out in the night, before he knew where he was. Mr. Stryver was lying back on his sofa, winking at his ceiling.

Thirteen

THE FELLOW OF NO DELICACY

IF SYDNEY CARTON EVER SHONE ANYWHERE, HE CERTAINLY never shone in the house of Dr. Manette. He had been there often, during a whole year, and had always been the same moody and morose lounger there. When he cared to talk, he talked well; but, the cloud of caring for nothing, which overshadowed him with such a fatal darkness, was very rarely pierced by the light within him.

And yet he did care something for the streets that environed that house, and for the senseless stones that made their pavements. Many a night he vaguely and unhappily wandered there, when wine had brought no transitory gladness to him; many a dreary daybreak revealed his solitary figure lingering there, and still lingering there when the first beams of the sun brought into strong relief, removed beauties of architecture in spires of churches and lofty buildings, as perhaps the quiet time brought some sense of better things, else forgotten and unattainable, into his mind. Of late, the neglected bed in the Temple court had known him more scantily than ever; and often when he had thrown himself upon it no longer than a few minutes he had got up again, and haunted that neighborhood.

On a day in August, when Mr. Stryver (after notifying to his jackal that "he had thought better of that marrying matter") had carried his delicacy into Devonshire, and when the sight and scent of flowers in the city streets had some waifs of goodness in them for the worst, of health for the sickliest, and of youth for the oldest, Sydney's feet still trod those stones. From being irresolute and purposeless, his feet became animated by an intention, and in the working out of that intention, they took him to the Doctor's door.

He was shown upstairs, and found Lucie at her work, alone. She had never been quite at her ease with him, and received him with some little embarrassment as he seated himself near her table. But, looking up at his face in the interchange of the first few commonplaces, she observed a change in it.

"I fear you are not well, Mr. Carton!"

"No. But the life I lead, Miss Manette, is not conducive to health. What is to be expected of, or by, such profligates?"

"Is it not—forgive me; I have begun the question on my lips—a pity to live no better life?"

"God knows it is a shame!"

"Then why not change it?"

Looking gently at him again, she was surprised and saddened to see that there were tears in his eyes. There were tears in his voice too, as he answered:

"It is too late for that. I shall never be better than I am. I shall sink lower, and be worse."

He leaned an elbow on her table, and covered his eyes with his hand. The table trembled in the silence that followed.

She had never seen him softened, and was much distressed. He knew her to be so, without looking at her, and said:

"Pray forgive me, Miss Manette. I break down before the knowledge of what I want to say to you. Will you hear me?"

"If it will do you any good. Mr. Carton, if it would make you happier, it would make me very glad!"

"God bless you for your sweet compassion!"

He unshaded his face after a little while, and spoke steadily.

"Don't be afraid to hear me. Don't shrink from anything I say. I am like one who died young. All my life might have been."

"No, Mr. Carton. I am sure that the best part of it might still be; I am sure that you might be much, much worthier of yourself."

"Say of you, Miss Manette; and although I know better—although in the mystery of my own wretched heart I know better—I shall never forget it!"

She was pale and trembling. He came to her relief with a fixed despair of himself which made the interview unlike any other that could have been holden.

"If it had been possible, Miss Manette, that you could have returned the love of the man you see before you—self-flung away, wasted, drunken, poor creature of misuse as you know him to be—he would have been conscious this day and hour, in spite of his happiness, that he would bring you to misery, bring you to sorrow and repentance, blight you, disgrace you, pull you down with him. I know very well that you can have no tenderness for me; I ask for none; I am even thankful that it cannot be."

"Without it, can I not save you, Mr. Carton? Can I not recall you—forgive me again!—to a better course? Can I in no way repay your confidence? I know this is a confidence," she modestly said, after a little hesitation, and in earnest tears, "I know you would say this to no one else. Can I turn it to no good account for yourself, Mr. Carton?"

He shook his head.

"To none. No, Miss Manette, to none. If you will hear me through a very little more, all you can ever do for me is done. I wish you to know that you have been the last dream of my soul. In my degradation, I have not been so degraded but that the sight of you with your father, and of this home made such a home by you, has stirred old shadows that I thought had died out of me. Since I knew you, I have been troubled by a remorse that I thought would never reproach me again, and have heard whispers from old voices impelling me upward, that I thought were silent forever. I have had unformed ideas of striving afresh, beginning anew, shaking off sloth and sensuality, and fighting out the abandoned fight. A dream, all a dream, that ends in nothing, and leaves the sleeper where he lay down, but I wish you to know that you inspired it."

"Will nothing of it remain? O, Mr. Carton, think again! Try again!"

"No, Miss Manette; all through it, I have known myself to be quite undeserving. And yet I have had the weakness, and have still the weakness, to wish you to know, with what a sudden mastery you kindled me, heap of ashes that I am, into fire—a fire, however, inseparable in its nature from myself, quickening nothing, lighting nothing, doing no service, idly burning away."

"Since it is my misfortune, Mr. Carton, to have made you more unhappy than you were before you knew me—"

"Don't say that, Miss Manette, for you would have reclaimed me, if anything could. You will not be the cause of my becoming worse."

"Since the state of your mind that you describe, is, at all events, attributable to some influence of mine—this is what I mean, if I can make it plain—can I use no influence to serve you? Have I no power for good, with you, at all?"

"The utmost good that I am capable of now, Miss Manette, I have come here to realize. Let me carry through the rest of my misdirected life, the remembrance that I opened my heart to you, last of all the world; and that there was something left in me at this time which you could deplore and pity."

"Which I entreated you to believe, again and again, most fervently, with all my heart, was capable of better things, Mr. Carton!"

"Entreat me to believe it no more, Miss Manette. I have proved myself, and I know better. I distress you; I draw fast to an end. Will you let me believe, when I recall this day, that the last confidence of my life was reposed in your pure and innocent breast, and that it lies there alone, and will be shared by no one?"

"If that will be a consolation to you, yes."

"Not even by the dearest one ever to be known to you?"

"Mr. Carton," she answered, after an agitated pause, "the secret is yours, not mine; and I promise to respect it."

"Thank you. And again, God bless you!"

He put her hand to his lips, and moved toward the door.

"Be under no apprehension, Miss Manette, of my ever resuming this conversation by so much as a passing word. I will never refer to it again. If I were dead, that could not be surer than it is henceforth. In the hour of my death, I shall hold sacred the one good remembrance—and shall thank and bless you for it—that my last avowal of myself was made to you, and that my name, and faults, and miseries, were gently carried in your heart. May it otherwise be light and happy!"

He was so unlike what he had ever shown himself to be, and it was so sad to think how much he had thrown away, and how much he every day kept down and perverted, that Lucie Manette wept mournfully for him as he stood looking back at her.

"Be comforted!" he said. "I am not worth such feeling, Miss Manette. An hour or two hence, and the low companions and low habits that I scorn but yield to, will render me less worth such tears as those, than any wretch who creeps along the streets. Be comforted! But, within myself I shall always be, toward you, what I am now, though outwardly I shall be what you have heretofore seen me. The last supplication but one I make to you, is, that you will believe this of me."

"I will, Mr. Carton."

"My last supplication of all, is this; and with it, I will relieve you of a visitor with whom I well know you have nothing in unison, and between whom and you there is an impassable space. It is useless to say it, I know, but it rises out of my soul. For you, and for any dear to you, I would do anything. If my career were of that better kind that there was any opportunity or capacity of sacrifice in it, I would embrace any sacrifice for you and for those dear to you. Try to hold me in your mind, at some quiet times, as ardent and sincere in this one thing. The time will come, the time will not be long in coming, when new ties will be formed about you—ties that will bind you yet more tenderly and strongly to the home you so adorn—the dearest ties that will ever grace and gladden you. O Miss Manette, when the little picture of a happy father's face looks up in yours, when you see your own bright beauty springing up anew at your feet, think now and then that there is a man who would give his life, to keep a life you love beside you!"

He said "Farewell!" and "A last God bless you!" and left her.

Fourteen

THE HONEST TRADESMAN

To the eyes of Mr. Jeremiah Cruncher, sitting on his stool in Fleet Street with his grisly urchin beside him, a vast number and variety of objects in movement were every day presented. Who could sit upon anything in Fleet Street during the busy hours of the day, and not be dazed and deafened by two immense processions, one ever tending westward with the sun, the other ever tending eastward from the sun, both ever tending to the plains beyond the range of red and purple where the sun goes down!

With his straw in his mouth, Mr. Cruncher sat watching the two streams, like the heathen rustic who has for several centuries been on duty watching one stream—saving that Jerry had no expectation of their ever running dry. Nor would it have been an expectation of a hopeful kind, since a small part of his income was derived from the pilotage of timid women (mostly of a full habit and past the middle term of life) from Tellson's side of the tides to the opposite shore. Brief as such companionship was in every separate instance, Mr. Cruncher never failed to become so interested in the lady as to express a strong desire to have the honor of drinking her very good health. And it was from the gifts bestowed upon him toward the execution of this benevolent purpose, that he recruited his finances, as just now observed.

Time was, when a poet sat upon a stool in a public place, and mused in the sight of men. Mr. Cruncher, sitting on a stool in a public place but not being a poet, mused as little as possible, and looked about him.

It fell out that he was thus engaged in a season when crowds were few, and belated women few, and when his affairs in general were so unprosperous as to awaken a strong suspicion in his breast that Mrs. Cruncher must have been "flopping" in some pointed manner, when an unusual concourse pouring down Fleet Street westward, attracted his attention. Looking that way, Mr. Cruncher made out that some kind of funeral was coming along, and that there was popular objection to this funeral, which engendered uproar.

"Young Jerry," said Mr. Cruncher, turning to his offspring, "it's a buryin'."

"Hooroar, father!" cried Young Jerry.

The young gentleman uttered this exultant sound with mysterious significance. The elder gentleman took the cry so ill, that he watched his opportunity, and smote the young gentleman on the ear.

"What d'ye mean? What are you hooroaring at? What do you want to conwey to your own father, you young Rip? This boy is a getting too many for *me!*" said Mr. Cruncher, surveying him. "Him and his hooroars! Don't let me hear no more of you, or you shall feel some more of me. D'ye hear?"

"I warn't doing no harm," Young Jerry protested, rubbing his cheek.

"Drop it then," said Mr. Cruncher; "I won't have none of *your* no harms. Get atop of that there seat, and look at the crowd."

His son obeyed, and the crowd approached; they were bawling and hissing round a dingy hearse and dingy mourning coach, in which mourning coach there was only one mourner, dressed in the dingy trappings that were considered essential to the dignity of the position. The position appeared by no means to please him, however, with an increasing rabble surrounding the coach, deriding him, making grimaces at him, and incessantly groaning and calling out: "Yah! Spies! Tst! Yaha! Spies!" with many compliments too numerous and forcible to repeat.

Funerals had at all times a remarkable attraction for Mr. Cruncher; he always pricked up his senses, and became excited, when a funeral passed Tellson's. Naturally, therefore, a funeral with this uncommon attendance excited him greatly, and he asked of the first man who ran against him:

"What is it, brother? What's it about?"

"*I* don't know," said the man. "Spies! Yaha! Tst! Spies!"

He asked another man. "Who is it?"

"*I* don't know," returned the man, clapping his hands to his mouth nevertheless, and vociferating in a surprising heat and with the greatest ardor, "Spies! Yaha! Tst, tst! Spi-ies!"

At length, a person better informed on the merits of the case, tumbled against him, and from this person he learned that the funeral was the funeral of one Roger Cly.

"Was he a spy?" asked Mr. Cruncher.

"Old Bailey spy," returned his informant. "Yaha! Tst! Yah! Old Bailey Spi-i-es!"

"Why, to be sure!" exclaimed Jerry, recalling the Trial at which he had assisted, "I've seen him. Dead, is he?"

"Dead as mutton," returned the other, "and can't be too dead. Have 'em out, there! Spies! Pull 'em out, there! Spies!"

The idea was so acceptable in the prevalent absence of any idea, that the crowd caught it up with eagerness, and loudly repeating the suggestion to have 'em out, and to pull 'em out, mobbed the two vehicles so closely that they came to a stop. On the crowd's opening the coach-doors, the one mourner scuffled out of himself and was in their hands for a moment; but he was so alert, and made such good use of his time, that in another moment he was scouring away up a by-street, after shedding his cloak, hat, long hatband, white pocket-handkerchief, and other symbolical tears.

These, the people tore to pieces and scattered far and wide with great enjoyment, while the tradesmen hurriedly shut up their shops; for a crowd in those times stopped at nothing, and was a monster much dreaded. They had already got the length of opening the hearse to take the coffin out, when some brighter genius proposed instead, its being escorted to its destination amidst general rejoicing. Practical suggestions being much needed, this suggestion, too, was received with acclamation, and the coach was immediately filled with eight inside and a dozen out, while as many people got on the roof of the hearse as could by any exercise of ingenuity stick upon it. Among the first of these volunteers was Jerry Cruncher himself, who modestly concealed his spiky head from the observation of Tellson's, in the further corner of the mourning coach.

The officiating undertakers made some protest against these changes in the ceremonies; but, the river being alarmingly near, and several voices remarking on the efficacy of cold immersion in bringing refractory members of the profession to reason, the protest was faint and brief. The remodeled procession started, with a chimney-sweep driving the hearse—advised by the regular driver, who was perched beside him, under close inspection for the purpose—and with a pieman, also attended by his cabinet minister, driving the mourning coach. A bear-leader, a popular street character of the time, was impressed as an additional ornament, before the cavalcade had gone far down the Strand; and his bear, who was black and very mangy, gave quite an Undertaking air to that part of the procession in which he walked.

Thus, with beer-drinking, pipe-smoking, song-roaring, and infinite caricaturing of woe, the disorderly procession went its way, recruiting at every step, and all the shops shutting up before it. Its destination was the old church of Saint Pancras, far off in the fields. It got there in course of time; insisted on pouring into the burial-ground; finally, accomplished the interment of the deceased Roger Cly in its own way, and highly to its own satisfaction.

The dead man disposed of, and the crowd being under the necessity of providing some other entertainment for itself, another brighter genius (or perhaps the same) conceived the humor of impeaching casual passersby, as Old Bailey spies, and wreaking vengeance on them. Chase was given to some scores of inoffensive persons who had never been near the Old Bailey in their lives, in the realization of this fancy, and they were roughly hustled and maltreated. The transition to the sport of window-breaking, and thence to the plundering of public houses, was easy and natural. At last, after several hours, when sundry summer-houses had been pulled down, and some area railings had been torn up, to arm the more belligerent spirits, a rumor got about that the Guards were coming. Before this rumor, the crowd gradually melted away, and perhaps the Guards came, and perhaps they never came, and this was the usual progress of a mob.

Mr. Cruncher did not assist at the closing sports, but had remained behind in the churchyard, to confer and condole with the undertakers. The place had a soothing influence on him. He procured a pipe from a neighboring public-house, and smoked it, looking in at the railings, and maturely considering the spot.

"Jerry," said Mr. Cruncher, apostrophizing himself in his usual way, "you see that there Cly that day, and you see with your own eyes that he was a young 'un and a straight made 'un."

Having smoked his pipe out, and ruminated a little longer, he turned himself about, that he might appear, before the hour of closing, on his station at Tellson's. Whether his meditations on mortality had touched his liver, or whether his general health had been previously at all amiss, or whether he desired to show a little attention to an eminent man, is not so much to the purpose, as that he made a short call upon his medical adviser—a distinguished surgeon—on his way back.

Young Jerry relieved his father with dutiful interest, and reported No job in his absence. The bank closed, the ancient clerks came out, the usual watch was set, and Mr. Cruncher and his son went home to tea.

"Now, I tell you where it is!" said Mr. Cruncher to his wife, on entering. "If, as a honest tradesman, my wenturs goes wrong tonight, I shall make sure that you've been praying agin me, and I shall work you for it the same as if I seen you do it."

The dejected Mrs. Cruncher shook her head.

"Why, you're at it afore my face!" said Mr. Cruncher, with signs of angry apprehension.

"I am saying nothing."

"Well, then; don't meditate nothing. You might as well flop as meditate. You may as well go agin me one way as another. Drop it altogether."

"Yes, Jerry."

"Yes, Jerry," repeated Mr. Cruncher, sitting down to tea. "Ah! It *is* yes, Jerry. That's about it. You may say yes, Jerry."

Mr. Cruncher had no particular meaning in these sulky corroborations, but made use of them, as people not unfrequently do, to express general ironical dissatisfaction.

"You and your yes, Jerry," said Mr. Cruncher, taking a bite out of his bread and butter, and seeming to help it down with a large invisible oyster out of his saucer. "Ah! I think so. I believe you."

"You are going out tonight?" asked his decent wife, when he took another bite.

"Yes, I am."

"May I go with you, father?" asked his son, briskly.

"No, you mayn't. I'm a going—as your mother knows—a fishing. That's where I'm going to. Going a fishing."

"Your fishing-rod gets rather rusty; don't it, father?"

"Never you mind."

"Shall you bring any fish home, father?"

"If I don't, you'll have short commons tomorrow," returned that gentleman, shaking his head; "that's questions enough for you; I ain't a going out, till you've been long a-bed."

He devoted himself during the remainder of the evening to keeping a most viligant watch on Mrs. Cruncher, and sullenly holding her in conversation that she might be prevented from meditating any petitions to his disadvantage. With this view, he urged his son to hold her in conversation also, and led the unfortunate woman a hard life by dwelling on any causes of complaint he could bring against her, rather than he would leave her for a moment to her own reflections. The devoutest person could have rendered no greater homage to the efficacy of an honest prayer than he did in this distrust of his wife. It was as if a professed unbeliever in ghosts should be frightened by a ghost story.

"And mind you!" said Mr. Cruncher. "No games tomorrow! If I, as a honest tradesman, succeed in providing a jinte of meat or two, none of your not touching of it, and sticking to bread. If I, as a honest tradesman, am able to provide a little beer, none of your declaring on water. When you go to Rome, do as Rome does. Rome will be a ugly customer to you, if you don't. I'm your Rome, you know."

Then he began grumbling again:

"With your flying into the face of your own wittles and drink! I don't know how scarce you mayn't make the wittles and drink here, by your flopping tricks and your unfeeling conduct. Look at your boy: he is your'n, ain't he? He's as thin as a lath. Do you call yourself a mother, and not know that a mother's first duty is to blow her boy out?"

This touched Young Jerry on a tender place; who adjured his mother to perform her first duty, and, whatever else she did or neglected, above all things to lay especial stress on the discharge of that maternal function so affectingly and delicately indicated by his other parent.

Thus the evening wore away with the Cruncher family, until Young Jerry was ordered to bed, and his mother laid under similar injunctions, obeyed them. Mr. Cruncher beguiled the earlier watches of the night with solitary pipes, and did not start upon his excursion until nearly one o'clock. Toward that small and ghostly hour, he rose up from his chair, took a key out of his pocket, opened a locked cupboard, and brought forth a sack, a crowbar of convenient size, a rope and chain, and other fishing tackle of that nature. Disposing these articles about him in a skillful manner, he bestowed a parting defiance on Mrs. Cruncher, extinguished the light, and went out.

Young Jerry, who had only made a feint of undressing when he went to bed, was not long after his father. Under cover of the darkness he followed out of the room, followed down the stairs, followed down the court, followed out into the streets. He was in no uneasiness concerning his getting into the house again, for it was full of lodgers, and the door stood ajar all night.

Impelled by a laudable ambition to study the art and mystery of his father's honest calling, Young Jerry, keeping as close to house-fronts, walls, and doorways, as his eyes were close to one another, held his honored parent in view. The honored parent steering northward, had not gone far, when he was joined by another disciple of Izaak Walton, and the two trudged on together.

Within half an hour from the first starting, they were beyond the winking lamps, and the more than winking watchmen, and were out upon a lonely road. Another fisherman was picked up here—and that so silently, that if Young Jerry had been superstitious, he might have supposed the second follower of the gentle craft to have, all of a sudden, split himself in two.

The three went on, and Young Jerry went on, until the three stopped under a bank overhanging the road. Upon the top of the bank was a low brick wall surmounted by an iron railing. In the shadow of bank and wall, the three turned out of the road, and up a blind lane, of which the wall—there, risen to some eight or ten feet high—formed one side. Crouching down in a corner, peeping up the lane, the next object that Young Jerry saw, was the form of his honored parent, pretty well defined against a watery and clouded moon, nimbly scaling an iron gate. He was soon over, and then the second fisherman got over, and then the third. They all dropped softly on the ground within the gate, and lay there a little—listening perhaps. Then, they moved away on their hands and knees.

It was now Young Jerry's turn to approach the gate: which he did, holding his breath. Crouching down again in a corner there, and looking in, he made out the three fishermen creeping through some rank grass; and all the gravestones in the churchyard—it was a large churchyard that they were in— looking on like ghosts in white, while the church tower itself looked on like the ghost of a monstrous giant. They did not creep far, before they stopped and stood upright. And then they began to fish.

They fished with a spade, at first. Presently the honored parent appeared to be adjusting some instrument like a great corkscrew. Whatever tools they worked with, they worked hard, until the awful striking of the church-clock so terrified Young Jerry, that he made off, with his hair as stiff as his father's.

But, his long-cherished desire to know more about these matters, not only stopped him in his running away, but lured him back again. They were still fishing perseveringly, when he peeped in at the gate for the second time; but, now they seemed to have got a bite. There was a screwing and complaining sound down below, and their bent figures were strained, as if by a weight. By slow degrees the weight broke away the earth upon it, and came to the surface. Young Jerry very well knew what it would be; but, when he saw it, and saw his honored parent about to wrench it open, he was so frightened, being new to the sight, that he made off again, and never stopped until he had run a mile or more.

He would not have stopped then, for anything less necessary than breath, it being a spectral sort of race that he ran, and one highly desirable to get to the end of. He had a strong idea that the coffin he had seen was running after him; and, pictured as hopping on behind him, bolt upright upon its narrow end, always on the point of overtaking him and hopping on at his side—perhaps taking his arm—it was a pursuer to shun. It was an inconsistent and ubiquitous fiend too, for, while it was making the whole night behind him dreadful, he darted out into the roadway to avoid dark alleys, fearful of its coming hopping out of them like a dropsical boy's-Kite without tail and wings. It hid in doorways too, rubbing its horrible shoulders against doors, and drawing them up to its ears as if it were laughing. It got into shadows on the road, and lay cunningly on its back to trip him up. All this time, it was incessantly hopping on behind and gaining on him, so that when the boy got to his own door he had reason for being half-dead. And even then it would not leave him, but followed him upstairs with a bump on every stair, scrambled into bed with him, and bumped down, dead and heavy, on his breast when he fell asleep.

From his oppressed slumber, Young Jerry in his closet was awakened, after daybreak and before sunrise, by the presence of his father in the family room. Something had gone wrong with him; at least, so Young Jerry inferred, from the circumstance of his holding Mrs. Cruncher by the ears, and knocking the back of her head against the headboard of the bed.

"I told you I would," said Mr. Cruncher, "and I did."

"Jerry, Jerry, Jerry!" his wife implored.

"You oppose yourself to the profit of the business," said Jerry, "and me and my partners suffer. You was to honor and obey; why the devil don't you?"

"I try to be a good wife, Jerry," the poor woman protested, with tears.

"Is it being a good wife to oppose your husband's business? Is it honoring your husband to dishonor his business? Is it obeying your husband to disobey him on the wital subject of his business?"

"You hadn't taken to the dreadful business then, Jerry?"

"It's enough for you," retorted Mr. Cruncher, "to be the wife of a honest tradesman, and not to occupy your female mind with calculations when he took to his trade or when he didn't. A honoring and obeying wife would let his trade alone altogether. Call yourself a religious woman? If you're a religious woman, give me a irreligious one! You have no more nat'ral sense of duty than the bed of this here Thames river has of a pile, and similarly it must be knocked into you."

The altercation was conducted in a low tone of voice, and terminated in the honest tradesman's kicking off his clay-soiled boots and lying down at his length on the floor. After taking a timid peep at him lying on his back, with his rusty hands under his head for a pillow, his son lay down too, and fell asleep again.

There was no fish for breakfast, and not much of anything else. Mr. Cruncher was out of spirits, and out of temper, and kept an iron pot-lid by him as a projectile for the correction of Mrs. Cruncher, in case he should observe any symptoms of her saying Grace. He was brushed and washed at the usual hour, and set off with his son to pursue his ostensible calling.

Young Jerry walking with the stool under his arm at his father's side along sunny and crowded Fleet Street, was a very different Young Jerry from him of the previous night, running home through darkness and solitude from his grim pursuer. His cunning was fresh with the day, and his qualms were gone with the night—in which particulars it is not improbable that he had compeers in Fleet Street and the City of London, that fine morning.

"Father," said Young Jerry, as they walked along: taking care to keep at arm's length and to have the stool well between them: "what's a Resurrection-Man?"

Mr. Cruncher came to stop on the pavement before he answered, "How should I know?"

"I thought you knowed everything, father," said the artless boy.

"Hem! Well," returned Mr. Cruncher, going on again, and lifting off his hat to give his spikes free play, "he's a tradesman."

"What's his goods, father?" asked the brisk Young Jerry.

"His goods," said Mr. Cruncher, after turning it over in his mind, "is a branch of Scientific goods."

"Persons' bodies, ain't it, father?" asked the lively boy.

"I believe it is something of that sort," said Mr. Cruncher.

"Oh, father, I should so like to be a Resurrection-Man when I'm quite growed up!"

Mr. Cruncher was soothed, but shook his head in a dubious and moral way. "It depends upon how you develop your talents. Be careful to develop your talents, and never to say no more than you can help to nobody, and there's no telling at the present time what you may not come to be fit for." As Young Jerry, thus encouraged, went on a few yards in advance, to plant the stool in the shadow of the Bar, Mr. Cruncher added to himself: "Jerry, you honest tradesman, there's hopes wot that boy will yet be a blessing to you, and a recompense to you for his mother!"

Fifteen

KNITTING

THERE HAD BEEN EARLIER DRINKING THAN USUAL IN THE wine-shop of Monsieur Defarge. As early as six o'clock in the morning, sallow faces peeping through its barred windows had descried other faces within, bending over measures of wine. Monsieur Defarge sold a very thin wine at the best of times, but it would seem to have been an unusually thin wine that he sold at this time. A sour wine, moreover, or a souring, for its influence on the mood of those who drank it was to make them gloomy. No vivacious bacchanalian flame leaped out of the pressed grape of Monsieur Defarge; but, a smoldering fire that burnt in the dark, lay hidden in the dregs of it.

This had been the third morning in succession, on which there had been early drinking at the wine-shop of Monsieur Defarge. It had begun on Monday, and here was Wednesday come. There had been more of early brooding than drinking; for many men had listened, and whispered, and slunk about there from the time of the opening of the door, who could not have laid a piece of money on the counter to save their souls. These were to the full as interested in the place, however, as if they could have commanded whole barrels of wine; and they glided from seat to seat, and from corner to corner, swallowing talk in lieu of drink, with greedy looks.

Notwithstanding an unusual flow of company, the master of the wine-shop was not visible. He was not missed; for nobody who crossed the threshold looked for him, nobody asked for him, nobody wondered to see only Madame Defarge in her seat, presiding over the distribution of wine, with a bowl of battered small coins before her, as much defaced and beaten out of their original impress as the small coinage of humanity from whose ragged pockets they had come.

A suspended interest and a prevalent absence of mind, were perhaps observed by the spies who looked in at the wine-shop, as they looked in at every place, high and low, from the king's palace to the criminal's jail. Games at cards languished, players at dominoes musingly built towers with them, drinkers drew figures on the tables with spilt drops of wine, Madame Defarge herself picked out the pattern on her sleeve with her toothpick, and saw and heard something inaudible and invisible a long way off.

Thus Saint Antoine in this vinous feature of his, until midday. It was high noontide, when two dusty men passed through his streets and under his swinging lamps; of whom, one was Monsieur Defarge, the other, a mender of roads in a blue cap. All adust and athirst, the two entered the wine-shop. Their arrival had lighted a kind of fire in the breast of Saint Antoine, fast spreading as they came along, which stirred and flickered in flames of faces at most doors and windows. Yet, no one had followed them, and no man spoke when they entered the wine-shop, though the eyes of every man there were turned upon them.

"Good day, gentlemen!" said Monsieur Defarge.

It may have been a signal for loosening the general tongue. It elicited an answering chorus of "Good day!"

"It is bad weather, gentlemen," said Defarge, shaking his head.

Upon which every man looked at his neighbor, and then all cast down their eyes and sat silent, except one man, who got up and went out.

"My wife," said Defarge aloud, addressing Madame Defarge; "I have traveled certain leagues with this good mender of roads, called Jacques. I met him—by accident—a day and a half's journey out of Paris. He is a good child, this mender of roads, called Jacques. Give him to drink, my wife."

A second man got up and went out. Madame Defarge set wine before the mender of roads called Jacques, who doffed his blue cap to the company, and drank. In the breast of his blouse he carried some coarse dark bread; he ate of this between whiles, and sat munching and drinking near Madame Defarge's counter. A third man got up and went out.

Defarge refreshed himself with a draught of wine—but he took less than was given to the stranger, as being himself a man to whom it was no rarity—and stood waiting until the countryman had made his breakfast. He looked at no one present, and no one now looked at him; not even Madame Defarge, who had taken up her knitting, and was at work.

"Have you finished your repast, friend?" he asked, in due season.

"Yes, thank you."

"Come then! You shall see the apartment that I told you you could occupy. It will suit you to a marvel."

Out of the wine-shop into the street, out of the street into a courtyard, out of the courtyard up a steep staircase, out of the staircase into a garret—formerly the garret where a white-haired man sat on a low bench, stooping forward, and very busy, making shoes.

No white-haired man was there now; but, the three men were there who had gone out of the wine-shop singly. And between them and the white-haired man afar off, was the one small link, that they had once looked in at him through the chinks in the wall.

Defarge closed the door carefully, and spoke in a subdued voice:

"Jacques One, Jacques Two, Jacques Three! This is the witness encountered by appointment, by me, Jacques Four. He will tell you all. Speak, Jacques Five!"

The mender of roads, blue cap in hand, wiped his swarthy forehead with it, and said, "Where shall I commence, Monsieur?"

"Commence," was Monsieur Defarge's not unreasonable reply, "at the commencement."

"I saw him then, messieurs," began the mender of roads, "a year ago this running summer, underneath the carriage of the Marquis, hanging by the chain. Behold the manner of it. I leaving my work on the road, the sun going to bed, the carriage of the Marquis slowly ascending the hill, he hanging by the chain—like this."

Again the mender of roads went through the whole performance; in which he ought to have been perfect by that time, seeing that it had been the infallible resource and indispensable entertainment of his village during a whole year.

Jacques One struck in, and asked if he had ever seen the man before?

"Never," answered the mender of roads, recovering his perpendicular.

Jacques Three demanded how he afterwards recognized him then?

"By his tall figure," said the mender of roads, softly, and with his finger at his nose. "When Monsieur the Marquis demands that evening, 'Say, what is he like?' I make response, 'Tall as a spectre.'"

"You should have said, short as a dwarf," returned Jacques Two.

"But what did I know? The deed was not then accomplished, neither did he confide in me. Observe! Under those circumstances, even, I do not offer my testimony. Monsieur the Marquis indicates me with his finger, standing near our little fountain, and says, 'To me! Bring that rascal!' My faith, messieurs, I offer nothing."

"He is right there, Jacques," murmured Defarge, to him who had interrupted. "Go on!"

"Good," said the mender of roads, with an air of mystery. "The tall man is lost, and he is sought—how many months? Nine, ten, eleven?"

"No matter, the number," said Defarge. "He is well hidden, but at last he is unluckily found. Go on!"

"I am again at work upon the hillside, and the sun is again about to go to bed. I am collecting my tools to descend to my cottage down in the village below, where it is already dark, when I raise my eyes, and see coming over the hill, six soldiers. In the midst of them is a tall man with his arms bound—tied to his sides, like this!"

With the aid of his indispensable cap, he represented a man with his elbows bound fast at his hips, with cords that were knotted behind him.

"I stand aside, messieurs, by my heap of stones, to see the soldiers and their prisoner pass (for it is a solitary road, that, where any spectacle is well worth looking at), and at first, as they approach, I see no more than that they are six soldiers, with a tall man bound, and that they are almost black, to my sight—except on the side of the sun going to bed, where they have a red edge, messieurs. Also, I see that their long shadows are on the hollow ridge on the opposite side of the road, and are on the hill above it, and are like the shadows of giants. Also, I see that they are covered with dust, and that the dust moves with them as they come, tramp, tramp! But when they advance quite near to me, I recognize the tall man, and he recognizes me. Ah, but he would be well content to precipitate himself over the hillside once again, as on the evening when he and I first encountered, close to the same spot!"

He described it as if he were there, and it was evident that he saw it vividly; perhaps he had not seen much in his life.

"I do not show the soldiers that I recognize the tall man; he does not show the soldiers that he recognizes me; we do it, and we know it, with our eyes. 'Come on!' says the chief of that company, pointing to the village, 'bring him fast to his tomb!' and they bring him faster. I follow. His arms are swelled because of being bound so tight, his wooden shoes are large and clumsy, and he is lame. Because he is lame, and consequently slow, they drive him with their guns—like this!"

He imitated the action of a man's being impelled forward by the butt-ends of muskets.

"As they descend the hill like madmen running a race, he falls. They laugh and pick him up again. His face is bleeding and covered with dust, but he cannot touch it; thereupon, they laugh again. They bring him into the village; all the village runs to look; they take him past the mill, and up to the prison; all the village sees the prison gate open in the darkness of night, and swallow him—like this!"

He opened his mouth as wide as he could, and shut it with a sounding snap of his teeth. Observant of his unwillingness to mar the effect by opening it again, Defarge said, "Go on, Jacques."

"All the village," pursued the mender of roads, on tiptoe and in a low voice, "withdraws; all the village whispers by the fountain; all the village sleeps; all the village dreams of that unhappy one, within the locks and bars of the prison on the crag, and never to come out of it, except to perish. In the morning, with my tools upon my shoulder, eating my morsel of black bread as I go, I make a circuit by the prison, on my way to my work. There, I see him, high up, behind the bars of a lofty iron cage, bloody and dusty as last night, looking through. He has no hand free, to wave to me; I dare not call to him; he regards me like a dead man."

Defarge and the three glanced darkly at one another. The looks of all of them were dark, repressed, and revengeful, as they listened to the country-man's story; the manner of all of them, while it was secret, was authoritative too. They had the air of a rough tribunal; Jacques One and Two sitting on the old pallet-bed, each with his chin resting on his hand, and his eyes intent on the road mender; Jacques Three, equally intent, on one knee behind them, with his agitated hand always gliding over the network of fine nerves about his mouth and nose; Defarge standing between them and the narrator whom he had stationed in the light of the window, by turns looking from him to them and from them to him.

"Go on, Jacques," said Defarge.

"He remains up there in his iron cage, some days. The village looks at him by stealth, for it is afraid. But it always looks up, from a distance, at the prison on the crag; and in the evening when the work of the day is achieved, and it assembles to gossip at the fountain, all faces are turned toward the prison. Formerly, they were turned toward the posting-house; now, they are turned toward the prison. They whisper at the fountain, that although condemned to death he will not be executed; they say that petitions have been presented in Paris, showing that he was enraged and made mad by the death of his child; they say that a petition has been presented to the King himself. What do I know? It is possible. Perhaps yes, perhaps no."

"Listen then, Jacques," Number One of that name sternly interposed. "Know that a petition was presented to the King and Queen. All here, yourself excepted, saw the King take it, in his carriage in the street, sitting beside the Queen. It is Defarge whom you see here, who, at the hazard of his life, darted out before the horses, with the petition in his hand."

"And once again listen, Jacques!" said the kneeling Number Three: his fingers ever wandering over and over those fine nerves, with a strikingly greedy air, as if he hungered for something—that was neither food nor drink; "the guard, horse and foot, surrounded the petitioner, and struck him blows. You hear?"

"I hear, messieurs."

"Go on, then," said Defarge.

"Again; on the other hand, they whisper at the fountain," resumed the countryman, "that he is brought down into our country to be executed on the spot, and that he will very certainly be executed. They even whisper that because he has slain Monseigneur, and because Monseigneur was the father of his tenants—serfs—what you will—he will be executed as a parricide. One old man says at the fountain, that his right hand, armed with the knife, will be burnt off before his face; that, into wounds which will be made in his arms, his breast, and his legs, there will be poured boiling oil, melted lead, hot resin, wax, and sulphur; finally, that he will be torn limb from limb by four strong horses. That old man says, all this was actually done to a prisoner who made an attempt on the life of the last King, Louis Fifteen. But how do I know if he lies? I am not a scholar."

"Listen once again then, Jacques!" said the man with the restless hand and the craving air. "The name of that prisoner was Damiens, and it was all done in open day, in the open streets of this city of Paris; and nothing was more noticed in the vast concourse that saw it done, than the crowd of ladies of quality and fashion, who were full of eager attention to the last—to the last, Jacques, prolonged until nightfall, when he had lost two legs and an arm, and still breathed! And it was done—why, how old are you?"

"Thirty-five," said the mender of roads, who looked sixty.

"It was done when you were more than ten years old; you might have seen it."

"Enough!" said Defarge, with grim impatience. "Long live the Devil! Go on."

"Well. Some whisper this, some whisper that; they speak of nothing else: even the fountain appears to fall to that tune. At length, on Sunday night, when all the village is asleep, come soldiers, winding down from the prison, and their guns ring on the stones of the little street. Workmen dig, workmen hammer, soldiers laugh and sing; in the morning, by the fountain, there is raised a gallows forty feet high, poisoning the water."

The mender of roads looked *through* rather than *at* the low ceiling, and pointed as if he saw the gallows somewhere in the sky.

"All work is stopped, all assemble there, nobody leads the cows out, the cows are there with the rest. At midday, the roll of drums. Soldiers have marched into the prison in the night, and he is in the midst of many soldiers. He is bound as before, and in his mouth there is a gag—tied so, with a tight string, making him look almost as if he laughed." He suggested it, by creasing his face with his two thumbs, from the corners of his mouth to his ears. "On the top of the gallows is fixed the knife, blade upward, with its point in the air. He is hanged there forty feet high—and is left hanging, poisoning the water."

They looked at one another, as he used his blue cap to wipe his face, on which the perspiration had started afresh while he recalled the spectacle.

"It is frightful, messieurs. How can the women and the children draw water! Who can gossip of an evening, under that shadow! Under it, have I said? When I left the village, Monday evening as the sun was going to bed, and looked back from the hill, the shadow struck across the church, across the mill, across the prison—seemed to strike across the earth, messieurs, to where the sky rests upon it!"

The hungry man gnawed one of his fingers as he looked at the other three, and his finger quivered with the craving that was on him.

"That's all, messieurs. I left at sunset (as I had been warned to do), and I walked on, that night and half next day, until I met (as I was warned I should) this comrade. With him, I came on, now riding and now walking, through the rest of yesterday and through last night. And here you see me!"

After a gloomy silence, the first Jacques said, "Good! You have acted and recounted, faithfully. Will you wait for us a little, outside the door?"

"Very willingly," said the mender of roads. Whom Defarge escorted to the top of the stairs, and leaving seated there, returned.

The three had risen, and their heads were together when he came back to the garret.

"How say you, Jacques?" demanded Number One. "To be registered?"

"To be registered, as doomed to destruction," returned Defarge.

"Magnificent!" croaked the man with the craving.

"The chateau, and all the race?" inquired the first.

"The chateau and all the race," returned Defarge. "Extermination."

The hungry man repeated, in a rapturous croak, "Magnificent!" and began gnawing another finger.

"Are you sure," asked Jacques Two, of Defarge, "that no embarrassment can arise from our manner of keeping the register? Without doubt it is safe, for no one beyond ourselves can decipher it; but shall we always be able to decipher it—or, I ought to say, will she?"

"Jacques," returned Defarge, drawing himself up, "if madame my wife undertook to keep the register in her memory alone, she would not lose a word of it—not a syllable of it. Knitted, in her own stitches and her own symbols, it will always be as plain to her as the sun. Confide in Madame Defarge. It would be easier for the weakest poltroon that lives, to erase himself from existence, than to erase one letter of his name or crimes from the knitted register of Madame Defarge."

There was a murmur of confidence and approval, and then the man who hungered, asked: "Is this rustic to be sent back soon? I hope so. He is very simple; is he not a little dangerous?"

"He knows nothing," said Defarge; "at least nothing more than would easily elevate himself to a gallows of the same height. I charge myself with him; let him remain with me; I will take care of him, and set him on his road. He wishes to see the fine world—the King, the Queen, and Court; let him see them on Sunday."

"What?" exclaimed the hungry man, staring. "Is it a good sign, that he wishes to see Royalty and Nobility?"

"Jacques," said Defarge, "judiciously show a cat, milk, if you wish her to thirst for it. Judiciously show a dog his natural prey if you wish him to bring it down one day."

Nothing more was said, and the mender of roads, being found already dozing on the topmost stair, was advised to lay himself down on the pallet-bed and take some rest. He needed no persuasion, and was soon asleep.

Worse quarters than Defarge's wine-shop, could easily have been found in Paris for a provincial slave of that degree. Saving for a mysterious dread of madame, by which he was constantly haunted, his life was very new and agreeable. But, madame sat all day at her counter, so expressly unconscious of him, and so particularly determined not to perceive that his being there had any connection with anything below the surface, that he shook in his wooden shoes whenever his eye lighted on her. For, he contended with himself that it was impossible to foresee what that lady might pretend next; and he felt assured that if she should take it into her brightly ornamented head to pretend that she had seen him do a murder and afterward flay the victim, she would infallibly go through with it until the play was played out.

Therefore, when Sunday came, the mender of roads was not enchanted (though he said he was) to find that madame was to accompany monseigneur and himself to Versailles. It was additionally disconcerting to have madame knitting all the way there, in a public conveyance; it was additionally disconcerting yet, to have madame in the crowd in the afternoon, still with her knitting in her hands as the crowd waited to see the carriage of the King and Queen.

"You work hard, madame," said a man near her.

"Yes," answered Madame Defarge; "I have a good deal to do."

"What do you make, madame?"

"Many things."

"For instance—"

"For instance," returned Madame Defarge, composedly, "shrouds."

The man moved a little further away, as soon as he could, and the mender of roads fanned himself with his blue cap: feeling it mightily close and oppressive. If he needed a King and Queen to restore him, he was fortunate in having his remedy at hand; for, soon the large-faced King and the fair-faced Queen came in their golden coach, attended by the shining Bull's Eye of their Court, a glittering multitude of laughing ladies and fine lords; and in jewels and silks and powder and splendor and elegantly spurning figures and handsomely disdainful faces of both sexes, the mender of roads bathed himself, so much to his temporary intoxication, that he cried Long live the King, Long live the Queen, Long live everybody and everything! as if he had never heard of ubiquitous Jacques in his time. Then, there were gardens, courtyards, terraces, fountains, green banks, more King and Queen, more Bull's Eye, more lords and ladies, more Long live they all! until he absolutely wept with sentiment. During the whole of this scene, which lasted some three hours, he had plenty of shouting and weeping and sentimental company, and throughout Defarge held him by the collar, as if to restrain him from flying at the objects of his brief devotion and tearing them to pieces.

"Bravo!" said Defarge, clapping him on the back when it was over, like a patron; "you are a good boy!"

The mender of roads was now coming to himself, and was mistrustful of having made a mistake in his late demonstrations; but no.

"You are the fellow we want," said Defarge, in his ear; "you make these fools believe that it will last forever. Then, they are the more insolent, and it is the nearer ended."

"Hey!" cried the mender of roads, reflectively; "that's true."

"These fools know nothing. While they despise your breath, and would stop it forever and ever, in you or in a hundred like you rather than in one of their own horses or dogs, they only know what your breath tells them. Let it deceive them, then, a little longer; it cannot deceive them too much."

Madame Defarge looked superciliously at the client, and nodded in confirmation.

"As to you," said she, "you would shout and shed tears for anything, if it made a show and a noise. Say! Would you not?"

"Truly, madame, I think so. For the moment."

"If you were shown a great heap of dolls, and were set upon them to pluck them to pieces and despoil them for your own advantage, you would pick out the richest and gayest. Say! Would you not?"

"Truly yes, madame."

"Yes. And if you were shown a flock of birds unable to fly, and were set upon them to strip them of their feathers for your own advantage, you would set upon the birds of the finest feathers; would you not?"

"It is true, madame."

"You have seen both dolls and birds today," said Madame Defarge, with a wave of her hand toward the place where they had last been apparent; "now, go home!"

Sixteen

STILL KNITTING

MADAME DEFARGE AND MONSIEUR HER HUSBAND RE-turned amicably to the bosom of Saint Antoine, while a speck in a blue cap toiled through the darkness, and through the dust, and down the weary miles of avenue by the wayside, slowly tending toward that point of the compass where the chateau of Monsieur the Marquis, now in his grave, listened to the whispering trees. Such ample leisure had the stone faces, now, for listening to the trees and to the fountain, that the few village scarecrows who, in their quest for herbs to eat and fragments of dead stick to burn, strayed within sight of the great stone courtyard and terrace staircase, had it borne in upon their starved fancy that the expression of the faces was altered. A rumor just lived in the village—had a faint and bare existence there, as its people had—that when the knife struck home, the faces changed, from faces of pride to faces of anger and pain; also, that when that dangling figure was hauled up forty feet above the fountain, they changed again, and bore a cruel look of being avenged, which they would henceforth bear forever. In the stone face over the great window of the bedchamber where the murder was done, two fine dints were pointed out in the sculptured nose, which everybody recognized, and which nobody had seen of old; and on the scarce occasion when two or three ragged peasants emerged from the crowd to take a hurried peep at Monsieur the Marquis petrified, a skinny finger would not have pointed to it for a minute, before they all started away among the moss and leaves, like the more fortunate hares who could find a living there.

Chateau and hut, stone face and dangling figure, the red stain on the stone floor and the pure water in the village well—thousands of acres of land—a whole province of France—all France itself—lay under the night sky, concentrated into a faint hairbreadth line. So does a whole world with all its greatnesses and littlenesses, lie in a twinkling star. And as mere human knowledge can split a ray of light and analyze the manner of its composition, so, sublimer intelligences may read in the feeble shining of this earth of ours, every thought and act, every vice and virtue, of every responsible creature on it.

The Defarges, husband and wife, came lumbering under the starlight, in their public vehicle, to that gate of Paris whereunto their journey naturally tended. There was the usual stoppage at the barrier guardhouse, and the usual lanterns came glancing forth for the usual examination and inquiry. Monsieur Defarge alighted: knowing one or two of the soldiery there, and one of the police. The latter he was intimate with, and affectionately embraced.

When Saint Antoine had again enfolded the Defarges in his dusky wings, and they, having finally alighted near the Saint's boundaries, were picking their way on foot through the black mud and offal of his streets, Madame Defarge spoke to her husband:

"Say then, my friend; what did Jacques of the police tell thee?"

"Very little tonight, but all he knows. There is another spy commissioned for our quarter. There may be many more, for all that he can say, but he knows of one."

"Eh well!" said Madame Defarge, raising her eyebrows with a cool business air. "It is necessary to register him. How do they call that man?"

"He is English."

"So much the better. His name?"

"Barsad," said Defarge, making it French by pronunciation. But, he had been so careful to get it accurately, that he then spelt it with perfect correctness.

"Barsad," repeated madame. "Good. Christian name?"

"John."

"John Barsad," repeated madame, after murmuring it once to herself. "Good. His appearance; is it known?"

"Age, about forty years; height, about five feet nine; black hair; complexion dark; generally, rather handsome visage; eyes dark, face thin, long, and sallow; nose aquiline, but not straight, having a peculiar inclination towards the left cheek; expression, therefore, sinister."

"Eh, my faith. It is a portrait!" said madame, laughing. "He shall be registered tomorrow."

They turned into the wine-shop, which was closed (for it was midnight), and where Madame Defarge immediately took her post at her desk, counted the small moneys that had been taken during her absence, examined the stock, went through the entries in the book, made other entries of her own, checked the serving man in every possible way, and finally dismissed him to bed. Then she turned out the contents of the bowl of money for the second time, and began knotting them up in her handkerchief, in a chain of separate knots, for safekeeping through the night. All this while, Defarge, with his pipe in his mouth, walked up and down, complacently admiring, but never interfering; in which condition, indeed, as to the business and his domestic affairs, he walked up and down through life.

The night was hot, and the shop, close shut and surrounded by so foul a neighborhood, was ill-smelling. Monsieur Defarge's olfactory sense was by no means delicate, but the stock of wine smelt much stronger than it ever tasted, and so did the stock of rum and brandy and aniseed. He whiffed the compound of scents away, as he put down his smoked-out pipe.

"You are fatigued," said madame, raising her glance as she knotted the money. "There are only the usual odors."

"I am a little tired," her husband acknowledged.

"You are a little depressed, too," said madame, whose quick eyes had never been so intent on the accounts, but they had had a ray or two for him. "Oh, the men, the men!"

"But my dear," began Defarge.

"But my dear!" repeated madame, nodding firmly: "but my dear! You are faint of heart tonight, my dear!"

"Well, then," said Defarge, as if a thought were wrung out of his breast, "it *is* a long time."

"It is a long time," repeated his wife; "and when is it not a long time? Vengeance and retribution require a long time; it is the rule."

"It does not take a long time to strike a man with lightning," said Defarge.

"How long," demanded madame, composedly, "does it take to make and store the lightning? Tell me?"

Defarge raised his forehead thoughtfully, as if there were something in that, too.

"It does not take a long time," said madame, "for an earthquake to swallow a town. Eh well! Tell me how long it takes to prepare the earthquake?"

"A long time, I suppose," said Defarge.

"But when it is ready, it takes place, and grinds to pieces everything before it. In the meantime, it is always preparing, though it is not seen or heard. That is your consolation. Keep it."

She tied a knot with flashing eyes, as if it throttled a foe.

"I tell thee," said madame, extending her right hand, for emphasis, "that although it is a long time on the road, it is on the road and coming. I tell thee it never retreats, and never stops. I tell thee it is always advancing. Look around and consider the lives of all the world that we know, consider the faces of all the world that we know, consider the rage and discontent to which the Jacquerie addresses itself with more and more of certainty every hour. Can such things last? Bah! I mock you."

"My brave wife," returned Defarge, standing before her with his head a little bent, and his hands clasped at his back, like a docile and attentive pupil before his catechist, "I do not question all this. But it has lasted a long time, and it is possible—you know well, my wife, it is possible—that it may not come, during our lives."

"Eh well! How then?" demanded madame, tying another knot, as if there were another enemy strangled.

"Well!" said Defarge, with a half complaining and half apologetic shrug. "We shall not see the triumph."

"We shall have helped it," returned madame, with her extended hand in strong action. "Nothing that we do, is done in vain. I believe, with all my soul, that we shall see the triumph. But even if not, even if I knew certainly not, show me the neck of an aristocrat and tyrant, and still I would—"

Then madame, with her teeth set, tied a very terrible knot indeed.

"Hold!" cried Defarge, reddening a little as if he felt charged with cowardice; "I too, my dear, will stop at nothing."

"Yes! But it is your weakness that you sometimes need to see your victim and your opportunity, to sustain you. Sustain yourself without that. When the time comes, let loose a tiger and a devil; but wait for the time with the tiger and the devil chained—not shown—yet always ready."

Madame enforced the conclusion of this piece of advice by striking her little counter with her chain of money as if she knocked its brains out, and then gathering the heavy handkerchief under her arm in a serene manner, and observing that it was time to go to bed.

Next noontide saw the admirable woman in her usual place in the wine-shop, knitting away assiduously. A rose lay beside her, and if she now and then glanced at the flower, it was with no infraction of her usual preoccupied air. There were a few customers, drinking or not drinking, standing or seated, sprinkled about. The day was very hot, and heaps of flies, who were extending their inquisitive and adventurous perquisitions into all the glutinous little glasses near madame, fell dead at the bottom. Their decease made no impression on the other flies out promenading, who looked at them in the coolest manner (as if they themselves were elephants, or something as far removed), until they met the same fate. Curious to consider how heedless flies are!—perhaps they thought as much at Court that sunny summer day.

A figure entering at the door threw a shadow on Madame Defarge which she felt to be a new one. She laid down her knitting, and began to pin the rose in her head-dress, before she looked at the figure.

It was curious. The moment Madame Defarge took up the rose, the customers ceased talking, and began gradually to drop out of the wine-shop.

"Good day, madame," said the newcomer.

"Good day, monsieur."

She said it aloud, but added to herself, as she resumed her knitting: "Hah! Good day, age about forty, height about five feet nine, black hair, generally rather handsome visage, complexion dark, eyes dark, thin, long and sallow face, aquiline nose but not straight, having a peculiar inclination toward the left cheek, which imparts a sinister expression! Good day, one and all!"

"Have the goodness to give me a little glass of old cognac, and a mouthful of cool fresh water, madame."

Madame complied with a polite air.

"Marvelous cognac this, madame!"

It was the first time it had ever been so complimented, and Madame Defarge knew enough of its antecedents to know better. She said, however, that the cognac was flattered, and took up her knitting. The visitor watched her fingers for a few moments, and took the opportunity of observing the place in general.

"You knit with great skill, madame."

"I am accustomed to it."

"A pretty pattern, too!"

"*You* think so?" said madame, looking at him with a smile.

"Decidedly. May one ask what it is for?"

"Pastime," said madame, looking at him with a smile, while her fingers moved nimbly.

"Not for use?"

"That depends. I may find a use for it one day. If I do—well," said madame, drawing a breath and nodding her head with a stern kind of coquetry, "I'll use it!"

It was remarkable; but the taste of Saint Antoine seemed to be decidedly opposed to a rose on the head-dress of Madame Defarge. Two men had entered separately, and had been about to order drinks, when, catching sight of that novelty, they faltered, made a pretense of looking about as if for some friend who was not there, and went away. Nor, of those who had been there when this visitor entered, was there one left. They had all dropped off. The spy had kept his eyes open, but had been able to detect no sign. They had lounged away in a poverty-stricken, purposeless, accidental manner, quite natural and unimpeachable.

"JOHN," thought madame, checking off her work as her fingers knitted, and her eyes looked at the stranger. "Stay long enough, and I shall knit 'BARSAD' before you go."

"You have a husband, madame?"

"I have."

"Children?"

"No children."

"Business seems bad?"

"Business is very bad; the people are so poor."

"Ah, the unfortunate, miserable people! So oppressed, too—as you say."

"As *you* say," madame retorted, correcting him and deftly knitting an extra something into his name that boded him no good.

"Pardon me; certainly it was I who said so, but you naturally think so. Of course."

"*I* think?" returned madame, in a high voice. "I and my husband have enough to do to keep this wine-shop open, without thinking. All we think, here, is how to live. That is the subject *we* think of, and it gives us, from morning to night, enough to think about, without embarrassing our heads concerning others. *I* think for others? No, no."

The spy, who was there to pick up any crumbs he could find or make, did not allow his baffled state to express itself in his sinister face; but, stood with an air of gossiping gallantry, leaning his elbow on Madame Defarge's little counter, and occasionally sipping his cognac.

"A bad business this, madame, of Gaspard's execution. Ah! the poor Gaspard!" With a sigh of great compassion.

"My faith!" returned madame, coolly and lightly, "if people use knives for such purposes, they have to pay for it. He knew beforehand what the price of his luxury was; he has paid the price."

"I believe," said the spy, dropping his soft voice to a tone that invited confidence, and expressing an injured revolutionary susceptibility in every muscle of his wicked face: "I believe there is much compassion and anger in this neighborhood, touching the poor fellow? Between ourselves."

"Is there?" asked madame, vacantly.

"Is there not?"

"—Here is my husband!" said Madame Defarge.

As the keeper of the wine-shop entered at the door, the spy saluted him by touching his hat, and saying, with an engaging smile, "Good day, Jacques!" Defarge stopped short, and stared at him.

"Good day, Jacques!" the spy repeated; with not quite so much confidence, or quite so easy a smile under the stare.

"You deceive yourself, monsieur," returned the keeper of the wine-shop. "You mistake me for another. That is not my name. I am Ernest Defarge."

"It is all the same," said the spy, airily, but discomfited too; "good day!"

"Good day!" answered Defarge, drily.

"I was saying to madame, with whom I had the pleasure of chatting when you entered, that they tell me there is—and no wonder!—much sympathy and anger in Saint Antoine, touching the unhappy fate of poor Gaspard."

"No one has told me so," said Defarge, shaking his head; "I know nothing of it."

Having said it, he passed behind the little counter, and stood with his hand on the back of his wife's chair, looking over that barrier at the person to whom they were both opposed, and whom either of them would have shot with the greatest satisfaction.

The spy, well used to his business, did not change his unconscious attitude, but drained his little glass of cognac, took a sip of fresh water, and asked
for another glass of cognac. Madame Defarge poured it out for him, took to
her knitting again, and hummed a little song over it.

"You seem to know this quarter well; that is to say, better than I do?"
observed Defarge.

"Not at all, but I hope to know it better. I am so profoundly interested in
its miserable inhabitants."

"Hah!" muttered Defarge.

"The pleasure of conversing with you, Monsieur Defarge, recalls to me,"
pursued the spy, "that I have the honor of cherishing some interesting associations with your name."

"Indeed?" said Defarge, with much indifference.

"Yes, indeed. When Doctor Manette was released, you his old domestic
had the charge of him, I know. He was delivered to you. You see I am
informed of the circumstances?"

"Such is the fact, certainly," said Defarge. He had had it conveyed to
him, in an accidental touch of his wife's elbow as she knitted and warbled,
that he would do best to answer, but always with brevity.

"It was to you," said the spy, "that his daughter came; and it was from
your care that his daughter took him, accompanied by a neat brown monsieur; how is he called?—in a little wig—Lorry—of the bank of Tellson and
Company—over to England."

"Such is the fact," repeated Defarge.

"Very interesting remembrances!" said the spy. "I have known Doctor
Manette and his daughter, in England."

"Yes?" said Defarge.

"You don't hear much about them now?" said the spy.

"No," said Defarge.

"In effect," madame struck in, looking up from her work and her little
song, "we never hear about them. We received the news of their safe arrival,
and perhaps another letter or perhaps two; but since then, they have gradually
taken their road in life—we, ours—and we have held no correspondence."

"Perfectly so, madame," replied the spy. "She is going to be married."

"Going?" echoed madame. "She was pretty enough to have been married
long ago. You English are cold, it seems to me."

"Oh! You know I am English."

"I perceive your tongue is," returned madame; "and what the tongue is,
I suppose the man is."

He did not take the identification as a compliment; but he made the best
of it, and turned it off with a laugh. After sipping his cognac to the end, he
added:

"Yes, Miss Manette is going to be married. But not to an Englishman: to
one who, like herself, is French by birth. And speaking of Gaspard (ah, poor

Gaspard! It was cruel, cruel!), it is a curious thing that she is going to marry the nephew of Monsieur the Marquis, for whom Gaspard was exalted to that height of so many feet; in other words, the present Marquis. But he lives unknown in England, he is no Marquis there; he is Mr. Charles Darnay. D'Aulnais is the name of his mother's family."

Madame Defarge knitted steadily, but the intelligence had a palpable effect upon her husband. Do what he would behind the little counter, as to the striking of a light and the lighting of his pipe, he was troubled, and his hand was not trustworthy. The spy would have been no spy if he had failed to see it, or to record it in his mind.

Having made, at least, this one hit, whatever it might prove to be worth, and no customers coming in to help him to any other, Mr. Barsad paid for what he had drunk, and took his leave: taking occasion to say, in a genteel manner, before he departed, that he looked forward to the pleasure of seeing Monsieur and Madame Defarge again. For some minutes after he had emerged into the outer presence of Saint Antoine, the husband and wife remained exactly as he had left them, lest he should come back.

"Can it be true," said Defarge, in a low voice, looking down at his wife as he stood smoking with his hand on the back of her chair, "what he has said of Ma'amselle Manette?"

"As he has said it," returned madame, lifting her eyebrows a little, "it is probably false. But it may be true."

"If it is—" Defarge began, and stopped.

"If it is?" repeated his wife.

"—And if it does come, while we live to see it triumph—I hope, for her sake, Destiny will keep her husband out of France."

"Her husband's destiny," said Madame Defarge, with her usual composure, "will take him where he is to go, and will lead him to the end that is to end him. That is all I know."

"But it is very strange—now, at least is it not very strange"—said Defarge, rather pleading with his wife to induce her to admit it, "that, after all our sympathy for monsieur her father and herself, her husband's name should be proscribed under your hand at this moment, by the side of that infernal dog's who has just left us?"

"Stranger things than that, will happen when it does come," answered madame. "I have them both here, of a certainty; and they are both here for their merits; that is enough."

She rolled up her knitting when she had said those words, and presently took the rose out of the handkerchief that was wound about her head. Either Saint Antoine had an instinctive sense that the objectionable decoration was gone, or Saint Antoine was on the watch for its disappearance; howbeit, the Saint took courage to lounge in, very shortly afterward, and the wine-shop recovered its habitual aspect.

In the evening, at which season of all others, Saint Antoine turned himself inside out, and sat on doorsteps and window-ledges, and came to the corners of vile streets and courts, for a breath of air, Madame Defarge with her work in her hand was accustomed to pass from place to place and from group to group: a missionary—there were many like her—such as the world will do well never to breed again. All the women knitted. They knitted worthless things; but, the mechanical work was a mechanical substitute for eating and drinking; the hands moved for the jaws and the digestive apparatus; if the bony fingers had been still, the stomachs would have been more famine-pinched.

But, as the fingers went, the eyes went, and the thoughts. And as Madame Defarge moved on from group to group, all three went quicker and fiercer among every little knot of women that she had spoken with, and left behind.

Her husband smoked at his door, looking after her with admiration. "A great woman," said he, "strong woman, a grand woman, a frightfully grand woman!"

Darkness closed around, and then came the ringing of church bells and the distant beating of the military drums of the Royal Guard, as the women sat knitting, knitting. Darkness encompassed them. Another darkness was closing in as surely, when the church bells, then ringing pleasantly in many an airy steeple over France, should be melted into thunder cannon; when the military drums should be beating to drown a wretched voice, that night all potent as the voice of Power and Plenty, Freedom and Life. So much was closing in about the women who sat knitting, knitting, that they their very selves were closing in around a structure yet unbuilt, where they were to sit knitting, knitting, counting dropping heads.

S e v e n t e e n

ONE NIGHT

NEVER DID THE SUN GO DOWN WITH A BRIGHTER GLORY on the quiet corner of Soho, than one memorable evening when the Doctor and his daughter sat under the plane-tree together. Never did the moon rise with a milder radiance over great London, than on that night when it found them still seated under the tree, and shone upon their faces through its leaves.

Lucie was to be married tomorrow. She had reserved this last evening for her father, and they sat alone under the plane-tree.

"You are happy, my dear father?"

"Quite, my child."

They had said little, though they had been there a long time. When it was yet light enough to work and read, she had neither engaged herself in her usual work, nor had she read to him. She had employed herself in both ways, at his side under the tree, many and many a time; but, this time was not quite like any other, and nothing could make it so.

"And I am very happy tonight, dear father. I am deeply happy in the love that Heaven has so blessed—my love for Charles, and Charles's love for me. But, if my life were not to be still consecrated to you, or if my marriage were so arranged as that it would part us, even by the length of a few of these streets, I should be more unhappy and self-reproachful now, than I can tell you. Even as it is—"

Even as it was, she could not command her voice.

In the sad moonlight, she clasped him by the neck, and laid her face upon his breast. In the moonlight which is always sad, as the light of the sun itself is—as the light called human life is—as its coming and its going.

"Dearest dear! Can you tell me, this last time, that you feel quite, quite sure no new affections of mine, and no new duties of mine, will ever interpose between us? *I* know it well, but do you know it? In your own heart, do you feel quite certain?"

Her father answered with a cheerful firmness of conviction he could scarcely have assumed, "Quite sure, my darling! More than that," he added, as he tenderly kissed her: "my future is far brighter, Lucie, seen through your marriage, than it could have been—nay, than it ever was—without it."

"If I could hope *that*, my father!—"

"Believe it, love! Indeed it is so. Consider how natural and how plain it is, my dear, that it should be so. You, devoted and young, cannot freely appreciate the anxiety I have felt that your life should not be wasted—"

She moved her hand toward his lips, but he took it in his, and repeated the word.

"—wasted, my child—should not be wasted, struck aside from the natural order of things—for my sake. Your unselfishness cannot entirely comprehend how much my mind has gone on this; but, only ask yourself, how could my happiness be perfect, while yours was incomplete?"

"If I had never seen Charles, my father, I should have been quite happy with you."

He smiled at her unconscious admission that she would have been unhappy without Charles, having seen him, and replied:

"My child, you did see him, and it is Charles. If it had not been Charles, it would have been another. Or, if it had been no other, I should have been the cause, and then the dark part of my life would have cast its shadow beyond myself, and would have fallen on you."

It was the first time, except at the trial, of her ever hearing him refer to the period of his suffering. It gave her a strange and new sensation while his words were in her ears; and she remembered it long afterward.

"See!" said the Doctor of Beauvais, raising his hand toward the moon. "I have looked at her, from my prison-window, when I could not bear her light. I have looked at her when it has been such torture to me to think of her shining upon what I had lost, that I have beaten my head against my prison-walls. I have looked at her, in a state so dull and lethargic, that I have thought of nothing but the number of horizontal lines I could draw across her at the full, and the number of perpendicular lines with which I could intersect them." He added, in his inward and pondering manner, as he looked at the moon, "It was twenty either way, I remember, and the twentieth was difficult to squeeze in."

The strange thrill with which she heard him go back to that time, deepened as he dwelt upon it; but, there was nothing to shock her in the manner of his reference. He only seemed to contrast his present cheerfulness and felicity with the dire endurance that was over.

"I have looked at her, speculating thousands of times upon the unborn child from whom I had been rent. Whether it was alive. Whether it had been born alive, or the poor mother's shock had killed it. Whether it was a son who would someday avenge his father. (There was a time in my imprisonment, when my desire for vengeance was unbearable.) Whether it was a son who would never know his father's story; who might even live to weigh the possibility of his father's having disappeared of his own will and act. Whether it was a daughter who would grow to be a woman."

She drew closer to him, and kissed his cheek and his hand.

"I have pictured my daughter, to myself, as perfectly forgetful of me—rather, altogether ignorant of me, and unconscious of me. I have cast up the years of her age, year after year. I have seen her married to a man who knew nothing of my fate. I have altogether perished from the remembrance of the living, and in the next generation my place was a blank."

"My father! Even to hear that you had such thoughts of a daughter who never existed, strikes to my heart as if I had been that child."

"You, Lucie? It is out of the consolation and restoration you have brought to me, that these remembrances arise, and pass between us and the moon on this last night.—What did I say just now?"

"She knew nothing of you. She cared nothing for you."

"So! But on other moonlight nights, when the sadness and the silence have touched me in a different way—have affected me with something as like a sorrowful sense of peace, as any emotion that had pain for its foundations could—I have imagined her as coming to me in my cell, and leading me out into the freedom beyond the fortress. I have seen her image in the moonlight, often, as I now see you; except that I never held her in my arms; it stood between the little grated window and the door. But, you understand that that was not the child I am speaking of?"

"The figure was not; the—the—image; the fancy?"

"No. That was another thing. It stood before my disturbed sense of sight, but it never moved. The phantom that my mind pursued was another and more real child. Of her outward appearance I know no more than that she was like her mother. The other had that likeness too—as you have—but was not the same. Can you follow me, Lucie? Hardly, I think. I doubt you must have been a solitary prisoner to understand these perplexed distinctions."

His collected and calm manner could not prevent her blood from running cold, as he thus tried to anatomize his old condition.

"In that more peaceful state, I have imagined her, in the moonlight, coming to me and taking me out to show me that the home of her married life was full of her loving remembrance of her lost father. My picture was in her room, and I was in her prayers. Her life was active, cheerful, useful; but my poor history pervaded it all."

"I was that child, my father. I was not half so good, but in my love that was I."

"And she showed me her children," said the Doctor of Beauvais, "and they had heard of me, and had been taught to pity me. When they passed a prison of the State, they kept far from its frowning walls, and looked up at its bars, and spoke in whispers. She could never deliver me; I imagined that she always brought me back after showing me such things. But then, blessed with the relief of tears, I fell upon my knees, and blessed her."

"I am that child, I hope, my father. O my dear, my dear, will you bless me as fervently tomorrow?"

"Lucie, I recall these old troubles in the reason that I have tonight for loving you better than words can tell, and thanking God for my great happiness. My thoughts, when they were wildest, never rose near the happiness that I have known with you, and that we have before us."

He embraced her, solemnly commended her to Heaven, and humbly thanked Heaven for having bestowed her on him. By-and-by, they went into the house.

There was no one bidden to the marriage but Mr. Lorry; there was even to be no bridesmaid but the gaunt Miss Pross. The marriage was to make no change in their place of residence; they had been able to extend it, by taking to themselves the upper rooms, formerly belonging to the apocryphal invisible lodger, and they desired nothing more.

Doctor Manette was very cheerful at the little supper. They were only three at table, and Miss Pross made the third. He regretted that Charles was not there; was more than half disposed to object to the loving little plot that kept him away; and drank to him affectionately.

So, the time came for him to bid Lucie good night, and they separated. But, in the stillness of the third hour of the morning, Lucie came downstairs again, and stole into his room; not free from unshaped fears, beforehand.

All things, however, were in their places; all was quiet; and he lay asleep, his white hair picturesque on the untroubled pillow, and his hands lying quiet on the coverlet. She put her needless candle in the shadow at a distance, crept up to his bed, and put her lips to his; then, leaned over him, and looked at him.

Into his handsome face, the bitter waters of captivity had worn; but, he covered up their tracks with a determination so strong, that he held the mastery of them, even in his sleep. A more remarkable face in its quiet, resolute, and guarded struggle with an unseen assailant was not to be beheld in all the wide dominions of sleep, that night.

She timidly laid her hand on his dear breast, and put up a prayer that she might ever be as true to him as her love aspired to be, and as his sorrows deserved. Then, she withdrew her hand, and kissed his lips once more, and went away. So, the sunrise came, and the shadows of the leaves of the plane-tree moved upon his face, as softly as her lips had moved in praying for him.

E i g h t e e n

NINE DAYS

THE MARRIAGE DAY WAS SHINING BRIGHTLY, AND THEY were ready outside the closed door of the Doctor's room, where he was speaking with Charles Darnay. They were ready to go to church; the beautiful bride, Mr. Lorry, and Miss Pross—to whom the event, through a gradual process of reconcilement to the inevitable, would have been one of absolute bliss, but for the yet lingering consideration that her brother, Solomon, should have been the bridegroom.

"And so," said Mr. Lorry, who could not sufficiently admire the bride, and who had been moving round her to take in every point of her quiet pretty dress; "and so it was for this, my sweet Lucie, that I brought you across the Channel, such a baby! Lord bless me! How little I thought what I was doing. How lightly I valued the obligation I was conferring on my friend Mr. Charles!"

"You didn't mean it," remarked the matter-of-fact Miss Pross, "and therefore how could you know it? Nonsense!"

"Really? Well; but don't cry," said the gentle Mr. Lorry.

"I am not crying," said Miss Pross; "*you* are."

"I, my Pross?" (By this time Mr. Lorry dared to be pleasant with her, on occasion.)

"You were just now; I saw you do it, and I don't wonder at it. Such a present of plate as you have made 'em, is enough to bring tears into anybody's eyes. There's not a fork or a spoon in the collection," said Miss Pross, "that I didn't cry over, last night after the box came, till I couldn't see it."

"I am highly gratified," said Mr. Lorry, "though, upon my honor, I had no intention of rendering those trifling articles of remembrance invisible to anyone. Dear me! This is an occasion that makes a man speculate on all he has lost. Dear, dear, dear! To think that there might have been a Mrs. Lorry, any time these fifty years almost!"

"Not at all!" From Miss Pross.

"You think there never might have been a Mrs. Lorry?" asked the gentleman of that name.

"Pooh!" rejoined Miss Pross; "you were a bachelor in your cradle."

"Well!" observed Mr. Lorry, beamingly adjusting his little wig, "that seems probable, too."

"And you were cut out for a bachelor," pursued Miss Pross, "before you were put in your cradle."

"Then, I think," said Mr. Lorry, "that I was very unhandsomely dealt with, and that I ought to have had a voice in the selection of my pattern. Enough! Now, my dear Lucie," drawing his arm soothingly round her waist, "I hear them moving in the next room, and Miss Pross and I, as two formal folks of business, are anxious not to lose the final opportunity of saying something to you that you wish to hear. You leave your good father, my dear, in hands as earnest and as loving as your own; he shall be taken every conceivable care of: during the next fortnight, while you are in Warwickshire and thereabouts, even Tellson's shall go to the wall (comparatively speaking) before him. And when, at the fortnight's end, he comes to join you and your beloved husband, on your other fortnight's trip in Wales, you shall say that we have sent him to you in the best health and in the happiest frame. Now, I hear Somebody's step coming to the door. Let me kiss my dear girl with an old-fashioned bachelor blessing, before Somebody comes to claim his own."

For a moment, he held the fair face from him to look at the well-remembered expression on the forehead, and then laid the bright golden hair against his little brown wig, with a genuine tenderness and delicacy, which, if such things be old-fashioned, were as old as Adam.

The door of the Doctor's room opened, and he came out with Charles Darnay. He was so deadly pale—which had not been the case when they went in together—that no vestige of color was to be seen in his face. But, in the composure of his manner he was unaltered, except that to the shrewd glance of Mr. Lorry it disclosed some shadowy indication that the old air of avoidance and dread had lately passed over him, like a cold wind.

He gave his arm to his daughter, and took her downstairs to the chariot which Mr. Lorry had hired in honor of the day. The rest followed in another carriage, and soon, in a neighboring church, where no strange eyes looked on, Charles Darnay and Lucie Manette were happily married.

Besides the glancing tears that shone among the smiles of the little group when it was done, some diamonds, very bright and sparkling, glanced on the bride's hand, which were newly released from the dark obscurity of one of Mr. Lorry's pockets. They returned home to breakfast, and all went well, and in due course the golden hair that had mingled with the poor shoemaker's white locks in the Paris garret, were mingled with them again in the morning sunlight, on the threshold of the door at parting.

It was a hard parting, though it was not for long. But her father cheered her, and said at last, gently disengaging himself from her enfolding arms, "Take her, Charles! She is yours!"

And her agitated hand waved to them from a chaise window, and she was gone.

The corner being out of the way of the idle and curious, and the preparations having been very simple and few, the Doctor, Mr. Lorry, and Miss Pross, were left quite alone. It was when they turned into the welcome shade of the cool, old hall, that Mr. Lorry observed a great change to have come over the Doctor; as if the golden arm uplifted there, had struck him a poisoned blow.

He had naturally repressed much, and some revulsion might have been expected in him when the occasion for repression was gone. But, it was the old, scared, lost look that troubled Mr. Lorry; and through his absent manner of clasping his head and drearily wandering away into his own room when they got upstairs, Mr. Lorry was reminded of Defarge the wine-shop keeper, and the starlight ride.

"I think," he whispered to Miss Pross, after anxious consideration, "I think we had best not speak to him just now, or at all disturb him. I must look in at Tellson's; so I will go there at once and come back presently. Then, we will take him a ride into the country, and dine there, and all will be well."

It was easier for Mr. Lorry to look in at Tellson's than to look out of Tellson's. He was detained two hours. When he came back, he ascended the old staircase alone, having asked no question of the servant; going thus into the Doctor's rooms, he was stopped by a low sound of knocking.

"Good God!" he said, with a start. "What's that?"

Miss Pross, with a terrified face, was at his ear. "O me, O me! All is lost!" cried she, wringing her hands. "What is to be told to Ladybird? He doesn't know me, and is making shoes!"

Mr. Lorry said what he could to calm her, and went himself into the Doctor's room. The bench was turned toward the light, as it had been when he had seen the shoemaker at his work before, and his head was bent down, and he was very busy.

"Doctor Manette. My dear friend, Doctor Manette!"

The Doctor looked at him for a moment—half inquiringly, half as if he were angry at being spoken to—and bent over his work again.

He had laid aside his coat and waistcoat; his shirt was open at the throat, as it used to be when he did that work; and even the old haggard, faded surface of face had come back to him. He worked hard—impatiently—as if in some sense of having been interrupted.

Mr. Lorry glanced at the work in his hand, and observed that it was a shoe of the old size and shape. He took up another that was lying by him, and asked what it was?

"A young lady's walking shoe," he muttered, without looking up. "It ought to have been finished long ago. Let it be."

"But, Doctor Manette. Look at me!"

He obeyed, in the old mechanically submissive manner, without pausing in his work.

"You know me, my dear friend? Think again. This is not your proper occupation. Think, dear friend!"

Nothing would induce him to speak more. He looked up, for an instant at a time, when he was requested to do so; but, no persuasion would extract a word from him. He worked, and worked, and worked in silence, and words fell on him as they would have fallen on an echoless wall, or on the air. The only ray of hope that Mr. Lorry could discover, was, that he sometimes furtively looked up without being asked. In that there seemed a faint expression of curiosity or perplexity—as though he were trying to reconcile some doubts in his mind.

Two things at once impressed themselves on Mr. Lorry, as important above all others; the first, that this must be kept secret from Lucie; the second, that it must be kept secret from all who knew him. In conjunction with Miss Pross, he took immediate steps towards the latter precaution, by giving out that the Doctor was not well, and required a few days of complete rest. In aid of the kind deception to be practiced on his daughter, Miss Pross was to write, describing his having been called away professionally, and referring to an imaginary letter of two or three hurried lines in his own hand, represented to have been addressed to her by the same post.

These measures, advisable to be taken in any case, Mr. Lorry took in the hope of his coming to himself. If that should happen soon, he kept another course in reserve; which was, to have a certain opinion that he thought the best, on the Doctor's case.

In the hope of his recovery, and of resort to this third course being thereby rendered practicable, Mr. Lorry resolved to watch him attentively, with as little appearance as possible of doing so. He therefore made arrangements to absent himself from Tellson's for the first time in his life, and took his post by the window in the same room.

He was not long in discovering that it was worse than useless to speak to him, since, on being pressed, he became worried. He abandoned that attempt in the first day, and resolved merely to keep himself always before him, as a silent protest against the delusion into which he had fallen, or was falling. He remained, therefore, in his seat near the window, reading and writing, and expressing in as many pleasant and natural ways as he could think of, that it was a free place.

Doctor Manette took what was given him to eat and drink, and worked on, that first day, until it was too dark to see—worked on, half an hour after Mr. Lorry could not have seen, for his life, to read or write. When he put his tools aside as useless, until morning, Mr. Lorry rose and said:

"Will you go out?"

He looked down at the floor on either side of him in the old manner, looked up in the old manner, and repeated in the old low voice,

"Out?"

"Yes; for a walk with me. Why not?"

He made no effort to say why not, and said not a word more. But, Mr. Lorry thought he saw, as he leaned forward on his bench in the dusk, with his elbows on his knees and his head in his hands, that he was in some misty way asking himself, "Why not?" The sagacity of the man of business perceived an advantage here, and determined to hold it.

Miss Pross and he divided the night into two watches, and observed him at intervals from the adjoining room. He paced up and down for a long time before he lay down; but, when he did finally lay himself down, he fell asleep. In the morning, he was up betimes, and went straight to his bench and to work.

On the second day, Mr. Lorry saluted him cheerfully by his name, and spoke to him on topics that had been of late familiar to them. He returned no reply, but it was evident that he heard what was said, and that he thought about it, however confusedly. This encouraged Mr. Lorry to have Miss Pross in with her work, several times during the day; at those times, they quietly spoke of Lucie, and of her father then present, precisely in the usual manner, and as if there were nothing amiss. This was done without any demonstrative accompaniment, not long enough or often enough to harass him; and it lightened Mr. Lorry's friendly heart to believe that he looked up oftener, and that he appeared to be stirred by some perception of inconsistencies surrounding him.

When it fell dark again, Mr. Lorry asked him as before:

"Dear Doctor, will you go out?"

As before, he repeated, "Out?"

"Yes; for a walk with me. Why not?"

This time, Mr. Lorry feigned to go out when he could extract no answer from him, and, after remaining absent for an hour, returned. In the meanwhile, the Doctor had removed to the seat in the window, and had sat there looking down at the plane-tree; but, on Mr. Lorry's return, he slipped away to his bench.

The time went very slowly on, and Mr. Lorry's hope darkened, and his heart grew heavier again, and grew yet heavier and heavier every day. The third day came and went, the fourth, the fifth. Five days, six days, seven days, eight days, nine days.

With a hope ever darkening, and with a heart always growing heavier and heavier, Mr. Lorry passed through this anxious time. The secret was well kept, and Lucie was unconscious and happy; but he could not fail to observe that the shoemaker, whose hand had been a little out at first, was growing dreadfully skillful, and that he had never been so intent on his work, and that his hands had never been so nimble and expert, as in the dusk of the ninth evening.

N i n e t e e n

AN OPINION

WORN OUT BY ANXIOUS WATCHING, MR. LORRY FELL asleep at his post. On the tenth morning of his suspense, he was startled by the shining of the sun into the room where a heavy slumber had overtaken him when it was dark night.

He rubbed his eyes and roused himself; but he doubted, when he had done so, whether he was not still asleep. For, going to the door of the Doctor's room and looking in, he perceived that the shoemaker's bench and tools were put aside again, and that the Doctor himself sat reading at the window. He was in his usual morning dress, and his face (which Mr. Lorry could distinctly see), though still very pale, was calmly studious and attentive.

Even when he had satisfied himself that he was awake, Mr. Lorry felt giddily uncertain for some few moments whether the late shoemaking might not be a disturbed dream of his own; for, did not his eyes show him his friend before him in his accustomed clothing and aspect, and employed as usual; and was there any sign within their range, that the change of which he had so strong an impression had actually happened?

It was but the inquiry of his first confusion and astonishment, the answer being obvious. If the impression were not produced by a real corresponding, and sufficient cause, how came he, Jarvis Lorry, there? How came he to have fallen asleep, in his clothes, on the sofa in Doctor Manette's consulting-room, and to be debating these points outside the Doctor's bedroom door in the early morning?

Within a few minutes, Miss Pross stood whispering at his side. If he had had any particle of doubt left, her talk would of necessity have resolved it; but he was by that time clearheaded, and had none. He advised that they should let the time go by until the regular breakfast-hour, and should then meet the Doctor as if nothing unusual had occurred. If he appeared to be in his customary state of mind, Mr. Lorry would then cautiously proceed to seek direction and guidance from the opinion he had been, in his anxiety, so anxious to obtain.

Miss Pross submitting herself to his judgment, the scheme was worked out with care. Having abundance of time for his usual methodical toilette, Mr. Lorry presented himself at the breakfast-hour in his usual white linen and with his usual neat leg. The Doctor was summoned in the usual way, and came to breakfast.

So far as it was possible to comprehend him without overstepping those delicate and gradual approaches which Mr. Lorry felt to be the only safe advance, he at first supposed that his daughter's marriage had taken place yesterday. An incidental allusion, purposely thrown out, to the day of the week, and the day of the month, set him thinking and counting, and evidently made him uneasy. In all other respects, however, he was so composedly himself, that Mr. Lorry determined to have the aid he sought. And that aid was his own.

Therefore, when the breakfast was done and cleared away, and he and the Doctor were left together, Mr. Lorry said, feelingly:

"My dear Manette, I am anxious to have your opinion, in confidence, on a very curious case in which I am deeply interested; that is to say, it is very curious to me; perhaps, to your better information, it may be less so."

Glancing at his hands, which were discolored by his late work, the Doctor looked troubled, and listened attentively. He had already glanced at his hands more than once.

"Doctor Manette," said Mr. Lorry, touching him affectionately on the arm, "the case is the case of a particularly dear friend of mine. Pray give your mind to it, and advise me well for his sake—and above all, for his daughter's—his daughter's, my dear Manette."

"If I understand," said the Doctor, in a subdued tone, "some mental shock—?"

"Yes!"

"Be explicit," said the Doctor. "Spare no detail."

Mr. Lorry saw that they understood one another, and proceeded.

"My dear Manette, it is the case of an old and a prolonged shock, of great acuteness and severity, to the affections, the feelings, the—the—as you express it—the mind. The mind. It is the case of a shock under which the sufferer was borne down, one cannot say for how long, because I believe he cannot calculate the time himself, and there are no other means of getting at it. It is the case of a shock from which the sufferer recovered, by a process that he cannot trace himself—as I once heard him publicly relate in a striking manner. It is the case of a shock from which he has recovered, so completely, as to be a highly intelligent man, capable of close application of mind, and great exertion of body, and of constantly making fresh additions to his stock of knowledge, which was already very large. But, unfortunately, there has been," he paused, and took a deep breath—"a slight relapse."

The Doctor, in a low voice, asked, "Of how long duration?"

"Nine days and nights."

"How did it show itself? I infer," glancing at his hands again, "in the resumption of some old pursuit connected with the shock?"

"That is the fact."

"Now, did you ever see him," asked the Doctor, distinctly and collectedly, though in the same low voice, "engaged in that pursuit originally?"

"Once."

"And when the relapse fell on him, was he in most respects—or in all respects—as he was then?"

"I think in all respects."

"You spoke of his daughter. Does his daughter know of the relapse?"

"No. It has been kept from her, and I hope will always be kept from her. It is known only to myself, and to one other who may be trusted."

The Doctor grasped his hand, and murmured, "That was very kind. That was very thoughtful!" Mr. Lorry grasped his hand in return, and neither of the two spoke for a little while.

"Now, my dear Manette," said Mr. Lorry, at length, in his most considerate and most affectionate way, "I am a mere man of business, and unfit to cope with such intricate and difficult matters. I do not possess the kind of information necessary; I do not possess the kind of intelligence; I want guiding. There is no man in this world on whom I could so rely for right guidance, as on you. Tell me, how does this relapse come about? Is there danger of another? Could a repetition of it be prevented? How should a repetition of it be treated? How does it come about at all? What can I do for my friend? No man ever can have been more desirous in his heart to serve a friend, than I am to serve mine, if I knew how. But I don't know how to originate in such a case. If your sagacity, knowledge, and experience could put me on the right track, I might be able to do so much; unenlightened and undirected, I can do so little. Pray discuss it with me; pray enable me to see it a little more clearly, and teach me how to be a little more useful."

Doctor Manette sat meditating after these earnest words were spoken, and Mr. Lorry did not press him.

"I think it probable," said the Doctor, breaking silence with an effort, "that the relapse you have described, my dear friend, was not quite unforeseen by its subject."

"Was it dreaded by him?" Mr. Lorry ventured to ask.

"Very much." He said it with an involuntary shudder.

"You have no idea how such an apprehension weighs on the sufferer's mind, and how difficult—how almost impossible—it is, for him to force himself to utter a word upon the topic that oppresses him."

"Would he," asked Mr. Lorry, "be sensibly relieved if he could prevail upon himself to impart that secret brooding to anyone, when it is on him?"

"I think so. But it is, as I have told you, next to impossible. I even believe it—in some cases—to be quite impossible."

"Now," said Mr. Lorry, gently laying his hand on the Doctor's arm again, after a short silence on both sides, "to what would you refer this attack?"

"I believe," returned Doctor Manette, "that there had been a strong and extraordinary revival of the train of thought and remembrance that was the first cause of the malady. Some intense associations of a most distressing nature were vividly recalled, I think. It is probable that there had long been a dread lurking in his mind, that those associations would be recalled—say, under certain circumstances—say, on a particular occasion. He tried to prepare himself in vain; perhaps the effort to prepare himself made him less able to bear it."

"Would he remember what took place in the relapse?" asked Mr. Lorry, with natural hesitation.

The Doctor looked desolately round the room, shook his head, and answered, in a low voice, "Not at all."

"Now, as to the future," hinted Mr. Lorry.

"As to the future," said the Doctor, recovering firmness, "I should have great hope. As it pleased heaven in its mercy to restore him so soon, I should have great hope. He, yielding under the pressure of a complicated something, long dreaded and long vaguely foreseen and contended against, and recovering after the cloud had burst and passed, I should hope that the worst was over."

"Well, well! That's good comfort. I am thankful!" said Mr. Lorry.

"I am thankful!" repeated the Doctor, bending his head with reverence.

"There are two other points," said Mr. Lorry, "on which I am anxious to be instructed. I may go on?"

"You cannot do your friend a better service." The Doctor gave him his hand.

"To the first, then. He is of a studious habit, and unusually energetic; he applies himself with great ardor to the acquisition of professional knowledge, to the conducting of experiments, to many things. Now, does he do too much?"

"I think not. It may be the character of his mind, to be always in singular need of occupation. That may be, in part, natural to it; in part, the result of affliction. The less it was occupied with healthy things, the more it would be in danger of turning in the unhealthy direction. He may have observed himself, and made the discovery."

"You are sure that he is not under too great a strain?"

"I think I am quite sure of it."

"My dear Manette, if he were overworked now—"

"My dear Lorry, I doubt if that could easily be. There has been a violent stress in one direction, and it needs a counterweight."

"Excuse me, as a persistent man of business. Assuming for a moment that he *was* overworked; it would show itself in some renewal of this disorder?"

"I do not think so. I do not think," said Doctor Manette, with the firmness of self-conviction, "that anything but the one train of association would renew it. I think that, henceforth, nothing but some extraordinary jarring of that chord could renew it. After what has happened, and after his recovery, I find it difficult to imagine any such violent sounding of that string again. I trust, and I almost believe, that the circumstances likely to renew it are exhausted."

He spoke with the diffidence of a man who knew how slight a thing would overset the delicate organization of the mind, and yet with the confidence of a man who had slowly won his assurance out of personal endurance and distress. It was not for his friend to abate that confidence. He professed himself more relieved and encouraged than he really was, and approached his second and last point. He felt it to be the most difficult of all; but, remembering his old Sunday-morning conversation with Miss Pross, and remembering what he had seen in the last nine days, he knew that he must face it.

"The occupation resumed under the influence of this passing affliction so happily recovered from," said Mr. Lorry, clearing his throat, "we will call—Blacksmith's work, Blacksmith's work. We will say, to put a case and for the sake of illustration, that he had been used, in his bad time, to work at a little forge. We will say that he was unexpectedly found at his forge again. Is it not a pity that he should keep it by him?"

The Doctor shaded his forehead with his hand, and beat his foot nervously on the ground.

"He has always kept it by him," said Mr. Lorry, with an anxious look at his friend. "Now, would it not be better that he should let it go?"

Still, the Doctor, with shaded forehead, beat his foot nervously on the ground.

"You do not find it easy to advise me?" said Mr. Lorry. "I quite understand it to be a nice question. And yet I think—" And there he shook his head, and stopped.

"You see," said Doctor Manette, turning to him after an uneasy pause, "it is very hard to explain, consistently, the innermost workings of this poor

A TALE OF TWO CITIES   157

man's mind. He once yearned so frightfully for that occupation, and it was so welcome when it came; no doubt it relieved his pain so much, by substituting the perplexity of the fingers for the perplexity of the brain, and by substituting, as he became more practiced, the ingenuity of the hands for the ingenuity of the mental torture; that he has never been able to bear the thought of putting it quite out of his reach. Even now, when, I believe, he is more hopeful of himself than he has ever been, and even speaks of himself with a kind of confidence, the idea that he might need that old employment, and not find it, gives him a sudden sense of terror, like that which one may fancy strikes to the heart of a lost child."

He looked like his illustration, as he raised his eyes to Mr. Lorry's face.

"But may not—mind! I ask for information, as a plodding man of business who only deals with such material objects as guineas, shillings, and bank-notes—may not the retention of the thing involve the retention of the idea? If the thing were gone, my dear Manette, might not the fear go with it? In short, is it not a concession to the misgiving, to keep the forge?"

There was another silence.

"You see, too," said the Doctor, tremulously, "it is such an old companion."

"I would not keep it," said Mr. Lorry, shaking his head; for he gained in firmness as he saw the Doctor disquieted. "I would recommend him to sacrifice it. I only want your authority. I am sure it does no good. Come! Give me your authority, like a dear good man. For his daughter's sake, my dear Manette!"

Very strange to see what a struggle there was within him!

"In her name, then, let it be done; I sanction it. But, I would not take it away while he was present. Let it be removed when he is not there; let him miss his old companion after an absence."

Mr. Lorry readily engaged for that, and the conference was ended. They passed the day in the country, and the Doctor was quite restored. On the three following days, he remained perfectly well, and on the fourteenth day, he went away to join Lucie and her husband. The precaution that had been taken to account for his silence, Mr. Lorry had previously explained to him, and he had written to Lucie in accordance with it, and she had no suspicions.

On the night of the day on which he had left the house, Mr. Lorry went into his room with a chopper, saw, chisel, and hammer, attended by Miss Pross carrying a light. There, with closed doors, and in a mysterious and guilty manner, Mr. Lorry hacked the shoemaker's bench to pieces, while Miss Pross held the candle as if she were assisting at a murder—for which, indeed, in her grimness, she was no unsuitable figure. The burning of the body (previously reduced to pieces convenient for the purpose), was commenced without delay in the kitchen fire; and the tools, shoes, and leather, were buried in the garden. So wicked do destruction and secrecy appear to honest minds, that Mr. Lorry and Miss Pross, while engaged in the commission of their deed and in the removal of its traces, almost felt, and almost looked, like accomplices in a horrible crime.

A PLEA

W HEN THE NEWLY-MARRIED PAIR CAME HOME, THE FIRST person who appeared, to offer his congratulations, was Sydney Carton. They had not been at home many hours, when he presented himself. He was not improved in habits, or in looks, or in manner; but there was a certain rugged air of fidelity about him, which was new to the observation of Charles Darnay.

He watched his opportunity of taking Darnay aside into a window, and of speaking to him when no one overheard.

"Mr. Darnay," said Carton, "I wish we might be friends."

"We are already friends, I hope."

"You are good enough to say so, as a fashion of speech; but, I don't mean any fashion of speech. Indeed, when I say I wish we might be friends, I scarcely mean quite that, either."

Charles Darnay—as was natural—asked him, in all good-humor and good-fellowship, what he did mean?

"Upon my life," said Carton, smiling, "I find that easier to comprehend in my own mind, than to convey to yours. However, let me try. You remember a certain famous occasion when I was more drunk than—than usual?"

"I remember a certain famous occasion when you forced me to confess that you had been drinking."

"I remember it too. The curse of those occasions is heavy upon me, for I always remember them. I hope it may be taken into account one day, when all days are at an end for me! Don't be alarmed; I am not going to preach."

"I am not at all alarmed. Earnestness in you is anything but alarming to me."

"Ah!" said Carton, with a careless wave of his hand, as if he waved that away. "On the drunken occasion in question (one of a large number, as you know), I was insufferable about liking you, and not liking you. I wish you would forget it."

"I forgot it long ago."

"Fashion of speech again! But, Mr. Darnay, oblivion is not so easy to me, as you represent it to be to you. I have by no means forgotten it, and a light answer does not help me to forget it."

"If it was a light answer," returned Darnay, "I beg your forgiveness for it. I had no other object than to turn a slight thing, which, to my surprise, seems to trouble you too much, aside. I declare to you on the faith of a gentleman, that I have long dismissed it from my mind. Good Heaven, what was there to dismiss! Have I had nothing more important to remember, in the great service you rendered me that day?"

"As to the great service," said Carton, "I am bound to avow to you, when you speak of it in that way, that it was mere professional claptrap. I don't know that I cared what became of you, when I rendered it. Mind! I say when I rendered it; I am speaking of the past."

"You make light of the obligation," returned Darnay, "but I will not quarrel with *your* light answer."

"Genuine truth, Mr. Darnay, trust me! I have gone aside from my purpose; I was speaking about our being friends. Now, you know me; you know I am incapable of all the higher and better flights of men. If you doubt it, ask Stryver, and he'll tell you so."

"I prefer to form my own opinion, without the aid of his."

"Well! At any rate you know me as a dissolute dog, who has never done any good, and never will."

"I don't know that you 'never will.'"

"But I do, and you must take my word for it. Well! If you could endure to have such a worthless fellow, and a fellow of such indifferent reputation, coming and going at odd times, I should ask that I might be permitted to come and go as a privileged person here; that I might be regarded as a useless (and I would add, if it were not for the resemblance I detected between you and me), an unornamental, piece of furniture, tolerated for its old service and taken no notice of. I doubt if I should abuse the permission. It is a hundred to one if I should avail myself of it four times in a year. It would satisfy me, I dare say, to know that I had it."

"Will you try?"

"That is another way of saying that I am placed on the footing I have indicated. I thank you, Darnay. I may use that freedom with your name?"

"I think so, Carton, by this time."

They shook hands upon it, and Sydney turned away. Within a minute afterwards, he was, to all outward appearance, as unsubstantial as ever.

When he was gone, and in the course of an evening passed with Miss Pross, the Doctor, and Mr. Lorry, Charles Darnay made some mention of this conversation in general terms, and spoke of Sydney Carton as a problem of carelessness and recklessness. He spoke of him, in short, not bitterly or meaning to bear hard upon him, but as anybody might who saw him as he showed himself.

He had no idea that this could dwell in the thoughts of his fair young wife; but, when he afterwards joined her in their own room, he found her waiting for him with the old pretty lifting of the forehead strongly marked.

"We are thoughtful tonight!" said Darnay, drawing his arm about her.

"Yes, dearest Charles," with her hand on his breast, and the inquiring and attentive expression fixed upon him; "we are rather thoughtful tonight, for we have something on our mind tonight."

"What is it, my Lucie?"

"Will you promise not to press one question on me, if I beg you not to ask it?"

"Will I promise? What will I not promise to my Love?"

What, indeed, with his hand putting aside the golden hair from the cheek, and his other hand against the heart that beat for him!

"I think, Charles, poor Mr. Carton deserves more consideration and respect than you expressed for him tonight."

"Indeed, my own? Why so?"

"That is what you are not to ask me! But I think—I know—he does."

"If you know it, it is enough. What would you have me do, my Life?"

"I would ask you, dearest, to be very generous with him always, and very lenient on his faults, when he is not by. I would ask you to believe that he has a heart he very, very seldom reveals, and that there are deep wounds in it. My dear, I have seen it bleeding."

"It is a painful reflection to me," said Charles Darnay, quite astounded, "that I should have done him any wrong. I never thought this of him."

"My husband, it is so. I fear he is not to be reclaimed; there is scarcely a hope that anything in his character or fortunes is reparable now. But, I am sure that he is capable of good things, gentle things, even magnanimous things."

She looked so beautiful in the purity of her faith in this lost man, that her husband could have looked at her as she was for hours.

"And, O my dearest Love!" she urged, clinging nearer to him, laying her head upon his breast, and raising her eyes to his, "remember how strong we are in our happiness, and how weak he is in our misery!"

The supplication touched him home. "I will always remember it, dear Heart! I will remember it as long as I live."

He bent over the golden head, and put the rosy lips to his, and folded her in his arms. If one forlorn wanderer then pacing the dark streets, could have heard her innocent disclosure, and could have seen the drops of pity kissed away by her husband from the soft, blue eyes so loving of that husband, he might have cried to the night—and the words would not have parted from his lips for the first time—

"God bless her for her sweet compassion!"

ECHOING FOOTSTEPS

A WONDERFUL CORNER FOR ECHOES, IT HAS BEEN RE-marked, that corner where the Doctor lived. Ever busily winding the golden thread which bound her husband, and her father, and herself, and her old directress and companion, in a life of quiet bliss, Lucie sat in the still house in the tranquilly resounding corner, listening to the echoing footsteps of years.

At first, there were times, though she was a perfectly happy young wife, when her work would slowly fall from her hands, and her eyes would be dimmed. For, there was something coming in the echoes, something light, afar off, and scarcely audible yet, that stirred her heart too much. Fluttering hopes and doubts—hopes, of a love as yet unknown to her; doubts of her remaining upon earth, to enjoy that new delight—divided her breast. Among the echoes then, there would arise the sound of footsteps at her own early grave; and thoughts of the husband who would be left so desolate, and who would mourn for her so much, swelled to her eyes and broke like waves.

That time passed, and her little Lucie lay on her bosom. Then, among the advancing echoes, there was the tread of her tiny feet and the sound of her prattling words. Let greater echoes resound as they would, the young mother at the cradle side could always hear those coming. They came, and the shady house was sunny with a child's laugh, and the Divine friend of children, to whom in her trouble she had confided hers, seemed to take her child in His arms, as He took the child of old, and made it a sacred joy to her.

Ever busily winding the golden thread that bound them all together, weaving the service of her happy influence through the tissue of all their lives, and making it predominate nowhere, Lucie heard in the echoes of years none but friendly and soothing sounds. Her husband's step was strong and prosperous among them; her father's firm and equal. Lo, Miss Pross, in harness of string, awakening the echoes, as an unruly charger whip-corrected, snorting and pawing the earth under the plane-tree in the garden!

Even when there were sounds of sorrow among the rest, they were not harsh nor cruel. Even when golden hair, like her own, lay in a halo on a pillow round the worn face of a little boy, and he said, with a radiant smile, "Dear papa and mamma, I am very sorry to leave you both, and to leave my pretty sister; but I am called, and I must go!" those were not tears all of agony that wetted his young mother's cheek, as the spirit departed from her embrace that had been entrusted to it. Suffer them and forbid them not. They see my Father's face. O Father, blessed words!

Thus, the rustling of an Angel's wings got blended with the other echoes, and they were not wholly of earth, but had in them that breath of Heaven. Sighs of the winds that blew over a little garden-tomb were mingled with them also, and both were audible to Lucie, in a hushed murmur—like the breathing of a summer sea asleep upon a sandy shore—as the little Lucie, comically studious at the task of the morning, or dressing a doll at her mother's footstool, chattered in the tongues of the Two Cities that were blended in her life.

The echoes rarely answered to the actual tread of Sydney Carton. Some half-dozen times a year, at most, he claimed his privilege of coming in uninvited, and would sit among them through the evening as he had once done often. He never came there heated with wine. And one other thing regarding him was whispered in the echoes, which has been whispered by all true echoes for ages and ages.

No man ever really loved a woman, lost her, and knew her with a blameless though an unchanged mind, when she was a wife and a mother, but her children had a strange sympathy with him—an instinctive delicacy of pity for him. What fine hidden sensibilities are touched in such a case, no echoes tell; but, it is so, and it was so here. Carton was the first stranger to whom little Lucie held out her chubby arms and he kept his place with her as she grew. The little boy had spoken of him, almost at the last. "Poor Carton! Kiss him for me!"

Mr. Stryver shouldered his way through the law, like some great engine forcing itself through turbid waters, and dragged his useful friend in his wake, like a boat towed astern. As the boat so favored is usually in a rough plight and mostly under water, so, Sydney had a swamped life of it. But, easy and strong custom, unhappily so much easier and stronger in him than any stimulating sense of desert or disgrace, made it the life he was to lead; and he no more thought of emerging from his state of lion's jackal, than any real jackal may be supposed to think of rising to be a lion. Stryver was rich; had married a florid widow with property and three boys, who had nothing particularly shining about them but the straight hair of their dumpling heads.

These three young gentlemen, Mr. Stryver, exuding patronage of the most offensive quality from every pore, had walked before him like three sheep to the quiet corner in Soho, and had offered as pupils to Lucie's husband: delicately saying, "Halloa! here are three lumps of bread-and-cheese towards your matrimonial picnic, Darnay!" The polite rejection of the three lumps of bread-and-cheese had quite bloated Mr. Stryver with indignation, which he afterward turned to account in the training of the young gentlemen, by directing them to beware of the pride of beggars, like that tutor-fellow. He was also in the habit of declaiming to Mrs. Stryver, over his full-bodied wine, on the arts Mrs. Darnay had once put in practice to "catch" him, and on the diamond-cut-diamond arts in himself, madam, which had rendered him "not to be caught." Some of his King's Bench familiars, who were occasionally parties to the full-bodied wine and the lie, excused him for the latter by saying that he had told it so often, that he believed it himself— which is surely such an incorrigible aggravation of an originally bad offense, as to justify any such offender's being carried off to some suitably retired spot, and there hanged out of the way.

These were among the echoes to which Lucie, sometimes pensive, sometimes amused and laughing, listened in the echoing corner, until her little daughter was six years old. How near to her heart, the echoes of her child's tread came, and those of her own dear father's, always active and self-possessed, and those of her dear husband's, need not be told. Nor, how the slightest echo of their united home, directed by herself with such a wise and elegant thrift, that it was more abundant than any waste, was music to her. Nor, how there were echoes all about her, sweet in her ears, of the many times her father had told her that he found her more devoted to him married (if that could be) than single, and of the many times her husband had said to her that no cares and duties seemed to divide her love for him or her help to him, and asked her, "What is the magic secret, my darling, of your being everything to all of us, as if there were only one of us, yet never seeming to be hurried, or to have too much to do?"

But, there were other echoes, from a distance, that rumbled menacingly in the corner all through this space of time. And it was now, about little Lucie's sixth birthday, that they began to have an awful sound, as of a great storm in France with a dreadful sea rising.

On a night in mid-July, one thousand seven hundred and eighty-nine, Mr. Lorry came in late, from Tellson's, and sat himself down by Lucie and her husband in the dark window. It was a hot, wild night, and they were all three reminded of the old Sunday night when they had looked at the lightning from the same place.

"I began to think," said Mr. Lorry, pushing his brown wig back, "that I should have to pass the night at Tellson's. We have been so full of business all day, that we have not known what to do first, or which way to turn. There is such an uneasiness in Paris, that we have actually a run of confidence upon us! Our customers over there seem not to be able to confide their property to us fast enough. There is positively a mania among some of them for sending it to England."

"That has a bad look," said Darnay.

"A bad look, you say, my dear Darnay? Yes, but we don't know what reason there is in it. People are so unreasonable! Some of us at Tellson's are getting old, and we really can't be troubled out of the ordinary course without due occasion."

"Still," said Darnay, "you know how gloomy and threatening the sky is."

"I know that, to be sure," assented Mr. Lorry, trying to persuade himself that his sweet temper was soured, and that he grumbled, "but I am determined to be peevish after my long day's botheration. Where is Manette?"

"Here he is," said the Doctor, entering the dark room at the moment.

"I am quite glad you are at home; for these hurries and foreboding, by which I have been surrounded all day long, have made me nervous without reason. You are not going out, I hope?"

"No; I am going to play backgammon with you, if you like," said the Doctor.

"I don't think I do like, if I may speak my mind. I am not fit to be pitted against you tonight. Is the tea-board still there, Lucie? I can't see."

"Of course, it has been kept for you."

"Thank ye, my dear. The precious child is safe in bed?"

"And sleeping soundly."

"That's right; all safe and well! I don't know why anything should be otherwise than safe and well here, thank God; but I have been so put out all day, and I am not as young as I was! My tea, my dear? Thank ye. Now, come and take your place in the circle, and let us sit quiet, and hear the echoes about which you have your theory."

"Not a theory; it was a fancy."

"A fancy, then, my wise pet," said Mr. Lorry, patting her hand. "They are very numerous and very loud, though, are they not? Only hear them!"

Headlong, mad, and dangerous footsteps to force their way into anybody's life, footsteps not easily made clean again if once stained red, the footsteps raging in Saint Antoine afar off, as the little circle sat in the dark London window.

Saint Antoine had been, that morning, a vast dusky mass of scarecrows heaving to and fro, with frequent gleams of light above the billowy heads, where steel blades and bayonets shone in the sun. A tremendous roar arose from the throat of Saint Antoine, and a forest of naked arms struggled in the air like shriveled branches of trees in a winter wind: all the fingers convulsively clutching at every weapon or semblance of a weapon that was thrown up from the depths below, no matter how far off.

Who gave them out, whence they last came, where they began, through what agency they crookedly quivered and jerked, scores at a time, over the heads of the crowd, like a kind of lightning, no eye in the throng could have told; but, muskets were being distributed—so were cartridges, powder, and ball, bars of iron and wood, knives, axes, pikes, every weapon that distracted ingenuity could discover or devise. People who could lay hold of nothing else, set themselves with bleeding hands to force stones and bricks out of their places in walls. Every pulse and heart in Saint Antoine was on high fever strain and at high fever heat. Every living creature there, held life as of no account, and was demented with a passionate readiness to sacrifice it.

As a whirlpool of boiling waters has a center point, so, all this raging circled round Defarge's wine-shop, and every human drop in the caldron had a tendency to be sucked toward the vortex where Defarge himself, already begrimed with gunpowder and sweat, issued orders, issued arms, thrust this man back, dragged this man forward, disarmed one to arm another, labored and strove in the thickest of the uproar.

"Keep near to me, Jacques Three," cried Defarge; "and do you, Jacques One and Two, separate and put yourselves at the head of as many of these patriots as you can. Where is my wife?"

"Eh, well! Here you see me!" said madame, composed as ever, but not knitting today. Madame's resolute right hand was occupied with an axe, in place of the usual softer implements, and in her girdle were a pistol and a cruel knife.

"Where do you go, my wife?"

"I go," said madame, "with you at present. You shall see me at the head of women, by-and-by."

"Come, then!" cried Defarge, in a resounding voice. "Patriots and friends, we are ready! The Bastille!"

With a roar that sounded as if all the breath in France had been shaped into the detested word, the living sea rose, wave on wave, depth on depth, and overflowed the city to that point. Alarm bells ringing, drums beating, the sea raging and thundering on its new beach, the attack begun.

Deep ditches, double drawbridge, massive stone walls, eight great towers, cannon, muskets, fire and smoke. Through the fire and through the smoke—in the fire and in the smoke, for the sea cast him up against a cannon, and on the instant he became a cannonier—Defarge of the wine-shop worked like a manful soldier, Two fierce hours.

Deep ditch, single drawbridge, massive stone walls, eight great towers, cannon, muskets, fire and smoke. One drawbridge down! "Work, comrades all, work! Work, Jacques One, Jacques Two, Jacques One Thousand, Jacques Two Thousand, Jacques Five-and-Twenty Thousand; in the name of all the Angels or the Devils—which you prefer—work!" Thus Defarge of the wine-shop, still at his gun, which had long grown hot.

"To me, women!" cried madame his wife. "What! We can kill as well as the men when the place is taken!" And to her, with a shrill, thirsty cry, trooping women variously armed, but all armed alike in hunger and revenge.

Cannon, muskets, fire, and smoke; but, still the deep ditch, the single drawbridge, the massive stone walls, and the eight great towers. Slight displacements of the raging sea, made by the falling wounded. Flashing weapons, blazing torches, smoking wagon-loads of wet straw, hard work at neighboring barricades, in all directions, shrieks, volleys, execrations, bravery without stint, boom smash and rattle, and the furious sounding of the living sea; but, still the deep ditch, and the single drawbridge, and the massive stone walls, and the eight great towers, and still Defarge of the wine-shop at his gun, grown doubly hot by the service of Four fierce hours.

A white flag from within the fortress, and a parley—this dimly percepti-
ble through the raging storm, nothing audible in it—suddenly the sea rose
immeasurably wider and higher, and swept Defarge of the wine-shop over the
lowered drawbridge, past the massive stone outer walls, in among the eight
great towers surrendered!

So resistless was the force of the ocean bearing him on, that even to draw
his breath or turn his head was as impracticable as if he had been struggling
in the surf at the South Sea, until he was landed in the outer courtyard of the
Bastille. There, against an angle of a wall, he made a struggle to look about
him. Jacques Three was nearly at his side; Madame Defarge, still heading
some of her women, was visible in the inner distance, and her knife was in
her hand. Everywhere was tumult, exultation, deafening and maniacal bewilderment, astounding noise, yet furious dumb-show.

"The Prisoners!"

"The Records!"

"The secret cells!"

"The instruments of torture!"

"The Prisoners!"

Of all these cries, and ten thousand incoherencies, "The Prisoners!" was
the cry most taken up by the sea that rushed in, as if there were an eternity of
people, as well as of time and space. When the foremost billows rolled past,
bearing the prison officers with them, and threatening them all with instant
death if any secret nook remained undisclosed, Defarge laid his strong hand
on the breast of one of these men—a man with a gray head who had a lighted
torch in his hand—separated him from the rest, and got him between himself and the wall.

"Show me the North Tower!" said Defarge. "Quick!"

"I will, faithfully," replied the man, "if you will come with me. But there
is no one there."

"What is the meaning of One Hundred and Five, North Tower?" asked
Defarge. "Quick!"

"The meaning, monsieur?"

"Does it mean a captive, or a place of captivity? Or do you mean that I
shall strike you dead?"

"Kill him!" croaked Jacques Three, who had come close up.

"Monsieur, it is a cell."

"Show it me!"

"Pass this way, then."

Jacques Three, with his usual craving on him, and evidently disappointed
by the dialogue taking a turn that did not seem to promise bloodshed, held
by Defarge's arm as he held by the turnkey's. Their three heads had been close
together during this brief discourse, and it had been as much as they could do
to hear one another, even then: so tremendous was the noise of the living

ocean, in its irruption into the Fortress, and its inundation of the courts and passages and staircases. All around outside, too, it beat the walls with a deep, hoarse roar, from which, occasionally, some partial shouts of tumult broke and leaped into the air like spray.

Through gloomy vaults where the light of day had never shone, past hideous doors of dark dens and cages, down cavernous flights of steps, and again up steep rugged ascents of stone and brick, more like dry waterfalls than staircases, Defarge, the turnkey, and Jacques Three, linked hand and arm, went, with all the speed they could make. Here and there, especially at first, the inundation started on them and swept by; but, when they had done descending, and were winding and climbing up a tower, they were alone. Hemmed in here by the massive thickness of walls and arches, the storm within the fortress and without was only audible to them in a dull, subdued way, as if the noise out of which they had come had almost destroyed their sense of hearing.

The turnkey stopped at a low door, put a key in a clashing lock, swung the door slowly open, and said, as they all bent their heads and passed in: "One Hundred and Five, North Tower!"

There was a small, heavily-grated, unglazed window high in the wall, with a stone screen before it, so that the sky could be only seen by stooping low and looking up. There was a small chimney, heavily barred across, a few feet within. There was a heap of old feathery wood ashes on the hearth. There were a stool, and table, and a straw bed. There were the four blackened walls, and a rusted iron ring in one of them.

"Pass that torch slowly along these walls, that I may see them," said Defarge to the turnkey.

The man obeyed, and Defarge followed the light closely with his eyes.

"Stop! Look here, Jacques!"

"A. M.!" croaked Jacques Three, as he read greedily.

"Alexandre Manette," said Defarge in his ear, following the letters with his swart forefinger, deeply engrained with gunpowder. "And here he wrote 'a poor physician.' And it was he, without doubt, who scratched a calendar on this stone. What is that in your hand? A crowbar? Give it me!"

He had still the linstock of his gun in his own hand. He made a sudden exchange of the two instruments, and turning on the worm-eaten stool and table, beat them to pieces in a few blows.

"Hold the light higher!" he said, wrathfully, to the turnkey. "Look among those fragments with care, Jacques. And see! Here is my knife," throwing it to him; "rip open that bed, and search the straw. Hold the light higher, you!"

With a menacing look at the turnkey he crawled upon the hearth, and, peering up the chimney, struck and prised at its sides with the crowbar, and worked at the iron grating across it. In a few minutes, some mortar and dust came dropping down, which he averted his face to avoid; and in it, and in the old wood-ashes, and in a crevice in the chimney into which his weapon had slipped or wrought itself, he groped with a cautious touch.

"Nothing in the wood, and nothing in the straw, Jacques?"

"Nothing."

"Let us collect them together, in the middle of the cell. So! Light them, you!"

The turnkey fired the little pile, which blazed high and hot. Stooping again to come out at the low-arched door, they left it burning, and retraced their way to the courtyard; seeming to recover their sense of hearing as they came down, until they were in the raging flood once more.

They found it surging and tossing, in quest of Defarge himself. Saint Antoine was clamorous to have its wine-shop keeper foremost in the guard upon the governor who had defended the Bastille and shot the people. Otherwise, the governor would not be marched to the Hôtel de Ville for judgment. Otherwise, the governor would escape, and the people's blood (suddenly of some value, after many years of worthlessness) be unavenged.

In the howling universe of passion and contention that seemed to encompass this grim old officer, conspicuous in his gray coat and red decoration, there was but one quite steady figure, and that was a woman's. "See, there is my husband!" she cried, pointing him out. "See Defarge!" She stood immovable close to the grim old officer, and remained immovable close to him; remained immovable close to him through the streets, as Defarge and the rest bore him along; remained immovable close to him when he got near his destination, and began to be struck at from behind; remained immovable close to him when the long-gathering rain of stabs and blows fell heavy; was so close to him when he dropped dead under it, that, suddenly animated, she put her foot upon his neck, and with her cruel knife—long ready—hewed off his head.

The hour was come, when Saint Antoine was to execute his horrible idea of hoisting up men for lamps to show what he could be and do. Saint Antoine's blood was up, and the blood of tyranny and domination by the iron hand was down—down on the steps of the Hôtel de Ville where the governor's body lay—down on the sole of the shoe of Madame Defarge where she had trodden on the body to steady it for mutilation. "Lower the lamp yonder!" cried Saint Antoine, after glaring round for a new means of death; "here is one of his soldiers to be left on guard!" The swinging sentinel was posted, and the sea rushed on.

The sea of black and threatening waters, and of destructive upheaving of wave against wave, whose depths were yet unfathomed and whose forces were yet unknown. The remorseless sea of turbulently swaying shapes, voices of vengeance, and faces hardened in the furnaces of suffering until the touch of pity could make no mark on them.

But, in the ocean of faces, where every fierce and furious expression was in vivid life, there were two groups of faces—each seven in number—so fixedly contrasting with the rest, that never did sea roll which bore more memorable wrecks with it. Seven faces of prisoners, suddenly released by the storm that had burst their tomb, were carried high overhead: all scared, all lost, all wondering and amazed, as if the Last Day were come, and those who rejoiced around them were lost spirits. Other seven faces there were, carried higher, seven dead faces, whose drooping eyelids and half-seen eyes awaited the Last Day. Impassive faces, yet with a suspended—not an abolished— expression on them; faces, rather, in a fearful pause, as having yet to raise the dropped lids of the eyes, and bear witness with the bloodless lips, "THOU DIDST IT!"

Seven prisoners released, seven gory heads on pikes, the keys of the accursed fortress of the eight strong towers, some discovered letters and other memorials of prisoners of old time, long dead of broken hearts,—such, and suchlike, the loudly echoing footsteps of Saint Antoine escort through the Paris streets in mid-July, one thousand seven hundred and eighty-nine. Now, Heaven defeat the fancy of Lucie Darnay, and keep these feet far out of her life! For, they are headlong, mad, and dangerous; and in the years so long after the breaking of the cask at Defarge's wine-shop door, they are not easily purified when once stained red.

Twenty - two

THE SEA STILL RISES

HAGGARD SAINT ANTOINE HAD HAD ONLY ONE EXULTANT week, in which to soften his modicum of hard and bitter bread to such extent as he could, with the relish of fraternal embraces and congratulations, when Madame Defarge sat at her counter, as usual, presiding over the customers. Madame Defarge wore no rose in her head, for the great brotherhood of Spies had become, even in one short week, extremely chary of trusting themselves to the saint's mercies. The lamps across his streets had a portentously elastic swing with them.

Madame Defarge, with her arms folded, sat in the morning light and heat, contemplating the wine-shop and the street. In both, there were several knots of loungers, squalid and miserable, but now with a manifest sense of power enthroned on their distress. The raggedest nightcap, awry on the wretchedest head, had this crooked significance in it: "I know how hard it has grown for me, the wearer of this, to support life in myself; but do you know how easy it has grown for me, the wearer of this, to destroy life in you?" Every lean bare arm, that had been without work before, had this work always ready for it now, that it could strike. The fingers of the knitting women were vicious, with the experience that they could tear. There was a change in the appearance of Saint Antoine; the image had been hammering into this for hundreds of years, and the last finishing blows had told mightily on the expression.

Madame Defarge sat observing it, with such suppressed approval as was to be desired in the leader of the Saint Antoine women. One of her sisterhood knitted beside her. The short, rather plump wife of a starved grocer, and the mother of two children withal, this lieutenant had already earned the complimentary name of The Vengeance.

"Hark!" said The Vengeance. "Listen, then! Who comes?"

As if a train of powder laid from the outermost bound of the Saint Antoine Quarter to the wine-shop door, had been suddenly fired, a fast-spreading murmur came rushing along.

"It is Defarge," said madame. "Silence, patriots!"

Defarge came in breathless, pulled off a red cap he wore, and looked around him. "Listen, everywhere!" said madame again. "Listen to him!" Defarge stood, panting, against a background of eager eyes and open mouths, formed outside the door; all those within the wine-shop had sprung to their feet.

"Say then, my husband. What is it?"

"News from the other world!"

"How, then?" cried madame, contemptuously. "The other world?"

"Does everybody here recall old Foulon, who told the famished people that they might eat grass, and who died, and went to Hell?"

"Everybody!" from all throats.

"The news is of him. He is among us!"

"Among us!" from the universal throat again. "And dead?"

"Not dead! He feared us so much—and with reason—that he caused himself to be represented as dead, and had a grand mock-funeral. But they have found him alive, hiding in the country, and have brought him in. I have seen him but now, on his way to the Hôtel de Ville, a prisoner. I have said that he had reason to fear us. Say all! *Had* he reason?"

Wretched old sinner of more than threescore years and ten, if he had never known it yet, he would have known it in his heart of hearts if he could have heard the answering cry.

A moment of profound silence followed. Defarge and his wife looked steadfastly at one another. The Vengeance stooped, and the jar of a drum was heard as she moved it at her feet behind the counter.

"Patriots!" said Defarge, in a determined voice, "are we ready?"

Instantly Madame Defarge's knife was in her girdle; the drum was beating in the streets, as if it and a drummer had flown together by magic; and The Vengeance, uttering terrific shrieks, and flinging her arms about her head like all the forty Furies at once, was tearing from house to house, rousing the women.

The men were terrible, in the bloody-minded anger with which they looked from windows, caught up what arms they had, and came pouring down into the streets; but, the women were a sight to chill the boldest. From such household occupations as their bare poverty yielded, from their children, from their aged and their sick crouching on the bare ground famished and naked, they ran out with streaming hair, urging one another, and themselves, to madness with the wildest cries and actions. Villain Foulon taken, my sister! Old Foulon taken, my mother! Miscreant Foulon taken, my daughter! Then, a score of others ran into the midst of these, beating their breasts, tearing their hair, and screaming, Foulon alive! Foulon who told the starving people they might eat grass! Foulon who told my old father that he might eat grass, when I had no bread to give him! Foulon who told my baby it might suck grass, when these breasts were dry with want! O mother of God, this Foulon! O Heaven, our suffering! Hear me, my dead baby and my withered father: I swear on my knees, on these stones, to avenge you on Foulon! Husbands, and brothers, and young men, Give us the blood of Foulon, Give us the head of Foulon, Give us the heart of Foulon, Give us the body and soul of Foulon, Rend Foulon to pieces, and dig him into the ground, that grass may grow from him! With these cries, numbers of the women, lashed into blind frenzy, whirled about, striking and tearing at their own friends until they dropped into a passionate swoon, and were only saved by the men belonging to them from being trampled underfoot.

Nevertheless, not a moment was lost; not a moment! This Foulon was at the Hôtel de Ville, and might be loosed. Never, if Saint Antoine knew his own sufferings, insults, and wrongs! Armed men and women flocked out of the Quarter so fast, and drew even these last dregs after them with such a force of suction, that within a quarter of an hour there was not a human creature in Saint Antoine's bosom but a few old crones and the wailing children.

No. They were all by that time choking the Hall of examination where this old man, ugly and wicked, was, and overflowing into the adjacent open space and streets. The Defarges, husband and wife, The Vengeance, and Jacques Three, were in the first press, and at no great distance from him in the Hall.

"See!" cried madame, pointing with her knife. "See the old villain bound with ropes. That was well done to tie a bunch of grass upon his back. Ha, ha! That was well done. Let him eat it now!" Madame put her knife under her arm, and clapped her hands as at a play.

The people immediately behind Madame Defarge, explaining the cause of her satisfaction to those behind them, and those again explaining to others, and those to others, the neighboring streets resounded with the clapping of hands. Similarly, during two or three hours of drawl, and the winnowing of many bushels of words, Madame Defarge's frequent expressions of impatience were taken up, with marvelous quickness, at a distance; the more readily, because certain men who had by some wonderful exercise of agility climbed up the external architecture to look in from the windows, knew Madame Defarge well, and acted as a telegraph between her and the crowd outside the building.

At length, the sun rose so high that it struck a kindly ray as of hope or protection, directly down upon the old prisoner's head. The favor was too much to bear; in an instant the barrier of dust and chaff that had stood surprisingly long, went to the winds, and Saint Antoine had got him!

It was known directly, to the furthest confines of the crowd. Defarge had but sprung over a railing and a table, and folded the miserable wretch in a deadly embrace—Madame Defarge had but followed and turned her hand in one of the ropes with which he was tied—The Vengeance and Jacques Three were not yet up with them, and the men at the windows had not yet swooped into the Hall, like birds of prey from their high perches—when the cry seemed to go up, all over the city, "Bring him out! Bring him to the lamp!"

Down, and up, and head foremost on the steps of the building; now, on his knees; now, on his feet; now, on his back; dragged, and struck at, and stifled by the bunches of grass and straw that were thrust into his face by hundreds of hands; torn, bruised, panting, bleeding, yet always entreating and beseeching for mercy; now, full of vehement agony of action, with a small clear space about him as the people drew one another back that they might see; now, a log of dead wood drawn through a forest of legs; he was hauled to the nearest street corner where one of the fatal lamps swung, and there Madame Defarge let him go—as a cat might have done to a mouse—and silently and composedly looked at him while they made ready, and while he besought her: the women passionately screeching at him all the time, and the men sternly calling out to have him killed with grass in his mouth. Once, he went aloft, and the rope broke, and they caught him shrieking; twice, he went aloft, and the rope broke, and they caught him shrieking; then, the rope was merciful, and held him, and his head was soon upon a pike, with grass enough in the mouth for all Saint Antoine to dance at the sight of.

Nor was this the end of the day's bad work, for Saint Antoine so shouted and danced his angry blood up, that it boiled again, on hearing when the day closed in that the son-in-law of the dispatched, another of the people's enemies and insulters, was coming into Paris under a guard five hundred strong, in cavalry alone. Saint Antoine wrote his crimes on flaring sheets of paper, seized him—would have torn him out of the breast of an army to bear

Foulon company—set his head and heart on pikes, and carried the three spoils of the day, in Wolf-procession, through the streets.

Not before dark night did the men and women come back to the children, wailing and breadless. Then, the miserable bakers' shops were beset by long files of them, patiently waiting to buy bad bread; and while they waited with stomachs faint and empty, they beguiled the time by embracing one another on the triumphs of the day, and achieving them again in gossip. Gradually, these strings of ragged people shortened and frayed away; and then poor lights began to shine in high windows, and slender fires were made in the streets, at which neighbors cooked in common, afterward supping at their doors.

Scanty and insufficient suppers those, and innocent of meat, as of most other sauce to wretched bread. Yet, human fellowship infused some nourishment into the flinty viands, and struck some sparks of cheerfulness out of them. Fathers and mothers who had had their full share in the worst of the day, played gently with their meager children; and lovers, with such a world around them and before them, loved and hoped.

It was almost morning, when Defarge's wine-shop parted with its last knot of customers, and Monsieur Defarge said to madame his wife, in husky tones, while fastening the door:

"At last it is come, my dear!"

"Eh well!" returned madame. "Almost."

Saint Antoine slept, the Defarges slept: even The Vengeance slept with her starved grocer, and the drum was at rest. The drum's was the only voice in Saint Antoine, that blood and hurry had not changed. The Vengeance as custodian of the drum, could have wakened him up and had the same speech out of him as before the Bastille fell, or old Foulon was seized; not so with the hoarse tones of the men and women in Saint Antoine's bosom.

Twenty-three

FIRE RISES

T HERE WAS A CHANGE ON THE VILLAGE WHERE THE FOUN-tain fell, and where the mender of roads went forth daily to hammer out of the stones on the highway, such morsels of bread as might serve for patches to hold his poor ignorant soul and his poor reduced body, together. The prison on the crag was not so dominant as of yore; there were soldiers to guard it, but not many; there were officers to guard the soldiers, but not one of them knew what his men would do—beyond this: that it would probably not be what he was ordered.

Far and wide, lay a ruined country, yielding nothing but desolation. Every green leaf, every blade of grass and blade of grain, was as shriveled and poor as the miserable people. Everything was bowed down, dejected, oppressed, and broken. Habitations, fences, domesticated animals, men, women, children, and the soil that bore them—all worn out.

Monseigneur (often a most worthy individual gentleman) was a national blessing, gave a chivalrous tone to things, was a polite example of luxurious and shining life, and a great deal more to equal purpose; nevertheless, Monseigneur as a class had, somehow or other, brought things to this. Strange that creation, designed expressly for Monseigneur, should be so soon wrung dry and squeezed out! There must be something shortsighted in the eternal arrangements, surely! Thus it was, however; and the last drop of blood having been extracted from the flints, and the last screw of the rack having been turned so often that its purchase crumbled, and it now turned and turned with nothing to bite, Monseigneur began to run away from a phenomenon so low and unaccountable.

But, this was not the change on the village, and on many a village like it. For scores of years gone by, Monseigneur had squeezed it and wrung it, and had seldom graced it with his presence except for the pleasures of the chase—now, found in hunting the people; now, found in hunting the beasts, for whose preservation Monseigneur made edifying spaces of barbarous and barren wilderness. No. The change consisted in the appearance of strange faces of low caste, rather than in the disappearance of the high-caste, chiseled, and otherwise beatified and beatifying features of Monseigneur.

For, in these times, as the mender of roads worked, solitary, in the dust, not often troubling himself to reflect that dust he was and to dust he must return, being for the most part too much occupied in thinking how little he had for supper and how much more he would eat if he had it—in these times, as he raised his eyes from his lonely labor, and viewed the prospect, he would see some rough figure approaching on foot, the like of which was once a rarity in those parts, but was now a frequent presence. As it advanced, the mender of roads would discern without surprise, that it was a shaggy-haired man, of almost barbarian aspect, tall, in wooden shoes that were clumsy even to the eyes of a mender of roads, grim, rough, swart, steeped in the mud and dust of many highways, dank with the marshy moisture of many low grounds, sprinkled with the thorns and leaves and moss of many byways through woods.

Such a man came upon him, like a ghost, at noon in the July weather, as he sat on his heap of stones under a bank, taking such shelter as he could get from a shower of hail.

The man looked at him, looked at the village in the hollow at the mill, and at the prison on the crag. When he had identified these objects in what benighted mind he had, he said, in a dialect that was just intelligible:

"How goes it, Jacques?"

"All well, Jacques."

"Touch then!"

They joined hands, and the man sat down on the heap of stones.

"No dinner?"

"Nothing but supper now," said the mender of roads, with a hungry face.

"It is the fashion," growled the man. "I meet no dinner anywhere."

He took out a blackened pipe, filled it, lighted it with flint and steel, pulled at it until it was in a bright glow: then, suddenly held it from him and dropped something into it from between his finger and thumb, that blazed and went out in a puff of smoke.

"Touch then." It was the turn of the mender of roads to say it this time, after observing these operations. They again joined hands.

"Tonight?" said the mender of roads.

"Tonight," said the man, putting the pipe in his mouth.

"Where?"

"Here."

He and the mender of roads sat on the heap of stones looking silently at one another, with the hail driving in between them like a pigmy charge of bayonets, until the sky began to clear over the village.

"Show me!" said the traveler then, moving to the brow of the hill.

"See!" returned the mender of roads, with extended finger. "You go down here, and straight through the street, and past the fountain—"

"To the Devil with all that!" interrupted the other, rolling his eyes over the landscape. "*I* go through no streets and past no fountains. Well?"

"Well! About two leagues beyond the summit of that hill above the village."

"Good. When do you cease to work?"

"At sunset."

"Will you wake me, before departing? I have walked two nights without resting. Let me finish my pipe, and I shall sleep like a child. Will you wake me?"

"Surely."

The wayfarer smoked his pipe out, put it in his breast, slipped off his great wooden shoes, and lay down on his back on the heap of stones. He was fast asleep directly.

As the road-mender plied his dusty labor, and the hail-clouds, rolling away, revealed bright bars and streaks of sky which were responded to by silver gleams upon the landscape, the little man (who wore a red cap now, in place of his blue one) seemed fascinated by the figure on the heap of stones. His eyes were so often turned towards it, that he used his tools mechanically, and, one would have said, to very poor account. The bronze face, the shaggy black hair and beard, the coarse woollen red cap, the rough medley dress of homespun stuff and hairy skins of beasts, the powerful frame attenuated by spare living, and the sullen and desperate compression of the lips in sleep, inspired the mender of roads with awe. The traveler had traveled far, and his feet were footsore, and his ankles chafed and bleeding; his great shoes, stuffed with leaves and grass, had been heavy to drag over the many long leagues, and his clothes were chafed into holes, as he himself was into sores. Stooping down beside him, the road-mender tried to get a peep at secret weapons in his breast or where not; but in vain, for he slept with his arms crossed upon him, and set as resolutely as his lips. Fortified towns with their stockades, guardhouses, gates, trenches, and drawbridges, seemed, to the mender of roads, to be so much air as against this figure. And when he lifted his eyes from it to the horizon and looked around, he saw in his small fancy similar figures, stopped by no obstacle, tending to centers all over France.

The man slept on, indifferent to showers of hail and intervals of brightness, to sunshine on his face and shadow, to the pattering lumps of dull ice on his body and the diamonds into which the sun changed them, until the sun was low in the west, and the sky was glowing. Then the mender of roads having got his tools together and all things ready to go down into the village, roused him.

"Good!" said the sleeper, rising on his elbow. "Two leagues beyond the summit of the hill?"

"About."

"About. Good!"

The mender of roads went home, with the dust going on before him according to the set of the wind, and was soon at the fountain, squeezing himself in among the lean kine brought there to drink, and appearing even to whisper to them in his whispering to all the village. When the village had taken its poor supper, it did not creep to bed, as it usually did, but came out of doors again, and remained there. A curious contagion of whispering was upon it, and also, when it gathered together at the fountain in the dark, another curious contagion of looking expectantly at the sky in one direction only. Monsieur Gabelle, chief functionary of the place, became uneasy; went out on his housetop alone, and looked in that direction too; glanced down from behind his chimneys at the darkening faces by the fountain below, and sent word to the sacristan who kept the keys of the church, that there might be need to ring the tocsin by-and-by.

The night deepened. The trees environing the old chateau, keeping its solitary state apart, moved in a rising wind, as though they threatened the pile of building massive and dark in the gloom. Up the two terrace flights of steps the rain ran wildly, and beat at the great door, like a swift messenger rousing those within; uneasy rushes of wind went through the hall, among the old spears and knives, and passed lamenting up the stairs, and shook the curtains of the bed where the last Marquis had slept. East, West, North, and South, through the woods, four heavy-treading, unkempt figures crushed the high grass and cracked the branches, striding on cautiously to come together in the courtyard. Four lights broke out there, and moved away in different directions, and all was black again.

But, not for long. Presently, the chateau began to make itself strangely visible by some light of its own, as though it were growing luminous. Then, a flickering streak played behind the architecture of the front, picking out transparent places, and showing where balustrades, arches, and windows were. Then it soared higher, and grew broader and brighter. Soon, from a score of the great windows, flames burst forth, and the stone faces, awakened, stared out of fire.

A faint murmur arose about the house from the few people who were left there, and there was a saddling of a horse and riding away. There was spurring and splashing through the darkness, and bridle was drawn in the space by the village fountain, and the horse in a foam stood at Monsieur Gabelle's door. "Help, Gabelle! Help, everyone!" The tocsin rang impatiently, but other help (if that were any) there was none. The mender of roads, and two hundred and fifty particular friends, stood with folded arms at the fountain, looking at the pillar of fire in the sky. "It must be forty feet high," said they, grimly; and never moved.

The rider from the chateau, and the horse in a foam, clattered away through the village, and galloped up the stony steep, to the prison on the crag. At the gate, a group of officers were looking at the fire; removed from them, a group of soldiers. "Help, gentlemen-officers! The chateau is on fire; valuable objects may be saved from the flames by timely aid! Help, help!" The officers looked toward the soldiers who looked at the fire; gave no orders; and answered, with shrugs and biting of lips, "It must burn."

As the rider rattled down the hill again and through the street, the village was illuminating. The mender of roads, and the two hundred and fifty particular friends, inspired as one man and woman by the idea of lighting up, had darted into their houses, and were putting candles in every dull little pane of glass. The general scarcity of everything occasioned candles to be borrowed in a rather peremptory manner of Monsieur Gabelle; and in a moment of reluctance and hesitation on that functionary's part, the mender of roads, once so submissive to authority, had remarked that carriages were good to make bonfires with, and that post-horses would roast.

The chateau was left to itself to flame and burn. In the roaring and raging of the conflagration, a red-hot wind, driving straight from the infernal regions, seemed to be blowing the edifice away. With the rising and falling of the blaze, the stone faces showed as if they were in torment. When the great masses of stone and timber fell, the face with the two dints in the nose became obscured: anon struggled out of the smoke again, as if it were the face of the cruel Marquis, burning at the stake and contending with the fire.

The chateau burned; the nearest trees, laid hold of by the fire, scorched and shriveled; trees at a distance, fired by the four fierce figures, begirt the blazing edifice with a new forest of smoke. Molten lead and iron boiled in the marble basin of the fountain; the water ran dry; the extinguisher tops of the towers vanished like ice before the heat, and trickled down into four rugged wells of flame. Great rents and splits branched out in the solid walls, like crystallization; stupefied birds wheeled about, and dropped into the furnace; four fierce figures trudged away, East, West, North, and South, along the night-enshrouded roads guided by the beacon they had lighted, toward their next destination. The illuminated village had seized hold of the tocsin, and, abolishing the lawful ringer, rang for joy.

Not only that; but the village, light-headed with famine, fire, and bell-ringing, and bethinking itself that Monsieur Gabelle had to do with the collection of rent and taxes—though it was but a small installment of taxes, and no rent at all, that Gabelle had got in those latter days—became impatient for an interview with him, and, surrounding his house, summoned him to come forth for personal conference. Whereupon, Monsieur Gabelle did heavily bar his door, and retire to hold counsel with himself. The result of that conference was that Gabelle again withdrew himself to his housetop behind his stack of chimneys: this time resolved, if his door was broken in (he was a small Southern man of retaliative temperament), to pitch himself, head foremost over the parapet, and crush a man or two below.

Probably, Monsieur Gabelle passed a long night up there, with the distant chateau for fire and candle, and the beating at his door, combined with the joy-ringing, for music; not to mention his having an ill-omened lamp slung across the road before his posting-house gate, which the village showed a lively inclination to displace in his favor. A trying suspense, to be passing a whole summer night on the brink of the black ocean, ready to take that plunge into it upon which Monsieur Gabelle had resolved! But, the friendly dawn appearing at last, and the rush-candles of the village guttering out, the people happily dispersed, and Monsieur Gabelle came down, bringing his life with him for that while.

Within a hundred miles, and in the light of other fires, there were other functionaries less fortunate, that night and other nights, whom the rising sun found hanging across once-peaceful streets, where they had been born and bred; also, there were other villages and townspeople less fortunate than the mender of roads and his fellows, upon whom the functionaries and soldiery turned with success, and whom they strung up in their turn. But the fierce figures were steadily wending East, West, North, and South, be that as it would; and whosoever hung, fire burned. The altitude of the gallows that would turn to water and quench it, no functionary, by any stretch of mathematics, was able to calculate successfully.

Twenty-four

DRAWN TO THE LOADSTONE ROCK

IN SUCH RISINGS OF FIRE AND RISINGS OF SEA—THE FIRM earth shaken by the rushes of an angry ocean which had now no ebb but was always on the flow, higher and higher, to the terror and wonder of the beholders on the shore—three years of tempest were consumed. Three more birthdays of little Lucie had been woven by the golden thread into the peaceful tissue of the life of her home.

Many a night and many a day had its inmates listened to the echoes in the corner, with hearts that failed them when they heard the thronging feet. For, the footsteps had become to their minds as the footsteps of a people, tumultuous under a red flag and with their country declared in danger, changed into wild beasts, by terrible enchantment long persisted in.

Monseigneur, as a class, had dissociated himself from the phenomenon of his not being appreciated: of his being so little wanted in France, as to incur considerable danger of receiving his dismissal from it, and this life together. Like the fabled rustic who raised the Devil with infinite pains, and was so terrified at the sight of him that he could ask the Enemy no question, but immediately fled; so, Monseigneur, after boldly reading the Lord's Prayer backward for a great number of years, and performing many other potent spells for compelling the Evil One, no sooner beheld him in his terrors than he took to his noble heels.

The shining Bull's Eye of the Court was gone, or it would have been the mark for a hurricane of national bullets. It had never been a good eye to see with—had long had the mote in it of Lucifer's pride, Sardanapalus's luxury, and a mole's blindness—but it had dropped out and was gone. The Court, from that exclusive inner circle to its outermost rotten ring of intrigue, corruption, and dissimulation, was all gone together. Royalty was gone; had been besieged in its Palace and "suspended," when the last tidings came over.

The August of the year one thousand seven hundred and ninety-two was come, and Monseigneur was by this time scattered far and wide.

As was natural, the headquarters and great gathering-place of Monseigneur, in London, was Tellson's Bank. Spirits are supposed to haunt the places where their bodies most resorted, and Monseigneur without a guinea haunted the spot where his guineas used to be. Moreover, it was the spot to which such French intelligence as was most to be relied upon came quickest. Again: Tellson's was a munificent house, and extended great liberality to old customers who had fallen from their high estate. Again: those nobles who had seen the coming storm in time, and, anticipating plunder or confiscation, had made provident remittances to Tellson's, were always to be heard of there by their needy brethren. To which must be added that every newcomer from France reported himself and his tidings at Tellson's, almost as a matter of course. For such variety of reasons, Tellson's was at that time, as to French intelligence, a kind of High Exchange; and this was so well known to the public, and the inquiries made there were in consequence so numerous, that Tellson's sometimes wrote the latest news out in a line or so and posted it in the Bank windows, for all who ran through Temple Bar to read.

On a steaming, misty afternoon, Mr. Lorry sat at his desk, and Charles Darnay stood leaning on it, talking with him in a low voice. The penitential den once set apart for interviews with the House, was now the news-Exchange, and was filled to overflowing. It was within half an hour or so of the time of closing.

"But, although you are the youngest man that ever lived," said Charles Darnay, rather hesitating, "I must still suggest to you—"

"I understand. That I am too old?" said Mr. Lorry.

"Unsettled weather, a long journey, uncertain means of traveling, a disorganized country, a city that may not be even safe for you."

"My dear Charles," said Mr. Lorry, with cheerful confidence, "you touch some of the reasons for my going: not for my staying away. It is safe enough for me; nobody will care to interfere with an old fellow of hard upon fourscore when there are so many people there much better worth interfering with. As to its being a disorganized city, if it were not a disorganized city there would be no occasion to send somebody from our House here to our House there, who knows the city and the business, of old, and is in Tellson's confidence. As to the uncertain traveling, the long journey, and the winter weather, if I were not prepared to submit myself to a few inconveniences for the sake of Tellson's, after all these years, who ought to be?"

"I wish I were going myself," said Charles Darnay, somewhat restlessly, and like one thinking aloud.

"Indeed! You are a pretty fellow to object and advise!" exclaimed Mr. Lorry. "You wish you were going yourself? And you a Frenchman born? You are a wise counselor."

"My dear Mr. Lorry, it is because I am a Frenchman born, that the thought (which I did not mean to utter here, however) has passed through my mind often. One cannot help thinking, having had some sympathy for the miserable people, and having abandoned something to them," he spoke here in his former thoughtful manner, "that one might be listened to, and might have the power to persuade to some restraint. Only last night, after you had left us, when I was talking to Lucie—"

"When you were talking to Lucie," Mr. Lorry repeated. "Yes. I wonder you are not ashamed to mention the name of Lucie! Wishing you were going to France at this time of day!"

"However, I am not going," said Charles Darnay, with a smile. "It is more to the purpose that you say you are."

"And I am, in plain reality. The truth is, my dear Charles," Mr. Lorry glanced at the distant House, and lowered his voice, "you can have no conception of the difficulty with which our business is transacted, and of the peril in which our books and papers over yonder are involved. The Lord above knows what the compromising consequence would be to numbers of people, if some of our documents were seized or destroyed; and they might be, at any time, you know, for who can say that Paris is not set afire today, or sacked tomorrow! Now, a judicious selection from these with the least possible delay, and the burying of them, or otherwise getting them out of harm's way, is within the power (without loss of precious time) of scarcely anyone but myself, if anyone. And shall I hang back, when Tellson's knows this and says this—Tellson's, whose bread I have eaten these sixty years—because I am a little stiff about the joints? Why, I am a boy, sir, to half a dozen old codgers here!"

"How I admire the gallantry of your youthful spirit, Mr. Lorry."

"Tut! Nonsense, sir! And, my dear Charles," said Mr. Lorry, glancing at the House again, "you are to remember, that getting things out of Paris at this present time, no matter what things, is next to an impossibility. Papers and precious matters were this very day brought to us here (I speak in strict confidence; it is not businesslike to whisper it, even to you), by the strangest bearers you can imagine, every one of whom had his head hanging on by a single hair as he passed the Barriers. At another time, our parcels would come and go, as easily as in businesslike Old England; but now, everything is stopped."

"And do you really go tonight?"

"I really go tonight, for the case has become too pressing to admit of delay."

"And do you take no one with you?"

"All sorts of people have been proposed to me, but I will have nothing to say to any of them. I intend to take Jerry. Jerry has been my bodyguard on Sunday nights for a long time past, and I am used to him. Nobody will suspect Jerry of being anything but an English bulldog, or of having any design in his head but to fly at somebody who touches his master."

"I must say again that I heartily admire your gallantry and youthfulness."

"I must say again, nonsense, nonsense! When I have executed this little commission, I shall, perhaps, accept Tellson's proposal to retire and live at my ease. Time enough, then, to think about growing old."

This dialogue had taken place at Mr. Lorry's usual desk, with Monseigneur swarming within a yard or two of it, boastful of what he would do to avenge himself on the rascal-people before long. It was too much the way of Monseigneur under his reverses as a refugee, and it was much too much the way of native British orthodoxy, to talk of this terrible Revolution as if it were the one only harvest ever known under the skies that had not been sown—as if nothing had ever been done, or omitted to be done, that had led to it—as if observers of the wretched millions in France, and of the misused and perverted resources that should have made them prosperous, had not seen it inevitably coming, years before, and had not in plain words recorded what they saw. Such vaporing, combined with the extravagant plots of Monseigneur for the restoration of a state of things that had utterly exhausted itself, and worn out Heaven and earth as well as itself, was hard to be endured without some remonstrance by any sane man who knew the truth. And it was such vaporing all about his ears, like a troublesome confusion of blood in his own head, added to a latent uneasiness in his mind, which had already made Charles Darnay restless, and which still kept him so.

Among the talkers was Stryver, of the King's Bench Bar, far on his way to state promotion, and, therefore, loud on the theme; broaching to Monseigneur his devices for blowing the people up and exterminating them from the face of the earth, and doing without them: and for accomplishing many similar objects akin in their nature to the abolition of eagles, by sprinkling salt on the tails of the race. Him, Darnay heard with a particular feeling of objection; and Darnay stood divided between going away that he might hear no more, and remaining to interpose his word, when the thing that was to be went on to shape itself out.

The House approached Mr. Lorry, and laying a soiled and unopened letter before him, asked if he had yet discovered any traces of the person to whom it was addressed? The House laid the letter down so close to Darnay that he saw the direction—the more quickly because it was his own right name. The address, turned into English, ran: "Very pressing. To Monsieur heretofore the Marquis St. Evrémonde, of France, Confided to the cares of Messrs. Tellson and Co., Bankers, London, England."

On the marriage morning, Doctor Manette had made it his one urgent and express request to Charles Darnay, that the secret of this name should be—unless he, the Doctor, dissolved the obligation—kept inviolate between them. Nobody else knew it to be his name; his own wife had no suspicion of the fact; Mr. Lorry could have none.

"No," said Mr. Lorry, in reply to the House; "I have referred it, I think, to everybody now here, and no one can tell me where this gentleman is to be found."

The hands of the clock verging upon the hour of closing the Bank, there was a general set of the current of talkers past Mr. Lorry's desk. He held the letter out inquiringly; and Monseigneur looked at it, in the person of this plotting and indignant refugee; and Monseigneur looked at it, in the person of that plotting and indignant refugee; and This, That, and The Other, all had something disparaging to say, in French or in English, concerning the Marquis who was not to be found.

"Nephew, I believe—but in any case degenerate successor—of the polished Marquis who was murdered," said one. "Happy to say, I never knew him."

"A craven who abandoned his post," said another—this Monseigneur had been got out of Paris, legs uppermost and half suffocated, in a load of hay—"some years ago."

"Infected with the new doctrines," said a third, eyeing the direction through his glass in passing; "set himself in opposition to the last Marquis, abandoned the estates when he inherited them, and left them to the ruffian herd. They will recompense him now, I hope, as he deserves."

"Hey?" cried the blatant Stryver. "Did he though? Is that the sort of fellow? Let us look at his infamous name. D—n the fellow!"

Darnay, unable to restrain himself any longer, touched Mr. Stryver on the shoulder, and said:

"I know the fellow."

"Do you, by Jupiter?" said Stryver. "I am sorry for it."

"Why?"

"Why, Mr. Darnay? D'ye hear what he did? Don't ask why, in these times."

"But I do ask why."

"Then I tell you again, Mr. Darnay, I am sorry for it. I am sorry to hear you putting any such extraordinary questions. Here is a fellow, who, infected by the most pestilent and blasphemous code of deviltry that ever was known, abandoned his property to the vilest scum of the earth that ever did murder by wholesale, and you ask me why I am sorry that a man who instructs youth knows him? Well, but I'll answer you. I am sorry, because I believe there is contamination in such a scoundrel. That's why."

Mindful of the secret, Darnay with great difficulty checked himself, and said: "You may not understand the gentleman."

"I understand how to put *you* in a corner, Mr. Darnay," said Bully Stryver, "and I'll do it. If this fellow is a gentleman, I *don't* understand him. You may tell him so, with my compliments. You may also tell him, from me, that after abandoning his worldly goods and position to this butcherly mob, I wonder he is not at the head of them. But, no, gentlemen," said Stryver, looking all round, and snapping his fingers, "I know something of human nature, and I tell you that you'll never find a fellow like this fellow, trusting himself to the mercies of such precious *protégés*. No, gentlemen; he'll always show 'em a clean pair of heels very early in the scuffle, and sneak away."

With those words, and a final snap of his fingers, Mr. Stryver shouldered himself into Fleet Street, amidst the general approbation of his hearers. Mr. Lorry and Charles Darnay were left alone at the desk, in the general departure from the Bank.

"Will you take charge of the letter?" said Mr. Lorry. "You know where to deliver it?"

"I do."

"Will you undertake to explain that we suppose it to have been addressed here, on the chance of our knowing where to forward it, and that it has been here some time?"

"I will do so. Do you start for Paris from here?"

"From here, at eight."

"I will come back, to see you off."

Very ill at ease with himself, and with Stryver and most other men, Darnay made the best of his way into the quiet of the Temple, opened the letter and read it. These were its contents:

Prison of the Abbaye, Paris, June 21, 1792

MONSIEUR HERETOFORE THE MARQUIS,

After having long been in danger of my life at the hands of the village, I have been seized, with great violence and indignity, and brought a long journey on foot to Paris. On the road I have suffered a great deal. Nor is that all; my house has been destroyed—razed to the ground.

The crime for which I am imprisoned, Monsieur heretofore the Marquis, and for which I shall be summoned before the tribunal, and shall lose my life (without your so generous help), is, they tell me, treason against the majesty of the people, in that I have acted against them for an emigrant. It is in vain I represent that I have acted for them, and not against, according to your commands. It is in vain I represent that, before the sequestration of emigrant property, I had remitted the imposts they had ceased to pay; that I had collected no rent; that I had had recourse to no process. The only response is, that I have acted for an emigrant, and where is that emigrant?

Ah! most gracious Monsieur heretofore the Marquis, where is that emigrant! I cry in my sleep where is he! I demand of Heaven will he not come to deliver me! No answer. Ah! Monsieur heretofore the Marquis, I send my desolate cry across the sea, hoping it may perhaps reach your ears through the great bank of Tellson known at Paris!

For the love of Heaven, of justice, of generosity, of the honor of your noble name, I supplicate you, Monsieur heretofore the Marquis, to succor and release me. My fault is, that I have been true to you. O Monsieur heretofore the Marquis, I pray you be you true to me!

From this prison here of horror, whence I every hour tend nearer and nearer to destruction, I send you, Monsieur heretofore the Marquis, the assurance of my dolorous and unhappy service.

Your afflicted
Gabelle

The latent uneasiness in Darnay's mind was roused to vigorous life by this letter. The peril of an old servant and a good one, whose only crime was fidelity to himself and his family, stared him so reproachfully in the face, that, as he walked to and fro in the Temple considering what to do, he almost hid his face from the passersby.

He knew very well, that in his horror of the deed which had culminated the bad deeds and bad reputation of the old family house, in his resentful suspicions of his uncle, and in the aversion with which his conscience regarded the crumbling fabric that he was supposed to uphold, he had acted imperfectly. He knew very well that in his love for Lucie, his renunciation of his social place, though by no means new to his own mind, had been hurried and incomplete. He knew that he ought to have systematically worked it out and supervised it, and that he had meant to do it, and that it had never been done.

The happiness of his own chosen English home, the necessity of being always actively employed, the swift changes and troubles of the time which had followed on one another so fast, that the events of this week annihilated the immature plans of last week, and the events of the week following made all new again; he knew very well, that to the force of these circumstances he had yielded:—not without disquiet, but still without continuous and accumulating resistance. That he had watched the times for a time of action, and that they had shifted and struggled until the time had gone by, and the nobility were trooping from France by every highway and byway, and their property was in course of confiscation and destruction, and their very names were blotting out, was as well known to himself as it could be to any new authority in France that might impeach him for it.

But, he had oppressed no man, he had imprisoned no man; he was so far from having harshly exacted payment of his dues, that he had relinquished them of his own will, thrown himself on a world with no favor in it, won his own private place there, and earned his own bread. Monsieur Gabelle had held the impoverished and involved estate on written instructions to spare the people, to give them what little there was to give—such fuel as the heavy creditors would let them have in the winter, and such produce as could be saved from the same grip in the summer—and no doubt he had put the fact in plea and proof, for his own safety, so that it could not but appear now.

This favored the desperate resolution Charles Darnay had begun to make, that he would go to Paris.

Yes. Like the mariner in the old story, the winds and streams had driven him within the influence of the Loadstone Rock, and it was drawing him to itself, and he must go. Everything that arose before his mind drifted him on, faster and faster, more and more steadily, to the terrible attraction. His latent uneasiness had been, that bad aims were being worked out in his own unhappy land by bad instruments, and that he who could not fail to know that he was better than they, was not there, trying to do something to stay bloodshed, and assert the claims of mercy and humanity. With this uneasiness half stifled, and half reproaching him, he had been brought to the pointed comparison of himself with the brave old gentleman in whom duty was so strong; upon that comparison (injurious to himself), had instantly followed the sneers of Monseigneur, which had stung him bitterly, and those of Stryver, which above all, were coarse and galling, for old reasons. Upon those, had followed Gabelle's letter: the appeal of an innocent prisoner, in danger of death, to his justice, honor, and good name.

His resolution was made. He must go to Paris.

Yes. The Loadstone Rock was drawing him, and he must sail on, until he struck. He knew of no rock; he saw hardly any danger. The intention with which he had done what he had done, even although he had left it incompleted, presented it before him in an aspect that would be gratefully acknowledged in France on his presenting himself to assert it. Then, that glorious vision of doing good, which is so often the sanguine mirage of so many good minds, arose before him, and he even saw himself in the illusion with some influence to guide this raging Revolution that was running so fearfully wild.

As he walked to and fro with his resolution made, he considered that neither Lucie nor her father must know of it until he was gone. Lucie should be spared the pain of separation; and her father, always reluctant to turn his thoughts toward the dangerous ground of old, should come to the knowledge of the step, as a step taken, and not in the balance of suspense and doubt. How much of the incompleteness of his situation was referable to her father, through the painful anxiety to avoid reviving old associations of France in his mind, he did not discuss with himself. But, that circumstance too, had its influence in his course.

He walked to and fro, with thoughts very busy, until it was time to return to Tellson's, and take leave of Mr. Lorry. As soon as he arrived in Paris he would present himself to this old friend, but he must say nothing of his intention now.

A carriage with post-horses was ready at the Bank door, and Jerry was booted and equipped.

"I have delivered that letter," said Charles Darnay to Mr. Lorry. "I would not consent to your being charged with any written answer, but perhaps you will take a verbal one?"

"That I will, and readily," said Mr. Lorry, "if it is not dangerous."

"Not at all. Though it is to a prisoner in the Abbaye."

"What is his name?" said Mr. Lorry, with his open pocket-book in his hand.

"Gabelle."

"Gabelle. And what is the message to the unfortunate Gabelle in prison?"

"Simply, 'that he has received the letter, and will come.' "

"Any time mentioned?"

"He will start upon his journey tomorrow night."

"Any person mentioned?"

"No."

He helped Mr. Lorry to wrap himself in a number of coats and cloaks, and went out with him from the warm atmosphere of the old bank, into the misty air of Fleet Street. "My love to Lucie, and to little Lucie," said Mr. Lorry at parting, "and take precious care of them till I come back." Charles Darnay shook his head and doubtfully smiled, as the carriage rolled away.

That night—it was the fourteenth of August—he sat up late, and wrote two fervent letters; one was to Lucie, explaining the strong obligation he was under to go to Paris, and showing her, at length, the reasons that he had, for feeling confident that he could become involved in no personal danger there; the other was to the Doctor, confiding Lucie and their dear child to his care, and dwelling on the same topics with the strongest assurances. To both, he wrote that he would despatch letters in proof of his safety, immediately after his arrival.

It was a hard day, that day of being among them, with the first reservation of their joint lives on his mind. It was a hard matter to preserve the innocent deceit of which they were profoundly unsuspicious. But, an affectionate glance at his wife, so happy and busy, made him resolute not to tell her what impended (he had been half moved to do it, so strange it was to him to act in anything without her quiet aid), and the day passed quickly. Early in the evening he embraced her, and her scarcely less dear namesake, pretending that he would return by-and-by (an imaginary engagement took him out, and he had secreted a valise of clothes ready), and so he emerged into the heavy mist of the heavy street, with a heavier heart.

The unseen force was drawing him fast to itself, now, and all the tides and winds were setting straight and strong toward it. He left his two letters with a trusty porter, to be delivered half an hour before midnight, and no sooner; took horse for Dover; and began his journey. "For the love of Heaven, justice, of generosity, of the honor of your noble name!" was the poor prisoner's cry with which he strengthened his sinking heart, as he left all that was dear on earth behind him, and floated away for the Loadstone Rock.

THE TRACK
OF A STORM

One

IN SECRET

T HE TRAVELER FARED SLOWLY ON HIS WAY, WHO FARED
towards Paris from England in the autumn of the year one thousand
seven hundred and ninety-two. More than enough of bad roads, bad
equipages, and bad horses, he would have encountered to delay him, though
the fallen and unfortunate King of France had been upon his throne in all his
glory; but, the changed times were fraught with other obstacles than these.
Every town gate and village taxing-house had its band of citizen-patriots,
with their national muskets in a most explosive state of readiness, who
stopped all comers and goers, cross-questioned them, inspected their papers,
looked for their names in lists of their own, turned them back, or sent them
on, or stopped them and laid them in hold, as their capricious judgment or
fancy deemed best for the dawning Republic One and Indivisible, of Liberty,
Equality, Fraternity, or Death.

A very few French leagues of his journey were accomplished, when
Charles Darnay began to perceive that for him along these country roads

there was no hope of return until he should have been declared a good citizen at Paris. Whatever might befall now, he must on to his journey's end. Not a mean village closed upon him, not a common barrier dropped across the road behind him, but he knew it to be another iron door in the series that was barred between him and England. The universal watchfulness so encompassed him, that if he had been taken in a net, or were being forwarded to his destination in a cage, he could not have felt his freedom more completely gone.

This universal watchfulness not only stopped him on the highway twenty times in a stage, but retarded his progress twenty times in a day, by riding after him and taking him back, riding before him and stopping him by anticipation, riding with him and keeping him in charge. He had been days upon his journey in France alone, when he went to bed tired out, in a little town on the high road, still a long way from Paris.

Nothing but the production of the afflicted Gabelle's letter from his prison of the Abbaye would have got him on so far. His difficulty at the guardhouse in this small place had been such, that he felt his journey to have come to a crisis. And he was, therefore, as little surprised as a man could be, to find himself awakened at the small inn to which he had been remitted until morning, in the middle of the night.

Awakened by a timid local functionary and three armed patriots in rough red caps and with pipes in their mouths, who sat down on the bed.

"Emigrant," said the functionary, "I am going to send you on to Paris, under an escort."

"Citizen, I desire nothing more than to get to Paris, though I could dispense with the escort."

"Silence!" growled a red-cap, striking at the coverlet with the butt-end of his musket. "Peace, aristocrat!"

"It is as the good patriot says," observed the timid functionary. "You are an aristocrat, and must have an escort—and must pay for it."

"I have no choice," said Charles Darnay.

"Choice! Listen to him!" cried the same scowling red-cap. "As if it was not a favor to be protected from the lamp-iron!"

"It is always as the good patriot says," observed the functionary. "Rise and dress yourself, emigrant."

Darnay complied, and was taken back to the guardhouse where other patriots in rough red caps were smoking, drinking, and sleeping, by a watchfire. Here he paid a heavy price for his escort, and hence he started with it on the wet, wet roads at three o'clock in the morning.

The escort were two mounted patriots in red caps and tricolored cockades, armed with national muskets and sabres, who rode one on either side of him. The escorted governed his own horse, but a loose line was attached to his bridle, the end of which one of the patriots kept girded round his wrist. In this state they set forth, with the sharp rain driving in their faces:

clattering at a heavy dragoon trot over the uneven town pavement, and out upon the mire-deep roads. In this state they traversed without change, except of horses and pace, all the mire-deep leagues that lay between them and the capital.

They traveled in the night, halting an hour or two after daybreak, and lying by until the twilight fell. The escort were so wretchedly clothed, that they twisted straw round their bare legs, and thatched their ragged shoulders to keep the wet off. Apart from personal discomfort of being so attended, and apart from such considerations of present danger as arose from one of the patriots being chronically drunk, and carrying his musket very recklessly, Charles Darnay did not allow the restraint that was laid upon him to awaken any serious fears in his breast; for, he reasoned with himself that it could have no reference to the merits of an individual case that was not yet stated, and of representations, confirmable by the prisoner in the Abbaye, that were not yet made.

But, when they came to the town of Beauvais—which they did at eventide, when the streets were filled with people—he could not conceal from himself that the aspect of affairs was very alarming. An ominous crowd gathered to see him dismount at the posting-yard, and many voices called out loudly, "Down with the emigrant!"

He stopped in the act of swinging himself out of his saddle, and, resuming it as his safest place, said:

"Emigrant, my friends! Do you not see me here, in France, of my own will?"

"You are a cursed emigrant," cried a farrier, making at him in a furious manner through the press, hammer in hand; "and you are a cursed aristocrat!"

The postmaster interposed himself between this man and the rider's bridle (at which he was evidently making), and soothingly said, "Let him be; let him be! He will be judged at Paris."

"Judged!" repeated the farrier, swinging his hammer. "Ay! and condemned as a traitor." At this, the crowd roared approval.

Checking the postmaster, who was for turning his horse's head to the yard (the drunken patriot sat composedly in his saddle looking on, with the line round his wrist), Darnay said, as soon as he could make his voice heard:

"Friends, you deceive yourselves, or you are deceived. I am not a traitor."

"He lies!" cried the smith. "He is a traitor since the decree. His life is forfeit to the people. His cursed life is not his own!"

At the instant, when Darnay saw a rush in the eyes of the crowd, which another instant would have brought upon him, the postmaster turned his horse into the yard, the escort rode in close upon his horse's flanks, and the postmaster shut and barred the crazy double gates. The farrier struck a blow upon them with his hammer, and the crowd groaned; but, no more was done.

"What is this decree that the smith spoke of?" Darnay asked the postmaster, when he had thanked him, and stood beside him in the yard.

"Truly, a decree for selling the property of emigrants."

"When passed?"

"On the fourteenth."

"The day I left England!"

"Everybody says it is but one of several, and that there will be others—if there are not already—banishing all emigrants, and condemning all to death who return. That is what he meant when he said your life was not your own."

"But there are no such decrees yet?"

"What do I know!" said the postmaster, shrugging his shoulders; "there may be, or there will be. It is all the same. What would you have?"

They rested on some straw in a loft until the middle of the night, and then rode forward again when all the town was asleep. Among the many wild changes observable on familiar things which made this wild ride unreal, not the least was the seeming rarity of sleep. After long and lonely spurring over dreary roads, they would come to a cluster of poor cottages, not steeped in darkness, but all glittering with lights, and would find the people, in a ghostly manner in the dead of the night, circling hand in hand round a shriveled tree of Liberty, or all drawn up together singing a Liberty song. Happily, however, there was sleep in Beauvais that night to help them out of it, and they passed on once more into solitude and loneliness: jingling through the untimely cold and wet, among impoverished fields that had yielded no fruits of the earth that year, diversified by the blackened remains of burnt houses, and by the sudden emergence from ambuscade, and sharp reining up across their way, of patriot patrols on the watch on all the roads.

Daylight at last found them before the wall of Paris. The barrier was closed and strongly guarded when they rode up to it.

"Where are the papers of this prisoner?" demanded a resolute-looking man in authority, who was summoned out by the guard.

Naturally struck by the disagreeable word, Charles Darnay requested the speaker to take notice that he was a free traveler and French citizen, in charge of an escort which the disturbed state of the country had imposed upon him, and which he had paid for.

"Where," repeated the same personage, without taking any heed of him whatever, "are the papers of this prisoner?"

The drunken patriot had them in his cap, and produced them. Casting his eyes over Gabelle's letter, the same personage in authority showed some disorder and surprise, and looked at Darnay with a close attention.

He left escort and escorted without saying a word, however, and went into the guardroom; meanwhile, they sat upon their horses outside the gate. Looking about him while in this state of suspense, Charles Darnay observed that the gate was held by a mixed guard of soldiers and patriots, the latter far outnumbering the former; and that while ingress into the city for peasants' carts bringing in supplies, and for similar traffic and traffickers, was easy enough, egress, even for the homeliest people, was very difficult. A numerous medley of men and women, not to mention beasts and vehicles of various sorts, was waiting to issue forth; but, the previous identification was so strict that they filtered through the barrier very slowly. Some of these people knew their turn for examination to be so far off, that they lay down on the ground to sleep or smoke, while others talked together, or loitered about. The red cap and tricolor cockade were universal, both among men and women.

When he had sat in his saddle some half-hour, taking note of these things, Darnay found himself confronted by the same man in authority, who directed the guard to open the barrier. Then he delivered to the escort, drunk and sober, a receipt for the escorted, and requested him to dismount. He did so, and the two patriots, leading his tired horse, turned and rode away without entering the city.

He accompanied his conductor into a guardroom, smelling of common wine and tobacco, where certain soldiers and patriots, asleep and awake, drunk and sober, and in various neutral states between sleeping and waking, drunkenness and sobriety, were standing and lying about. The light in the guardhouse, half derived from the waning oil-lamps of the night, and half from the overcast day, was in a correspondingly uncertain condition. Some registers were lying open on a desk, and an officer of a coarse, dark aspect presided over these.

"Citizen Defarge," said he to Darnay's conductor, as he took a slip of paper to write on. "Is this the emigrant Evrémonde?"

"This is the man."

"Your age, Evrémonde?"

"Thirty-seven."

"Married, Evrémonde?"

"Yes."

"Where married?"

"In England."

"Without doubt. Where is your wife, Evrémonde?"

"In England."

"Without doubt. You are consigned, Evrémonde, to the prison of La Force."

"Just Heaven!" exclaimed Darnay. "Under what law, and for what offense?"

The officer looked up from his slip of paper for a moment.

"We have new laws, Evrémonde, and new offenses, since you were here." He said it with a hard smile, and went on writing.

"I entreat you to observe that I have come here voluntarily, in response to that written appeal of a fellow-citizen which lies before you. I have come here, to clear him and to clear myself. I demand no more than the opportunity to do so without delay. Is not that my right?"

"Emigrants have no rights, Evrémonde," was the stolid reply. The officer wrote until he had finished, read over to himself what he had written, sanded it, and handed it to Defarge, with the words "In secret."

Defarge motioned with the paper to the prisoner that he must accompany him. The prisoner obeyed, and a guard of two armed patriots attended them.

"Is it you," said Defarge, in a low voice, as they went down the guardhouse steps and turned into Paris, "who married the daughter of Doctor Manette, once a prisoner in the Bastille that is no more?"

"Yes," replied Darnay, looking at him with surprise.

"My name is Defarge, and I keep a wine-shop in the Quarter Saint Antoine. Possibly you have heard of me?"

"My wife came to your house to reclaim her father? Yes!"

The word "wife" seemed to serve as a gloomy reminder to Citizen Defarge, to say with sudden impatience, "In the name of that sharp female newly born and called La Guillotine, why did you come to France?"

"You heard me say why, a minute ago. Do you not believe it is the truth?"

"A bad truth for you," said Defarge, speaking with knitted brows, and looking straight before him.

"Indeed, I am lost here. All here is so unprecedented, so changed, so sudden and unfair, that I am absolutely lost. Will you render me a little help?"

"None." Defarge spoke, always looking straight before him.

"Will you answer me a single question?"

"Perhaps. According to its nature. You can say what it is."

"In this prison that I am going to so unjustly, shall I have some free communication with the world outside?"

"You will see."

"I am not to be buried there, prejudged, and without any means of presenting my case?"

"You will see. But, what then? Other people have been similarly buried in worse prisons, before now."

"But never by me, Citizen Defarge."

Citizen Defarge glanced darkly at him for answer, and walked on in a steady and set silence. The deeper he sank into this silence, the fainter hope there was—or so Darnay thought—of his softening in any slight degree. He, therefore, made haste to say:

"It is of the utmost importance to me (you know, Citizen, even better than I, of how much importance) that I should be able to communicate to Mr. Lorry of Tellson's Bank, an English gentleman who is now in Paris, the simple fact, without comment, that I have been thrown into the prison of La Force. Will you cause that to be done for me?"

"I will do," Defarge doggedly rejoined, "nothing for you. My duty is to my country and the people. I am the sworn servant of both, against you. I will do nothing for you."

Charles Darnay felt it hopeless to entreat him further, and his pride was touched besides. As they walked on in silence, he could not but see how used the people were to the spectacle of prisoners passing along the streets. The very children scarcely noticed him. A few passers turned their heads, and a few shook their fingers at him as an aristocrat; otherwise, that a man in good clothes should be going to prison was no more remarkable than that a laborer in working clothes should be going to work. In one narrow, dark, and dirty street through which they passed, an excited orator, mounted on a stool, was addressing an excited audience on the crimes against the people, of the king and the royal family. The few words that he caught from this man's lips, first made it known to Charles Darnay that the king was in prison, and that the foreign ambassadors had one and all left Paris. On the road (except at Beauvais) he had heard absolutely nothing. The escort and the universal watchfulness had completely isolated him.

That he had fallen among far greater dangers than those which had developed themselves when he left England, he of course knew now. That perils had thickened about him fast, and might thicken faster and faster yet, he of course knew now. He could not but admit to himself that he might not have made this journey, if he could have foreseen the events of a few days. And yet his misgivings were not so dark as, imagined by the light of this later time, they would appear. Troubled as the future was, it was the unknown future, and in its obscurity there was ignorant hope. The horrible massacre, days and nights long, which, within a few rounds of the clock, was to set a great mark of blood upon the blessed garnering time of harvest, was as far out of his knowledge as if it had been a hundred thousand years away. The "sharp female newly-born, and called La Guillotine," was hardly known to him, or to the generality of people, by name. The frightful deeds that were to be soon done were probably unimagined at that time in the brains of the doers. How could they have a place in the shadowy conceptions of a gentle mind?

Of unjust treatment in detention and hardship, and in cruel separation from his wife and child, he foreshadowed the likelihood, or the certainty; but, beyond this, he dreaded nothing distinctly. With this on his mind, which was enough to carry into a dreary prison courtyard, he arrived at the prison of La Force.

A man with a bloated face opened the strong wicket, to whom Defarge presented "The Emigrant Evrémonde."

"What the Devil! How many more of them!" exclaimed the man with the bloated face.

Defarge took his receipt without noticing the exclamation, and withdrew, with his two fellow-patriots.

"What the Devil, I say again!" exclaimed the gaoler, left with his wife. "How many more!"

The gaoler's wife, being provided with no answer to the question, merely replied, "One must have patience, my dear!" Three turnkeys who entered responsive to a bell she rang, echoed the sentiment, and one added, "For the love of Liberty!" which sounded in that place like an inappropriate conclusion.

The prison of La Force was a gloomy prison, dark and filthy, and with a horrible smell of foul sleep in it. Extraordinary how soon the noisome flavor of imprisoned sleep becomes manifest in all such places that are ill cared for!

"In secret, too," grumbled the gaoler, looking at the written paper. "As if I was not already full to bursting!"

He stuck the paper on a file, in an ill-humor, and Charles Darnay awaited his further pleasure for half an hour: sometimes, pacing to and fro in the strong arched room; sometimes, resting on a stone seat: in either case detained to be imprinted on the memory of the chief and his subordinates.

"Come!" said the chief, at length taking up his keys, "come with me, emigrant."

Through the dismal prison twilight, his new charge accompanied him by corridor and staircase, many doors clanging and locking behind them, until they came into a large, low, vaulted chamber, crowded with prisoners of both sexes. The women were seated at a long table, reading and writing, knitting, sewing, and embroidering; the men were for the most part standing behind their chairs, or lingering up and down the room.

In the instinctive association of prisoners with shameful crime and disgrace, the newcomer recoiled from this company. But, the crowning unreality of his long unreal ride, was, their all at once rising to receive him, with every refinement of manner known to the time, and with all the engaging graces and courtesies of life.

So strangely clouded were these refinements by the prison manners and gloom, so spectral did they become in the inappropriate squalor and misery through which they were seen, that Charles Darnay seemed to stand in a company of the dead. Ghosts all! The ghost of beauty, the ghost of stateliness, the ghost of elegance, the ghost of pride, the ghost of frivolity, the ghost of wit, the ghost of youth, the ghost of age, all waiting their dismissal from the desolate shore, all turning on him eyes that were changed by the death they had died in coming there.

It struck him motionless. The gaoler standing at his side, and the other gaolers moving about, who would have been well enough as to appearance in the ordinary exercise of their functions, looked so extravagantly coarse contrasted with sorrowing mothers and blooming daughters who were there— with the apparitions of the coquette, the young beauty, and the mature woman delicately bred—that the inversion of all experience and likelihood which the scene of shadows presented, was heightened to its utmost. Surely, ghosts all. Surely, the long unreal ride some progress of disease that had brought him to these gloomy shades.

"In the name of the assembled companions in misfortune," said a gentleman of courtly appearance and address, coming forward, "I have the honor of giving you welcome to La Force, and of condoling with you on the calamity that has brought you among us. May it soon terminate happily! It would be an impertinence elsewhere, but it is not so here, to ask your name and condition?"

Charles Darnay roused himself, and gave the required information, in words as suitable as he could find.

"But I hope," said the gentleman, following the chief gaoler with his eyes, who moved across the room, "that you are not in secret?"

"I do not understand the meaning of the term, but I have heard them say so."

"Ah, what a pity! We so much regret it! But take courage; several members of our society have been in secret, at first, and it has lasted but a short time." Then he added, raising his voice, "I grieve to inform the society—in secret."

There was a murmur of commiseration as Charles Darnay crossed the room to a grated door where the gaoler awaited him, and many voices—among which, the soft and compassionate voices of women were conspicuous—gave him good wishes and encouragement. He turned at the grated door, to render the thanks of his heart; it closed under the gaoler's hand; and the apparitions vanished from his sight forever.

The wicket opened on a stone staircase, leading upward. When they had ascended forty steps (the prisoner of half an hour already counted them), the gaoler opened a low black door, and they passed into a solitary cell. It struck cold and damp, but it was not dark.

"Yours," said the gaoler.

"Why am I confined alone?"

"How do I know!"

"I can buy pen, ink, and paper?"

"Such are not my orders. You will be visited, and can ask then. At present, you may buy your food, and nothing more."

There were in the cell, a chair, a table, and a straw mattress. As the gaoler made a general inspection of these objects, and of the four walls, before going out, a wandering fancy wandered through the mind of the prisoner leaning against the wall opposite to him, that this gaoler was so unwholesomely bloated, both in face and person, as to look like a man who had been drowned and filled with water. When the gaoler was gone, he thought, in the same wandering way, "Now am I left, as if I were dead." Stopping then, to look down at the mattress, he turned from it with a sick feeling, and thought, "And here in these crawling creatures is the first condition of the body after death.

"Five paces by four and a half, five paces by four and a half, five paces by four and a half." The prisoner walked to and fro in his cell, counting its measurement, and the roar of the city arose like muffled drums with a wild swell of voices added to them. "He made shoes, he made shoes, he made shoes." The prisoner counted the measurement again, and paced faster, to draw his mind with him from that latter repetition. "The ghosts that vanished when the wicket closed. There was one among them, the appearance of a lady dressed in black, who was leaning in the embrasure of a window, and she had a light shining upon her golden hair, and she looked like **** Let us ride on again, for God's sake, through the illuminated villages with the people all awake! **** He made shoes, he made shoes, he made shoes. **** Five paces by four and a half." With such scraps tossing and rolling upward from the depths of his mind, the prisoner walked faster and faster, obstinately counting and counting; and the roar of the city changed to this extent—that it still rolled in like muffled drums, but with the wail of voices that he knew, in the swell that rose above them.

T w o

THE GRINDSTONE

Tellson's Bank, established in the Saint Germain Quarter of Paris, was in a wing of a large house, approached by a courtyard and shut off from the street by a high wall and a strong gate. The house belonged to a great nobleman who had lived in it until he made a flight from the troubles, in his own cook's dress, and got across the borders. A mere beast of the chase flying from hunters, he was still in his metempsychosis no other than the same Monseigneur, the preparation of whose chocolate for whose lips had once occupied three strong men besides the cook in question.

Monseigneur gone, and the three strong men absolving themselves from the sin of having drawn his high wages, by being more than ready and willing to cut his throat on the altar of the dawning Republic One and Indivisible of Liberty, Equality, Fraternity, or Death, Monseigneur's house had been first sequestrated, and then confiscated. For, all things moved so fast, and decree followed decree with that fierce precipitation, that now upon the third night of the autumn month of September, patriot emissaries of the law were in possession of Monseigneur's house, and had marked it with the tricolor, and were drinking brandy in its state apartments.

A place of business in London like Tellson's place of business in Paris, would soon have driven the House out of its mind and into the Gazette. For, what would staid British responsibility and respectability have said to orange-trees in boxes in a Bank courtyard, and even to a Cupid over the counter? Yet such things were. Tellson's had whitewashed the Cupid, but he was still to be seen on the ceiling, in the coolest linen, aiming (as he very often does) at money from morning to night. Bankruptcy must inevitably have come of this young Pagan, in Lombard Street, London, and also of a curtained alcove in the rear of the immortal boy, and also of a looking-glass let into the wall, and also of clerks not at all old who danced in public on the slightest provocation. Yet, a French Tellson's could get on with these things exceedingly well, and, as long as the times held together, no man had taken fright at them, and drawn out his money.

What money would be drawn out of Tellson's, henceforth, and what would lie there, lost and forgotten; what plate and jewels would tarnish in Tellson's hiding-places, while the depositors rusted in prisons, and when they should have violently perished; how many accounts with Tellson's, never to be balanced in this world, must be carried over into the next; no man could have said, that night, anymore than Mr. Jarvis Lorry could, though he thought heavily of these questions. He sat by a newly lighted wood fire (the blighted and unfruitful year was prematurely cold), and on his honest and courageous face there was a deeper shade than the pendent lamp could throw, or any object in the room distortedly reflect—a shade of horror.

He occupied rooms in the Bank, in his fidelity to the house of which he had grown to be a part, like strong root-ivy. It chanced that they derived a kind of security from the patriotic occupation of the main building, but the true-hearted old gentleman never calculated about that. All such circumstances were indifferent to him, so that he did his duty. On the opposite side of the courtyard, under a colonnade, was extensive standing for carriages—where, indeed, some carriages of Monseigneur yet stood. Against two of the pillars were fastened two great flaring flambeaux, and, in the light of these, standing out in the open air, was a large grindstone: a roughly mounted thing which appeared to have hurriedly been brought there from some neighboring smithy, or other workshop. Rising and looking out of window at these harmless objects, Mr. Lorry shivered, and retired to his seat by the fire. He had opened, not only the glass window, but the lattice blind outside it, and he had closed both again, and he shivered through his frame.

From the street beyond the high wall and the strong gate, there came the usual night hum of the city, with now and then an indescribable ring to it, weird and unearthly, as if some unwonted sounds of a terrible nature were going up to heaven.

"Thank God," said Mr. Lorry, clasping his hands, "that no one near and dear to me is in this dreadful town tonight. May He have mercy on all who are in danger!"

Soon afterward, the bell at the great gate sounded, and he thought, "They have come back!" and sat listening. But, there was no loud irruption into the courtyard, as he had expected, and he heard the gate clash again, and all was quiet.

The nervousness and dread that were upon him inspired that vague uneasiness respecting the Bank which a great charge would naturally awaken, with such feelings roused. It was well guarded, and he got up to go among the trusty people who were watching it, when his door suddenly opened, and two figures rushed in, at sight of which he fell back in amazement.

Lucie and her father! Lucie with her arms stretched out to him, and with that old look of earnestness so concentrated and intensified, that it seemed as though it had been stamped upon her face expressly to give force and power to it in this one passage of her life.

"What is this!" cried Mr. Lorry, breathless and confused. "What is the matter? Lucie! Manette! What has happened? What has brought you here? What is it?"

With the look fixed upon him, in her paleness and wildness, she panted out in his arms, imploringly, "Oh my dear friend! My husband!"

"Your husband, Lucie?"

"Charles."

"What of Charles?"

"Here."

"Here, in Paris?"

"Has been here some days—three or four—I don't know how many—I can't collect my thoughts. An errand of generosity brought him here unknown to us; he was stopped at the barrier, and sent to prison."

The old man uttered an irrepressible cry. Almost at the same moment, the bell of the great gate rang again, and a loud noise of feet and voices came pouring into the courtyard.

"What is that noise?" said the Doctor, turning toward the window. "Don't look!" cried Mr. Lorry. "Don't look out! Manette, for your life, don't touch the blind!"

The Doctor turned, with his hand upon the fastening of the window, and said, with a cool bold smile:

"My dear friend, I have a charmed life in this city. I have been a Bastille prisoner. There is no patriot in Paris—in Paris?—in France—who, knowing me to have been a prisoner in the Bastille would touch me, except to overwhelm me with embraces, or carry me in triumph. My old pain has given me a power that has brought us through the barrier, and gained us news of Charles there, and brought us here. I knew it would be so; I knew I could help Charles out of all danger; I told Lucie so.—What is that noise?" His hand was again upon the window.

"Don't look!" cried Mr. Lorry, absolutely desperate. "No, Lucie, my dear, nor you!" He got his arm around her, and held her. "Don't be so terrified, my love. I solemnly swear to you that I know of no harm having happened to Charles; that I had no suspicion even, of his being in this fatal place. What prison is he in?"

"La Force."

"La Force! Lucie, my child, if ever you were brave and serviceable in your life—and you were always both—you will compose yourself now, to do exactly as I bid you; for, more depends upon it than you can think, or I can say. There is no help for you in any action on your part tonight; you cannot possibly stir out. I say this, because what I must bid you to do for Charles's sake, is the hardest thing to do of all. You must instantly be obedient, still, and quiet. You must let me put you in a room at the back here. You must leave your father and me alone for two minutes, and as there are Life and Death in the world, you must not delay."

"I will be submissive to you. I see in your face that you know I can do nothing else than this. I know you are true."

The old man kissed her, and hurried her into his room, and turned the key; then, came hurrying back to the Doctor, and opened the window and partly opened the blind, and put his hand upon the Doctor's arm, and looked out with him into the courtyard.

Looked out upon a throng of men and women: not enough in number, or near enough, to fill the courtyard: not more than forty or fifty in all. The people in possession of the house had let them in at the gate, and they had rushed in to work at the grindstone; it had evidently been set up there for their purpose, as in a convenient and retired spot.

But, such awful workers, and such awful work!

The grindstone had a double handle, and, turning at it madly were two men, whose faces, as their long hair flapped back when the whirlings of the grindstone brought their faces up, were more horrible and cruel than the visages of the wildest savages in their most barbarous disguise. False eyebrows and false mustaches were stuck upon them, and their hideous countenances were all bloody and sweaty, and all awry with howling, and all staring and glaring with beastly excitement and want of sleep. As these ruffians turned and turned, their matted locks now flung forward over their eyes, now flung backward over their necks, some women held wine to their mouths that they might drink; and what with dropping blood, and what with dropping wine, and what with the stream of sparks struck out of the stone, all their wicked atmosphere seemed gore and fire. The eye could not detect one creature in the group free from the smear of blood. Shouldering one another to get next at the sharpening-stone were men stripped to the waist, with the stain all over their limbs and bodies; men in all sorts of rags, with the stain upon those rags; men devilishly set off with spoils of women's lace and silk and ribbon, with the stain dyeing those trifles through and through. Hatchets, knives, bayonets, swords, all brought to be sharpened, were all red with it. Some of the hacked swords were tied to the wrists of those who carried them, with strips of linen and fragments of dress: ligatures various in kind, but all deep of the one color. And as the frantic wielders of these weapons snatched them from the stream of sparks and tore away into the streets, the same red hue was red in their frenzied eyes;—eyes which any unbrutalized beholder would have given twenty years of life, to petrify with a well-directed gun.

All this was seen in a moment, as the vision of a drowning man, or of any human creature at any very great pass, could see a world if it were there. They drew back from the window, and the Doctor looked for explanation in his friend's ashy face.

"They are," Mr. Lorry whispered the words glancing fearfully round at the locked room, "murdering the prisoners. If you are sure of what you say; if you really have the power you think you have—as I believe you have—make yourself known to these devils, and get taken to La Force. It may be too late, I don't know, but let it not be a minute later!"

Doctor Manette pressed his hand, hastened bareheaded out of the room, and was in the courtyard when Mr. Lorry regained the blind.

His streaming white hair, his remarkable face, and the impetuous confidence of his manner, as he put the weapons aside like water, carried him in an instant to the heart of the concourse at the stone. For a few moments there was a pause, and a hurry, and a murmur, and the unintelligible sound of his voice; and then Mr. Lorry saw him, surrounded by all, and in the midst of a line of twenty men long, all linked shoulder to shoulder, and hand to shoulder, hurried out with cries of—"Live the Bastille prisoner! Help for the Bastille prisoner's kindred in La Force! Room for the Bastille prisoner in front there! Save the prisoner Evrémonde at La Force!" and a thousand answering shouts.

He closed the lattice again with a fluttering heart, closed the window and the curtain, hastened to Lucie, and told her that her father was assisted by the people, and gone in search of her husband. He found her child and Miss Pross with her; but it never occurred to him to be surprised by their appearance until a long time afterward, when he sat watching them in such quiet as the night knew.

Lucie had, by that time, fallen into a stupor on the floor at his feet, clinging to his hand. Miss Pross had laid the child down on his own bed, and her head had gradually fallen on the pillow beside her pretty charge. O the long, long night, with the moans of the poor wife. And O the long, long night, with no return of her father and no tidings!

Twice more in the darkness the bell at the great gate sounded, and the irruption was repeated, and the grindstone whirled and spluttered. "What is it?" cried Lucie, affrighted.

"Hush! The soldiers' swords are sharpened there," said Mr. Lorry. "The place is national property now, and used as a kind of armory, my love."

Twice more in all; but, the last spell of work was feeble and fitful. Soon afterward the day began to dawn, and he softly detached himself from the clasping hand, and cautiously looked out again. A man, so besmeared that he might have been a sorely wounded soldier creeping back to consciousness on a field of slain, was rising from the pavement by the side of the grindstone, and looking about him with a vacant air. Shortly, this worn-out murderer descried in the imperfect light one of the carriages of Monseigneur, and, staggering to that gorgeous vehicle, climbed in at the door, and shut himself up to take his rest on its dainty cushions.

The great grindstone, Earth, had turned when Mr. Lorry looked out again, and the sun was red on the courtyard. But, the lesser grindstone stood alone there in the calm morning air, with a red upon it that the sun had never given, and would never take away.

Three

THE SHADOW

ONE OF THE FIRST CONSIDERATIONS WHICH AROSE IN THE business mind of Mr. Lorry when business hours came round, was this:—that he had no right to imperil Tellson's by sheltering the wife of an emigrant prisoner under the Bank roof. His own possessions, safety, life, he would have hazarded for Lucie and her child, without a moment's demur; but, the great trust he held was not his own, and as to that business charge he was a strict man of business.

At first, his mind reverted to Defarge, and he thought of finding out the wine-shop again and taking counsel with its master in reference to the safest dwelling-place in the distracted state of the city. But, the same consideration that suggested him, repudiated him; he lived in the most violent Quarter, and doubtless was influential there, and deep in its dangerous workings.

Noon coming, and the Doctor not returning, and every minute's delay tending to compromise Tellson's, Mr. Lorry advised with Lucie. She said that her father had spoken of hiring a lodging for a short term, in that Quarter, near the Banking-house. As there was no business objection to this, and as he foresaw that even if it were all well with Charles, and he were to be released, he could not hope to leave the city, Mr. Lorry went out in quest of such a lodging, and found a suitable one, high up in a removed by-street, where the closed blinds in all the other windows of a high melancholy square of buildings marked deserted homes.

To this lodging he at once removed Lucie and her child, and Miss Pross: giving them what comfort he could, and much more than he had himself. He left Jerry with them, as a figure to fill a doorway that would bear considerable knocking on the head, and returned to his own occupations. A disturbed and doleful mind he brought to bear upon them, and slowly and heavily the day lagged on with him.

It wore itself out, and wore him out with it, until the Bank closed. He was again alone in his room of the previous night, considering what to do next, when he heard a foot upon the stair. In a few moments, a man stood in his presence, who, with a keenly observant look at him, addressed him by his name.

"Your servant," said Mr. Lorry. "Do you know me?"

He was a strongly made man with dark curling hair, from forty-five to fifty years of age. For answer he repeated, without any change of emphasis, the words:

"Do you know me?"

"I have seen you somewhere."

"Perhaps at my wine-shop?"

Much interested and agitated, Mr. Lorry said: "You come from Doctor Manette?"

"Yes. I come from Doctor Manette."

"And what says he? What does he send me?"

Defarge gave into his anxious hand, an open scrap of paper. It bore the words in the Doctor's writing:

"Charles is safe, but I cannot safely leave this place yet. I have obtained the favor that the bearer has a short note from Charles to his wife. Let the bearer see his wife."

It was dated from La Force, within an hour.

"Will you accompany me," said Mr. Lorry, joyfully relieved after reading this note aloud, "to where his wife resides?"

"Yes," returned Defarge.

Scarcely noticing, as yet, in what a curiously reserved and mechanical way Defarge spoke, Mr. Lorry put on his hat and they went down into the courtyard. There, they found two women; one knitting.

"Madame Defarge, surely!" said Mr. Lorry, who had left her in exactly the same attitude some seventeen years ago.

"It is she," observed her husband.

"Does madame go with us?" inquired Mr. Lorry, seeing that she moved as they moved.

"Yes. That she may be able to recognize the faces and know the persons. It is for their safety."

Beginning to be struck by Defarge's manner, Mr. Lorry looked dubiously at him, and led the way. Both the women followed; the second woman being The Vengeance.

They passed through the intervening streets as quickly as they might, ascended the staircase of the new domicile, were admitted by Jerry, and found Lucie weeping, alone. She was thrown into a transport by the tidings Mr.

Lorry gave her of her husband, and clasped the hand that delivered his note—little thinking what it had been doing near him in the night, and might, but for a chance, have done to him.

DEAREST—Take courage. I am well, and your father has influence around me. You cannot answer this. Kiss our child for me.

That was all the writing. It was so much, however, to her who received it, that she turned from Defarge to his wife, and kissed one of the hands that knitted. It was a passionate, loving, thankful, womanly action, but the hand made no response—dropped cold and heavy, and took to its knitting again.

There was something in its touch that gave Lucie a check. She stopped in the act of putting the note in her bosom, and, with her hands yet at her neck, looked terrified at Madame Defarge. Madame Defarge met the lifted eyebrows and forehead with a cold, impassive stare.

"My dear," said Mr. Lorry, striking in to explain; "there are frequent risings in the streets; and, although it is not likely they will ever trouble you, Madame Defarge wishes to see those whom she has the power to protect at such times, to the end that she may know them—that she may identify them. I believe," said Mr. Lorry, rather halting in his reassuring words, as the stony manner of all the three impressed itself upon him more and more, "I state the case, Citizen Defarge?"

Defarge looked gloomily at his wife, and gave no other answer than a gruff sound of acquiescence.

"You had better, Lucie," said Mr. Lorry, doing all he could to propitiate, by tone and manner, "have the dear child here, and our good Pross. Our good Pross, Defarge, is an English lady and knows no French."

The lady in question, whose rooted conviction that she was more than a match for any foreigner, was not to be shaken by distress and danger, appeared with folded arms, and observed in English to The Vengeance whom her eyes first encountered, "Well, I am sure, Boldface! I hope *you* are pretty well!" She also bestowed a British cough on Madame Defarge; but, neither of the two took much heed of her.

"Is that his child?" said Madame Defarge, stopping in her work for the first time, and pointing her knitting-needle at little Lucie as if it were the finger of Fate.

"Yes, madame," answered Mr. Lorry; "this is our poor prisoner's darling daughter, and only child."

The shadow attendant on Madame Defarge and her party seemed to fall so threatening and dark on the child, that her mother instinctively kneeled on the ground beside her, and held her to her breast. The shadow attendant on Madame Defarge and her party seemed then to fall, threatening and dark, on both the mother and the child.

"It is enough, my husband," said Madame Defarge. "I have seen them. We may go."

But, the suppressed manner had enough of menace in it—not visible and presented, but indistinct and withheld—to alarm Lucie into saying, as she laid her appealing hand on Madame Defarge's dress:

"You will be good to my poor husband. You will do him no harm. You will help me to see him if you can?"

"Your husband is not my business here," returned Madame Defarge, looking down at her with perfect composure. "It is the daughter of your father who is my business here."

"For my sake, then, be merciful to my husband. For my child's sake! She will put her hands together and pray you to be merciful. We are more afraid of you than of these others."

Madame Defarge received it as a compliment, and looked at her husband. Defarge, who had been uneasily biting his thumbnail and looking at her, collected his face into a sterner expression.

"What is it that your husband says in that little letter?" asked Madame Defarge, with a lowering smile. "Influence; he says something touching influence?"

"That my father," said Lucie, hurriedly taking the paper from her breast, but with her alarmed eyes on her questioner, and not on it, "has much influence around him."

"Surely it will release him!" said Madame Defarge. "Let it do so."

"As a wife and mother," cried Lucie, most earnestly, "I implore you to have pity on me, and not to exercise any power that you possess, against my innocent husband, but to use it in his behalf. Oh sister woman, think of me! As a wife and mother!"

Madame Defarge looked coldly as ever at the suppliant, and said, turning to her friend, The Vengeance:

"The wives and mothers we have been used to see, since we were as little as this child, and much less, have not been geatly considered? We have known *their* husbands and fathers laid in prison and kept from them, often enough? All our lives, we have seen our sister women suffer, in themselves and in their children, poverty, nakedness, hunger, thirst, sickness, misery, oppression and neglect of all kinds?"

"We have seen nothing else," returned The Vengeance.

"We have borne this a long time," said Madame Defarge, turning her eyes again upon Lucie. "Judge you! Is it likely that the trouble of one wife and mother would be much to us now?"

She resumed her knitting and went out. The Vengeance followed. Defarge went last, and closed the door.

"Courage, my dear Lucie," said Mr. Lorry, as he raised her. "Courage, courage! So far all goes well with us—much, much better than it has of late gone with many poor souls. Cheer up, and have a thankful heart."

"I am not thankless, I hope, but that dreadful woman seems to throw a shadow on me and on all my hopes."

"Tut, tut!" said Mr. Lorry; "what is this despondency in the brave little breast? A shadow, indeed! No substance in it, Lucie."

But the shadow of the manner of these Defarges was dark upon himself, for all that, and in his secret mind it troubled him greatly.

F o u r

CALM IN A STORM

DOCTOR MANETTE DID NOT RETURN UNTIL THE MORNING of the fourth day of his absence. So much of what had happened in that dreadful time as could be kept from the knowledge of Lucie, was so well concealed from her, that not until long afterward, when France and she were far apart, did she know that eleven hundred defenseless prisoners of both sexes and all ages, had been killed by the populace; that four days and nights had been darkened by this deed of horror; and that the air around her had been tainted by the slain. She only knew that there had been an attack upon the prisons, that all political prisoners had been in danger, and that some had been dragged out by the crowd and murdered.

To Mr. Lorry, the Doctor communicated under an injunction of secrecy on which he had no need to dwell, that the crowd had taken him through a scene of carnage to the prison of La Force. That, in the prison he had found a self-appointed Tribunal sitting, before which the prisoners were brought singly, and by which they were rapidly ordered to be put forth to be massacred, or to be released, or (in a few cases) to be sent back to their cells. That, presented by his conductors to this Tribunal, he had announced himself by name and profession as having been for eighteen years a secret and unaccused prisoner in the Bastille; that one of the body so sitting in judgment had risen and identified him, and that this man was Defarge.

That, hereupon he had ascertained, through the registers on the table, that his son-in-law was among the living prisoners, and had pleaded hard to the tribunal—of whom some members were asleep and some awake, some dirty with murder and some clean, some sober and some not—for his life and liberty. That, in the first frantic greetings lavished on himself as a notable sufferer under the overthrown system, it had been accorded to him to have Charles Darnay brought before the lawless Court, and examined. That he seemed on the point of being at once released, when the tide in his favor met with some unexplained check (not intelligible to the Doctor), which led to a few words of secret conference. That, the man sitting as President had then informed Doctor Manette that the prisoner must remain in custody, but should, for his sake, be held inviolate in safe custody. That, immediately, on a signal, the prisoner was removed to the interior of the prison again; but that he, the Doctor, had then so strongly pleaded for permission to remain and assure himself that his son-in-law was, through no malice or mischance, delivered to the concourse whose murderous yells outside the gate had often drowned the proceedings; that he had obtained the permission, and had remained in that Hall of Blood until the danger was over.

The sights he had seen there, with brief snatches of food and sleep by intervals, shall remain untold. The mad joy over the prisoners who were saved, had astounded him scarcely less than the mad ferocity against those who were cut to pieces. One prisoner there was, he said, who had been discharged into the street free, but at whom a mistaken savage had thrust a pike as he passed out. Being besought to go to him and dress the wound, the Doctor had passed out at the same gate, and had found him in the arms of a company of Samaritans, who were seated on the bodies of their victims. With an inconsistency as monstrous as anything in this awful nightmare, they had helped the healer, and tended the wounded man with the gentlest solicitude—had made a litter for him and escorted him carefully from the spot— had then caught up their weapons and plunged anew into a butchery so dreadful, that the Doctor had covered his eyes with his hands, and swooned away in the midst of it.

As Mr. Lorry received these confidences, and as he watched the face of his friend now sixty-two years of age, a misgiving arose within him that such dread experiences would revive the old danger. But, he had never seen his friend in his present aspect; he had never at all known him in his present character. For the first time the Doctor felt, now, that his suffering was strength and power. For the first time, he felt that in that sharp fire, he had slowly forged the iron which could break the prison door of his daughter's husband, and deliver him. "It all tended to a good end, my friend; it was not mere waste and ruin. As my beloved child was helpful in restoring me to myself, I will be helpful now in restoring the dearest part of herself to her; by the aid of heaven I will do it!" Thus, Doctor Manette. And when Jarvis Lorry saw the kindled eyes, the resolute face, the calm strong look and bearing of the man whose life always seemed to him to have been stopped, like a clock, for so many years, and then set going again with an energy which had lain dormant during the cessation of its usefulness, he believed greater things than the Doctor had at that time to contend with, would have yielded before his persevering purpose.

While he kept himself in his place, as a physician whose business was with all degrees of mankind, bond and free, rich and poor, bad and good, he used his personal influence so wisely, that he was soon the inspecting physician of three prisons, and among them of La Force. He could now assure Lucie that her husband was no longer confined alone, but was mixed with the general body of prisoners; he saw her husband weekly, and brought sweet messages to her, straight from his lips; sometimes her husband himself sent a letter to her, (though never by the Doctor's hand), but she was not permitted to write to him: for, among the many wild suspicions of plots in the prisons, the wildest of all pointed at emigrants who were known to have made friends or permanent connections abroad.

This new life of the Doctor's was an anxious life, no doubt; still, the sagacious Mr. Lorry saw that there was a new sustaining pride in it. Nothing unbecoming tinged the pride; it was a natural and worthy one; but he observed it as a curiosity. The Doctor knew, that up to that time, his imprisonment had been associated in the minds of his daughter and his friend, with his personal affliction, deprivation, and weakness. Now that this was changed, and he knew himself to be invested through that old trial, with forces to which they both looked for Charles's ultimate safety and deliverance, he became so far exalted by the change, that he took the lead and direction, and required them as the weak, to trust to him as the strong. The preceding relative positions of himself and Lucie were reversed, yet only as the liveliest gratitude and affection could reverse them, for he could have had no pride but in rendering some service to her who had rendered so much to him. "All curious to see," thought Mr. Lorry, in his amiably shrewd way, "but all natural and right; so, take the lead, my dear friend, and keep it; it couldn't be in better hands."

But, though the Doctor tried hard, and never ceased trying to get Charles Darnay set at liberty, or at least to get him brought to trial, the public current of the time set too strong and fast for him. The new Era began; the king was tried, doomed, and beheaded; the Republic of Liberty, Equality, Fraternity, or Death, declared for victory or death against the world in arms; the black flag waved night and day from the great towers of Notre Dame; three hundred thousand men, summoned to rise against the tyrants of the earth, rose from all the varying soils of France, as if the dragon's teeth had been sown broadcast, and had yielded fruit equally on hill and plain, on rock, in gravel, and alluvial mud, under the bright sky of the South, and under the clouds of the North, in fell and forest, in the vineyards and the olive-grounds, and among the cropped grass and the stubble of the corn, along the fruitful banks of the broad rivers, and in the sand of the seashore. What private solicitude could rear itself against the deluge of the Year One of Liberty—the deluge rising from below, not falling from above, and with the windows of Heaven shut, not opened!

There was no pause, no pity, no peace, no interval of relenting rest, no measurement of time. Though days and nights circled as regularly as when time was young, and the evening and morning were the first day, other count of time there was none. Hold of it was lost in the raging fever of a nation, as it is in the fever of one patient. Now, breaking the unnatural silence of a whole city, the executioner showed the people the head of the king—and now, it seemed almost in the same breath, the head of his fair wife, which had had eight weary months of imprisoned widowhood and misery, to turn it gray.

And yet, observing the strange law of contradiction which obtains in all such cases, the time was long, while it flamed by so fast. A revolutionary tribunal in the capital, and forty or fifty thousand revolutionary committees all over the land; a law of the Suspected, which struck away all security for liberty or life, and delivered over any good and innocent person to any bad and guilty one; prisons gorged with people who had committed no offense, and could obtain no hearing; these things became the established order and nature of appointed things, and seemed to be ancient usage before they were many weeks old. Above all, one hideous figure grew as familiar as if it had been before the general gaze from the foundations of the world—the figure of the sharp female called La Guillotine.

It was the popular theme for jests; it was the best cure for headache; it infallibly prevented the hair from turning gray; it imparted a peculiar delicacy to the complexion; it was the National Razor which shaved close: who kissed La Guillotine, looked through the little window and sneezed into the sack. It was the sign of the regeneration of the human race. It superseded the Cross. Models of it were worn on breasts from which the Cross was discarded, and it was bowed down to and believed in where the Cross was denied.

It sheared off heads so many, that it, and the ground it most polluted, were a rotten red. It was taken to pieces, like a toy puzzle for a young Devil, and was put together again when the occasion wanted it. It hushed the eloquent, struck down the powerful, abolished the beautiful and good. Twenty-two friends of high public mark, twenty-one living and one dead, it had lopped the heads off, in one morning, in as many minutes. The name of the strong man of Old Scripture had descended to the chief functionary who worked it; but, so armed, he was stronger than his namesake, and blinder, and tore away the gates of God's own Temple every day.

Among these terrors, and the brood belonging to them, the Doctor walked with a steady head; confident in his power, cautiously persistent in his end, never doubting that he would save Lucie's husband at last. Yet the current of the time swept by, so strong and deep, and carried the time away so fiercely, that Charles had lain in prison one year and three months when the Doctor was thus steady and confident. So much more wicked and distracted had the Revolution grown in that December month, that the rivers of the South were encumbered with the bodies of the violently drowned by night, and prisoners were shot in lines and squares under the southern wintry sun. Still, the Doctor walked among the terrors with a steady hand. No man better known than he in Paris at that day; no man in a stranger situation. Silent, humane, indispensable in hospital and prison, using his art equally among assassins and victims, he was a man apart. In the exercise of his skill, the appearance and the story of the Bastille Captive removed him from all other men. He was not suspected or brought in question, any more than if he had indeed been recalled to life some eighteen years before, or were a Spirit moving among mortals.

Five

THE WOOD-SAWYER

O NE YEAR AND THREE MONTHS. DURING ALL THAT TIME Lucie was never sure, from hour to hour, but that the Guillotine would strike off her husband's head next day. Every day, through the stony streets, the tumbrils now jolted heavily, filled with Condemned. Lovely girls; bright women, brown-haired, black-haired, and gray; youths; stalwart men and old; gentle born and peasant born; all red wine for La Guillotine, all daily brought into light from the dark cellars of the loathsome prisons, and carried to her through the streets to slake her devouring thirst. Liberty, equality, fraternity, or death; the last much the easiest to bestow, O Guillotine!

If the suddenness of her calamity, and the whirling wheels of the time, had stunned the Doctor's daughter into awaiting the result in idle despair, it would but have been with her as it was with many. But, from the hour when she had taken the white head to her fresh young bosom in the garret of Saint Antoine, she had been true to her duties. She was truest to them in the season of trial, as all the quietly loyal and good will always be.

As soon as they were established in their new residence, and her father had entered on the routine of his avocations, she arranged the little household as exactly as if her husband had been there. Everything had its appointed place and its appointed time. Little Lucie she taught as regularly as if they had all been united in their English home. The slight devices with which she cheated herself in the show of a belief that they would soon be reunited—the little preparations for his speedy return, the setting aside of his chair and his books—these, and the solemn prayer at night for one dear prisoner especially, among the many unhappy souls in prison, and the shadow of death—were almost the only outspoken reliefs of her heavy mind.

She did not greatly alter in appearance. The plain dark dresses, akin to mourning dresses, which she and her child wore, were as neat and as well attended to as the brighter clothes of happy days. She lost her color, and the old and intent expression was a constant, not an occasional, thing: otherwise, she remained very pretty and comely. Sometimes, at night on kissing her father, she would burst into the grief she had repressed all day, and would say that her sole reliance, under Heaven, was on him. He always resolutely answered:—"Nothing can happen to him without my knowledge, and I know that I can save him, Lucie."

They had not made the round of their changed life many weeks, when her father said to her, on coming home one evening:—

"My dear, there is an upper window in the prison, to which Charles can sometimes gain access at three in the afternoon. When he can get to it— which depends on many uncertainties and incidents—he might see you in the street, he thinks, if you stood in a certain place that I can show you. But you will not be able to see him, my poor child, and even if you could, it would be unsafe for you to make a sign of recognition."

"O show me the place, my father, and I will go there every day."

From that time, in all weathers, she waited there two hours. As the clock struck two, she was there, and at four she turned resignedly away. When it was not too wet or inclement for her child to be with her, they went together; at other times she was alone; but she never missed a single day.

It was the dark and dirty corner of a small winding street. The hovel of a cutter of wood into lengths for burning, was the only house at that end; all else was wall. On the third day of her being there, he noticed her.

"Good day, citizeness."

"Good day, citizen."

This mode of address was now prescribed by decree. It had been established voluntarily some time ago, among the more thorough patriots; but, was now law for everybody.

"Walking here again, citizeness?"

"You see me, citizen!"

The wood-sawyer, who was a little man with a redundancy of gesture, (he had once been a mender of roads), cast a glance at the prison, pointed at the prison, and putting his ten fingers before his face to represent bars, peeped through them jocosely.

"But it's not my business," said he. And went on sawing his wood.

Next day, he was looking out for her, and accosted her the moment she appeared.

"What? Walking here again, citizeness?"

"Yes, citizen."

"Ah! A child too! Your mother, is it not, my little citizeness?"

"Do I say yes, mamma?" whispered little Lucie, drawing close to her.

"Yes, dearest."

"Yes, citizen."

"Ah! But it's not my business. My work is my business. See my saw! I call it my Little Guillotine. La, la, la! La, la, la! And off his head comes!"

The billet fell as he spoke, and he threw it into a basket.

"I call myself the Samson of the firewood guillotine. See here again! Loo, loo, loo! Loo, loo, loo! And off *her* head comes! Now, a child. Tickle, tickle; Pickle, pickle! And off *its* head comes! All the family!"

Lucie shuddered as he threw two more billets into his basket, but it was impossible to be there while the wood-sawyer was at work, and not be in his sight. Thenceforth, to secure his goodwill, she always spoke to him first, and often gave him drink-money, which he readily received.

He was an inquisitive fellow, and sometimes when she had quite forgotten him in gazing at the prison roof and grates, and in lifting her heart up to her husband, she would come to herself to find him looking at her, with his knee on his bench and his saw stopped in its work. "But it's not my business!" he would generally say at those times, and briskly fall to his sawing again.

In all weathers, in the snow and frost of winter, in the bitter winds of spring, in the hot sunshine of summer, in the rain of autumn, again in the snow and frost of winter, Lucie passed two hours of every day at this place; and every day, on leaving it, she kissed the prison wall. Her husband saw her, (so she learned from her father), it might be once in five or six times; it might be twice or thrice running: it might be, not for a week or a fortnight together. It was enough that he could and did see her when the chances served, and on that possibility she would have waited out the day, seven days a week.

These occupations brought her round to the December month, wherein her father walked among the terrors with a steady head. On a lightly snowing afternoon she arrived at the usual corner. It was a day of some wild rejoicing, and a festival. She had seen the houses, as she came along, decorated with little pikes, and with little red caps stuck upon them; also, with tricolored ribbons; also, with the standard inscription, (tricolored letters were the favorite), Republic One and Indivisible. Liberty, Equality, Fraternity, or Death!

The miserable shop of the wood-sawyer was so small, that its whole surface furnished very indifferent space for this legend. He had got somebody to scrawl it up for him, however, who had squeezed Death in with most inappropriate difficulty. On his housetop, he displayed pike and cap, as a good citizen must, and in a window he had stationed his saw, inscribed as his "Little Saint Guillotine"—for the great sharp female was by that time popularly canonized. His shop was shut and he was not there, which was a relief to Lucie, and left her quite alone.

But, he was not far off, for presently she heard a troubled movement and a shouting coming along, which filled her with fear. A moment afterward, and a throng of people came pouring round the corner by the prison wall, in the midst of whom was the wood-sawyer, hand in hand with The Vengeance. There could not be fewer than five hundred people, and they were dancing like five thousand demons. There was no other music than their own singing. They danced to the popular Revolution song, keeping a ferocious time that was like a gnashing of teeth in unison. Men and women danced together, women danced together, men danced together, as hazard had brought them together. At first, they were a mere storm of coarse red caps and coarse woollen rags; but, as they filled the place, and stopped to dance about Lucie, some ghastly apparition of a dance-figure gone raving mad arose among them. They advanced, retreated, struck at one another's hands, clutched at one another's heads, spun round alone, caught one another and spun round in pairs, until many of them dropped. While those were down, the rest linked hand in hand, and all spun round together; then the ring broke, and in separate rings of two and four they turned and turned until they all stopped at once, began again, struck, clutched, and tore, and then reversed the spin, and all spun round another way. Suddenly they stopped again, paused, struck out the time afresh, formed into lines the width of the public way, and, with their heads low down and their hands high up, swooped screaming off. No fight could have been half so terrible as this dance. It was so emphatically a fallen sport—a some-thing once innocent delivered over to all devilry—a healthy pastime changed into a means of angering the blood, bewildering the senses, and steeling the heart. Such grace as was visible in it, made it the uglier, showing how warped and perverted all things good by nature were become. The maidenly bosom bared to this, the pretty almost-child's head thus distracted, the delicate foot mincing in this slough of blood and dirt, were types of the disjointed time.

This was the Carmagnole. As it passed, leaving Lucie frightened and bewildered in the doorway of the wood-sawyer's house, the feathery snow fell as quietly and lay as white and soft, as if it had never been.

"O my father!" for he stood before her when she lifted up the eyes she had momentarily darkened with her hand; "such a cruel, bad sight!"

"I know, my dear, I know. I have seen it many times. Don't be frightened! Not one of them would harm you."

"I am not frightened for myself, my father. But when I think of my hus-band, and the mercies of these people—"

"We will set him above their mercies very soon. I left him climbing to the window, and I came to tell you. There is no one here to see. You may kiss your hand toward that highest shelving roof."

"I do so, Father, and I send my soul with it."

"You cannot see him, my poor dear?"

"No, father," said Lucie, yearning and weeping as she kissed her hand, "no."

A footstep in the snow. Madame Defarge. "I salute you, citizeness," from the Doctor. "I salute you, citizen." This in passing. Nothing more. Madame Defarge gone, like a shadow over the white road.

"Give me your arm, my love. Pass from here with an air of cheerfulness and courage, for his sake. That was well done"; they had left the spot; "it shall not be in vain. Charles is summoned for tomorrow."

"For tomorrow!"

"There is no time to lose. I am well prepared, but there are precautions to be taken, that could not be taken until he was actually summoned before the Tribunal. He has not received the notice yet, but I know that he will presently be summoned for tomorrow, and removed to the Conciergerie; I have timely information. You are not afraid?"

She could scarcely answer, "I trust in you."

"Do so, implicitly. Your suspense is nearly ended, my darling; he shall be restored to you within a few hours; I have encompassed him with every protection. I must see Lorry."

He stopped. There was a heavy lumbering of wheels within hearing. They both knew too well what it meant. One. Two. Three. Three tumbrils faring away with their dread loads over the hushing snow.

"I must see Lorry," the Doctor repeated, turning her another way.

The stanch old gentleman was still in his trust: had never left it. He and his books were in frequent requisition as to property confiscated and made national. What he could save for the owners, he saved. No better man living to hold fast by what Tellson's had in keeping, and to hold his peace.

A murky red and yellow sky, and a rising mist from the Seine, denoted the approach of darkness. It was almost dark when they arrived at the Bank. The stately residence of Monseigneur was altogether blighted and deserted. Above a heap of dust and ashes in the court, ran the letters: National Property. Republic One and Indivisible. Liberty, Equality, Fraternity, or Death.

Who could that be with Mr. Lorry—the owner of the riding-coat upon the chair—who must not be seen? From whom newly arrived, did he come out, agitated and surprised, to take his favorite in his arms? To whom did he appear to repeat her faltering words, when, raising his voice and turning his head toward the door of the room from which he had issued, he said: "Removed to the Conciergerie, and summoned for tomorrow?"

S i x

TRIUMPH

THE DREAD TRIBUNAL OF FIVE JUDGES, PUBLIC PROSECUtor, and determined Jury, sat every day. Their lists went forth every evening, and were read out by the gaolers of the various prisons to their prisoners. The standard gaoler-joke was, "Come out and listen to the Evening Paper, you inside there!"

"Charles Evrémonde, called Darnay!"

So, at last began, the Evening Paper at La Force.

When a name was called, its owner stepped apart into a spot reserved for those who were announced as being thus fatally recorded. Charles Evrémonde, called Darnay, had reason to know the usage; he had seen hundreds pass away so.

His bloated gaoler, who wore spectacles to read with, glanced over them to assure himself that he had taken his place, and went through the list, making a similar short pause at each name. There were twenty-three names, but only twenty were responded to; for one of the prisoners so summoned had died in gaol and been forgotten, and two had already been guillotined and forgotten. The list was read, in the vaulted chamber where Darnay had seen the associated prisoners on the night of his arrival. Every one of those had perished in the massacre; every human creature he had since cared for and parted with, had died on the scaffold.

There were hurried words of farewell and kindness, but the parting was soon over. It was the incident of every day, and the society of La Force were engaged in the preparation of some games of forfeits and a little concert, for that evening. They crowded to the grates and shed tears there; but, twenty places in the projected entertainments had to be refilled, and the time was, at best, short to the lock-up hour, when the common rooms and corridors would be delivered over to the great dogs who kept watch there through the night. The prisoners were far from insensible or unfeeling; their ways arose out of a condition of the time. Similarly, though with a subtle difference, a species of fervor or intoxication, known, without doubt, to have led some persons to brave the guillotine unnecessarily, and to die by it, was not mere boastfulness, but a wild infection of the wildly shaken public mind. In seasons of pestilence, some of us will have a secret attraction to the disease—a terrible passing inclination to die of it. And all of us have like wonders hidden in our breasts, only needing circumstances to evoke them.

The passage to the Conciergerie was short and dark; the night in its vermin-haunted cells was long and cold. Next day, fifteen prisoners were put to the bar before Charles Darnay's name was called. All the fifteen were condemned, and the trials of the whole occupied an hour and a half.

"Charles Evrémonde, called Darnay," was at length arraigned.

His Judges sat upon the bench in feathered hats; but the rough red cap and tricolored cockade was the head-dress otherwise prevailing. Looking at the Jury and the turbulent audience he might have thought that the usual order of things was reversed, and that the felons were trying the honest men. The lowest, cruelest, and worst populace of a city, never without its quantity of low, cruel, and bad, were the directing spirits of the scene: noisily commenting, applauding, disapproving, anticipating, and precipitating the result, without a check. Of the men, the greater part were armed in various ways; of the women, some wore knives, some daggers, some ate and drank as they looked on, many knitted. Among these last, was one, with a spare piece of knitting under her arm as she worked. She was in a front row, by the side of a man whom he had never seen since his arrival at the Barrier, but whom he directly remembered as Defarge. He noticed that she once or twice whispered in his ear, and that she seemed to be his wife; but, what he most noticed in the two figures was, that although they were posted as close to himself as they could be, they never looked toward him. They seemed to be waiting for something with a dogged determination, and they looked at the Jury, but at nothing else. Under the President sat Doctor Manette, in his usual quiet dress. As well as the prisoner could see, he and Mr. Lorry were the only men there, unconnected with the Tribunal, who wore their usual clothes, and had not assumed the coarse garb of the Carmagnole.

Charles Evrémonde, called Darnay, was accused by the public prosecutor as an emigrant, whose life was forfeit to the Republic, under the decree which banished all emigrants on pain of Death. It was nothing that the decree bore date since his return to France. There he was, and there was the decree; he had been taken in France, and his head was demanded.

"Take off his head!" cried the audience. "An enemy to the Republic!"

The President rang his bell to silence those cries, and asked the prisoner whether it was not true that he had lived many years in England?

Undoubtedly it was.

Was he not an emigrant then? What did he call himself?

Not an emigrant, he hoped, within the sense and spirit of the law.

"Why not?" the President desired to know.

Because he had voluntarily relinquished a title that was distasteful to him, and a station that was distasteful to him, and had left his country—he submitted before the word emigrant in the present acceptation by the Tribunal was in use—to live by his own industry in England, rather than on the industry of the overladen people of France.

What proof had he of this?

He handed in the names of two witnesses: Theophile Gabelle, and Alexandre Manette.

But he had married in England? the President reminded him.

True, but not an English woman.

A citizeness of France?

Yes. By birth.

Her name and family?

"Lucie Manette, only daughter of Doctor Manette, the good physician who sits there."

This answer had a happy effect upon the audience. Cries in exaltation of the well-known good physician rent the hall. So capriciously were the people moved, that tears immediately rolled down several ferocious countenances which had been glaring at the prisoner a moment before, as if with impatience to pluck him out into the streets and kill him.

On these few steps of his dangerous way, Charles Darnay had set his foot according to Doctor Manette's reiterated instructions. The same cautious counsel directed every step that lay before him, and had prepared every inch of his road.

The President asked why had he returned to France when he did, and not sooner?

He had not returned sooner, he replied, simply because he had no means of living in France, save those he had resigned; whereas, in England, he lived by giving instruction in the French language and literature. He had returned when he did, on the pressing and written entreaty of a French citizen, who represented that his life was endangered by his absence. He had come back, to save a citizen's life, and to bear his testimony, at whatever personal hazard, to the truth. Was that criminal in the eyes of the Republic?

The populace cried enthusiastically, "No!" and the President rang his bell to quiet them. Which it did not, for they continued to cry "No!" until they left off, of their own will.

The President required the name of that citizen? The accused explained that the citizen was his first witness. He also referred with confidence to the citizen's letter, which had been taken from him at the Barrier, but which he did not doubt would be found among the papers then before the President.

The Doctor had taken care that it should be there—had assured him that it would be there—and at this stage of the proceedings it was produced and read. Citizen Gabelle was called to confirm it, and did so. Citizen Gabelle hinted, with infinite delicacy and politeness, that in the pressure of business imposed on the Tribunal by the multitudes of enemies of the Republic with which it had to deal, he had been slightly overlooked in his prison of the Abbaye—in fact, had rather passed out of the Tribunal's patriotic remembrance—until three days ago; when he had been summoned before it, and had been set at liberty on the jury's declaring themselves satisfied that the accusation against him was answered, as to himself, by the surrender of the citizen Evrémonde, called Darnay.

Doctor Manette was next questioned. His high personal popularity, and the clearness of his answers, made a great impression; but, as he proceeded as he showed that the accused was his first friend on his release from his long imprisonment; that the accused had remained in England, always faithful and devoted to his daughter and himself in their exile; that, so far from being in favor with the aristocrat government there, he had actually been tried for his life by it, as the foe of England and friend of the United States—as he brought these circumstances into view, with the greatest discretion and with the straightforward force of truth and earnestness, the Jury and the populace became one. At last, when he appealed by name to Monsieur Lorry, an English gentleman then and there present, who, like himself, had been a witness on that English trial and could corroborate his account of it, the Jury declared that they had heard enough, and that they were ready with their votes if the President were content to receive them.

At every vote (the jurymen voted aloud and individually), the populace set up a shout of applause. All the voices were in the prisoner's favor, and the President declared him free.

Then, began one of those extraordinary scenes with which the populace sometimes gratified their fickleness, or their better impulses toward generosity and mercy, or which they regarded as some set-off against their swollen account of cruel rage. No man can decide now to which of these motives such extraordinary scenes were referable; it is probable, to a blending of all the three, with the second predominating. No sooner was the acquittal pronounced, than tears were shed as freely as blood at another time, and such fraternal embraces were bestowed upon the prisoner by as many of both sexes as could rush at him, that after his long and unwholesome confinement he was in danger of fainting from exhaustion; none the less he knew very well, that the very same people, carried by another current, would have rushed at him with the very same intensity, to rend him to pieces and strew him over the streets.

His removal, to make way for other accused persons who were to be tried, rescued him from these caresses for the moment. Five were to be tried together, next, as enemies of the Republic, forasmuch as they had not assisted it by word or deed. So quick was the Tribunal to compensate itself and the nation for a chance lost, that these five came down to him before he left the place, condemned to die within twenty-four hours. The first of them told him so, with the customary prison sign of Death—a raised finger—and they all added in words, "Long live the Republic!"

The five had had, it is true, no audience to lengthen their proceedings, for when he and Doctor Manette emerged from the gate, there was a great crowd about it, in which there seemed to be every face he had seen in Court—except two, for which he looked in vain. On his coming out, the concourse made at him anew, weeping, embracing, and shouting, all by turns and all together, until the very tide of the river on the bank of which the mad scene was acted, seemed to run mad, like the people on the shore.

They put him into a great chair they had among them, and which they had taken either out of the court itself, or one of its rooms or passages. Over the chair they had thrown a red flag, and to the back of it they had bound a pike with a red cap on its top. In this car of triumph, not even the Doctor's entreaties could prevent his being carried to his home on men's shoulders, with a confused sea of red caps heaving about him, and casting up to sight from the stormy deep such wrecks of faces, that he more than once misdoubted his mind being in confusion, and that he was in the tumbril on his way to the Guillotine.

In wild, dreamlike procession, embracing whom they met, and pointing him out, they carried him on. Reddening the snowy streets with the prevailing Republican color, in winding and tramping through them, as they had reddened them below the snow with a deeper dye, they carried him thus into the courtyard of the building where he lived. Her father had gone on before, to prepare her, and when her husband stood upon his feet, she dropped insensible in his arms.

As he held her to his heart and turned her beautiful head between his face and the brawling crowd, so that his tears and her lips might come together unseen, a few of the people fell to dancing. Instantly, all the rest fell to dancing, and the courtyard overflowed with the Carmagnole. Then, they elevated into the vacant chair a young woman from the crowd to be carried as the Goddess of Liberty, and then swelling and overflowing out into the adjacent streets, and along the river's bank, and over the bridge, the Carmagnole absorbed them every one and whirled them away.

After grasping the Doctor's hand, as he stood victorious and proud before him; after grasping the hand of Mr. Lorry, who came panting in breathless from his struggle against the waterspout of the Carmagnole; after kissing little Lucie, who was lifted up to clasp her arms round his neck; and after embracing the ever zealous and faithful Pross who lifted her, he took his wife in his arms and carried her up to their rooms.

"Lucie! My own! I am safe."

"O dearest Charles! let me thank God for this on my knees as I have prayed to Him."

They all reverently bowed their heads and hearts. When she was again in his arms, he said to her:

"And now speak to your father, dearest. No other man in all this France could have done what he has done for me."

She laid her head upon her father's breast as she had lain his poor head on her own breast, long, long ago. He was happy in the return he had made her, he was recompensed for his suffering, he was proud of his strength. "You must not be weak, my darling," he remonstrated; "don't tremble so. I have saved him."

S e v e n

A KNOCK AT THE DOOR

"I HAVE SAVED HIM." IT WAS NOT ANOTHER OF THE DREAMS in which he had often come back; he was really here. And yet his wife trembled, and a vague but heavy fear was upon her.

All the air around was so thick and dark, the people were so passionately revengeful and fitful, the innocent were so constantly put to death on vague suspicion and black malice, it was so impossible to forget that many as blameless as her husband, and as dear to others as he was to her, every day shared the fate from which he had been clutched, that her heart could not be as lightened of its load as she felt it ought to be. The shadows of the wintry afternoon were beginning to fall, and even now the dreadful carts were rolling through the streets. Her mind pursued them, looking for him among the Condemned; and then she clung to his real presence, and trembled more.

Her father, cheering her, showed a compassionate superiority to this woman's weakness, which was wonderful to see. No garret, no shoemaking, no One Hundred and Five, North Tower, now! He had accomplished the task he had set himself, his promise was redeemed, he had saved Charles. Let them all lean upon him.

Their housekeeping was of a very frugal kind; not only because that was the safest way of life, involving the least offense to the people, but because they were not rich, and Charles, throughout his imprisonment, had had to pay heavily for his bad food, and for his guard, and toward the living of the poorer prisoners. Partly on this account, and partly to avoid a domestic spy, they kept no servant; the citizen and citizeness who acted as porters at the courtyard gate rendered them occasional service; and Jerry (almost wholly transferred to them by Mr. Lorry) had become their daily retainer, and had his bed there every night.

It was an ordinance of the Republic One and Indivisible of Liberty, Equality, Fraternity, or Death, that on the door or doorpost of every house, the name of every inmate must be legibly inscribed in letters of a certain size, at a certain convenient height from the ground. Mr. Jerry Cruncher's name, therefore, duly embellished the doorpost down below; and, as the afternoon shadows deepened, the owner of that name himself appeared, from over-looking a painter whom Doctor Manette had employed to add to the list the name of Charles Evrémonde, called Darnay.

In the universal fear and distrust that darkened the time, all the usual harmless ways of life were changed. In the Doctor's little household, as in very many others, the articles of daily consumption that were wanted were purchased every evening, in small quantities, and at various small shops. To avoid attracting notice, and to give as little occasion as possible for talk and envy, was the general desire.

For some months past, Miss Pross and Mr. Cruncher had discharged the office of purveyors: the former carrying the money; the latter the basket. Every afternoon, at about the time when the public lamps were lighted, they fared forth on this duty, and made and brought home such purchases as were need-ful. Although Miss Pross, through her long association with a French family, might have known as much of their language as of her own, if she had had a mind, she had no mind in that direction; consequently she knew no more of "that nonsense," (as she was pleased to call it), than Mr. Cruncher did. So her manner of marketing was to plump a noun-substantive at the head of a shopkeeper without any introduction in the nature of an article, and, if it happened not to be the name of the thing she wanted, to look round for that thing, lay hold of it, and hold on by it until the bargain was concluded. She always made a bargain for it, by holding up, as a statement of its just price, one finger less than the merchant held up, whatever his number might be.

"Now, Mr. Cruncher," said Miss Pross, whose eyes were red with felicity; "if you are ready, I am."

Jerry hoarsely professed himself at Miss Pross's service. He had worn all his rust off long ago, but nothing would file his spiky head down.

"There's all manner of things wanted," said Miss Pross, "and we shall have a precious time of it. We want wine, among the rest. Nice toasts these Redheads will be drinking, wherever we buy it."

"It will be much the same to your knowledge, miss, I should think," retorted Jerry, "whether they drink your health or the Old Un's."

"Who's he?" said Miss Pross.

Mr. Cruncher, with some difference, explained himself as meaning "Old Nick's."

"Ha!" said Miss Pross, "it doesn't need an interpreter to explain the meaning of these creatures. They have but one, and it's Midnight Murder and Mischief!"

"Hush, dear! Pray, pray, be cautious!" cried Lucie.

"Yes, yes, yes, I'll be cautious," said Miss Pross; "but I may say among ourselves, that I do hope there will be no oniony and tobaccoey smotherings in the form of embracings going on in the streets. Now, Ladybird, never you stir from that fire till I come back! Take care of the dear husband you have recovered, and don't move your pretty head from his shoulder as you have it now, till you see me again! May I ask a question, Doctor Manette, before I go?"

"I think you may take that liberty," the Doctor answered, smiling.

"For gracious sake don't talk about liberty; we have quite enough of that," said Miss Pross.

"Hush, dear! Again?" Lucie remonstrated.

"Well, my sweet," said Miss Pross, nodding her head emphatically, "the short and the long of it is, that I am a subject of His Most Gracious Majesty King George the Third"; Miss Pross courtesied at the name; "and as such, my maxim is, Confound their politics, Frustrate their knavish tricks, On him our hopes we fix, God save the King!"

Mr. Cruncher, in an access of loyalty, growlingly repeated the words after Miss Pross, like somebody at church.

"I am glad you have so much of the Englishman in you, though I wish you had never taken that cold in your voice," said Miss Pross, approvingly. "But the question, Doctor Manette. Is there"—it was the good creature's way to affect to make light of anything that was a great anxiety with them all, and to come at it in this chance manner—"is there any prospect, yet, of our getting out of this place?"

"I fear not yet. It would be dangerous for Charles yet."

"Heigh-ho-hum!" said Miss Pross, cheerfully repressing a sigh, as she glanced at her darling's golden hair in the light of the fire, "then we must have patience and wait: that's all. We must hold up our heads and fight low, as my brother Solomon used to say. Now, Mr. Cruncher!—Don't you move, Lady-bird!"

They went out leaving Lucie, and her husband, her father and the child, by a bright fire. Mr. Lorry was expected back presently from the Banking House. Miss Pross had lighted the lamp, but had put it aside in a corner, that they might enjoy the firelight undisturbed. Little Lucie sat by her grand-father, with her hands clasped through his arm; and he, in a tone not rising much above a whisper, began to tell her a story of a great and powerful Fairy who had opened a prison wall and let out a captive who had once done the Fairy a service. All was subdued and quiet, and Lucie was more at ease than she had been.

"What is that?" she cried, all at once.

"My dear!" said her father, stopping in his story, and laying his hand on hers, "command yourself. What a disordered state you are in! The least thing—nothing—startles you. *You,* your father's daughter?"

"I thought, my father," said Lucie, excusing herself, with a pale face and in a faltering voice, "that I heard strange feet upon the stairs."

"My love, the staircase is as still as Death."

As he said the word, a blow was struck upon the door.

"O Father, Father. What can this be! Hide, Charles. Save him!"

"My child," said the Doctor, rising and laying his hand upon her shoul-der. "I have *saved* him. What weakness is this, my dear! Let me go to the door."

He took the lamp in his hand, crossed the two intervening outer rooms, and opened it. A rude clattering of feet over the floors, and four rough men in red caps, armed with sabres and pistols, entered the room.

"The Citizen Evrémonde, called Darnay," said the first.

"Who seeks him?" answered Darnay.

"I seek him. We seek him. I know you, Evrémonde; I saw you before the Tribunal today. You are again the prisoner of the Republic."

The four surrounded him, where he stood with his wife and child cling-ing to him.

"Tell me how and why am I again a prisoner?"

"It is enough that you return straight to the Conciergerie, and will know tomorrow. You are summoned for tomorrow."

Doctor Manette, whom this visitation had so turned into stone, that he stood with the lamp in his hand, as if he were a statue made to hold it, moved after these words were spoken, put the lamp down, and confronting the speaker, and taking him, not ungently, by the loose front of his red woollen shirt, said:—

"You know him, you have said. Do you know me?"

"Yes, I know you, Citizen Doctor."

"We all know you, Citizen Doctor," said the other three.

He looked abstractedly from one to another, and said, in a lower voice, after a pause:

"Will you answer his question to me? How does this happen?"

"Citizen Doctor," said the first, reluctantly, "he has been denounced to the section of Saint Antoine. This citizen," pointing out the second who had entered, "is from Saint Antoine."

The citizen here indicated nodded his head, and added:

"He is accused by Saint Antoine."

"Of what?" asked the Doctor.

"Citizen Doctor," said the first, with his former reluctance, "ask no more. If the Republic demands sacrifices from you, without doubt you, as a good patriot, will be happy to make them. The Republic goes before all. The people is supreme. Evrémonde, we are pressed."

"One word," the Doctor entreated. "Will you tell me who denounced him?"

"It is against rule," answered the first; "but you can ask Him of Saint Antoine here."

The Doctor turned his eyes upon that man, who moved uneasily on his feet, pulled his beard a little, and at length said:—

"Well! Truly it is against rule. But he is denounced—and gravely—by the Citizen and Citizeness Defarge. And by one other."

"What other?"

"Do *you* ask, Citizen Doctor?"

"Yes!"

"Then," said he of Saint Antoine, with a strange look, "you will be answered tomorrow. Now, I am dumb!"

E i g h t

A HAND AT CARDS

HAPPILY UNCONSCIOUS OF THE NEW CALAMITY AT HOME, Miss Pross threaded her way along the narrow streets and crossed the river by the bridge of the Pont-Neuf, reckoning in her mind the number of indispensable purchases she had to make. Mr. Cruncher, with the basket, walked at her side. They both looked to the right and to the left into most of the shops they passed, had a wary eye for all gregarious assemblages of people, and turned out of their road to avoid any very excited group of talkers. It was a raw evening, and the misty river, blurred to the eye with blazing lights and to the ear with harsh noises, showed where the barges were stationed in which the smiths worked, making guns for the Army of the Republic. Woe to the man who played tricks with *that* Army, or got undeserved promotion in it! Better for him that his beard had never grown, for the National Razor shaved him close.

Having purchased a few small articles of grocery, and a measure of oil for the lamp, Miss Pross bethought herself of the wine they wanted. After peeping into several wine-shops, she stopped at the sign of The Good Republican Brutus of Antiquity, not far from the National Palace, once (and twice) the Tuileries, where the aspect of things rather took her fancy. It had a quieter look than any other place of the same description they had passed, and, though red with patriotic caps, was not so red as the rest. Sounding Mr. Cruncher and finding him of her opinion, Miss Pross resorted to The Good Republican Brutus of Antiquity, attended by her cavalier.

Slightly observant of the smoky lights; of the people, pipe in mouth, playing with limp cards and yellow dominoes; of the one bare-breasted, bare-armed, soot-begrimed workman, reading a journal aloud, and of the others listening to him; of the weapons worn, or laid aside to be resumed; of the two or three customers fallen forward asleep, who in the popular, high-shouldered shaggy black spencer, looked, in that attitude, like slumbering bears or dogs; the two outlandish customers approached the counter, and showed what they wanted.

As their wine was measuring out, a man parted from another man in a corner, and rose to depart. In going, he had to face Miss Pross. No sooner did he face her, than Miss Pross uttered a scream, and clapped her hands.

In a moment the whole company were on their feet. That somebody was assassinated by somebody vindicating a difference of opinion, was the likeliest occurrence. Everybody looked to see somebody fall, but only saw a man and a woman standing staring at each other; the man with all the outward aspect of a Frenchman and a thorough Republican; the woman, evidently English.

What was said in this disappointing anticlimax, by the disciples of The Good Republican Brutus of Antiquity, except that it was something very voluble and loud, would have been as so much Hebrew or Chaldean to Miss Pross and her protector, though they had been all ears. But, they had no ears for anything in their surprise. For, it must be recorded, that not only was Miss Pross lost in amazement and agitation; but, Mr. Cruncher—though it seemed on his own separate and individual account—was in a state of the greatest wonder.

"What is the matter?" said the man who had caused Miss Pross to scream; speaking in a vexed, abrupt voice, (though in a low tone), and in English.

"Oh, Solomon, dear Solomon!" cried Miss Pross, clapping her hands again. "After not setting eyes upon you or hearing of you for so long a time, do I find you here!"

"Don't call me Solomon. Do you want to be the death of me?" asked the man, in a furtive, frightened way.

"Brother, brother!" cried Miss Pross, bursting into tears. "Have I ever been so hard with you that you ask me such a cruel question!"

"Then hold your meddlesome tongue," said Solomon, "and come out, if you want to speak to me. Pay for your wine, and come out. Who's this man?"

Miss Pross, shaking her loving and dejected head at her by no means affectionate brother, said, through her tears, "Mr. Cruncher."

"Let him come out, too," said Solomon. "Does he think me a ghost?"

Apparently, Mr. Cruncher did, to judge from his looks. He said not a word, however, and Miss Pross, exploring the depths of her reticule through her tears, with great difficulty, paid for her wine. As she did so, Solomon turned to the followers of The Good Republican Brutus of Antiquity, and offered a few words of explanation in the French language, which caused them all to relapse into their former places and pursuits.

"Now," said Solomon, stopping at the dark street corner, "what do you want?"

"How dreadfully unkind in a brother nothing has ever turned my love away from," cried Miss Pross, "to give me such a greeting, and show me no affection."

"There. Con-found it! There!" said Solomon, making a dab at Miss Pross's lips with his own. "Now are you content?"

Miss Pross only shook her head and wept in silence.

"If you expect me to be surprised," said her brother Solomon, "I am not surprised; I knew you were here; I know of most people who are here. If you really don't want to endanger my existence—which I half believe you do—go your ways as soon as possible, and let me go mine. I am busy. I am an official."

"My English brother Solomon," mourned Miss Pross, casting up her tear-fraught eyes, "that had the makings in him of one of the best and greatest of men in his native country, an official among foreigners, and such foreigners! I would almost sooner have seen the dear boy lying in his—"

"I said so!" cried her brother, interrupting. "I knew it! You want to be the death of me. I shall be rendered Suspected, by my own sister. Just as I am getting on!"

"The gracious and merciful Heavens forbid!" cried Miss Pross. "Far rather would I never see you again, dear Solomon, though I have ever loved you truly, and ever shall. Say but one affectionate word to me, and tell me there is nothing angry or estranged between us, and I will detain you no longer."

Good Miss Pross! As if the estrangement between them had come of any culpability of hers. As if Mr. Lorry had not known it for a fact, years ago, in the quiet corner in Soho, that this precious brother had spent her money and left her!

He was saying the affectionate word, however, with a far more grudging condescension and patronage than he could have shown if their relative merits and positions had been reversed (which is invariably the case, all the world over), when Mr. Cruncher, touching him on the shoulder, hoarsely and unexpectedly interposed with the following singular question:—

"I say! Might I ask the favor? As to whether your name is John Solomon, or Solomon John?"

The official turned towards him with sudden distrust. He had not previously uttered a word.

"Come!" said Mr. Cruncher. "Speak out, you know." (Which, by the way, was more than he could do himself.) "John Solomon, or Solomon John? She calls you Solomon, and she must know, being your sister. And *I* know you're John, you know. Which of the two goes first? And regarding that name of Pross, likewise? That warn't your name over the water."

"What do you mean?"

"Well, I don't know all I mean, for I can't call to mind what your name was over the water."

"No?" sneered Solomon.

"No. But I'll swear it was a name of two syllables."

"Indeed!"

"Yes. T'other one's was one syllable. I know you. You was a spy-witness at the Bailey. What in the name of the Father of Lies—own father to yourself—was you called at that time?"

"Barsad," said another voice, striking in.

"That's the name for a thousand pound!" cried Jerry.

The speaker who struck in was Sydney Carton. He had his hands behind him, under the skirts of his riding-coat, and he stood at Mr. Cruncher's elbow as negligently as he might have stood at the Old Bailey itself.

"Don't be alarmed, my dear Miss Pross. I arrived at Mr. Lorry's, to his surprise, yesterday evening; we agreed that I would not present myself elsewhere until all was well, or unless I could be useful; I present myself here, to beg a little talk with your brother. I wish you had a better employed brother than Mr. Barsad. I wish for your sake, Mr. Barsad was not a Sheep of the Prisons."

Sheep was a cant word of the time for a spy, under the gaolers. The spy, who was pale, turned paler, and asked him how he dared—

"I'll tell you," said Sydney. "I lighted on you, Mr. Barsad, coming out of the prison of the Conciergerie while I was contemplating the walls, an hour or more ago. You have a face to be remembered, and I remember faces well. Made curious by seeing you in that connection, and having a reason to which you are no stranger, for associating you with the misfortunes of a friend now very unfortunate, I walked in your direction. I walked into the wine-shop here, close after you, and sat near you. I had no difficulty in deducing from your unreserved conversation, and the rumor openly going about among your admirers, the nature of your calling. And gradually, what I had done at random seemed to shape itself into a purpose, Mr. Barsad."

"What purpose?" the spy asked.

"It would be troublesome, and might be dangerous, to explain in the street. Could you favor me, in confidence, with some minutes of your company—at the office of Tellson's Bank, for instance?"

"Under a threat?"

"Oh! Did I say that?"

"Then, why should I go there?"

"Really, Mr. Barsad, I can't say, if you can't."

"Do you mean that you won't say, sir?" the spy irresolutely asked.

"You apprehend me very clearly, Mr. Barsad. I won't."

Carton's negligent recklessness of manner came powerfully in aid of his quickness and skill, in such a business as he had in his secret mind, and with such a man as he had to do with. His practiced eye saw it, and made the most of it.

"Now, I told you so," said the spy, casting a reproachful look at his sister; "if any trouble comes of this, it's your doing."

"Come, come, Mr. Barsad!" exclaimed Sydney. "Don't be ungrateful. But for my great respect for your sister, I might not have led up so pleasantly to a little proposal that I wish to make for our mutual satisfaction. Do you go with me to the Bank?"

"I'll hear what you have got to say. Yes, I'll go with you."

"I propose that we first conduct your sister safely to the corner of her own street. Let me take your arm, Miss Pross. This is not a good city, at this time, for you to be out in, unprotected; and as your escort knows Mr. Barsad, I will invite him to Mr. Lorry's with us. Are we ready? Come then!"

Miss Pross recalled soon afterward, and to the end of her life remembered, that as she pressed her hands on Sydney's arm and looked up in his face, imploring him to do no hurt to Solomon, there was a braced purpose in the arm and a kind of inspiration in the eyes, which not only contradicted his light manner, but changed and raised the man. She was too much occupied then, with fears for the brother who so little deserved her affection, and with Sydney's friendly reassurances, adequately to heed what she observed.

They left her at the corner of the street, and Carton led the way to Mr. Lorry's, which was within a few minutes' walk. John Barsad, or Solomon Pross, walked at his side.

Mr. Lorry had just finished his dinner, and was sitting before a cheery little log or two of fire—perhaps looking into their blaze for the picture of that younger elderly gentleman from Tellson's, who had looked into the red coals at the Royal George at Dover, now a good many years ago. He turned his head as they entered, and showed the surprise with which he saw a stranger.

"Miss Pross's brother, sir," said Sydney. "Mr. Barsad."

"Barsad?" repeated the old gentleman, "Barsad! I have an association with the name—and with the face."

"I told you, you had a remarkable face, Mr. Barsad," observed Carton, coolly. "Pray sit down."

As he took a chair himself, he supplied the link that Mr. Lorry wanted, by saying to him with a frown, "Witness at that trial." Mr. Lorry immediately remembered, and regarded his new visitor with an undisguised look of abhorrence.

"Mr. Barsad has been recognized by Miss Pross as the affectionate brother you have heard of," said Sydney, "and has acknowledged the relationship. I pass to worse news. Darnay has been arrested again."

Struck with consternation, the old gentleman exclaimed: "What do you tell me! I left him safe and free within these two hours, and am about to return to him!"

"Arrested for all that. When was it done, Mr. Barsad?"

"Just now, if at all."

"Mr. Barsad is the best authority possible, sir," said Sydney; "and I have it from Mr. Barsad's communication to a friend and brother sheep over a bottle of wine, that the arrest has taken place. He left the messengers at the gate, and saw them admitted by the porter. There is no earthly doubt that he is retaken."

Mr. Lorry's business eye read in the speaker's face that it was loss of time to dwell upon the point. Confused, but sensible that something might depend upon his presence of mind, he commanded himself, and was silently attentive.

"Now, I trust," said Sydney to him, "that the name and influence of Doctor Manette may stand him in as good stead tomorrow—you said he would be before the Tribunal again tomorrow, Mr. Barsad?—"

"Yes; I believe so."

"—In as good stead tomorrow as today. But it may not be so. I own to you, I am shaken, Mr. Lorry, by Doctor Manette's not having the power to prevent this arrest."

"He may not have known of it beforehand," said Mr. Lorry.

"But that very circumstance would be alarming, when we remember how identified he is with his son-in-law."

"That's true," Mr. Lorry acknowledged, with his troubled hand at his chin, and his troubled eyes on Carton.

"In short," said Sydney, "this is a desperate time, when desperate games are played for desperate stakes. Let the Doctor play the winning game; I will play the losing one. No man's life here is worth purchase. Anyone carried home by the people today, may be condemned tomorrow. Now, the stake I have resolved to play for, in case of the worst, is a friend in the Conciergerie. And the friend I purpose to myself to win is Mr. Barsad."

"You need have good cards, sir," said the spy.

"I'll run them over. I'll see what I hold. Mr. Lorry, you know what a brute I am; I wish you'd give me a little brandy."

It was put before him, and he drank off a glassful—drank off another glassful—pushed the bottle thoughtfully away.

"Mr. Barsad," he went on, in the tone of one who really was looking over a hand at cards: "Sheep of the prisons, emissary of Republican committees, now turnkey, now prisoner, always spy and secret informer, so much the more valuable here for being English that an Englishman is less open to suspicion of subornation in those characters than a Frenchman, represents himself to his employers under a false name. That's a very good card. Mr. Barsad, now in the employ of the Republican French government, was formerly in the employ of the aristocratic English government, the enemy of France and freedom. That's an excellent card. Inference clear as day in this region of suspicion, that Mr. Barsad, still in the pay of the aristocratic English government, is the spy of Pitt, the treacherous foe of the Republic, crouching in its bosom, the English traitor and agent of all mischief so much spoken of and so difficult to find. That's a card not to be beaten. Have you followed my hand, Mr. Barsad?"

"Not to understand your play," returned the spy, somewhat uneasily.

"I play my Ace, Denunciation of Mr. Barsad to the nearest Section Committee. Look over your hand, Mr. Barsad, and see what you have. Don't hurry."

He drew the bottle near, poured out another glassful of brandy, and drank it off. He saw that the spy was fearful of his drinking himself into a fit state for the immediate denunciation of him. Seeing it, he poured out and drank another glassful.

"Look over your hand carefully, Mr. Barsad. Take time."

It was a poorer hand than he suspected. Mr. Barsad saw losing cards in it that Sydney Carton knew nothing of. Thrown out of his honorable employment in England, through too much unsuccessful hard swearing there—not because he was wanted there: our English reasons for vaunting our superiority to secrecy and spies are of very modern date—he knew that he had crossed the Channel, and accepted service in France: first, as a tempter and an eavesdropper among his own countrymen there: gradually, as a tempter and an eavesdropper among the natives. He knew that under the overthrown government he had been a spy upon Saint Antoine and Defarge's wine-shop; had received from the watchful police such heads of information concerning Doctor Manette's imprisonment, release, and history, as should serve him for an introduction to familiar conversation with the Defarges; and tried them on Madame Defarge, and had broken down with them signally. He always remembered with fear and trembling, that that terrible woman had knitted when he talked with her, and had looked ominously at him as her fingers moved. He had since seen her, in the Section of Saint Antoine, over and over again produce her knitted registers, and denounce people whose lives the guillotine then surely swallowed up. He knew, as everyone employed as he was, did, that he was never safe; that flight was impossible; that he was tied fast under the shadow of the axe; and that in spite of his utmost tergiversation and treachery in furtherance of the reigning terror, a word might bring it down upon him. Once denounced, and on such grave grounds as had just now been suggested to his mind, he foresaw that the dreadful woman of whose unrelenting character he had seen many proofs, would produce against him that fatal register, and would quash his last chance of life. Besides that all secret men are men soon terrified, here were surely cards enough of one black suit, to justify the holder in growing rather livid as he turned them over.

"You scarcely seem to like your hand," said Sydney, with the greatest composure. "Do you play?"

"I think, sir," said the spy, in the meanest manner, as he turned to Mr. Lorry, "I may appeal to a gentleman of your years and benevolence, to put it to this other gentleman, so much your junior, whether he can under any circumstances reconcile it to his station to play that Ace of which he has spoken. I admit that *I* am a spy, and that it is considered a discreditable station— though it must be filled by somebody; but this gentleman is no spy, and why should he so demean himself as to make himself one?"

"I play my Ace, Mr. Barsad," said Carton, taking the answer on himself, and looking at his watch, "without any scruple, in a very few minutes."

"I should have hoped, gentlemen both," said the spy, always striving to hook Mr. Lorry into the discussion, "that your respect for my sister—"

"I could not better testify my respect for your sister than by finally relieving her of her brother," said Sydney Carton.

"You think not, sir?"

"I have thoroughly made up my mind about it."

The smooth manner of the spy, curiously in dissonance with his ostentatiously rough dress, and probably with his usual demeanor, received such a check from the inscrutability of Carton—who was a mystery to wiser and honester men than he—that it faltered here and failed him. While he was at a loss, Carton said, resuming his former air of contemplating cards:

"And indeed, now I think again, I have a strong impression that I have another good card here, not yet enumerated. That friend and fellow-sheep, who spoke of himself as pasturing in the country prisons; who was he?"

"French. You don't know him," said the spy, quickly.

"French, eh?" repeated Carton, musing, and not appearing to notice him at all, though he echoed the word. "Well; he may be."

"Is, I assure you," said the spy; "though it's not important."

"Though it's not important," repeated Carton in the same mechanical way—"though it's not important—No, it's not important—No. Yet I know the face."

"I think not. I am sure not. It can't be," said the spy.

"It—can't—be," muttered Sydney Carton, retrospectively, and filling his glass (which fortunately was a small one) again. "Can't—be. Spoke good French. Yet like a foreigner, I thought?"

"Provincial," said the spy.

"No. Foreign?" cried Carton, striking his open hand on the table, as a light broke clearly on his mind. "Cly! Disguised, but the same man. We had that man before us at the Old Bailey."

"Now, there you are hasty, sir," said Barsad, with a smile that gave his aquiline nose an extra inclination to one side; "there you really give me an advantage over you. Cly (who I will unreservedly admit, at this distance of time, was a partner of mine) has been dead several years. I attended him in his last illness. He was buried in London, at the church of Saint Pancras-in-the-fields. His unpopularity with the blackguard multitude at the moment prevented my following his remains, but I helped to lay him in his coffin."

Here Mr. Lorry became aware, from where he sat, of a most remarkable goblin shadow on the wall. Tracing it to its source, he discovered it to be caused by a sudden extraordinary rising and stiffening of all the risen and stiff hair on Mr. Cruncher's head.

"Let us be reasonable," said the spy, "and let us be fair. To show you how mistaken you are, and what an unfounded assumption yours is, I will lay before you a certificate of Cly's burial, which I happen to have carried in my pocket-book," (with a hurried hand he produced and opened it), "ever since. There it is. Oh, look at it, look at it! You may take it in your hand; it's no forgery."

Here Mr. Lorry perceived the reflection on the wall to elongate, and Mr. Cruncher rose and stepped forward. His hair could not have been more violently on end, if it had been that moment dressed by the cow with the crumpled horn in the house that Jack built.

Unseen by the spy, Mr. Cruncher stood at his side, and touched him on the shoulder like a ghostly bailiff.

"That there Roger Cly, master," said Mr. Cruncher, with a taciturn and iron-bound visage. "So *you* put him in his coffin?"

"I did."

"Who took him out of it?"

Barsad leaned back in his chair, and stammered, "What do you mean?"

"I mean," said Mr. Cruncher, "that he warn't never in it. No! Not he! I'll have my head took off, if he was ever in it."

The spy looked round at the two gentlemen; they both looked in unspeakable astonishment at Jerry.

"I tell you," said Jerry, "that you buried paving-stones and earth in that there coffin. Don't go and tell *me* that you buried Cly. It was a take-in. Me and two more knows it."

"How do you know it?"

"What's that to you? Ecod!" growled Mr. Cruncher, "it's you I have got a old grudge agin, is it, with your shameful impositions upon tradesmen! I'd catch hold of your throat and choke you for half a guinea." Sydney Carton, who, with Mr. Lorry, had been lost in amazement at this turn of the business, here requested Mr. Cruncher to moderate and explain himself.

"At another time, sir," he returned, evasively, "the present time is ill-convenient for explainin'. What I stand to, is, that he knows well wot that there Cly was never in that there coffin. Let him say he was, in so much as a word of one syllable, and I'll either catch hold of his throat and choke him for half a guinea";—Mr. Cruncher dwelt upon this as quite a liberal offer; "or I'll out and announce him."

"Humph! I see one thing," said Carton. "I hold another card, Mr. Barsad. Impossible, here in raging Paris, with Suspicion filling the air, for you to outlive denunciation, when you are in communication with another aristocratic spy of the same antecedents as yourself, who, moreover, has the mystery about him of having feigned death and come to life again! A plot in the prisons, of the foreigners against the Republic. A strong card—a certain Guillotine card! Do you play?"

"No!" returned the spy. "I throw up. I confess that we were so unpopular with the outrageous mob, that I only got away from England at the risk of being ducked to death, and that Cly was so ferreted up and down that he never would have got away at all but for that sham. Though how this man knows it was a sham, is a wonder of wonders to me."

"Never you trouble your head about this man," retorted the contentious Mr. Cruncher; "you'll have trouble enough with giving your attention to that gentleman. And look here! Once more!"—Mr. Cruncher could not be restrained from making rather an ostentatious parade of his liberality—"I'd catch hold of your throat and choke you for half a guinea."

The Sheep of the prisons turned from him to Sydney Carton and said, with more decision, "It has come to a point. I go on duty soon, and can't overstay my time. You told me you had a proposal; what is it? Now, it is of no use asking too much of me. Ask me to do anything in my office, putting my head in great extra danger, and I had better trust my life to the chances of a refusal than the chances of consent. In short, I should make that choice. You talk of desperation. We are all desperate here. Remember! I may denounce you if I think proper, and I can swear my way through stone walls, and so can others. Now, what do you want with me?"

"Not very much. You are a turnkey at the Conciergerie?"

"I tell you once for all, there is no such thing as an escape possible," said the spy, firmly.

"Why need you tell me what I have not asked? You are a turnkey at the Conciergerie?"

"I am sometimes."

"You can be when you choose?"

"I can pass in and out when I choose."

Sydney Carton filled another glass with brandy, poured it slowly out upon the hearth, and watched it as it dropped. It being all spent, he said, rising:

"So far, we have spoken before these two, because it was as well that the merits of the cards should not rest solely between you and me. Come into the dark room here and let us have one final word alone."

N i n e

THE GAME MADE

WHILE SYDNEY CARTON AND THE SHEEP OF THE PRISONS were in the adjoining dark room, speaking so low that not a sound was heard, Mr. Lorry looked at Jerry in considerable doubt and mistrust. That honest tradesman's manner of receiving the look, did not inspire confidence; he changed the leg on which he rested, as often as if he had fifty of those limbs, and were trying them all; he examined his fingernails with a very questionable closeness of attention; and whenever Mr. Lorry's eye caught his, he was taken with that peculiar kind of short cough requiring the hollow of a hand before it, which is seldom, if ever, known to be an infirmity attendant on perfect openness of character.

"Jerry," said Mr. Lorry. "Come here."

Mr. Cruncher came forward sideways, with one of his shoulders in advance of him.

"What have you been besides a messenger?"

After some cogitation, accompanied with an intent look at his patron, Mr. Cruncher conceived the luminous idea of replying, "Agricultooral character."

"My mind misgives me much," said Mr. Lorry, angrily shaking his forefinger at him, "that you have used the respectable and great house of Tellson's as a blind, and that you have had an unlawful occupation of an infamous description. If you have, don't expect me to befriend you, when you get back to England. If you have, don't expect me to keep your secret. Tellson's shall not be imposed upon."

"I hope, sir," pleaded the abashed Mr. Cruncher, "that a gentleman like yourself, wot I've had the honor of odd-jobbing till I'm gray at it, would think twice about harming of me, even if it wos so—I don't say it is, but even if it wos. And which it is to be took into account that if it wos, it wouldn't, even then, be all o' one side. There'd be two sides to it. There might be medical doctors at the present hour, a picking up their guineas where a honest tradesman don't pick up his fardens—fardens! no, nor yet his half fardens—half fardens! no, nor yet his quarter—a banking away like smoke at Tellson's, and a cocking their medical eyes at that tradesman on the sly, a going in and going out to their own carriages—ah! equally like smoke, if not more so. Well, that 'ud be imposing, too, on Tellson's. For you cannot sarse the goose and not the gander. And here's Mrs. Cruncher, or leastways wos in the Old England times, and would be tomorrow, if cause given, a floppin' agin the business to that degree as is ruinating—stark ruinating! Whereas them medical doctors' wives don't flop—catch 'em at it! Or, if they flop, their floppings goes in favor of more patients, and how can you rightly have one without t'other? Then, wot with undertakers, and wot with parish clerks, and wot with sextons, and wot with private watchmen (all awaricious, and all in it), a man wouldn't get much by it, even if it wos so. And wot little a man did get, would never prosper with him, Mr. Lorry. He'd never have no good of it; he'd want all along to be out of the line, if he could see his way out, being once in—even if it wos so."

"Ugh!" cried Mr. Lorry, rather relenting, nevertheless. "I am shocked at the sight of you."

"Now, wot I would humbly offer to you, sir," pursued Mr. Cruncher, "even if it wos so, which I don't say it is—"

"Don't prevaricate," said Mr. Lorry.

"No, I will *not*, sir," returned Mr. Cruncher, as if nothing were further from his thoughts or practice—"which I don't say it is—wot I would humbly offer to you, sir, would be this. Upon that there stool, at that there Bar, sets that there boy of mine, brought up and growed up to be a man, wot will errand you, message you, general-light-job you, till your heels is where your head is, if such should be your wishes. If it wos so, which I still don't say it is (for I will not prewaricate to you, sir), let that there boy keep his father's place, and take care of his mother; don't blow upon that boy's father—do not do it, sir—and let that father go into the line of the reg'lar diggin', and make amends for what he would have un-dug—if it wos so—by diggin' of 'em in with a will, and with conwictions respectin' the future keepin' of 'em safe. That, Mr. Lorry," said Mr. Cruncher, wiping his forehead with his arm, as an announcement that he had arrived at the peroration of his discourse, "is wot I would respectfully offer to you, sir. A man don't see all this here goin' on dreadful round him, in the way of subjects without heads, dear me, plentiful enough fur to bring the price down to porterage and hardly that without havin' his serious thoughts of things. And these here would be mine, if it wos so, entreatin' of you fur to bear in mind that wot I said just now, I up and said in the good cause when I might have kep' it back."

"That at least is true," said Mr. Lorry. "Say no more now. It may be that I shall yet stand your friend, if you deserve it, and repent in action—not in words. I want no more words."

Mr. Cruncher knuckled his forehead, as Sydney Carton and the spy returned from the dark room. "Adieu, Mr. Barsad!" said the former; "our arrangement thus made, you have nothing to fear from me."

He sat down in a chair on the hearth, over against Mr. Lorry. When they were alone, Mr. Lorry asked him what he had done?

"Not much. If it should go ill with the prisoner, I have ensured access to him, once."

Mr. Lorry's countenance fell.

"It is all I could do," said Carton. "To propose too much would be to put this man's head under the axe, and, as he himself said, nothing worse could happen to him if he were denounced. It was obviously the weakness of the position. There is no help for it."

"But access to him," said Mr. Lorry, "if it should go ill before the tribunal, will not save him."

"I never said it would."

Mr. Lorry's eyes gradually sought the fire; his sympathy with his darling, and the heavy disappointment of this second arrest, gradually weakened them; he was an old man now, overborne with anxiety of late, and his tears fell.

"You are a good man and a true friend," said Carton, in an altered voice. "Forgive me if I notice that you are affected. I could not see my father weep, and sit by, careless. And I could not respect your sorrow more, if you were my father. You are free from that misfortune, however."

Though he said the last words, with a slip into his usual manner, there was a true feeling and respect both in his tone and in his touch, that Mr. Lorry, who had never seen the better side of him, was wholly unprepared for. He gave him his hand, and Carton gently pressed it.

"To return to poor Darnay," said Carton. "Don't tell Her of this interview, or this arrangement. It would not enable Her to go to see him. She might think it was contrived, in case of the worst, to convey to him the means of anticipating the sentence."

Mr. Lorry had not thought of that, and he looked quickly at Carton to see if it were in his mind. It seemed to be; he returned the look, and evidently understood it.

"She might think a thousand things," he said, "and any of them would only add to her trouble. Don't speak of me to her. As I said to you when I first came, I had better not see her. I can put my hand out to do any little helpful work for her that my hand can find to do, without that. You are going to her, I hope? She must be very desolate tonight."

"I am going now, directly."

"I am glad of that. She has such a strong attachment to you and reliance on you. How does she look?"

"Anxious and unhappy, but very beautiful."

"Ah!"

It was a long, grieving sound, like a sigh—almost like a sob. It attracted Mr. Lorry's eyes to Carton's face, which was turned to the fire. A light, or a shade (the old gentleman could not have said which), passed from it as swiftly as a change would sweep over a hillside on a wild, bright day, and he lifted his foot to put back one of the little flaming logs, which was tumbling forward. He wore the white riding-coat and top-boots, then in vogue, and the light of the fire touching their light surfaces made him look very pale, with his long brown hair, all untrimmed, hanging loose about him. His indifference to fire was sufficiently remarkable to elicit a word of remonstrance from Mr. Lorry; his boot was still upon the hot embers of the flaming log, when it had broken under the weight of his foot.

"I forgot it," he said.

Mr. Lorry's eyes were again attracted to his face. Taking note of the wasted air which clouded the naturally handsome features, and having the expression of prisoners' faces fresh in his mind, he was strongly reminded of that expression.

"And your duties here have drawn to an end, sir?" said Carton, turning to him.

"Yes. As I was telling you last night, when Lucie came in so unexpectedly, I have at length done all that I can do here. I hoped to have left them in perfect safety, and then to have quitted Paris. I have my Leave to Pass. I was ready to go."

They were both silent.

"Yours is a long life to look back upon, sir?" said Carton, wistfully.

"I am in my seventy-eighth year."

"You have been useful all your life; steadily and constantly occupied; trusted, respected, and looked up to?"

"I have been a man of business, ever since I have been a man. Indeed, I may say that I was a man of business when a boy."

"See what a place you fill at seventy-eight. How many people will miss you when you leave it empty!"

"A solitary old bachelor," answered Mr. Lorry, shaking his head. "There is nobody to weep for me."

"How can you say that? Wouldn't She weep for you? Wouldn't her child?"

"Yes, yes, thank God. I didn't quite mean what I said."

"It *is* a thing to thank God for; is it not?"

"Surely, surely."

"If you could say, with truth, to your own solitary heart, tonight, 'I have secured to myself the love and attachment, the gratitude or respect, of no human creature; I have won myself a tender place in no regard; I have done nothing good or serviceable to be remembered by!' your seventy-eight years would be seventy-eight heavy curses; would they not?"

"You say truly, Mr. Carton; I think they would be."

Sydney turned his eyes again upon the fire, and, after a silence of a few moments, said:

"I should like to ask you: Does your childhood seem far off? Do the days when you sat at your mother's knee, seem days of very long ago?"

Responding to his softened manner, Mr. Lorry answered:

"Twenty years back, yes; at this time of my life, no. For, as I draw closer and closer to the end, I travel in the circle, nearer and nearer to the beginning. It seems to be one of the kind smoothings and preparings of the way. My heart is touched now, by many remembrances that had long fallen asleep, of my pretty young mother (and I so old!), and by many associations of the days when what we call the World was not so real with me, and my faults were not confirmed in me."

"I understand the feeling!" exclaimed Carton, with a bright flush. "And you are the better for it?"

"I hope so."

Carton terminated the conversation here, by rising to help him on with his outer coat. "But you," said Mr. Lorry, reverting to the theme, "you are young."

"Yes," said Carton. "I am not old, but my young way was never the way to age. Enough of me."

"And of me, I am sure," said Mr. Lorry. "Are you going out?"

"I'll walk with you to her gate. You know my vagabond and restless habits. If I should prowl about the streets a long time, don't be uneasy; I shall reappear in the morning. You go to the Court tomorrow?"

"Yes, unhappily."

"I shall be there, but only as one of the crowd. My spy will find a place for me. Take my arm, sir."

Mr. Lorry did so, and they went downstairs and out in the streets. A few minutes brought them to Mr. Lorry's destination. Carton left him there; but lingered at a little distance, and turned back to the gate again when it was shut, and touched it. He had heard of her going to the prison every day. "She came out here," he said, looking about him, "turned this way, must have trod on these stones often. Let me follow in her steps."

It was ten o'clock at night when he stood before the prison of La Force, where she had stood hundreds of times. A little wood-sawyer, having closed his shop, was smoking his pipe at his shop-door.

"Good night, citizen," said Sydney Carton, pausing in going by; for, the man eyed him inquisitively.

"Good night, citizen."

"How goes the Republic?"

"You mean the Guillotine. Not ill. Sixty-three today. We shall mount to a hundred soon. Samson and his men complain sometimes, of being exhausted. Ha, ha, ha! He is so droll, that Samson. Such a Barber!"

"Do you often go to see him—"

"Shave? Always. Every day. What a barber! You have seen him at work?"

"Never."

"Go and see him when he has a good batch. Figure this to yourself, citizen; he shaved the sixty-three today, in less than two pipes! Less than two pipes. Word of honor!"

As the grinning little man held out the pipe he was smoking, to explain how he timed the executioner, Carton was so sensible of a rising desire to strike the life out of him, that he turned away.

"But you are not English," said the wood-sawyer, "though you wear English dress?"

"Yes," said Carton, pausing again, and answering over his shoulder.

"You speak like a Frenchman."

"I am an old student here."

"Aha, a perfect Frenchman! Good night, Englishman."

"Good night, citizen."

"But go and see that droll dog," the little man persisted, calling after him. "And take a pipe with you!"

Sydney had not gone far out of sight, when he stopped in the middle of the street under a glimmering lamp, and wrote with his pencil on a scrap of paper. Then, traversing with the decided step of one who remembered the way well, several dark and dirty streets—much dirtier than usual, for the best public thoroughfares remained uncleansed in those times of terror—he stopped at a chemist's shop, which the owner was closing with his own hands. A small, dim, crooked shop, kept in a tortuous, uphill thoroughfare, by a small, dim, crooked man.

Giving this citizen, too, good night, as he confronted him at his counter, he laid the scrap of paper before him. "Whew!" the chemist whistled softly, as he read it. "Hi! hi! hi!"

Sydney Carton took no heed, and the chemist said:

"For you, citizen?"

"For me."

"You will be careful to keep them separate, citizen? You know the consequences of mixing them?"

"Perfectly."

Certain small packets were made and given to him. He put them, one by one, in the breast of his inner coat, counted out the money for them, and deliberately left the shop. "There is nothing more to do," said he, glancing upward at the moon, "until tomorrow. I can't sleep."

It was not a reckless manner, the manner in which he said these words aloud under the fast-sailing clouds, nor was it more expressive of negligence than defiance. It was the settled manner of a tired man, who had wandered and struggled and got lost, but who at length struck into his road and saw its end.

Long ago, when he had been famous among his earliest competitors as a youth of great promise, he had followed his father to the grave. His mother had died, years before. These solemn words, which had been read at his father's grave, arose in his mind as he went down the dark streets, among the heavy shadows, with the moon and the clouds sailing on high above him. "I am the resurrection and the life, saith the Lord: he that believeth in me, though he were dead, yet shall he live: and whosoever liveth and believeth in me, shall never die."

In a city dominated by the axe, alone at night, with natural sorrow rising in him for the sixty-three who had been that day put to death, and for to-morrow's victims then awaiting their doom in the prisons, and still of to-morrow's and tomorrow's, the chain of association that brought the words home, like a rusty old ship's anchor from the deep, might have been easily found. He did not seek it, but repeated them and went on.

With a solemn interest in the lighted windows where the people were going to rest, forgetful through a few calm hours of the horrors surrounding them; in the towers of the churches, where no prayers were said, for the pop-ular revulsion had even traveled that length of self-destruction from years of priestly impostors, plunderers, and profligates; in the distant burial-places, reserved, as they wrote upon the gates, for Eternal Sleep; in the abounding gaols; and in the streets along which the sixties rolled to a death which had become so common and material, that no sorrowful story of a haunting Spirit ever arose among the people out of all the working of the Guillotine; with a solemn interest in the whole life and death of the city settling down to its short, nightly pause in fury; Sydney Carton crossed the Seine again for the lighter streets.

Few coaches were abroad, for riders in coaches were liable to be sus-pected, and gentility hid its head in red nightcaps, and put on heavy shoes, and trudged. But, the theaters were all well filled, and the people poured cheerfully out as he passed, and went chatting home. At one of the theater doors, there was a little girl with a mother, looking for a way across the street through the mud. He carried the child over, and before the timid arm was loosed from his neck asked her for a kiss.

"I am the resurrection and the life, saith the Lord: he that believeth in me, though he were dead, yet shall he live: and whosoever liveth, and believeth in me, shall never die."

Now, that the streets were quiet, and the night wore on, the words were in the echoes of his feet, and were in the air. Perfectly calm and steady, he sometimes repeated them to himself as he walked; but, he heard them always.

The night wore out, and, as he stood upon the bridge listening to the water as it splashed the river-walls of the Island of Paris, where the pic-turesque confusion of houses and cathedral shone bright in the light of the moon, the day came coldly, looking like a dead face out of the sky. Then, the night, with the moon and the stars, turned pale and died, and for a little while it seemed as if Creation were delivered over to Death's dominion. But, the glorious sun, rising, seemed to strike those words, that burden of the night, straight and warm to his heart in its long bright rays. And looking along them, with reverently shaded eyes, a bridge of light appeared to span the air between him and the sun, while the river sparkled under it.

The strong tide, so swift, so deep, and certain, was like a congenial friend in the morning stillness. He walked by the stream, far from the houses, and in the light and warmth of the sun, fell asleep on the bank. When he awoke and was afoot again, he lingered there yet a little longer, watching an eddy that turned and turned purposeless, until the stream absorbed it, and carried it on to the sea. "Like me!"

A trading-boat, with a sail of the softened color of a dead leaf, then glided into his view, floated by him, and died away. As its silent track in the water disappeared, the prayer that had broken up out of his heart for a merciful consideration of all his poor blindness and errors, ended in the words, "I am the resurrection and the life."

Mr. Lorry was aleady out when he got back, and it was easy to surmise where the good old man was gone. Sydney Carton drank nothing but a little coffee, ate some bread, and, having washed and changed to refresh himself, went out to the place of trial.

The court was all astir and abuzz, when the black sheep—whom many fell away from in dread—pressed him into an obscure corner among the crowd. Mr. Lorry was there, and Doctor Manette was there. She was there, sitting beside her father.

When her husband was brought in, she turned a look upon him, so sustaining, so encouraging, so full of admiring love and pitying tenderness, yet so courageous for his sake, that it called the healthy blood into his face, brightened his glance, and animated his heart. If there had been any eyes to notice the influence of her look on Sydney Carton, it would have been seen to be the same influence exactly.

Before that unjust Tribunal, there was little or no order of procedure, insuring to any accused person any reasonable hearing. There could have been no such Revolution, if all laws, forms, and ceremonies had not first been so monstrously abused, that the suicidal vengeance of the Revolution was to scatter them all to the winds.

Every eye was turned to the jury. The same determined patriots and good Republicans as yesterday and the day before, and tomorrow and the day after. Eager and prominent among them, one man with a craving face, and his fingers perpetually hovering about his lips, whose appearance gave great satisfaction to the spectators. A life-thirsting, cannibal-looking, bloody-minded juryman, the Jacques Three of Saint Antoine. The whole jury, as a jury of dogs impanelled to try the deer.

Every eye then turned to the five judges and the public prosecutor. No favorable leaning in that quarter today. A fell, uncompromising, murderous business-meaning there. Every eye then sought some other eye in the crowd, and gleamed at it approvingly; and heads nodded at one another, before bending forward with a strained attention.

Charles Evrémonde, called Darnay. Released yesterday. Reaccused and retaken yesterday. Indictment delivered to him last night. Suspected and denounced enemy of the Republic, Aristocrat, one of a family of tyrants, one of a race proscribed, for that they had used their abolished privileges to the infamous oppression of the people. Charles Evrémonde, called Darnay, in right of such proscription absolutely Dead in law.

To this effect, in as few or fewer words, the Public Prosecutor.

The President asked, was the accused openly denounced or secretly?

"Openly, President."

"By whom?"

"Three voices. Ernest Defarge, wine-vendor of Saint Antoine."

"Good."

"Therese Defarge, his wife."

"Good."

"Alexandre Manette, physician."

A great uproar took place in the court, and in the midst of it, Doctor Manette was seen, pale and trembling, standing where he had been seated.

"President, I indignantly protest to you that this is a forgery and a fraud. You know the accused to be the husband of my daughter. My daughter, and those dear to her, are far dearer to me than my life. Who and where is the false conspirator who says that I denounce the husband of my child?"

"Citizen Manette, be tranquil. To fail in submission to the authority of the Tribunal, would be to put yourself out of Law. As to what is dearer to you than life, nothing can be so dear to a good citizen as the Republic."

Loud acclamations hailed this rebuke. The President rang his bell, and with warmth resumed.

"If the Republic should demand of you the sacrifice of your child herself, you would have no duty but to sacrifice her. Listen to what is to follow. In the meanwhile, be silent!"

Frantic acclamations were again raised. Doctor Manette sat down, with his eyes looking around, and his lips trembling; his daughter drew closer to him. The craving man on the jury rubbed his hands together, and restored the usual hand to his mouth.

Defarge was produced, when the Court was quiet enough to admit of his being heard, and rapidly expounded the story of the imprisonment, and of his having been a mere boy in the Doctor's service, and of the release, and of the state of the prisoner when released and delivered to him. This short examination followed, for the court was quick with its work.

"You did good service at the taking of the Bastille, citizen?"

"I believe so."

Here, an excited woman screeched from the crowd: "You were one of the best patriots there. Why not say so? You were a cannonier that day there, and you were among the first to enter the accursed fortress when it fell. Patriots, I speak the truth!"

It was The Vengeance who, amidst the warm commendations of the audience, thus assisted the proceedings. The President rang his bell; but, The Vengeance, warming with encouragement, shrieked, "I defy that bell!" wherein she was likewise much commended.

"Inform the Tribunal of what you did that day within the Bastille, citizen."

"I knew," said Defarge, looking down at his wife, who stood at the bottom of the steps on which he was raised, looking steadily up at him; "I knew that this prisoner, of whom I speak, had been confined in a cell known as One Hundred and Five, North Tower. I knew it from himself. He knew himself by no other name than One Hundred and Five, North Tower, when he made shoes under my care. As I serve my gun that day, I resolve, when the place shall fall, to examine that cell. It falls. I mount to the cell, with a fellow-citizen who is one of the Jury, directed by a gaoler. I examine it, very closely. In a hole in the chimney, where a stone has been worked out and replaced, I find a written paper. This is that written paper. I have made it my business to examine some specimens of the writing of Doctor Manette. This is the writing of Doctor Manette. I confide this paper, in the writing of Doctor Manette, to the hands of the President."

"Let it be read."

In a dead silence and stillness—the prisoner under trial looked lovingly at his wife, his wife only looking from him to look with solicitude at her father, Doctor Manette keeping his eyes fixed on the reader, Madame Defarge never taking hers from the prisoner, Defarge never taking his from his feasting wife, and all the other eyes there intent upon the Doctor, who saw none of them—the paper was read, as follows.

Ten

THE SUBSTANCE
OF THE SHADOW

"I, ALEXANDRE MANETTE, UNFORTUNATE PHYSICIAN, NATIVE of Beauvais, and afterward resident in Paris, write this melancholy paper in my doleful cell in the Bastille, during the last month of the year 1767. I write it at stolen intervals, under every difficulty. I design to secrete it in the wall of the chimney, where I have slowly and laboriously made a place of concealment for it. Some pitying hand may find it there, when I and my sorrows are dust.

"These words are formed by the rusty iron point with which I write with difficulty in scrapings of soot and charcoal from the chimney, mixed with blood, in the last month of the tenth year of my captivity. Hope has quite departed from my breast. I know from terrible warnings I have noted in myself that my reason will not long remain unimpaired; but I solemnly declare that I am at this time in the possession of my right mind—that my memory is exact and circumstantial—and that I write the truth as I shall answer for these, my last recorded words, whether they be ever read by men or not, at the Eternal Judgment seat.

"One cloudy moonlight night, in the third week of December (I think the twenty-second of the month) in the year 1757, I was walking on a retired part of the quay by the Seine for the refreshment of the frosty air, at an hour's distance from my place of residence in the Street of the School of Medicine, when a carriage came along behind me, driven very fast. As I stood aside to let that carriage pass, apprehensive that it might otherwise run me down, a head was put out at the window, and a voice called to the driver to stop.

"The carriage stopped as soon as the driver could rein in his horses, and the same voice called to me by my name. I answered. The carriage was then so far in advance of me that the two gentlemen had time to open the door and alight before I came up with it. I observed that they were both wrapped in cloaks, and appeared to conceal themselves. As they stood side by side near the carriage-door, I also observed that they both looked of about my own age, or rather younger, and that they were greatly alike, in stature, manner, voice, and (as far as I could see) face too.

" 'You are Doctor Manette?' said one.

" 'I am.'

" 'Doctor Manette, formerly of Beauvais,' said the other; 'the young physician, originally an expert surgeon, who within the last year or two has made a rising reputation in Paris?'

" 'Gentlemen,' I returned, 'I am that Doctor Manette of whom you speak so graciously.'

" 'We have been to your residence,' said the first, 'and not being so fortunate as to find you there, and being informed that you were probably walking in this direction, we followed, in the hope of overtaking you. Will you please to enter the carriage?'

"The manner of both was imperious, and they both moved, as these words were spoken, so as to place me between themselves and the carriage-door. They were armed. I was not.

" 'Gentlemen,' said I, 'pardon me; but I usually inquire who does me the honor to seek my assistance, and what is the nature of the case to which I am summoned.'

"The reply to this was made by him who had spoken second. 'Doctor, your clients are people of condition. As to the nature of the case, our confidence in your skill assures us that you will ascertain it for yourself better than we can describe it. Enough. Will you please to enter the carriage?'

"I could do nothing but comply, and I entered it in silence. They both entered after me—the last springing in, after putting up the steps. The carriage turned about, and drove on at its former speed.

"I repeat this conversation exactly as it occurred. I have no doubt that it is, word for word, the same. I describe everything exactly as it took place, constraining my mind not to wander from the task. Where I make the broken marks that follow here, I leave off for the time, and put my paper in its hiding-place. . . .

"The carriage left the streets behind, passed the North Barrier, and emerged upon the country road. At two-thirds of a league from the Barrier—I did not estimate the distance at that time, but afterwards when I traversed it—it struck out of the main avenue, and presently stopped at a solitary house. We all three alighted, and walked, by a damp soft footpath in a garden where a neglected fountain had overflowed, to the door of the house. It was not opened immediately, in answer to the ringing of the bell, and one of my two conductors struck the man who opened it, with his heavy riding-glove, across the face.

"There was nothing in this action to attract my particular attention, for I had seen common people struck more commonly than dogs. But, the other of the two, being angry likewise, struck the man in like manner with his arm; the look and bearing of the brothers were then so exactly alike, that I then first perceived them to be twin brothers.

"From the time of our alighting at the outer gate (which we found locked, and which one of the brothers had opened to admit us, and had relocked), I had heard cries proceeding from an upper chamber. I was conducted to this chamber straight, the cries growing louder as we ascended the stairs, and I found a patient in a high fever of the brain, lying on a bed.

"The patient was a woman of great beauty, and young; assuredly not much past twenty. Her hair was torn and ragged, and her arms were bound to her sides with sashes and handkerchiefs. I noticed that these bonds were all portions of a gentleman's dress. On one of them, which was a fringed scarf for a dress of ceremony, I saw the armorial bearings of a noble, and the letter *E*.

"I saw this, within the first minute of my contemplation of the patient; for, in her restless strivings she had turned over on her face on the edge of the bed, had drawn the end of the scarf into her mouth, and was in danger of suffocation. My first act was to put out my hand to relieve her breathing; and in moving the scarf aside, the embroidery in the corner caught my sight.

"I turned her gently over, placed my hands upon her breast to calm her and keep her down, and looked into her face. Her eyes were dilated and wild, and she constantly uttered piercing shrieks, and repeated the words,

'My husband, my father, and my brother!' and then counted up to twelve, and said, 'Hush!' For an instant, and no more, she would pause to listen, and then the piercing shrieks would begin again, and she would repeat the cry, 'My husband, my father, and my brother!' and would count up to twelve, and say 'Hush!' There was no variation in the order, or the manner. There was no cessation, but the regular moment's pause, in the utterance of these sounds.

" 'How long,' I asked, 'has this lasted?'

"To distinguish the brothers, I will call them the elder and the younger; by the elder, I mean him who exercised the most authority. It was the elder who replied, 'Since about this hour last night.'

" 'She has a husband, a father, and a brother?'

" 'A brother.'

" 'I do not address her brother?'

"He answered with great contempt, 'No.'

" 'She has some recent association with the number twelve?'

"The younger brother impatiently rejoined, 'With twelve o'clock.'

" 'See, gentlemen,' said I, still keeping my hands upon her breast, 'how useless I am, as you have brought me! If I had known what I was coming to see, I could have come provided. As it is, time must be lost. There are no medicines to be obtained in this lonely place.'

"The elder brother looked to the younger, who said haughtily, 'There is a case of medicines here'; and brought it from a closet, and put it on the table. . . .

"I opened some of the bottles, smelled them, and put the stoppers to my lips. If I had wanted to use anything save narcotic medicines that were poisons in themselves, I would not have administered any of those.

" 'Do you doubt them?' asked the younger brother.

" 'You see, monsieur, I am going to use them,' I replied, and said no more.

"I made the patient swallow, with great difficulty, and after many efforts, the dose that I desired to give. As I intended to repeat it after a while, and as it was necessary to watch its influence, I then sat down by the side of the bed. There was a timid and suppressed woman in attendance (wife of the man downstairs), who had retreated into a corner. The house was damp and decayed, indifferently furnished—evidently, recently occupied and temporarily used. Some thick old hangings had been nailed up before the windows, to deaden the sound of the shrieks. They continued to be uttered in their regular succession, with the cry, 'My husband, my father, and my brother!' the counting up to twelve, and 'Hush!' The frenzy was so violent, that I had not unfastened the bandages restraining the arms; but I had looked to them to see that they were not painful. The only spark of encouragement in the case was that my hand upon the sufferer's breast had this much soothing influence, that for a few minutes at a time it tranquilized the figure. It had no effect upon the cries: no pendulum could be more regular.

"For the reason that my hand had this effect (I assume), I had sat by the side of the bed for half an hour, with the two brothers looking on, before the elder said:

" 'There is another patient.'

"I was startled and asked, 'Is it a pressing case?'

" 'You had better see,' he carelessly answered; and took up a light. . . .

"The other patient lay in a back room across a second staircase, which was a species of loft over a stable. There was a low plastered ceiling to a part of it; the rest was open, to the ridge of the tiled roof, and there were beams across. Hay and straw were stored in that portion of the place, fagots for firing, and a heap of apples in sand. I had to pass through that part, to get at the other. My memory is circumstantial and unshaken. I try it with these details, and I see them all, in this my cell in the Bastille, near the close of the tenth year of my captivity, as I saw them all that night.

"On some hay on the ground, with a cushion thrown under his head, lay a handsome peasant boy—a boy of not more than seventeen at the most. He lay on his back, with his teeth set, his right hand clenched on his breast, and his glaring eyes looking straight upward. I could not see where his wound was, as I kneeled on one knee over him; but I could see that he was dying of a wound from a sharp point.

" 'I am a doctor, my poor fellow,' said I. 'Let me examine it.'

" 'I do not want it examined,' he answered; 'let it be.'

"It was under his hand, and I soothed him to let me move his hand away. The wound was a sword-thrust, received from twenty to twenty-four hours before, but no skill could have saved him if it had been looked to without delay. He was then dying fast. As I turned my eyes to the elder brother, I saw him looking down at this handsome boy whose life was ebbing out, as if he were a wounded bird, or hare, or rabbit; not at all as if he were a fellow-creature.

" 'How has this been done, monsieur?' said I.

" 'A crazed young common dog! A serf! Forced my brother to draw upon him, and has fallen by my brother's sword—like a gentleman.'

"There was no touch of pity, sorrow, or kindred humanity in this answer. The speaker seemed to acknowledge that it was inconvenient to have that different order of creature dying there, and that it would have been better if he had died in the usual obscure routine of his vermin kind. He was quite incapable of any compassionate feeling about the boy, or about his fate.

"The boy's eyes had slowly moved to him as he had spoken, and they now slowly moved to me.

" 'Doctor, they are very proud, these Nobles; but we common dogs are proud too, sometimes. They plunder us, outrage us, beat us, kill us; but we have a little pride left, sometimes. She— Have you seen her?'

"The shrieks and the cries were audible there, though subdued by the distance. He referred to them, as if she were lying in our presence.

"I said, 'I have seen her.'

" 'She is my sister, Doctor. They have had their shameful rights, these Nobles, in the modesty and virtue of our sisters, many years, but we have had good girls among us. I know it, and have heard my father say so. She was a good girl. She was betrothed to a good young man, too; a tenant of his. We were all tenants of his—that man's who stands there. The other is his brother, the worst of a bad race.'

"It was with the greatest difficulty that the boy gathered bodily force to speak; but his spirit spoke with a dreadful emphasis.

" 'We were so robbed by that man who stands there, as all we common dogs are by those superior Beings—taxed by him without mercy, obliged to work for him without pay, obliged to grind our corn at his mill, obliged to feed scores of his tame birds on our wretched crops, and forbidden for our lives to keep a single tame bird of our own, pillaged and plundered to that degree that when we chanced to have a bit of meat, we ate it in fear, with the door barred and the shutters closed, that his people should not see it and take it from us—I say, we were so robbed, and hunted, and were made so poor, that our father told us it was a dreadful thing to bring a child into the world, and that what we should most pray for was that our women might be barren and our miserable race die out!'

"I had never before seen the sense of being oppressed—bursting forth like a fire. I had supposed that it must be latent in the people somewhere; but, I had never seen it break out, until I saw it in the dying boy.

" 'Nevertheless, Doctor, my sister married. He was ailing at that time, poor fellow, and she married her lover, that she might tend and comfort him in our cottage—our dog hut, as that man would call it. She had not been married many weeks, when that man's brother saw her and admired her, and asked that man to lend her to him—for what are husbands among us! He was willing enough, but my sister was good and virtuous, and hated his brother with a hatred as strong as mine. What did the two then, to persuade her husband to use his influence with her, to make her willing?'

"The boy's eyes, which had been fixed on mine, slowly turned to the looker-on, and I saw in the two faces that all he said was true. The two opposing kinds of pride confronting one another I can see even in this Bastille; the gentleman's all negligent indifference; the peasant's, all trodden-down sentiment and passionate revenge.

" 'You know, Doctor, that it is among the Rights of these Nobles to harness us common dogs to carts, and drive us. They so harnessed him and drove him. You know that it is among their Rights to keep us in their grounds all night, quieting the frogs, in order that their noble sleep may not be disturbed. They kept him out in the unwholesome mists at night, and ordered him back into his harness in the day. But he was not persuaded. No! Taken out of harness one day at noon, to feed—if he could find food—he sobbed twelve times, once for every stroke of the bell, and died on her bosom.'

" 'Nothing human could have held life in the boy but his determination to tell all his wrong. He forced back the gathering shadows of death, as he forced his clenched right hand to remain clenched, and to cover his wound.

" 'Then, with that man's permission and even with his aid, his brother took her away; in spite of what I know she must have told his brother—and what that is, will not be long unknown to you, Doctor, if it is now—his brother took her away—for his pleasure and diversion, for a little while. I saw her pass me on the road. When I took the tidings home our father's heart burst; he never spoke one of the words that filled it. I took my young sister (for I have another) to a place beyond the reach of this man, and where, at least, she will never be *his* vassal. Then I tracked the brother here, and last night climbed in—a common dog, but sword in hand.—Where is the loft window? It was somewhere here.'

"The room was darkening to his sight; the world was narrowing around him. I glanced about me, and saw that the hay and straw were trampled over the floor, as if there had been a struggle.

" 'She heard me, and ran in. I told her not to come near us till he was dead. He came in and first tossed me some pieces of money; then struck at me with a whip. But I, though a common dog, so struck at him as to make him draw. Let him break into as many pieces as he will the sword that he stained with my common blood; he drew to defend himself—thrust at me with all his skill for his life.'

"My glance had fallen, but a few moments before, on the fragments of a broken sword, lying among the hay. That weapon was a gentleman's. In another place lay an old sword that seemed to have been a soldier's.

" 'Now, lift me up, Doctor; lift me up. Where is he?'

" 'He is not here,' I said, supporting the boy, and thinking that he referred to the brother.

" 'He! Proud as these Nobles are, he is afraid to see me. Where is the man who was here? Turn my face to him.'

"I did so, raising the boy's head against my knee. But, invested for the moment with extraordinary power, he raised himself completely: obliging me to rise too, or I could not have still supported him.

" 'Marquis,' said the boy, turning to him with his eyes opened wide, and his right hand raised, 'in the days when all these things are to be answered for, I summon you and yours, to the last of your bad race, to answer for them. I mark this cross of blood upon you, as a sign that I do it. In the days when all these things are to be answered for, I summon your brother, the worst of the bad race, to answer for them separately. I mark this cross of blood upon him, as a sign that I do it.'

"Twice, he put his hand to the wound in his breast, and with his forefinger drew a cross in the air. He stood for an instant with the finger yet raised, and, as it dropped, he dropped with it, and I laid him down dead. . . .

"When I returned to the bedside of the young woman I found her raving in precisely the same order and continuity. I knew that this might last for many hours and that it would probably end in the silence of the grave.

"I repeated the medicines I had given her, and I sat at the side of the bed until the night was far advanced. She never abated the piercing quality of her shrieks, never stumbled in the distinctness or the order of her words. They were always 'My husband, my father, and my brother! One, two, three, four, five, six, seven, eight, nine, ten, eleven, twelve. Hush!'

"This lasted twenty-six hours from the time when I first saw her. I had come and gone twice, and was again sitting by her, when she began to falter. I did what little could be done to assist that opportunity, and by-and-by she sank into a lethargy, and lay like the dead.

"It was as if the wind and rain had lulled at last, after a long and fearful storm. I released her arms, and called the woman to assist me to compose her figure and the dress she had torn. It was then that I knew her condition to be that of one in whom the first expectations of being a mother have arisen; and it was then that I lost the little hope I had had of her.

" 'Is she dead?' asked the Marquis, whom I will still describe as the elder brother, coming booted into the room from his horse.

" 'Not dead,' said I; 'but like to die.'

" 'What strength there is in these common bodies!' he said, looking down at her with some curiosity.

" 'There is prodigious strength,' I answered him, 'in sorrow and despair.'

"He first laughed at my words, and then frowned at them. He moved a chair with his foot near to mine, ordered the woman away, and said in a subdued voice:

" 'Doctor, finding my brother in this difficulty with these hinds, I recommended that your aid should be invited. Your reputation is high, and, as a young man with your fortune to make, you are probably mindful of your interest. The things that you see here are things to be seen, and not spoken of.'

"I listened to the patient's breathing, and avoided answering.

" 'Do you honor me with your attention, Doctor?'

" 'Monsieur,' said I, 'in my profession, the communications of patients are always received in confidence.' I was guarded in my answer, for I was troubled in my mind with what I had heard and seen.

"Her breathing was so difficult to trace, that I carefully tried the pulse and the heart. There was life, and no more. Looking round as I resumed my seat, I found both the brothers intent upon me. . . .

"I write with so much difficulty, the cold is so severe, I am so fearful of being detected and consigned to an underground cell and total darkness, that I must abridge this narrative. There is no confusion or failure in my memory;

it can recall, and could detail, every word that was ever spoken between me and those brothers.

"She lingered for a week. Towards the last, I could understand some few syllables that she said to me, by placing my ear close to her lips. She asked me where she was, and I told her; who I was, and I told her. It was in vain that I asked her for her family name. She faintly shook her head upon the pillow, and kept her secret, as the boy had done.

"I had no opportunity of asking her any question, until I had told the brothers she was sinking fast, and could not live another day. Until then, though no one was ever presented to her consciousness save the woman and myself, one or other of them had always jealously sat behind the curtain at the head of the bed when I was there. But when it came to that, they seemed careless what communication I might hold with her; as if—the thought passed through my mind—I were dying too.

"I always observed that their pride bitterly resented the younger brother's (as I call him) having crossed swords with a peasant, and that peasant a boy. The only consideration that appeared to affect the mind of either of them was the consideration that this was highly degrading to the family, and was ridiculous. As often as I caught the younger brother's eyes, their expression reminded me that he disliked me deeply, for knowing what I knew from the boy. He was smoother and more polite to me than the elder; but I saw this. I also saw that I was an incumbrance in the mind of the elder too.

"My patient died, two hours before midnight—at a time, by my watch, answering almost to the minute when I had first seen her. I was alone with her, when her forlorn young head drooped gently on one side, and all her earthly wrongs and sorrows ended.

"The brothers were waiting in a room downstairs, impatient to ride away. I had heard them, alone at the bedside, striking their boots with their riding-whips, and loitering up and down.

" 'At last she is dead?' said the elder, when I went in.

" 'She is dead,' said I.

" 'I congratulate you, my brother,' were his words as he turned round.

"He had before offered me money, which I had postponed taking. He now gave me a rouleau of gold. I took it from his hand, but laid it on the table. I had considered the question, and had resolved to accept nothing.

" 'Pray excuse me,' said I. 'Under the circumstances, no.'

"They exchanged looks, but bent their heads to me as I bent mine to them, and we parted without another word on either side. . . .

"I am weary, weary, weary—worn down by misery. I cannot read what I have written with this gaunt hand.

"Early in the morning, the rouleau of gold was left at my door in a little box, with my name on the outside. From the first, I had curiously considered what I ought to do. I decided, that day, to write privately to the Minister, stating the nature of the two cases to which I had been summoned, and the place to which I had gone: in effect, stating all the circumstances. I knew what Court influence was, and what the immunities of the Nobles were, and I expected that the matter would never be heard of; but I wished to relieve my own mind. I had kept the matter a profound secret, even from my wife; and this, too, I resolved to state in my letter. I had no apprehension whatever of my real danger; but I was conscious that there might be danger for others, if others were compromised by possessing the knowledge that I possessed.

"I was much engaged that day, and could not complete my letter that night. I rose long before my usual time next morning to finish it. It was the last day of the year. The letter was lying before me just completed, when I was told that a lady waited, who wished to see me. . . .

"I am growing more and more unequal to the task I have set myself. It is so cold, so dark, my senses are so benumbed, and the gloom upon me is so dreadful.

"The lady was young, engaging, and handsome, but not marked for long life. She was in great agitation. She presented herself to me as the wife of the Marquis St. Evrémonde. I connected the title by which the boy had addressed the elder brother, with the initial letter embroidered on the scarf, and had no difficulty in arriving at the conclusion that I had seen that nobleman very lately.

"My memory is still accurate, but I cannot write the words of our conversation. I suspect that I am watched more closely than I was, and I know not at what times I may be watched. She had in part suspected, and in part discovered, the main facts of the cruel story, of her husband's share in it, and my being resorted to. She did not know that the girl was dead. Her hope had been, she said in great distress, to show her, in secret, a woman's sympathy. Her hope had been to avert the wrath of Heaven from a House that had long been hateful to the suffering many.

"She had reasons for believing that there was a young sister living, and her greatest desire was to help that sister. I could tell her nothing but that there was such a sister; beyond that, I knew nothing. Her inducement to come to me, relying on my confidence, had been the hope that I could tell her the name and place of abode. Whereas, to this wretched hour I am ignorant of both. . . .

"These scraps of paper fail me. One was taken from me, with a warning, yesterday. I must finish my record today.

"She was a good, compassionate lady, and not happy in her marriage. How could she be! The brother distrusted and disliked her, and his influence was all opposed to her; she stood in dread of him, and in dread of her husband too. When I handed her down to the door, there was a child, a pretty boy from two to three years old, in her carriage.

" 'For his sake, Doctor,' she said, pointing to him in tears, 'I would do all I can to make what poor amends I can. He will never prosper in his inheritance otherwise. I have a presentiment that if no other innocent atonement is made for this, it will one day be required of him. What I have left to call my own—it is little beyond the worth of a few jewels—I will make it the first charge of his life to bestow, with the compassion and lamenting of his dead mother, on this injured family, if the sister can be discovered.'

"She kissed the boy, and said, caressing him, 'It is for thine own dear sake. Thou wilt be faithful, little Charles?' The child answered her bravely, 'Yes!' I kissed her hand, and she took him in her arms, and went away caressing him. I never saw her more.

"As she had mentioned her husband's name in the faith that I knew it, I added no mention of it to my letter. I sealed my letter, and, not trusting it out of my own hands, delivered it myself that day.

"That night, the last night of the year, towards nine o'clock, a man in a black dress rang at my gate, demanded to see me, and softly followed my servant, Ernest Defarge, a youth, upstairs. When my servant came into the room where I sat with my wife—Oh my wife, beloved of my heart! My fair, young, English wife!—we saw the man, who was supposed to be at the gate, standing silent behind him.

"An urgent case in the Rue St. Honoré, he said. It would not detain me, he had a coach in waiting.

"It brought me here, it brought me to my grave. When I was clear of the house, a black muffler was drawn tightly over my mouth from behind, and my arms were pinioned. The two brothers crossed the road from a dark corner, and identified me with a single gesture. The Marquis took from his pocket the letter I had written, showed it me, burnt it in the light of a lantern that was held, and extinguished the ashes with his foot. Not a word was spoken. I was brought here, I was brought to my living grave.

"If it had pleased God to put it in the hard heart of either of the brothers, in all these frightful years, to grant me any tidings of my dearest wife—so much as to let me know by a word whether alive or dead—I might have thought that He had not quite abandoned them. But, now I believe that the mark of the red cross is fatal to them, and that they have no part in His mercies. And them and their descendants, to the last of their race, I, Alexander Manette, unhappy prisoner, do this last night of the year 1767, in my unbearable agony, denounce to the times when all these things shall be answered for. I denounce them to Heaven and to earth."

A terrible sound arose when the reading of this document was done. A sound of craving and eagerness that had nothing articulate in it but blood. The narrative called up the most revengeful passions of the time, and there was not a head in the nation but must have dropped before it.

Little need, in presence of that tribunal and that auditory, to show how the Defarges had not made the paper public, with the other captured Bastille memorials borne in procession, and had kept it, biding their time. Little need to show that this detested family name had long been anathematized by Saint Antoine, and was wrought into the fatal register. The man never trod ground whose virtues and services would have sustained him in that place that day, against such denunciation.

And all the worse for the doomed man, that the denouncer was a well-known citizen, his own attached friend, the father of his wife. One of the frenzied aspirations of the populace was for imitations of the questionable public virtues of antiquity, and for sacrifices and self-immolations on the people's altar. Therefore when the President said (else had his own head quivered on his shoulders), that the good physician of the Republic would deserve better still of the Republic by rooting out an obnoxious family of aristocrats, and would doubtless feel a sacred glow and joy in making his daughter a widow and her child an orphan, there was wild excitement, patriotic fervor, not a touch of human sympathy.

"Much influence around him, has that Doctor?" murmured Madame Defarge, smiling to The Vengeance. "Save him now, my Doctor, save him!"

At every juryman's vote, there was a roar. Another and another. Roar and roar.

Unanimously voted. At heart and by descent an Aristocrat, an enemy of the Republic, a notorious oppressor of the People. Back to the Conciergerie, and Death within four-and-twenty hours!

E l e v e n

DUSK

THE WRETCHED WIFE OF THE INNOCENT MAN THUS DOOMED to die fell under the sentence as if she had been mortally stricken. But she uttered no sound; and so strong was the voice within her, representing that it was she of all the world who must uphold him in his misery and not augment it, that it quickly raised her, even from that shock.

The judges having to take part in a public demonstration out of doors, the tribunal adjourned. The quick noise and movement of the court's emptying itself by many passages had not ceased, when Lucie stood stretching out her arms toward her husband, with nothing in her face but love and consolation.

"If I might touch him! If I might embrace him once! Oh, good citizens, if you would have so much compassion for us!"

There was but a jailer left, along with two of the four men who had taken him last night, and Barsad. The people had all poured out to the show in the streets. Barsad proposed to the rest, "Let her embrace him then; it is but a moment." It was silently acquiesced in, and they passed her over the seats in the hall to a raised place, where he, by leaning over the dock, could fold her in his arms.

"Farewell, dear darling of my soul. My parting blessing on my love. We shall meet again, where the weary are at rest!"

They were her husband's words, as he held her to his bosom.

"I can bear it, dear Charles. I am supported from above: don't suffer for me. A parting blessing for our child."

"I send it to her by you. I kiss her by you. I say farewell to her by you."

"My husband. No! A moment!" He was tearing himself apart from her. "We shall not be separated long. I feel that this will break my heart by-and-by; but I will do my duty while I can, and when I leave her, God will raise up friends for her, as He did for me."

Her father had followed her, and would have fallen on his knees to both of them, but that Darnay put out a hand and seized him, crying:

"No, no! What have you done, what have you done, that you should kneel to us! We know now what a struggle you made of old. We know now what you underwent when you suspected my descent, and when you knew it. We know now the natural antipathy you strove against, and conquered, for her dear sake. We thank you with all our hearts, and all our love and duty. Heaven be with you!"

Her father's only answer was to draw his hands through his white hair, and wring them with a shriek of anguish.

"It could not be otherwise," said the prisoner. "All things have worked together as they have fallen out. It was the always vain endeavor to discharge my poor mother's trust that first brought my fatal presence near you. Good could never come of such evil, a happier end was not in nature to so unhappy a beginning. Be comforted, and forgive me. Heaven bless you!"

As he was drawn away, his wife released him, and stood looking after him with her hands touching one another in the attitude of prayer, and with a radiant look upon her face, in which there was even a comforting smile. As he went out at the prisoners' door, she turned, laid her head lovingly on her father's breast, tried to speak to him, and fell at his feet.

Then, issuing from the obscure corner from which he had never moved, Sydney Carton came and took her up. Only her father and Mr. Lorry were with her. His arm trembled as it raised her, and supported her head. Yet, there was an air about him that was not all pity—that had a flush of pride in it.

"Shall I take her to a coach? I shall never feel her weight."

He carried her lightly to the door, and laid her tenderly down in a coach. Her father and their old friend got into it, and he took his seat beside the driver.

When they arrived at the gateway where he had paused in the dark not many hours before, to picture to himself on which of the rough stones of the street her feet had trodden, he lifted her again, and carried her up the staircase to their rooms. There, he laid her down on a couch, where her child and Miss Pross wept over her.

"Don't recall her to herself," he said, softly, to the latter; "she is better so; don't revive her to consciousness, while she only faints."

"Oh, Carton, Carton, dear Carton!" cried little Lucie, springing up and throwing her arms passionately round him, in a burst of grief. "Now that you have come, I think you will do something to help mamma, something to save papa! Oh, look at her, dear Carton! Can you, of all the people who love her, bear to see her so?"

He bent over the child, and laid her blooming cheek against his face. He put her gently from him, and looked at her unconscious mother.

"Before I go," he said, and paused—"I may kiss her?"

It was remembered afterwards that when he bent down and touched her face with his lips, he murmured some words. The child, who was nearest to him, told them afterwards, and told her grandchildren when she was a handsome old lady, that she heard him say, "A life you love."

When he had gone out into the next room, he turned suddenly on Mr. Lorry and her father, who were following, and said to the latter:

"You had great influence but yesterday, Doctor Manette; let it at least be tried. These judges, and all the men in power, are very friendly to you, and very recognizant of your services; are they not?"

"Nothing connected with Charles was concealed from me. I had the strongest assurances that I should save him; and I did." He returned the answer in great trouble, and very slowly.

"Try them again. The hours between this and tomorrow afternoon are few and short, but try."

"I intend to try. I will not rest a moment."

"That's well. I have known such energy as yours do great things before now—though never," he added, with a smile and a sigh together, "such great things as this. But try! Of little worth as life is when we misuse it, it is worth that effort. It would cost nothing to lay down if it were not."

"I will go," said Doctor Manette, "to the Prosecutor and the President straight, and I will go to others whom it is better not to name. I will write too, and— But stay! There is a celebration in the streets, and no one will be accessible until dark."

"That's true. Well! It is a forlorn hope at the best, and not much the forlorner for being delayed till dark. I should like to know how you speed; though, mind! I expect nothing! When are you likely to have seen these dread powers, Doctor Manette?"

"Immediately after dark, I should hope. Within an hour or two from this."

"It will be dark soon after four. Let us stretch the hour or two. If I go to Mr. Lorry's at nine, shall I hear what you have done, either from our friend or from yourself?"

"Yes."

"May you prosper!"

Mr. Lorry followed Sydney to the outer door, and, touching him on the shoulder as he was going away, caused him to turn.

"I have no hope," said Mr. Lorry, in a sorrowful whisper.

"Nor have I."

"If anyone of these men, or all of these men, were disposed to spare him—which is a large supposition; for what is his life, or any man's to them!—I doubt if they durst spare him after the demonstration in the court."

"And so do I. I heard the fall of the axe in that sound."

Mr. Lorry leaned his arm upon the doorpost, and bowed his face upon it.

"Don't despond," said Carton, very gently; "don't grieve. I encouraged Doctor Manette in this idea, because I felt that it might one day be consolatory to her. Otherwise, she might think 'his life was wantonly thrown away or wasted,' and that might trouble her."

"Yes, yes, yes," returned Mr. Lorry, drying his eyes, "you are right. But he will perish; there is no real hope."

"Yes. He will perish; there is no real hope," echoed Carton. And walked with a settled step, downstairs.

Twelve

DARKNESS

SYDNEY CARTON PAUSED IN THE STREET, NOT QUITE decided where to go. "At Tellson's Banking-house at nine," he said with a musing face. "Shall I do well, in the meantime, to show myself? I think so. It is best that these people should know there is such a man as I here; it is a sound precaution, and may be a necessary preparation. But care, care, care! Let me think it out!"

Checking his steps, which had begun to tend towards an object, he took a turn or two in the already darkening street, and traced the thought in his mind to its possible consequences. His first impression was confirmed. "It is best," he said, finally resolved, "that these people should know there is such a man as I here." And he turned his face towards Saint Antoine.

Defarge had described himself, that day, as the keeper of a wine-shop in the Saint Antoine suburb. It was not difficult, for one who knew the city well, to find his house without asking any question. Having ascertained its situation, Carton came out of those closer streets again, and dined at a place of refreshment and fell sound asleep after dinner. For the first time in many years, he had no strong drink. Since last night he had taken nothing but a little light thin wine, and last night he had dropped the brandy slowly down on Mr. Lorry's hearth like a man who had done with it.

It was as late as seven o'clock when he awoke refreshed, and went out into the streets again. As he passed along towards Saint Antoine, he stopped at a shop-window where there was a mirror, and slightly altered the disordered arrangement of his loose cravat, and his coat-collar, and his wild hair. This done he went on direct to Defarge's, and went in.

There happened to be no customer in the shop but Jacques Three, of the restless fingers and the croaking voice. This man, whom he had seen upon the Jury, stood drinking at the little counter, in conversation with the Defarges, man and wife. The Vengeance assisted in the conversation, like a regular member of the establishment.

As Carton walked in, took his seat and asked (in very indifferent French) for a small measure of wine, Madame Defarge cast a careless glance at him, and then a keener, and then a keener, and then advanced to him herself, and asked him what it was he had ordered.

He repeated what he had already said.

"English?" asked Madame Defarge, inquisitively raising her dark eyebrows.

After looking at her, as if the sound of even a single French word were slow to express itself to him, he answered, in his former strong foreign accent, "Yes, madame, yes. I am English!"

Madame Defarge returned to her counter to get the wine, and as he took up a Jacobin journal and feigned to pore over it puzzling out its meaning, he heard her say, "I swear to you, like Evrémonde!"

Defarge brought him the wine, and gave him Good evening.

"How?"

"Good evening."

"Oh! Good evening, citizen," filling his glass. "Ah! and good wine. I drink to the Republic."

Defarge went back to the counter, and said, "Certainly, a little like." Madame sternly retorted, "I tell you a good deal like." Jacques Three pacifically remarked, "He is so much in your mind, see you, madame." The amiable Vengeance added, with a laugh, "Yes, my faith! And you are looking forward with so much pleasure to seeing him once more tomorrow!"

Carton followed the lines and words of his paper with a slow forefinger, and with a studious and absorbed face. They were all leaning their arms on the counter close together, speaking low. After a silence of a few moments, during which they all looked towards him without disturbing his outward attention from the Jacobin editor, they resumed their conversation.

"It is true what madame says," observed Jacques Three. "Why stop? There is great force in that. Why stop?"

"Well, well," reasoned Defarge, "but one must stop somewhere. After all, the question is still where?"

"At extermination," said madame.

"Magnificent!" croaked Jacques Three. The Vengeance, also, highly approved.

"Extermination is good doctrine, my wife," said Defarge, rather troubled; "in general, I say nothing against it. But this Doctor has suffered much; you have seen him today; you have observed his face when the paper was read."

"I have observed his face!" repeated madame, contemptuously and angrily. "Yes. I have observed his face. I have observed his face to be not the face of a true friend of the Republic. Let him take care of his face!"

"And you have observed, my wife," said Defarge, in a deprecatory manner, "the anguish of his daughter, which must be dreadful anguish to him!"

"I have observed his daughter!" repeated madame; "yes, I have observed his daughter more times than one. I have observed her today, and I have observed her other days. I have observed her in the court, and I have observed her in the street by the prison. Let me but lift my finger—!" She seemed to raise it (the listener's eyes were always on his paper), and to let it fall with a rattle on the ledge before her, as if the axe had dropped.

"The citizeness is superb!" croaked the Juryman.

"She is an Angel!" said The Vengeance, and embraced her.

"As to thee," pursued madame, implacably, addressing her husband, "if it depended on thee—which, happily, it does not—thou wouldst rescue this man even now."

"No!" protested Defarge. "Not if to lift this glass would do it! But I would leave the matter there. I say, stop there."

"See you then, Jacques," said Madame Defarge, wrathfully; "and see you too, my little Vengeance; see you both! Listen! For other crimes as tyrants and oppressors, I have this race a long time on my register, doomed to destruction and extermination. Ask my husband, is that so."

"It is so," asserted Defarge, without being asked.

"In the beginning of the great days, when the Bastille falls, he finds this paper of today, and he brings it home, and in the middle of the night when this place is clear and shut, we read it, here on this spot, by the light of this lamp. Ask him, is that so."

"It is so," asserted Defarge.

"That night I tell him, when the paper is read through, and the lamp is burned out, and the day is gleaming in above those shutters and between those iron bars, that I have now a secret to communicate. Ask him, is that so."

"It is so," asserted Defarge again.

"I communicate to him that secret. I smite this bosom with these two hands as I smite it now, and I tell him, 'Defarge, I was brought up among the fishermen of the seashore, and that injured family is mine. Defarge, that sister was my sister, that husband was my sister's husband, that unborn child was their child, that brother was my brother, that father was my father, those dead are my dead, and that summons to answer for those things descends to me!' Ask him is that so."

"It is so," assented Defarge once more.

"Then tell Wind and Fire where to stop," returned madame; "but don't tell me."

Both her hearers derived a horrible enjoyment from the deadly nature of her wrath—the listener could feel how white she was, without seeing her—and both highly commended it. Defarge, a weak minority, interposed a few words for the memory of the compassionate wife of the Marquis; but only elicited from his own wife a repetition of her last reply. "Tell the Wind and the Fire where to stop; not me!"

Customers entered, and the group was broken up. The English customer paid for what he had had, perplexedly counted his change, and asked, as a stranger, to be directed toward the National Palace. Madame Defarge took him to the door, and put her arm on his in pointing out the road. The English customer was not without his reflections then, that it might be a good deed to seize that arm, lift it, and strike under it sharp and deep.

But, he went on his way, and was soon swallowed up in the shadow of the prison wall. At the appointed hour, he emerged from it to present himself in Mr. Lorry's room again, where he found the old gentleman walking to and fro in restless anxiety. He said he had been with Lucie until just now, and had only left her for a few minutes, to come and keep his appointment. Her father had not been seen, since he quitted the Banking-house toward four o'clock. She had some faint hopes that his mediation might save Charles, but they were very slight. He had been more than five hours gone: where could he be?

Mr. Lorry waited until ten; but, Doctor Manette not returning, and he being unwilling to leave Lucie any longer, it was arranged that he should go back to her, and come to the Banking-house again at midnight. In the meanwhile, Carton would wait alone by the fire for the Doctor.

He waited and waited, and the clock struck twelve; but Doctor Manette did not come back. Mr. Lorry returned, and found no tidings of him, and brought none. Where could he be?

They were discussing this question, and were almost building up some weak structure of hope on his prolonged absence, when they heard him on the stairs. The instant he entered the room, it was plain that all was lost.

Whether he had really been to anyone, or whether he had been all that time traversing the streets, was never known. As he stood staring at them, they asked him no question, for his face told them everything.

"I cannot find it," said he, "and I must have it. Where is it?"

His head and throat were bare, and as he spoke with a helpless look straying all around, he took his coat off and let it drop on the floor.

"Where is my bench? I have been looking everywhere for my bench, and I can't find it. What have they done with my work? Time presses: I must finish those shoes."

They looked at one another, and their hearts died within them.

"Come, come!" said he, in a whimpering miserable way; "let me get to work. Give me my work."

Receiving no answer, he tore his hair and beat his feet upon the ground like a distracted child.

"Don't torture a poor, forlorn wretch," he implored them, with a dreadful cry; "but give me my work! What is to become of us if those shoes are not done tonight?"

Lost, utterly lost!

It was so clearly beyond hope to reason with him or try to restore him, that—as if by agreement—they each put a hand upon his shoulder, and soothed him to sit down before the fire, with a promise that he should have his work presently. He sank into the chair, and brooded over the embers and shed tears. As if all that had happened since the garret time were a momentary fancy or a dream, Mr. Lorry saw him shrink into the exact figure that Defarge had had in keeping.

Affected, and impressed with terror as they both were, by this spectacle of ruin, it was not a time to yield to such emotions. His lonely daughter, bereft of her final hope and reliance, appealed to them both too strongly. Again, as if by agreement, they looked at one another with one meaning in their faces. Carton was the first to speak:

"The last chance is gone: it was not much. Yes; he had better be taken to her. But before you go, will you for a moment, steadily attend to me? Don't ask me why I make the stipulations I am going to make, and exact the promise I am going to exact; I have a reason—a good one."

"I do not doubt it," answered Mr. Lorry. "Say on."

The figure in the chair between them was all the time monotonously rocking itself to and fro, and moaning. They spoke in such a tone as they would have used if they had been watching by a sickbed in the night.

Carton stooped to pick up the coat which lay almost entangling his feet. As he did so, a small case in which the Doctor was accustomed to carry the list of his day's duties, fell lightly on the floor. Carton took it up, and there was a folded paper in it. "We should look at this!" he said. Mr. Lorry nodded his consent. He opened it, and exclaimed, "Thank God!"

"What is it?" asked Mr. Lorry, eagerly.

"A moment! Let me speak of it in its place. First," he put his hand in his coat, and took another paper from it, "that is the certificate which enables me to pass out of this city. Look at it. You see—Sydney Carton, an Englishman?"

Mr. Lorry held it open in his hand, gazing in his earnest face.

"Keep it for me until tomorrow. I shall see him tomorrow, you remember, and I had better not take it into the prison."

"Why not?"

"I don't know; I prefer not to do so. Now take this paper that Doctor Manette has carried about him. It is a similar certificate, enabling him and his daughter and her child, at any time to pass the Barrier and the frontier. You see?"

"Yes!"

"Perhaps he obtained it as his last and utmost precaution against evil, yesterday. When is it dated? But no matter; don't stay to look; put it up carefully with mine and your own. Now, observe! I never doubted until within this hour or two, that he had or could have such a paper. It is good until recalled. But it may be soon recalled, and, I have reason to think will be."

"They are not in danger?"

"They are in great danger. They are in danger of denunciation by Madame Defarge. I know it from her own lips. I have overheard words of that woman's, tonight, which have presented their danger to me in strong colors. I have lost no time, and since then I have seen the spy. He confirms me. He knows that a wood-sawyer, living by the prison-wall, is under the control of the Defarges, and has been rehearsed by Madame Defarge as to his having seen *Her*"—he never mentioned Lucie's name—"making signs and signals to prisoners. It is easy to foresee that the pretense will be the common one, a prison plot, and that it will involve her life—and perhaps her child's—and perhaps her father's—for both have been seen with her at that place. Don't look so horrified. You will save them all."

"Heaven grant I may, Carton! But how?"

"I am going to tell you how. It will depend on you, and it could depend on no better man. This new denunciation will certainly not take place until after tomorrow; probably not until two or three days afterward: more probably a week afterward. You know it is a capital crime to mourn for, or sympathize with, a victim of the guillotine. She and her father would unquestionably be guilty of this crime, and this woman (the inveteracy of whose pursuit cannot be described) would wait to add that strength to her case, and make herself doubly sure. You follow me?"

"So attentively, and with so much confidence in what you say, that for the moment I lose sight," touching the back of the Doctor's chair, "even of this distress."

"You have money, and can buy the means of traveling to the seacoast as quickly as the journey can be made. Your preparations have been completed for some days to return to England. Early tomorrow have your horses ready, so that they may be in starting trim at two o'clock in the afternoon."

"It shall be done!"

His manner was so fervent and inspiring, that Mr. Lorry caught the flame, and was quick as youth.

"You are a noble heart. Did I say we could depend upon no better man? Tell her, tonight, what you know of her danger as involving her child and her father. Dwell upon that, for she would lay her own fair head beside her husband's cheerfully." He faltered for an instant; then went on as before. "For the sake of her child and her father, press upon her the necessity of leaving Paris, with them and you, at that hour. Tell her that it was her husband's last arrangement. Tell her that more depends upon it than she dare believe, or hope. You think that her father, even in this sad state, will submit himself to her; do you not?"

"I am sure of it."

"I thought so. Quietly and steadily have all these arrangements made in the courtyard here, even to the taking of your own seat in the carriage. The moment I come to you take me in, and drive away."

"I understand that I wait for you under all circumstances?"

"You have my certificate in your hand with the rest, you know, and will reserve my place. Wait for nothing but to have my place occupied, and then for England!"

"Why, then," said Mr. Lorry, grasping his eager but so firm and steady hand, "it does not all depend on one old man, but I shall have a young and ardent man at my side."

"By the help of Heaven you shall! Promise me solemnly that nothing will influence you to alter the course on which we now stand pledged to one another."

"Nothing, Carton."

"Remember these words tomorrow: change the course, or delay in it—for any reason—and no life can possibly be saved, and many lives must inevitably be sacrificed."

"I will remember them. I hope to do my part faithfully."

"And I hope to do mine. Now, good-bye!"

Though he said it with a grave smile of earnestness, and though he even put the old man's hand to his lips, he did not part from him then. He helped him so far to arouse the rocking figure before the dying embers as to get a cloak and hat put upon it, and to tempt it forth to find where the bench and work were hidden that it still moaningly besought to have. He walked on the other side of, it and protected it to the courtyard of the house where the afflicted heart—so happy in the memorable time when he had revealed his own desolate heart to it—outwatched the awful night. He entered the courtyard and remained there for a few moments alone, looking up at the light in the window of her room. Before he went away, he breathed a blessing toward it, and a farewell.

FIFTY-TWO

I N THE BLACK PRISON OF THE CONCIERGERIE THE DOOMED of the day awaited their fate. They were in number as the weeks of the year. Fifty-two were to roll that afternoon on the life-tide of the city to the boundless, everlasting sea. Before their cells were quit of them, new occupants were appointed; before their blood ran into the blood spilled yesterday, the blood that was to mingle with theirs tomorrow was already set apart.

Two score and twelve were told off. From the Farmer-General of seventy, whose riches could not buy his life, to the seamstress of twenty, whose poverty and obscurity could not save her. Physical diseases, engendered in the vices and neglects of men, will seize on victims of all degrees; and the frightful moral disorder, born of unspeakable suffering, intolerable oppression, and heartless indifference, smote equally without distinction.

Charles Darnay, alone in a cell, had sustained himself with no flattering delusion since he came to it from the Tribunal. In every line of the narrative he had heard read, he had heard his condemnation. He had fully comprehended that no personal influence could possibly save him—that he was virtually sentenced by the millions, and that units could avail him nothing.

Nevertheless, it was not easy, with the face of his beloved wife fresh before him, to compose his mind to what it must bear. His hold on life was strong, and it was very, very hard to loosen; by gradual efforts and degrees unclosed a little here, it clenched the tighter there, and when he brought his strength to bear on that hand and it yielded, this was closed again. There was a hurry, too, in all his thoughts, a turbulent and heated working of his heart, that contended against resignation. If, for a moment, he did feel resigned, then his wife and child, who had to live after him, seemed to protest and to make it a selfish thing.

But all this was at first. Before long the consideration that there was no disgrace in the fate he must meet, and that numbers went the same road wrongfully, and trod it firmly, every day, sprang up to stimulate him. Next followed the thought that much of the future peace of mind enjoyable by the dear ones depended on his quiet fortitude. So, by degrees he calmed into the better state, when he could raise his thoughts much higher, and draw comfort down.

Before it had set in dark on the night of his condemnation he had traveled thus far on his last way. Being allowed to purchase the means of writing, and a light, he sat down to write until such time as the prison lamps should be extinguished.

He wrote a long letter to Lucie, showing her that he had known nothing of her father's imprisonment, until he had heard of it from herself, and that he had been as ignorant as she of his father's and uncle's responsibility for that misery until the paper had been read. He had already explained to her that his concealment from herself of the name he had relinquished was the one condition—fully intelligible now—that her father had attached to their betrothal, and was the one promise he had still exacted on the morning of their marriage. He entreated her, for her father's sake, never to seek to know whether her father had become oblivious of the existence of the paper, or had had it recalled to him (for the moment, or for good), by the story of the Tower, on that old Sunday under the dear old plane-tree in the garden. If he had preserved any definite remembrance of it, there could be no doubt that he had supposed it destroyed with the Bastille, when he had found no mention of it among the relics of prisoners which the populace had discovered there, and which had been described to all the world. He besought her—though he added that he knew it was needless—to console her father, by impressing him, through every tender means she could think of, with the truth that he had done nothing for which he could justly reproach himself, but had uniformly forgotten himself for their joint sakes. Next to her preservation of his own last grateful love and blessing, and her overcoming of her sorrow, to devote herself to their dear child, he adjured her, as they would meet in Heaven, to comfort her father.

To her father himself, he wrote in the same strain; but he told her father that he expressly confided his wife and child to his care. And he told him this, very strongly, with the hope of rousing him from any despondency or dangerous retrospect toward which he foresaw he might be tending.

To Mr. Lorry, he commended them all, and explained his worldly affairs. That done, with many added sentences of grateful friendship and warm attachment, all was done. He never thought of Carton. His mind was so full of the others, that he never once thought of him.

He had time to finish these letters before the lights were put out. When he lay down on his straw bed, he thought he had done with this world.

But it beckoned him back in his sleep, and showed itself in shining forms. Free and happy, back in the old house in Soho (though it had nothing in it like the real house), unaccountably released and light of heart, he was with Lucie again, and she told him it was all a dream, and he had never gone away. A pause of forgetfulness, and then he had even suffered, and had come back to her, dead and at peace, and yet there was no difference in him. Another pause of oblivion, and he awoke in the somber morning, unconscious where he was or what had happened, until it flashed upon his mind, "This is the day of my death!"

Thus, had he come through the hours to the day when the fifty-two heads were to fall. And now, while he was composed and hoped that he could meet the end with quiet heroism, a new action began in his waking thoughts, which was very difficult to master.

He had never seen the instrument that was to terminate his life. How high it was from the ground, how many steps it had, where he would be stood, how he would be touched, whether the touching hands would be dyed red, which way his face would be turned, whether he would be the first, or might be the last: these and many similar questions, in no wise directed by his will, obtruded themselves over and over again, countless times. Neither were they connected with fear; he was conscious of no fear. Rather, they originated in a strange besetting desire to know what to do when the time came; a desire gigantically disproportionate to the few split moments to which it referred; a wondering that was more like the wondering of some other spirit within his than his own.

The hours went on as he walked to and fro, and the clocks struck the numbers he would never hear again. Nine gone forever, ten gone forever, eleven gone forever, twelve coming on to pass away. After a hard contest with that eccentric action of thought which had last perplexed him, he had got the better of it. He walked up and down, softly repeating their names to himself. The worst of the strife was over. He could walk up and down, free from distracting fancies, praying for himself and for them.

Twelve gone forever.

He had been apprised that the final hour was Three, and he knew he would be summoned sometime earlier, inasmuch as the tumbrils jolted heavily and slowly through the streets. Therefore, he resolved to keep Two before his mind as the hour, and so to strengthen himself in the interval that he might be able, after that time, to strengthen others.

Walking regularly to and fro with his arms folded on his breast, a very different man from the prisoner who had walked to and fro at La Force, he heard One struck away from him without surprise. The hour had measured like most other hours. Devoutly thankful to Heaven for his recovered self-possession, he thought, "There is but another now," and turned to walk again.

Footsteps in the stone passage outside the door. He stopped.

The key was put in the lock, and turned. Before the door was opened, or as it opened, a man said in a low voice, in English: "He has never seen me here; I have kept out of his way. Go you in alone; I wait near. Lose no time!"

The door was quickly opened and closed, and there stood before him face to face, quiet, intent upon him, with the light of a smile on his features, and a cautionary finger on his lip, Sydney Carton.

There was something so bright and remarkable in his look, that, for the first moment, the prisoner misdoubted him to be an apparition of his own imagining. But he spoke, and it was his voice; he took the prisoner's hand, and it was his real grasp.

"Of all the people upon earth, you least expected to see me!" he said.

"I could not believe it to be you. I can scarcely believe it now. You are not"—the apprehension came suddenly into his mind—"a prisoner?"

"No. I am accidentally possessed of a power over one of the keepers here, and in virtue of it I stand before you. I come from her—your wife, dear Darnay."

The prisoner wrung his hand.

"I bring you a request from her."

"What is it?"

"A most earnest, pressing, and emphatic entreaty, addressed to you in the most pathetic tones of the voice so dear to you, that you well remember."

The prisoner turned his face partly aside.

"You have no time to ask me why I bring it, or what it means; I have no time to tell you. You must comply with it—take off those boots you wear, and draw on these of mine."

There was a chair against the wall of the cell, behind the prisoner. Carton, pressing forward, had already, with the speed of lightning, got him down into it, and stood over him, barefoot.

"Draw on those boots of mine. Put your hands to them; put your will to them. Quick!"

"Carton, there is no escaping from this place; it never can be done. You will only die with me. It is madness."

"It would be madness if I asked you to escape; but do I? When I ask you to pass out at that door, tell me it is madness and remain here. Change that cravat for this of mine, that coat for this of mine. While you do it, let me take this ribbon from your hair, and shake out your hair like this of mine!"

With wonderful quickness, and with a strength both of will and action, that appeared quite supernatural, he forced all these changes upon him. The prisoner was like a young child in his hands.

"Carton! Dear Carton! It is madness. It cannot be accomplished, it never can be done, it has been attempted, and has always failed. I implore you not to add your death to the bitterness of mine."

"Do I ask you, my dear Darnay, to pass the door? When I ask that, refuse. There are pen and ink and paper on this table. Is your hand steady enough to write?"

"It was when you came in."

"Steady it again, and write what I shall dictate. Quick, friend, quick!"

Pressing his hand to his bewildered head, Darnay sat down at the table. Carton, with his right hand in his breast, stood close beside him.

"Write exactly as I speak."

"To whom do I address it?"

"To no one." Carton still had his hand in his breast.

"Do I date it?"

"No."

The prisoner looked up at each question. Carton, standing over him with his hand in his breast, looked down.

" 'If you remember,' " said Carton, dictating, " 'the words that passed between us, long ago, you will readily comprehend this when you see it. You do remember them, I know. It is not in your nature to forget them.' "

He was drawing his hand from his breast; the prisoner chancing to look up in his hurried wonder as he wrote, the hand stopped, closing upon something.

"Have you written 'forget them'?" Carton asked.

"I have. Is that a weapon in your hand?"

"No; I am not armed."

"What is it in your hand?"

"You shall know directly. Write on; there are but a few words more." He dictated again. " 'I am thankful that the time has come, when I can prove them. That I do so is no subject for regret or grief.' " As he said these words with his eyes fixed on the writer, his hand slowly and softly moved down close to the writer's face.

The pen dropped from Darnay's fingers on the table, and he looked about him vacantly.

"What vapor is that?" he asked.

"Vapor?"

"Something that crossed me?"

"I am conscious of nothing; there can be nothing here. Take up the pen and finish. Hurry, hurry!"

As if his memory were impaired, or his faculties disordered, the prisoner made an effort to rally his attention. As he looked at Carton with clouded eyes and with an altered manner of breathing, Carton—his hand again in his breast—looked steadily at him.

"Hurry, hurry!"

The prisoner bent over the paper once more.

" 'If it had been otherwise'; " Carton's hand was again watchfully and softly stealing down; " 'I never should have used the longer opportunity. If it had been otherwise'; " the hand was at the prisoner's face; " 'I should but have had so much the more to answer for. If it had been otherwise—' " Carton looked at the pen and saw it was trailing off into unintelligible signs.

Carton's hand moved back to his breast no more. The prisoner sprang up with a reproachful look, but Carton's hand was close and firm at his nostrils, and Carton's left arm caught him round the waist. For a few seconds he faintly struggled with the man who had come to lay down his life for him; but within a minute or so, he was stretched insensible on the ground.

Quickly, but with hands as true to the purpose as his heart was, Carton dressed himself in the clothes the prisoner had laid aside, combed back his hair, and tied it with the ribbon the prisoner had worn. Then, he softly called, "Enter there! Come in!" and the spy presented himself.

"You see?" said Carton, looking up at him as he kneeled on one knee beside the insensible figure, putting the paper in the breast: "is your hazard very great?"

"Mr. Carton," the spy answered, with a timid snap of his fingers, "my hazard is not *that,* in the thick of business here, if you are true to the whole of your bargain."

"Don't fear me. I will be true to the death."

"You must be, Mr. Carton, if the tale of fifty-two is to be right. Being made right by you in that dress, I shall have no fear."

"Have no fear! I shall soon be out of the way of harming you, and the rest will soon be far from here, please God! Now, get assistance and take me to the coach."

"You?" said the spy nervously.

"Him, man, with whom I have exchanged. You go out at the gate by which you brought me in?"

"Of course."

"I was weak and faint when you brought me in, and I am fainter now you take me out. The parting interview has overpowered me. Such a thing has happened here, often, and too often. Your life is in your own hands. Quick! Call assistance!"

"You swear not to betray me?" said the trembling spy, as he paused for a last moment.

"Man, man!" returned Carton, stamping his foot; "have I sworn by no solemn vow already, to go through with this, that you waste the precious moments now? Take him yourself to the courtyard you know of, place him yourself in the carriage, show him yourseif to Mr. Lorry, tell him yourself to give him no restorative but air, and to remember my words of last night, and his promise of last night, and drive away!"

The spy withdrew, and Carton seated himself at the table, resting his forehead on his hands. The spy returned immediately, with two men.

"How, then?" said one of them, contemplating the fallen figure. "So afflicted to find that his friend has drawn a prize in the lottery of Saint Guillotine?"

"A good patriot," said the other, "could hardly have been more afflicted if the Aristocrat had drawn a blank."

They raised the unconscious figure, placed it on a litter they had brought to the door, and bent to carry it away.

"The time is short, Evrémonde," said the spy, in a warning voice.

"I know it well," answered Carton. "Be careful of my friend, I entreat you, and leave me."

"Come, then, my children," said Barsad. "Lift him, and come away!"

The door closed, and Carton was left alone. Straining his powers of listening to the utmost, he listened for any sound that might denote suspicion or alarm. There was none. Keys turned, doors clashed, footsteps passed along distant passages: no cry was raised, or hurry made, that seemed unusual. Breathing more freely in a little while, he sat down at the table, and listened again until the clock struck Two.

Sounds that he was not afraid of, for he divined their meaning, then began to be audible. Several doors were opened in succession, and finally his own. A gaoler, with a list in his hand, looked in, merely saying, "Follow me, Evrémonde!" and he followed into a large dark room at a distance. It was a dark winter day, and what with the shadows within, and what with the shadows without, he could but dimly discern the others who were brought there to have their arms bound. Some were standing; some seated. Some were lamenting, and in restless motion; but, these were few. The great majority were silent and still, looking fixedly at the ground.

As he stood by the wall in a dim corner, while some of the fifty-two were brought in after him, one man stopped in passing, to embrace him, as having a knowledge of him. It thrilled him with a great dread of discovery; but the man went on. A very few moments after that, a young woman, with a slight girlish form, a sweet spare face in which there was no vestige of color, and large widely-opened patient eyes, rose from the seat where he had observed her sitting, and came to speak to him.

"Citizen Evrémonde," she said, touching him with her cold hand, "I am a poor little seamstress, who was with you in La Force."

He murmured for answer, "True. I forget what you were accused of?"

"Plots. Though the just Heaven knows I am innocent of any. Is it likely? Who would think of plotting with a poor little weak creature like me?"

The forlorn smile with which she said it so touched him, that tears started from his eyes.

"I am not afraid to die, Citizen Evrémonde, but I have done nothing! I am not unwilling to die, if the Republic which is to do so much good for us poor, will profit by my death; but I do not know how that can be, Citizen Evrémonde. Such a poor weak little creature!"

As the last thing on earth that his heart was to warm and soften to, it warmed and softened to this pitiable girl.

"I heard you were released, Citizen Evrémonde. I hoped it was true?"

"It was. But, I was again taken and condemned."

"If I may ride with you, Citizen Evrémonde, will you let me hold your hand? I am not afraid, but I am little and weak, and it will give me more courage."

As the patient eyes were lifted to his face, he saw a sudden doubt in them, and then astonishment. He pressed the work-worn, hunger-worn young fingers, and touched his lips.

"Are you dying for him?" she whispered.

"And his wife and child. Hush! Yes."

"Oh, you will let me hold your brave hand, stranger?"

"Hush! Yes, my poor sister; to the last."

The same shadows that are falling on the prison are falling, in that same hour of the early afternoon, on the Barrier with the crowd about it, when a coach going out of Paris drives up to be examined.

"Who goes here? Whom have we within? Papers!"

The papers are handed out, and read.

"Alexandre Manette. Physician. French. Which is he?"

This is he; this helpless, inarticulately-murmuring, wandering old man pointed out.

"Apparently the Citizen-Doctor is not in his right mind? The Revolution-fever will have been too much for him?"

Greatly too much for him.

"Hah! Many suffer with it. Lucie. His daughter. English. Which is she?"

This is she.

"Apparently it must be. Lucie, the wife of Evrémonde; is it not?"

It is.

"Hah! Evrémonde has an assignation elsewhere. Lucie, her child. English. This is she?"

She and no other.

"Kiss me, child of Evrémonde. Now, thou hast kissed a good Republican; something new in thy family; remember it! Sydney Carton. Advocate. English. Which is he?"

He lies here, in this corner of the carriage. He, too, is pointed out.

"Apparently the English advocate is in a swoon?"

It is hoped he will recover in the fresher air. It is represented that he is not in strong health, and has separated sadly from a friend who is under the displeasure of the Republic.

"Is that all? It is not a great deal, that! Many are under the displeasure of the Republic, and must look out at the little window. Jarvis Lorry. Banker. English. Which is he?"

"I am he. Necessarily, being the last."

It is Jarvis Lorry who has replied to all the previous questions. It is Jarvis Lorry who has alighted and stands with his hands on the coach-door, replying to a group of officials. They leisurely walk round the carriage and leisurely mount the box, to look at what little luggage it carries on the roof; the country-people hanging about press nearer to the coach-doors and greedily stare in; a little child, carried by its mother, has its short arm held out for it, that it may touch the wife of an aristocrat who has gone to the Guillotine.

"Behold your papers, Jarvis Lorry, countersigned."

"One can depart, citizen?"

"One can depart. Forward, my postillions! A good journey!"

"I salute you, citizens.—And the first danger passed!"

These are again the words of Jarvis Lorry, as he clasps his hands, and looks upward. There is terror in the carriage, there is weeping, there is the heavy breathing of the insensible traveler.

"Are we not going too slowly? Can they not be induced to go faster?" asks Lucie, clinging to the old man.

"It would seem like flight, my darling. I must not urge them too much; it would rouse suspicion."

"Look back, look back, and see if we are pursued!"

"The road is clear, my dearest. So far, we are not pursued."

Houses in twos and threes pass by us, solitary farms, ruinous buildings, dye-works, tanneries, and the like, open country, avenues of leafless trees. The hard uneven pavement is under us, the soft deep mud is on either side. Sometimes we strike into the skirting mud, to avoid the stones that clatter us and shake us and sometimes we stick in ruts and sloughs there. The agony of our impatience is then so great, that in our wild alarm and hurry, we are for getting out and running—hiding—doing anything but stopping.

Out of the open country, in again among ruinous buildings, solitary farms, dye-works, tanneries, and the like, cottages in twos and threes, avenues of leafless trees. Have these men deceived us, and taken us back by another road? Is not this the same place twice over? Thank Heaven, no. A village. Look back, look back, and see if we are pursued! Hush; the posting-house.

Leisurely, our four horses are taken out; leisurely, the coach stands in the little street, bereft of horses, and with no likelihood upon it of ever moving again; leisurely, the new horses come into visible existence, one by one; leisurely, the new postillions follow, sucking and plaiting the lashes of their whips; leisurely, the old postillions count their money, make wrong additions, and arrive at dissatisfied results. All the time, our overfraught hearts are beating at a rate that would far outstrip the fastest gallop of the fastest horses ever foaled.

At length the new postillions are in their saddles, and the old are left behind. We are through the village, up the hill, and down the hill, and on the low watery grounds. Suddenly, the postillions exchange speech with animated gesticulation, and the horses are pulled up, almost on their haunches. We are pursued?

"Ho! Within the carriage there. Speak then!"

"What is it?" asks Mr. Lorry, looking out the window.

"How many did they say?"

"I do not understand you."

"—At the last post. How many to the Guillotine today?"

"Fifty-two."

"I said so! A brave number! My fellow-citizen here would have it forty-two; ten more heads are worth having. The Guillotine goes handsomely. I love it. Hi forward! Whoop then!"

The night comes on dark. He moves more; he is beginning to revive, and to speak intelligibly; he thinks they are still together; he asks him, by his name, what he has in his hand. O pity us, kind Heaven, and help us! Look out, look out, and see if we are pursued.

The wind is rushing after us, and the clouds are flying after us, and the moon is plunging after us, and the whole wild night is in pursuit of us; but, so far, we are pursued by nothing else.

F o u r t e e n

THE KNITTING DONE

IN THAT SAME JUNCTURE OF TIME WHEN THE FIFTY-TWO awaited their fate, Madame Defarge held darkly ominous council with The Vengeance and Jacques Three of the Revolutionary Jury. Not in the wine-shop did Madame Defarge confer with these ministers, but in the shed of the wood-sawyer, erst a mender of roads. The sawyer himself did not participate in the conference, but abided at a little distance, like an outer satellite who was not to speak until required, or to offer an opinion until invited.

"But our Defarge," said Jacques Three, "is undoubtedly a good Republican? Eh?"

"There is no better," the voluble Vengeance protested in her shrill notes, "in France."

"Peace, little Vengeance," said Madame Defarge, laying her hand with a slight frown on her lieutenant's lips, "hear me speak. My husband, fellow-citizen, is a good Republican and a bold man; he has deserved well of the Republic, and possesses its confidence. But my husband has his weaknesses, and he is so weak as to relent towards this Doctor."

"It is a great pity," croaked Jacques Three, dubiously shaking his head, with his cruel fingers at his hungry mouth; "it is not quite like a good citizen; it is a thing to regret."

"See you," said madame, "I care nothing for this Doctor, I. He may wear his head or lose it, for any interest I have in him; it is all one to me. But, the Evrémonde people are to be exterminated, and the wife and child must follow the husband and father."

"She has a fine head for it," croaked Jacques Three. "I have seen blue eyes and golden hair there, and they looked charming when Samson held them up." Ogre that he was, he spoke like an epicure.

Madame Defarge cast down her eyes, and reflected a little.

"The child also," observed Jacques Three, with a meditative enjoyment of his words, "has golden hair and blue eyes. And we seldom have a child there. It is a pretty sight!"

"In a word," said Madame Defarge, coming out of her short abstraction, "I cannot trust my husband in this matter. Not only do I feel, since last night, that I dare not confide to him the details of my projects; but also I feel that if I delay, there is danger of his giving warning, and then they might escape."

"That must never be," croaked Jacques Three; "no one must escape. We have not half enough as it is. We ought to have six score a day."

"In a word," Madame Defarge went on, "my husband has not my reason for pursuing this family to annihilation, and I have not his reason for regarding this Doctor with any sensibility. I must act for myself, therefore. Come hither, little citizen."

The wood-sawyer, who held her in the respect, and himself in the submission, of mortal fear, advanced with his hand to his red cap.

"Touching those signals, little citizen," said Madame Defarge, sternly, "that she made to the prisoners; you are ready to bear witness to them this very day?"

"Ay, ay, why not?" cried the sawyer. "Every day, in all weathers, from two to four, always signaling, sometimes with the little one, sometimes without. I know what I know. I have seen with my eyes."

He made all manner of gestures while he spoke, as if in incidental imitation of some few of the great diversity of signals that he had never seen.

"Clearly plots," said Jacques Three. "Transparently!"

"There is no doubt of the Jury?" inquired Madame Defarge, letting her eyes turn to him with a gloomy smile.

"Rely upon the patriotic Jury, dear citizeness. I answer for my fellow-Jurymen."

"Now, let me see," said Madame Defarge, pondering again. "Yet once more! Can I spare this Doctor to my husband? I have no feeling either way. Can I spare him?"

"He would count as one head," observed Jacques Three, in a low voice. "We really have not heads enough; it would be a pity, I think."

"He was signaling with her when I saw her," argued Madame Defarge; "I cannot speak of one without the other; and I must not be silent, and trust the case wholly to him, this little citizen here. For, I am not a bad witness."

The Vengeance and Jacques Three vied with each other in their fervent protestations that she was the most admirable and marvelous of witnesses. The little citizen, not to be outdone, declared her to be a celestial witness.

"He must take his chance," said Madame Defarge. "No, I cannot spare him! You are engaged at three o'clock; you are going to see the batch of today executed.—You?"

The question was addressed to the wood-sawyer, who hurriedly replied in the affirmative: seizing the occasion to add that he was the most ardent of

Republicans, and that he would be in effect the most desolate of Republicans, if anything prevented him from enjoying the pleasure of smoking his afternoon pipe in the contemplation of the droll national barber. He was so very demonstrative herein, that he might have been suspected (perhaps was, by the dark eyes that looked contemptuously at him out of Madame Defarge's head) of having his small individual fears for his own personal safety, every hour in the day.

"I," said madame, "am equally engaged at the same place. After it is over—say at eight tonight—come you to me, in Saint Antoine, and we will give information against these people at my Section."

The wood-sawyer said he would be proud and flattered to attend the citizeness. The citizeness looking at him, he became embarrassed, evaded her glance as a small dog would have done, retreated among his wood, and hid his confusion over the handle of the saw.

Madame Defarge beckoned the Juryman and The Vengeance a little nearer to the door, and there expounded her further views to them thus:

"She will now be at home, awaiting the moment of his death. She will be mourning and grieving. She will be in a state of mind to impeach the justice of the Republic. She will be full of sympathy with its enemies. I will go to her."

"What an admirable woman; what an adorable woman!" exclaimed Jacques Three, rapturously. "Ah, my cherished!" cried The Vengeance; and embraced her.

"Take you my knitting," said Madame Defarge, placing it in her lieutenant's hands, "and have it ready for me in my usual seat. Keep me my usual chair. Go you there, straight, for there will probably be a greater concourse than usual, today."

"I willingly obey the orders of my chief," said The Vengeance with alacrity, and kissing her cheek. "You will not be late?"

"I shall be there before the commencement."

"And before the tumbrils arrive. Be sure you are there, my soul," said The Vengeance, calling after her, for she had already turned into the street, "before the tumbrils arrive!"

Madame Defarge slightly waved her hand, to imply that she heard, and might be relied upon to arrive in good time, and so went through the mud and round the corner of the prison wall. The Vengeance and the Juryman, looking after her as she walked away, were highly appreciative of her fine figure, and her superb moral endowments.

There were many women at that time, upon whom the time laid a dreadfully disfiguring hand; but, there was not one among them more to be dreaded than this ruthless woman, now taking her way along the streets. Of a strong and fearless character, and shrewd sense and readiness, of great determination, of that kind of beauty which not only seems to impart to its possessor firmness and animosity, but to strike into others an instinctive recognition of those qualities; the troubled time would have heaved her up under any circumstances. But imbued from her childhood with a brooding sense of wrong, and an inveterate hatred of a class, opportunity had developed her into a tigress. She was absolutely without pity. If she had ever had the virtue in her, it had quite gone out of her.

It was nothing to her that an innocent man was to die for the sins of his forefathers; she saw, not him, but them. It was nothing to her, that his wife was to be made a widow and his daughter an orphan; that was insufficient punishment, because they were her natural enemies and her prey, and as such had no right to live. To appeal to her was made hopeless by her having no sense of pity, even for herself. If she had been laid low in the streets, in any of the many encounters in which she had been engaged, she would not have pitied herself: nor, if she had been ordered to the axe tomorrow, would she have gone to it with any softer feeling than a fierce desire to change places with the man who sent her there.

Such a heart Madame Defarge carried under her rough robe. Carelessly worn, it was a becoming robe enough, in a certain weird way, and her dark hair looked rich under her coarse red cap. Lying hidden in her bosom was a loaded pistol. Lying hidden at her waist was a sharpened dagger. Thus accoutred, and walking with the confident tread of such a character, and with the supple freedom of a woman who had habitually walked in her girlhood, barefoot and bare-legged, on the brown sea-sand, Madame Defarge took her way along the streets.

Now, when the journey of the traveling coach, at that very moment waiting for the completion of its load, had been planned out last night, the difficulty of taking Miss Pross in it had much engaged Mr. Lorry's attention. It was not merely desirable to avoid overloading the coach, but it was of the highest importance that the time occupied in examining it and its passengers, should be reduced to the utmost, since their escape might depend on the saving of only a few seconds here and there. Finally, he had proposed, after anxious consideration, that Miss Pross and Jerry, who were at liberty to leave the city, would leave it at three o'clock in the lightest-wheeled conveyance known to that period. Unencumbered with luggage, they would soon overtake the coach, and, passing it and preceding it on the road, would order its horses in advance, and greatly facilitate its progress during the precious hours of the night, when delay was the most to be dreaded.

Seeing in this arrangement the hope of rendering real service in that pressing emergency, Miss Pross hailed it with joy. She and Jerry had beheld the coach start, had known who it was that Solomon brought, had passed some ten minutes in tortures of suspense, and were now concluding their arrangements to follow the coach, even as Madame Defarge, taking her way through the streets, now drew nearer and nearer to the else-deserted lodging in which they held their consultation.

"Now what do you think, Mr. Cruncher," said Miss Pross, whose agitation was so great that she could hardly speak, or stand, or move, or live; "what do you think of our not starting from this courtyard? Another carriage having already gone from here today, it might awaken suspicion."

"My opinion, Miss," returned Mr. Cruncher, "is as you're right. Likewise wot. I'll stand by you, right or wrong."

"I am so distracted with fear and hope for our precious creatures," said Miss Pross, wildly crying, "that I am incapable of forming any plan. Are *you* capable of forming any plan, my dear, good Mr. Cruncher?"

"Respectin' a future spear o' life, miss," returned Mr. Cruncher, "I hope so. Respectin' any present use o' this here blessed old head o' mine, I think not. Would you do me the favor, Miss, to take notice o' two promises and wows wot it is my wishes fur to record in this here crisis?"

"Oh, for gracious' sake!" cried Miss Pross, still wildly crying, "record them at once, and get them out of the way, like an excellent man."

"First," said Mr. Cruncher, who was all in a tremble, and who spoke with an ashy and solemn visage, "them poor things well out o' this, never no more will I do it, never no more!"

"I am quite sure, Mr. Cruncher," returned Miss Pross, "that you never will do it again, whatever it is, and I beg you not to think it necessary to mention more particularly what it is."

"No, Miss," returned Jerry, "it shall not be named to you. Second: them poor things well out o' this, and never no more will I interfere with Mrs. Cruncher's flopping, never no more!"

"Whatever housekeeping arrangement that may be," said Miss Pross, striving to dry her eyes and compose herself, "I have no doubt it is best that Mrs. Cruncher should have it entirely under her own superintendence.—O my poor darlings!"

"I go so far as to say, Miss, moreover," proceeded Mr. Cruncher, with a most alarming tendency to hold forth as from a pulpit—"and let my words be took down and took to Mrs. Cruncher through yourself—that wot my opinions respectin' flopping has undergone a change, and that wot I only hope with all my heart as Mrs. Cruncher may be a flopping at the present time."

"There, there, there! I hope she is, my dear man," cried the distracted Miss Pross, "and I hope she finds it answering her expectations."

"Forbid it," proceeded Mr. Cruncher, with additional solemnity, additional slowness, and additional tendency to hold forth and hold out, "as anything wot I have ever said or done should be wisited on my earnest wishes for them poor creeturs now! Forbid it as we shouldn't all flop (if it was anyways conwenient) to get 'em out o' this here dismal risk! Forbid it, Miss! Wot I say, for—BID it!" This was Mr. Cruncher's conclusion after a protracted but vain endeavor to find a better one.

And still Madame Defarge, pursuing her way along the streets, came nearer and nearer.

"If we ever get back to our native land," said Miss Pross, "you may rely upon my telling Mrs. Cruncher as much as I may be able to remember and understand of what you have so impressively said; and at all events you may be sure that I shall bear witness to your being thoroughly in earnest at this dreadful time. Now, pray let us think! My esteemed Mr. Cruncher, let us think!"

Still, Madame Defarge, pursuing her way along the streets, came nearer and nearer.

"If you were to go before," said Miss Pross, "and stop the vehicle and horses from coming here, and were to wait somewhere for me, wouldn't that be best?"

Mr. Cruncher thought it might be best.

"Where could you wait for me?" asked Miss Pross.

Mr. Cruncher was so bewildered that he could think of no locality but Temple Bar. Alas! Temple Bar was hundreds of miles away, and Madame Defarge was drawing very near indeed.

"By the cathedral door," said Miss Pross. "Would it be much out of the way, to take me in, near the great cathedral door between the two towers?"

"No, Miss," answered Mr. Cruncher.

"Then, like the best of men," said Miss Pross, "go to the post-house straight, and make that change."

"I am doubtful," said Mr. Cruncher, hesitating and shaking his head, "about leaving of you, you see. We don't know what may happen."

"Heaven knows we don't," returned Miss Pross, "but have no fear of me. Take me in at the cathedral, at Three o'clock, or as near it as you can, and I am sure it will be better than our going from here. I feel certain of it. There! Bless you, Mr. Cruncher! Think—not of me, but of the lives that may depend on both of us!"

This exordium, and Miss Pross's two hands in quite agonized entreaty clasping his, decided Mr. Cruncher. With an encouraging nod or two, he immediately went out to alter the arrangements, and left her by herself to follow as she had proposed.

The having originated a precaution which was already in course of execution was a great relief to Miss Pross. The necessity of composing her appearance so that it should attract no special notice in the streets was another relief. She looked at her watch, and it was twenty minutes past two. She had no time to lose, but must get ready at once.

Afraid, in her extreme perturbation, of the loneliness of the deserted rooms, and of half-imagined faces peeping from behind every open door in them, Miss Pross got a basin of cold water and began laving her eyes, which were swollen and red. Haunted by her feverish apprehensions, she could not bear to have her sight obscured for a minute at a time by the dripping water, but constantly paused and looked around to see that there was no one watching her. In one of those pauses she recoiled and cried out, for she saw a figure standing in the room.

The basin fell to the ground broken, and the water flowed to the feet of Madame Defarge. By wild, wild ways, and through much staining blood, those feet had come to meet that water.

Madame Defarge looked coldly at her, and said, "The wife of Evrémonde; where is she?"

It flashed upon Miss Pross's mind that the doors were all standing open, and would suggest the flight. Her first act was to shut them. There were four in the room, and she shut them all. She then placed herself before the door of the chamber which Lucie had occupied.

Madame Defarge's dark eyes followed her through this rapid movement, and rested on her when it was finished. Miss Pross had nothing beautiful about her; years had not tamed the wildness, or softened the grimness, of her appearance; but, she too, was a determined woman in her different way, and she measured Madame Defarge with her eyes, every inch.

"You might, from your appearance, be the wife of Lucifer," said Miss Pross, in her breathing. "Nevertheless, you shall not get the better of me. I am an Englishwoman."

Madame Defarge looked at her scornfully, but still with something of Miss Pross's own perception that they two were at bay. She saw a tight, hard, wiry woman before her, as Mr. Lorry had seen in the same figure a woman with a strong hand, in the years gone by. She knew full well that Miss Pross was the family's devoted friend; Miss Pross knew full well that Madame Defarge was the family's malevolent enemy.

"On my way yonder," said Madame Defarge, with a slight movement of her hand towards the fatal spot, "where they reserve my chair and my knitting for me, I am come to make my compliments to her in passing. I wish to see her."

"I know that your intentions are evil," said Miss Pross, "and you may depend upon it, I'll hold my own against them."

Each spoke in her own language; neither understood the other's words; both were very watchful, and intent to deduce, from look and manner, what the unintelligible words meant.

"It will do her no good to keep herself concealed from me at this moment," said Madame Defarge. "Good patriots will know what that means. Let me see her. Go tell her that I wish to see her. Do you hear?"

"If those eyes of yours were bed-winches," returned Miss Pross, "and I was an English four-poster, they shouldn't loose a splinter of me. No, you wicked foreign woman; I am your match."

Madame Defarge was not likely to follow these idiomatic remarks in detail; but she so far understood them as to perceive that she was set at naught.

"Woman imbecile and piglike!" said Madame Defarge, frowning. "I take no answer from you. I demand to see her. Either tell her that I demand to see her, or stand out of the way of the door and let me go to her!" This, with an angry explanatory wave of her right arm.

"I little thought," said Miss Pross, "that I should ever want to understand your nonsensical language; but I would give all I have, to the very clothes I wear, to know whether you suspect the truth, or any part of it."

Neither of them for a single moment released the other's eyes. Madame Defarge had not moved from the spot where she stood when Miss Pross first became aware of her; but she now advanced one step.

"I am a Briton," said Miss Pross, "I am desperate. I don't care an English Twopence for myself. I know that the longer I keep you here, the greater hope there is for my Ladybird. I'll not leave a handful of that dark hair upon your head, if you lay a finger on me!"

Thus Miss Pross, with a shake of her head and a flash of her eyes between every rapid sentence, and every rapid sentence a whole breath. Thus Miss Pross, who had never struck a blow in her life.

But her courage was of that emotional nature that it brought the irrepressible tears into her eyes. This was a courage that Madame Defarge so little comprehended, as to mistake for weakness. "Ha, ha!" she laughed, "you poor wretch! What are you worth! I address myself to that Doctor." Then she raised her voice and called out, "Citizen Doctor! Wife of Evrémonde! Child of Evrémonde! Any person but this miserable fool, answer the Citizeness Defarge!"

Perhaps the following silence, perhaps some latent disclosure in the expression of Miss Pross's face, perhaps a sudden misgiving apart from either suggestion, whispered to Madame Defarge that they were gone. Three of the doors she opened swiftly, and looked in.

"Those rooms are all in disorder, there has been hurried packing, there are odds and ends upon the ground. There is no one in that room behind you! Let me look."

"Never!" said Miss Pross, who understood the request as perfectly as Madame Defarge understood the answer.

"If they are not in that room, they are gone, and can be pursued and brought back," said Madame Defarge to herself.

"As long as you don't know whether they are in that room or not, you are uncertain what to do," said Miss Pross to *herself*; "and you shall not know that, if I can prevent your knowing it; and know that, or not know that, you shall not leave here while I can hold you."

"I have been in the streets from the first, nothing has stopped me, I will tear you to pieces, but I will have you from that door," said Madame Defarge.

"We are alone at the top of a high house in a solitary courtyard, we are not likely to be heard, and I pray for bodily strength to keep you here, while every minute you are here is worth a hundred thousand guineas to my darling," said Miss Pross.

Madame Defarge made at the door. Miss Pross, on the instinct of the moment, seized her round the waist in both her arms, and held her tight. It was in vain for Madame Defarge to struggle and to strike; Miss Pross, with the vigorous tenacity of love, always so much stronger than hate, clasped her tight, and even lifted her from the floor in the struggle that they had. The two hands of Madame Defarge buffeted and tore her face; but, Miss Pross, with her head down, held her round the waist, and clung to her with more than the hold of a drowning woman.

Soon, Madame Defarge's hands ceased to strike, and felt at her encircled waist. "It is under my arm," said Miss Pross, in smothered tones, "you shall not draw it. I am stronger than you, I bless Heaven for it. I'll hold you till one or other of us faints or dies!"

Madame Defarge's hands were at her bosom. Miss Pross looked up, saw what it was, struck at it, struck out a flash and a crash, and stood alone—blinded with smoke.

All this was in a second. As the smoke cleared, leaving an awful stillness, it passed out on the air, like the soul of the furious woman whose body lay lifeless on the ground.

In the first fright and horror of her situation, Miss Pross passed the body as far from it as she could, and ran down the stairs to call for fruitless help. Happily, she bethought herself of the consequences of what she did, in time to check herself and go back. It was dreadful to go in at the door again; but she did go in, and even went near it, to get the bonnet and other things that she must wear. These she put on, out on the staircase, first shutting and locking the door, and taking away the key. She then sat down on the stairs a few moments to breathe and to cry, and then got up and hurried away.

By good fortune she had a veil on her bonnet, or she could hardly have gone along the streets without being stopped. By good fortune, too, she was naturally so peculiar in appearance as not to show disfigurement like any other woman. She needed both advantages, for the marks of gripping fingers were deep in her face, and her hair was torn, and her dress (hastily composed with unsteady hands) was clutched and dragged a hundred ways.

In crossing the bridge, she dropped the door key in the river. Arriving at the cathedral some few minutes before her escort, and waiting there, she thought, what if the key were already taken in a net, what if it were identified, what if the door were opened and the remains discovered, what if she were stopped at the gate, sent to prison, and charged with murder! In the midst of these fluttering thoughts, the escort appeared, took her in, and took her away.

"Is there any noise in the streets?" she asked him.

"The usual noises," Mr. Cruncher replied; and looked surprised by the question and by her aspect.

"I don't hear you," said Miss Pross. "What do you say?"

It was in vain for Mr. Cruncher to repeat what he said; Miss Pross could not hear him. "So I'll nod my head," thought Mr. Cruncher, amazed, "at all events she'll see that." And she did.

"Is there any noise in the streets now?" asked Miss Pross again, presently.

Again Mr. Cruncher nodded his head.

"I don't hear it."

"Gone deaf in a hour?" said Mr. Cruncher, ruminating, with his mind much disturbed; "wot's come to her?"

"I feel," said Miss Pross, "as if there had been a flash and a crash, and that crash was the last thing I should ever hear in this life."

"Blest if she ain't in a queer condition!" said Mr. Cruncher, more and more disturbed. "Wot can she have been a takin', to keep her courage up? Hark! There's the roll of them dreadful carts! You can hear that, Miss?"

"I can hear," said Miss Pross, seeing that he spoke to her, "nothing. Oh, my good man, there was first a great crash, and then a great stillness, and that stillness seems to be fixed and unchangeable, never to be broken anymore as long as my life lasts."

"If she don't hear the roll of those dreadful carts, now very nigh their journey's end," said Mr. Cruncher, glancing over his shoulder, "it's my opinion that indeed she never will hear anything else in this world."

And indeed she never did.

F i f t e e n

THE FOOTSTEPS DIE
OUT FOREVER

ALONG THE PARIS STREETS, THE DEAD-CARTS RUMBLE, hollow and harsh. Six tumbrils carry the day's wine to La Guillotine. All the devouring and insatiate monsters imagined since imagination could record itself, are fused in the one realization, Guillotine. And yet there is not in France, with its rich variety of soil and climate, a blade, a leaf, a root, a sprig, a peppercorn, which will grow to maturity under conditions more certain than those that have produced this horror. Crush humanity out of shape once more, under similar hammers, and it will twist itself into the same tortured forms. Sow the same seed of rapacious license and oppression over again, and it will surely yield the same fruit according to its kind.

Six tumbrils roll along the streets. Change these back again to what they were, thou powerful enchanter, Time, and they shall be seen to be the carriages of absolute monarchs, the equipages of feudal nobles, the toilettes of flaring Jezebels, the churches that are not my father's house but dens of thieves, the huts of millions of starving peasants! No; the great magician who majestically works out the appointed order of the Creator never reverses his transformations. "If thou be changed into this shape by the will of God," say the seers to the enchanted, in the wise Arabian stories, "then remain so! But, if thou wear this form through mere passing conjuration, then resume thy former aspect!" Changeless and hopeless, the tumbrils roll along.

As the somber wheels of the six carts go round, they seem to plow up a long crooked furrow among the populace in the streets. Ridges of faces are thrown to this side and to that, and the plows go steadily onward. So used are the regular inhabitants of the houses to the spectacle, that in many windows there are no people, and in some the occupation of the hands is not so much as suspended, while the eyes survey the faces in the tumbrils. Here and there, the inmate has visitors to see the sight; then he points his finger, with something of the complacency of a curator or authorized exponent, to this cart and to this, and seems to tell who sat here yesterday, and who sat there the day before.

Of the riders in the tumbrils, some observe these things, and all things on their last roadside, with an impassive stare; others, with a lingering interest in the ways of life and men. Some, seated with drooping heads, are sunk in silent despair; again, there are some so heedful of their looks that they cast upon the multitude such glances as they have seen in theaters, and in pictures. Several close their eyes, and think, or try to get their straying thoughts together. Only one, and he a miserable creature, of a crazed aspect, is so shattered and made drunk by horror, that he sings, and tries to dance. Not one of the whole number appeals, by look or gesture, to the pity of the people.

There is a guard of sundry horsemen riding abreast of the tumbrils, and faces are often turned up to some of them, and they are asked some questions. It would seem to be always the same question, for, it is always followed by a press of people towards the third cart. The horsemen abreast of that cart frequently point out one man in it with their swords. The leading curiosity is to know which is he; he stands at the back of the tumbril with his head bent down, to converse with a mere girl who sits on the side of the cart, and holds his hand. He has no curiosity or care for the scene about him, and always speaks to the girl. Here and there in the long street of St. Honoré, cries are raised against him. If they move him at all, it is only to a quiet smile, as he shakes his hair a little more loosely about his face. He cannot easily touch his face, his arms being bound.

On the steps of a church, awaiting the coming-up of the tumbrils, stands the spy and prison-sheep. He looks into the first of them: not there. He looks into the second: not there. He already asks himself, "Has he sacrificed me?" when his face clears, as he looks into the third.

"Which is Evrémonde?" says a man behind him.

"That. At the back there."

"With his hand in the girl's?"

"Yes."

The man cries, "Down, Evrémonde! To the Guillotine all aristocrats; Down, Evrémonde!"

"Hush, hush!" the spy entreats him, timidly.

"And why not, citizen?"

"He is going to pay the forfeit; it will be paid in five minutes more. Let him be at peace."

But the man continuing to exclaim, "Down, Evrémonde!" the face of Evrémonde is for a moment turned towards him. Evrémonde then sees the spy, and looks attentively at him, and goes his way.

The clocks are on the stroke of three, and the furrow plowed among the populace is turning round, to come on into the place of execution, and end. The ridges thrown to this side and to that, now crumble in and close behind the last plow as it passes on, for all are following to the Guillotine. In front of it, seated in chairs, as in a garden of public diversion, are a number of women, busily knitting. On one of the foremost Chairs stands The Vengeance, looking about for her friend.

"Therese!" she cries, in her shrill tones. "Who has seen her? Therese Defarge!"

"She never missed before," says a knitting-woman of the sisterhood.

"No; nor will she miss now," cries The Vengeance, petulantly. "Therese!"

"Louder," the woman recommends.

Aye! Louder, Vengeance, much louder, and still she will scarcely hear thee. Louder yet, Vengeance, with a little oath or so added, and yet it will hardly bring her. Send other women up and down to seek her, lingering somewhere; and yet, although the messengers have done dread deeds, it is questionable whether of their own will they will go far enough to find her!

"Bad Fortune!" cries The Vengeance, stamping her foot in the chair, "and here are the tumbrils! And Evrémonde will be dispatched in a wink, and she not here! See her knitting in my hand, and her empty chair ready for her. I cry with vexation and disappointment!"

As The Vengeance descends from her elevation to do it, the tumbrils begin to discharge their loads. The ministers of Saint Guillotine are robed and ready. Crash!—A head is held up, and the knitting-women who scarcely lifted their eyes to look at it a moment ago when it could think and speak, count One.

The second tumbril empties and moves on; the third comes up. Crash!— And the knitting-women, never faltering or pausing in their work, count Two.

The supposed Evrémonde descends, and the seamstress is lifted out next after him. He has not relinquished her patient hand in getting out, but still holds it as he promised. He gently places her with her back to the crashing engine that constantly whirrs up and falls, and she looks into his face and thanks him.

"But for you, dear stranger, I should not be so composed, for I am naturally a poor little thing, faint of heart; nor should I have been able to raise my thoughts to Him who was put to death, that we might have hope and comfort here today. I think you were sent to me by Heaven."

"Or you to me," says Sydney Carton. "Keep your eyes upon me, dear child, and mind no other object."

"I mind nothing while I hold your hand. I shall mind nothing when I let it go, if they are rapid."

"They will be rapid. Fear not!"

The two stand in the fast-thinning throng of victims, but they speak as if they were alone. Eye to eye, voice to voice, hand to hand, heart to heart, these two children of the Universal Mother, else so wide apart and differing, have come together on the dark highway, to repair home together, and to rest in her bosom.

"Brave and generous friend, will you let me ask you one last question? I am very ignorant, and it troubles me—just a little."

"Tell me what it is."

"I have a cousin, an only relative and an orphan like myself, whom I love very dearly. She is five years younger than I, and she lives in a farmer's house in the south country. Poverty parted us, and she knows nothing of my fate—for I cannot write—and if I could, how should I tell her! It is better as it is."

"Yes, yes; better as it is."

"What I have been thinking as we came along, and what I am still thinking now, as I look into your kind, strong face, which gives me much support, is this:—If the Republic really does good to the poor, and they come to be less hungry, and in all ways to suffer less, she may live a long time! she may even live to be old."

"What then, my gentle sister?"

"Do you think"—the uncomplaining eyes in which there is so much endurance, fill with tears, and the lips part a little more and tremble—"that it will seem long to me, while I wait for her in the better land where I trust both you and I will be mercifully sheltered?"

"It cannot be, my child; there is no Time there, and no trouble there."

"You comfort me so much! I am so ignorant. Am I to kiss you now? Is the moment come?"

"Yes."

She kisses his lips; he kisses hers; they solemnly bless each other. The spare hand does not tremble as he releases it: nothing worse than a sweet, bright constancy is in the patient face. She goes next before him—is gone; the knitting-women count Twenty-two.

"I am the Resurrection and the Life, saith the Lord; he that believeth in me, though he were dead, yet shall he live: and whosoever liveth and believeth in me shall never die."

The murmuring of many voices, the upturning of many faces, the pressing on of many footsteps in the outskirts of the crowd, so that it swells forward in a mass, like one great heave of water, all flashes away. Twenty-three.

They said of him, about the city that night, that it was the peacefullest man's face ever beheld there. Many added that he looked sublime and prophetic.

One of the most remarkable sufferers by the same axe—a woman—had asked at the foot of the same scaffold, not long before, to be allowed to write down the thoughts that were inspiring her. If he had given an utterance to his, and they were prophetic, they would have been these:

"I see Barsad, and Cly, Defarge, The Vengeance, the Juryman, the Judge, long ranks of the new oppressors who have risen on the destruction of the old, perishing by this retributive instrument, before it shall cease out of its present use. I see a beautiful city and a brilliant people rising from this abyss, and, in their struggles to be truly free, in their triumphs and defeats through long, long years to come, I see the evil of this time and of the previous time of which this is the natural birth, gradually making expiation for itself and wearing out.

"I see the lives for which I lay down my life, peaceful, useful, prosperous and happy, in that England which I shall see no more. I see Her with a child upon her bosom, who bears my name. I see her father, aged and bent, but otherwise restored, and faithful to all men in his healing office, and at peace. I see the good old man, so long their friend, in ten years' time enriching them with all he has, and passing tranquilly to his reward.

"I see that I hold a sanctuary in their hearts, and in the hearts of their descendants, generations hence. I see her, an old woman, weeping for me on the anniversary of this day. I see her and her husband, their course done, living side by side in their last earthly bed, and I know that each was not more honored and held sacred in the other's soul, than I was in the souls of both.

"I see that child who lay upon her bosom and who bore my name, a man winning his way up in that path of life which once was mine. I see him winning it so well, that my name is made illustrious there by the light of his. I see the blots I threw upon it faded away. I see him, foremost of just judges and honored men, bringing a boy of my name, with a forehead that I know and golden hair, to this place—then fair to look upon, with not a trace of this day's disfigurement—and I hear him tell the child my story, with a tender and faltering voice.

"It is a far, far better thing that I do, than I have ever done; it is a far, far better rest that I go to, than I have ever known."

GREAT
EXPECTATIONS

One

M Y FATHER'S FAMILY NAME BEING PIRRIP, AND MY CHRIS-
tian name Philip, my infant tongue could make of both names
nothing longer or more explicit than Pip. So I called myself Pip, and came
to be called Pip.

I give Pirrip as my father's family name, on the authority of his tombstone and my sister—Mrs. Joe Gargery, who married the blacksmith. As I
never saw my father or my mother, and never saw any likeness of either of
them (for their days were long before the days of photographs), my first fancies regarding what they were like were unreasonably derived from their
tombstones. The shape of the letters on my father's gave me an odd idea that
he was a square, stout, dark man with curly black hair. From the character
and turn of the inscription, *"Also Georgiana wife of the above,"* I drew a childish conclusion that my mother was freckled and sickly. To five little stone
lozenges, each about a foot and a half long, which were arranged in a neat row
beside their grave, and were sacred to the memory of five little brothers of

mine—who gave up trying to get a living exceedingly early in that universal struggle—I am indebted for a belief I religiously entertained that they had all been born on their backs with their hands in their trowsers-pockets, and had never taken them out in this state of existence.

Ours was the marsh country, down by the river, within, as the river wound, twenty miles of the sea. My first distinct impression of the identity of things seems to me to have been gained on a memorable raw, damp after-noon toward evening. At such a time I found out for certain that this bleak place overgrown with nettles was the churchyard; and that Tobias Pirrip, late of this Parish, and also Georgiana, wife of the above, were dead and buried; and that Alexander, Bartholomew, Abraham, George, and Robert, infant children of the aforesaid, were also dead and buried; and that the dark, flat wilderness beyond the churchyard, intersected with dikes and mounds and gates, with scattered cattle feeding on it, was the marshes; and that the low leaden line beyond was the river; and that the distant savage lair from which the wind was rushing, was the sea; and that the small bundle of shivers grow-ing afraid of it all and beginning to cry, was Pip.

"Hold your noise!" cried a terrible voice, as a man started up from among the graves at the side of the church-porch. "Hold your noise, you little devil, or I'll cut your throat!"

A fearful man, all in gray, with a great iron on his leg. A man with no hat, and with broken shoes, and with an old rag tied round his head. A man who had been soaked in water and smothered in mud, and lamed by stones, and cut by flints, and stung by nettles, and torn by briers; who limped, and shiv-ered, and glared, and growled; and whose teeth chattered in his head as he seized me by the chin.

"Don't cut my throat, sir!" I pleaded in terror. "Pray don't do it, sir!"

"Tell us your name!" said the man. "Quick!"

"Pip, sir."

"Once more," said the man. "Give it mouth!"

"Pip. Pip, sir."

"Show us where you live," said the man. "Pint out the place!"

I pointed to where our village lay on the flat in-shore among the alder-trees and pollards, a mile or more from the church.

The man, after looking at me for a moment, turned me upside-down, and emptied my pockets. There was nothing in them but a piece of bread. When the church came to itself—for he was so sudden and strong that he made it go head over heels before me, and I saw the steeple under my legs—when the church came to itself, I say, I was seated on a high tombstone trem-bling, while he ate the bread ravenously.

"You young dog!" said the man, licking his lips at me, "what fat cheeks you ha' got!"

I believe they were fat, though I was at that time undersized for my years, and not strong.

"Damned if I couldn't eat 'em," said the man, with a threatening shake of his head, "and if I han't half a mind to' t!"

I earnestly expressed my hope that he wouldn't, and held tighter to the tombstone on which he had put me; partly to keep myself upon it, partly to keep myself from crying.

"Now then, lookie here!" said the man. "Where's your mother?"

"There, sir!" said I.

He started, made a short run, and stopped and looked over his shoulder.

"There, sir!" I timidly explained. "Also Georgiana. That's my mother."

"Oho!" said he, coming back. "And is that your father alonger your mother?"

"Yes, sir," said I; "him too; late of this parish."

"Ha!" he muttered then, considering. "Who d'ye live with—supposin' you're kindly let to live, which I han't made up my mind about?"

"My sister, sir—Mrs. Joe Gargery—wife of Joe Gargery, the blacksmith, sir."

"Blacksmith, eh?" said he. And looked down at his leg.

After darkly looking at his leg and at me several times, he came closer to my tombstone, took me by both arms, and tilted me back as far as he could hold me; so that his eyes looked most powerfully down into mine, and mine looked most helplessly up into his.

"Now lookie here," he said, "the question being whether you're to be let to live. You know what a file is?"

"Yes, sir."

"And you know what wittles is?"

"Yes, sir."

After each question he tilted me over a little more, so as to give me a greater sense of helplessness and danger.

"You get me a file." He tilted me again. "And you get me wittles." He tilted me again. "You bring 'em both to me." He tilted me again. "Or I'll have your heart and liver out." He tilted me again.

I was dreadfully frightened, and so giddy that I clung to him with both hands, and said, "If you would kindly please to let me keep upright, sir, perhaps I shouldn't be sick, and perhaps I could attend more."

He gave me a most tremendous dip and roll, so that the church jumped over its own weathercock. Then he held me by the arms, in an upright position on the top of the stone, and went on in these fearful terms:

"You bring me, tomorrow morning early, that file, and them wittles. You bring the lot to me at that old Battery over yonder. You do this, and you never dare to say a word or dare to make a sign concerning your haven't seen such a person as me, or any person, and you shall be let to live. You fail, or you go from my words in any partickler, no matter how small the partickler, and your heart and your liver shall be tore out, roasted, and ate. Now I ain't alone, as you may think I am. There's a young man hid with me, in comparison with which young man I am a Angel o'light. That young man hears the words I speak. That young man has a secret way pecooliar to himself, of getting at a boy, and at his heart, and at his liver. It is in wain for a boy to attempt to hide himself from that young man. A boy may lock his door, may be warm in bed, may tuck himself up, may draw the clothes over his head, may think himself comfortable and safe; but that young man will softly creep and creep his way to him and tear him open. I am akeepin that young man from harmin' of you at the present moment, with great difficulty. I find it very hard to hold that young man off of your inside. Now, what do you say?"

I said that I would get him the file, and I would get him what broken bits of food I could, and I would come to him at the Battery, early in the morning.

"Say Lord strike you dead if you don't?" said the man.

I said so, and he took me down.

"Now," he pursued, "you remember what you've undertook, and you remember that young man, and you get home!"

"Goo-good night, sir," I faltered.

"Much of that!" said he, glancing about him over the cold wet flat. "I wish I was a frog. Or a eel!"

At the same time he hugged his shuddering body in both his arms—clasping himself, as if to hold himself together—and limped toward the low church wall. As I saw him go, picking his way among the nettles, and among the brambles that bound the evergreen mounds, he looked in my young eyes, as if he were eluding the hands of the dead people, stretching up cautiously out of their graves, to get a twist upon his ankle and pull him in.

When he came to the low church wall, he got over it, like a man whose legs were numbed and stiff, and then turned round to look for me. When I saw him turning, I set my face toward home, and made the best use of my legs. But presently I looked over my shoulder, and saw him going on again toward the river, still hugging himself in both arms, and picking his way with his sore feet among the great stones dropped into the marshes here and there, for stepping-places when the rains were heavy, or the tide was in.

The marshes were just a long black horizontal line then, as I stopped to look after him; and the river was just another horizontal line not nearly so broad nor yet so black; and the sky was just a row of long angry red lines, and dense black lines intermixed. On the edge of the river I could faintly make out the only two black things in all the prospect that seemed to be standing upright; one of these was the beacon by which the sailors steered—like an unhooped cask upon a pole—an ugly slimy thing when you were near it; the other, a gibbet with some chains hanging to it which had once held a pirate. The man was limping on toward this latter, as if he were the pirate coming to life and come down, and going back to hook himself up again. It gave me a terrible turn when I thought so; and as I saw the black cattle lifting their heads to gaze after him, I wondered whether they thought so too. I looked all around for the horrible young man, and could see no signs of him. But now I was frightened again, and ran home without stopping.

T w o

MY SISTER, MRS. JOE GARGERY, WAS MORE THAN TWENTY years older than I, and had established a great reputation with herself and the neighbors because she had brought me up "by hand." Having at that time to find out for myself what the expression meant, and knowing her to have a hard and heavy hand, and to be much in the habit of laying it upon her husband, as well as upon me, I supposed that Joe Gargery and I were both brought up by hand.

She was not a good-looking woman, my sister; and I had a general impression that she must have made Joe Gargery marry her by hand. Joe was a fair man, with curls of flaxen hair on each side of his smooth face, and eyes of such a very undecided blue that they seemed to have somehow got mixed with their own whites. He was a mild, good-natured, sweet-tempered, easy-going, foolish, dear fellow—a sort of Hercules in strength, and also in weakness.

My sister, Mrs. Joe, with black hair and eyes, had such a prevailing redness of skin that I sometimes used to wonder whether it was possible she washed herself with a nutmeg-grater instead of soap. She was tall and bony, and almost always wore a coarse apron, fastened over her figure behind with two loops, and having a square, impregnable bib in front that was stuck full of pins and needles. She made it a powerful merit in herself, and a strong reproach against Joe, that she wore this apron so much. Though I really see no reason now why she should have worn it at all; or why, if she did wear it at all, she should not have taken it off every day of her life.

Joe's forge adjoined our house, which was a wooden house, as many of the dwellings in our country were—most of them, at that time. When I ran home from the churchyard, the forge was shut up, and Joe was sitting alone in the kitchen. Joe and I being fellow-sufferers, and having confidence as such, Joe imparted a confidence to me the moment I raised the latch of the door and peeped in at him opposite to it, sitting in the chimney-corner.

"Mrs. Joe has been out a dozen times, looking for you, Pip; and she's out now, making it a baker's dozen."

"Is she?"

"Yes, Pip," said Joe; "and what's worse, she's got Tickler with her."

At this dismal intelligence I twisted the only button on my waistcoat round and round, and looked in great depression at the fire. Tickler was a wax-ended piece of cane, worn smooth by collision with my tickled frame.

"She sat down," said Joe, "and she got up, and she made a grab at Tickler, and she ram-paged out. That's what she did," said Joe, slowly clearing the fire between the bars with the poker; "she ram-paged out, Pip."

"Has she been gone long, Joe?" I always treated him as a larger species of child, and as no more than my equal.

"Well," said Joe, looking up at the Dutch clock, "she's been on the Rampage, this last spell, about five minutes, Pip. She's a coming! Get behind the door, old chap, and have the jack-towel betwixt you."

I took the advice. My sister, Mrs. Joe, throwing the door wide open, and finding an obstruction behind it, immediately divined the cause, and applied Tickler to further investigation. She concluded by showing me. I often served her as a connubial missile at Joe, who, glad to get hold of me on any terms, passed me on into the chimney and quietly fenced me up there with his great legs.

"Where have you been, you young monkey?" said Mrs. Joe, stamping her foot. "Tell me directly what you've been doing to wear me away with fret and fright and worrit, or I'd have you out of that corner if you was fifty Pips and he was five hundred Gargerys."

"I have only been to the churchyard," said I, from my stool, crying and rubbing myself.

"Churchyard!" repeated my sister. "If it warn't for me you'd have been to the churchyard long ago, and staid there. Who brought you up by hand?"

"You did," said I.

"And why did I do it, I should like to know!" exclaimed my sister.

I whimpered, "I don't know."

"*I* don't!" said my sister. "I'd never do it again! I know that. I may truly say I've never had this apron of mine off since born you were. It's bad enough to be a blacksmith's wife (and him a Gargery), without being your mother."

My thoughts strayed from that question as I looked disconsolately at the fire. For the fugitive out on the marshes with the ironed leg, the mysterious young man, the file, the victuals, and the dreadful pledge I was under to commit a larceny on those sheltering premises, rose before me in the avenging coals.

"Hah!" said Mrs. Joe, restoring Tickler to his station. "Churchyard, indeed! You may well say churchyard, you two." One of us, by-the-by, had not said it at all. "You'll drive *me* to the churchyard betwixt you one of these days, and oh, a pr-r-recious pair you'd be without me!"

As she applied herself to set the tea-things, Joe peeped down at me over his leg, as if he were mentally casting me and himself up, and calculating what kind of pair we practically should make, under the grievous circumstances foreshadowed. After that, he sat feeling his right-side flaxen curls and whisker, and following Mrs. Joe about with his blue eyes, as his manner always was at squally times.

My sister had a trenchant way of cutting our bread-and-butter for us, that never varied. First, with her left hand she held the loaf, hard and fast, against her bib—where it sometimes got a pin into it, and sometimes a needle, which we afterward got into our mouths. Then she took some butter (not too much) on a knife and spread it on the loaf in an apothecary kind of way, as if she were making a plaster—using both sides of the knife with a slapping dexterity, and trimming and molding the butter off round the crust. Then she gave the knife a final smart wipe on the edge of the plaster, and then sawed a very thick round off the loaf, which she finally, before separating from the loaf, hewed into two halves: of which Joe got one, and I the other.

On the present occasion, though I was hungry, I dared not eat my slice. I felt that I must have something in reserve for my dreadful acquaintance and his ally, the still more dreadful young man. I knew Mrs. Joe's housekeeping to be of the strictest kind, and that my larcenous researches in the dead of night might find nothing available in the safe, therefore I resolved to put my hunk of bread-and-butter down the leg of my trowsers.

The effort of resolution necessary to the achievement of this purpose I found to be quite awful. It was as if I had to make up my mind to leap from the top of a high house, or plunge into a great depth of water. And it was made the more difficult by the unconscious Joe. In our above-mentioned freemasonry as fellow-sufferers, and in his good-natured companionship with me, it was our evening habit to compare the way we bit through our slices by silently holding them up to each other's admiration now and then—which in general led us to new exertions. Tonight Joe several times invited me, by the display of his fast-diminishing slice, to enter upon our usual friendly competition; but he found me each time with my yellow mug of tea on one knee, and my untouched bread-and-butter on the other. At last, I desperately considered that the thing I contemplated must be done, and that it had best be done in the least improbable manner consistent with the circumstances. I took advantage of a moment when Joe had just looked aside, and got my bread-and-butter down my leg.

Joe was evidently made uncomfortable by what he supposed to be my loss of appetite, and took a thoughtful semicircular bite out of his slice, which he didn't seem to enjoy. He rolled it about in his mouth much longer than usual, pondering over it a good deal, and after all gulped it down like a pill. He was about to take another bite, and had just got his head on one side for a good purchase on it, when his eye fell on me, and he saw that my bread-and-butter was gone.

The wonder and consternation with which Joe stopped on the threshold of his bite and stared at me were too evident to escape my sister's observation.

"What's the matter now?" said she smartly, as she put down her cup.

"I say, you know!" muttered Joe, shaking his head at me in very serious remonstrances. "Pip, old chap! You'll do yourself a mischief. It'll stick somewhere. You can't have chawed it, Pip."

"What's the matter *now?*" repeated my sister more, sharply than before.

"If you can cough any trifle on it up, Pip, I'd recommend you to do it," said Joe, all aghast. "Manners is manners, but still your elth's your elth."

By this time my sister was quite desperate, so she pounced on Joe, and taking him by the two whiskers, knocked his head for a little while against the wall behind him: while I sat in the corner looking guiltily on.

"Now, perhaps you'll mention what's the matter," said my sister, out of breath, "you staring great stuck pig."

Joe looked at her in a helpless way; then took a helpless bite and looked at me again.

"You know, Pip," said Joe, solemnly, with his last bite in his cheek, and speaking in a confidential tone, as if we were quite alone, "you and me is always friends, and I'd be the last to tell upon you any time. But such a"—he moved his chair and looked about the floor between us, and then again at me—"such a honcommon Bolt as that!"

"Been bolting his food, has he?" cried my sister.

"You know, old chap," said Joe, looking at me, and not Mrs. Joe, with his bite still in his cheek, "I Bolted, myself, when I was your age—frequent—and as a boy I've been among a many Bolters; but I never see your equal yet, Pip, and it's a mercy you ain't choked dead."

My sister made a dive at me, and fished me up by the hair: saying nothing more than the awful words, "you come along and be dosed."

Some medical beast had revived Tar-water in those days as a fine medicine, and Mrs. Joe always kept a supply of it in the cupboard; having a belief in its virtues correspondent to its horrible nastiness. At the best of times, so much of this elixir was administered to me as a choice restorative, that I was conscious of going about, smelling like a new fence. On this particular evening the urgency of my case demanded a pint of this mixture, which was poured down my throat, for my greater comfort, while Mrs. Joe held my head under her arm as a boot would be held in a boot-jack. Joe got off with half-a-pint, but was made to take that (much to his disturbance, as he sat slowly biting and meditating before the fire), "because he had had a turn." Judging for myself, I should say he certainly had one afterward, if he had had none before.

Conscience is a dreadful thing when it accuses man or boy; but when, in the case of a boy, that secret burden cooperates with another secret burden down the leg of his trowsers, it is (as I can testify) a great punishment. The guilty knowledge that I was going to rob Mrs. Joe—I never thought I was going to rob Joe, for I never thought of any of the housekeeping property as his—united to the necessity of always keeping one hand on the bread-and-butter as I sat, or when I was ordered about the kitchen on any small errand, almost drove me out of my mind. Then, as the March winds made the fire glow and flare, I thought I heard the fierce voice outside of the man with the iron on his leg who had sworn me to secrecy, declaring that he couldn't and wouldn't starve until tomorrow, but must be fed now. At other times, I thought, what if the young man who was with so much difficulty restrained from imbruing his hands in me, should either yield to his constitutional impatience, or should mistake the time, and should think himself accredited to my heart and liver tonight, instead of tomorrow! If ever anybody's hair stood on end with terror, mine must have done so then. But, perhaps, nobody's ever did?

It was Christmas eve, and I had to stir the pudding for next day, with the copper-stick, from seven to eight by the Dutch clock. I tried it with the load upon my leg (and that made me think afresh of the man with the iron on *his* leg), and found the tendency of exercise to bring the bread-and-butter out at my ancle, quite unmanageable and unconquerable. Happily I slipped away, and deposited that part of my conscience in my garret bedroom.

"Hark!" said I, when I had done my stirring, and was taking a final warm in the chimney corner before being sent up to bed; "was that guns, Joe?"

"Ah!" said Joe. "There's another conwict off."

"What does that mean, Joe?" said I.

Mrs. Joe, who always took explanations upon herself, said, snappishly, "Escaped. Escaped." Administering the definition like Tar-water.

While Mrs. Joe sat with her head bending over her needlework, I put my mouth into the forms of saying to Joe, "What's a convict?" Joe put *his* mouth into the forms of returning such a highly elaborate answer, that I could make out nothing of it but the single word "Pip."

"There was one off last night," said Joe, aloud, "after sunset-gun. And they fired warning of him. And now, it appears, they're firing warning of another."

"*Who's* firing?" said I.

"Drat that child," interposed my sister, frowning at me over her work, "what a questioner he is. Ask no questions, and you'll be told no lies."

It was not very polite to herself, I thought, to imply that I should be told lies by her, even if I did ask questions. But she never was polite, unless there was company.

At this point Joe greatly augmented my curiosity by taking the utmost pains to open his mouth very wide, and put it into the form of a word that looked to me like "sulks." Therefore I naturally pointed to Mrs. Joe, and put my mouth into the form of saying "her?" But Joe wouldn't hear of that at all and again opened his mouth very wide, and shook the form of a most emphatic word out of it. But I could make nothing of the word.

"Mrs. Joe," said I, as a last resource, "I should like to know—if you wouldn't much mind—where the firing comes from?"

"Lord bless the boy!" exclaimed my sister, as if she didn't quite mean that, but rather the contrary. "From the Hulks!"

"Oh-ho!" said I, looking at Joe. "Hulks!"

Joe gave a reproachful cough, as much as to say, "Well, I told you so."

"And please what's Hulks?" said I.

"That's the way with this boy!" exclaimed my sister, pointing me out with her needle and thread, and shaking her head. "Answer him one question, and he'll ask you a dozen directly. Hulks are prison-ships, right 'cross th' meshes." We always used that name for marshes, in our country.

"I wonder who's put into prison-ships, and why they're put there?" said I, in a general way, and with desperation.

It was too much for Mrs. Joe, who immediately rose. "I tell you what, young man," said she, "I didn't bring you up by hand to badger people's lives out. It would be blame to me, and not praise, if I had. People are put in the Hulks because they murder, and because they rob, and do all sorts of bad; and they almost always begin by asking questions. Now you get along to bed!"

I was never allowed a candle to light me to bed, and, as I went upstairs in the dark, with my head tingling from Mrs. Joe's thimble, having played the tambourine upon it to accompany her last words, I felt fearfully sensible of the great convenience that the Hulks were handy for me. I was clearly on my way there. I had begun by asking questions, and I was going to rob Mrs. Joe.

Since that time, which is far enough away now, I have often thought that few people know what secrecy there is in the young, under terror. No matter how unreasonable the terror, so that it be terror. I was in mortal terror of the young man who wanted my heart and liver; I was in mortal terror of my interlocutor with the ironed leg; I was in mortal terror of myself, from whom an awful promise had been extracted; I had no hope of deliverance through my all-powerful sister, who repulsed me at every turn; I am afraid to think, even now, of what I might have done, upon requirement, in the secrecy of my terror.

If I slept at all that night, it was only to imagine myself drifting down the river on a strong spring tide to the Hulks; a ghostly pirate calling out to me through a speaking trumpet, as I passed the gibbet-station, that I had better come ashore, and be hanged there at once, and not put it off. I was afraid to sleep, even if I had been inclined, for I knew that at the first faint dawn of morning I must rob the pantry. There was no getting a light by easy friction then; to have got one I must have struck it out of flint and steel, and have made a noise like the very pirate himself rattling his chains.

As soon as the great black velvet pall outside my little window was shot with gray, I got up and went downstairs: every board upon the way, and every crack in every board, calling after me, "Stop thief!" and "Get up, Mrs. Joe!" In the pantry, which was far more abundantly supplied than usual, owing to the season, I was very much alarmed by a hare hanging up by the heels, whom I rather thought I caught, when my back was half turned, waking. I had no time for verification, no time for selection, no time for anything, for I had no time to spare. I stole some bread, some rind of cheese, about half a jar of mince-meat (which I tied up in my pocket-handkerchief with my last night's slice), some brandy from a stone bottle (which I decanted into a glass bottle I had secretly used for making that intoxicating fluid, Spanish-liquorice-water, up in my room: diluting the stone bottle from a jug in the kitchen cupboard), a meat bone with very little on it, and a beautiful round, compact pork-pie. I was nearly going away without the pie, but I was tempted to mount upon a shelf to look what it was that was put away so carefully in a covered earthenware dish in a corner, and I found it was the pie, and I took it in the hope that it was not intended for early use, and would not be missed for some time.

There was a door in the kitchen communicating with the forge; I unlocked and unbolted that door, and got a file from among Joe's tools. Then I put the fastenings as I had found them, opened the door at which I had entered when I ran home last night, shut it, and ran for the misty marshes.

Three

IT WAS A RIMY MORNING, AND VERY DAMP. I HAD SEEN THE damp lying on the outside of my little window, as if some goblin had been crying there all night, and using the window for a pocket-handkerchief. Now I saw the damp lying on the bare hedges and spare grass, like a coarser sort of spiders' webs; hanging itself from twig to twig and blade to blade. On every rail and gate wet lay clammy; and the marsh mist was so thick that the wooden finger on the post, directing people to our village—a direction which they never accepted, for they never came there—was invisible to me until I was quite close under it. Then, as I looked up at it, while it dripped, it seemed, to my oppressed conscience, like a phantom devoting me to the Hulks.

The mist was heavier yet when I got out upon the marshes, so that, instead of my running at everything, everything seemed to run at me. This was very disagreeable to a quiet mind. The gates and dikes and banks came bursting at me through the mist, as if they cried as plainly as could be, "A boy with a pork-pie! Stop him!" The black cattle came upon me with like suddenness, staring out of their eyes, and smoking out of their nostrils, "Halloa, young thief!" One black ox, with a white cravat on—who had to my awakened conscience something of a clerical air—fixed me so steadily with his eyes, and moved his blunt head round in such an accusatory manner as I moved round, that I called out to him, "I couldn't help it! It wasn't for myself

I took it!" Upon which he put down his head, blew a cloud of smoke out of his nose, and vanished with a kick-up of his hind leg and flourish of his tail.

All this time I was getting on toward the river; but however fast I went, I couldn't warm my feet, to which the damp cold seemed riveted, as the iron was riveted to the leg of the man I was running to meet. I knew my way to the Battery pretty straight, for I had been down there on a Sunday with Joe, and Joe had, sitting on an old gun, told me that when I was 'prentice to him regularly bound, we would have such larks there as should recompense us for our constraint at home. However, in the confusion of the mist, I found myself at last too far to the right, and consequently had to try back along the riverside, on the bank of loose stones above the mud and the stakes that staked the tide out, to come at the Battery. Making my way along here with all dispatch, I had just crossed a ditch which I knew to be very near the Battery, and had just scrambled up the mound beyond the ditch, when I saw the man sitting before me. His back was toward me, and he had got his arms folded, and was nodding forward heavy with sleep.

I thought he would be more glad if I came upon him with his breakfast in that unexpected manner, so I went forward softly and touched him on the shoulder. He instantly jumped up, and it was not the man, but another man!

And yet he was dressed in coarse gray, too, and had a great iron on his leg, and was lame, and hoarse, and cold, and was everything that the other man was; except that he had not the same face, and had a flat, broad-brimmed, low-crowned felt hat on. All this I saw in a moment, for I had only a moment to see it in; he swore an oath at me, made a hit at me—it was a round weak blow that missed me and almost knocked himself down, for it made him stumble—and then he ran into the mist, tumbling twice as he went, and I lost him.

"It's the young man!" I thought. I felt my heart shoot as I identified him; and I dare say I should have felt a pain in my liver, too, if I had known where it was.

I was soon at the Battery after that, and there was the man—hugging himself and limping to and fro, as if he had never all night left off hugging and limping—waiting for me. He was awfully cold, to be sure. I half expected to see him drop down before my face and die of cold. His eyes looked so awfully hungry, too, that when I handed him the file it occurred to me he would have tried to eat it, if he had not seen my bundle. He did not turn me upside down, this time, to get at what I had, but left me right side upward while I opened the bundle and emptied my pockets.

"What's in the bottle, boy?" said he.

"Brandy," said I.

He was already handing mince-meat down his throat in the most curious manner, more like a man who was putting it away somewhere in a violent hurry than a man who was eating it—but he left off to take some of the liquor, shivering all the while so violently that it was quite as much as he could do to keep the neck of the bottle between his teeth.

"I think you have got the ague," said I.

"I'm much of your opinion, boy," said he.

"It's bad about here. You've been lying out on the meshes, and they're dreadful aguish. Rheumatic, too."

"I'll eat my breakfast afore they're the death of me," said he. "I'd do that, if I was going to be strung up to that there gallows as there is over there directly arterward. I'll beat the shivers so far, *I'll* bet you a guinea."

He was gobbling mince-meat, meat, bone, bread, cheese, and pork-pie. All at once: staring distrustfully while he did so at the mist all round us, and often stopping—even stopping his jaws—to listen. Some real or fancied sound, some clink upon the river or breathing of beasts upon the marsh, now gave him a start, and he said, suddenly:

"You're not a false imp? You brought no one with you?"

"No, sir! No!"

"Nor give no one the office to follow you?"

"No!"

"Well," said he, "I believe you. You'd be but a fierce young hound indeed, if at your time of life you could help to hunt a wretched warmint, hunted as near death and dunghill as this poor wretched warmint is!"

Something clicked in his throat, as if he had works in him like a clock, and was going to strike. And he smeared his ragged, rough sleeve over his eyes.

Pitying his desolation, and watching him as he gradually settled down upon the pie, I made bold to say, "I am glad you enjoy it."

"Did you speak?"

"I said I was glad you enjoyed it."

"Thankee, my boy. I do."

I had often watched a large dog of ours eating his food; and I now noticed a decided similarity between the dog's way of eating and the man's. The man took strong, sharp, sudden bites, just like the dog. He swallowed, or rather snapped up, every mouthful too soon and too fast; and he looked sideways here and there while he ate, as if he thought there was danger of somebody's coming to take the pie away. He was altogether too unsettled in his mind over it to appreciate it comfortably, I thought, or to have anybody to dine with him, without making a chop with his jaws at the visitor. In all of which particulars he was very like the dog.

"You won't leave any of it for him," said I, timidly, after a silence during which I had hesitated as to the politeness of making the remark. "There's no more to be got where that came from." It was the certainty of this fact that impelled me to offer the hint.

"Leave for him? Who's him?" said my friend, stopping in his crunching of pie-crust.

"The young man. That you spoke of. That was hid with you."

"Oh, ah!" he returned, with something like a gruff laugh. "Him? Yes, yes! *He* don't want no wittles."

"I thought he looked as if he did," said I.

The man stopped eating, and regarded me with the closest scrutiny and the greatest surprise.

"Looked? When?"

"Just now!"

"Where?"

"Yonder," said I, pointing; "over there, where I found him nodding asleep, and thought it was you."

He held me by the collar and stared at me so, that I began to think his first idea about cutting my throat had revived.

"Dressed like you, you know, only with a hat," I explained, trembling; "and—and"—I was very anxious to put it delicately—"and with—the same reason for wanting to borrow a file. Didn't you hear the gun last night?"

"Then there *was* firing!" he said to himself.

"I wonder you shouldn't have been sure of that," I returned, "for we heard it up at home, and that's further away, and we were shut in besides."

"Why, see now!" said he. "When a man's alone on these flats, with a light head and a light stomach, perishin' of cold and want, he hears nothin' all night but guns firin', and voices callin'. Hears? He sees the soldiers with their red coats, lighted up by the torches carried afore, closin' in round him. Hears his number called, hears himself challenged, hears the rattle of the muskets, hears the orders, 'Make ready! Present!—Cover him steady, men!' and is laid hands on, and there's nothing! Why, if I see one pursuing party last night—coming up in order, Damn 'em, with their tramp, tramp—I see a hundred. And as to firin'! Why, I see the mist shake with the cannon, when it was broad day.—But this man"—he had said all the rest as if he had forgotten my being there—"did you notice anything in him?"

"He had a bruised face," said I, recalling what I hardly knew I knew.

"Not here?" exclaimed the man, striking his left cheek with the flat of his hand.

"Yes! There!"

"Where is he?" He crammed what little food was left into the breast of his gray jacket. "Show me the way he went. I'll pull him down like a bloodhound. Curse this iron on my sore leg! Give us hold of the file, boy."

I indicated in what direction. The mist had shrouded the other man, and he looked up at it for an instant. But he was going down on the rank wet grass, filing at his iron like a madman, and not minding me or minding his own leg, which had an old chafe upon it and was bloody, but which he handled as roughly as if it had no more feeling in it than the file. I was very much afraid of him again, now that he had worked himself into this fierce hurry, and I was likewise very much afraid of keeping away from home any longer. I told him I must go, but he took no notice, so I thought the best thing I could do was to slip off. The last I saw of him, his head was bent over his knee, and he was working hard at his fetter, muttering impatient imprecations at it and at his leg. The last I heard of him, I stopped in the mist to listen, and the file was still going.

F o u r

I FULLY EXPECTED TO FIND A CONSTABLE IN THE KITCHEN, waiting to take me up. But not only was there no constable there, but no discovery had yet been made of the robbery. Mrs. Joe was prodigiously busy in getting the house ready for the festivities of the day, and Joe had been put upon the kitchen doorstep to keep him out of the dust-pan—an article into which his destiny always led him sooner or later when my sister was vigorously reaping the floors of her establishment.

"And where the deuce ha' *you* been?" was Mrs. Joe's Chistmas salutation, when I and my conscience showed ourselves.

I said I had been down to hear the Carols. "Ah! well!" observed Mrs. Joe. "You might ha' done worse." "Not a doubt of it," I thought.

"Perhaps if I warn't a blacksmith's wife, and (what's the same thing) a slave with her apron never off, *I* should have been to hear the Carols," said Mrs. Joe. "I'm rather partial to Carols myself, and that's the best of reasons for my never hearing any."

Joe, who had ventured into the kitchen after me as the dust-pan had retired before us, drew the back of his hand across his nose with a conciliatory air when Mrs. Joe darted a look at him, and, when her eyes were withdrawn, secretly crossed his two forefingers, and exhibited them to me, as our token that Mrs. Joe was in a cross temper. This was so much her normal state, that Joe and I would often, for weeks together, be, as to our fingers, like monumental Crusaders as to their legs.

We were to have a superb dinner, consisting of a leg of pickled pork, and greens, and a pair of roast stuffed fowls. A handsome mince-pie had been made yesterday morning (which accounted for the mince-meat not being missed), and the pudding was already on the boil. These extensive arrangements occasioned us to be cut off unceremoniously in respect of breakfast, "for I an't," said Mrs. Joe, "I an't a going to have no cramming and gorging and washing up now, with what I've got before me, I promise you!"

So we had our slices served out, as if we were two thousand troops on a forced march, instead of a man and boy at home; and we took gulps of milk and water, with apologetic countenances, from a jug on the dresser. In the meantime Mrs. Joe put clean white curtains up, and tacked a new flowered flounce across the wide chimney to replace the old one, and uncovered the little state parlor across the passage, which was never uncovered at any other time, but passed the rest of the year in a cool haze of silver paper, which even extended to the four little white crockery poodles on the mantle shelf, each with a black nose, and a basket of flowers in his mouth, and each the counterpart of the other. Mrs. Joe was a very clean housekeeper, but had an exquisite art of making her cleanliness more uncomfortable and unacceptable than dirt itself. Cleanliness is next to Godliness, and some people do the same by their religion.

My sister having so much to do, was going to church vicariously; that is to say, Joe and I were going. In his working clothes Joe was a well-knit, characteristic-looking blacksmith; in his holiday clothes, he was more like a scarecrow in good circumstances than anything else. Nothing that he wore then fitted him or seemed to belong to him, and everything that he wore then grazed him. On the present festive occasion he emerged from his room, when the blithe bells were going, the picture of misery in a full suit of Sunday penitentials. As to me, I think my sister must have had some general idea that I was a young offender whom an Accoucheur Policeman had taken up (on my birthday), and delivered over to her to be dealt with according to the outraged majesty of the law. I was always treated as if I had insisted on being born in opposition to the dictates of reason, religion, and morality, and against the dissuading arguments of my best friends; even when I was taken to have a new suit of clothes, the tailor had orders to make them like a kind of Reformatory, and on no account to let me have the use of my limbs.

Joe and I going to church, therefore, must have been a moving spectacle for compassionate minds. Yet what I suffered outside was nothing to what I underwent within. The terrors that had assailed me whenever Mrs. Joe had gone near the pantry or out of the room, were only to be equaled by the remorse with which my mind dwelt on what my hands had done. Under the weight of my wicked secret I pondered whether the Church would be powerful enough to shield me from the vengeance of the terrible young man, if I divulged it to that establishment. I conceived the idea that the time when the bans were read and when the clergyman said, "Ye are now to declare it!" would be the time for me to rise and propose a private audience in the vestry. I am far from being quite sure that I might not have astonished our small congregation by resorting to this extreme measure, but for its being Christmas Day and no Sunday.

Mr. Wopsle, the clerk at church, was to dine with us; and Mr. Hubble the wheel-wright and Mrs. Hubble; and Uncle Pumblechook (Joe's uncle, but Mrs. Joe appropriated him), who was a well-to-do corn-chandler in the nearest town, and drove his own chaise-cart. The dinner hour was half-past one. When Joe and I got home we found the table laid, and Mrs. Joe dressed, and the dinner dressing, and the front door unlocked (it never was at any other time) for the company to enter by, and everything most splendid. And still, not a word of the robbery.

The time came without bringing with it any relief to my feelings, and the company came. Mr. Wopsle, united to a Roman nose and a large bald forehead, had a deep sonorous voice which he was proud of; indeed it was understood among his acquaintance that if you could only give him his head he would read the clergyman into fits; he himself confessed that if the Church was "thrown open," meaning to competition, he would not despair of making his mark in it. The Church not being "thrown open," he was, as I have said, our clerk. But he finished the Amens tremendously; and when he gave out the psalm—always giving us the whole verse—he looked all round the congregation first, as much as to say, "You have heard my friend overhead; oblige me with your opinion of this!"

I opened the door to the company—making believe that it was a habit of ours to open that door—and I opened it first to Mr. Wopsle, next to Mr. and Mrs. Hubble, and last of all to Uncle Pumblechook. N. B. I was not allowed to call him uncle under the severest penalties.

"Mrs. Joe," said Uncle Pumblechook, who was a large, hard-breathing, middle-aged, slow man, with a mouth like a fish, dull staring eyes, and sandy hair standing upright on his head, so that he looked as if he had just been choked, and had that very moment come to, "I have brought you, as the compliments of the season—I have brought you, Mum, a bottle of sherry wine, and I have brought you, Mum, a bottle of port wine."

Every Christmas Day he presented himself, as a profound novelty, with exactly the same words, and carrying the two bottles like dumb-bells. Every Christmas Day, Mrs. Joe replied, as she now replied, "Oh, Un—cle Pum—ble—chook! This is kind!" Every Christmas Day, he retorted, as he now retorted, "It's no more than your merits. And how are you all—bobbish? And how's Sixpennorth of half pence?" meaning me.

We dined on these occasions in the kitchen, and adjourned, for the nuts and oranges and apples, to the parlor; which was a change very like Joe's change from his working clothes to his Sunday's dress. My sister was uncommonly lively on the present occasion, and indeed was generally more gracious in the society of Mrs. Hubble than in any other company. I remember Mrs. Hubble as a little, sharp-eared person in curly sky-blue, who held a conventionally juvenile position, because she had married Mr. Hubble—I don't know at what remote period—when she was much younger than he. I remember Mr. Hubble as a tough, high-shouldered, stooping old man, of a sawdusty fragrance, with his legs extraordinarily wide apart, so that in my short and early days I always saw some miles of open country between them when I met him coming up the lane.

Among this good company I should have felt myself, even if I hadn't robbed the pantry, in a false position. Not because I was squeezed in at an acute angle of the tablecloth with the table in my chest, and the Pumblechookian elbow in my eye; not because I was not allowed to speak (I didn't want to speak), nor because I was regaled with the scaly tips of the drumsticks of the fowls, and with those corners of obscure pork of which the pig, when living, had had the least reason to be vain. No; I should not have minded that, if they would only have left me alone. But they wouldn't leave me alone. They seemed to think the opportunity lost, if they failed to point the conversation at me every now and then, and stick the point into me. I might have been an unfortunate little bull in a Spanish arena: I got so smartingly touched up by these moral goads.

It began the moment we sat down to dinner. Mr. Wopsle said grace with theatrical declamation, as it now appears to me, something like a religious cross of the Ghost in Hamlet with Richard the Third—and ended with the very proper aspiration that we might be truly grateful. Upon which my sister instantly fixed me with her eye, and said, in a low, reproachful voice, "Do you hear that? Be grateful."

"Especially," said Mr. Pumblechook, "be grateful, boy, to them which brought you up by hand."

Mrs. Hubble shook her head, and contemplating me with a mournful presentiment that I should come to no good, asked, "Why is it that the young are never grateful?" This mystery seemed too much for the company until Mr. Hubble tersely solved it by saying, "Naturally wicious." Everybody then murmured "Ah!" and "True!" and looked at me in a particularly unpleasant and personal manner.

Joe's station and influence were something feebler (if possible) when there was company than when there was none. But he always aided and abetted me when he could, in some way of his own, and he always did so at dinnertime by giving me gravy, if there were any. There being plenty of gravy today, Joe spooned into my plate, at this point, about half-a-pint.

A little later on in the dinner, Mr. Wopsle reviewed the sermon with some severity, and intimated in the usual hypothetical case of the Church being "thrown open," what kind of sermon *he* would have given them. After favoring them with some heads of that discourse, he remarked that he considered the subject of the day's homily ill chosen; which was the less excusable, he added, when there were so many subjects "going about."

"True again," said Uncle Pumblechook. "You've hit it—plenty of subjects going about, for them that know how to put salt upon their tails. That's what's wanted. A man needn't go far to find a subject if he's ready with his salt box. Why," added Mr. Pumblechook, after a short interval of deep reflection, "look at Pork alone. There's a subject! If you want subject, look at Pork!"

"True, sir. Many a moral for the young," returned Mr. Wopsle; and I knew he was going to bring me in before he said it, "might be deducted from that text."

("You listen to this," said my sister to me, in a severe parenthesis.)

Joe gave me some more gravy.

"Swine," pursued Mr. Wopsle, in his deepest voice, and pointing his fork at my blushes as if he were mentioning my Christian name—"Swine were the companions of the prodigal. The gluttony of Swine is set before us as an example to the young." (I thought this pretty well in him who had been praising up the pork for being so plump and juicy.) "What is detestable in a pig is more detestable in a boy."

"Or girl," suggested Mr. Hubble.

"Of course, or girl," assented Mr. Wopsle, rather irritably; "but there is no girl present."

"Besides," said Mr. Pumblechook, turning sharp on me, "think what you've got to be grateful for. If you'd been born a squeaker—"

"He was, if ever a child was," said my sister, most emphatically.

Joe gave me some more gravy.

"Well, but I mean a four-footed squeaker," said Mr. Pumblechook. "If you had been born such, would you have been here now? Not you—"

"Unless in that form," said Mr. Wopsle, nodding toward the dish.

"But I don't mean in that form, sir," returned Mr. Pumblechook, who had an objection to being interrupted; "I mean enjoying himself with his elders and betters, and improving himself with their conversation, and rolling in the lap of luxury. Would he have been doing that? No, he wouldn't. And what would have been your destination?" turning on me again. "You would have been disposed of for so many shillings, according to the market price of the article, and Dunstable, the butcher, would have come up to you as you lay in your straw, and he would have whipped you under his left arm, and with his right he would have tucked up his frock to get a penknife from out of his waistcoat-pocket, and he would have shed your blood and had your life. No bringing up by hand then. Not a bit of it!"

Joe offered me more gravy, which I was afraid to take.

"He was a world of trouble to you, ma'am," said Mrs. Hubble, commiserating my sister.

"Trouble?" echoed my sister; "trouble?" And then entered on a fearful catalogue of all the illnesses I had been guilty of, and all the acts of sleeplessness I had committed, and all the high places I had tumbled from, and all the low places I had tumbled into, and all the injuries I had done myself, and all the times she had wished me in my grave, and I had contumaciously refused to go there.

I think the Romans must have aggravated one another very much with their noses. Perhaps they became the restless people they were in consequence. Anyhow, Mr. Wopsle's Roman nose so aggravated me, during the recital of my misdemeanors, that I should have liked to pull it until he howled. But all I had endured up to this time was nothing in comparison with the awful feeling that took possession of me when the pause was broken which ensued upon my sister's recital, and in which pause everybody had looked at me (as I felt deeply conscious) with indignation and abhorrence.

"Yet," said Mr. Pumblechook, leading the company gently back to the theme from which they had strayed, "Pork—regarded as biled—is rich, too; ain't it?"

"Have a little brandy, uncle?" said my sister.

O Heavens, it had come at last! He would find it was weak, he would say it was weak, and I was lost! I held tight to the leg of the table with both hands, and awaited my fate.

My sister went for the stone bottle, came back with the stone bottle, and poured his brandy out, no one else taking any. The wretched man trifled with his glass—took it up, looked at it through the light, put it down—prolonged my misery. All this time Mrs. Joe and Joe were busily clearing the table for the pie and pudding.

I couldn't keep my eyes off him. Always holding tight by the leg of the table with my hands and feet, I saw the miserable creature finger his glass playfully, take it up, smile, throw his head back, and drink the brandy off. Instantly afterward the company were seized with unspeakable consternation, owing to his springing to his feet, turning round several times in an appalling spasmodic, hooping-cough dance, and rushing out at the door; he then became visible through the window, violently stamping and expectorating, making the most hideous faces, and apparently out of his mind.

I held on tight, while Mrs. Joe and Joe ran to him. I didn't know how I had done it, but I had no doubt I had murdered him somehow. In my dreadful situation it was a relief when he was brought back, and surveying the company all round, as if *they* had disagreed with him, sank down into his chair with the one significant gasp, "Tar!"

I had filled up the bottle from the tar-water jug. I knew he would be worse by-and-by. I moved the table, like a Medium of the present day, by the vigor of my unseen grasp upon it.

"Tar!" cried my sister, in amazement. "Why, however could it come there?"

But Uncle Pumblechook, who was omnipotent in that kitchen, wouldn't hear the word, wouldn't hear the subject mentioned, imperiously waved it all away with his hand, and asked for hot gin and water. My sister, who had begun to be alarmingly meditative, had to employ herself actively in getting the gin, the hot water, the sugar, and the lemon-peel, and mixing them. For the time at least, I was saved. I still held on the leg of the table, but clutched it now with the fervor of gratitude.

By degrees I became calm enough to release my grasp and partake of pudding. Mr. Pumblechook partook of pudding. All partook of pudding. The course terminated, and Mr. Pumblechook had begun to beam under the genial influence of the gin and water. I began to think I should get over the day when my sister said to Joe, "Clear plates—cold."

I clutched the leg of the table again immediately, and pressed it to my bosom as if it had been the companion of my youth and friend of my soul. I foresaw what was coming, and I felt that this time I really was gone.

"You must taste," said my sister, addressing the guests with her best grace, "you must really taste, to finish with, such a delightful and delicious present of Uncle Pumblechook's!"

Must they! Let them not hope it!

"You must know," said my sister, rising, "it's a pie—a savory pork-pie."

The company murmured their compliments; and Uncle Pumblechook, sensible of having deserved well of his fellow-creatures, and having distinguished himself by his gift, said vivaciously, all things considered, "Well, Mrs. Joe, we'll do our best endeavors; let us have a cut at this same pie."

My sister went out to get it. I heard her steps proceed to the pantry. I saw Mr. Pumblechook balance his knife. I saw reawakening appetite in the Roman nostrils of Mr. Wopsle. I heard Mr. Hubble remark that "a bit of savory pork-pie would lay a-top of anything and do no harm," and I heard Joe say, "You shall have some, Pip." I have never been absolutely certain whether I uttered a shrill cry of terror merely in spirit, or in the bodily hearing of the company. I felt that I could bear no more, and that I must run away. I released the leg of the table, and ran for my life.

But I ran no further than the house door, for there I ran head foremost into a party of soldiers with their muskets, one of whom held out a pair of handcuffs to me, saying: "Here you are, look sharp, come on!"

Five

THE APPARITION OF A FILE OF SOLDIERS RINGING DOWN the butt end of their loaded muskets on our doorstep caused the dinner-party to rise from table confused, and caused Mrs. Joe reentering the kitchen empty-handed, to stop short and stare, after her first wondering lament of "Lord gracious, what's gone with the pie!"

The sergeant and I were in the kitchen when Mrs. Joe stood staring; at which crisis I partly recovered the use of my senses. It was the sergeant who had spoken to me, and he was now looking round at the company, with his handcuffs invitingly extended toward them in his right hand, and his left on my shoulder.

"Excuse me, ladies and gentlemen," said the sergeant, "but as I have mentioned at the door to this young shaver (which he hadn't), I am on a chase for the King, and I want the blacksmith."

"And pray what might you want with *him?*" retorted my sister, quick to resent his being wanted at all.

"Missus," returned the gallant sergeant, "speaking for myself, I should reply, the honor and pleasure of his wife's acquaintance; speaking for the King, I answer a little job done."

This was received as rather neat in the sergeant; insomuch that Mr. Pumblechook cried audibly, "Good again!"

"You see, blacksmith," said the sergeant, who had by this time picked out Joe with his eye, "we have had an accident with these, and find the lock of one of 'em goes wrong, and the coupling don't act pretty. As they are wanted for immediate service, will you throw your eye over them?"

Joe threw his eye over them, and pronounced that the job would necessitate the lighting of his forge fire, and would take nearer two hours than one. "Then will you set about it at once, blacksmith," said the sergeant, "as it's on his Majesty's service; and if my men can bear a hand anywhere, they'll make themselves useful." With that he called to his men, who came trooping into the kitchen one after another, and piled their arms in a corner. And there they stood about as soldiers do; now, with their hands loosely clasped before them; now, resting a knee or a shoulder; now, easing a belt or a pouch; now, opening the door to spit stiffly over their high stocks out into the yard.

All these things I saw without knowing that I saw them, for I was in mortal terror. But, beginning to perceive that the handcuffs were not for me, and that the military had so far got the better of the pie as to put it in the background for the moment, I collected a little more of my scattered wits.

"Would you give me the time?" said the sergeant, addressing himself to Mr. Pumblechook, as a man whose appreciative powers justified the inference that he was equal to the time.

"It's just gone half past two."

"That's not so bad," said the sergeant, reflecting; "even if I were forced to halt here nigh two hours, that'll do. How far might you call yourselves from the marshes here? Not above a mile, I reckon?"

"Just a mile," said Mrs. Joe.

"That'll do. We begin to close in upon 'em about dusk. A little before dusk, my orders are. That'll do."

"Convicts, sergeant?" said Mr. Wopsle, in a matter-of-course way.

"Ay!" returned the sergeant, "two. They're pretty well known to be out on the marshes still, and they won't try to get clear of 'em before dusk. Anybody here seen anything of any such game?"

Everybody, myself excepted, said no, with confidence. Nobody thought of me.

"Well," said the sergeant, "they'll find themselves trapped in a circle, I expect, sooner than they count on. Now, blacksmith! If you're ready, the King is."

Joe had got his coat and waistcoat and cravat off, and his leather apron on, and passed into the forge. One of the soldiers opened its wooden windows, another lighted the fire, another turned to at the bellows, the rest stood round the blaze, which was soon roaring. Then Joe began to hammer and clink, hammer and clink, and all looked on.

The interest of the impending pursuit not only absorbed the general attention, but even made my sister generous. She drew a pitcher of beer from the cask for the soldiers, and invited the sergeant to take a glass of brandy. But Mr. Pumblechook said, sharply, "Give him wine, mum. I'll engage there's no Tar in that"; so the sergeant thanked him and said that, as he preferred his drink without tar, he would take wine, if it was equally convenient. When it was given him he drank his Majesty's health and Compliments of the Season, and took it all at a mouthful and smacked his lips.

"Good stuff, eh, sergeant?" said Mr. Pumblechook.

"I'll tell you something," returned the sergeant; "I suspect that stuff's of *your* providing."

Mr. Pumblechook, with a fat sort of laugh, said, "Ay, ay? Why?"

"Because," returned the sergeant, clapping him on the shoulder, "you're a man that knows what's what."

"D'ye think so?" said Mr. Pumblechook, with his former laugh. "Have another glass."

"With you. Hob and nob," returned the sergeant. "The top of mine to the foot of yours, the foot of yours to the top of mine. Ring once, ring twice, the best tune on the Musical Glasses! Your health. May you live a thousand years, and never be a worse judge of the right sort than at the present moment of your life!"

The sergeant tossed off his glass again and seemed quite ready for more. I noticed that Mr. Pumblechook in his hospitality appeared to forget that he had made a present of the wine, but took the bottle from Mrs. Joe and had all the credit of handing it about in a gush of joviality. Even I got some. And he was so very free of the wine that he even called for the other bottle, and handed that about with the same liberality when the first was gone.

As I watched them while they all stood clustered about the forge enjoying themselves so much, I thought what terrible good sauce for a dinner my fugitive friend in the marshes was. They had not enjoyed themselves a quarter so much before the entertainment was brightened with the excitement he furnished. And now, when they were all in lively expectation of those two villains being taken, and when the bellows seemed to roar for them, the fire to flare for them, the smoke to hurry out in pursuit of them, Joe to hammer and clink for them, and all the murky shadows on the wall to stare at them in menace as the blaze rose and sank, and the red-hot sparks dropped and died, the pale afternoon outside almost seemed, in my pitying young fancy, to have turned pale on their account, poor wretches!

At last, Joe's job was done, and the ringing and roaring stopped. As Joe got on his coat, he mustered courage to propose that some of us should go down with the soldiers and see what came of the hunt. Mr. Pumblechook and Mr. Hubble declined, on the plea of a pipe and ladies' society; but Mr. Wopsle said he would go if Joe would. Joe said he was agreeable, and he would take me, if Mrs. Joe approved. We never should have got leave to go, I am sure, but for Mrs. Joe's curiosity to know all about it and how it ended. As it was, she merely stipulated, "If you bring the boy back with his head blown off by a musket, don't say it was my doing."

The sergeant took a polite leave of the ladies, and parted from Mr. Pumblechook as from a comrade: though I doubted if he were quite as fully sensible of that gentleman's merits under arid conditions as when something to drink was going. His men resumed their muskets and fell in. Mr. Wopsle, Joe, and I, received strict charge to keep in the rear, and to speak no word after we reached the marshes. When we were all out in the raw air and steadily moving toward our business, I treasonably whispered to Joe, "I hope, Joe, we sha'n't find them"; and Joe whispered to me, "I'd give a shilling if they had cut and run, Pip."

We were joined by no stragglers from our village, for the weather was cold and threatening, the way dreary, the footing bad, dusk coming on, and the people had good fires indoors and were keeping the day. A few faces hurried to glowing windows and looked after us, but none came out. We passed the finger-post, and held straight on to the churchyard. There we were stopped a few minutes by a signal from the sergeant's hand, while two or three of his men dispersed themselves among the graves, and examined the porch. They came in again without finding anything, and then we struck out on the open marshes, through the gate at the side of the churchyard. A bitter sleet came rattling against us on the east wind, and Joe took me on his back.

Now that we were out upon the dismal wilderness, where they little thought I had been within eight or nine hours and had seen both men hiding, I considered, for the first time, with great dread, if we should come upon them, would my particular convict suppose that it was I who had brought the soldiers there? He had asked me if I was a deceiving imp, and he had said I should be a fierce young hound if I joined the hunt against him. Would he believe that I was both imp and hound in treacherous earnest, and had betrayed him?

It was of no use asking myself this question now. There I was, on Joe's back, and there was Joe beneath me, charging out the ditches in the nimblest manner, and stimulating Mr. Wopsle not to tumble on his Roman nose, and to keep up with us. The soldiers were in front of us, extended into a pretty wide line with an interval between man and man. We were taking the exact course I had begun with, and from which I had diverged in the mist. Either the mist was not out again yet, or the wind had moved it. Under the low red glare of sunset the beacon, and the gibbet, and the mound of the Battery, and the opposite shore of the river, were plain enough, though all of a watery lead color.

With my heart thumping like a small blacksmith at Joe's broad shoulder, I looked all about for any sign of the convicts. I could see none, I could hear none. Mr. Wopsle had greatly alarmed me more than once by his blowing and hard breathing; but I knew the sounds by this time, and could dissociate them from the object of pursuit. I got a dreadful start, and thought I heard the file still going; but it was only a sheep-bell. The sheep stopped in their eating and looked timidly at us; and the cattle, their heads turned from the wind and sleet, stared angrily, as if they held us responsible for both these annoyances: but, except these things, and the shudder of the whole dying day, there was no break in the uniform stillness of the marshes.

The soldiers were moving on in the direction of the old Battery, and we were moving on a little way behind them, when, all of a sudden, we all stopped. For there had reached us, on the wings of the wind and rain, a long shout. It was repeated. It was at a distance toward the east, but it was long and loud. Nay, there seemed to be two shouts raised together—if one might judge from a confusion in the sound.

To this effect the sergeant and the nearest men were speaking under their breath when Joe and I came up. After another moment's listening, Joe (who was a good judge) agreed, and Mr. Wopsle (who was a bad judge) also agreed. The sergeant, a quick, decisive man, ordered that the sound should not be answered, but that the course should be changed, and that his men should make toward it "at the double." So we slanted to the right (where the East was), and Joe pounded away so wonderfully that I had to hold on tight to keep my seat.

It was a run indeed now, and what Joe called, in the only two words he spoke all the time, "a buster." Down banks and up banks, and over gates, and splashing into dikes: no man cared where he went. As we came nearer to the shouting, it became more and more apparent that it was made by more than one voice. Sometimes it seemed to stop altogether, and then the soldiers stopped. When it broke out again the soldiers made for it at a greater rate than ever, and we after them. After a while we had so run it down that we could hear one voice calling "Murder!" and another voice, "Convicts! Runaways! Guard! guard! This way for the runaway convicts!" Then both voices would seem to be stifled in a struggle, and then would break out again. And when it had come to this the soldiers ran like deer, and Joe too.

The sergeant ran in first, when we had run the noise quite down, and two of his men ran in close upon him. Their pieces were cocked and leveled when we all ran in.

"Here are lots more!" panted the sergeant, struggling with something at the bottom of a ditch. "Surrender, you two! and confound you for two wild beasts! Come asunder!"

Water was splashing, and mud was splashing, and oaths were being sworn, and blows were being struck, when half a dozen more men went down into the ditch to help the sergeant, and dragged out, separately, my convict and the other one. Both were bleeding and panting and execrating and struggling; but of course I knew them both directly.

"Mind!" said my convict, wiping blood from his face, with his ragged sleeves, and shaking torn hair from his fingers; "*I* took him! *I* giv' him up to you! Mind that!"

"It's not much to be particular about!" said the sergeant, coolly. "It'll do you small good, my man, being in the same plight yourself. Handcuffs there!"

"I don't expect it to do me any good. I don't want it to do me more good than it does now," said my convict, with a terrible laugh. "I took him. He knows it. That's enough for me."

The other convict was livid to look at, and, in addition to the old bruise on the left side of his face, seemed to be bruised and torn all over. He could not so much as get his breath to speak, until they were both separately handcuffed, but leaned upon a soldier to keep himself from falling.

"Take notice, guard, that he tried to murder me," were his first words.

"Tried to murder him?" said my convict, disdainfully. "Try, and not do it? I took him, and giv' him up; that's what I done. I not only prevented him getting off the marshes, but I dragged him here—dragged him this far on his way back. He's a gentleman, if you please, that villain. Now the Hulks has got its gentleman again, through me. Murder him? Worth my while, too, to murder him, when I could do worse and drag him back!"

The other one still gasped, "He tried—he tried—to—murder me. Bear—bear witness."

"Lookee here!" said my convict to the sergeant. "I got clear of the prisonship; I made a dash, and I done it. I could ha' got clear of these death-cold flats likewise—look at my leg; you won't find much iron on it—if I hadn't made discovery that *he* was there. Let *him* go free? Let *him* profit by the means as I found out? Let *him* make use of me afresh and again? Once more? No, no, no. If I had died at the bottom there"—and he made an emphatic motion at the ditch with his manacled hands—"I'd have held to him with that grip that you should have been safe to find him in my hold."

The other fugitive, who was evidently in extreme fear of his companion, repeated, "He tried to murder me. I should have been a dead man if you had not come up."

"He lies!" said my convict, with fierce energy. "He always lies. He's a liar born, and he'll die a liar. Look at his face; ain't it written there? Let him turn them eyes of his on me. I defy him to do it."

The other, with an effort at a scornful smile—which could not, however, collect the nervous working of his mouth into any set expression—looked at the soldiers, and looked about at the marshes and at the sky, but certainly did not look at the speaker.

"Do you see him?" pursued my convict. "Do you see what a villain he is? Do you see them groveling and wandering eyes? That's how he looked when we were tried together. He never looked at me."

The other, always working and working his dry lips and turning his eyes restlessly about him far and near, did at last turn them for a moment on the speaker, with the words, "You are not much to look at," and with a half-taunting glance at the bound hands. At that point my convict became so frantically exasperated that he would have rushed upon him but for the interposition of the soldiers. "Didn't I tell you," said the other convict then, "that he would murder me if he could?" And anyone could see that he shook, and that there broke out upon his lips curious white flakes, like thin snow.

"Enough of this parley," said the sergeant. "Light those torches."

As one of the soldiers, who carried a basket in lieu of a gun, went down on his knee to open it, my convict looked round him for the first time and saw me. I had alighted from Joe's back on the brink of the ditch when he came up, and had not moved since. I looked at him eagerly when he looked at me, and moved my hands and shook my head. I had been waiting for him to see me, that I might try to assure him of my innocence. It was not at all expressed to me that he even comprehended my intention, for he gave me a look that I did not understand, and it all passed in a moment. But if he had looked at me for an hour or a day, I could not have remembered his face ever afterward as having been more attentive.

The soldier with the basket soon got a light, and lighted three or four torches, and took one himself and distributed the others. It had been almost dark before, but now it seemed quite dark, and soon afterward very dark. Before we departed from that spot four of the soldiers, standing in a ring, fired twice into the air. Presently we saw other torches lighted at some distance behind us, and others on the marshes on the opposite bank of the river. "All right," said the sergeant. "March!"

We had not gone far when three cannon were fired ahead of us with a sound that seemed to burst something inside my ear. "You are expected on board," said the sergeant to my convict; "they know you are coming. Don't straggle, my men. Close up here."

The two were kept apart, and each walked surrounded by a separate guard. I had hold of Joe's hand now, and Joe carried one of the torches. Mr. Wopsle had been for going back, but Joe was resolved to see it out, so we went on with the party. There was a reasonably good path now, mostly on the edge of the river, with a divergence here and there where a dike came, with a miniature windmill on it, and a slimy sluice-gate. When I looked round I could see the other lights coming on after us. The torches we carried dropped great blotches of fire upon the track, and I could see these, too, smoking and flaring. I could see nothing else but black darkness. Our lights warmed the air about us with their pitchy blaze, and the two wretched men seemed to like that rather as they limped along in the midst of the muskets. We could not go fast because of their lameness, and they were so spent that two or three times we had to halt while they rested.

After an hour or so of this traveling we came to a rough wooden hut and a landing-place. There was a guard in the hut, and they challenged us, and the sergeant answered. Then we went into the hut, where there was a smell of tobacco and whitewash, and a bright fire, and a lamp, and a stand of muskets, and a drum, and a low wooden bedstead, like an immense mangle without the machinery, capable of holding about a dozen soldiers all at once. Three or four soldiers who lay upon it were not much interested in us, but just lifted their heads and took a stare, and then lay down again. The sergeant made some kind of report, and some entry in a book, and then the convict, whom I call the other convict, was drafted off with his guard to go on board first.

My convict never looked at me, except that once that I have mentioned. While we stood in the hut he stood before the fire looking at it, or putting up his miserable feet by turns upon the hob and looking at them as if he pitied them. Suddenly he turned to the sergeant, and remarked:

"I wish to say something respecting this escape. It may prevent some persons lying under suspicion alonger me."

"You can say what you like," returned the sergeant, standing looking at him with his arms folded; "but you have no call to say it here, you know. You'll have opportunity enough to say about it, and hear about it, before it's done with."

"I know that, but this is another pint, a separate pint. A man can't starve; at least I can't. I took some wittles up at the willage over yonder—where the church stands a'most out on the marshes."

"You mean stole?" said the sergeant.

"Ah! I'll tell you where from. From the blacksmith's."

"Halloa!" said the sergeant, staring at Joe.

"Halloa, Pip!" said Joe, staring at me.

"It was some broken wittles—that's what it was—and a dram of liquor, and a pie."

"Have you happened to miss such an article as a pie, blacksmith?" asked the sergeant, confidentially.

"Mrs. Joe did, at the very moment when you came in. Don't you know, Pip?"

"Oh!" said my convict to Joe, in a moody manner, and without the least glance at me. "So you're the blacksmith are you? Then I'm sorry to say I've eat your pie."

"God knows you're welcome to it—so far as it was ever mine," returned Joe, with a saving remembrance of Mrs. Joe. "We don't know what you have done; but we wouldn't have you starved to death for it, miserable fellow-creature, whatever it was.—Would us, Pip?"

The something that I had noticed before clicked in the man's throat again, and he turned his back. The boat had returned, and his guard were ready, so we followed him to the landing-place, made of rough stakes and stones, and saw him put into the boat, which was rowed by a crew of convicts like himself. No one appeared glad to see him, or sorry to see him, or spoke a word, except that somebody called as if to dogs, "Give way, you!" which was the signal for the dip of the oars. By the light of the torches we saw the black

Hulk lying out a little way from the mud of the shore, like a wicked Noah's ark; cribbed, and barred, and anchored by massive rusty chains, the prison-ship was ironed like the prisoners. We saw the boat go alongside, and we saw him taken up the side and disappear. Then the ends of the torches were flung hissing into the water, and went out, as if it were all over with him.

S i x

MY STATE OF MIND REGARDING THE PILFERING FROM which I had been so unexpectedly exonerated, did not impel me to frank disclosure; but I hope it had some dregs of good at the bottom of it.

I do not recall that I felt any tenderness of conscience in reference to Mrs. Joe when the fear of being found out was lifted off me. But I loved Joe—perhaps for no better reason in those early days than because the dear fellow let me love him—and, as to him, my inner self was not so easily composed. It was much upon my mind (particularly when I first saw him looking about for his file) that I ought to tell Joe the whole truth. Yet I did not, and for the reason that I mistrusted that if I did he would think me worse than I was. The fear of losing Joe's confidence, and of thenceforth sitting in the chimney corner at night staring drearily at my forever lost companion and friend, tied up my tongue. I morbidly represented to myself that if Joe knew it, I never afterward could see him at the fireside feeling his fair whisker, without thinking that he was meditating on it. That if Joe knew it, I never afterward could see him glance, however casually, at yesterday's meat or pudding when it came on today's table, without thinking that he was debating whether I had been in the pantry. That if Joe knew it, and at any subsequent period of our joint domestic life remarked that his beer was flat or thick, the conviction that he suspected Tar in it would bring a rush of blood to my face. In a word, I was too cowardly to do what I knew to be right, as I had been too cowardly to avoid doing what I knew to be wrong. I had had no intercourse with people at that time, and I imitated none of the host of people who act in this manner; quite an untaught genius, I made the discovery of the line of action for myself.

As I was sleepy before we were far away from the prison-ship, Joe took me on his back again and carried me home. He must have had a tiresome journey of it, for Mr. Wopsle, being knocked up, was in such a very bad temper that if the Church had been thrown open he probably would have excommunicated the whole expedition, beginning with Joe and myself. In his simple lay capacity he simply persisted in sitting down in the damp to such an insane extent, that, when his coat was taken off to be dried at the kitchen fire, the circumstantial evidence on his trowsers would have hanged him if it had been a capital offense.

By that time I was staggering on the kitchen floor like a little drunkard, through having been newly set upon my feet, and through having been fast asleep, and through waking in the heat and lights and noise of tongues. As I came to myself (with the aid of a heavy thump between the shoulders, and the restorative exclamation "Yah! Was there ever such a boy as this!" from my sister) I found Joe telling them about the convict's confession, and all the visitors suggesting different ways by which he had got into the pantry. Mr. Pumblechook made out, after carefully surveying the premises, that he had first got upon the roof of the forge, and had then got upon the roof of the house, and had then let himself down the kitchen chimney by a rope made of his bedding cut into strips; and as Mr. Pumblechook was very positive and drove his own chaise-cart—over everybody—it was agreed that it must be so. Mr. Wopsle, indeed, wildly cried out "No!" with the feeble malice of a tired man; but as he had no theory, and no coat on, he was unanimously set at naught—not to mention his smoking hard behind, as he stood with his back to the kitchen fire to draw the damp out, which was not calculated to inspire confidence.

This was all I heard that night before my sister clutched me, as a slumberous offense to the company's eyesight, and assisted me up to bed with such a strong hand that I seemed to have twenty boots on, and to be dangling them all against the edges of the stairs. My state of mind, as I have described it, began before I was up in the morning, and lasted long after the subject had died out, and had ceased to be mentioned saving on exceptional occasions.

S e v e n

AT THE TIME WHEN I STOOD IN THE CHURCHYARD, reading the family tombstones, I had just enough learning to be able to spell them out. My construction even of their simple meaning was not very correct, for I read "wife of the Above" as a complimentary reference to my father's exaltation to a better world; and if any one of my deceased relations had been referred to as "Below," I have no doubt I should have formed the worst opinions of that member of the family. Neither were my notions of the theological positions to which my Catechism bound me at all accurate, for I have a lively remembrance that I supposed my declaration that I was to "walk in the same all the days of my life" laid me under an obligation always to go through the village from our house in one particular direction, and never to vary it by turning down by the wheelwright's or up by the mill.

When I was old enough I was to be apprenticed to Joe, and until I could assume that dignity I was not to be what Mrs. Joe called "Pompeyed," or pampered. Therefore I was not only odd-boy about the forge, but if any neighbor happened to want an extra boy to frighten birds, or pick up stones, or do any such job, I was favored with the employment; but in order that our superior position might not be compromised thereby a money-box was kept on the kitchen mantle-shelf, into which it was publicly made known that all my earnings were dropped. I have an impression that they were to be contributed eventually toward the liquidation of the National Debt, but I know I had no hope of any personal participation in the treasure.

Mr. Wopsle's great aunt kept an evening school in the village; that is to say, she was an ancient woman of limited means and unlimited infirmity, who used to go to sleep from six to seven every evening, in the society of youth who paid three pence per week each for the improving opportunity of seeing her do it. She rented a three-roomed cottage, and Mr. Wopsle had the room upstairs, where we students used to overhear him reading aloud in a most dignified and terrific manner, and occasionally bumping on the ceiling. There was a fiction that Mr. Wopsle "examined" the scholars once a quarter. What he did on those occasions was to turn up his cuffs, stick up his hair, and give us Mark Antony's oration over the body of Cæsar. This was always followed by Collins's Ode on the Passions, wherein I particularly venerated Mr. Wopsle as Fear, whistling to keep his courage up. It was not with me then, as it was in later life, when I fell into the society of the Passions, and compared them with Collins and Wopsle, rather to the disadvantage of both gentlemen.

Mr. Wopsle's great aunt, besides keeping this Educational Institution, kept—in the same room—a little general shop. She had no idea what stock she had, or what the price of anything in it was; but there was a little greasy memorandum book kept in a drawer, which served as a Catalogue of Prices, and by this oracle Biddy arranged all the shop transactions. Biddy was Mr. Wopsle's great aunt's granddaughter; I confess myself quite unequal to the working out of the problem what relation she was to Mr. Wopsle. She was an orphan like myself; like, me, too, had been brought up by hand. She was most noticeable, I thought, in respect of her extremities; for her hair always wanted brushing, her hands always wanted washing, and her shoes always wanted mending and pulling up at the heel. This description must be received, however, with a weekday limitation. On Sundays she went to church elaborated.

Much of my unassisted self, and more by the help of Biddy than of Mr. Wopsle's great aunt, I struggled through the alphabet as if it had been a bramble-bush; getting considerably worried and scratched by every letter. After that I fell among those thieves, the nine figures, who seemed every evening to do something new to disguise themselves and baffle recognition. But at last I began, in a purblind groping way, to read, write, and cipher, on the very smallest scale.

One night I was sitting in the chimney corner with my slate, expending great efforts on the production of a letter to Joe. I think it must have been a full year after our hunt upon the marshes, for it was a long time after, and it was winter and a hard frost. With an alphabet on the hearth at my feet for reference, I contrived in an hour or two to print and smear this epistle:

mI deEer JO i opE U r krWitE wEll i opE i shAl soN B haBelL 4 2 teeDge U JO aN theN wE shOrl b sO glOdd aN wEn i M preNgtD 2 u JO woT larX an blEvE ME inF xn PiP.

There was no indispensable necessity for my communicating with Joe by letter, inasmuch as he sat beside me and we were alone. But I delivered this written communication (slate and all) with my own hand, and Joe received it as a miracle of erudition.

"I say, Pip, old chap!" cried Joe, opening his blue eyes wide, "what a scholar you are! An't you?"

"I should like to be," said I, glancing at the slate as he held it, with a misgiving that the writing was rather hilly.

"Why, here's a J," said Joe, "and a O equal to anythink! Here's a J and a O, Pip, and a J-O, Joe."

I had never heard Joe read aloud to any greater extent than this monosyllable, and I had observed at church last Sunday when I accidentally held our Prayer-book upside down, that it seemed to suit his convenience quite as well as if it had been all right. Wishing to embrace the present occasion of finding out whether in teaching Joe I should have to begin quite at the beginning, I said, "Ah! But read the rest, Joe."

"The rest, eh, Pip?" said Joe, looking at it with a slowly searching eye, "One, two, three. Why, here's three Js and three Os, and three J-O, Joes in it, Pip!"

I leaned over Joe, and, with the aid of my forefinger, read him the whole letter.

"Astonishing!" said Joe, when I had finished. "You ARE a scholar."

"How do you spell Gargery, Joe?" I asked him, with a modest patronage.

"I don't spell it at all," said Joe.

"But supposing you did?"

"It *can't* be supposed," said Joe. "But I'm oncommon fond of reading, too."

"Are you, Joe?"

"On-common. Give me," said Joe, "a good book, or a good newspaper, and sit me down afore a good fire, and I ask no better. Lord!" he continued, after rubbing his knees a little, "when you *do* come to a J and a O, and says you, 'Here, at last, is a J-O, Joe,' how interesting reading is!"

I derived from this last that Joe's education, like steam, was yet in its infancy. Pursuing the subject, I inquired:

"Didn't you ever go to school, Joe, when you were as little as me?"

"No, Pip."

"Why didn't you ever go to school, Joe, when you were as little as me?"

"Well, Pip," said Joe, taking up the poker and settling himself to his usual occupation when he was thoughtful, of slowly raking the fire between the lower bars, "I'll tell you. My father, Pip, he were given to drink, and when he were overtook with drink he hammered away at my mother most onmerciful. It were a'most the only hammering he did, indeed, 'xcepting at myself. And he hammered at me with a wigor only to be equaled by the wigor with which he didn't hammer at his anwil. You're a listening and understanding, Pip?"

"Yes, Joe."

"Consequence—my mother and me we ran away from my father several times; and then my mother she'd go out to work, and she'd say, 'Joe,' she'd say, 'now, please God, you shall have some schooling, child,' and she'd put me to school. But my father were that good in his hart that he couldn't abear to be without us. So he'd come with a most tremenjous crowd, and make such a row at the doors of the houses where we was, that they used to be obligated to have no more to do with us and to give us up to him. And then he took us home and hammered us. Which you see, Pip," said Joe, pausing in his meditative raking of the fire, and looking at me, "were a drawback on my learning."

"Certainly, poor Joe!"

"Though mind you, Pip," said Joe, with a judicial touch or two of the poker on the top bar, "rendering unto all their doo, and maintaining equal justice betwixt man and man, my father were that good in his hart, don't you see?"

I didn't see, but I didn't say so.

"Well!" Joe pursued, "somebody must keep the pot a biling, Pip, or the pot won't bile, don't you know?"

I saw that, and said so.

"'Consequence—my father didn't make objections to my going to work; so I went to work at my present calling, which were his too, if he would have followed it, and I worked tolerable hard, I assure *you*, Pip. In time I were able to keep him, and I kep him till he went off in a purple leptic fit. And it were my intentions to have had put upon his tombstone that Whatsume'er the failings on his part, Remember reader he were that good in his hart."

Joe recited this couplet with such manifest pride and careful perspicuity that I asked him if he had made it himself?

"I made it," said Joe, "my own self. I made it in a moment. It was like striking out a horseshoe complete in a single blow. I never was so much surprised in all my life—couldn't credit my own ed—to tell you the truth, hardly believed it *was* my own ed. As I was saying, Pip, it were my intentions to have had it cut over him; but poetry costs money, cut it how you will, small or large, and it were not done. Not to mention bearers, all the money that could be spared were wanted for my mother. She were in poor elth, and quite broke. She waren't long of following, poor soul, and her share of peace come round at last."

Joe's blue eyes turned a little watery; he rubbed, first one of them, and then the other, in a most uncongenial and uncomfortable manner, with the round knob on the top of the poker.

"It were but lonesome then," said Joe, "living here alone, and I got acquainted with your sister. Now, Pip," Joe looked firmly at me, as if he knew I was not going to agree with him, "your sister is a fine figure of a woman."

I could not help looking at the fire in an obvious state of doubt.

"Whatever family opinions, or whatever the world's opinions, on that subject may be, Pip, your sister is"—Joe tapped the top bar with the poker after every word following—"a—fine—figure—of—a—woman!"

I could think of nothing better to say than, "I am glad you think so, Joe."

"So am I," returned Joe, catching me up. "*I* am glad I think so, Pip. A little redness, or a little matter of Bone, here or there, what does it signify to Me?"

I sagaciously observed, if it didn't signify to him, to whom did it signify?

"Certainly!" assented Joe. "That's it. You're right, old chap! When I got acquainted with your sister, it were the talk how she was bringing you up by hand. Very kind of her too, all the folks said, and I said, along with all the folks. As to you," Joe pursued, with a countenance expressive of seeing something very nasty indeed: "if you could have been aware how small and flabby and mean you was, dear me, you'd have formed the most contemptible opinions of yourself!"

Not exactly relishing this, I said, "Never mind me, Joe."

"But I did mind you, Pip," he returned, with tender simplicity. "When I offered to your sister to keep company, and to be asked in church at such times as she was willing and ready to come to the forge, I said to her, 'And bring the poor little child. God bless the poor little child,' I said to your sister, 'there's room for *him* at the forge!' "

I broke out crying and begging pardon, and hugged Joe round the neck; who dropped the poker to hug me, and to say, "Ever the best of friends; an't us, Pip? Don't cry, old chap!"

When this little interruption was over, Joe resumed:

"Well, you see, Pip, and here we are! That's about where it lights; here we are! Now, when you take me in hand in my learning, Pip (and I tell you beforehand I am awful dull, most awful dull), Mrs. Joe mustn't see too much of what we're up to. It must be done, as I may say, on the sly. And why on the sly? I'll tell you why, Pip."

He had taken up the poker again, without which, I doubt if he could have proceeded in his demonstration.

"Your sister is given to government."

"Given to government, Joe?" I was startled, for I had some shadowy idea (and I am afraid I must add, hope) that Joe had divorced her in favor of the Lords of the Admiralty, or Treasury.

"Given to government," said Joe. "Which I meantersay the government of you and myself."

"Oh!"

"And she an't over partial to having scholars on the premises," Joe continued, "and in partickler would not be over partial to my being a scholar, for fear as I might rise. Like a sort of rebel, don't you see?"

I was going to retort with an inquiry, and had got so far as "Why—" when Joe stopped me.

"Stay a bit. I know what you're going to say, Pip; stay a bit! I don't deny that your sister comes the Mogul over us, now and again. I don't deny that she do throw us falls, and that she do drop down upon us heavy. At such times as your sister is on the Ram-page, Pip," Joe sank his voice to a whisper and glanced at the door, "candor compels fur to admit that she is a Buster."

Joe pronounced this word as if it began with at least twelve capital Bs.

"Why don't I rise? That were your observation when I broke it off, Pip?"

"Yes, Joe."

"Well," said Joe, passing the poker into his left hand, that he might feel his whisker; and I had no hope of him when he took to that placid occupation; "your sister's a mastermind. A mastermind."

"What's that?" I asked, in some hope of bringing him to a stand. But Joe was readier with his definition than I had expected, and completely stopped me by arguing circularly and answering with a fixed look, "Her."

"And I ain't a mastermind," Joe resumed, when he had unfixed his look, and got back to his whisker. "And last of all, Pip—and this I want to say very serious to you, old chap—I see so much in my poor mother of a woman drudging, and slaving, and breaking her honest heart, and never getting no peace in her mortal days, that I'm dead afeerd of going wrong in the way of not doing what's right by a woman, and I'd fur rather of the two go wrong the t'other way, and be a little ill-conwenienced myself. I wish it was only me that got put out, Pip; I wish there warn't no Tickler for you, old chap; I wish I could take it all on myself; but this is the up-and-down-and-straight on it, Pip, and I hope you'll overlook shortcomings."

Young as I was, I believe that I dated a new admiration of Joe from that night. We were equals afterward, as we had been before; but afterward at quiet times, when I sat looking at Joe and thinking about him, I had a new sensation of feeling conscious that I was looking up to Joe in my heart.

"However," said Joe, rising to replenish the fire, "here's the Dutch-clock a working himself up to being equal to striking Eight of 'em, and she's not come home yet! I hope Uncle Pumblechook's mare mayn't have set a forefoot on a piece o' ice, and gone down."

Mrs. Joe made occasional trips with Uncle Pumblechook on market days, to assist him in buying such household stuffs and goods as required a woman's judgment; Uncle Pumblechook being a bachelor and reposing no confidences in his domestic servant. This was market-day, and Mrs. Joe was out on one of these expeditions.

Joe made the fire and swept the hearth, and then we went out to listen for the chaise-cart. It was a dry, cold night, and the wind blew keenly, and the frost was white and hard. A man would die tonight of lying out on the marshes, I thought; and then I looked at the stars, and considered how awful it would be for a man to turn his face up to them as he froze to death, and see no help or pity in the whole glittering multitude.

"Here comes the mare," said Joe, "ringing like bells!"

The sound of her iron shoes upon the hard road was quite musical, as she came along at a much brisker trot than usual. We got a chair out ready for Mrs. Joe's alighting, and stirred up the fire that they might see a bright window, and took a final survey of the kitchen that nothing might be out of its place. When we had completed these preparations they drove up, wrapped to the eyes. Mrs. Joe was soon landed, and Uncle Pumblechook was soon down covering the mare with a cloth, and we were soon all in the kitchen, carrying so much cold air in with us that it seemed to drive all the heat out of the fire.

"Now," said Mrs. Joe, unwrapping herself with haste and excitement, and throwing her bonnet back on her shoulders where it hung by the strings, "if this boy an't grateful this night, he never will be!"

I looked as grateful as any boy possibly could who was wholly uninformed why he ought to assume that expression.

"It's only to be hoped," said my sister, "that he won't be Pompeyed. But I have my fears."

"She an't in that line, mum," said Mr. Pumblechook. "She knows better."

She? I looked at Joe, making the motion with my lips and eyebrows, "She?" Joe looked at me, making the motion with *his* lips and eyebrows, "She?" My sister catching him in the act, he drew the back of his hand across his nose with his usual conciliatory air on such occasions, and looked at her.

"Well?" said my sister in her snappish way. "Is the house a-fire?"

—"Which some individual," Joe politely hinted, "mentioned—she."

"And she is a she, I suppose?" said my sister. "Unless you call Miss Havisham a he. And I doubt if even you'll go so far as that."

"Miss Havisham, uptown?" said Joe.

"Is there any Miss Havisham, downtown?" returned my sister. "She wants this boy to go and play there. And of course he's going. And he had better play there," said my sister, shaking her head at me as an encouragement to be extremely light and sportive, "or I'll work him."

I had heard of Miss Havisham uptown—everybody for miles round had heard of Miss Havisham uptown—as an immensely rich and grim old lady, who lived in a large and dismal house barricaded against robbers, and who led a life of seclusion.

"Well to be sure!" said Joe, astounded. "I wonder how she come to know Pip!"

"Noodle!" cried my sister. "Who said she knew him?"

—"Which some individual," Joe again politely hinted, "mentioned that she wanted him to go and play there."

"And couldn't she ask Uncle Pumblechook if he knew of a boy to go and play there? Isn't it just barely possible that Uncle Pumblechook may be a tenant of hers, and that he may sometimes—we won't say quarterly or half-yearly, for that would be requiring too much of you—but sometimes—go there to pay his rent? And couldn't she then ask Uncle Pumblechook if he knew of a boy to go and play there? And couldn't Uncle Pumblechook, being always considerate and thoughtful for us—though you may not think it, Joseph," in a tone of the deepest reproach, as if he were the most callous of nephews, "then mention this boy, standing Prancing here"—which I solemnly declare I was not doing—"that I have forever been a willing slave to?"

"Good again!" cried Uncle Pumblechook. "Well put! Prettily pointed! Good indeed! Now Joseph, you know the case."

"No, Joseph," said my sister, still in a reproachful manner, while Joe apologetically drew the back of his hand across and across his nose, "you do not yet—though you may not think it—know the case. You may consider that you do, but you do *not*, Joseph. For you do not know that Uncle Pumblechook, being sensible that for anything we can tell this boy's fortune may be made by his going to Miss Havisham's, has offered to take him into town tonight in his own chaise-cart, and to keep him tonight, and to take him with his own hands to Miss Havisham's tomorrow morning. And Lor-a-mussy me!" cried my sister, casting off her bonnet in sudden desperation, "here I stand talking to mere Mooncalfs, with Uncle Pumblechook waiting, and the mare catching cold at the door, and the boy grimed with crock and dirt from the hair of his head to the sole of his foot!"

With that she pounced upon me, like an eagle on a lamb, and my face was forced into wooden bowls in sinks, and my head was put under taps of water-butts, and I was soaped, and kneaded, and toweled, and thumped, and harrowed, and rasped, until I really was quite beside myself. (I may here remark that I conceive myself to be better acquainted than any living authority with the ridgy effect of a wedding-ring, passing unsympathetically over the human countenance.)

When my ablutions were completed, I was put into clean linen of the stiffest character, like a young penitent in sackcloth, and was trussed up in my tightest and fearfulest suit. I was then delivered over to Mr. Pumblechook, who formally received me as if he were the Sheriff, and who let off upon me the speech which I knew he had been dying to make all along; "Boy, be forever grateful to all friends, but especially to them which brought you up by hand!"

"Good-bye, Joe!"

"God bless you, Pip, old chap!"

I had never parted from him before, and what with my feelings and what with soapsuds I could at first see no stars from the chaise-cart. But they twinkled out one by one, without throwing any light on the questions why on earth I was going to play at Miss Havisham's, and what on earth I was expected to play at.

Eight

MR. PUMBLECHOOK'S PREMISES IN THE HIGH STREET OF the market town were of a peppercorny and farinaceous character, as the premises of a corn chandler and seedsman should be. It appeared to me that he must be a very happy man indeed to have so many little drawers in his shop; and I wondered when I peeped into one or two on the lower tiers, and saw the tied-up brown paper packages inside, whether the flower-seeds and bulbs ever wanted of a fine day to break out of those jails and bloom.

It was in the early morning after my arrival that I entertained this speculation. On the previous night I had been sent straight to bed in an attic with a sloping roof, which was so low in the corner where the bedstead was that I calculated the tiles as being within a foot of my eyebrows. In the same early morning I discovered a singular affinity between seeds and corduroys. Mr. Pumblechook wore corduroys, and so did his shopman; and somehow there was a general air and flavor about the corduroys, so much in the nature of seeds, and a general air and flavor about the seeds, so much in the nature of corduroys, that I hardly knew which was which. The same opportunity served me for noticing that Mr. Pumblechook appeared to conduct his business by looking across the street at the saddler, who appeared to transact *his* business by keeping his eye on the coachmaker, who appeared to get on in life by putting his hands in his pockets and contemplating the baker, who in his turn folded his arms and stared at the grocer, who stood at his door and yawned at the chemist. The watchmaker, always poring over a little desk with a magnifying glass at his eye, and always inspected by a group in smock-frocks poring over him through the glass of his shop-window, seemed to be about the only person in the High Street whose trade engaged his attention.

Mr. Pumblechook and I breakfasted at eight o'clock in the parlor behind the shop, while the shopman took his mug of tea and hunch of bread-and-butter on a sack of pease in the front premises. I considered Mr. Pumblechook wretched company. Besides being possessed by my sister's idea that a mortifying and penitential character ought to be imparted to my diet— besides giving me as much crumb as possible in combination with as little butter, and putting such a quantity of warm water into my milk that it would have been more candid to have left the milk out altogether—his conversation consisted of nothing but arithmetic. On my politely bidding him Good morning, he said, pompously, "Seven times nine, boy!" And how should *I* be able to answer, dodged in that way, in a strange place, on an empty stomach! I was hungry, but before I had swallowed a morsel he began a running sum that lasted all through the breakfast. "Seven?" "And four?" "And eight?" "And six?" "And two?" "And ten?" And so on. And after each figure was disposed of, it was as much as I could do to get a bite or a sup before the next came; while he sat at his ease guessing nothing and eating bacon and hot roll in (if I may be allowed the expression) a gorging and gormandizing manner.

For such reasons I was very glad when ten o'clock came and we started for Miss Havisham's; though I was not at all at my ease regarding the manner in which I should acquaint myself under that lady's roof. Within a quarter of an hour we came to Miss Havisham's house, which was of old brick, and dismal, and had a great many iron bars to it. Some of the windows had been walled up; of those that remained all the lower were rustily barred. There was a courtyard in front, and that was barred; so we had to wait, after ringing the bell, until someone should come to open it. While we waited at the gate I peeped in (even then Mr. Pumblechook said, "And fourteen?" but I pretended not to hear him), and saw that at the side of the house there was a large brewery; no brewing was going on in it, and none seemed to have gone on for a long long time.

A window was raised, and a clear voice demanded "What name?" To which my conductor replied "Pumblechook." The voice returned "Quite right," and the window was shut again, and a young lady came across the courtyard with keys in her hand.

"This," said Mr. Pumblechook, "is Pip."

"This is Pip, is it?" returned the young lady, who was very pretty and seemed very proud; "Come in, Pip."

Mr. Pumblechook was coming in also, when she stopped him with the gate.

"Oh!" she said. "Did you wish to see Miss Havisham?"

"If Miss Havisham wishes to see me," returned Mr. Pumblechook, discomfited.

"Ah!" said the girl; "but you see she don't."

She said it so finally, and in such an undiscussible way, that Mr. Pumblechook, though in a condition of ruffled dignity, could not protest. But he eyed me severely—as if *I* had done anything to him!—and departed with the words reproachfully delivered: "Boy! Let your behavior here be a credit unto them which brought you up by hand!" I was not free from apprehension that he would come back to propound through the gate, "And sixteen?" But he didn't.

My young conductress locked the gate, and we went across the court-yard. It was paved and clean, but grass was growing in every crevice. The brewery buildings had a little lane of communication with it, and the wooden gates of that lane stood open, and all the brewery beyond stood open, away to the high enclosing wall, and all was empty and disused. The cold wind seemed to blow colder there than outside the gate, and it made a shrill noise in howling in and out at the open side of the brewery, like the noise of wind in the rigging of a ship at sea.

She saw me looking at it, and she said, "You could drink without hurt all the strong beer that's brewed there now, boy."

"I should think I could, miss," said I, in a shy way.

"Better not try to brew beer there now, or it would turn out sour, boy; don't you think so?"

"It looks like it, miss."

"Not that anybody means to try," she added, "for that's all done with, and the place will stand as idle as it is till it falls. As to strong beer, there's enough of it in the cellars already to drown the Manor House."

"Is that the name of this house, miss?"

"One of its names, boy."

"It has more than one, then, miss?"

"One more. Its other name was Satis; which is Greek, or Latin, or Hebrew, or all three—or all one to me—for enough."

"Enough House," said I; "that's a curious name, miss."

"Yes," she replied; "but it meant more than it said. It meant, when it was given, that whoever had this house could want nothing else. They must have been easily satisfied in those days, I should think. But don't loiter, boy."

Though she called me "boy" so often, and with a carelessness that was far from complimentary, she was of about my own age—or very little older. She seemed much older than I, of course, being a girl, and beautiful and self-possessed: and she was as scornful of me as if she had been one-and-twenty, and a queen.

We went into the house by a side door—the great front entrance had two chains across it outside—and the first thing I noticed was, that the passages were all dark, and that she had left a candle burning there. She took it up, and we went through more passages and up a staircase, and still it was all dark, and only the candle lighted us.

At last we came to the door of a room, and she said, "Go in."

I answered, more in shyness than politeness, "After you, miss."

To this, she returned: "Don't be ridiculous, boy; I am not going in." And scornfully walked away, and—what was worse—took the candle with her.

This was very uncomfortable, and I was half afraid. However, the only thing to be done being to knock at the door, I knocked, and was told from within to enter. I entered, therefore, and found myself in a pretty large room well lighted with wax candles. No glimpse of daylight was to be seen in it. It was a dressing-room, as I supposed from the furniture, though much of it was of forms and uses then quite unknown to me. But prominent in it was a draped table with a gilded looking-glass, and that I made out at first sight to be a fine lady's dressing-table.

Whether I should have made out this object so soon if there had been no fine lady sitting at it I cannot say. In an armchair, with an elbow resting on the table and her head leaning on that hand, sat the strangest lady I have ever seen, or shall ever see.

She was dressed in rich materials—satins, and lace, and silks—all of white. Her shoes were white. And she had a long white vail dependent from her hair, and she had bridal flowers in her hair, but her hair was white. Some bright jewels sparkled on her neck and on her hands, and some other jewels lay sparkling on the table. Dresses, less splendid than the dress she wore, and half-packed trunks, were scattered about. She had not quite finished dressing, for she had but one shoe on—the other was on the table near her hand—her vail was but half arranged, her watch and chain were not put on, and some lace for her bosom lay with those trinkets, and with her handkerchief, and gloves, and some flowers, and a prayer-book, all confusedly heaped about the looking-glass.

It was not in the first minute that I saw all these things, though I saw more of them in the first minute than might be supposed. But I saw that everything within my view which ought to be white had been white long ago, and had lost its luster, and was faded and yellow. I saw that the bride within the bridal dress had withered like the dress, and like the flowers, and had no brightness left but the brightness of her sunken eyes. I saw that the dress had been put upon the rounded figure of a young woman, and that the figure upon which it now hung loose had shrunk to skin and bone. Once, I had been taken to see some ghastly wax-work at the Fair, representing I know not what impossible personage lying in state. Once, I had been taken to one of our old marsh churches to see a skeleton in the ashes of a rich dress that had been dug out of a vault under the church pavement. Now, wax-work and skeleton seemed to have dark eyes that moved and looked at me. I should have cried out if I could.

"Who is it?" said the lady at the table.

"Pip, ma'am."

"Pip?"

"Mr. Pumblechook's boy, ma'am. Come—to play."

"Come nearer; let me look at you. Come close."

It was when I stood before her, avoiding her eyes, that I took note of the surrounding objects in detail, and saw that her watch had stopped at twenty minutes to nine, and that a clock in the room had stopped at twenty minutes to nine.

"Look at me," said Miss Havisham. "You are not afraid of a woman who has never seen the sun since you were born?"

I regret to state that I was not afraid of telling the enormous lie comprehended in the answer,

"No."

"Do you know what I touch here?" she said, laying her hands, one upon the other, on her left side.

"Yes, ma'am." (It made me think of the young man.)

"What do I touch?"

"Your heart."

"Broken!"

She uttered the word with an eager look, and with strong emphasis, and with a weird smile that had a kind of boast in it. Afterward, she kept her hands there for a little while, and slowly took them away as if they were heavy.

"I am tired," said Miss Havisham. "I want diversion, and I have done with men and women. Play!"

I think it will be conceded by my most disputatious reader that she could hardly have directed an unfortunate boy to do anything in the wide world more difficult to be done under the circumstances.

"I sometimes have sick fancies," she went on, "and I have a sick fancy that I want to see some play. There, there!" with an impatient movement of the fingers of her right hand; "play, play, play!"

For a moment, with the fear of my sister's working me before my eyes, I had a desperate idea of starting round the room in the assumed character of Mr. Pumblechook's chaise-cart. But I felt myself so unequal to the performance that I gave it up, and stood looking at Miss Havisham in what I suppose she took for a dogged manner, inasmuch as she said, when we had taken a good look at each other:

"Are you sullen and obstinate?"

"No, ma'am, I am very sorry for you, and very sorry I can't play just now. If you complain of me I shall get into trouble with my sister, so I would do it if I could; but it's so new here, and so strange, and so fine—and melancholy—" I stopped, fearing I might say too much, or had already said it, and we took another look at each other.

Before she spoke again she turned her eyes from me and looked at the dress she wore, and at the dressing-table, and finally at herself in the looking-glass.

"So new to him," she muttered, "so old to me; so strange to him, so familiar to me; so melancholy to both of us! Call Estella."

As she was still looking at the reflection of herself, I thought she was still talking to herself, and kept quiet.

"Call Estella," she repeated, flashing a look at me. "You can do that. Call Estella. At the door."

To stand in the dark in a mysterious passage of an unknown house bawling Estella to a scornful young lady neither visible nor responsive, and feeling it a dreadful liberty so to roar out her name, was almost as bad as playing to order. But she answered at last, and her light came along the dark passage like a star.

Miss Havisham beckoned her to come close, and took up a jewel from the table, and tried its effect upon her fair young bosom and against her pretty brown hair. "Your own, one day, my dear, and you will use it well. Let me see you play cards with this boy."

"With this boy! Why, he is a common laboring boy!"

I thought I overheard Miss Havisham answer—only it seemed so unlikely—"Well? You can break his heart."

"What do you play, boy?" asked Estella of myself, with the greatest disdain.

"Nothing but beggar my neighbor, miss."

"Beggar him," said Miss Havisham to Estella. So we sat down to cards.

It was then I began to understand that everything in the room had stopped, like the watch and the clock, a long time ago. I noticed that Miss Havisham put down the jewel exactly on the spot from which she had taken it up. As Estella dealt the cards, I glanced at the dressing-table again, and saw that the shoe upon it, once white, now yellow, had never been worn. I glanced down at the foot from which the shoe was absent, and saw that the silk stocking on it, once white, now yellow, had been trodden ragged. Without this arrest of everything, this standing still of all the pale decayed objects, not even the withered bridal dress on the collapsed form could have looked so like grave-clothes, or the long vail so like a shroud.

So she sat corpselike, as we played at cards; the frillings and trimmings on her bridal dress looking like earthy paper, as if they would crumble under a touch. I knew nothing then of the discoveries that are occasionally made of bodies buried in ancient times, which fall to powder in the moment of being distinctly seen; but I have often thought since that she must have looked as if the admission of the natural light of day would have struck her to dust.

"He calls the knaves Jacks, this boy?" said Estella, with disdain, before our first game was out. "And what coarse hands he has! And what thick boots!"

I had never thought of being ashamed of my hands before; but I began to consider them a very indifferent pair. Her contempt was so strong that it became infectious, and I caught it.

She won the game, and I dealt. I misdealt, as was only natural, when I knew she was lying in wait for me to do wrong, and she denounced me for a stupid, clumsy laboring boy.

"You say nothing of her," remarked Miss Havisham to me as she looked on. "She says many hard things of you, but you say nothing of her. What do you think of her?"

"I don't like to say," I stammered.

"Tell me in my ear," said Miss Havisham, bending down.

"I think she is very proud," I replied, in a whisper.

"Anything else?"

"I think she is very pretty."

"Anything else?"

"I think she is very insulting." (She was looking at me, then, with a look of supreme aversion.)

"Anything else?"

"I think I should like to go home."

"And never see her again, though she is so pretty?"

"I am not sure that I should not like to see her again, but I should like to go home now."

"You shall go soon," said Miss Havisham, aloud. "Play the game out." Saving for the one weird smile at first, I should have felt almost sure that Miss Havisham's face could not smile. It had dropped into a watchful and brooding expression—most likely when all the things about her had become transfixed—and it looked as if nothing could ever lift it up anymore. Her chest had dropped, so that she stooped; and her voice had dropped, so that she spoke low, and with a dead lull upon her; altogether she had the appearance of having dropped, body and soul, within and without, under the weight of a crushing blow.

I played the game to an end with Estella, and she beggared me. She threw the cards down on the table when she had won them all, as if she despised them for having been won of me.

"When shall I have you here again?" said Miss Havisham. "Let me think."

I was beginning to remind her that today was Wednesday, when she checked me with her former impatient movement of the fingers of her right hand.

"There, there! I know nothing of days of the week; I know nothing of weeks of the year. Come again after three days. You hear?"

"Yes, ma'am."

"Estella, take him down. Let him have something to eat, and let him roam and look about him while he eats it. Go, Pip."

I followed the candle down as I had followed the candle up, and she stood it in the place where we had found it. Until she opened the side entrance I had fancied, without thinking about it, that it must necessarily be nighttime. The rush of the daylight quite confounded me, and made me feel as if I had been in the candlelight of the strange room many hours.

"You are to wait here, you boy," said Estella, and disappeared and closed the door.

I took the opportunity of being alone in the courtyard to look at my coarse hands and my common boots. My opinion of those accessories was not favorable. They had never troubled me before, but they troubled me now, as vulgar appendages. I determined to ask Joe why he had ever taught me to call those picture-cards Jacks which ought to be called knaves. I wished Joe had been rather more genteelly brought up, and then I should have been so too.

She came back with some bread and meat and a little mug of beer. She put the mug down on the stones of the yard, and gave me the bread and meat without looking at me, as insolently as if I were a dog. I was so humiliated, hurt, spurned, offended, angry, sorry—I cannot hit upon the right name for the smart—God knows what its name was—that tears started to my eyes. The moment they sprang there the girl looked at me with a quick delight in having been the cause of them. It gave me power to force them back and to look at her; so she gave a contemptuous toss—but with a sense, I thought, of having made too sure that I was so wounded—and left me.

But when she was gone I looked about me for a place to hide my face in, and got behind one of the gates in the brewery-lane, and leaned my sleeve against the wall there, and leaned my forehead on it and cried. As I cried I kicked the wall and took a hard twist at my hair; so bitter were my feelings, and so sharp was the smart without a name, that needed counteraction.

My sister's bringing up had made me sensitive. In the little world in which children have their existence, whosoever brings them up, I am convinced there is nothing so finely perceived and so finely felt as injustice. It may be only small injustice that the child can be exposed to; but the child is small, and its world is small, and its rocking-horse stands as many hands high, according to scale, as a big-boned Irish hunter. Within myself I had sustained from my babyhood a perpetual conflict with injustice. I had known from the time when I could speak that my sister, in her capricious and violent coercion, was unjust to me. I had cherished a profound conviction that her bringing me up by hand gave her no right to bring me up by jerks. Through all my punishments, disgraces, fasts, and vigils, and other penitential performances, I had nursed this assurance; and to my communing so much with it, in a solitary and unprotected way, I, in great part, refer the fact that I was morally timid and very sensitive.

I got rid of my injured feelings for the time by kicking them into the brewery wall, and twisting them out of my hair, and then I smoothed my face with my sleeve and came from behind the gate. The bread and meat were acceptable, and the beer was warming and tingling, and I was soon in spirits to look about me.

To be sure, it was a deserted place, down to the pigeon-house in the brewery-yard, which had been blown crooked on its pole by some high wind, and would have made the pigeons think themselves at sea, if there had been any pigeons there to be rocked by it. But there were no pigeons in the dovecot, no horses in the stable, no pigs in the sty, no malt in the storehouse, no smells of grains and beer in the copper or the vat. All the uses and scents of the brewery might have evaporated with its last reek of smoke. In a by-yard there was a wilderness of empty casks, which had a certain sour remembrance of better days lingering about them; but it was too sour to be accepted as a sample of the beer that was gone—and in this respect I remember those recluses as being like most others.

Behind the farthest end of the brewery was a rank garden with an old red wall: not so high but that I could struggle up and hold on long enough to look over it, and see that the rank garden was the garden of the house, and that it was overgrown with tangled weeds, but that there was a track upon the green and yellow paths, as if someone sometimes walked there, and that Estella was walking away from me even then. But she seemed to be everywhere. For when I yielded to the temptation presented by the casks, and began to walk on them, I saw *her* walking on them at the end of the yard of casks. She had her back to me, and held her pretty brown hair spread out in her two hands, and never looked round, and passed out of my view directly. So in the brewery itself—by which I mean the large paved lofty place in which they used to make the beer, and where the brewing utensils still were. When I first went into it, and, rather oppressed by its gloom, stood near the door looking about me, I saw her pass among the extinguished fires, and ascend some light iron stairs, and go out by an iron gallery high overhead, as if she were going out into the sky.

It was in this place, and at this moment, that a strange thing happened to my fancy. I thought it a strange thing then, and I thought it stranger long afterward. I turned my eyes—a little dimmed by looking up at the frosty light—toward a great wooden beam in a low nook of the building near me on my right hand, and I saw a figure hanging there by the neck. A figure all in yellow white, with but one shoe to the feet; and it hung so that I could see that the faded trimmings of the dress were like earthy paper, and that the face was Miss Havisham's with the eyes open, and with a movement going over the whole countenance as if she were trying to call to me. In the terror of seeing the figure, and in the terror of being certain that it had not been there a moment before, I at first ran from it, and then ran toward it. And my terror was greatest of all when I found no figure there.

Nothing less than the frosty light of the cheerful sky, the sight of people passing beyond the bars of the courtyard gate, and the reviving influence of the rest of the bread and meat and beer, would have brought me round. Even with those aids I might not have come to myself as soon as I did, but that I saw Estella approaching with the keys to let me out. She would have some fair reason for looking down upon me, I thought, if she saw me frightened; and she should have no fair reason.

She gave me a triumphant glance in passing me, as if she rejoiced that my hands were so coarse and my boots were so thick, and she opened the gate and stood holding it. I was passing out without looking at her, when she touched me with a taunting hand.

"Why don't you cry?" said she.

"Because I don't want to," said I.

"You do," said she. "You have been crying, and you are near crying again."

She laughed contemptuously, pushed me out, and locked the gate upon me. I went straight to Mr. Pumblechook's, and was immensely relieved to find him not at home. So leaving word with the shopman on what day I was wanted at Miss Havisham's again, I set off on the four-mile walk to our forge; pondering, as I went along, on all I had seen, and deeply revolving that I was a common laboring boy, that my hands were coarse, that my boots were thick, that I had fallen into a despicable habit of calling knaves Jacks, that I was much more ignorant than I had considered myself last night, and, on the whole, that I was in a low-lived bad way.

N i n e

WHEN I REACHED HOME MY SISTER WAS VERY CURIOUS to know all about Miss Havisham's, and asked a number of questions. And I soon found myself getting heavily bumped in the nape of the neck and the small of the back, and having my face ignominiously shoved against the kitchen wall, because I did not answer those questions at sufficient length.

If a dread of not being understood be hidden in the breasts of other young people to anything like the extent to which it used to be hidden in mine—which I consider probable, as I have no particular reason to suspect myself of having been a monstrosity—it is the key to many reservations. I felt convinced that if I described Miss Havisham's as my eyes had seen it, I should not be understood. Not only that, but I felt convinced that Miss Havisham too would not be understood; and although she was perfectly incomprehensible to me, I entertained an impression that there would be something coarse and treacherous in my dragging her (to say nothing of Miss Estella) before the contemplation of Mrs. Joe. Consequently, I said as little as I could, and had my face shoved against the kitchen wall.

The worst of it was that that bullying old Pumblechook, preyed upon by a devouring curiosity to be informed of all I had seen and heard, came gaping over in his chaise-cart at tea-time to have the details divulged to him. And the mere sight of the torment, with his fishy eyes and mouth open, his sandy hair inquisitively on end, and his waistcoat heaving with windy arithmetic, made me vicious in my reticence.

"Well, boy," Uncle Pumblechook began, as soon as he was seated in the chair of honor by the fire. "How did you get on uptown?"

I answered, "Pretty well, sir," and my sister shook her fist at me.

"Pretty well?" Mr. Pumblechook repeated. "Pretty well is no answer. Tell us what you mean by pretty well, boy?"

Whitewash on the forehead hardens the brain into a state of obstinacy, perhaps. Anyhow, with whitewash from the wall on my forehead, my obstinacy was adamantine. I reflected for some time, and then answered, "I mean pretty well."

My sister, with an explanation of impatience, was going to fly at me—I had no shadow of defense, for Joe was busy in the forge—when Mr. Pumblechook interposed with, "No! Don't lose your temper. Leave this lad to me, ma'am; leave this lad to me." Mr. Pumblechook then turned me toward him, as if he were going to cut my hair or take out one of my teeth, or perform some such operation, and said:

"First (to get our thoughts in order): Forty-three pence?"

I calculated the consequences of replying "Four Hundred Pound," and, finding them against me, went as near the answer as I could—which was somewhat about eight pence off. Mr. Pumblechook then put me through my pence-table from "twelve pence make one shilling," up to "forty pence make three-and-four pence," and then triumphantly demanded, as if he had done for me, "*Now!* How much is forty-three pence?" To which I replied, after a long interval of reflection, "I don't know." And I was so aggravated that I almost doubt if I did know.

Mr. Pumblechook worked his head like a screw to screw it out of me, and said, "Is forty-three pence seven and sixpence three fardens, for instance?"

"Yes!" said I. And although my sister instantly boxed my ears, it was highly gratifying to me to see that the answer spoilt his joke, and brought him to a dead stop.

"Boy! What like is Miss Havisham?" Mr. Pumblechook began again when he had recovered; folding his arms tight on his chest and applying the screw.

"Very tall and dark," I told him.

"Is she, uncle?" asked my sister.

Mr. Pumblechook winked assent; from which I at once inferred that he had never seen Miss Havisham, for she was nothing of the kind.

"Good!" said Mr. Pumblechook, conceitedly. "This is the way to have him! We are beginning to hold our own, I think, Mum?"

"I am sure, uncle," returned Mrs. Joe, "I wish you had him always; you know so well how to deal with him."

"Now, boy! What was she a doing of when you went in today?" asked Mr. Pumblechook.

"She was sitting," I answered, "in a black velvet coach."

Mr. Pumblechook and Mrs. Joe stared at one another—as they well might—and both repeated, "In a black velvet coach?"

"Yes," said I. "And Miss Estella—that's her niece, I think—handed her in cake and wine at the coach window, on a gold plate. And we all had cake and wine on gold plates. And I got up behind the coach to eat mine, because she told me to."

"Was anybody else there?" asked Mr. Pumblechook.

"Four dogs," said I.

"Large or small?"

"Immense," said I. "And they fought for veal cutlets out of a silver basket."

Mr. Pumblechook and Mrs. Joe stared at one another again, in utter amazement. I was perfectly frantic—a reckless witness under the torture—and would have told them anything.

"Where *was* this coach, in the name of gracious?" asked my sister.

"In Miss Havisham's room." They stared again. "But there weren't any horses to it." I added this saving clause, in the moment of rejecting four richly caparisoned coursers which I had had wild thoughts of harnessing.

"Can this be possible, uncle?" asked Mrs. Joe. "What can the boy mean?"

"I'll tell you, Mum," said Mr. Pumblechook. "My opinion is, it's a sedan-chair. She's flighty, you know—very flighty—quite flighty enough to pass her days in a sedan-chair."

"Did you ever see her in it, uncle?" asked Mrs. Joe.

"How could I?" he returned, forced to the admission, "when I never see her in my life? Never clapped eyes upon her?"

"Goodness, uncle! And yet you have spoken to her?"

"Why, don't you know," said Mr. Pumblechook testily, "that when I have been there I have been took up to the outside of her door, and the door has stood ajar, and she has spoke to me that way. Don't say you don't know *that*, Mum. Howsoever, the boy went there to play. What did you play at, boy?"

"We played with flags," I said. (I beg to observe that I think of myself with amazement, when I recall the lies I told on this occasion.)

"Flags!" echoed my sister.

"Yes," said I. "Estella waved a blue flag, and I waved a red one, and Miss Havisham waved one sprinkled all over with little gold stars, out at the coach window. And then we all waved our swords and hurrahed."

"Swords!" repeated my sister. "Where did you get swords from?"

"Out of a cupboard," said I. "And I saw pistols in it—and jam—and pills. And there was no daylight in the room, but it was all lighted up with candles."

"That's true, Mum," said Mr. Pumblechook, with a grave nod. "That's the state of the case, for that much I've seen myself." And then they both stared at me, and I with an obtrusive show of artlessness on my countenance stared at them, and plaited the right leg of my trowsers with my right hand.

If they had asked me any more questions I should undoubtedly have betrayed myself, for I was even then on the point of mentioning that there was a balloon in the yard, and should have hazarded the statement but for my mind being divided between that phenomenon and a bear in the brewery. They were so much occupied, however, in discussing the marvels I had already presented for their consideration that I escaped. The subject still held them when Joe came in from his work to have a cup of tea, to whom my sister, more for the relief of her own mind than for the gratification of his, related my pretended experiences.

Now when I saw Joe open his blue eyes and roll them all round the kitchen in helpless astonishment, I was overtaken by penitence; but only as regarded him—not in the least as regarded the other two. Toward Joe, and Joe only, I considered myself a young monster while they sat debating what results would come to me from Miss Havisham's acquaintance and favor. They had no doubt that Miss Havisham would "do something" for me; their doubts related to the form that something would take. My sister stood out "for property." Mr. Pumblechook was in favor of a handsome premium for binding me apprentice to some genteel trade—say, the corn and seed trade for instance. Joe fell into the deepest disgrace with both, for offering the bright suggestion that I might only be presented with one of the dogs who had fought for the veal-cutlets. "If a fool's head can't express better opinions than that," said my sister, "and you have got any work to do you had better go and do it." So he went.

After Mr. Pumblechook had driven off, and when my sister was washing up, I stole into the forge to Joe, and remained by him until he had done for the night. Then I said, "Before the fire goes quite out, Joe, I should like to tell you something."

"Should you, Pip?" said Joe, drawing his shoeing-stool near the forge. "Then tell us. What is it, Pip?"

"Joe," said I, taking hold of his rolled up shirt-sleeve, and twisting it between my finger and thumb, "you remember all that about Miss Havisham's?"

"Remember?" said Joe. "I believe you! Wonderful!"

"It's a terrible thing, Joe; it an't true."

"What are you telling of, Pip?" cried Joe, falling back in the greatest amazement. "You don't mean to say it's—"

"Yes, I do; it's lies, Joe."

"But not all of it? Why sure you don't mean to say, Pip, that there was no black welwetco—eh?" For I stood shaking my head. "But at least there was dogs, Pip. Come, Pip," said Joe, persuasively, "if there warn't no weal-cutlets, at least there was dogs?"

"No, Joe."

"A dog?" said Joe. "A puppy? Come?"

"No, Joe, there was nothing at all of the kind."

As I fixed my eyes hopelessly on Joe, Joe contemplated me in dismay. "Pip, old chap! this won't do, old fellow! I say! where do you expect to go to?"

"It's terrible, Joe; an't it?"

"Terrible?" cried Joe. "Awful! What possessed you?"

"I don't know what possessed me, Joe," I replied, letting his shirtsleeve go, and sitting down in the ashes at his feet, hanging my head; "but I wish you hadn't taught me to call Knaves at cards Jacks; and I wish my boots weren't so thick nor my hands so coarse."

And then I told Joe that I felt very miserable, and that I hadn't been able to explain myself to Mrs. Joe and Pumblechook, who were so rude to me, and that there had been a beautiful young lady at Miss Havisham's who was dreadfully proud, and that she had said I was common, and that I knew I was common, and that I wished I was not common, and that the lies had come of it, somehow, though I didn't know how.

This was a case of metaphysics, at least as difficult for Joe to deal with as for me. But Joe took the case altogether out of the region of metaphysics, and by that means got the better of it.

"There's one thing you may be sure of, Pip," said Joe, after some rumination, "namely, that lies is lies. However they come, they didn't ought to come, and they come from the father of lies, and work round to the same. Don't you tell no more of 'em, Pip. That ain't the way to get out of being common, old chap. And as to being common, I don't make it out at all clear. You are oncommon in some things. You're oncommon small. Likewise you're an oncommon scholar."

"No, I am ignorant and backward, Joe."

"Why, see what a letter you wrote last night! Wrote in print even! I've seen letters—Ah! and from gentlefolks!—that I'll swear weren't wrote in print," said Joe.

"I have learned next to nothing, Joe. You think much of me. It's only that."

"Well, Pip," said Joe, "be it so or be it son't, you must be a common scholar afore you can be an oncommon one, I should hope! The king upon his throne, with his crown upon his ed, can't sit and write his acts of Parliament in print, without having begun, when he were a unpromoted Prince, with the alphabet—Ah!" added Joe, with a shake of the head that was full of meaning, "and begun at A too, and worked his way to Z. And *I* know what that is to do, though I can't say I've done it."

There was some hope in this piece of wisdom, and it rather encouraged me.

"Whether common ones as to callings and earnings," pursued Joe, reflectively, "mightn't be the better of continuing for to keep company with common ones, instead of going out to play with oncommon ones—which reminds me to hope that there were a flag perhaps?"

"No, Joe."

"(I'm sorry there weren't a flag, Pip.) Whether that might be or mightn't be, is a thing as can't be looked into now, without putting your sister on the Ram-page; and that's a thing not to be thought of as being done intentional. Lookee here, Pip, at what is said to you by a true friend. Which this to you the true friend say. If you can't get to the oncommon through going straight, you'll never do it through going crooked. So don't tell no more on 'em, Pip, and live well and die happy."

"You are not angry with me, Joe?"

"No, old chap. But bearing in mind that them were which I meantersay of a stunning and thundering sort—alluding to them which bordered on weal-cutlets and dog-fighting—a sincere well-wisher would adwise, Pip, their being dropped into your meditations when you go upstairs to bed. That's all, old chap, and don't never do it no more."

When I got up to my little room and said my prayers, I did not forget Joe's recommendation, and yet my young mind was in that disturbed and unthankful state, that I thought long after I laid me down, how common Estella would consider Joe, a mere blacksmith; how thick his boots, and how coarse his hands. I thought how Joe and my sister were then sitting in the kitchen, and how I'd come up to bed from the kitchen, and how Miss Havisham and Estella never sat in a kitchen, but were far above the level of such common doings. I fell asleep recalling what I "used to do" when I was at Miss Havisham's; as though I had been there weeks or months, instead of hours, and as though it were quite an old subject of remembrance, instead of one that had arisen only that day.

That was a memorable day to me, for it made great changes in me and in my fortunes. But it is the same with any life. Imagine one selected day struck out of it, and think how different its course would have been. Pause, you who read this, and think for a moment of the long chain of iron or gold, of thorns or flowers, that would never have bound you, but for the formation of the first link on one memorable day.

Ten

THE FELICITOUS IDEA OCCURRED TO ME A MORNING OR two later when I awoke, that the best step I could take toward making myself uncommon, was to get out of Biddy everything she knew, and to pay the strictest attention to Mr. Wopsle when he read aloud. In pursuance of this luminous conception I mentioned to Biddy when I went to Mr. Wopsle's great-aunt's at night, that I had a particular reason for wishing to get on in life, and that I should feel very much obliged to her if she would impart all her learning to me. Biddy, who was the most obliging of girls, immediately said she would, and indeed began to carry out her promise within five minutes.

The Educational scheme or Course established by Mr. Wopsle's great-aunt may be resolved into the following synopsis. The pupils ate apples and put straw up one another's backs, until Mr. Wopsle's great-aunt collected her energies, and made an indiscriminate totter at them with a birch-rod. After receiving the charge with every mark of derision, the pupils formed in line and buzzingly passed a ragged book from hand to hand. The book had an alphabet in it, some figures and tables, and a little spelling—that is to say, it had once. As soon as this volume began to circulate, Mr. Wopsle's great-aunt fell into a state of coma; arising either from sleep or a paroxysm of rheumatics. The pupils then entered among themselves upon a competitive examination on the subject of Boots, with the view of ascertaining who could tread the hardest upon whose toes. This mental exercise lasted until Biddy made a rush at them and distributed three defaced Bibles, shaped as if they had been unskillfully cut off the chump-end of something, more illegibly printed at the best than any curiosities of literature I have since met with, speckled all over with iron-mold, and having various specimens of the insect world smashed between their leaves. This part of the Course was usually lightened by several single combats between Biddy and refractory students. When the fights were over, Biddy gave out the number of a page, and then we all read aloud what we could—or what we couldn't—in a frightful chorus; Biddy leading with a high shrill monotonous voice, and none of us having the least notion what we were reading about. When this horrible din had lasted a certain time, it mechanically awoke Mr. Wopsle's great-aunt, who staggered at a boy and fortuitously pulled his ears. This was understood to terminate the Course for the evening, and we emerged into the air with shrieks of intellectual victory. It is fair to remark that there was no prohibition against any pupil's entertaining himself with a slate or even with the ink (when there was any), but that it was not easy to pursue that branch of study in the winter season, on account of the little general shop in which the classes were holden—and which was also Mr. Wopsle's great-aunt's sitting-room and bedchamber—being but faintly illuminated through the agency of one low-spirited dip-candle and no snuffers.

It appeared to me that it would take time to become uncommon under these circumstances: nevertheless I resolved to try it, and that very evening Biddy entered on our special agreement, by imparting some information from her little catalogue of Prices, under the head of moist sugar, and lending me, to copy at home, a German text or old English D which she had imitated from the heading of some newspaper, and which I supposed, until she told me what it was, to be a design for a buckle.

Of course there was a public-house in the village, and of course Joe liked sometimes to smoke his pipe there. I had received strict orders from my sister to call for him at the Three Jolly Bargemen, that evening, on my way from school, and bring him home at my peril. To the Three Jolly Bargemen, therefore, I directed my steps.

There was a bar at the Jolly Bargemen, with some alarmingly long chalk scores in it on the wall at the side of the door, which seemed to me to be never paid off. They had been there ever since I could remember, and had grown more than I had. But there was a quantity of chalk about our country, and perhaps the people neglected no opportunity of turning it to account.

It being Saturday night, I found the landlord looking rather grimly at these records; but as my business was with Joe and not with him, I merely wished him good evening, and passed into the common room at the end of the passage, where there was a bright large kitchen fire, and where Joe was smoking his pipe in company with Mr. Wopsle and a stranger. Joe greeted me as usual with "Halloa, Pip, old chap!" and the moment he said that, the stranger turned his head and looked at me.

He was a secret-looking man whom I had never seen before. His head was all on one side, and one of his eyes was half shut up, as if he were making aim at something with an invisible gun. He had a pipe in his mouth, and he took it out, and, after slowly blowing all his smoke away and looking hard at me all the time, nodded. So I nodded, and then he nodded again, and made room on the settle beside him that I might sit down there.

But as I was used to sit beside Joe whenever I entered that place of resort, I said "No, thank you, sir," and fell into the space Joe made for me on the opposite settle. The strange man, after glancing at Joe, and seeing that his attention was otherwise engaged, nodded to me again when I had taken my seat, and then rubbed his leg in a very odd way, as it struck me.

"You was saying," said the strange man, turning to Joe, "that you was a blacksmith."

"Yes, I said it, you know," said Joe.

"What'll you drink, Mr. —? You didn't mention your name, by-the-by."

Joe mentioned it now, and the strange man called him by it. "What'll you drink, Mr. Gargery? At my expense? To top up with?"

"Well," said Joe, "to tell you the truth, I ain't much in the habit of drinking at anybody's expense but my own."

"Habit? No," returned the stranger, "but once and away, and on a Saturday night too. Come! Put a name to it, Mr. Gargery."

"I wouldn't wish to be stiff company," said Joe. "Rum."

"Rum," repeated the stranger. "And will the other gentleman originate a sentiment?"

"Rum," said Mr. Wopsle.

"Three Rums here!" cried the stranger, calling to the landlord. "Glasses round!"

"This other gentleman," observed Joe, by way of introducing Mr. Wopsle, "is a gentleman that you would like to hear give it out. Our clerk at church."

"Aha!" said the stranger, quickly, and cocking his eye at me. "The lonely church, right out on the marshes, with the graves round it!"

"That's it," said Joe.

The stranger, with a comfortable kind of grunt over his pipe, put his legs up on the settle that he had all to himself. He wore a flapping broad-brimmed traveler's hat, and under it a handkerchief tied over his head in the manner of a cap; so that he showed no hair. As he looked at the fire, I thought I saw a cunning expression, followed by a half laugh, come into his face.

"I am not acquainted with this country, gentlemen, but it seems a solitary country toward the river."

"Most marshes is solitary," said Joe.

"No doubt, no doubt. Do you find any gipsies now, or tramps, or vagrants of any sort out on those lowlands?"

"No," said Joe; "none but a runaway convict now and then. And we don't find *them* easy. Eh, Mr. Wopsle?"

Mr. Wopsle, with a majestic remembrance of old discomfiture, assented; but not warmly.

"Seems you have been out after such?" asked the stranger.

"Once," returned Joe. "Not that we wanted to take them, you understand; we went out as lookers-on; me, and Mr. Wopsle, and Pip. Didn't us, Pip?"

"Yes, Joe."

The stranger looked at me again—still cocking his eye, as if he were expressly taking aim at me with his invisible gun—and said, "He's a likely young parcel of bones that. What is it you call him?"

"Pip," said Joe.

"Christened Pip?"

"No, not christened Pip."

"Surnamed Pip?"

"No," said Joe, "it's a kind of a family name what he gave himself when an infant, and is called by."

"Son of yours?"

"Well," said Joe, meditatively—not, of course, that it could be in anywise necessary to consider about it, but because it was the way at the Jolly Bargemen to seem to consider deeply about everything that was discussed over pipes; "well—no. No, he ain't."

"Nevvy?" said the strange man.

"Well," said Joe, with the same appearance of profound cogitation, "he is not—no, not to deceive you, he is *not*—my nevvy."

"What the Blue Blazes is he?" asked the stranger. Which appeared to me to be an inquiry of unnecessary strength.

Mr. Wopsle struck in upon that; as one who knew all about relationships, having professional occasion to bear in mind what female relations a man might not marry; and expounded the ties between me and Joe. Having his hand in, Mr. Wopsle introduced a most terrifically snarling passage from Richard the Third, and seemed to think he had done quite enough to account for it when he added "—as the poet says."

And here I may remark that when Mr. Wopsle referred to me, he considered it a necessary part of such reference to rumple my hair and poke it into my eyes. I cannot conceive why anybody of his standing who visited at our house should always have put me through the same inflammatory process under similar circumstances. Yet I do not call to mind that I was ever in my earlier youth the subject of remark in our social family circle, but some large-handed person took these ophthalmic steps to patronize me.

All this while the strange man looked at nobody but me, and looked at me as if he were determined to have a shot at me at last, and bring me down. But he said nothing after offering his Blue Blazes observation until the glasses of rum-and-water were brought; and then he made his shot, and a most extraordinary one it was.

It was not a verbal remark, but a proceeding in dumb-show, and was pointedly addressed to me. He stirred his rum-and-water pointedly at me, and he tasted his rum-and-water pointedly at me. And he stirred it and he tasted it, not with a spoon that was brought to him, but *with a file.*

He did this so that nobody but I saw the file; and when he had done it he wiped the file and put it in a breast-pocket. I knew it to be Joe's file, and I knew that he knew my convict the moment I saw the instrument. I sat gazing at him, spellbound. But he now reclined on his settle, taking very little notice of me, and talking principally about turnips.

There was a delicious sense of cleaning-up and making a quiet pause before going on in life afresh, in our village on Saturday nights, which stimulated Joe to dare to stay out half an hour longer on Saturdays than at other times. The half-hour and the rum-and-water running out together, Joe got up to go, and took me by the hand.

"Stop half a moment, Mr. Gargery," said the strange man. "I think I've got a bright new shilling somewhere in my pocket, and if I have the boy shall have it."

He looked it out from a handful of small change, folded it in some crumpled paper, and gave it to me. "Yours!" said he. "Mind! your own."

I thanked him, staring at him far beyond the bounds of good manners, and holding tight to Joe. He gave Joe good night, and he gave Mr. Wopsle good night (who went out with us), and he gave me only a look with his aiming eye—no, not a look, for he shut it up, but wonders may be done with an eye by hiding it.

On the way home, if I had been in a humor for talking, the talk must have been all on my side, for Mr. Wopsle parted from us at the door of the Jolly Bargemen, and Joe went all the way home with his mouth wide open, to rinse the rum out with as much air as possible. But I was in a manner stupefied by this turning up of my old misdeed and old acquaintance, and could think of nothing else.

My sister was not in a very bad temper when we presented ourselves in the kitchen, and Joe was encouraged by that unusual circumstance to tell her about the bright shilling. "A bad 'un, I'll be bound," said Mrs. Joe, triumphantly, "or he wouldn't have given it to the boy! Let's look at it."

I took it out of the paper, and it proved to be a good one. "But what's this?" said Mrs. Joe, throwing down the shilling and catching up the paper. "Two One-Pound notes?"

Nothing less than two fat sweltering one-pound notes, that seemed to have been on terms of the warmest intimacy with all the cattle-markets in the county. Joe caught up his hat again, and ran with them to the Jolly Bargemen, to restore them to their owner. While he was gone, I sat down on my usual stool and looked vacantly at my sister, feeling pretty sure that the man would not be there.

Presently Joe came back, saying that the man was gone, but that he, Joe, had left word at the Three Jolly Bargemen concerning the notes. Then my sister sealed them up in a piece of paper, and put them under some dried rose-leaves in an ornamental teapot on the top of a press in the state parlor. There they remained, a nightmare to me, many and many a night and day.

I had sadly broken sleep when I got to bed, through thinking of the strong man taking aim at me with his invisible gun, and of the guiltily-coarse and common thing it was to be on secret terms of conspiracy with convicts— a feature in my low career that I had previously forgotten. I was haunted by the file too. A dread possessed me that, when I least expected it, the file would reappear. I coaxed myself to sleep by thinking of Miss Havisham's next Wednesday; and in my sleep I saw the file coming at me out of a door, without seeing who held it, and I screamed myself awake.

Eleven

A T THE APPOINTED TIME I RETURNED TO MISS HAVISHAM'S, and my hesitating ring at the gate brought out Estella. She locked it after admitting me, as she had done before, and again preceded me into the dark passage where her candle stood. She took no notice of me until she had the candle in her hand, when she looked over her shoulder, superciliously saying, "You are to come this way today," and took me to quite another part of the house.

The passage was a long one, and seemed to pervade the whole square basement of the Manor House. We traversed but one side of the square, however, and at the end of it she stopped and put her candle down and opened a door. Here the daylight reappeared, and I found myself in a small paved courtyard, the opposite side of which was formed by a detached dwelling-house, that looked as if it had once belonged to the manager or head clerk of the extinct brewery. There was a clock in the outer wall of this house. Like the clock in Miss Havisham's room, and like Miss Havisham's watch, it had stopped at twenty minutes to nine.

We went in at the door which stood open, and into a gloomy room with a low ceiling on the ground-floor at the back. There was some company in the room, and Estella said to me as she joined it, "You are to go and stand there, boy, till you are wanted." "There" being the window, I crossed to it, and stood "there" in a very uncomfortable state of mind, looking out.

It opened to the ground, and looked into a most miserable corner of the neglected garden, upon a rank ruin of cabbage stalks, and one box-tree that had been clipped round long ago, like a pudding, and had a new growth at the top of it out of shape and of a different color, as if that part of the pudding had stuck to the saucepan and got burned. This was my homely thought, as I contemplated the box-tree. There had been some light snow overnight, and it lay nowhere else to my knowledge; but it had not quite melted from the cold shadow of this bit of garden, and the wind caught it up in little eddies and threw it at the window, as if it pelted me for coming there.

I divined that my coming had stopped conversation in the room, and that its other occupants were looking at me: I could see nothing of the room except the shining of the fire in the window-glass, but I stiffened in all my joints with the consciousness that I was under close inspection.

There were three ladies in the room, and one gentleman. Before I had been standing at the window five minutes they somehow conveyed to me that they were all toadies and humbugs, but that each of them pretended not to know that the others were toadies and humbugs, because the admission that he or she did know it would have made him or her out to be a toady and humbug.

They all had a listless and dreary air of waiting somebody's pleasure, and the most talkative of the ladies had to speak quite rigidly to suppress a yawn. This lady, whose name was Camilla, very much reminded me of my sister, with the difference that she was older and (as I found when I caught sight of her) of a blunter cast of features. Indeed, when I knew her better, I began to think it was a Mercy she had any features at all, so very black and high was the dead wall of her face.

"Poor dear soul!" said this lady with an abruptness of manner quite my sister's. "Nobody's enemy but his own!"

"It would be much more commendable to be somebody else's enemy," said the gentleman; "far more natural."

"Cousin John," observed another lady, "we are to love our neighbor."

"Sarah Pocket," returned Cousin John, "if a man is not his own neighbor, who is?"

Miss Pocket laughed, and Camilla laughed, and said (checking a yawn), "The idea!" But I thought they seemed to think it rather a good idea too. The other lady, who had not spoken yet, said, gravely and emphatically, "*Very* true!"

"Poor soul!" Camilla presently went on (I knew they had all been look-ing at me in the meantime), "he is so very strange! Would anyone believe that when Tom's wife died, he actually could not be induced to see the importance of the children's having the deepest of trimmings to their mourning? 'Good Lord!' says he, 'Camilla, what can it signify so long as the poor bereaved lit-tle things are in black?' So like Matthew! The idea!"

"Good points in him; good points in him!" said Cousin John; "Heaven forbid I should deny good points in him! but he never had, and he never will have, any sense of the proprieties."

"You know I was obliged," said Camilla—"I was obliged to be firm. I said, 'It WILL NOT DO for the credit of the family.' I told him that, without deep trimmings, the family was disgraced. I cried about it from breakfast till dinner. I injured my digestion. And at last he flung out in his violent way, and said with a D, 'Then do as you like.' Thank Goodness it will always be a consolation to me to know that I instantly went out in a pouring rain and bought the things."

"*He* paid for them, did he not?" asked Estella.

"It's not the question, my dear child, who paid for them," returned Camilla; "*I* bought them. And I shall often think of that with peace when I wake up in the night."

The ringing of a distant bell, combined with the echoing of some cry or call along the passage by which I had come, interrupted the conversation, and caused Estella to say to me, "Now, boy!" On my turning round, they all looked at me with the utmost contempt, and, as I went out, I heard Sarah Pocket say, "Well! I am sure! What next?" and Camilla add, with indignation, "Was there ever such a fancy? The i—de—a!"

As we were going with our candle along the dark passage Estella stopped all of a sudden, and facing round said, in her taunting manner, with her face quite close to mine,

"Well?"

"Well, Miss?" I answered, almost falling over her, and checking myself.

She stood looking at me, and of course, I stood looking at her.

"Am I pretty?"

"Yes; I think you are very pretty."

"Am I insulting?"

"Not so much as you were last time," said I.

"Not so much so!"

"No."

She fired when she asked the last question, and she slapped my face with such force as she had when I answered it.

"Now?" said she, "you little coarse monster, what do you think of me now?"

"I shall not tell you."

"Because you are going to tell upstairs. Is that it?"

"No," said I, "that's not it."

"Why don't you cry again, you little wretch?"

"Because I'll never cry for you again," said I. Which was, I suppose, as false a declaration as ever was made; for I was inwardly crying for her then, and I know what I know of the pain she cost me afterward.

We went on our way upstairs after this episode; and, as we were going up, we met a gentleman groping his way down.

"Who have we here?" asked the gentleman, stopping and looking at me.

"A boy," said Estella.

He was a burly man of an exceedingly dark complexion, with an exceedingly large head and a correspondingly large hand. He took my chin in his large hand and turned up my face to have a look at me by the light of the candle. He was prematurely bald on the top of his head, and had bushy black eyebrows that wouldn't lie down, but stood up bristling. His eyes were set very deep in his head, and were disagreeably sharp and suspicious. He had a very large watch-chain, and very strong black dots where his beard and whiskers would have been if he had let them. He was nothing to me, and I could have had no foresight then that he ever would be anything to me, but it happened that I had this opportunity of observing him well.

"Boy of the neighborhood? Hey?" said he.

"Yes, sir," said I.

"How do *you* come here?"

"Miss Havisham sent for me, sir," I explained.

"Well! Behave yourself. I have a pretty large experience of boys, and you're a bad set of fellows. Now mind!" said he, biting the side of his great forefinger as he frowned at me, "you behave yourself!"

With these words he released me—which I was glad of, for his hand smelled of scented soap—and went his way downstairs. I wondered whether he could be a doctor; but no, I thought he couldn't be a doctor, or he would have a quieter and more persuasive manner. There was not much time to consider the subject, for we were soon in Miss Havisham's room, where she and everything else were just as I had left them. Estella left me standing near the door, and I stood there until Miss Havisham cast her eyes upon me from the dressing table.

"So!" she said, without being startled or surprised, "the days have worn away, have they?"

"Yes, ma'am. Today is—"

"There, there, there!" with the impatient movement of her fingers. "I don't want to know. Are you ready to play?"

I was obliged to answer in some confusion, "I don't think I am, ma'am."

"Not at cards again?" she demanded, with a searching look.

"Yes, ma'am; I could do that if I was wanted."

"Since this house strikes you old and grave, boy," said Miss Havisham, impatiently, "and you are unwilling to play, are you willing to work?"

I could answer this inquiry with a better heart than I had been able to find for the other question, and I said I was quite willing.

"Then go into that opposite room," said she, pointing at the door behind me with her withered hand, "and wait there till I come."

I crossed the staircase landing, and entered the room she indicated. From that room, too, the daylight was completely excluded, and it had an airless smell that was oppressive. A fire had been lately kindled in the damp old-fashioned grate, and it was more disposed to go out than to burn up, and the reluctant smoke which hung in the room seemed colder than the clearer air—like our own marsh mist. Certain wintry branches of candles on the high chimney-piece faintly lighted the chamber: or it would be more expressive to say, faintly disturbed and troubled its darkness. It was spacious, and I dare say had once been handsome, but every discernible thing in it was covered with dust and mold and dropping to pieces. The most prominent object was a long table with a tablecloth spread on it, as if a feast had been in preparation when the house and the clocks all stopped together. An epergne or center-piece of some kind was in the middle of this cloth; it was so heavily overhung with cobwebs that its form was quite undistinguishable, and as I looked along the yellow expanse out of which I remember its seeming to grow like a black fungus, I saw speckled-legged spiders with blotchy bodies running home to it, and running out from it, as if some circumstance of the greatest public importance had just transpired in the spider community.

I heard the mice too rattling behind the panels, as if the same occurrence were important to their interests. But the black beetles took no notice of the agitation, and groped about the hearth in a ponderous elderly way, as if they were short-sighted and hard of hearing and not on terms with one another.

These crawling things had fascinated my attention and I was watching them from a distance, when Miss Havisham laid a hand upon my shoulder. In her other hand she had a crutch-headed stick on which she leaned, and she looked like the Witch of the place.

"This," said she, pointing to the long table with her stick, "is where I will be laid when I am dead. They shall come and look at me here."

With some vague misgiving that she might get upon the table then and there and die at once, the complete realization of the ghastly waxwork at the Fair, I shrank under her touch.

"What do you think that is?" she asked me, again pointing with her stick; "that, where those cobwebs are?"

"I can't guess what it is, ma'am!"

"It's a great cake. A bride-cake. Mine!"

She looked all round the room in a glaring manner, and then said, leaning on me while her hand twitched my shoulder, "Come, come, come! Walk me, walk me!"

I made out from this that the work I had to do was to walk Miss Havisham round and round the room. Accordingly I started at once, and she leaned upon my shoulder, and we went away at a pace that might have been an imitation (founded on my first impulse under that roof) of Mr. Pumble-chook's chaise-cart.

She was not physically strong, and after a little time she said "Slower!" Still we went at an impatient fitful speed and as we went, she twitched the hand upon my shoulder and worked her mouth, and led me to believe that we were going fast because her thoughts went fast. After awhile she said, "Call Estella!" so I went out on the landing and roared that name as I had done on the previous occasion. When her light appeared I returned to Miss Havisham, and we started away again round and round the room.

If only Estella had come to be a spectator of our proceedings I should have felt sufficiently discontented; but as she brought with her the three ladies and the gentleman whom I had seen below, I didn't know what to do. In my politeness I would have stopped, but Miss Havisham twitched my shoulder, and we posted on—with a shame-faced consciousness on my part that they would think it was all my doing.

"Dear Miss Havisham," said Miss Sarah Pocket. "How well you look!"

"I do not," returned Miss Havisham. "I am yellow skin and bone."

Camilla brightened when Miss Pocket met with this rebuff; and she mur-mured, as she plaintively contemplated Miss Havisham, "Poor dear soul! Certainly not to be expected to look well, poor thing. The idea!"

"And how are *you?*" said Miss Havisham to Camilla. As we were close to Camilla then, I would have stopped as a matter of course, only Miss Hav-isham wouldn't stop. We swept on, and I felt that I was highly obnoxious to Camilla.

"Thank you, Miss Havisham," she returned, "I am as well as can be expected."

"Why, what's the matter with you?" asked Miss Havisham, with exceed-ing sharpness.

"Nothing worth mentioning," replied Camilla. "I don't wish to make a display of my feelings, but I have habitually thought of you more in the night than I am quite equal to."

"Then don't think of me," retorted Miss Havisham.

"Very easily said!" remarked Camilla, amiably repressing a sob, while a hitch came into her upper lip, and her tears overflowed. "Raymond is a wit-ness what ginger and sal volatile I am obliged to take in the night. Raymond is a witness what nervous jerkings I have in my legs. Chokings and nervous jerkings, however, are nothing new to me when I think with anxiety of those I love. If I could be less affectionate and sensitive I should have a better diges-tion and an iron set of nerves. I am sure I wish it could be so. But as to not thinking of you in the night—The idea!" Here a burst of tears.

The Raymond referred to I understood to be the gentleman present, and him I understood to be Mr. Camilla. He came to the rescue at this point, and said, in a consolatory and complimentary voice, "Camilla, my dear, it is well known that your family feelings are gradually undermining you to the extent of making one of your legs shorter than the other."

"I am not aware," observed the grave lady whose voice I had heard but once, "that to think of any person is to make a great claim upon that person, my dear."

Miss Sarah Pocket, whom I now saw to be a little dry brown corrugated old woman, with a small face that might have been made of walnut shells, and a large mouth like a cat's without the whiskers, supported this position by saying, "No, indeed, my dear. Hem!"

"Thinking is easy enough," said the grave lady.

"What is easier, you know?" assented Miss Sarah Pocket.

"Oh, yes, yes!" cried Camilla, whose fermenting feelings appeared to rise from her legs to her bosom. "It's all very true! It's a weakness to be so affectionate, but I can't help it. No doubt my health would be much better if it was otherwise, still I wouldn't change my disposition if I could. It's the cause of much suffering, but it's a consolation to know I possess it when I wake up in the night." Here another burst of feeling.

Miss Havisham and I had never stopped all this time, but kept going round and round the room, now brushing against the skirts of the visitors, and now giving them the whole length of the dismal chamber.

"There's Matthew!" said Camilla. "Never mixing with my natural ties, never coming here to see how Miss Havisham is! I have taken to the sofa with my stay-lace cut, and have lain there hours insensible, with my head over the side, and my hair all down, and my feet I don't know where—"

("Much higher than your head, my love," said Mr. Camilla.)

"I have gone off into that state hours and hours on account of Matthew's strange and inexplicable conduct, and nobody has thanked me."

"Really I must say I should think not!" interposed the grave lady.

"You see, my dear," added Miss Sarah Pocket (a blandly vicious personage), "the question to put to yourself is, who did you expect to thank you, my love?"

"Without expecting any thanks, or anything of the sort," resumed Camilla, "I have remained in that state, hours and hours, and Raymond is a witness of the extent to which I have choked, and what the total inefficacy of ginger has been, and I have been heard at the pianoforte-tuner's across the street, where the poor, mistaken children have even supposed it to be pigeons cooing at a distance—and now to be told—" Here Camilla put her hand to her throat, and began to be quite chemical as to the formation of new combinations there.

When this same Matthew was mentioned Miss Havisham stopped me and herself and stood looking at the speaker. This change had a great influence in bringing Camilla's chemistry to a sudden end.

"Matthew will come and see me at last," said Miss Havisham, sternly, "when I am laid on that table. That will be his place—there," striking the table with her stick, "at my head! And yours will be there! And your husband's there! And Sarah Pocket's there! And Georgiana's there! Now you all know where to take your stations when you come to feast upon me. And now go!"

At the mention of each name she had struck the table with her stick in a new place. She now said, "Walk me, walk me!" and we went on again.

"I suppose there's nothing to be done," exclaimed Camilla, "but comply and depart. It's something to have seen the object of one's love and duty for even so short a time. I shall think of it with a melancholy satisfaction when I wake up in the night. I wish Matthew could have that comfort, but he sets it at defiance. I am determined not to make a display of my feelings, but it's very hard to be told one wants to feast on one's relations, and to be told to go. The bare idea!"

Mr. Camilla interposing, as Mrs. Camilla laid her hand upon her heaving bosom, that lady assumed an unnatural fortitude of manner which I supposed to be expressive of an intention to drop and choke when out of view, and kissing her hand to Miss Havisham, was escorted forth. Sarah Pocket and Georgiana contended who should remain last, but Sarah was too knowing to be outdone, and ambled round Georgiana with that artful slipperiness, that the latter was obliged to take precedence. Sarah Pocket then made her separate effect of departing with, "Bless you, Miss Havisham dear!" and with a smile of forgiving pity on her walnut-shell countenance for the weaknesses of the rest.

While Estella was away lighting them down, Miss Havisham still walked with her hand on my shoulder, but more and more slowly. At last she stopped before the fire, and said, after muttering and looking at it some seconds:

"This is my birthday, Pip."

I was going to wish her many happy returns, when she lifted her stick.

"I don't suffer it to be spoken of. I don't suffer those who were here just now or anyone to speak of it. They come here on the day, but they dare not refer to it."

Of course I made no further effort to refer to it.

"On this day of the year, long before you were born, this heap of decay," stabbing with her crutched stick at the pile of cobwebs on the table but not touching it, "was brought here. It and I have worn away together. The mice have gnawed at it, and sharper teeth than teeth of mice have gnawed at me."

She held the head of her stick against her heart as she stood looking at the table; she in her once white dress, all yellow and withered; the once white cloth all yellow and withered; everything around in a state to crumble under a touch.

"When the ruin is complete," said she, with a ghastly look, "and when they lay me dead in my bride's dress on the bride's table—which shall be done, and which will be the finished curse upon him—so much the better if it is on this day!"

She stood looking at the table as if she stood looking at her own figure lying there. I remained quiet. Estella returned, and she too remained quiet. It seemed to me that we continued thus for a long time. In the heavy air of the room, and the heavy darkness that brooded in its remoter corners, I even had an alarming fancy that Estella and I would presently begin to decay.

At length, not coming out of her distraught state by degrees but in an instant, Miss Havisham said, "Let me see you two play cards; why have you not begun?" With that, we returned to her room, and sat down as before; I was beggared as before; and again, as before, Miss Havisham watched us all the time, directed my attention to Estella's beauty, and made me notice it the more by trying her jewels on Estella's breast and hair.

Estella, for her part, likewise treated me as before; except that she did not condescend to speak. When we had played some half dozen games a day was appointed for my return, and I was taken down into the yard to be fed in the former doglike manner. There, too, I was again left to wander about as I liked.

It is not much to the purpose whether a gate in that garden wall which I had scrambled up to peep over on the last occasion was, on that last occasion, open or shut. Enough that I saw no gate then, and that I saw one now. As it stood open, and as I knew that Estella had let the visitors out—for she had returned with the keys in her hand—I strolled into the garden and strolled all over it. It was quite a wilderness, and there were old melon-frames and cucumber-frames in it, which seemed in their decline to have produced a spontaneous growth of feeble attempts at pieces of old hats and boots, with now and then a weedy offshoot into the likeness of a battered saucepan.

When I had exhausted the garden, and a greenhouse with nothing in it but a fallen down grapevine and some bottles, I found myself in the dismal corner upon which I had looked out of the window. Never questioning for a moment that the house was now empty, I looked in at another window, and found myself, to my great surprise, exchanging a broad stare with a pale young gentleman with red eyelids and very light hair.

This pale young gentleman quickly disappeared, and reappeared beside me. He had been at his books when I had found myself staring at him, and I now saw that he was inky.

"Halloa!" said he, "young fellow!" Halloa being a general observation which I have usually observed to be best answered by itself, I said "Halloa!" politely omitting young fellow.

"Who let you in?" said he.

"Miss Estella."

"Who gave you leave to prowl about?"

"Miss Estella."

"Come and fight," said the pale young gentleman.

What could I do but follow him? I have often asked myself the question since; but what else could I do? His manner was so final, and I was so astonished, that I followed where he led, as if I had been under a spell.

"Stop a minute, though," he said, wheeling round before we had gone many paces. "I ought to give you a reason for fighting, too. There it is!" In a most irritating manner he instantly slapped his hands against one another, daintily flung one of his legs up behind him, pulled my hair, slapped his hands again, dipped his head, and ran it into my stomach.

The bull-like proceeding last mentioned, besides that it was unquestionably to be regarded in the light of a liberty, was particularly disagreeable just after bread and meat. I therefore hit out at him, and was going to hit out again, when he said, "Aha! Would you?" and began dancing backward and forward in a manner quite unparalleled within my limited experience.

"Laws of the game!" said he. Here he skipped from his left leg onto his right. "Regular rules!" Here he skipped from his right leg onto his left. "Come to the ground, and go through the preliminaries!" Here he dodged backward and forward, and did all sorts of things, while I looked helplessly at him.

I was secretly afraid of him when I saw him so dexterous; but I felt morally and physically convinced that his light head of hair could have had no business in the pit of my stomach, and that I had a right to consider it irrelevant when so obtruded on my attention. Therefore I followed him, without a word, to a retired nook of the garden formed by the junction of two walls and screened by some rubbish. On his asking me if I was satisfied with the ground, and on my replying Yes, he begged my leave to absent himself for a moment and quickly returned with a bottle of water and a sponge dipped in vinegar. "Available for both," he said, placing these against the wall. And then fell to pulling off, not only his jacket and waistcoat, but his shirt too, in a manner at once lighthearted, businesslike, and bloodthirsty.

Although he did not look very healthy—having pimples on his face, and a breaking out at his mouth—these dreadful preparations quite appalled me. I judged him to be about my own age, but he was much taller, and he had a way of spinning himself about that was full of appearance and highly impressive. For the rest he was a young gentleman in a gray suit (when not denuded for battle), with his elbows, knees, wrists, and heels considerably in advance of the rest of him as to development.

My heart failed me when I saw him squaring at me with every demonstration of mechanical nicety, and eying my anatomy as if he were minutely choosing his bone. I never have been so surprised in my life as I was when I let out the first blow, and saw him lying on his back looking up at me with a bloody nose and his face exceedingly foreshortened.

But he was on his feet directly, and after sponging himself with a great show of dexterity, began squaring again. The second greatest surprise I have ever had in my life was seeing him on his back again, looking up at me out of a black eye.

His spirit inspired me with great respect. He seemed to have no strength, and he never once hit me hard, and he was always knocked down; but he would be up again in a moment, sponging himself or drinking out of the water-bottle, with the greatest satisfaction in seconding himself according to form, and then came at me with an air and a show that made me believe he really was going to do for me at last. He got heavily bruised, for I am sorry to record that the more I hit him the harder I hit him, but he came up again and again and again, until at last he got a bad fall with the back of his head against the wall. Even after that crisis in our affairs he got up and turned round and round confusedly a few times, not knowing where I was, but finally went on his knees to his sponge and threw it up: at the same time panting out, "That means you have won."

He seemed so brave and innocent, that, although I had not proposed the contest, I felt but a gloomy satisfaction in my victory. Indeed, I go so far as to hope that I regarded myself while dressing as a species of savage young wolf, or other wild beast. However, I got dressed, darkly wiping my face at intervals, and I said, "Can I help you?" and he said, "No, thankee," and I said, "Good afternoon," and *he* said, "Same to you."

When I got into the courtyard I found Estella waiting with the keys. But she neither asked me where I had been, nor why I had kept her waiting; and there was a bright flush upon her face as though something had happened to delight her. Instead of going straight to the gate, too, she stepped back into the passage, and beckoned me.

"Come here! You may kiss me, if you like."

I kissed her cheek as she turned it to me. I think I would have gone through a great deal to kiss her cheek. But I felt that the kiss was given to the coarse, common boy, as a piece of money might have been, and that it was worth nothing.

What with the birthday visitors, and what with the cards, and what with the fight, my stay had lasted so long, that when I neared home the light on the spit of sand off the point on the marshes was gleaming against a black night-sky, and Joe's furnace was flinging a path of fire across the road.

T w e l v e

MY MIND GREW VERY UNEASY ON THE SUBJECT OF THE pale young gentleman. The more I thought of the fight, and recalled the pale young gentleman on his back in various stages of puffy and in-crimsoned countenance, the more certain it appeared that something would be done to me. I felt that the pale young gentleman's blood was on my head, and that the Law would avenge it. Without having any definite idea of the penalties I had incurred, it was clear to me that village boys could not go stalking about the country, ravaging the houses of gentlefolks and pitching into the studious youth of England, without laying themselves open to severe punishment. For some days I even kept close at home, and looked out at the kitchen-door with the greatest caution and trepidation before going on an errand, lest the officers of the County Jail should pounce upon me. The pale young gentleman's nose had stained my trowsers, and I tried to wash out that evidence of my guilt in the dead of night. I had cut my knuckles against the pale young gentleman's teeth, and I twisted my imagination into a thousand tangles, as I devised incredible ways of accounting for that damnatory circumstance when I should be haled before the Judges.

When the day came round for my return to the scene of the deed of violence, my terrors reached their height. Whether myrmidons of Justice, specially sent down from London, would be lying in ambush behind the gate? Whether Miss Havisham, preferring to take personal vengeance for an outrage done to her house, might rise in those grave-clothes of hers, draw a pistol, and shoot me dead? Whether suborned boys—a numerous band of mercenaries—might be engaged to fall upon me in the brewery, and knock me about until I was no more? It was high testimony to my confidence in the spirit of the pale young gentleman, that I never imagined *him* accessory to these retaliations; they always came into my mind as the acts of injudicious relatives of his, goaded on by the state of his visage and an indignant sympathy with the family features.

However, go to Miss Havisham's I must, and go I did. And behold! nothing came of the late struggle. It was not alluded to in any way, and no pale young gentleman was to be discovered on the premises. I found the same gate open, and I explored the garden, and even looked in at the windows of the detached house; but my view was suddenly stopped by the closed shutters within, and all was lifeless and deserted. Only in the corner where the combat had taken place could I detect any evidence of the young gentleman's existence. There were traces of his gore in that spot, and I covered them with garden-mold from the eye of man.

On the broad landing between Miss Havisham's own room and that other room in which the long table was laid out, I saw a garden-chair—a light chair on wheels that you pushed from behind. It had been placed there since my last visit, and I entered, that same day, on a regular occupation of pushing Miss Havisham in this chair (when she was tired of walking with her hand upon my shoulder) round her own room, and across the landing, and round the other room. Over and over and over again, we would make these journeys, and sometimes they would last as long as three hours at a stretch. I insensibly fall into a general mention of these journeys as numerous, because it was at once settled that I should return every alternate day at noon for these purposes, and because I am now going to sum up a period of at least eight or ten months.

As we began to be more used to one another, Miss Havisham talked more to me, and asked me such questions as what had I learned and what was I going to be? I told her I was going to be apprenticed to Joe, I believed; and I enlarged upon my knowing nothing and wanting to know everything, in the hope that she might offer some help toward that desirable end. But she did not; on the contrary, she seemed to like my being ignorant. Neither did she ever give me any money—or anything but my daily dinner—nor ever stipulate that I should be paid for my services.

Estella was always about, and always let me in and out, but never told me I might kiss her again. Sometimes, she would coldly tolerate me; sometimes, she would condescend to me; sometimes, she would be quite familiar with me; sometimes, she would tell me energetically that she hated me. Miss Havisham would often ask me in a whisper, or when we were alone, "Does she grow prettier and prettier, Pip?" And when I said yes (for indeed she did), would seem to enjoy it greedily in secret. Also, when we played at cards Miss Havisham would look on, with a miserly relish of Estella's moods, whatever they were. And sometimes, when her moods were so many and so contradictory of one another that I was puzzled what to say or do, Miss Havisham would embrace her with lavish fondness, murmuring something in her ear that sounded like "Break their hearts my pride and hope, break their hearts and have no mercy!"

There was a song Joe used to hum fragments of at the forge, of which the burden was Old Clem. This was not a very ceremonious way of rendering homage to a patron saint; but I believe Old Clem stood in that relation toward smiths. It was a song that imitated the measure of beating upon iron, and was a mere lyrical excuse for the introduction of Old Clem's respected name. Thus, you were to hammer boys round—Old Clem! With a thump and a sound—Old Clem! Beat it out, beat it out—Old Clem! With a clink for the stout—Old Clem! Blow the fire, blow the fire—Old Clem! Roaring dryer, soaring higher—Old Clem! One day soon after the appearance of the chair, Miss Havisham suddenly saying to me, with the impatient movement of her fingers, "There, there, there! Sing!" I was surprised into crooning this ditty as I pushed her over the floor. It happened so to catch her fancy, that she took it up in a low brooding voice as if she were singing in her sleep. After that, it became customary with us to have it as we moved about, and Estella would often join in; though the whole strain was so subdued, even when there were three of us, that it made less noise in the grim old house than the lightest breath of wind.

What could I become with these surroundings? How could my character fail to be influenced by them? Is it to be wondered at if my thoughts were dazed, as my eyes were, when I came out into the natural light from the misty yellow rooms!

Perhaps I might have told Joe about the pale young gentleman, if I had not previously been betrayed into those enormous inventions to which I have confessed. Under the circumstances, I felt that Joe could hardly fail to discern in the pale young gentleman an appropriate passenger to be put into the black velvet coach; therefore I said nothing of him. Besides, that shrinking from having Miss Havisham and Estella discussed, which had come upon me in the beginning, grew much more potent as time went on. I reposed complete confidence in no one but Biddy; but I told poor Biddy everything. Why it came natural to me to do so, and why Biddy had a deep concern in everything I told her, I did not know then, though I think I know now. Shade of poor Biddy, forgive me!

Meanwhile councils went on in the kitchen at home, fraught with almost insupportable aggravation to my exasperated spirit. That ass, Pumblechook, used often to come over of a night for the purpose of discussing my prospects with my sister; and I really do believe (to this hour with less penitence than I ought to feel), that if these hands could have taken a linch-pin out of his chaise-cart they would have done it. The miserable man was a man of that confined stolidity of mind that he could not discuss my prospects without having me before him—as it were, to operate upon—and he would drag me up from my stool (usually by the collar) where I was quiet in a corner, and, standing me before the fire as if I was going to be cooked, would begin by saying, "Now, mum, here is this boy! Here is this boy which you brought up by hand. Hold up your head, boy, and be forever grateful unto them which so did do. Now, mum, with respections to this boy!" And then he would rumple my hair the wrong way—which, from my earliest remembrance, as already hinted, I have in my soul denied the right of any fellow-creature to do—and would hold me before him by the sleeve; a spectacle of imbecility only to be equaled by himself.

Then he and my sister would pair off in such nonsensical speculations about Miss Havisham, and about what she would do with me and for me, that I used to want—quite painfully—to burst in spiteful tears, fly at Pumblechook, and pommel him all over. In these dialogues, my sister spoke of me as if she were morally wrenching one of my teeth out at every reference; while Pumblechook himself, self-constituted my patron, would sit supervising me with a depreciatory eye, like the architect of my fortunes who thought himself engaged in a very unremunerative job.

In these discussions Joe bore no part. But he was often talked at, while they were in progress, by reason of Mrs. Joe's perceiving that he was not favorable to my being taken from the forge. I was fully old enough now to be apprenticed to Joe; and when Joe sat with the poker on his knees thought-fully raking out the ashes between the lower bars, my sister would so distinctly construe that innocent action into opposition on his part, that she would dive at him, take the poker out of his hands, shake him and put it away. There was a most irritating end to every one of these debates. All in a moment, with nothing to lead up to it, my sister would stop herself in a yawn, and would swoop upon me, with "Come! There's enough of *you! You* get along to bed; you've given trouble enough for one night, I hope!" As if I had besought them as a favor to bother my life out.

Well! We went on in this way for a long time, and it seemed likely that we should continue to go on in this way for a long time, when one day Miss Havisham stopped short as she and I were walking, she leaning on my shoulder; and said, with some displeasure,

"You are growing tall, Pip!"

I thought it best to hint, through the medium of a meditative look, that this might be occasioned by circumstances over which I had no control.

She said no more at the time; but she presently stopped and looked at me again; and presently again; and after that looked frowning and moody. On the next day of my attendance when our usual exercise was over, and I had landed her at her dressing-table, she staid me with a movement of her impatient fingers:

"Tell me the name again of that blacksmith of yours."

"Joe Gargery, ma'am."

"Meaning the master you were to be apprenticed to?"

"Yes, Miss Havisham."

"You had better be apprenticed at once. Would Gargery come here with you, and bring your indentures, do you think?"

I signified that I had no doubt he would take it as an honor to be asked.

"Then let him come."

"At any particular time, Miss Havisham?"

"There, there! I know nothing about times. Let him come soon, and come alone with you."

When I got home at night, and delivered this message for Joe, my sister "went on the Ram-page," as Joe expressed it, in a more alarming degree than at any previous period. She asked me and Joe whether we supposed she was door mats under our feet, and how we dared to use her so, and what company we graciously thought she *was* fit for? When she had exhausted a torrent of such inquiries, she threw a candlestick at Joe, burst into a loud sobbing, got out the dustpan—which was always a very bad sign—put on her coarse apron, and began cleaning up to a terrible extent. Not satisfied with a dry cleaning, she took to a pail and scrubbing brush, and cleaned us out of house and home, so that we stood shivering in the backyard. It was ten o'clock at night before we ventured to creep in again, and then she asked Joe why he hadn't married a Negress Slave at once? Joe offered no answer, poor fellow! but stood feeling his whisker and looking dejectedly at me, as if he thought it really might have been a better speculation.

Thirteen

IT WAS A TRIAL TO MY FEELINGS ON THE NEXT DAY BUT ONE, to see Joe arraying himself in his Sunday clothes to accompany me to Miss Havisham's. However, as he thought his court-suit necessary to the occasion, it was not for me to tell him that he looked far better in his working dress; the rather, because I knew he made himself so dreadfully uncomfortable, entirely on my account, and that it was for me he pulled up his shirt-collar so very high behind that it made the hair on the crown of his head stand up like a tuft of feathers.

At breakfast-time my sister declared her intention of going to town with us, and being left at Uncle Pumblechook's, and called for "when we had done with our fine ladies"—a way of putting the case, from which Joe appeared inclined to augur the worst. The forge was shut up for the day, and Joe inscribed in chalk upon the door (as it was his custom to do on the very rare occasions when he was not at work) the monosyllable HOUT, accompanied by a sketch of an arrow supposed to be flying in the direction he had taken.

We walked to town, my sister leading the way in a very large beaver bonnet, and carrying a basket like the Great Seal of England in plaited straw, a pair of pattens, and an umbrella, though it was a fine bright day. I am not quite clear whether these articles were carried penitentially or ostentatiously; but I rather think they were displayed as articles of property—much as Cleopatra, or any other sovereign lady on the Ram-page, might exhibit her wealth in a pageant or procession.

When we came to Pumblechook's my sister bounced in and left us. As it was almost noon Joe and I held straight on to Miss Havisham's house. Estella opened the gate as usual, and the moment she appeared Joe took his hat off and stood weighing it by the brim in both his hands—as if he had some urgent reason in his mind for being particular to half a quarter of an ounce.

Estella took no notice of either of us, but led us the way that I knew so well. I followed next to her, and Joe came last. When I looked back at Joe in the long passage he was still weighing his hat with the greatest care, and was coming after us in long strides on the tips of his toes.

Estella told me we were both to go in, so I took Joe by the coat-cuff and conducted him into Miss Havisham's presence. She was seated at her dressing-table, and looked round at us immediately.

"Oh!" said she to Joe. "You are the husband of the sister of this boy?"

I could hardly have imagined dear old Joe looking so unlike himself or so like some extraordinary bird; standing, as he did, speechless, with his tuft of feathers ruffled, and his mouth open, as if he wanted a worm.

"You are the husband," repeated Miss Havisham, "of the sister of this boy?"

It was very aggravating, but throughout the interview Joe persisted in addressing Me instead of Miss Havisham.

"Which I meantersay, Pip," Joe now observed in a manner that was at once expressive of forcible argumentation, strict confidence, and great politeness, "as I hup and married your sister, and I were at the time what you might call (if you was any ways inclined) a single man."

"Well!" said Miss Havisham. "And you have reared the boy, with the intention of taking him for your apprentice; is that so, Mr. Gargery?"

"You know, Pip," replied Joe, "as you and me were ever friends, and it were look'd for'ard to betwixt us, as being calc'lated to lead to larks. Not but what, Pip, if you had ever made objections to the business—such as its being open to black and sut, or such like—not but what they would have been attended to; don't you see?"

"Has the boy," said Miss Havisham, "ever made any objection? Does he like the trade?"

"Which it is well beknown to yourself, Pip," returned Joe, strengthening his former mixture of argumentation, confidence, and politeness, "that it were the wish of your own hart." (I saw the idea suddenly break upon him that he would adapt his epitaph to the occasion, before he went on to say) "And there were no objection on your part, and, Pip, it were the great wish of your hart!"

It was quite in vain for me to endeavor to make him sensible that he ought to speak to Miss Havisham. The more I made faces and gestures to him to do it, the more confidential, argumentative, and polite he persisted in being to Me.

"Have you brought his indentures with you?" asked Miss Havisham.

"Well, Pip, you know," replied Joe, as if that were a little unreasonable, "you yourself see me put 'em in my 'at, and therefore you know as they are here." With which he took them out, and gave them, not to Miss Havisham, but to me. I am afraid I was ashamed of the dear, good fellow—I *know* I was ashamed of him—when I saw that Estella stood at the back of Miss Havisham's chair, and that her eyes laughed mischievously. I took the indentures out of his hand and gave them to Miss Havisham.

"You expected," said Miss Havisham, as she looked them over, "no premium with the boy?"

"Joe!" I remonstrated, for he made no answer at all. "Why don't you—"

"Pip," returned Joe, cutting me short as if he were hurt, "which I mean-tersay that were not a question requiring a answer betwixt yourself and me, and which you know the answer to be full well No. You know it to be No, Pip, and wherefore should I say it?"

Miss Havisham glanced at him as if she understood what he really was, better than I had thought possible, seeing what he was there; and took up a little bag from the table beside her.

"Pip has earned a premium here," she said, "and here it is. There are five-and-twenty guineas in this bag. Give it to your master, Pip."

As if he were absolutely out of his mind with the wonder awakened in him by her strange figure and the strange room, Joe, even at this pass, persisted in addressing me.

"This is very liberal on your part, Pip," said Joe, "and it is as such received and grateful welcome, though never looked for, far nor near nor nowheres. And now, old chap," said Joe, conveying to me a sensation, first of burning and then of freezing, for I felt as if that familiar expression were applied to Miss Havisham; "and now, old chap, may we do our duty! May you and me do our duty, both on us by one and another, and by them which your liberal present—have—conweyed—to be—for the satisfaction of mind—of—them as never—" here Joe showed that he felt he had fallen into frightful difficulties, until he triumphantly rescued himself with the words, "and from myself far be it!" These words had such a round and convincing sound to him that he said them twice.

"Good-bye, Pip!" said Miss Havisham. "Let them out, Estella."

"Am I to come again, Miss Havisham?" I asked.

"No. Gargery is your master now. Gargery! One word!"

Thus calling him back as I went out of the door, I heard her say to Joe in a distinct emphatic voice, "The boy has been a good boy here, and that is his reward. Of course, as an honest man, you will expect no other and no more."

How Joe got out of the room I have never been able to determine; but I know that when he did get out he was insanely proceeding upstairs instead of coming down, and was deaf to all remonstrances until I went after him and laid hold of him. In another minute we were outside the gate, and it was locked, and Estella was gone.

When we stood in the daylight alone again, Joe backed up against a wall, and said to me, "Astonishing!" And there he remained so long, saying "Astonishing" at intervals, so often, that I began to think his senses were never coming back. At length he prolonged his remark into "Pip, I do assure *you* that this is as-TON-ishing!" and so, by degrees, became conversational and able to walk away.

I have reason to think that Joe's intellects were brightened by the encounter they had passed through, and that on our way to Pumblechook's he invented a subtle and deep design. My reason is to be found in what took place in Mr. Pumblechook's parlor: where, on our presenting ourselves, my sister sat in conference with that detested seedsman.

"Well?" cried my sister, addressing us both at once. "And what's happened to *you?* I wonder you condescend to come back to such poor society as this, I am sure I do!"

"Miss Havisham," said Joe, with a fixed look at me, like an effort of remembrance, "made it wery partick'ler that we should give her—were it compliments or respects, Pip?"

"Compliments," I said.

"Which that were my own belief," answered Joe—"her compliments to Mrs. J. Gargery."

"Much good they'll do me!" observed my sister; but rather gratified too.

"And wishing," pursued Joe, with another fixed look at me, like another effort of remembrance, "that the state of Miss Havisham's elth were sitch as would have—allowed, were it, Pip?"

"Of her having the pleasure," I added.

"Of ladies' company," said Joe. And drew a long breath.

"Well!" cried my sister, with a mollified glance at Mr. Pumblechook. "She might have had the politeness to send that message at first, but it's better late than never. And what did she give young Rantipole here?"

"She giv' him," said Joe, "nothing." Mrs. Joe was going to break out, but Joe went on.

"What she giv'," said Joe, "she giv' to his friends. 'And by his friends,' were her explanation, 'I mean into the hands of his sister Mrs. J. Gargery.' Them were her words; 'Mrs. J. Gargery.' She mayn't have know'd," added Joe, with an appearance of reflection, "whether it were Joe, or Jorge."

My sister looked at Pumblechook, who smoothed the elbows of his wooden armchair, and nodded at her and at the fire, as if he had known all about it beforehand.

"And how much have you got?" asked my sister, laughing. Positively laughing!

"What would present company say to ten pound?" demanded Joe.

"They'd say," returned my sister, curtly, "pretty well. Not too much, but pretty well."

"It's more than that, then," said Joe.

That fearful Impostor, Pumblechook, immediately nodded, and said, as he rubbed the arms of his chair: "It's more than that, mum."

"Why, you don't mean to say—" began my sister.

"Yes, I do, mum," said Pumblechook; "but wait a bit. Go on, Joseph. Good in you! Go on!"

"What would present company say," proceeded Joe, "to twenty pound?"

"Handsome would be the word," returned my sister.

"Well, then," said Joe, "it's more than twenty pound."

That abject Hypocrite, Pumblechook, nodded again, and said, with a patronizing laugh, "It's more than that, mum. Good again! Follow her up, Joseph!"

"Then to make an end of it," said Joe, delightedly handing the bag to my sister; "it's five-and-twenty pound."

"It's five-and-twenty pound, mum," echoed that basest of swindlers, Pumblechook, rising to shake hands with her; "and it's no more than your merits (as I said when my opinion was asked), and I wish you joy of the money!"

If the Villain had stopped here his case would have been sufficiently awful, but he blackened his guilt by proceeding to take me into custody, with a right of patronage that left his former criminality far behind.

"Now you see, Joseph and wife," said Pumblechook, as he took me by the arm above the elbow, "I am one of them that always go right through with what they've begun. This boy must be bound out of hand. That's *my* way. Bound out of hand."

"Goodness knows, Uncle Pumblechook," said my sister (grasping the money), "we're deeply beholden to you."

"Never mind me, mum," returned that diabolical corn-chandler. "A pleasure's a pleasure all the world over. But this boy, you know; we must have him bound. I said I'd see to it—to tell you the truth."

The Justices were sitting in the Town Hall near at hand, and we at once went over to have me bound apprentice to Joe in the Magisterial presence. I say we went over but I was pushed over by Pumblechook, exactly as if I had that moment picked a pocket or fired a rick; indeed, it was the general impression in Court that I had been taken red-handed, for, as Pumblechook shoved me before him through the crowd, I heard some people say, "What's he done?" and others, "He's a young 'un too, but looks bad, don't he?" One person of mild and benevolent aspect even gave me a tract ornamented with a woodcut of a malevolent young man in a perfect sausage-shop of fetters, and entitled, TO BE READ IN MY CELL.

The Hall was a queer place, I thought, with higher pews in it than a church—and with people hanging over the pews looking on—and with mighty Justices (one with a powdered head) leaning back in chairs, with folded arms, or taking snuff, or going to sleep, or writing, or reading the newspapers—and with some shining black portraits on the walls, which my unartistic eye regarded as a composition of hard bake and sticking-plaster. Here, in a corner, my indentures were duly signed and attested, and I was "bound"; Mr. Pumblechook holding me all the while as if we had looked in on our way to the scaffold to have those little preliminaries disposed of.

When we had come out again, and had got rid of the boys who had been put into great spirits by the expectation of seeing me publicly tortured, and who were much disappointed to find that my friends were merely rallying round me, we went back to Pumblechook's. And there my sister became so excited by the twenty-five guineas, that nothing would serve her but we must have a dinner out of that windfall at the Blue Boar, and that Pumblechook must go over in his chaise-cart and bring the Hubbles and Mr. Wopsle.

It was agreed to be done; and a most melancholy day I passed. For it inscrutably appeared to stand to reason, in the minds of the whole company, that I was an excrescence on the entertainment. And to make it worse, they all asked me from time to time—in short, whenever they had nothing else to do—why I didn't enjoy myself. And what could I possibly do then but say I *was* enjoying myself—when I wasn't?

However, they were grown up and had their own way, and they made the most of it. That swindling Pumblechook, exalted into the beneficent contriver of the whole occasion, actually took the top of the table; and, when he addressed them on the subject of my being bound, and fiendishly congratulated them on my being liable to imprisonment if I played at cards, drank strong liquors, kept late hours or bad company, or indulged in other vagaries which the form of my indentures appeared to contemplate as next to inevitable, he placed me standing on a chair beside him to illustrate his remarks.

My only other remembrances of the great festival are, that they wouldn't let me go to sleep, but whenever they saw me dropping off, woke me up and told me to enjoy myself. That, rather late in the evening Mr. Wopsle gave us Collins's Ode, and threw his blood-stain'd sword in thunder down with such effect that a waiter came in and said: "The Commercials underneath sent up their compliments, and it wasn't the Tumbler's Arms." That, they were all in excellent spirits on the road home, and sang O Lady Fair! Mr. Wopsle taking the bass, and asserting with a tremendously strong voice (in reply to the inquisitive bore who leads that piece of music in a most impertinent manner, by wanting to know all about everybody's private affairs), that *he* was the man with his white locks flowing, and that he was upon the whole the weakest pilgrim going.

Finally, I remember that when I got into my little bedroom I was truly wretched, and had a strong conviction on me that I should never like Joe's trade. I had liked it once, but once was not now.

Fourteen

I T IS A MOST MISERABLE THING TO FEEL ASHAMED OF HOME. There may be black ingratitude in the thing, and the punishment may be retributive and well deserved; but that it is a miserable thing, I can testify.

Home had never been a very pleasant place to me, because of my sister's temper. But Joe had sanctified it, and I had believed in it. I had believed in the best parlor as a most elegant saloon; I had believed in the front door as a mysterious portal of the Temple of State whose solemn opening was attended with a sacrifice of roast fowls; I had believed in the kitchen as a chaste though not magnificent apartment; I had believed in the forge as the glowing road to manhood and independence. Within a single year all this was changed. Now it was all coarse and common, and I would not have had Miss Havisham and Estella see it on any account.

How much of my ungracious condition of mind may have been my own fault, how much Miss Havisham's, how much my sister's, is now of no moment to me or to anyone. The change was made in me; the thing was done. Well or ill done, excusably or inexcusably, it was done.

Once it had seemed to me that when I should at last roll up my shirt-sleeves and go into the forge, Joe's 'prentice, I should be distinguished and happy. Now the reality was in my hold, I only felt that I was dusty with the dust of small coal, and that I had a weight upon my daily remembrance to which the anvil was a feather. There have been occasions in my later life (I suppose as in most lives) when I have felt for a time as if a thick curtain had fallen on all its interest and romance, to shut me out from anything save dull endurance anymore. Never has that curtain dropped so heavy and blank as when my way in life lay stretched out straight before me through the newly-entered road of apprenticeship to Joe.

I remember that at a later period of my "time" I used to stand about the churchyard on Sunday evenings when night was falling, comparing my own perspective with the windy marsh view, and making out some likeness between them by thinking how flat and low both were, and how on both there came an unknown way and a dark mist and then the sea. I was quite as dejected on the first working-day of my apprenticeship as in that after-time; but I am glad to know that I never breathed a murmur to Joe while my indentures lasted. It is about the only thing I *am* glad to know of myself in that connection.

For, though it includes what I proceed to add, all the merit of what I proceed to add was Joe's. It was not because I was faithful, but because Joe was faithful, that I never ran away and went for a soldier or a sailor. It was not because I had a strong sense of the virtue of industry, but because Joe had a strong sense of the virtue of industry, that I worked with tolerable zeal against the grain. It is not possible to know how far the influence of any amiable honest-hearted duty-doing man flies out into the world; but it is very possible to know how it has touched one's self in going by, and I know right well that any good that intermixed itself with my apprenticeship came of plain contented Joe, and not of restlessly aspiring discontented me.

What I wanted who can say? How can *I* say when I never knew? What I dreaded was, that in some unlucky hour I, being at my grimiest and commonest, should lift up my eyes and see Estella looking in at one of the wooden windows of the forge. I was haunted by the fear that she would, sooner or later, find me out, with a black face and hands, doing the coarsest part of my work, and would exult over me and despise me. Often after dark, when I was pulling the bellows for Joe and we were singing Old Clem, and when the thought how we used to sing it at Miss Havisham's would seem to show me Estella's face in the fire with her pretty hair fluttering in the wind and her eyes scorning me—often at such a time I would look toward those panels of black night in the wall which the wooden windows then were, and would fancy that I saw her just drawing her face away, and would believe that she had come at last.

After that, when we went in to supper, the place and the meal would have a more homely look than ever, and I would feel more ashamed of home than ever in my own ungracious breast.

Fifteen

AS I WAS GETTING TOO BIG FOR MR. WOPSLE'S GREAT-aunt's room, my education under that preposterous female terminated. Not, however, until Biddy had imparted to me everything she knew, from the little catalogue of prices to a comic song she had once bought for a half-penny. Although the only coherent parts of the latter piece of literature were the open lines,

> When I went to Lunnon town sirs
> Too rul loo rul
> Too rul loo rul
>
> Wasn't I done very brown sirs
> Too rul loo rul
> Too rul loo rul

—still, in my desire to be wiser, I got this composition by heart with the utmost gravity; nor do I recollect that I questioned its merit, except that I thought (as I still do) the amount of Too rul somewhat in excess of the poetry. In my hunger for information I made proposals to Mr. Wopsle to bestow some intellectual crumbs upon me: with which he kindly complied. As it turned out, however, that he only wanted me for a dramatic lay figure, to be contradicted and embraced and wept over and bullied and clutched and stabbed and knocked about in a variety of ways, I soon declined that course of instruction; though not until Mr. Wopsle in his poetic fury had severely mauled me.

Whatever I acquired I tried to impart to Joe. This statement sounds so well that I cannot in my conscience let it pass unexplained. I wanted to make Joe less ignorant and common, that he might be worthier of my society and less open to Estella's reproach.

The old Battery out on the marshes was our place of study, and a broken slate and a short piece of slate-pencil were our educational implements: to which Joe always added a pipe of tobacco. I never knew Joe to remember anything from one Sunday to another, or to acquire, under my tuition, any piece of information whatever. Yet he would smoke his pipe at the Battery with a far more sagacious air than anywhere else—I would even say with a learned air—as if he considered himself to be advancing immensely. Dear fellow, I hope he did.

It was pleasant and quiet out there, with the sails on the river passing beyond the earthwork, and sometimes, when the tide was low, looking as if they belonged to sunken ships that were still sailing on at the bottom of the water. Whenever I watched the vessels standing out to sea with their white sails spread, I somehow thought of Miss Havisham and Estella; and whenever the light struck aslant afar off, upon a cloud of sail or green hillside or water-line, it was just the same. Miss Havisham and Estella and the strange house and the strange life appeared to have something to do with everything that was picturesque.

One Sunday when Joe, greatly enjoying his pipe, had so plumed himself on being "most awful dull," that I had given him up for the day, I lay on the earthwork for some time with my chin on my hand descrying traces of Miss Havisham and Estella all over the prospect, in the sky and in the water, until at last I resolved to mention a thought concerning them that had been much in my head.

"Joe," said I; "don't you think I ought to make Miss Havisham a visit?"

"Well, Pip," returned Joe, slowly considering. "What for?"

"What for, Joe? What is any visit made for?"

"There is some wisits p'r'aps," said Joe, "as forever remains open to the question, Pip. But in regard of wisiting Miss Havisham. She might think you wanted something—expected something of her."

"Don't you think I might say that I did not, Joe?"

"You might, old chap," said Joe. "And she might credit it. Similarly she mightn't."

Joe felt, as I did, that he had made a point there, and he pulled hard at his pipe to keep himself from weakening it by repetition.

"You see, Pip," Joe pursued, as soon as he was past that danger, "Miss Havisham done the handsome thing by you. When Miss Havisham done the handsome thing by you, she called me back to say to me as that were all."

"Yes, Joe. I heard her."

"ALL," Joe repeated, very emphatically.

"Yes, Joe. I tell you, I heard her."

"Which I meantersay, Pip, it might be that her meaning were—Make a end on it!—As you was!—Me to the North and you to the South!—Keep in sunders!"

I had thought of that too, and it was very far from comforting to me to find that he had thought of it; for it seemed to render it more probable.

"But, Joe."

"Yes, old chap."

"Here am I, getting on in the first year of my time, and since the day of my being bound I have never thanked Miss Havisham, or asked after her, or shown that I remember her."

"That's true, Pip; and unless you was to turn her out a set of shoes all four round—and which I meantersay as even a set of shoes all four round might not act acceptable as a present, in a total vacancy of hoofs—"

"I don't mean that sort of remembrance, Joe; I don't mean a present."

But Joe had got the idea of a present in his head and must harp upon it. "Or even," said he, "if you was helped to knocking her up a new chain for the front door—or say a gross or two of shark-headed screws for general use—or some light fancy article, such as a toasting-fork when she took her muffins—or a gridiron when she took a sprat or such like—"

"I don't mean any present at all, Joe," I interposed.

"Well," said Joe, still harping on it as though I had particularly pressed it, "if I was yourself, Pip, I wouldn't. No, I would *not*. For what's a door-chain when she's got one always up? And shark-headers is open to misrepresentations. And if it was a toasting-fork, you'd go into brass and do yourself no credit. And the oncommonest workman can't show himself oncommon in a gridiron—for a gridiron is a gridiron," said Joe, steadfastly impressing it upon me, as if he were endeavoring to rouse me from a fixed delusion, "and you may haim at what you like, but a gridiron it will come out, either by your leave or again your leave, and you can't help yourself—"

"My dear Joe," I cried, in desperation, taking hold of his coat, "don't go on in that way. I never thought of making Miss Havisham any present."

"No, Pip," Joe assented, as if he had been contending for that all along; "and what I say to you is, you are right, Pip."

"Yes, Joe; but what I wanted to say was, that as we are rather slack just now, if you could give me a half-holiday tomorrow, I think I would go up town and make a call on Miss Est—Havisham."

"Which her name," said Joe, gravely, "ain't Estavisham, Pip, unless she have been rechristened."

"I know, Joe, I know. It was a slip of mine. What do you think of it, Joe?"

In brief, Joe thought that if I thought well of it, he thought well of it. But he was particular in stipulating that if I were not received with cordiality, or if

I were not encouraged to repeat my visit as a visit which had no ulterior object but was simply one of gratitude for a favor received, then this experimental trip should have no successor. By these conditions I promised to abide.

Now Joe kept a journeyman at weekly wages whose name was Orlick. He pretended that his Christian name was Dolge—a clear impossibility—but he was a fellow of that obstinate disposition that I believe him to have been the prey of no delusion in this particular, but willfully to have imposed that name upon the village as an affront to its understanding. He was a broad-shouldered, loose-limbed, swarthy fellow of great strength, never in a hurry, and always slouching. He never even seemed to come to his work on purpose, but would slouch in as if by mere accident; and when he went to the Jolly Bargemen to eat his dinner, or went away at night, he would slouch out like Cain or the Wandering Jew, as if he had no idea where he was going and no intention of ever coming back. He lodged at a sluice-keeper's out on the marshes, and on working days would come slouching from his hermitage, with his hands in his pockets and his dinner loosely tied in a bundle round his neck and dangling on his back. On Sundays he mostly lay all day on sluice gates, or stood against ricks and barns. He always slouched, locomotively, with his eyes on the ground; and, when accosted or otherwise required to raise them, he looked up in a half resentful, half puzzled way, as though the only thought he ever had, was, that it was rather an odd and injurious fact that he should never be thinking.

This morose journeyman had no liking for me. When I was very small and timid, he gave me to understand that the Devil lived in a black corner of the forge, and that he knew the fiend very well; also that it was necessary to make up the fire once in every seven years with a live boy, and that I might consider myself fuel. When I became Joe's 'prentice, he was perhaps confirmed in some suspicion that I should displace him; howbeit, he liked me still less. Not that he ever said anything, or did anything openly importing hostility; I only noticed that he always beat his sparks in my direction, and that whenever I sang Old Clem he came in out of time.

Dolge Orlick was at work and present, next day, when I reminded Joe of my half-holiday. He said nothing at the moment, for he and Joe had just got a piece of hot iron between them and I was at the bellows; but by-and-by he said, leaning on his hammer:

"Now, master! Sure you're not a going to favor only one of us. If Young Pip has a half-holiday, do as much for Old Orlick." I suppose he was about five-and-twenty, but he usually spoke of himself as an ancient person.

"Why, what'll you do with a half-holiday, if you get it?" said Joe.

"What'll *I* do with it? What'll *he* do with it? I'll do as much with it as *him,* said Orlick.

"As to Pip, he's going uptown," said Joe.

"Well, then, as to Old Orlick, *he's* going uptown," retorted that worthy. "Two can go uptown. Tan't only one wot can go uptown."

"Don't lose your temper," said Joe.

"Shall if I like," growled Orlick. "Some and their up-towning? Now, master! Come. No favoring in this shop. Be a man."

The master refusing to entertain the subject until the journeyman was in a better temper, Orlick plunged at the furnace, drew out a red-hot bar, made at me with it as if he were going to run it through my body, whisked it round my head, laid it on the anvil, hammered it out—as if it were I, I thought, and the sparks were my spirting blood—and finally said, when he had hammered himself hot and the iron cold, and he again leaned on his hammer:

"Now, master!"

"Are you all right now?" demanded Joe.

"Ah! I am all right," said gruff Old Orlick.

"Then, as in general you stick to your work as well as most men," said Joe, "let it be a half-holiday for all."

My sister had been standing silent in the yard, within hearing—she was a most unscrupulous spy and listener—and she instantly looked in at one of the windows.

"Like you, you fool!" said she to Joe, "giving holidays to great idle hulkers like that. You are a rich man, upon my life, to waste wages in that way. I wish *I* was his master!"

"You'd be everybody's master, if you durst," retorted Orlick, with an ill-favored grin.

("Let her alone," said Joe.)

"I'd be a match for all noodles and all rogues," returned my sister, beginning to work herself into a mighty rage. "And I couldn't be a match for the noodles without being a match for your master, who's the dunderheaded king of the noodles. And I couldn't be a match for the rogues, without being a match for you, who are the blackest-looking and the worst rogue between this and France. Now!"

"You're a foul shrew, Mother Gargery," growled the journeyman. "If that makes a judge of rogues, you ought to be a good 'un."

("Let her alone, will you?" said Joe.)

"What did you say?" cried my sister, beginning to scream. "What did you say? What did that fellow Orlick say to me, Pip? What did he call me, with my husband standing by? O! O! O!" Each of these exclamations was a shriek; and I must remark of my sister, what is equally true of all the violent women I have ever seen, that passion was no excuse for her, because it is undeniable that, instead of lapsing into passion, she consciously and deliberately took extraordinary pains to force herself into it, and became blindly furious by regular stages; "what was the name he gave me before the base man who swore to defend me? O! Hold me! O!"

"Ah-h-h!" growled the journeyman, between his teeth, "I'd hold you, if you was my wife. I'd hold you under the pump, and choke it out of you."

("I tell you, let her alone," said Joe.)

"O! To hear him!" cried my sister, with a clap of her hands and a scream together—which was her next stage. "To hear the names he's giving me! That Orlick! In my own house! Me, a married woman! With my husband standing by! O! O!" Here my sister, after a fit of clappings and screamings, beat her hands upon her bosom and upon her knees, and threw her cap off and pulled her hair down—which were the last stages on her road to frenzy. Being by this time a perfect Fury and a complete success, she made a dash at the door, which I had fortunately locked.

What could the wretched Joe do now, after his disregarded parenthetical interruptions, but stand up to his journeyman, and ask him what he meant by interfering betwixt himself and Mrs. Joe; and further, whether he was man enough to come on? Old Orlick felt that the situation admitted of nothing less than coming on, and was on his defense straightway; so, without so much as pulling off their singed and burned aprons, they went at one another like two giants. But if any man in that neighborhood could stand up long against Joe I never saw the man. Orlick, as if he had been of no more account than the pale young gentleman, was very soon among the coal-dust and in no hurry to come out of it. Then Joe unlocked the door and picked up my sister, who had dropped insensible at the window (but who had seen the fight first, I think), and who was carried into the house and laid down, and who was recommended to revive, and would do nothing but struggle and clench her hands in Joe's hair. Then came that singular calm and silence which succeed all uproars; and then, with the vague sensation which I have always connected with that lull—namely, that it was Sunday, and somebody was dead—I went upstairs to dress myself.

When I came down again I found Joe and Orlick sweeping up, without any other traces of discomposure than a slit in one of Orlick's nostrils, which was neither expressive nor ornamental. A pot of beer had appeared from the Jolly Bargemen, and they were sharing it by turns in a peaceable manner. The lull had a sedative and philosophic influence on Joe, who followed me out into the road to say, as a parting observation that might do me good, "On the Ram-page, Pip, and off the Ram-page, Pip—such is Life!"

With what absurd emotions (for we think the feelings that are very serious in a man quite comical in a boy) I found myself again going to Miss Havisham's matters little here. Nor how I passed and repassed the gate many times before I could make up my mind to ring; nor how I debated whether I should go away without ringing; nor how I should undoubtedly have gone, if my time had been my own to come back.

Miss Sarah Pocket came to the gate. No Estella.

"How, then? You here again?" said Miss Pocket. "What do you want?"

When I said that I only came to see how Miss Havisham was, Sarah evidently deliberated whether or no she should send me about my business. But unwilling to hazard the responsibility, she let me in, and presently brought the sharp message that I was to "come up."

Everything was unchanged, and Miss Havisham was alone. "Well?" said she, fixing her eyes upon me. "I hope you want nothing? You'll get nothing."

"No, indeed, Miss Havisham. I only wanted you to know that I am doing very well in my apprenticeship, and am always much obliged to you."

"There, there!" with the old restless fingers. "Come now and then; come on your birthday. Ay!" she cried suddenly, turning herself and her chair toward me, "you are looking round for Estella? Hey?"

I had been looking round, in fact, for Estella; and I stammered that I hoped she was well.

"Abroad," said Miss Havisham; "educating for a lady; far out of reach; prettier than ever; admired by all who see her. Do you feel that you have lost her?"

There was such a malignant enjoyment in her utterance of the last words, and she broke into such a disagreeable laugh, that I was at a loss what to say. She spared me the trouble of considering by dismissing me. When the gate was closed upon me by Sarah, of the walnut-shell countenance, I felt more than ever dissatisfied with my home and with my trade and with everything; and that was all I took by *that* motion.

As I was loitering along the High Street, looking in disconsolately at the shop-windows, and thinking what I should buy if I were a gentleman, who should come out of the bookshop but Mr. Wopsle. Mr. Wopsle had in his hand the affecting tragedy of George Barnwell, in which he had that moment invested sixpence, with the view of heaping every word of it on the head of Pumblechook, with whom he was going to drink tea. No sooner did he see me than he appeared to consider that a special Providence had put a 'prentice in his way to be read at; and he laid hold of me, and insisted on my accompanying him to the Pumblechookian parlor. As I knew it would be miserable at home, and as the nights were dark and the way was dreary, and almost any companionship on the road was better than none, I made no great resistance; consequently we turned into Pumblechook's just as the street and the shops were lighting up.

As I never assisted at any other representation of George Barnwell, I don't know how long it may usually take; but I know very well that it took until past nine o'clock that night, and that when Mr. Wopsle got into Newgate I thought he never would go to the scaffold, he became so much slower than at any former period of his disgraceful career. I thought it a little too much that he should complain of being cut short in his flower after all, as if he had not been running to seed, leaf after leaf, ever since he was taken up. This, however, was a mere question of length and wearisomeness. What stung me was the identification of the whole affair with my unoffending self. When Barnwell began to go wrong, I declare that I felt positively apologetic, Pumblechook's indignant stare so taxed me with it. Wopsle, too, took pains to present me in the worst light. At once ferocious and maudlin, I was made to murder my uncle with no extenuating circumstances whatever; Millwood put me down in argument on every occasion; it became sheer monomania in my master's daughter to care a button for me; and all I can say for my gasping and procrastinating conduct on the fatal morning is, that it was worthy of the general feebleness of my character. Even after I was happily hanged, and Wopsle had closed the book, Pumblechook sat staring at me, and shaking his head, and saying, "Take warning, boy! take warning!" as if it were a well-known fact that, in my private capacity, I contemplated murdering a near relation, provided I could only induce one to have the weakness to become my benefactor.

It was a very dark night when it was all over, and when I set out with Mr. Wopsle on the walk home. Beyond town we found a heavy mist out, and it fell wet and thick. The turnpike lamp was a blur, quite out of the lamp's usual place apparently, and its rays looked solid substance on the fog. We were noticing this, and saying how that the mist rose with a change of wind from a certain quarter of our marshes, when we came upon a man slouching under the lee of the turnpike house.

"Halloa!" we said, stopping. "Orlick, there?"

"Ah!" he answered, slouching out. "I was standing by a minute, on the chance of company."

"You are late," I remarked.

Orlick not unnaturally answered, "Well? And *you're* late."

"We have been," said Mr. Wopsle, exalted with his late performance—"we have been indulging, Mr. Orlick, in an intellectual evening."

Old Orlick growled, as if he had nothing to say about that, and we all went on together. I asked him presently whether he had been spending his half-holiday up and down town?

"Yes," said he, "all of it. I come in behind yourself. I didn't see you, but I must have been pretty close behind you. By-the-by, the guns is going again."

"At the Hulks?" said I.

"Ay! There's some of the birds flown from the cages. The guns have been going since dark, about. You'll hear one presently."

In effect, we had not walked many yards further when the well-remembered boom came towards us, deadened by the mist, and heavily rolled away along the low grounds by the river, as if it were pursuing and threatening the fugitives.

"A good night for cutting off in," said Orlick. "We'd be puzzled how to bring down a jailbird on the wing tonight."

The subject was a suggestive one to me, and I thought about it in silence. Mr. Wopsle, as the ill-requited uncle of the evening's tragedy, fell to meditating aloud in his garden at Camberwell. Orlick, with his hands in his pockets, slouched heavily at my side. It was very dark, very wet, very muddy, and so we splashed along. Now and then the sound of the signal cannon broke upon us again, and again rolled sulkily along the course of the river. I kept myself to myself and my thoughts. Mr. Wopsle died amiably at Camberwell, and exceedingly game on Bosworth Field, and in the greatest agonies at Glastonbury. Orlick sometimes growled, "Beat it out, beat it out—old Clem! With a clink for the stout—old Clem!" I thought he had been drinking, but he was not drunk.

Thus we came to the village. The way by which we approached it took us past the Three Jolly Bargemen, which we were surprised to find—it being eleven o'clock—in a state of commotion, with the door wide open, and unwonted lights, that had been hastily caught up and put down, scattered about. Mr. Wopsle dropped in to ask what was the matter (surmising that a convict had been taken), but came running out in a great hurry.

"There's something wrong," said he, without stopping, "up at your place, Pip. Run all!"

"What is it?" I asked, keeping up with him. So did Orlick, at my side.

"I can't quite understand. The house seems to have been violently entered when Joe was out. Supposed by convicts. Somebody has been attacked and hurt."

We were running too fast to admit of more being said, and we made no stop until we got into our kitchen. It was full of people; the whole village was there, or in the yard; and there was a surgeon, and there was Joe, and there were a group of women, all on the floor in the midst of the kitchen. The unemployed bystanders drew back when they saw me, and so I became aware of my sister—lying without sense or movement on the bare boards where she had been knocked down by a tremendous blow on the back of the head, dealt by some unknown hand when her face was turned toward the fire—destined never to be on the Ram-page again while she was wife of Joe.

S i x t e e n

WITH MY HEAD FULL OF GEORGE BARNWELL, I WAS AT first disposed to believe that *I* must have had some hand in the attack upon my sister, or at all events that as her near relation, popularly known to be under obligations to her, I was a more legitimate object of suspicion than anyone else. But when, in the clearer light of next morning, I began to reconsider the matter and to hear it discussed around me on all sides, I took another view of the case which was more reasonable.

Joe had been at the Three Jolly Bargemen, smoking his pipe, from a quarter after eight o'clock to a quarter before ten. While he was there my sister had been seen standing at the kitchen door, and had exchanged Good night with a farm-laborer going home. The man could not be more particular as to the time at which he saw her (he got into dense confusion when he tried to be) than that it must have been before nine. When Joe went home at five minutes before ten he found her struck down on the floor, and promptly called in assistance. The fire had not then burned unusually low, nor was the snuff of the candle very long; the candle, however, had been blown out.

Nothing had been taken away from any part of the house. Neither, beyond the blowing out of the candle—which stood on a table between the door and my sister, and was behind her when she stood facing the fire and was struck—was there any disarrangement of the kitchen, excepting such as she herself had made in falling and bleeding. But there was one remarkable piece of evidence on the spot. She had been struck with something blunt and heavy on the head and spine; after the blows were dealt, something heavy had been thrown down at her with considerable violence as she lay on her face. And on the ground beside her, when Joe picked her up, was a convict's leg-iron which had been filed asunder.

Now Joe, examining this iron with a smith's eye, declared it to have been filed asunder some time ago. The hue and cry going off to the Hulks, and people coming thence to examine the iron, Joe's opinion was corroborated. They did not undertake to say when it had left the prison-ships; to which it undoubtedly had once belonged; but they claimed to know for certain that that particular manacle had not been worn by either of two convicts who had escaped last night. Further, one of those two was already retaken, and had not freed himself of his iron.

Knowing what I knew, I set up an inference of my own here. I believed the iron to be my convict's iron—the iron I had seen and heard him filing at on the marshes—but my mind did not accuse him of having put it to its latest use. For I believed one of two other persons to have become possessed of it, and to have turned it to this cruel account. Either Orlick or the strange man who had shown me the file.

Now as to Orlick, he had gone to town exactly as he told us when we picked him up at the turnpike; he had been seen about town all the evening, he had been in divers companies in several public houses, and he had come back with myself and Mr. Wopsle. There was nothing against him save the quarrel; and my sister had quarreled with him, and with everybody else about her, ten thousand times. As to the strange man, if he had come back for his two bank-notes there could have been no dispute about them, because my sister was fully prepared to restore them. Besides, there had been no altercation; the assailant had come in so silent and suddenly that she had been felled before she could look round.

It was horrible to think that I had provided the weapon, however undesignedly, but I could hardly think otherwise. I suffered unspeakable trouble while I considered and reconsidered whether I should at last dissolve that spell of my childhood, and tell Joe all the story. For months afterward I every day settled the question finally in the negative, and reopened and reargued it next morning. The contention came, after all, to this; the secret was such an old one now, had so grown into me and become a part of myself, that I could not tear it away. In addition to the dread that, having led up to so much mischief, it would be now more likely than ever to alienate Joe from me if he believed it, I had the further restraining dread that he would not believe it, but would assort it with the fabulous dogs and veal cutlets as a monstrous invention. However, I temporized with myself, of course—for, was I not wavering between right and wrong, when the thing is always done?—and resolved to make a full disclosure if I should see any such new occasion as a new chance of helping in the discovery of the assailant.

The Constables, and the Bow Street men from London—for this happened in the days of the extinct red-waistcoated police—were about the house for a week or two, and did pretty much what I have heard and read of like authorities doing in other such cases. They took up several obviously wrong people, and they ran their heads very hard against wrong ideas, and persisted in trying to fit the circumstances to the ideas, instead of trying to extract ideas from the circumstances. Also, they stood about the door of the Jolly Bargemen, with knowing and reserved looks, that filled the whole neighborhood with admiration; and they had a mysterious manner of taking their drink, that was almost as good as taking the culprit. But not quite, for they never did it.

Long after these constitutional powers had dispersed my sister lay very ill in bed. Her sight was disturbed, so that she saw objects multiplied, and grasped at visionary teacups and wineglasses instead of realities; her hearing was greatly impaired; her memory also; and her speech was unintelligible. When at last she came round so far as to be helped downstairs, it was still necessary to keep my slate always by her, that she might indicate in writing what she could not indicate in speech. As she was (very bad handwriting apart) a more than indifferent speller, and as Joe was a more than indifferent reader, extraordinary complications arose between them, which I was always called in to solve. The administration of mutton instead of medicine, the substitution of Tea for Joe, and the baker for bacon, were among the mildest of my own mistakes.

However, her temper was greatly improved and she was patient. A tremulous uncertainty of the action of all her limbs soon became a part of her regular state, and afterward, at intervals of two or three months, she would often put her hands to her head and would then remain for about a week at a time in some gloomy aberration of mind. We were at a loss to find a suitable attendant for her, until a circumstance happened conveniently to relieve us. Mr. Wopsle's great-aunt conquered a confirmed habit of living into which she had fallen, and Biddy became a part of our establishment.

It may have been about a month after my sister's reappearance in the kitchen when Biddy came to us with a small speckled box containing the whole of her worldly effects, and became a blessing to the household. Above all, she was a blessing to Joe, for the dear old fellow was sadly cut up by the constant contemplation of the wreck of his wife, and had been accustomed, while attending on her all the evening, to turn to me every now and then, and say, with his blue eyes moistened, "Such a fine figure of a woman as she once were, Pip!" Biddy instantly taking the cleverest charge of her, as though she had studied her from infancy, Joe became able in some sort to appreciate the greater quiet of his life, and to get down to the Jolly Bargemen now and then, for a change that did him good. It was characteristic of the police people that they had all more or less suspected poor Joe (though he never knew it), and that they had to a man concurred in regarding him as one of the deepest spirits they had ever encountered.

Biddy's first triumph in her new office was to solve a difficulty that had completely vanquished me. I had tried hard at it, but had made nothing of it. Thus it was:

Again and again and again my sister had traced upon the slate a character that looked like a curious T, and then, with the utmost eagerness, had called our attention to it as something she particularly wanted. I had in vain tried everything producible that began with a T, from tar to toast and tub. At length it had come into my head that the sign looked like a hammer, and on my lustily calling that word in my sister's ear she had begun to hammer on the table, and expressed a qualified assent. Thereupon I had brought in all our hammers, one after another, but without avail. Then I bethought me of a crutch, the shape being much the same, and I borrowed one of a cripple in the village, and displayed it to my sister with considerable confidence. But she shook her head to that extent when she was shown it, that we were terrified lest, in her weak and shattered state, she should dislocate her neck.

When my sister found that Biddy was very quick to understand her, this mysterious sign immediately reappeared on the slate. Biddy looked thoughtfully at it, heard my explanation, looked thoughtfully at my sister, looked thoughtfully at Joe (who was always represented on the slate by his initial letter), and ran into the forge, followed by Joe and me.

"Why, of course!" cried Biddy, with an exultant face. "Don't you see? It's *him!*"

Orlick, without a doubt! She had lost his name, and could only signify him by his hammer. We told him why we wanted him to come into the kitchen, and he slowly laid down his hammer, wiped his brow with his arm, took another wipe at it with his apron, and came slouching out, with a curious loose, vagabond bend in the knees that strongly distinguished him.

I confess that I expected to see my sister denounce him, and that I was disappointed by the different result. She manifested the greatest anxiety to be on good terms with him; was evidently much pleased by his being at length produced, and motioned that she would have him given something to drink. She watched his countenance as if she were particularly wishful to be assured that he took kindly to his reception; she showed every possible desire to conciliate him; and there was an air of humble propitiation in all she did, such as I have seen pervade the bearing of a frightened child toward a hard master. After that day, a day rarely passed without her drawing the hammer on her slate, and without Orlick's slouching in and standing doggedly before her, as if he knew no more than I did what to make of it.

S e v e n t e e n

I NOW FELL INTO A REGULAR ROUTINE OF APPRENTICESHIP life, which was varied, beyond the limits of the village and the marshes, by no more remarkable circumstance than the arrival of my birthday and my paying another visit to Miss Havisham. I found Miss Sarah Pocket still on duty at the gate; I found Miss Havisham just as I had left her; and she spoke of Estella in the very same way, if not in the very same words. The interview lasted but a few minutes, and she gave me a guinea when I was going, and told me to come again on my next birthday. I may mention at once that this became an annual custom. I tried to decline taking the guinea on the first occasion, but with no better effect than causing her to ask me, very angrily, if I expected more? Then, and after that, I took it.

So unchanging was the dull old house, the yellow light in the darkened room, the faded spectre in the chair by the dressing-table glass, that I felt as if the stopping of the clocks had stopped Time in that mysterious place, and, while I and everything else outside it grew older, it stood still. Daylight never entered the house as to my thoughts and remembrances of it, any more than as to the actual fact. It bewildered me, and under its influence I continued at heart to hate my trade and to be ashamed of home.

Imperceptibly I became conscious of a change in Biddy, however. Her shoes came up at the heel, her hair grew bright and neat, her hands were always clean. She was not beautiful—she was common, and could not be like Estella—but she was pleasant and wholesome and sweet-tempered. She had not been with us more than a year (I remember her being newly out of mourning at the time it struck me), when I observed to myself one evening that she had curiously thoughtful and attentive eyes; eyes that were very pretty and very good.

It came of my lifting up my own eyes from a task I was poring at—writing some passages from a book, to improve myself in two ways at once by a sort of stratagem—and seeing Biddy observant of what I was about. I laid down my pen, and Biddy stopped in her needlework without laying it down.

"Biddy," said I, "how do you manage it? Either I am very stupid or you are very clever."

"What is it that I manage? I don't know," returned Biddy, smiling.

She managed our whole domestic life, and wonderfully too; but I did not mean that, though that made what I did mean more surprising.

"How do you manage, Biddy," said I, "to learn everything that I learn, and always to keep up with me?" I was beginning to be rather vain of my knowledge, for I spent my birthday guineas on it, and set aside the greater part of my pocket-money for similar investment; though I have no doubt now that the little I knew was extremely dear at the price.

"I might as well ask you," said Biddy, "how *you* manage?"

"No; because when I come in from the forge of a night, anyone can see me turning to at it. But you never turn to at it, Biddy."

"I suppose I must catch it—like a cough," said Biddy, quietly; and went on with her sewing.

Pursuing my idea as I leaned back in my wooden chair and looked at Biddy sewing away with her head on one side, I began to think her rather an extraordinary girl. For I called to my mind now that she was equally accomplished in the terms of our trade, and the names of our different sorts of work, and our various tools. In short, whatever I knew, Biddy knew. Theoretically, she was already as good a blacksmith as I, or better.

"You are one of those, Biddy," said I, "who make the most of every chance. You never had a chance before you came here, and see how improved you are!"

Biddy looked at me for an instant, and went on with her sewing. "I was your first teacher though; wasn't I?" said she, as she sewed.

"Biddy!" I exclaimed in amazement. "Why, you are crying!"

"No, I am not," said Biddy, looking up and laughing. "What put that in your head?"

What could have put it in my head but the glistening of a tear as it dropped on her work? I sat silent, recalling what a drudge she had been until Mr. Wopsle's great-aunt successfully overcame that bad habit of living, so highly desirable to be got rid of by some people. I recalled the hopeless circumstances by which she had been surrounded in the miserable little shop and the miserable little noisy evening school, with that miserable old bundle of incompetence always to be dragged and shouldered. I reflected that even in those untoward times there must have been latent in Biddy what was now developed or developing; for in my first uneasiness and discontent I had turned to her, as a matter of course, to help me. Biddy sat quietly sewing, shedding no more tears, and while I looked at her, and thought about it all, it occurred to me that perhaps I had not been sufficiently grateful to Biddy. I might have been too reserved, and should have patronized her more (though I did not use that precise word in my meditations) with my confidence.

"Yes, Biddy," I observed, when I had done turning it over, "you were my first teacher, and that at a time when we little thought of ever being together like this, in this kitchen."

"Ah, poor thing!" replied Biddy; and it was like her self-forgetfulness to transfer the remark to my sister, and to get up and be busy about her, making her more comfortable; "that's sadly true!"

"Well," said I, "we must talk together a little more, as we used to do. And I must consult you a little more, as I used to do. Let us have a quiet walk on the marshes next Sunday, Biddy, and a long chat."

My sister was never left alone now; but Joe more than readily undertook the care of her on that Sunday afternoon, and Biddy and I went out together. It was summer time and lovely weather. When we had passed the village and the church and the churchyard, and were out on the marshes, and began to see the sails of the ships as they sailed on, I began to combine Miss Havisham and Estella with the prospect, in my usual way. When we came to the riverside and sat down on the bank, with the water rippling at our feet, making it all more quiet than it would have been without that sound, I resolved that it was a good time and place for the admission of Biddy into my inner confidence.

"Biddy," said I, after binding her to secrecy, "I want to be a gentleman."

"Oh, I wouldn't, if I was you!" she returned. "I don't think it would answer."

"Biddy," said I, with some severity. "I have particular reasons for wanting to be a gentleman."

"You know best, Pip; but don't you think you are happier as you are?"

"Biddy," I exclaimed, impatiently, "I am not at all happy as I am. I am disgusted with my calling and with my life. I have never taken to either since I was bound. Don't be absurd!"

"Was I absurd?" said Biddy, quietly raising her eyebrows; "I am sorry for that; I didn't mean to be. I only want you to do well, and to be comfortable."

"Well, then, understand once for all that I never shall or can be comfortable—or anything but miserable—there, Biddy!—unless I can lead a very different sort of life from the life I lead now."

"That's a pity!" said Biddy, shaking her head with a sorrowful air.

Now, I too had so often thought it a pity, that, in the singular kind of quarrel with myself which I was always carrying on, I was half inclined to shed tears of vexation and distress when Biddy gave utterance to her sentiment and my own. I told her she was right, and I knew it was much to be regretted, but still it was not to be helped.

"If I could have settled down"; I said to Biddy, plucking up the short grass within reach, much as I had once upon a time pulled my feelings out of my hair and kicked them into the brewery wall: "if I could have settled down and been but half as fond of the forge as I was when I was little, I know it would have been much better for me. You and I and Joe would have wanted nothing then, and Joe and I would perhaps have gone partners when I was out of my time, and I might even have grown up to keep company with you, and we might have sat on this very bank on a fine Sunday, quite different people. I should have been good enough for *you*; shouldn't I, Biddy?"

Biddy sighed as she looked at the ships sailing on, and returned for answer, "Yes; I am not over particular." It scarcely sounded flattering, but I knew she meant well.

"Instead of that," said I, plucking up more grass and chewing a blade or two, "see how I am going on. Dissatisfied and uncomfortable, and—what would it signify to me, being coarse and common, if nobody had told me so!"

Biddy turned her face suddenly toward mine, and looked far more attentively at me than she had looked at the sailing ships.

"It was neither a very true nor a very polite thing to say," she remarked, directing her eyes to the ships again. "Who said it?"

I was disconcerted, for I had broken away without seeing where I was going. It was not to be shuffled off now, however, and I answered, "The beautiful young lady at Miss Havisham's, and she's more beautiful than anybody ever was, and I admire her dreadfully, and I want to be a gentleman on her account." Having made which lunatic confession I began to throw my torn-up grass in the river, as if I had some thoughts of following it.

"Do you want to be a gentleman to spite her or to gain her over?" Biddy quietly asked me, after a pause.

"I don't know," I moodily answered.

"Because, if it is to spite her," Biddy pursued, "I should think—but you know best—that might be better and more independently done by caring nothing for her words. And if it is to gain her over, I should think—but you know best—she was not worth gaining."

Exactly what I myself had thought many times. Exactly what was perfectly manifest to me at the moment. But how could I, a poor dazed village lad, avoid that wonderful inconsistency into which the best and wisest of men fall every day?

"It may be all quite true," said I to Biddy, "but I admire her dreadfully."

In short, I turned over on my face when I came to that and got a good grasp on the hair on each side of my head, and wrenched it well. All the while knowing the madness of my heart to be so very mad and misplaced, that I was quite conscious it would have served my face right if I had lifted it up by my hair and knocked it against the pebbles as a punishment for belonging to such an idiot.

Biddy was the wisest of girls, and she tried to reason no more with me. She put her hand, which was a comfortable hand though roughened by work, upon my hands, one after another, and gently took them out of my hair. Then she softly patted my shoulder in a soothing way, while with my face upon my sleeve I cried a little—exactly as I had done in the brewery yard—and felt vaguely convinced that I was very much ill-used by somebody, or by everybody; I can't say which.

"I am glad of one thing," said Biddy, "and that is, that you have felt you could give me your confidence, Pip. And I am glad of another thing, and that is, that of course you know you may depend upon my keeping it and always so far deserving it. If your first teacher (dear! such a poor one, and so much in need of being taught herself!) had been your teacher at the present time, she thinks she knows what lesson she would set. But it would be a hard one to learn, and you have got beyond her, and it's of no use now." So, with a quiet sigh for me, Biddy rose from the bank, and said, with a fresh and pleasant change of voice, "Shall we walk a little further, or go home?"

"Biddy," I cried, jumping up, putting my arm round her neck, and giving her a kiss, "I shall always tell you everything."

"Till you're a gentleman," said Biddy.

"You know I never shall be, so that's always. Not that I have any occasion to tell you anything, for you know everything I know—as I told you at home the other night."

"Ah!" said Biddy, quite in a whisper, as she looked away at the ships. And then repeated, with her former pleasant change: "Shall we walk a little further, or go home?"

I said to Biddy we would walk a little further, and we did so, and the summer afternoon toned down into the summer evening, and it was very beautiful. I began to consider whether I was not more naturally and wholesomely situated, after all, in these circumstances, than playing beggar my neighbor by candlelight in the room with the stopped clocks, and being despised by Estella. I thought it would be very good for me if I could get her out of my head, with all the rest of those remembrances and fancies, and could go to work determined to relish what I had to do, and stick to it, and make the best of it. I asked myself the question whether I did not surely know that if Estella were beside me at that moment instead of Biddy she would make me miserable? I was obliged to admit that I did know it for a certainty, and I said to myself, "Pip, what a fool you are!"

We talked a good deal as we walked, and all that Biddy said seemed right. Biddy was never insulting or capricious, or Biddy today and somebody else tomorrow; she would have derived only pain, and not pleasure, from giving me pain; she would far rather have wounded her own breast than mine. How could it be, then, that I did not like her much the better of the two?

"Biddy," said I, when we were walking homeward, "I wish you could put me right."

"I wish I could," said Biddy.

"If I could only get myself to fall in love with you—you don't mind my speaking so openly to such an old acquaintance?"

"Oh dear, not at all!" said Biddy. "Don't mind me."

"If I could only get myself to do it, *that* would be the thing for me."

"But you never will, you see," said Biddy.

It did not appear quite so unlikely to me that evening as it would have done if we had discussed it a few hours before. I therefore observed I was not quite sure of that. But Biddy said she *was,* and she said it decisively. In my heart I believed her to be right; and yet I took it rather ill, too, that she should be so positive upon the point.

When we came near the churchyard we had to cross an embankment, and get over a stile near a sluice-gate. There started up, from the gate, or from the rushes, or from the ooze (which was quite in his stagnant way), Old Orlick.

"Hulloa!" he growled; "where are you two going?"

"Where should we be going, but home?"

"Well, then," said he, "I'm jiggered if I don't see you home!"

This penalty of being jiggered was a favorite supposititious case of his. He attached no definite meaning to the word that I am aware of, but used it, like his own pretended Christian name, to affront mankind, and convey an idea of something savagely damaging. When I was younger, I had a general belief that if he had jiggered me personally he would have done it with a sharp and twisted hook.

Biddy was much against his going with us, and said to me in a whisper, "Don't let him come; I don't like him." As I did not like him either, I took the liberty of saying that we thanked him, but we didn't want seeing home. He received that piece of information with a yell of laughter, and dropped back, but came slouching after us at a little distance.

Curious to know whether Biddy suspected him of having had a hand in that murderous attack of which my sister had never been able to give any account, I asked her why she did not like him?

"Oh!" she replied, glancing over her shoulder as he slouched after us, "because I—I am afraid he likes me."

"Did he ever tell you he liked you?" I asked, indignantly.

"No," said Biddy, glancing over her shoulder again, "he never told me so; but he dances at me whenever he can catch my eye."

However novel and peculiar this testimony of attachment, I did not doubt the accuracy of the interpretation. I was very hot indeed upon old Orlick's daring to admire her; as hot as if it were an outrage on myself.

"But it makes no difference to you, you know," said Biddy, calmly.

"No, Biddy, it makes no difference to me; only I don't like it; I don't approve of it."

"Nor I either," said Biddy. "Though *that* makes no difference to you."

"Exactly," said I; "but I must tell you I should have no opinion of you, Biddy, if he danced at you with your own consent."

I kept an eye on Orlick after that night, and, whenever circumstances were favorable to his dancing at Biddy, got before him to obscure that demonstration. He had struck root in Joe's establishment by reason of my sister's sudden fancy for him, or I should have tried to get him dismissed. He quite understood and reciprocated my good intentions, as I had reason to know thereafter.

And now, because my mind was not confused enough before, I complicated its confusion fifty thousand-fold, by having states and seasons when I was clear that Biddy was immeasurably better than Estella, and that the plain honest working life to which I was born had nothing in it to be ashamed of, but offered me sufficient means of self-respect and happiness. At those times I would decide conclusively that my disaffection to dear old Joe and the forge was gone, and that I was growing up in a fair way to be partners with Joe and to keep company with Biddy, when all in a moment some confounding remembrance of the Havisham days would fall upon me like a destructive missile and scatter my wits again. Scattered wits take a long time picking up; and often, before I had got them well together again, they would be dispersed in all directions by one stray thought, that perhaps after all Miss Havisham was going to make my fortune when my time was out.

If my time had run out, it would have left me still at the height of my perplexities, I dare say. It never did run out, however, but was brought to a premature end, as I proceed to relate.

E i g h t e e n

IT WAS IN THE FOURTH YEAR OF MY APPRENTICESHIP TO JOE, and it was a Saturday night. There was a group assembled round the fire at the Three Jolly Bargemen, attentive to Mr. Wopsle as he read the newspaper aloud. Of that group I was one.

A highly popular murder had been committed, and Mr. Wopsle was imbrued in blood to the eyebrows. He gloated over every abhorrent adjective in the description, and identified himself with every witness at the Inquest. He faintly moaned, "I am done for," as the victim, and he barbarously bellowed, "I'll serve you out," as the murderer. He gave the medical testimony, in pointed imitation of our local practitioner; and he piped and shook, as the aged turnpike-keeper who had heard blows, to an extent so very paralytic as to suggest a doubt regarding the mental competency of that witness. The coroner, in Mr. Wopsle's hands, became Timon of Athens; the beadle, Coriolanus. He enjoyed himself thoroughly and we all enjoyed ourselves, and were delightfully comfortable. In this cozy state of mind we came to the verdict, Willful Murder.

Then, and not sooner, I became aware of a strange gentleman leaning over the back of the settle opposite me, looking on. There was an expression of contempt on his face, and he bit the side of a great forefinger as he watched the group of faces. "Well!" said the stranger to Mr. Wopsle, when the reading was done, "you have settled it all to your own satisfaction, I have no doubt?"

Everybody stared and looked up, as if it were the murderer. He looked at everybody coldly and sarcastically.

"Guilty, of course?" said he. "Out with it. Come!"

"Sir," returned Mr. Wopsle, "without having the honor of your acquaintance, I do say Guilty." Upon this we all took courage to unite in a confirmatory murmur.

"I know you do," said the stranger; "I knew you would, I told you so. But now I'll ask you a question. Do you know, or do you not know, that the law of England supposes every man to be innocent until he is proved—proved—to be guilty?"

"Sir," Mr. Wopsle began to reply, "as an Englishman myself, I—"

"Come!" said the stranger, biting his forefinger at him. "Don't evade the question. Either you know it or you don't know it. Which is it to be?"

He stood with his head on one side, and himself on one side, in a bullying, interrogative manner, and he threw his forefinger at Mr. Wopsle—as it were to mark him out—before biting it again.

"Now!" said he. "Do you know it, or don't you know it?"

"Certainly I know it," replied Mr. Wopsle.

"Certainly you know it. Then why didn't you say so at first? Now I'll ask you another question"; taking possession of Mr. Wopsle, as if he had a right to him. "*Do* you know that none of these witnesses have yet been cross-examined?"

Mr. Wopsle was beginning, "I can only say—" when the stranger stopped him.

"What? You won't answer the question, yes or no? Now I'll try you again." Throwing his finger at him again. "Attend to me. Are you aware, or are you not aware, that none of these witnesses have yet been cross-examined? Come, I only want one word from you. Yes or no?"

Mr. Wopsle hesitated, and we all began to conceive rather a poor opinion of him.

"Come!" said the stranger, "I'll help you. You don't deserve help, but I'll help you. Look at that paper you hold in your hand. What is it?"

"What is it?" repeated Mr. Wopsle, eying it, much at a loss.

"Is it," pursued the stranger in his most sarcastic and suspicious manner, "the printed paper you have just been reading from?"

"Undoubtedly."

"Undoubtedly. Now turn to that paper, and tell me whether it distinctly states that the prisoner expressly said that his legal advisers instructed him altogether to reserve his defense?"

"I read that just now," Mr. Wopsle pleaded.

"Never mind what you read just now, sir; I don't ask you what you read. You may read the Lord's Prayer backward, if you like—and, perhaps, have done it before today. Turn to the paper. No, no, no, my friend; not to the top of the column; you know better than that; to the bottom, to the bottom." (We all began to think Mr. Wopsle full of subterfuge.) "Well? Have you found it?"

"Here it is," said Mr. Wopsle.

"Now follow that passage with your eye, and tell me whether it distinctly states that the prisoner expressly said that he was instructed by his legal advisers wholly to reserve his defense? Come! Do you make that of it?"

Mr. Wopsle answered, "Those are not the exact words."

"Not the exact words!" repeated the gentleman, bitterly. "Is that the exact substance?"

"Yes!" said Mr. Wopsle.

"Yes," repeated the stranger, looking round at the rest of the company with his right hand extended toward the witness, Wopsle. "And now I ask you what you say to the conscience of that man who, with that passage before his eyes, can lay his head upon his pillow after having pronounced a fellow-creature guilty, unheard?"

We all began to suspect that Mr. Wopsle was not the man we had thought him, and that he was beginning to be found out.

"And that same man, remember," pursued the gentleman, throwing his finger at Mr. Wopsle heavily; "that same man might be summoned as a jury-man upon this very trial, and, having thus deeply committed himself, might return to the bosom of his family and lay his head upon his pillow, after deliberately swearing that he would well and truly try the issue joined between Our Sovereign Lord the King and the prisoner at the bar, and would a true verdict give according to the evidence, so help him God!"

We were all deeply persuaded that the unfortunate Wopsle had gone too far, and had better stop in his reckless career while there was yet time.

The strange gentleman, with an air of authority not to be disputed, and with a manner expressive of knowing something secret about every one of us that would effectually do for each individual if he chose to disclose it, left the back of the settle, and came into the space between the two settles, in front of the fire, where he remained standing; his left hand in his pocket, and he biting the forefinger of his right.

"From information I have received," said he, looking round at us as we all quailed before him, "I have reason to believe there is a blacksmith among you, by name Joseph—or Joe—Gargery. Which is the man?"

"Here is the man," said Joe.

The strange gentleman beckoned him out of his place, and Joe went.

"You have an apprentice," pursued the stranger, "commonly known as Pip? Is he here?"

"I am here!" I cried.

The stranger did not recognize me, but I recognized him as the gentleman I had met on the stairs on the occasion of my second visit to Miss Havisham. His appearance was too remarkable for me to have forgotten. I had known him the moment I saw him looking over the settle, and now that I stood confronting him with his hand upon my shoulder, I checked off again in detail, his large head, his dark complexion, his deep-set eyes, his bushy black eyebrows, his large watch-chain, his strong black dots of beard and whisker, and even the smell of scented soap on his great hand.

"I wish to have a private conference with you two," said he, when he had surveyed me at his leisure. "It will take a little time. Perhaps we had better go to your place of residence. I prefer not to anticipate my communication here; you will impart as much or as little of it as you please to your friends afterward; I have nothing to do with that."

Amidst a wondering silence we three walked out of the Jolly Bargemen, and in a wondering silence walked home. While going along, the strange gentleman occasionally looked at me, and occasionally bit the side of his finger. As we neared home, Joe, vaguely acknowledging the occasion as an impressive and ceremonious one, went on ahead to open the front door. Our conference was held in the state-parlor, which was feebly lighted by one candle. It began with the strange gentleman's sitting down at the table, drawing the candle to him, and looking over some entries in his pocket-book. He then put up the pocket-book, and set the candle a little aside: after peering round it into the darkness at Joe and me, to ascertain which was which.

"My name," he said, "is Jaggers, and I am a lawyer in London. I am pretty well known. I have unusual business to transact with you, and I commence by explaining that it is not of my originating. If my advice had been asked, I should not have been here. It was not asked, and you see me here. What I have to do, as the confidential agent of another, I do. No less, no more."

Finding that he could not see us very well from where he sat, he got up, and threw one leg over the back of a chair, and leaned upon it; thus having one foot on the seat of the chair, and one foot on the ground.

"Now, Joseph Gargery, I am the bearer of an offer to relieve you of this young fellow, your apprentice. You would not object to cancel his indentures, at his request and for his good? You would not want anything for so doing?"

"Lord forbid that I should want anything for not standing in Pip's way!" said Joe, staring.

"Lord forbidding is pious, but not to the purpose," returned Mr. Jaggers. "The question is, Would you want anything? Do you want anything?"

"The answer is," returned Joe, sternly, "no."

I thought Mr. Jaggers glanced at Joe as if he considered him a fool for his disinterestedness. But I was too much bewildered between breathless curiosity and surprise to be sure of it.

"Very well," said Mr. Jaggers. "Recollect the admission you have made, and don't try to go from it presently."

"Who's a going to try?" retorted Joe.

"I don't say anybody is. Do you keep a dog?"

"Yes, I do keep a dog."

"Bear in mind then, that Brag is a good dog, but Holdfast is a better. Bear that in mind, will you?" repeated Mr. Jaggers, shutting his eyes and nodding his head at Joe, as if he were forgiving him something. "Now I return to this young fellow. And the communication I have got to make is, that he has great expectations."

Joe and I gasped, and looked at one another.

"I am instructed to communicate to him," said Mr. Jaggers, throwing his finger at me, sideways, "that he will come into a handsome property. Further, that it is the desire of the present possessor of that property that he be immediately removed from his present sphere of life and from this place, and be brought up as a gentleman—in a word, as a young fellow of great expectations."

My dream was out; my wild fancy was surpassed by sober reality; Miss Havisham was going to make my fortune on a grand scale.

"Now, Mr. Pip," pursued the lawyer, "I address the rest of what I have to say to you. You are to understand first, that it is the request of the person from whom I take my instructions, that you always bear the name of Pip. You will have no objection, I dare say, to your great expectations being encumbered with that easy condition. But if you have any objection, this is the time to mention it."

My heart was beating so fast, and there was such a singing in my ears, that I could scarcely stammer I had no objection.

"I should think not! Now you are to understand, secondly, Mr. Pip, that the name of the person who is your liberal benefactor remains a profound secret until the person chooses to reveal it. I am empowered to mention that it is the intention of the person to reveal it at firsthand by word of mouth to yourself. When that intention may be carried out I cannot say; no one can say. It may be years hence; even many years. Now, you are distinctly to understand that you are most positively prohibited from making any inquiry on this head, or any allusion or reference, however distant, to any individual whomsoever as *the* individual in all the communications you may have with me. If you have a suspicion in your own breast, keep that suspicion in your own breast. It is not the least to the purpose what the reasons of this prohibition are; there may be the strongest and gravest reasons, or they may be mere whim. That is not for you to inquire into. The condition is laid down. Your acceptance of it, and your observance of it as binding, is the only remaining condition that I am charged with, by the person from whom I take my instructions, and for whom I am not otherwise responsible. That person is the person from whom you derive your expectations, and the secret is solely held by that person and by me. Again, not a very difficult condition with which to encumber such a rise in fortune; but if you have any objection to it, this is the time to mention it. Speak out."

Once more I stammered with difficulty that I had no objection.

"I should think not! Now, Mr. Pip, I have done with stipulations." Though he called me Mr. Pip, and began rather to make up to me, he still could not get rid of a certain air of bullying suspicion; and even now he occasionally shut his eyes and threw his finger at me while he spoke, as much as to express that he knew all kinds of things to my disparagement, if he only chose to mention them. "We come next to mere details of arrangement. You must know that, although I have used the term 'expectations' more than once, you are not endowed with expectations only. There is already lodged in my hands a sum of money amply sufficient for your suitable education and maintenance. You will please consider me your guardian. Oh!" for I was going to thank him, "I tell you at once I am paid for my services, or I shouldn't render them. It is considered that you must be better educated in accordance with your altered position, and that you will be alive to the importance and necessity of at once entering on that advantage."

I said I had always longed for it.

"Never mind what you have always longed for, Mr. Pip," he retorted; "keep to the record. If you long for it now, that's enough. Am I answered that you are ready to be placed at once under some proper tutor? Is that it?"

I stammered yes, that was it.

"Good. Now your inclinations are to be consulted. I don't think that wise, mind, but it's my trust. Have you ever heard of any tutor whom you would prefer to another?"

I had never heard of any tutor but Biddy and Mr. Wopsle's great-aunt; so I replied in the negative.

"There is a certain tutor, of whom I have some knowledge, who I think might suit the purpose," said Mr. Jaggers. "I don't recommend him, observe; because I never recommend anybody. The gentleman I speak of is one Mr. Matthew Pocket."

Ah! I caught at the name directly. Miss Havisham's relation. The Matthew whom Mr. and Mrs. Camilla had spoken of. The Matthew whose place was to be at Miss Havisham's head when she lay dead in her bride's dress on the bride's table.

"You know the name?" said Mr. Jaggers, looking shrewdly at me, and then shutting up his eyes while he waited for my answer.

My answer was, that I had heard of the name.

"Oh!" said he. "You have heard of the name. But the question is, what do you say of it?"

I said, or tried to say, that I was much obliged to him for his recommendation—

"No, my young friend!" he interrupted, shaking his great head very slowly. "Recollect yourself!"

Not recollecting myself, I began again that I was much obliged to him for his recommendation—

"No, my young friend," he interrupted, shaking his head and frowning and smiling both at once; "no, no, no; it's very well done, but it won't do; you are too young to fix me with it. Recommendation is not the word, Mr. Pip. Try another."

Correcting myself, I said that I was much obliged to him for his mention of Mr. Matthew Pocket—

"*That's* more like it!" cried Mr. Jaggers.

—And (I added) I would gladly try that gentleman.

"Good. You had better try him in his own house. The way shall be prepared for you, and you can see his son first, who is in London. When will you come to London?"

I said (glancing at Joe, who stood looking on motionless), that I supposed I could come directly.

"First," said Mr. Jaggers, "you should have some new clothes to come in, and they should not be working clothes. Say this day week. You'll want some money. Shall I leave you twenty guineas?"

He produced a long purse, with the greatest coolness, and counted them out on the table and pushed them over to me. This was the first time he had taken his leg from the chair. He sat astride of the chair when he had pushed the money over, and sat swinging his purse and eying Joe.

"Well, Joseph Gargery! You look dumbfounded?"

"I *am!*" said Joe, in a very decided manner.

"It was understood that you wanted nothing for yourself, remember?"

"It were understood," said Joe. "And it are understood. And it ever will be similar according."

"But what," said Mr. Jaggers, swinging his purse, "what if it was in my instructions to make you a present, as compensation?"

"As compensation what for?" Joe demanded.

"For the loss of his services."

Joe laid his hand upon my shoulder with the touch of a woman. I have often thought him since like the steam-hammer, that can crush a man or pat an eggshell, in his combination of strength with gentleness. "Pip is that hearty welcome," said Joe, "to go free with his services to honor and fortun', as no words can tell him. But if you think as Money can make compensation to me for the loss of the little child—what come to the forge—and ever the best of friends!" O dear, good Joe, whom I was so ready to leave and so unthankful to, I see you again, with your muscular blacksmith's arm before your eyes, and your broad chest heaving, and your voice dying away. O dear good faithful tender Joe, I feel the loving tremble of your hand upon my arm as solemnly this day as if it had been the rustle of an angel's wing!

But I encouraged Joe at the time. I was lost in the mazes of my future fortunes, and could not retrace the by-paths we had trodden together. I begged Joe to be comforted, for (as he said) we had ever been the best of friends, and (as I said) we ever would be so. Joe scooped his eyes with his disengaged wrist, as if he were bent on gouging himself, but said not another word.

Mr. Jaggers had looked on at this as one who recognized in Joe the village idiot, and in me his keeper. When it was over, he said, weighing in his hand the purse he had ceased to swing,

"Now, Joseph Gargery, I warn you this is your last chance. No half measures with me. If you mean to take a present that I have it in charge to make you, speak out, and you shall have it. If, on the contrary, you mean to say——" Here, to his great amazement, he was stopped by Joe's suddenly working round him with every demonstration of a fell pugilistic purpose.

"Which I meantersay," cried Joe, "that if you come into my place bullbaiting and badgering me, come out! Which I meantersay as such if you're a man, come on! Which I meantersay that what I say I meantersay, and stand or fall by!"

I drew Joe away, and he immediately became placable; merely stating to me, in an obliging manner, and as a polite expostulatory notice to anyone whom it might concern, that he were not a-going to be bull-baited and badgered in his own place. Mr. Jaggers had risen when Joe demonstrated, and had backed to near the door. Without evincing any inclination to come in again, he there delivered his valedictory remarks. They were these:

"Well, Mr. Pip, I think the sooner you leave here—as you are to be a gentleman—the better. Let it stand for this day week, and you shall receive my printed address in the meantime. You can take a hackney-coach at the stagecoach office in London, and come straight to me. Understand that I express no opinion, one way or other, on the trust I undertake. I am paid for undertaking it, and I do so. Now, understand that, finally. Understand that!"

He was throwing his finger at both of us, and I think would have gone on, but for his seeming to think Joe dangerous, and going off.

Something came into my head which induced me to run after him, as he was going down to the Jolly Bargemen where he had left a hired carriage.

"I beg your pardon, Mr. Jaggers."

"Halloa!" said he, facing round, "what's the matter?"

"I wish to be quite right, Mr. Jaggers, and to keep to your directions; so I thought I had better ask. Would there be any objection to my taking leave of anyone I know about here before I go away?"

"No," said he, looking as if he hardly understood me.

"I don't mean in the village only, but uptown?"

"No," said he. "No objection."

I thanked him and ran home again, and there I found that Joe had already locked the front door, and vacated the state-parlor, and was seated by the kitchen fire with a hand on each knee, gazing intently at the burning coals. I too sat down before the fire and gazed at the coals, and nothing was said for a long time.

My sister was in her cushioned chair in her corner, and Biddy sat at her needlework before the fire, and Joe sat next Biddy, and I sat next Joe in the corner opposite my sister. The more I looked into the glowing coals the more incapable I became of looking at Joe; the longer the silence lasted the more unable I felt to speak.

At length I got out, "Joe, have you told Biddy?"

"No, Pip," returned Joe, still looking at the fire, and holding his knees tight, as if he had private information that they intended to make off somewhere; "which I left it to yourself, Pip."

"I would rather you told, Joe."

"Pip's a gentleman of fortun', then," said Joe, "and God bless him in it!"

Biddy dropped her work and looked at me. Joe held his knees and looked at me. I looked at both of them. After a pause they both heartily congratulated me; but there was a certain touch of sadness in their congratulations that I rather resented.

I took it upon myself to impress Biddy (and through Biddy, Joe) with the grave obligation I considered my friends under, to know nothing and say nothing about the maker of my fortune. It would all come out in good time, I observed, and in the meanwhile nothing was to be said save that I had come into great expectations from a mysterious patron. Biddy nodded her head thoughtfully at the fire as she took up her work again, and said she would be very particular, and Joe, still detaining his knees, said, "Ay, ay, I'll be ekervally partickler, Pip"; and then they congratulated me again, and went on to express so much wonder at the notion of my being a gentleman that I didn't half like it.

Infinite pains were then taken by Biddy to convey to my sister some idea of what had happened. To the best of my belief those efforts entirely failed. She laughed and nodded her head a great many times, and even repeated after Biddy the words "Pip" and "Property." But I doubt if they had more meaning in them than an election cry, and I cannot suggest a darker picture of her state of mind.

I never could have believed it without experience, but as Joe and Biddy became more at their cheerful ease again I became quite gloomy. Dissatisfied with my fortune of course I could not be; but it is possible that I may have been, without quite knowing it, dissatisfied with myself.

Anyhow, I sat with my elbow on my knee and my face upon my hand, looking into the fire, as those two talked about my going away, and about what they should do with me, and all that. And whenever I caught one of them looking at me, though never so pleasantly (and they often looked at me—particularly Biddy), I felt in a manner offended: as if they were expressing some mistrust of me. Though Heaven knows they never did by word or sign.

At those times I would get up and look out at the door; for our kitchen door opened at once upon the night, and stood open on summer evenings to air the room. The very stars to which I then raised my eyes, I am afraid I took to be but poor and humble stars for glittering on the rustic objects among which I had passed my life.

"Saturday night," said I, when we sat at our supper of bread-and-cheese and beer. "Five more days, and then the day before *the* day! They'll soon go."

"Yes, Pip," observed Joe, whose voice sounded hollow in his beer mug. "They'll soon go."

"Soon, soon go," said Biddy.

"I have been thinking, Joe, that when I go downtown on Monday, and order my new clothes, I shall tell the tailor that I'll come and put them on there or that I'll have them sent to Mr. Pumblechook's. It would be very disagreeable to be stared at by all the people here."

"Mr. and Mrs. Hubble might like to see you in your new figure too, Pip," said Joe, industriously cutting his bread, with his cheese on it, in the palm of his left hand, and glancing at my untasted supper as if he thought of the time when we used to compare slices. "So might Wopsle. And the Jolly Bargemen might take it as a compliment."

"That's just what I don't want, Joe. They would make such a business of it—such a coarse and common business—that I couldn't bear myself."

"Ah, that indeed, Pip!" said Joe. "If you couldn't abear yourself—"

Biddy asked me here, as she sat holding my sister's plate, "Have you thought about when you'll show yourself to Mr. Gargery, and your sister, and me? You will show yourself to us, won't you?"

"Biddy," I returned, with some resentment, "you are so exceedingly quick that it's difficult to keep up with you."

("She always were quick," observed Joe.)

"If you had waited another moment, Biddy, you would have heard me say that I shall bring my clothes here in a bundle one evening—most likely on the evening before I go away."

Biddy said no more. Handsomely forgiving her, I soon exchanged an affectionate good night with her and Joe, and went up to bed. When I got into my little room I sat down and took a long look at it, as a mean little room that I should soon be parted from and raised above, forever. It was furnished with fresh young remembrances too, and even at the same moment I fell into much the same confused division of mind between it and the better rooms to which I was going, as I had been in so often between the forge and Miss Havisham's, and Biddy and Estella.

The sun had been shining brightly all day on the roof of my attic, and the room was warm. As I put the window open and stood looking out, I saw Joe come slowly forth at the dark door below and take a turn or two in the air; and then I saw Biddy come and bring him a pipe and light it for him. He never smoked so late, and it seemed to hint to me that he wanted comforting, for some reason or other.

He presently stood at the door immediately beneath me, smoking his pipe, and Biddy stood there too, quietly talking to him, and I knew that they talked of me, for I heard my name mentioned in a loving tone by both of them more than once. I would not have listened for more, if I could have heard more: so I drew away from the window, and sat down in my one chair by the bedside, feeling it very sorrowful and strange that this first night of my bright fortunes should be the loneliest I had ever known.

Looking toward the window, I saw light wreaths from Joe's pipe floating there, and I fancied it was like a blessing from Joe—not obtruded on me or paraded before me, but pervading the air we shared together. I put my light out and crept into bed; and it was an uneasy bed now, and I never slept the old sound sleep in it anymore.

Nineteen

MORNING MADE A CONSIDERABLE DIFFERENCE IN MY general prospect of Life, and brightened it so much that it scarcely seemed the same. What lay heaviest on my mind was the consideration that six days intervened between me and the day of departure; for I could not divest myself of a misgiving that something might happen to London in the meanwhile, and that, when I got there, it would be either greatly deteriorated or clean gone.

Joe and Biddy were very sympathetic and pleasant when I spoke of our approaching separation; but they only referred to it when I did. After breakfast Joe brought out my indentures from the press in the best parlor, and we put them in the fire, and I felt that I was free. With all the novelty of my emancipation on me, I went to church with Joe, and thought perhaps the clergyman wouldn't have read that about the rich man and the kingdom of Heaven if he had known all.

After an early dinner I strolled out alone, purposing to finish off the marshes at once, and get them done with. As I passed the church, I felt (as I had felt during service in the morning) a sublime compassion for the poor creatures who were destined to go there, Sunday after Sunday, all their lives through, and to lie obscurely at last among the low green mounds. I promised myself that I would do something for them one of these days, and formed a plan in outline for bestowing a dinner of roast beef and plum-pudding, a pint of ale, and a gallon of condescension, upon everybody in the village.

If I had often thought before, with something allied to shame, of my companionship with the fugitive whom I had once seen limping among those graves, what were my thoughts on this Sunday, when the place recalled the wretch, ragged and shivering, with his felon iron and badge! My comfort was that it happened a long time ago, and that he had doubtless been transported a long way off, and that he was dead to me, and might be veritably dead into the bargain.

No more low, wet grounds, no more dikes and sluices, no more of these grazing cattle—though they seemed, in their dull manner, to wear a more respectful air now, and to face round, in order that they might stare as long as possible at the possessor of such great expectations—farewell, monotonous acquaintances of my childhood, henceforth I was for London and greatness: not for smith's work in general and for you! I made my exultant way to the old Battery, and, lying down there to consider the question whether Miss Havisham intended me for Estella, fell asleep.

When I awoke I was much surprised to find Joe sitting beside me smoking his pipe. He greeted me with a cheerful smile on my opening my eyes, and said:

"As being the last time, Pip, I thought I'd foller."

"And, Joe, I am very glad you did so."

"Thankee, Pip," said Joe.

"You may be sure, dear Joe," I went on, after we had shaken hands, "that I shall never forget you."

"No, no, Pip!" said Joe, in a comfortable tone, "*I'm* sure of that. Ay, ay, old chap! Bless you, it were only necessary to get it well round in a man's mind to be certain on it. But it took a bit of time to get it well round; the change come so oncommon plump; didn't it?"

Somehow I was not best pleased with Joe's being so mightily secure of me. I should have liked him to have betrayed emotion, or to have said, "It does you credit, Pip," or something of that sort. Therefore I made no remark on Joe's first head: merely saying, as to his second, that the tidings had indeed come suddenly, but that I had always wanted to be a gentleman, and had often and often speculated on what I would do if I were one.

"Have you though!" said Joe. "Astonishing!"

"It's a pity now, Joe," said I, "that you did not get on a little more, when we had our lessons here; isn't it?"

"Well, I don't know," returned Joe. "I'm so awful dull. I'm only master of my own trade. It were always a pity as I was so awful dull; but it's no more of a pity now than it was—say this day twelvemonth—don't you see?"

What I had meant was, that when I came into my property and was able to do something for Joe, it would have been much more agreeable if he had been better qualified for a rise in station. He was so perfectly innocent of my meaning, however, that I thought I would mention it to Biddy in preference.

So, when we had walked home and had had tea, I took Biddy into our little garden by the side of the lane, and, after throwing out in a general way for the elevation of her spirits, that I should never forget her, said I had a favor to ask of her.

"And it is, Biddy," said I, "that you will not omit any opportunity of helping Joe on a little."

"How helping him on?" asked Biddy, with a steady sort of glance.

"Well! Joe is a dear good fellow—in fact, I think he is the dearest fellow that ever lived—but he is rather backward in some things. For instance, Biddy, in his learning and his manners."

Although I was looking at Biddy as I spoke, and although she opened her eyes very wide when I had spoken, she did not look at me.

"Oh, his manners! Won't his manners do then?" asked Biddy, plucking a black currant leaf.

"My dear Biddy, they do very well here—"

"Oh! they *do* very well here?" interposed Biddy, looking closely at the leaf in her hand.

"Hear me out—but if I were to remove Joe into a higher sphere, as I shall hope to remove him when I come into my property, they would hardly do him justice."

"And don't you think he knows that?" asked Biddy.

It was such a very provoking question (for it had never in the most distant manner occurred to me), that I said, snappishly, "Biddy, what do you mean?"

Biddy, having rubbed the leaf to pieces between her hands—and the smell of a black currant bush has ever since recalled to me that evening in the little garden by the side of the lane—said, "Have you ever considered that he may be proud?"

"Proud!" I repeated, with disdainful emphasis.

"Oh! there are many kinds of pride," said Biddy, looking full at me and shaking her head; "pride is not all of one kind—"

"Well! What are you stopping for?" said I.

"Not all of one kind," resumed Biddy. "He may be too proud to let anyone take him out of a place that he is competent to fill, and fills well and with respect. To tell you the truth, I think he is; though it sounds bold in me to say so, for you must know him far better than I do."

"Now, Biddy," said I, "I am very sorry to see this in you. I did not expect to see this in you. You are envious, Biddy, and grudging. You are dissatisfied on account of my rise in fortune, and you can't help showing it."

"If you have the heart to think so," returned Biddy, "say so. Say so over and over again, if you have the heart to think so."

"If you have the heart to be so, you mean, Biddy," said I, in a virtuous and superior tone; "don't put it off upon me. I am very sorry to see it, and it's a—it's a bad side of human nature. I did intend to ask you to use any little opportunities you might have after I was gone of improving dear Joe. But after this I ask you nothing. I am extremely sorry to see this in you, Biddy," I repeated. "It's a—it's a bad side of human nature."

"Whether you scold me or approve of me," returned poor Biddy, "you may equally depend upon my trying to do all that lies in my power here at all times. And whatever opinion you take away of me, shall make no difference in my remembrance of you. Yet a gentleman should not be unjust neither," said Biddy, turning away her head.

I again warmly repeated that it was a bad side of human nature (in which sentiment, waiving its application, I have since seen reason to think I was right), and I walked down the little path away from Biddy, and Biddy went into the house, and I went out at the garden gate and took a dejected stroll until supper-time; again feeling it very sorrowful and strange that this, the second night of my bright fortunes, should be as lonely and unsatisfactory as the first.

But morning once more brightened my view, and I extended my clemency to Biddy, and we dropped the subject. Putting on the best clothes I had, I went into town as early as I could hope to find the shops open, and presented myself before Mr. Trabb, the tailor, who was having his breakfast in the parlor behind his shop, and who did not think it worth his while to come out to me, but called me in to him.

"Well!" said Mr. Trabb, in a hail-fellow-well-met kind of way. "How are you, and what can I do for you?"

Mr. Trabb had sliced his hot roll into three feather beds, and was slipping butter in between the blankets, and covering it up. He was a prosperous old bachelor, and his open window looked into a prosperous little garden and orchard, and there was a prosperous iron safe let into the wall at the side of his fireplace, and I did not doubt that heaps of his prosperity were put away in it in bags.

"Mr. Trabb," said I, "it's an unpleasant thing to have to mention, because it looks like boasting; but I have come into a handsome property."

A change passed over Mr. Trabb. He forgot the butter in bed, got up from the bedside, and wiped his fingers on the tablecloth, exclaiming, "Lord bless my soul!"

"I am going up to my guardian in London," said I, casually drawing some guineas out of my pocket and looking at them; "and I want a fashionable suit of clothes to go in. I wish to pay for them," I added—otherwise I thought he might only pretend to make them—"with ready money."

"My dear sir," said Mr. Trabb, as he respectfully bent his body, opened his arms, and took the liberty of touching me on the outside of each elbow, "don't hurt me by mentioning that. May I venture to congratulate you? Would you do me the favor of stepping into the shop?"

Now Mr. Trabb's boy was the most audacious boy in all that countryside. When I had entered he was sweeping the shop, and he had sweetened his labors by sweeping over me. He was still sweeping when I came out into the shop with Mr. Trabb, and he knocked the broom against all possible corners and obstacles, to express (as I understood it) equality with any blacksmith, alive or dead.

"Hold that noise," said Mr. Trabb, with the greatest sternness, "or I'll knock your head off! Do me the favor to be seated, sir. Now this," said Mr. Trabb, taking down a roll of cloth, and tiding it out in a flowing manner over the counter, preparatory to getting his hand under it to show the gloss, "is a very sweet article. I can recommend it for your purpose, sir, because it really is extra super. But you shall see some others. Give me Number Four, you!" (To the boy, and with dreadful severity, foreseeing the danger of that miscreant's brushing me with it, or making some other sign of familiarity.)

Mr. Trabb never removed his stern eye from the boy until he had deposited number four on the counter and was at a safe distance again. Then he commanded him to bring number five and number eight. "And let me have none of your tricks here," said Mr. Trabb, "or you shall repent it, you young scoundrel, the longest day you have to live."

Mr. Trabb then bent over number four, and in a sort of deferential confidence recommended it to me as a light article for summer wear, an article much in vogue among the nobility and gentry, an article that it would ever be an honor to him to reflect upon a distinguished fellow-townsman's (if he might claim me for a fellow-townsman) having worn. "Are you bringing numbers five and eight, you vagabond," said Mr. Trabb to the boy after that; "or shall I kick you out of the shop and bring them myself?"

I selected the materials for a suit, with the assistance of Mr. Trabb's judgment, and reentered the parlor to be measured. For, although Mr. Trabb had my measure already, and had previously been quite contented with it, he said apologetically that it "wouldn't do under existing circumstances, sir— wouldn't do at all." So Mr. Trabb measured and calculated me, in the parlor, as if I were an estate and he the finest species of surveyor, and gave himself such a world of trouble that I felt that no suit of clothes could possibly remunerate him for his pains. When he had at last done, and had appointed to send the articles to Mr. Pumblechook's on the Thursday evening, he said, with his hand upon the parlor lock, "I know, sir, that London gentlemen cannot be expected to patronize local work, as a rule; but if you would give me a turn now and then in the quality of a townsman, I should greatly esteem it. Good morning, sir; much obliged. Door!"

The last word was flung at the boy, who had not the least notion what it meant. But I saw him collapse as his master rubbed me out with his hands, and my first decided experience of the stupendous power of money was, that it had morally laid upon his back Trabb's boy.

After this memorable event, I went to the hatter's, and the bootmaker's, and the hosier's, and felt rather like Mother Hubbard's dog, whose outfit required the services of so many trades. I also went to the coach-office, and took my place for seven o'clock on Saturday morning. It was not necessary to explain everywhere that I had come into a handsome property; but whenever I said anything to that effect, it followed that the officiating tradesman ceased to have his attention diverted through the window by the High Street, and concentrated his mind upon me. When I had ordered everything I wanted I directed my steps toward Pumblechook's, and as I approached that gentleman's place of business I saw him standing at his door.

He was waiting for me with great impatience. He had been out early with the chaise-cart, and had called at the forge and heard the news. He had prepared a collation for me in the Barnwell parlor, and he too ordered his shopman to "come out of the gangway" as my sacred person passed.

"My dear friend," said Mr. Pumblechook, taking me by both hands, when he and I and the collation were alone, "I give you joy of your good fortune. Well deserved, well deserved!"

This was coming to the point, and I thought it a sensible way of expressing himself.

"To think," said Mr. Pumblechook, after snorting admiration at me for some moments, "that I should have been the humble instrument of leading up to this, is a proud reward."

I begged Mr. Pumblechook to remember that nothing was to be ever said or hinted on that point.

"My dear young friend," said Mr. Pumblechook; "if you will allow me to call you so—"

I murmured "Certainly"; and Mr. Pumblechook took me by both hands again, and communicated a movement to his waistcoat that had an emotional appearance, though it was rather low down— "My dear young friend, rely upon my doing my little all in your absence, by keeping the fact before the mind of Joseph. Joseph!" said Mr. Pumblechook, in the way of a compassionate adjuration. "Joseph! Joseph!" Thereupon he shook his head and tapped it, expressing his sense of deficiency in Joseph.

"But my dear young friend," said Mr. Pumblechook, "you must be hungry, you must be exhausted. Be seated. Here is a chicken had round from the Boar, here is a tongue had round from the Boar, here's one or two little things that I hope you may not despise. But do I," said Mr. Pumblechook, getting up again the moment after he had sat down, "see afore me, him as I ever sported with in his times of happy infancy? And may I—may I—?"

This May I meant, might he shake hands? I consented, and he was fervent, and then sat down again.

"Here is wine," said Mr. Pumblechook. "Let us drink, Thanks to Fortune, and may she ever pick out her favorites with equal judgment! And yet I cannot," said Mr. Pumblechook, getting up again, "see afore me One—and likeways drink to One—without again expressing—May I—may I—?"

I said he might, and he shook hands with me again, and emptied his glass and turned it upside down. I did the same; and if I had turned myself upside down before drinking, the wine would not have gone more direct to my head.

Mr. Pumblechook helped me to the liver wing, and to the best slice of tongue (none of those out-of-the-way No Thoroughfares of Pork now), and took, comparatively speaking, no care of himself at all. "Ah! poultry, poultry! You little thought," said Mr. Pumblechook, apostrophizing the fowl in the dish, "when you was a young fledgeling, what was in store for you. You little thought you was to be refreshment beneath this humble roof for one as—call it a weakness, if you will," said Mr. Pumblechook, getting up again, "but may I? *may* I?"

It began to be unnecessary to repeat the form of saying he might, so he did it at once. How he ever did it so often without mortally wounding himself with my knife, I don't know.

"And your sister," he resumed, after a little steady eating, "which had the honor of bringing you up by hand! It's a sad picter, to reflect that she's no longer equal to fully understanding the honor. May—"

I saw he was about to come at me again, and I stopped him.

"We'll drink her health," said I.

"Ah!" cried Mr. Pumblechook, leaning back in his chair, quite flaccid with admiration, "that's the way you know 'em, sir!" (I don't know who Sir was, but he certainly was not I, and there was no third person present); "that's the way you know the noble-minded, sir! Ever forgiving and ever affable. It might," said the servile Pumblechook, putting down his untasted glass in a hurry and getting up again, "to a common person, have the appearance of repeating—but *may* I—?"

When he had done it, he resumed his seat and drank to my sister. "Let us never be blind," said Mr. Pumblechook, "to her faults of temper, but it is to be hoped she meant well."

At about this time I began to observe that he was getting flushed in the face; as to myself, I felt all face, steeped in wine and smarting.

I mentioned to Mr. Pumblechook that I wished to have my new clothes sent to his house, and he was ecstatic on my so distinguishing him. I mentioned my reason for desiring to avoid observation in the village, and he lauded it to the skies. There was nobody but himself, he intimated, worthy of my confidence, and—in short, might he? Then he asked me tenderly if I remembered our boyish games at sums, and how we had gone together to have me bound apprentice, and, in effect, how he had ever been my favorite fancy and my chosen friend? If I had taken ten times as many glasses of wine as I had, I should have known that he never had stood in that relation toward me, and should in my heart of hearts have repudiated the idea. Yet for all that, I remember feeling convinced that I had been much mistaken in him, and that he was a sensible, practical, good-hearted, prime fellow.

By degrees he fell to reposing such great confidence in me, as to ask my advice in reference to his own affairs. He mentioned that there was an opportunity for a great amalgamation and monopoly of the corn and seed trade on those premises, if enlarged, such as had never occurred before in that, or any other neighborhood. What alone was wanting to the realization of a vast fortune he considered to be More Capital. Those were the two little words, more capital. Now it appeared to him (Pumblechook) that if that capital were got into the business through a sleeping partner, sir: which sleeping partner would have nothing to do but walk in, by self or deputy, whenever he pleased, and examine the books—and walk in twice a year and take his profits away in his pocket, to the tune of fifty percent—it appeared to him that that might be an opening for a young gentleman of spirit combined with property, which would be worthy of attention. But what did I think? He had great confidence in my opinion, and what did I think? I gave it as my opinion, "Wait a bit!" The united vastness and distinctness of this view so struck him that he no longer asked if he might shake hands with me, but said he really must—and did.

We drank all the wine, and Mr. Pumblechook pledged himself over and over again to keep Joseph up to the mark (I don't know what mark), and to render me efficient and constant service (I don't know what service). He also made known to me for the first time in my life, and certainly after having kept his secret wonderfully well, that he had always said of me, "That boy is no common boy, and mark me, his fortun' will be no common fortun'." He said with a tearful smile that it was a singular thing to think of now, and I said so too. Finally, I went out into the air with a dim perception that there was something unwonted in the conduct of the sunshine, and found that I had slumberously got to the turnpike without having taken any account of the road.

There I was roused by Mr. Pumblechook's hailing me. He was a long way down the sunny street, and was making expressive gestures for me to stop. I stopped, and he came up breathless.

"No, my dear friend," said he, when he had recovered wind for speech. "Not if I can help it. This occasion shall not entirely pass without that affability on your part.—May I, as an old friend and well-wisher? *May* I?"

We shook hands for the hundredth time at least, and he ordered a young carter out of my way with the greatest indignation. Then he blessed me, and stood waving his hand to me until I had passed the crook in the road; and then I turned into a field and had a long nap under a hedge before I pursued my way home.

I had scant luggage to take with me to London, for little of the little I possessed was adapted to my new station. But I began packing that same afternoon, and wildly packed up things that I knew I should want next morning, in a fiction that there was not a moment to be lost.

So Tuesday, Wednesday, and Thursday passed, and on Friday morning I went to Mr. Pumblechook's to put on my new clothes and pay my visit to Miss Havisham. Mr. Pumblechook's own room was given up to me to dress in, and was decorated with clean towels expressly for the event. My clothes were rather a disappointment, of course. Probably every new and eagerly expected garment ever put on since clothes came in fell a trifle short of the wearer's expectation. But after I had had my new suit on some half an hour, and had gone through an immensity of posturing with Mr. Pumblechook's very limited dressing-glass, in the futile endeavor to see my legs, it seemed to fit me better. It being market morning at a neighboring town some ten miles off, Mr. Pumblechook was not at home. I had not told him exactly when I meant to leave, and was not likely to shake hands with him again before departing. This was all as it should be, and I went out in my new array: fearfully ashamed of having to pass the shopman, and suspicious after all that I was at a personal disadvantage, something like Joe in his Sunday suit.

I went circuitously to Miss Havisham's by all the back ways, and rang at the bell constrainedly, on account of the stiff long fingers of my gloves. Sarah Pocket came to the gate, and positively reeled back when she saw me so changed; her walnut-shell countenance likewise turned from brown to green and yellow.

"You?" said she. "You, good gracious? What do you want?"

"I am going to London, Miss Pocket," said I, "and want to say good-bye to Miss Havisham."

I was not expected, for she left me locked in the yard while she went to ask if I were to be admitted. After a very short delay she returned and took me up, staring at me all the way.

Miss Havisham was taking exercise in the room with the long spread table, leaning on her crutched stick. The room was lighted as of yore, and at the sound of our entrance she stopped and turned. She was then just abreast of the rotted bride-cake.

"Don't go, Sarah," she said. "Well, Pip?"

"I start for London, Miss Havisham, tomorrow"—I was exceedingly careful what I said—"and I thought you would kindly not mind my taking leave of you."

"This is a gay figure, Pip," said she, making her crutched stick play round me, as if she, the fairy godmother who had changed me, were bestowing the finishing gift.

"I have come into such good fortune since I saw you last, Miss Havisham," I murmured. "And I am so thankful for it, Miss Havisham!"

"Ay, ay!" said she, looking at the discomfited and envious Sarah with manifest delight. "I have seen Mr. Jaggers. *I* have heard about it, Pip. So you go tomorrow."

"Yes, Miss Havisham."

"And you are adopted by a rich person?"

"Yes, Miss Havisham."

"Not named?"

"No, Miss Havisham."

"And Mr. Jaggers is made your guardian?"

"Yes, Miss Havisham."

She quite gloated on these questions and answers, so keen was her enjoyment of Sarah Pocket's jealous dismay. "Well!" she went on; "you have a promising career before you. Be good—deserve it—and abide by Mr. Jaggers's instructions." She looked at me, and looked at Sarah, and Sarah's countenance wrung out of her watchful face a cruel smile. "Good-bye, Pip!—you will always keep the name of Pip!"

"Yes, Miss Havisham."

"Good-bye, Pip!"

She stretched out her hand, and I went down on my knee and put it to my lips. I had not considered how I should take leave of her; it came naturally to me at the moment to do this. She looked at Sarah Pocket with triumph in her weird eyes, and so I left my fairy godmother, with both her hands on her crutched stick, standing in the midst of the dimly lighted room beside the rotten bride-cake that was hidden in cobwebs.

Sarah Pocket conducted me down as if I were a Ghost who must be seen out. She could not get over my appearance, and was in the last degree confounded. I said "Good-bye, Miss Pocket"; but she merely stared, and did not seem collected enough to know that I had spoken. Clear of the house, I made the best of my way back to Pumblechook's, took off my new clothes, made them into a bundle, and went back home in my older dress, carrying it—to speak the truth, much more at my ease too, though I had the bundle to carry.

And now those six days which were to have run out so slowly, had run out fast and were gone; and tomorrow looked me in the face more steadily than I could look at it. As the six evenings had dwindled away to five, to four, to three, to two, I had become more and more appreciative of the society of Joe and Biddy. On this last evening I dressed myself out in my new clothes for their delight, and sat in my splendor until bedtime. We had a hot supper on the occasion, graced by the inevitable roast fowl, and some flip to finish with. We were all very low and none the higher for pretending to be in spirits.

I was to leave our village at five in the morning, carrying my little hand-portmanteau, and I had told Joe that I wished to walk away all alone. I am afraid—I am sore afraid—that this purpose originated in my sense of the contrast there would be between me and Joe if we went to the coach together. I had pretended with myself that there was nothing of this taint in the arrangement; but when I went up to my little room on this last night I felt compelled to admit that it might be so, and had an impulse upon me to go down again and entreat Joe to walk with me in the morning after all. I did not.

All night there were coaches in my broken sleep, going to wrong places instead of to London, and having in the traces, now dogs, now cats, now pigs, now men—never horses. Fantastic failures of journeys occupied me until the day dawned and the birds were singing. Then, I got up and partly dressed, and sat at the window to take a last look out, and in taking it fell asleep.

Biddy was astir so early to get my breakfast that, although I did not sleep an hour, I smelled the smoke of the kitchen fire when I started up with a terrible idea that it must be late in the afternoon. But long after that, and long after I had heard the clinking of the teacups and was quite ready, I wanted the resolution to go downstairs. After all, I remained up there, trying to cheat myself by repeatedly unlocking and unstrapping my small portmanteau and locking and strapping it up again, until Biddy called to me that I was late.

It was a hurried breakfast with no taste in it. I got up from the meal, saying with a sort of briskness, as if it had only just occurred to me, "Well! I suppose I must be off!" and then I kissed my sister, who was laughing and nodding and shaking in her usual chair, and kissed Biddy, and threw my arms around Joe's neck. Then I took up my little portmanteau and walked out. The last I saw of them was when I presently heard a scuffle behind me, and looking back, saw Joe throwing an old shoe after me and Biddy throwing another old shoe. I stopped then to wave my hat, and dear old Joe waved his strong right arm above his head, crying huskily, "Hooroar!" and Biddy put her apron to her face.

I walked away at a good pace, thinking it was easier to go than I had supposed it would be, and reflecting that it would never have done to have an old shoe thrown after the coach, in sight of all the High Street. I whistled and made nothing of it. But the village was very peaceful and quiet, and the light mists were solemnly rising, as if to show me the world, and I had been so innocent and little there, and all beyond was so unknown and great, that all in a moment with a strong heave and sob I broke into tears. It was by the fingerpost at the end of the village, and I laid my hand upon it, and said, "Good-bye my dear, dear friend!"

Heaven knows we need never be ashamed of shedding tears, for they are rain upon the blinding dust of earth, overlying our hard hearts. I was better after I had cried than before—more sorry, more aware of my own ingratitude, more gentle altogether. If I had cried before, I should have had Joe with me then.

So subdued I was by those tears, and by their breaking out again more than once in the course of the quiet walk, that when I was on the coach, and it was clear of the town, I deliberated with an aching heart whether I would not get down when we changed horses, and walk back, and have another evening at home, and a better parting. We changed, and I had not made up my mind, and still considered for my comfort that it would be quite practicable for me to get down and walk back, when we changed again. And while I was occupied with these deliberations, I would fancy an exact resemblance to Joe in some man coming along the road toward us, and my heart would beat high. As if he could possibly be there!

We changed again, and yet again, and it was now too late and too far to go back, and I went on. And the mists had all solemnly risen now, and the world was before me.

THIS IS THE END OF THE FIRST STAGE OF PIP'S EXPECTATIONS.

Tʜᴇ ᴊᴏᴜʀɴᴇʏ ꜰʀᴏᴍ ᴏᴜʀ ᴛᴏᴡɴ ᴛᴏ ᴛʜᴇ ᴍᴇᴛʀᴏᴘᴏʟɪs ᴡᴀs a journey of about five hours. It was a little past midday when the four-horse stagecoach by which I was a passenger got into the ravel of traffic frayed out about the Cross-Keys, Wood Street, Cheapside, London.

We Britons had at that time particularly settled that it was treasonable to doubt our having and our being the best of everything; otherwise, while I was scared by the immensity of London, I think I might have had some faint doubts whether it was not rather ugly, crooked, narrow, and smoky.

Mr. Jaggers had duly sent me his address; it was Little Britain, and he had written after it on his card, "just out of Smithfield, and close by the coach office." Nevertheless, a hackney-coachman, who seemed to have as many capes to his greasy greatcoat as he was years old, packed me up in his coach and hemmed me in with a folding and jingling barrier of steps, as if he were going to take me fifty miles. His getting on his box, which I remember to have been decorated with an old weather-stained pea-green hammer-cloth, moth-eaten into rags, was quite a work of time. Altogether, it was a wonderful equipage, with six great coronets outside, and ragged things behind for I don't know how many footmen to hold on by, and a harrow below them, to prevent amateur footmen from yielding to the temptation.

I had scarcely had time to enjoy the coach and to think how like a damp straw-yard it was, and yet how like a rag-shop, and to wonder why the horses' nose-bags were kept inside, when I observed the coachman beginning to get down, as if he were going to stop presently. And stop we presently did, in a gloomy street, at certain offices with an open door, whereon was painted Mʀ. Jᴀɢɢᴇʀs.

"How much?" I asked the coachman.

The coachman answered, "A shilling—unless you wish to make it more."

I naturally said I had no wish to make it more.

"Then it must be a shilling," observed the coachman. "I don't want to get into trouble. *I* know *him!*" He darkly closed an eye at Mr. Jaggers's name, and shook his head.

When he had got his shilling, and had in course of time completed the ascent to his box, and had got away (which appeared to relieve his mind), I went into the front office with my portmanteau in my hand, and asked, Was Mr. Jaggers at home?

"He is not," returned the clerk. "He is in Court at present. Am I addressing Mr. Pip?"

I signified that he was addressing Mr. Pip.

"Mr. Jaggers left word would you wait in his room. He couldn't say how long he might be, having a case on. But it stands to reason, his time being valuable, that he won't be longer than he can help."

With those words the clerk opened a door, and ushered me into an inner chamber at the back. Here we found a gentleman with one eye, in a velveteen suit and knee-breeches, who wiped his nose with his sleeve on being interrupted in the perusal of the newspaper. "Go and wait outside, Mike," said the clerk.

I began to say that I hoped I was not interrupting—when the clerk shoved this gentleman out with as little ceremony as I ever saw used, and tossing his fur cap out after him, left me alone.

Mr. Jaggers's room was lighted by a skylight only, and was a most dismal place; the skylight eccentrically patched, like a broken head, and the distorted adjoining houses looking as if they had twisted themselves to peep down at me through it. There were not so many papers about as I should have expected to see; and there were some odd objects about that I should not have expected to see—such as an old rusty pistol, a sword in a scabbard, several strange-looking boxes and packages, and two dreadful casts on a shelf of faces peculiarly swollen, and twitchy about the nose. Mr. Jaggers's own high-backed chair was of deadly black horsehair, with rows of brass nails round it like a coffin; and I fancied I could see how he leaned back in it, and bit his forefinger at the clients. The room was but small, and the clients seemed to have had a habit of backing up against the wall: for the wall, especially opposite to Mr. Jaggers's chair, was greasy with shoulders. I recalled, too, that the one-eyed gentleman had shuffled forth against the wall when I was the innocent cause of his being turned out.

I sat down in the cliental chair placed over against Mr. Jaggers's chair, and became fascinated by the dismal atmosphere of the place. I called to mind that the clerk had the same air of knowing something to everybody else's disadvantage as his master had. I wondered how many other clerks there were upstairs, and whether they all claimed to have the same detrimental mastery of their fellow-creatures. I wondered what was the history of all the odd litter about the room, and how it came there. I wondered whether the two swollen faces were of Mr. Jaggers's family, and, if he were so unfortunate as to have had a pair of such ill-looking relations, why he stuck them on that dusty perch for the blacks and flies to settle on, instead of giving them a place at home. Of course I had no experience of a London summer day, and my spirits may have been oppressed by the hot exhausted air, and by the dust and grit that lay thick on everything. But I sat wondering and waiting in Mr. Jaggers's close room, until I really could not bear the two casts on the shelf above Mr. Jaggers's chair, and got up and went out.

When I told the clerk that I would take a turn in the air while I waited, he advised me to go round the corner and I should come into Smithfield. So I came into Smithfield, and the shameful place, being all asmear with filth and fat and blood and foam, seemed to stick to me. So I rubbed it off with all possible speed by turning into a street where I saw the great black dome of Saint Paul's bulging at me from behind a grim stone building which a by-stander said was Newgate Prison. Following the wall of the jail, I found the roadway covered with straw to deaden the noise of passing vehicles; and from this, and from the quantity of people standing about, smelling strongly of spirits and beer, I inferred that the trials were on.

While I looked about me here, an exceedingly dirty and partially drunk minister of justice asked me if I would like to step in and hear a trial or so: informing me that he could give me a front place for half a crown, whence I should command a full view of the Lord Chief Justice in his wig and robes—mentioning that awful personage like waxwork, and presently offering him at the reduced price of eighteen pence. As I declined the proposal on the plea of an appointment, he was so good as to take me into a yard and show me where the gallows was kept, and also where people were publicly whipped, and then he showed me the Debtors' Door, out of which culprits came to be hanged: heightening the interest of that dreadful portal by giving me to understand that "four on 'em" would come out at that door the day after tomorrow at eight in the morning, to be killed in a row. This was horrible, and gave me a rather sickening idea of London: the more so as the Lord Chief Justice's pro-prietor wore (from his hat down to his boots, and up again to his pocket-handkerchief inclusive) mildewed clothes, which had evidently not belonged to him originally, and which, I took it into my head, he had bought cheap of the executioner. Under these circumstances I thought myself well rid of him for a shilling.

I dropped into the office to ask if Mr. Jaggers had come in yet, and I found he had not, and I strolled out again. This time I made the tour of Lit-tle Britain, and turned into Bartholomew Close; and now I became aware that other people were waiting about for Mr. Jaggers as well as I. There were two men of secret appearance lounging in Bartholomew Close, and thought-fully fitting their feet into the cracks of the pavement as they talked together, one of whom said to the other when they first passed me, that "Mr. Jaggers could do it if it was to be done." There was a knot of three men and two women standing at a corner, and one of the women was crying on her dirty shawl, and the other comforted her by saying, as she pulled her own shawl over her shoulders, "Jaggers is for him, 'Melia, and what more *could* you have?" There was a red-eyed little Jew who came into the Close while I was loitering there, in company with a second little Jew whom he sent upon an errand; and while the messenger was gone, I remarked this Jew, who was of a highly excitable temperament, performing a jig of anxiety under a lamppost, and accompanying himself, in a kind of frenzy, with the words, "Oh Jaggerth, Jaggerth, Jaggerth! all otherth ith Cag-Maggerth, give me Jaggerth!" These testimonies to the popularity of my guardian made a deep impression on me, and I admired and wondered more than ever.

At length, as I was looking out at the iron gate of Bartholomew Close into Little Britain, I saw Mr. Jaggers coming across the road toward me. All the others who were waiting saw him at the same time, and there was quite a rush at him. Mr. Jaggers, putting a hand on my shoulder and walking me on at his side without saying anything to me, addressed himself to his followers.

First, he took the two secret men.

"Now, I have nothing to say to you," said Mr. Jaggers, throwing his finger at them. "I want to know no more than I know. As to the result, it's a toss-up. I told you from the first it was a toss-up. Have you paid Wemmick?"

"We made the money up this morning, sir," said one of the men, submissively, while the other perused Mr. Jaggers's face.

"I don't ask you when you made it up, or where, or whether you made it up at all. Has Wemmick got it?"

"Yes, sir," said both the men together.

"Very well; then you may go. Now, I won't have it!" said Mr. Jaggers, waving his hand at them to put them behind him. "If you say a word to me I'll throw up the case."

"We thought, Mr. Jaggers—" one of the men began, pulling off his hat.

"That's what I told you not to do," said Mr. Jaggers. "*You* thought! I think for you; that's enough for you. If I want you, I know where to find you; I don't want you to find me. Now, I won't have it. I won't hear a word."

The two men looked at one another as Mr. Jaggers waved them behind again, and humbly fell back and were heard no more.

"And now *you!*" said Mr. Jaggers, suddenly stopping, and turning on the two women with the shawls, from whom the three men had meekly separated.—"Oh! Amelia, is it?"

"Yes, Mr. Jaggers."

"And do you remember," retorted Mr. Jaggers, "that but for me you wouldn't be here and couldn't be here?"

"Oh yes, sir!" exclaimed both women together. "Lord bless you, sir, well we knows that!"

"Then why," said Mr. Jaggers, "do you come here?"

"My Bill, sir!" the crying woman pleaded.

"Now, I tell you what!" said Mr. Jaggers. "Once for all. If you don't know that your Bill's in good hands, I know it. And if you come here, bothering about your Bill, I'll make an example of both your Bill and you, and let him slip through my fingers. Have you paid Wemmick?"

"Oh, yes, sir! Every farden."

"Very well. Then you have done all you have got to do. Say another word—one single word—and Wemmick shall give you your money back."

This terrible threat caused the two women to fall off immediately. No one remained now but the excitable Jew, who had already raised the skirts of Mr. Jaggers's coat to his lips several times.

"I don't know this man!" said Mr. Jaggers, in the most devastating strain. "What does this fellow want?"

"Ma thear Mithter Jaggerth. Hown brother to Habraham Latharuth!"

"Who's he?" said Mr. Jaggers. "Let go of my coat."

The suitor, kissing the hem of the garment again before relinquishing it, replied, "Habraham Latharuth, on thuthpithion of plate."

"You're too late," said Mr. Jaggers. "I am over the way."

"Holy father, Mithter Jaggerth!" cried my excitable acquaintance, turning white, "don't thay you're again Habraham Latharuth!"

"I am," said Mr. Jaggers, "and there's an end of it. Get out of the way."

"Mithter Jaggerth! Half a moment! My hown cuthen'th gone to Mithter Wemmick at thith prethent minute, to hoffer him hany termth. Mithter Jaggerth! Half a quarter of a moment! If you'd have the condethenthun to be bought off from the t'other thide—at any thuperior prithe!—money no object!—Mithter Jaggerth—Mithter—!"

My guardian threw his supplicant off with supreme indifference, and left him dancing on the pavement as if it were red-hot. Without further interruption we reached the front office, where we found the clerk and the man in velveteen with the fur cap.

"Here's Mike," said the clerk, getting down from his stool, and approaching Mr. Jaggers confidentially.

"Oh!" said Mr. Jaggers, turning to the man, who was pulling a lock of hair in the middle of his forehead, like the Bull in Cock Robin pulling at the bell-rope; "your man comes on this afternoon. Well?"

"Well, Mas'r Jaggers," returned Mike, in the voice of a sufferer from a constitutional cold; "arter a deal o' trouble, I've found one, sir, as might do."

"What is he prepared to swear?"

"Well, Mas'r Jaggers," said Mike, wiping his nose on his fur cap this time, "in a general way, anythink."

Mr. Jaggers suddenly became most irate. "Now I warned you before," said he, throwing his forefinger at the terrified client, "that if you ever presumed to talk in that way here I'd make an example of you. You infernal scoundrel, how dare you tell ME that?"

The client looked scared, but bewildered too, as if he were unconscious what he had done.

"Spooney!" said the clerk, in a low voice, giving him a stir with his elbow. "Softhead! Need you say it face to face?"

"Now, I ask you, you blundering booby," said my guardian, very sternly, "once more, and for the last time, what the man you have brought here is prepared to swear?"

Mike looked hard at my guardian, as if he were trying to learn a lesson from his face, and slowly replied, "Ayther to character, or to having been in his company and never left him all the night in question."

"Now, be careful. In what station of life is this man?"

Mike looked at his cap, and looked at the floor, and looked at the ceiling, and looked at the clerk, and even looked at me, before beginning to reply, in a nervous manner, "We've dressed him up like—" when my guardian blustered out:

"What? You WILL, will you?"

("Spooney!" added the clerk again, with another stir.)

After some helpless casting about, Mike brightened and began again: "He is dressed like a 'spectable pieman. A sort of a pastry-cook."

"Is he here?" asked my guardian.

"I left him," said Mike, "a settin on some doorsteps round the corner."

"Take him past that window, and let me see him."

The window indicated was the office-window. We all three went to it, behind the wire blind, and presently saw the client go by in an accidental manner, with a murderous-looking tall individual, in a short suit of white linen and a paper cap. This guileless confectioner was not by any means sober, and had a black eye in the green stage of recovery, which was painted over.

"Tell him to take his witness away directly," said my guardian to the clerk, in extreme disgust, "and ask him what he means by bringing such a fellow as that."

My guardian then took me into his own room, and while he lunched, standing, from a sandwich-box and a pocket-flask of sherry (he seemed to bully his very sandwich as he ate it), informed me what arrangements he had made for me. I was to go to "Barnard's Inn," to young Mr. Pocket's room, where a bed had been sent in for my accommodation; I was to remain with young Mr. Pocket until Monday; on Monday I was to go with him to his father's house on a visit, that I might try how I liked it. Also I was told what my allowance was to be—it was a very liberal one—and had handed to me from one of my guardian's drawers the cards of certain tradesmen with whom I was to deal for all kinds of clothes, and such other things as I could in reason want. "You will find your credit good, Mr. Pip," said my guardian, whose flask of sherry smelled like a whole caskful, as he hastily refreshed himself; "but I shall by this means be able to check your bills, and to pull you up if I find you outrunning the constable. Of course you'll go wrong somehow, but that's no fault of mine."

After I had pondered a little over this encouraging sentiment, I asked Mr. Jaggers if I could send for a coach? He said it was not worthwhile, I was so near my destination; Wemmick should walk round with me, if I pleased.

I then found that Wemmick was the clerk in the next room. Another clerk was rung down from upstairs to take his place while he was out, and I accompanied him into the street, after shaking hands with my guardian. We found a new set of people lingering outside, but Wemmick made a way among them by saying coolly yet decisively, "I tell you it's no use; he won't have a word to say to one of you"; and we soon got clear of them, and went on side by side.

Casting my eyes on Mr. Wemmick as we went along, to see what he was like in the light of day, I found him to be a dry man, rather short in stature, with a square wooden face, whose expression seemed to have been imperfectly chipped out with a dull-edged chisel. There were some marks in it that might have been dimples, if the material had been softer and the instrument finer, but which, as it was, were only dints. The chisel had made three or four of these attempts at embellishment over his nose, but had given them up without an effort to smooth them off. I judged him to be a bachelor from the frayed condition of his linen, and he appeared to have sustained a good many bereavements; for he wore at least four mourning rings, besides a brooch representing a lady and a weeping willow at a tomb with an urn on it. I noticed, too, that several rings and seals hung at his watch-chain, as if he were quite laden with remembrances of departed friends. He had glittering eyes—small, keen, and black—and thin white mottled lips. He had had them, to the best of my belief, from forty to fifty years.

"So you were never in London before?" said Mr. Wemmick to me.

"No," said I.

"*I* was new here once," said Mr. Wemmick. "Rum to think of now!"

"You are well acquainted with it now?"

"Why, yes," said Mr. Wemmick. "I know the moves of it."

"Is it a very wicked place?" I asked, more for the sake of saying something than for information.

"You may get cheated, robbed, and murdered in London. But there are plenty of people anywhere who'll do that for you."

"If there is bad blood between you and them," said I, to soften it off a little.

"Oh! I don't know about bad blood," returned Mr. Wemmick, "there's not much bad blood about. If there's anything to be got by it."

"That makes it worse."

"You think so?" returned Mr. Wemmick. "Much about the same, I should say."

He wore his hat on the back of his head and looked straight before him: walking in a self-contained way as if there were nothing in the streets to claim his attention. His mouth was such a post-office of a mouth that he had a mechanical appearance of smiling. We had got to the top of Holborn Hill before I knew that it was merely a mechanical appearance, and that he was not smiling at all.

"Do you know where Mr. Matthew Pocket lives?" I asked Mr. Wemmick.
"Yes," said he, nodding in the direction. "At Hornsey, north of London."
"Is that far?"
"Well! Say five miles."
"Do you know him?"
"Why, you are a regular examiner!" said Mr. Wemmick, looking at me with an approving air. "Yes, I know him. *I* know him!"

There was an air of toleration or depreciation about his utterance of these words that rather depressed me; and I was still looking sideways at his block of a face in search of any encouraging note to the text when he said here we were at Barnard's Inn. My depression was not alleviated by the announcement, for I had supposed that establishment to be a hotel kept by one Barnard, to which the Blue Boar in our town was a mere public-house. Whereas I now found Barnard to be a ghost, and his inn the dingiest collection of shabby buildings ever squeezed together in a rank corner as a club for Tomcats.

We entered this haven through a wicket-gate, and were disgorged by an introductory passage into a melancholy little square that looked to me like a very confined burying-ground. I thought it had the most dismal trees in it, and the most dismal sparrows, and the most dismal cats, and the most dismal houses (in number half a dozen or so), that I had ever seen. I thought the windows of the sets of chambers into which these houses were divided were in every stage of dilapidated blind and curtain, crippled flowerpot, cracked glass, dusty decay and miserable makeshift; while To Let To Let To Let glared at me from empty rooms, as if no new wretches ever came there, and the vengeance of the soul of Barnard were being slowly appeased by the gradual suicide of the present occupants and their unholy interment under the gravel. A frouzy mourning of soot and smoke (I thought) attired this forlorn creation of Barnard, and it had strewn ashes on its head and on all its members, and was undergoing penance and humiliation as a mere dust-hole. Thus far the sense of sight; while dry-rot and wet-rot and all the silent rots that rot in neglected roof and cellar, rot of rat and mouse and bug and coaching-stables near at hand besides, addressed themselves faintly to my sense of smell, and moaned, "Try Barnard's Mixture."

So imperfect was this realization of the first of my great expectations, that I looked in dismay at Mr. Wemmick. "Ah!" said he, mistaking me; "the retirement reminds you of the country. So it does me."

He led me into a corner and conducted me up a flight of stairs—which appeared to me to be slowly collapsing into sawdust, so that one of these days the upper lodgers would look out at their doors and find themselves without the means of coming down—to a set of chambers on the top floor. MR. POCKET, JUN., was painted on the door, and there was a label on the letterbox, "Return shortly."

"He hardly thought you'd come so soon," Mr. Wemmick explained. "You don't want me anymore?"

"No, thank you," said I.

"As I keep the cash," Mr. Wemmick observed, "we shall most likely meet pretty often. Good day."

"Good day."

I put out my hand, and Mr. Wemmick at first looked at it as if he thought I wanted something. Then he looked at me, and said, correcting himself,

"To be sure! Yes. You're in the habit of shaking hands?"

I was rather confused, thinking it must be out of the London fashion, but said yes.

"I have got so out of it!" said Mr. Wemmick—"except at last. Very glad, I'm sure, to make your acquaintance. Good day!"

When we had shaken hands and he was gone, I opened the staircase window, and had nearly beheaded myself, for the lines had rotted away, and it came down like the guillotine. Happily it was so quick that I had not put my head out. After this escape I was content to take a foggy view of the Inn through the window's incrusting dirt, and to stand dolefully looking out, saying to myself that London was decidedly overrated.

Mr. Pocket, Junior's, idea of Shortly was not mine, for I had nearly maddened myself with looking out for half an hour, and had written my name with my finger several times in the dirt of every pane in the window, before I heard footsteps on the stairs. Gradually there arose before me the hat, head, neckcloth, waistcoat, trowsers, boots, of a member of society of about my own standing. He had a paper-bag under each arm, and a pottle of strawberries in one hand, and was out of breath.

"Mr. Pip?" said he.

"Mr. Pocket?" said I.

"Dear me!" he exclaimed. "I am extremely sorry; but I knew there was a coach from your part of the country at midday, and I thought you would come by that one. The fact is, I have been out on your account—not that that is any excuse—for I thought, coming from the country, you might like a little fruit after dinner, and I went to Covent Garden Market to get it good."

For a reason that I had I felt as if my eyes would start out of my head. I acknowledged his attention incoherently, and began to think this was a dream.

"Dear me!" said Mr. Pocket, Junior. "This door sticks so!"

As he was fast making jam of his fruit by wrestling with the door while the paper-bags were under his arms, I begged him to allow me to hold them. He relinquished them with an agreeable smile, and combated with the door as if it were a wild beast. It yielded so suddenly at last that he staggered back upon me, and I staggered back upon the opposite door, and we both laughed. But still I felt as if my eyes must start out of my head, and as if this must be a dream.

"Pray come in," said Mr. Pocket, Junior. "Allow me to lead the way. I am rather bare here, but I hope you'll be able to make out tolerably well till Monday. My father thought you would get on more agreeably through tomorrow with me than with him, and might like to take a walk about London. I am sure I shall be very happy to show London to you. As to our table, you won't find that bad, I hope, for it will be supplied from our coffeehouse here, and (it is only right I should add) at your expense, such being Mr. Jaggers's directions. As to our lodging, it's not by any means splendid, because I have my own bread to earn, and my father hasn't anything to give me, and I shouldn't be willing to take it if he had. This is our sitting-room—just such chairs and tables and carpet and so forth, you see, as they could spare from home. You mustn't give me credit for the tablecloth and spoons and castors, they come for you from the coffeehouse. This is my little bedroom—rather musty, but Barnard's *is* musty. This is your bedroom; the furniture's hired for the occasion, but I trust it will answer the purpose; if you should want anything, I'll go and fetch it. The chambers are retired, and we shall be alone together; but we sha'n't fight, I dare say. But, dear me, I beg your pardon, you're holding the fruit all this time. Pray let me take these bags from you. I am quite ashamed."

As I stood opposite to Mr. Pocket, Junior, delivering him the bags, One, Two, I saw the starting appearance come into his own eyes that I knew to be in mine, and he said, falling back:

"Lord bless me, you're the prowling boy!"

"And you," said I, "are the pale young gentleman!"

Twenty-two

THE PALE YOUNG GENTLEMAN AND I STOOD CONTEMPLATing one another in Barnard's Inn until we both burst out laughing. "The idea of its being you!" said he. "The idea of its being *you!*" said I. And then we contemplated one another afresh, and laughed again. "Well!" said the pale young gentleman, reaching out his hand good-humoredly, "it's all over now, I hope, and it will be magnanimous in you if you'll forgive me for having knocked you about so."

I derived from this speech that Mr. Herbert Pocket (for Herbert was the pale young gentleman's name) still rather confounded his intention with his execution. But I made a modest reply, and we shook hands warmly.

"You hadn't come into your good fortune at that time?" said Herbert Pocket.

"No," said I.

"No," he acquiesced: "I heard it had happened very lately. *I* was rather on the lookout for good fortune then."

"Indeed?"

"Yes. Miss Havisham had sent for me, to see if she could take a fancy to me. But she couldn't—at all events, she didn't."

I thought it polite to remark that I was surprised to hear that.

"Bad taste," said Herbert, laughing, "but a fact. Yes, she had sent for me on a trial visit, and if I had come out of it successfully, I suppose I should have been provided for; perhaps I should have been what-you-may-called it to Estella."

"What's that?" I asked, with sudden gravity.

He was arranging his fruit in plates while we talked, which divided his attention, and was the cause of his making this lapse of a word. "Affianced," he explained, still busy with the fruit. "Betrothed. Engaged. What's-his-named. Any word of that sort."

"How did you bear your disappointment?" I asked.

"Pooh!" said he, "I didn't care much for it. *She's* a Tartar."

"Miss Havisham?"

"I don't say no to that, but I mean Estella. That girl's hard and haughty and capricious to the last degree, and has been brought up by Miss Havisham to wreak vengeance on all the male sex."

"What relation is she to Miss Havisham?"

"None," said he. "Only adopted."

"Why should she wreak revenge on all the male sex? What revenge?"

"Lord, Mr. Pip!" said he. "Don't you know?"

"No," said I.

"Dear me! It's quite a story, and shall be saved till dinner-time. And now let me take the liberty of asking you a question. How did you come there that day?"

I told him, and he was attentive until I had finished, and then burst out laughing again, and asked me if I was sore afterward? I didn't ask him if *he* was, for my conviction on that point was perfectly established.

"Mr. Jaggers is your guardian, I understand?" he went on.

"Yes."

"You know he is Miss Havisham's man of business and solicitor, and has her confidence when nobody else has?"

This was bringing me (I felt) toward dangerous ground. I answered with a constraint I made no attempt to disguise, that I had seen Mr. Jaggers in Miss Havisham's house on the very day of our combat, but never at any other time, and that I believed he had no recollection of having ever seen me there.

"He was so obliging as to suggest my father for your tutor, and he called on my father to propose it. Of course he knew about my father from his connection with Miss Havisham. My father is Miss Havisham's nephew; not that that implies familiar intercourse between them, for he is a bad courtier and will not propitiate her."

Herbert Pocket had a frank and easy way with him that was very taking. I had never seen anyone then, and I have never seen anyone since, who so strongly expressed to me, in every look and tone, a natural incapacity to do anything secret or mean. There was something wonderfully hopeful about his general air, and something that at the same time whispered to me that he would never be very successful or rich. I don't know how this was. I became imbued with the notion on that first occasion before we sat down to dinner, but I cannot define by what means.

He was still a pale young gentleman, and had a certain conquered languor about him in the midst of his spirits and briskness that did not seem indicative of natural strength. He had not a handsome face, but it was better than handsome: being extremely amiable and cheerful. His figure was a little ungainly, as in the days when my knuckles had taken such liberties with it; but it looked as if it would always be light and young. Whether Mr. Trabb's local work would have sat more gracefully on him than on me, may be a question; but I am conscious that he carried off his rather old clothes much better than I carried off my new suit.

As he was so communicative, I felt that reserve on my part would be a bad return, unsuited to our years. I therefore told him my small story, and laid stress on my being forbidden to inquire who my benefactor was. I further mentioned that as I had been brought up a blacksmith in a country place, and knew very little of the ways of politeness, I would take it as a great kindness in him if he would give me a hint whenever he saw me at a loss or going wrong.

"With pleasure," said he, "though I venture to prophesy that you'll want very few hints. I dare say we shall be often together, and I should like to banish any needless restraint between us. Will you do me the favor to begin at once to call me by my Christian name, Herbert?"

I thanked him, and said I would. I informed him in exchange that my Christian name was Philip.

"I don't take to Philip," said he, smiling, "for it sounds like a moral boy out of the spelling-book, who was so lazy that he fell into a pond, or so fat that he couldn't see out of his eyes, or so avaricious that he locked up his cake till the mice ate it, or so determined to go birds'-nesting that he got himself eaten by bears who lived handy in the neighborhood. I tell you what I should like. We are so harmonious, and you have been a blacksmith—would you mind it?"

"I shouldn't mind anything that you propose," I answered; "but I don't understand you."

"Would you mind Handel for a familiar name? There's a charming piece of music by Handel, called the Harmonious Blacksmith."

"I should like it very much."

"Then, my dear Handel," said he, turning round as the door opened, "here is the dinner, and I must beg of you to take the top of the table, because the dinner is of your providing."

This I would not hear of, so he took the top, and I faced him. It was a nice little dinner—seemed to me then a very Lord Mayor's Feast—and it acquired additional relish from being eaten under those independent circumstances, with no old people by, and with London all around us. This again was heightened by a certain gipsy character that set the banquet off; for, while the table was, as Mr. Pumblechook might have said, the lap of luxury—being entirely furnished forth from the coffeehouse—the circumjacent region of sitting-room was of a comparatively pastureless and shifty character: imposing on the waiter the wandering habits of putting the covers on the floor (where he fell over them), the melted butter in the armchair, the bread on the bookshelves, the cheese in the coal-scuttle, and the boiled fowl into my bed in the next room—where I found much of its parsley and butter in a state of congelation when I retired for the night. All this made the feast delightful, and when the waiter was not there to watch me my pleasure was without alloy.

When we had made some progress in the dinner I reminded Herbert of his promise to tell me about Miss Havisham.

"True," he replied. "I'll redeem it at once. Let me introduce the topic, Handel, by mentioning that in London it is not the custom to put the knife in the mouth—for fear of accidents—and that while the fork is reserved for that use, it is not put further in than is necessary. It is scarcely worth mentioning, only it's as well to do as other people do. Also, the spoon is not generally used over-hand, but under. This has two advantages. You get at your mouth better (which after all is the object), and you save a good deal of the attitude of opening oysters, on the part of the right elbow."

He offered these friendly suggestions in such a lively way that we both laughed, and I scarcely blushed.

"Now," he pursued, "concerning Miss Havisham. Miss Havisham, you must know, was a spoiled child. Her mother died when she was a baby, and her father denied her nothing. Her father was a country gentleman down in your part of the world, and was a brewer. I don't know why it should be a crack thing to be a brewer; but it is indisputable that while you cannot possibly be genteel and bake, you may be as genteel as never was and brew. You see it every day."

"Yet a gentleman may not keep a public-house; may he?" said I.

"Not on any account," returned Herbert; "but a public-house may keep a gentleman. Well! Mr. Havisham was very rich and very proud. So was his daughter."

"Miss Havisham was an only child?" I hazarded.

"Stop a moment, I am coming to that. No, she was not an only child; she had a half-brother. Her father privately married again—his cook, I rather think."

"I thought he was proud," said I.

"My good Handel, so he was. He married his second wife privately, because he was proud, and in course of time *she* died. When she was dead, I apprehend he first told his daughter what he had done, and then the son became a part of the family, residing in the house you are acquainted with. As the son grew a young man he turned out riotous, extravagant, undutiful—altogether bad. At last his father disinherited him; but he softened when he was dying, and left him well off, though not nearly so well off as Miss Havisham. Take another glass of wine, and excuse my mentioning that society as a body does not expect one to be so strictly conscientious in emptying one's glass as to turn it bottom upwards with the rim on one's nose."

I had been doing this, in an excess of attention to his recital. I thanked him and apologized. He said, "Not at all," and resumed.

"Miss Havisham was now an heiress, and you may suppose was looked after as a great match. Her half-brother had now ample means again, but what with debts and what with new madness wasted them most fearfully again. There were stronger differences between him and her than there had been between him and his father, and it is suspected that he cherished a deep and mortal grudge against her, as having influenced the father's anger. Now I come to the cruel part of the story—merely breaking off, my dear Handel, to remark that a dinner-napkin will not go into a tumbler."

Why I was trying to pack mine into my tumbler, I am wholly unable to say. I only know that I found myself, with a perseverance worthy of a much better cause, making the most strenuous exertions to compress it within those limits. Again I thanked him and apologized, and again he said, in the cheerfulest manner, "Not at all, I am sure!" and resumed.

"There appeared upon the scene—say at the races, or the public balls, or anywhere else you like—a certain man, who made love to Miss Havisham. I never saw him, for this happened five-and-twenty years ago, before you and I were, Handel, but I have heard my father mention that he was a showy man, and the kind of man for the purpose. But that he was not to be, without ignorance or prejudice, mistaken for a gentleman, my father most strongly asseverates; because it is a principle of his that no man who was not a true gentleman at heart ever was, since the world began, a true gentleman in manner. He says no varnish can hide the grain of the wood; and the more varnish you put on the more the grain will express itself. Well! This man pursued Miss Havisham closely, and professed to be devoted to her. I believe she had not shown much susceptibility up to that time; but all she possessed certainly came out then, and she passionately loved him. There is no doubt that she perfectly idolized him. He practiced on her affection in that systematic way, that he got great sums of money from her, and he induced her to buy her brother out of a share in the brewery (which had been weakly left him by his father) at an immense price, on the plea that when he was her husband he must hold and manage it all. Your guardian was not at that time in Miss Havisham's councils, and she was too haughty and too much in love to be advised by anyone. Her relations were poor and scheming, with the exception of my father; he was poor enough, but not time-serving or jealous. The only independent one among them, he warned her that she was doing too much for this man, and was placing herself too unreservedly in his power. She took the first opportunity of angrily ordering my father out of the house, in his presence, and my father has never seen her since."

I thought of her having said, "Matthew will come and see me at last when I am laid dead upon that table"; and I asked Herbert whether his father was so inveterate against her?

"It's not that," said he, "but she charged him before her intended husband with being disappointed in the hope of fawning upon her for his own advancement, and, if he were to go to her now, it would look true—even to him—and even to her after all. To return to the man, and make an end of him. The marriage day was fixed, the wedding dresses were bought, the wedding tour was planned out, the wedding guests were invited. The day came, but not the bridegroom. He wrote her a letter—"

"Which she received," I struck in, "when she was dressing for her marriage? At twenty minutes to nine?"

"At the hour and minute," said Herbert, nodding, "at which she afterward stopped all the clocks. What was in it, further than that it most heartlessly broke the marriage off, I can't tell you, because I don't know. When she recovered from a bad illness that she had, she laid the whole place waste, as you have seen it, and she has never since looked upon the light of day."

"Is that all the story?" I asked, after considering it.

"All I know of it; and indeed I only know so much through piecing it out for myself; for my father always avoids it, and, even when Miss Havisham invited me to go there, told me no more of it than it was absolutely requisite I should understand. But I have forgotten one thing. It has been supposed that the man to whom she gave her misplaced confidence acted throughout in concert with her half-brother; that it was a conspiracy between them; and that they shared the profits."

"I wonder he didn't marry her and get all the property," said I.

"He may have been married already, and her cruel mortification may have been a part of her half-brother's scheme," said Herbert. "Mind! I don't know that."

"What became of the two men?" I asked, after again considering the subject.

"They fell into deeper shame and degradation—if there can be deeper—and ruin."

"Are they alive now?"

"I don't know."

"You said just now that Estella was not related to Miss Havisham, but adopted. When adopted?"

Herbert shrugged his shoulders. "There has always been an Estella since I have heard of a Miss Havisham. I know no more. And now, Handel," said he, finally throwing off the story, as it were, "there is a perfectly open understanding between us. All that I know about Miss Havisham, you know."

"And all that I know," I retorted, "you know."

"I fully believe it. So there can be no competition or perplexity between you and me. And as to the condition on which you hold your advancement in life—namely, that you are not to inquire or discuss to whom you owe it—you may be very sure that it will never be encroached upon, or even approached by me, or by anyone belonging to me."

In truth, he said this with so much delicacy, that I felt the subject done with, even though I should be under his father's roof for years and years to come. Yet he said it with so much meaning, too, that I felt he as perfectly understood Miss Havisham to be my benefactress as I understood the fact myself.

It had not occurred to me before that he had led up to the theme for the purpose of clearing it out of our way; but we were so much the lighter and easier for having broached it, that I now perceived this to be the case. We were very gay and sociable, and I asked him, in the course of conversation, what he was? He replied, "A capitalist—an Insurer of Ships." I suppose he saw me glancing about the room in search of some tokens of Shipping, or capital, for he added, "In the City."

I had grand ideas of the wealth and importance of Insurers of Ships in the City, and I began to think with awe of having laid a young Insurer on his back, blackened his enterprising eye, and cut his responsible head open. But, again, there came upon me, for my relief, that odd impression that Herbert Pocket would never be very successful or rich.

"I shall not rest satisfied with merely employing my capital in insuring ships. I shall buy up some good Life Assurance shares, and cut into the Direction. I shall also do a little in the mining way. None of these things will interfere with my chartering a few thousand tons on my own account. I think I shall trade," said he, leaning back in his chair, "to the East Indies, for silks, shawls, spices, dyes, drugs, and precious woods. It's an interesting trade."

"And the profits are large?" said I.

"Tremendous!" said he.

I wavered again, and began to think here were greater expectations than my own.

"I think I shall trade, also," said he, putting his thumbs in his waistcoat pockets, "to the West Indies, for sugar, tobacco, and rum. Also to Ceylon, specially for elephants' tusks."

"You will want a good many ships," said I.

"A perfect fleet," said he.

Quite overpowered by the magnificence of these transactions, I asked him where the ships he insured mostly traded to at present?

"I haven't begun insuring yet," he replied. "I am looking about me."

Somehow, that pursuit seemed more in keeping with Barnard's Inn. I said (in a tone of conviction), "Ah-h!"

"Yes. I am in a counting-house, and looking about me."

"Is a counting-house profitable?" I asked.

"To—do you mean to the young fellow who's in it?" he asked, in reply.

"Yes; to you."

"Why, n-no: not to me." He said this with the air of one carefully reckoning up and striking a balance. "Not directly profitable. That is, it doesn't pay me anything, and I have to—keep myself."

This certainly had not a profitable appearance, and I shook my head as if I would imply that it would be difficult to lay by much accumulative capital from such a source of income.

"But the thing is," said Herbert Pocket, "that you look about you. *That's* the grand thing. You are in a counting-house, you know, and you look about you."

It struck me as a singular implication that you couldn't be out of a counting-house, you know, and look about you; but I silently deferred to his experience.

"Then the time comes," said Herbert, "when you see your opening. And you go in, and you swoop upon it, and you make your capital, and then there you are! When you have once made your capital, you have nothing to do but employ it!"

This was very like his way of conducting that encounter in the garden; very like. His manner of bearing his poverty, too, exactly corresponded to his manner of bearing that defeat. It seemed to me that he took all blows and buffets now with just the same air as he had taken mine then. It was evident that he had nothing around him but the simplest necessaries, for everything that I remarked upon turned out to have been sent in on my account from the coffeehouse or somewhere else.

Yet, having already made his fortune in his own mind, he was so unassuming with it that I felt quite grateful to him for not being puffed up. It was a pleasant addition to his naturally pleasant ways, and we got on famously. In the evening we went out for a walk in the streets, and went half-price to the Theater; and next day we went to church at Westminster Abbey, and in the afternoon we walked in the Parks; and I wondered who shod all the horses there, and wished Joe did.

On a moderate computation, it was many months, that Sunday, since I had left Joe and Biddy. The space interposed between myself and them partook of that expansion, and our marshes were any distance off. That I could have been at our old church in my old churchgoing clothes, on the very last Sunday that ever was, seemed a combination of impossibilities, geographical and social, solar and lunar. Yet in the London streets, so crowded with people and so brilliantly lighted in the dusk of evening, there were depressing hints of reproaches for that I had put the poor old kitchen at home so far away; and in the dead of night, the footsteps of some incapable impostor of a porter mooning about Barnard's Inn, under pretense of watching it, fell hollow on my heart.

On the Monday morning at a quarter before nine, Herbert went to the counting-house to report himself—to look about him, too, I suppose—and I bore him company. He was to come away in an hour or two to attend me to Hammersmith, and I was to wait about for him. It appeared to me that the eggs from which young Insurers were hatched were incubated in dust and heat, like the eggs of ostriches, judging from the places to which those incipient giants repaired on a Monday morning. Nor did the counting-house where Herbert assisted show in my eyes as at all a good Observatory, being a back second floor up a yard, of a grimy presence in all particulars, and with a look into another back second floor rather than a look out.

I waited about until it was noon, and I went upon 'Change, and I saw fluey men sitting there under the bills about shipping, whom I took to be great merchants, though I couldn't understand why they should all be out of spirits. When Herbert came, we went and had lunch at a celebrated house which I then quite venerated, but now believe to have been the most abject superstition in Europe, and where I could not help noticing, even then, that there was much more gravy on the tablecloths and knives and waiters' clothes than in the steaks. This collation disposed of at a moderate price (considering the grease, which was not charged for), we went back to Barnard's Inn and got my little portmanteau, and then took coach for Hammersmith. We arrived there at two or three o'clock in the afternoon, and had very little way to walk to Mr. Pocket's house. Lifting the latch of a gate, we passed direct into a little garden overlooking the river, where Mr. Pocket's children were playing about. And unless I deceive myself on a point where my interests or prepossessions are certainly not concerned, I saw at once that Mr. and Mrs. Pocket's children were not growing up or being brought up, but were tumbling up.

Mrs. Pocket was sitting on a garden chair under a tree, reading, with her legs upon another garden chair, and Mrs. Pocket's two nursemaids were looking about them while the children played. "Mamma," said Herbert, "this is young Mr. Pip." Upon which Mrs. Pocket received me with an appearance of amiable dignity, and I thought her a sweet woman.

"Master Alick and Miss Jane," cried one of the nurses to two of the children, "if you go a bouncing up against them bushes you'll fall over into the river and be drownded, and what'll your pa say then!"

At the same time this nurse picked up Mrs. Pocket's handkerchief, and said, "If that don't make six times you've dropped it, Mum!" Upon which Mrs. Pocket laughed, and said, "Thank you, Flopson"; and settling herself in one chair only, resumed her book. Her countenance immediately assumed a knitted and intent expression, as if she had been reading for a week; but before she could have read half a dozen lines she fixed her eyes upon me, and said, "I hope your mamma is quite well?" This unexpected inquiry put me into such a difficulty that I began saying in the absurdest way that if there had been any such person I had no doubt she would have been quite well, and would have been very much obliged, and would have sent her compliments, when the nurse came to my rescue.

"Well!" she cried, picking up the pocket-handkerchief, "if that don't make seven times! What ARE you a doing of this afternoon, Mum?" Mrs. Pocket received her property at first with a look of unutterable surprise, as if she had never seen it before, and then with a laugh of recognition, and said, "Thank you, Flopson," and forgot me, and went on reading.

I found, now I had leisure to count them, that there were no fewer than six little Pockets present in various stages of tumbling up. I had scarcely arrived at the total when a seventh was heard, as in the region of air, wailing dolefully.

"If there ain't Baby!" said Flopson, appearing to think it most surprising. "Make haste up, Millers!"

Millers, who was the other nurse, retired into the house, and by degrees the child's wailing was hushed and stopped, as if it were a young ventriloquist with something in its mouth. Mrs. Pocket read all the time, and I was curious to know what the book could be.

We were waiting, I supposed, for Mr. Pocket to come out to us; at any rate we waited there, and so I had an opportunity of observing the remarkable family phenomenon that whenever any of the children strayed near Mrs. Pocket in their play, they always tripped themselves up and tumbled over her—always very much to her momentary astonishment and their own more enduring lamentation. I was at a loss to account for this surprising circumstance, and could not help giving my mind to speculations about it, until by-and-by Millers came down with the baby, which baby was handed to Flopson, which Flopson was handing to Mrs. Pocket, when she too went fairly head-foremost over Mrs. Pocket, baby and all, and was caught by Herbert and myself.

"Gracious me, Flopson!" said Mrs. Pocket, "everybody's tumbling!"

"Gracious you, indeed, Mum!" returned Flopson, very red in the face; "what have you got there?"

"*I* got here, Flopson?" asked Mrs. Pocket.

"Why, if it ain't your footstool!" cried Flopson. "And if you keep it under your skirts like that, who's to help tumbling! Here! Take the baby, Mum, and give me your book."

Mrs. Pocket acted on the advice, and danced the infant a little in her lap, while the other children played about it prettily. This had lasted but a very short time, when Mrs. Pocket issued summary orders that they were all to be taken into the house for a nap. Thus I made the second discovery on that first occasion, that the nurture of the little Pockets consisted of alternately tumbling up and lying down.

Under these circumstances, when Flopson and Millers had got the children into the house like a little flock of sheep, and Mr. Pocket came out of it to make my acquaintance, I was not much surprised to find that Mr. Pocket was a gentleman with a rather perplexed expression of face, and with his hair disordered on his head, as if he didn't quite see his way to putting anything straight.

Twenty-three

MR. POCKET SAID HE WAS GLAD TO SEE ME, AND HE hoped I was not sorry to see him. "For I really am not," he added, with his son's smile, "an alarming personage." He was a young-looking man, in spite of his perplexities, and his manner seemed quite natural. I use the word natural in the sense of its being unaffected; there was something comic in his distraught way, as though it would have been downright ludicrous but for his own perception that it was very near being so. When he had talked with me a little he said to Mrs. Pocket, rather anxiously, "Belinda, I hope you have welcomed Mr. Pip?" And she looked up from her book, and said, "Yes." She then smiled upon me in an absent state of mind, and asked me if I liked the taste of orange-flower water? As the question had no bearing, near or remote, on any foregone or subsequent transaction, I consider it to have been thrown out, like her previous approaches, in general conversational hospitality.

I found out within a few hours, and may mention it at once, that Mrs. Pocket was the only daughter of a certain quite accidental deceased Knight, who had invented for himself a conviction that his deceased father would have been made a Baronet but for somebody's determined opposition, arising out of entirely personal motives—I forget whose, if I ever knew—the Sovereign's, the Prime Minister's, the Lord Chancellor's, the Archbishop of Canterbury's, anybody's—and had tacked himself on the nobles of the earth in right of this quite supposititious fact. I believe he had been knighted himself for storming the English grammar at the point of a pen in a desperate address engrossed on vellum, on the occasion of the laying of the first stone of some building or other, and handing some Royal Personage either the trowel or the mortar. Be that as it may, he had directed Mrs. Pocket to be brought up from her cradle as one who in the nature of things must marry a title, and who was to be guarded from the acquisition of plebeian domestic knowledge. So successful a watch and ward had been established over the young lady by this judicious parent that she had grown up highly ornamental, but perfectly helpless and useless. With her character thus happily formed, in the first bloom of her youth she had encountered Mr. Pocket, who was also in the first bloom of youth, and not quite decided whether to mount to the Woolsack, or to roof himself in with a Mitre. As his doing the one or the other was a mere question of time, he and Mrs. Pocket had taken Time by the forelock (at a season when, to judge from its length, it would seem to have wanted cutting), and had married without the knowledge of the judicious parent. The judicious parent having nothing to bestow or withhold but his blessing, had handsomely settled that dower upon them after a short struggle, and had informed Mr. Pocket that his wife was "a treasure for a Prince." Mr. Pocket had invested the Prince's treasure in the ways of the world ever since, and it was supposed to have brought him in but indifferent interest. Still Mrs. Pocket was in general the object of a queer sort of respectful pity, because she had not married a title; while Mr. Pocket was the object of a queer sort of forgiving reproach because he had never got one.

Mr. Pocket took me into the house and showed me my room, which was a pleasant one, and so furnished as that I could use it with comfort for my own private sitting-room. He then knocked at the doors of two other similar rooms, and introduced me to their occupants, by name Drummle and Startop. Drummle, an old-looking young man of a heavy order of architecture, was whistling. Startop, younger in years and appearance, was reading and holding his head, as if he thought himself in danger of exploding it with too strong a charge of knowledge.

Both Mr. and Mrs. Pocket had such a noticeable air of being in somebody else's hands, that I wondered who really was in possession of the house and let them live there, until I found this unknown power to be the servants. It was a smooth way of going on, perhaps, in respect of saving trouble; but it had the appearance of being expensive, for the servants felt it a duty they owed to themselves to be nice in their eating and drinking, and to keep a deal of company downstairs. They allowed a very liberal table to Mr. and Mrs. Pocket; yet it always appeared to me that by far the best part of the house to have boarded in would have been the kitchen—always supposing the boarder capable of self-defense, for, before I had been there a week a neighboring lady, with whom the family were personally unacquainted, wrote in to say that she had seen Millers slapping the baby. This greatly distressed Mrs. Pocket, who burst into tears on receiving the note, and said it was an extraordinary thing that the neighbors couldn't mind their own business.

By degrees I learned, and chiefly from Herbert, that Mr. Pocket had been educated at Harrow and at Cambridge, where he had distinguished himself; but that when he had had the happiness of marrying Mrs. Pocket, very early in life, he had impaired his prospects and taken up the calling of a Grinder. After grinding a number of dull blades—of whom it was remarkable that their fathers, when influential, were always going to help him to preferment, but always forgot to do it when the blades had left the Grindstone—he had wearied of that poor work and come to London. Here, after gradually failing in loftier hopes, he had "read" with divers who had lacked opportunities or neglected them, and had refurbished divers others for special occasions, and had turned his acquirements to the account of literary compilation and correction, and on such means, added to some very moderate private resources, still maintained the house I saw.

Mr. and Mrs. Pocket had a toady neighbor—a widow lady of that highly sympathetic nature that she agreed with everybody, blessed everybody, and shed smiles and tears on everybody according to circumstances. This lady's name was Mrs. Coiler, and I had the honor of taking her down to dinner on the day of my installation. She gave me to understand on the stairs that it was a blow to dear Mrs. Pocket that dear Mr. Pocket should be under the necessity of receiving gentlemen to read with him. That did not extend to Me, she told me in a gush of love and confidence (at that time I had known her something less than five minutes); if they were all like Me, it would be quite another thing.

"But dear Mrs. Pocket," said Mrs. Coiler, "after his early disappointment (not that dear Mr. Pocket was to blame in that), requires so much luxury and elegance—"

"Yes, ma'am," said I, to stop her, for I was afraid she was going to cry.

"And she is of so aristocratic a disposition—"

"Yes, ma'am," I said again with the same object as before.

"—that it *is* hard," said Mrs. Coiler, "to have dear Mr. Pocket's time and attention diverted from dear Mrs. Pocket."

I could not help thinking that it might be harder if the butcher's time and attention were diverted from dear Mrs. Pocket; but I said nothing, and indeed had enough to do in keeping a bashful watch upon my company-manners.

It came to my knowledge through what passed between Mrs. Pocket and Drummle while I was attentive to my knife and fork, spoon, glasses, and other instruments of self-destruction, that Drummle, whose Christian name was Bentley, was actually the next heir but one to a baronetcy. It further appeared that the book I had seen Mrs. Pocket reading in the garden was all about titles, and that she knew the exact date at which her grandpapa would have come into the book, if he ever had come at all. Drummle didn't say much, but in his limited way (he struck me as a sulky kind of a fellow) he spoke as one of the elect, and recognized Mrs. Pocket as a woman and a sister. No one but themselves and Mrs. Coiler, the toady neighbor, showed any interest in this part of the conversation, and it appeared to me that it was painful to Herbert; but it promised to last a long time, when the page came in with the announcement of a domestic affliction. It was, in effect, that the cook had "mislaid" the beef. To my unutterable amazement, I now, for the first time, saw Mr. Pocket relieve his mind by going through a performance that struck me as very extraordinary, but which made no effect on anybody else, and with which I soon became as familiar as the rest. He laid down the carving-knife and fork—being engaged in carving at the moment—put his two hands into his disturbed hair, and appeared to make an extraordinary effort to lift himself up by it. When he had done this, and had not lifted himself up at all, he quietly went on with what he was about.

Mrs. Coiler then changed the subject, and began to flatter me. I liked it for a few moments, but she flattered me so very grossly that the pleasure was soon over. She had a serpentine way of coming close at me when she pretended to be vitally interested in the friends and localities I had left, which was altogether snaky and fork-tongued; and when she made an occasional bounce upon Startop (who said very little), or upon Drummle (who said less), I rather envied them for being on the opposite side of the table.

After dinner the children were introduced, and Mrs. Coiler made admiring comments on their eyes, noses, and legs—a sagacious way of improving their minds. There were four little girls, and two little boys, besides the baby who might have been either, and the baby's next successor who was as yet neither. They were brought in by Flopson and Millers, much as though those two noncommissioned officers had been recruiting somewhere for children and had enlisted these; while Mrs. Pocket looked at the young Nobles that ought to have been, as if she rather thought she had had the pleasure of inspecting them before, but didn't quite know what to make of them.

"Here! Give me your fork, mum, and take the baby," said Flopson. "Don't take it that way, or you'll get its head under the table."

Thus advised, Mrs. Pocket took it the other way, and got its head upon the table; which was announced to all present by a prodigious concussion.

"Dear, dear! Give it me back, mum," said Flopson; "and Miss Jane come and dance to baby, do!"

One of the little girls—a mere mite, who seemed to have prematurely taken upon herself some charge of the others—stepped out of her place by me, and danced to and from the baby until it left off crying, and laughed. Then all the children laughed, and Mr. Pocket (who in the meantime had twice endeavored to lift himself up by the hair) laughed, and we all laughed and were glad.

Flopson, by dint of doubling the baby at the joints like a Dutch doll, then got it safely into Mrs. Pocket's lap, and gave it the nutcrackers to play with; at the same time recommending Mrs. Pocket to take notice that the handles of that instrument were not likely to agree with its eyes, and sharply charging Miss Jane to look after the same. Then the two nurses left the room, and had a lively scuffle on the staircase with a dissipated page who had waited at dinner, and who had clearly lost half his buttons at the gambling-table.

I was made very uneasy in my mind by Mrs. Pocket's falling into a discussion with Drummle respecting the dates of two baronetcies while she ate a sliced orange steeped in sugar and wine, and forgetting all about the baby on her lap, who did most appalling things with the nutcrackers. At length little Jane, perceiving its young brains to be imperiled, softly left her place, and with many small artifices coaxed the dangerous weapon away. Mrs. Pocket finishing her orange at about the same time, and not approving of this, said to Jane:

"You naughty child, how dare you? Go and sit down this instant!"

"Mamma dear," lisped the little girl, "baby ood have put hith eyeth out."

"How dare you tell me so!" retorted Mrs. Pocket. "Go and sit down in your chair this moment!"

Mrs. Pocket's dignity was so crushing that I felt quite abashed, as if I myself had done something to rouse it.

"Belinda," remonstrated Mr. Pocket from the other end of the table, "how can you be so unreasonable? Jane only interfered for the protection of baby."

"I will not allow anybody to interfere," said Mrs. Pocket. "I am surprised, Matthew, that you should expose me to the affront of interference."

"Good God!" cried Mr. Pocket, in an outbreak of desperation. "Are infants to be nutcrackered into their tombs, and is nobody to save them?"

"I will not be interfered with by Jane," said Mrs. Pocket, with a majestic glance at that innocent little offender. "I hope I know my poor grandpapa's position. Jane, indeed!"

Mr. Pocket got his hands in his hair again, and this time really did lift himself some inches out of his chair. "Hear this!" he helplessly exclaimed to the elements. "Babies are to be nutcrackered dead, for people's poor grandpapa's positions!" Then he let himself down again, and became silent.

We all looked awkwardly at the tablecloth while this was going on. A pause succeeded, during which the honest and irrepressible baby made a series of leaps and crows at little Jane, who appeared to me to be the only member of the family (irrespective of servants) with whom it had any decided acquaintance.

"Mr. Drummle," said Mrs. Pocket, "will you ring for Flopson? Jane, you undutiful little thing, go and lie down. Now, baby-darling, come with ma!"

The baby was the soul of honor, and protested with all its might. It doubled itself up the wrong way over Mrs. Pocket's arm, exhibited a pair of knitted shoes and dimpled ankles to the company in lieu of its soft face, and was carried out in the highest state of mutiny. And it gained its point after all, for I saw it through the window within a few minutes, being nursed by little Jane.

It happened that the other five children were left behind at the dinner table, through Flopson's having some private engagement and their not being anybody else's business. I thus became aware of the mutual relations between them and Mr. Pocket, which were exemplified in the following manner. Mr. Pocket, with the normal perplexity of his face heightened and his hair rumpled, looked at them for some minutes as if he couldn't make out how they came to be boarding and lodging in that establishment, and why they hadn't been billeted by Nature on somebody else. Then, in a distant Missionary way, he asked them certain questions—as why little Joe had that hole in his frill:

who said, Pa, Flopson was going to mend it when she had time—and how lit-tle Fanny came by that whitlow: who said, Pa, Millers was going to poultice it when she didn't forget. Then he melted into parental tenderness, and gave them a shilling apiece and told them to go and play; and then as they went out, with one very strong effort to lift himself up by the hair, he dismissed the hopeless subject.

In the evening there was rowing on the river. As Drummle and Startop had each a boat I resolved to set up mine, and to cut them both out. I was pretty good at most exercises in which country-boys are adepts, but as I was conscious of wanting elegance of style for the Thames—not to say for other waters—I at once engaged to place myself under the tuition of the winner of a prize-wherry who plied at our stairs, and to whom I was introduced by my new allies. This practical authority confused me very much by saying I had the arm of a blacksmith. If he could have known how nearly the compliment lost him his pupil I doubt if he would have paid it.

There was a supper-tray after we got home at night, and I think we should all have enjoyed ourselves but for a rather disagreeable domestic occurrence. Mrs. Pocket was extremely sweet, and Mr. Pocket was in good spirits, when a housemaid came in, and said, "If you please, sir, I should wish to speak to you."

"Speak to your master?" said Mrs. Pocket, whose dignity was roused again. "How can you think of such a thing! Go and speak to Flopson. Or speak to me at some other time."

"Begging your pardon, ma'am," returned the housemaid, "I should wish to speak at once, and to speak to master."

Hereupon Mr. Pocket went out of the room, and we made the best of ourselves until he came back.

"This is a pretty thing, Belinda!" said Mr. Pocket, returning with a coun-tenance expressive of grief and despair. "Here's the cook lying insensibly drunk on the kitchen-floor, with a large bundle of fresh butter made up in the cupboard ready to sell for grease!"

Mrs. Pocket instantly showed much amiable emotion, and said, "This is that odious Mary Anne's doing!"

"What do you mean, Belinda?" demanded Mr. Pocket.

"Mary Anne has told you," said Mrs. Pocket. "Did I not see her with my own eyes and hear her with my own ears, come into the room just now and ask to speak to you?"

"But has she not taken me downstairs, Belinda," returned Mr. Pocket, "and shown me the woman, and the bundle too?"

"And do you defend her, Matthew," said Mrs. Pocket, "for making mis-chief?"

Mr. Pocket uttered a dismal groan.

"Am I, grandpapa's granddaughter, to be nothing in the house?" said Mrs. Pocket. "Besides, the cook has always been a very nice respectful woman, and said, in the most natural manner, when she came to look after the situation, she felt I was born to be a Duchess."

There was a sofa where Mr. Pocket stood, and he dropped upon it in the attitude of the Dying Gladiator. Still in that attitude, he said, with a hollow voice, "Good night, Mr. Pip," when I deemed it advisable to go to bed and leave him.

Twenty-four

AFTER TWO OR THREE DAYS, WHEN I HAD ESTABLISHED myself in my room, and had gone backward and forward to London several times, and had ordered all I wanted of my tradesmen, Mr. Pocket and I had a long talk together. He knew more of my intended career than I knew myself, for he referred to his having been told by Mr. Jaggers that I was not designed for any profession, and that I should be well enough educated for my destiny if I could "hold my own" with the average of young men in prosperous circumstances. I acquiesced, of course, knowing nothing to the contrary.

He advised my attending certain places in London, for the acquisition of such mere rudiments as I wanted, and my investing him with the functions of explainer and director of all my studies. He hoped that with intelligent assistance I should meet with little to discourage me, and should soon be able to dispense with any aid but his. Through his way of saying this, and much more to similar purpose, he placed himself on confidential terms with me in an admirable manner; and I may state at once that he was always so zealous and honorable in fulfilling his compact with me, that he made me zealous and honorable in fulfilling mine with him. If he had shown indifference as a master, I have no doubt I should have returned the compliment as a pupil; he gave me no such excuse, and each of us did the other justice. Nor did I ever regard him as having anything ludicrous about him—or anything but what was serious, honest, and good—in his tutor communication with me.

When these points were settled, and so far carried out as that I had begun to work in earnest, it occurred to me that if I could retain my bedroom in Barnard's Inn, my life would be agreeably varied, while my manners would be none the worse for Herbert's society. Mr. Pocket did not object to this arrangement, but urged that before any step could possibly be taken in it, it must be submitted to my guardian. I felt that his delicacy arose out of the consideration that the plan would save Herbert some expense; so I went off to Little Britain, and imparted my wish to Mr. Jaggers.

"If I could buy the furniture now hired for me," said I, "and one or two other little things, I should be quite at home there."

"Go it!" said Mr. Jaggers, with a short laugh. "I told you you'd get on. Well! How much do you want?"

I said I didn't know how much.

"Come!" retorted Mr. Jaggers. "How much? Fifty pounds?"

"Oh, not nearly so much."

"Five pounds?" said Mr. Jaggers.

This was such a great fall that I said in discomfiture, "Oh! more than that."

"More than that, eh?" retorted Mr. Jaggers, lying in wait for me, with his hands in his pockets, his head on one side, and his eyes on the wall behind me; "how much more?"

"It is so difficult to fix a sum," said I, hesitating.

"Come!" said Mr. Jaggers. "Let's get at it. Twice five; will that do? Three times five; will that do? Four times five; will that do?"

I said I thought that would do handsomely.

"Four times five will do handsomely, will it?" said Mr. Jaggers, knitting his brows. "Now what do you make of four times five?"

"What do I make of it?"

"Ah!" said Mr. Jaggers; "how much?"

"I suppose you make it twenty pounds," said I, smiling.

"Never mind what *I* make it, my friend," observed Mr. Jaggers, with a knowing and contradictory toss of his head. "I want to know what *you* make it."

"Twenty pounds, of course."

"Wemmick!" said Mr. Jaggers, opening his office-door. "Take Mr. Pip's written order, and pay him twenty pounds."

This strongly marked way of doing business made a strongly marked impression on me, and that not of an agreeable kind. Mr. Jaggers never laughed; but he wore great bright creaking boots; and, in poising himself on these boots, with his large head bent down and his eyebrows joined together, awaiting an answer, he sometimes caused the boots to creak, as if *they* laughed in a dry and suspicious way. As he happened to go out now, and as Wemmick was brisk and talkative, I said to Wemmick that I hardly knew what to make of Mr. Jaggers's manner.

"Tell him that, and he'll take it as a compliment," answered Wemmick; "he don't mean that you *should* know what to make of it.—Oh!" for I looked surprised, "it's not personal; it's professional: only professional."

Wemmick was at his desk, lunching—and crunching—on a dry, hard biscuit; pieces of which he threw from time to time into his slit of a mouth, as if he were posting them.

"Always seems to me," said Wemmick, "as if he had set a man-trap and was watching it. Suddenly—click—you're caught!"

Without remarking that man-traps were not among the amenities of life, I said I supposed he was very skillful?

"Deep," said Wemmick, "as Australia." Pointing with his pen at the office floor, to express that Australia was understood for the purposes of the figure to be diametrically on the opposite spot of the globe. "If there was anything deeper," added Wemmick, bringing his pen to paper, "he'd be it."

Then I said I supposed that he had a fine business, and Wemmick said, "Ca-pi-tal!" Then I asked if there were many clerks? To which he replied:

"We don't run much into clerks, because there's only one Jaggers, and people won't have him at second-hand. There are only four of us. Would you like to see 'em? You are one of us, as I may say."

I accepted the offer. When Mr. Wemmick had put all his biscuit into the post, and had paid me my money from a cash-box in a safe, the key of which safe he kept somewhere down his back, and produced from his coat-collar like an iron pigtail, we went upstairs. The house was dark and shabby, and the greasy shoulders that had left their mark in Mr. Jaggers's room seemed to have been shuffling up and down the staircase for years. In the front first floor, a clerk who looked something between a publican and a rat-catcher— a large, pale, puffed, swollen man—was attentively engaged with three or four people of shabby appearance, whom he treated as unceremoniously as everybody seemed to be treated who contributed to Mr. Jaggers's coffers. "Getting evidence together," said Mr. Wemmick, as we came out, "for the Bailey." In the room over that, a little flabby terrier of a clerk with dangling hair (his cropping seemed to have been forgotten when he was a puppy) was similarly engaged with a man with weak eyes, whom Mr. Wemmick presented to me as a smelter who kept his pot always boiling, and would melt me anything I pleased—and who was in an excessive white-perspiration, as if he had been trying his art on himself. In a back room, a high-shouldered man, with a face-ache tied up in dirty flannel, who was dressed in old black clothes that bore the appearance of having been waxed, was stooping over his work of making fair copies of the notes of the other two gentlemen, for Mr. Jaggers's own use.

This was all the establishment. When we went downstairs again, Wemmick led me into my guardian's room, and said, "This you've seen already."

"Pray," said I, as the two odious casts with the twitchy leer upon them caught my sight again, "whose likenesses are those?"

"These?" said Wemmick, getting upon a chair, and blowing the dust off the horrible heads before bringing them down. "These are two celebrated ones. Famous clients of ours that got us a world of credit. This chap, (why you must have come down in the night and been peeping into the inkstand, to get this blot upon your eyebrow, you old rascal!) murdered his master, and, considering that he wasn't brought up to evidence, didn't plan it badly."

"Is it like him?" I asked, recoiling from the brute, as Wemmick spat upon his eyebrow and gave it a rub with his sleeve.

"Like him? It's himself, you know. The cast was made in Newgate, directly after he was taken down. You had a particular fancy for me, hadn't you, Old Artful?" said Wemmick. He then explained this affectionate apostrophe, by touching his brooch representing the lady and the weeping willow at the tomb with the urn upon it, and saying, "Had it made for me saying, express!"

"Is the lady anybody?" said I.

"No," returned Wemmick. "Only his game. (You liked your bit of game, didn't you?) No; deuce a bit of a lady in the case, Mr. Pip, except one—and she wasn't of this slender, ladylike sort, and you wouldn't have caught *her* looking after this urn—unless there was something to drink in it." Wemmick's attention being thus directed to his brooch, he put down the cast and polished the brooch with his pocket-handkerchief.

"Did that other creature come to the same end?" I asked. "He has the same look."

"You're right," said Wemmick, "it's the genuine look. Much as if one nostril was caught up with a horse-hair and a little fishhook. Yes, he came to the same end; quite the natural end here, I assure you. He forged wills, this blade did, if he didn't also put the supposed testators to sleep—and it looked precious like it. You were a gentlemanly Cove, too" (Mr. Wemmick was again apostrophizing), "and you said you could write Greek. Yah, Bounceable! What a liar you were! I never met such a liar as you!" Before putting his late friend on his shelf again, Wemmick touched the largest of his mourning rings and said, "Sent out to buy it for me only the day before."

While he was putting up the other cast and coming down from the chair, the thought crossed my mind that all his personal jewelry was derived from like sources. As he had shown no diffidence on the subject, I ventured on the liberty of asking him the question, when he stood before me, dusting his hands.

"Oh yes," he returned, "these are all gifts of that kind. One brings another, you see; that's the way of it. I always take 'em. They're curiosities. And they're property. They may not be worth much, but, after all, they're property and portable. It don't signify to you with your brilliant look-out, but as to myself, my guiding-star always is, 'Get hold of portable property.' "

When I had rendered homage to this light, he went on to say, in a friendly manner:

"If at any odd time, when you have nothing better to do, you wouldn't mind coming over to see me at Walworth, I could offer you a bed, and I should consider it an honor. I have not much to show you; but such two or three curiosities as I have got you might like to look over; and I am fond of a bit of garden and a summer-house."

I said I should be delighted to accept his hospitality.

"Thank'ee," said he; "then we'll consider that it's to come off, when convenient to you. Have you dined with Mr. Jaggers yet?"

"Not yet."

"Well," said Wemmick, "he'll give you wine, and good wine. I'll give you punch, and not bad punch. And now I'll tell you something. When you go to dine with Mr. Jaggers, look at his housekeeper."

"Shall I see something very uncommon?"

"Well," said Wemmick, "You'll see a wild beast tamed. Not so very uncommon, you'll tell me. I reply, that depends on the original wildness of the beast, and the amount of taming. It won't lower your opinion of Mr. Jaggers's powers. Keep your eye on it."

I told him I would do so with all the interest and curiosity that his preparation awakened. As I was taking my departure, he asked me if I would like to devote five minutes to seeing Mr. Jaggers "at it?"

For several reasons, and not least because I didn't clearly know what Mr. Jaggers would be found to be "at," I replied in the affirmative. We dived into the City, and came up in a crowded police-court, where a blood-relation (in the murderous sense) of the deceased with the fanciful taste in brooches was standing at the bar, uncomfortably chewing something; while my guardian had a woman under examination or cross-examination—I don't know which—and was striking her, and the bench, and everybody present with awe. If anybody, of whatsoever degree, said a word that he didn't approve of, he instantly required to have it "taken down." If anybody wouldn't make an admission, he said, "I'll have it out of you!" and if anybody made an admission, he said, "Now I have got you!" The magistrates shivered under a single bite of his finger. Thieves and thieftakers hung in dread rapture on his words, and shrank when a hair of his eyebrows turned in their direction. Which side he was on I couldn't make out, for he seemed to me to be grinding the whole place in a mill; I only know that when I stole out on tiptoe he was not on the side of the bench, for he was making the legs of the old gentleman who presided quite convulsive under the table, by his denunciations of his conduct as the representative of British law and justice in that chair that day.

Twenty-five

BENTLEY DRUMMLE, WHO WAS SO SULKY A FELLOW THAT HE even took up a book as if its writer had done him an injury, did not take up an acquaintance in a more agreeable spirit. Heavy in figure, movement, and comprehension—in the sluggish complexion of his face, and in the large, awkward tongue that seemed to loll about in his mouth as he himself lolled about in a room—he was idle, proud, niggardly, reserved, and suspicious. He came of rich people down in Somersetshire who had nursed this combination of qualities until they made the discovery that it was just of age and a blockhead. Thus Bentley Drummle had come to Mr. Pocket when he was a head taller than that gentleman, and half a dozen heads thicker than most gentlemen.

Startop had been spoiled by a weak mother and kept at home when he ought to have been at school; but he was devotedly attached to her, and admired her beyond measure. He had a woman's delicacy of feature, and was—"as you may see, though you never saw her," said Herbert to me— exactly like his mother. It was but natural that I should take to him much more kindly than to Drummle, and that even in the earliest evening of our boating he and I should pull homeward abreast of one another, conversing from boat to boat, while Bentley Drummle came up in our wake alone, under the overhanging banks and among rushes. He would always creep in shore like some uncomfortable amphibious creature, even when the tide would have sent him fast upon his way, and I always think of him as coming after us in the dark or by the backwater, when our own two boats were breaking the sunset or the moonlight in midstream.

Herbert was my most intimate companion and friend. I presented him with a half-share in my boat, which was the occasion of his often coming down to Hammersmith; and my possession of a half-share in his chambers often took me up to London. We used to walk between the two places at all hours, and I have an affection for the road yet (though it is not so pleasant a road as it was then), formed in the impressibility of untried youth and hope.

When I had been in Mr. Pocket's family a month or two Mr. and Mrs. Camilla turned up. Camilla was Mr. Pocket's sister. Georgiana, whom I had seen at Miss Havisham's on the same occasion, also turned up. She was a cousin—an indigestive single woman, who called her rigidity religion, and her liver love. These people hated me with the hatred of cupidity and disappointment. As a matter of course, they fawned upon me in my prosperity with the basest meanness. Toward Mr. Pocket, as a sort of grownup infant with no notion of his own interests, they showed the complacent forbearance I had heard them express. Mrs. Pocket they held in contempt; but they allowed the poor dear soul to have been heavily disappointed in life, because that shed a full reflected light upon themselves.

These were the surroundings among which I settled down, and applied myself to my education. I soon contracted expensive habits, and began to spend an amount of money that within a few short months I should have thought almost fabulous; but, through good and evil, I stuck to my books. There was no other merit in this than my having sense enough to feel my deficiencies. Between Mr. Pocket and Herbert I got on fast, and with one or the other always at my elbow to give me the directions I wanted, and clear obstructions out of my road, I must have been as great a dolt as Drummle if I had done less.

I had not seen Mr. Wemmick for some weeks, when I thought I would write him a note and propose to go home with him on a certain evening. He replied that it would give him much pleasure, and that he would expect me at the office at six o'clock. Thither I went, and there I found him putting the key on his safe down his back as the clock struck.

"Did you think of walking down to Walworth?" said he.

"Certainly," said I, "if you approve."

"Very much," was Wemmick's reply, "for I have had my legs under the desk all day, and shall be glad to stretch 'em. Now I'll tell you what I have got for supper, Mr. Pip. I have got a stewed steak—which is of home prepara-tion—and a cold roast fowl—which is from the cook-shop. I think it's ten-der, because the master of the shop was a juryman in some cases of ours the other day, and we let him down easy. I reminded him of it when I bought the fowl, and I said, 'Pick us out a good one, old fellow, because if we had cho-sen to keep you in the box another day or two we could easily have done it.' He said to that 'Let me make you a present of the best fowl in the shop.' I let him, of course. As far as it goes, it's property and portable. You don't object to an aged parent, I hope?"

I really thought he was still speaking of the fowl, until he added, "Because I have got an aged parent at my place." I then said what politeness required.

"So you haven't dined with Mr. Jaggers yet?" he pursued, as we walked along.

"Not yet."

"He told me so this afternoon when he heard you were coming to see me. I expect you'll have an invitation tomorrow. He's going to ask your pals, too. Three of 'em, ain't there?"

Although I was not in the habit of counting Drummle as one of my inti-mate associates, I said, "Yes."

"Well, he's going to ask the whole gang"—I hardly felt complimented by the word—"and whatever he gives you, he'll give you good. Don't look for-ward to variety, but you'll have excellence. And there's another rum thing in his house," proceeded Wemmick, after a moment's pause, as if the remark bestowed on the housekeeper was understood; "he never lets a door or win-dow be fastened at night."

"Is he never robbed?"

"That's it," returned Wemmick. "He says, and gives it out publicly, 'I want to see the man who'll rob *me*.' Lord bless you, I have heard him a hun-dred times if I have heard him once, say to regular cracksmen in our front office, 'You know where I live; now no bolt is ever drawn there; why don't you do a stroke of business with me? Come, can't I tempt you?' Not a man of 'em, sir, would be bold enough to try it on for love or money."

"They dread him so much?" said I.

"Dread him?" said Wemmick. "Ah! I believe you, they dread him. Not but what he's artful, even in his defiance of 'em. No silver, sir. Britannia metal, every spoon."

"So they wouldn't have much," I observed, "even if they—"

"Ah! but *he* would have much," said Wemmick, cutting me short, "and they know it. He'd have their lives, and the lives of scores of 'em. He'd have all he could get. And it's impossible to say what he couldn't get, if he gave his mind to it."

I was falling into meditation on my guardian's greatness, when Wemmick remarked:

"As to the absence of plate, that's only his natural depth. A river's its natural depth, and he's his natural depth. Look at his watch-chain. That's real enough."

"'Tis very massive," said I.

"Massive?" repeated Wemmick. "I think so. And his watch is a gold repeater, and worth a hundred pounds if it's worth a penny, Mr. Pip! There are about five hundred thieves in this town who know all about that watch: there's not a man, a woman, or a child among 'em who wouldn't identify the smallest link in that chain, and drop it as if it was red-hot if inveigled into touching it."

At first with such discourse, and afterward with conversation of a more general nature, did Mr. Wemmick and I beguile the time and the road until he gave me to understand that we had arrived in the district of Walworth.

It appeared to be a collection of back lanes, ditches, and little gardens, and to present the aspect of a mighty dull retirement. Wemmick's house was a little wooden cottage in the midst of plots of garden, and the top of it was cut out and painted like a battery mounted with guns.

"My own doing," said Wemmick. "Looks pretty, don't it?"

I highly commended it. I think it was the smallest house I ever saw; with the queerest Gothic windows (by far the greater part of them sham), and a Gothic door, almost too small to get in at.

"There's a real flagstaff, you see," said Wemmick, "and on Sundays I run up a real flag. Then look here. After I have crossed this bridge, I hoist it up— so—and cut off the communication."

The bridge was a plank, and it crossed a chasm about four feet wide and two deep. But it was very pleasant to see the pride with which he hoisted it up and made it fast; smiling as he did so with a relish, and not merely mechanically.

"At nine o'clock every night, Greenwich time," said Wemmick, "the gun fires. There he is, you see; and when you hear him go, I think you'll say he's a Stinger."

The piece of ordnance referred to was mounted into a separate fortress, lightly constructed of latticework. It was protected from the weather by an ingenious little tarpaulin contrivance in the nature of an umbrella.

"Then, at the back," said Wemmick, "out of sight, so as not to impede the idea of fortifications—for it's a principle with me, if you have an idea, carry it out and keep it up. I don't know whether that's your opinion—"

I said, decidedly.

"At the back, there's a pig, and there are fowls and rabbits; then I knock together my own little farm, you see, and grow cucumbers; and you'll judge at supper what sort of a salad I can raise. So, sir," said Wemmick, smiling again, but rather seriously too, "if you can suppose the little place besieged, it would hold out a devil of a time in point of provisions."

Then he conducted me to a bower about a dozen yards off, but which was approached by such ingenious twists of path that it took quite a long time to get at; and in this retreat our glasses were already set forth. Our punch was cooling in an ornamental lake, on whose margin the bower was raised. This piece of water (with an island in the middle which might have been the salad for supper) was of a circular form, and he had constructed a fountain in it, which, when you set a little mill going and took a cork out of a pipe, played to that powerful extent that it made the back of your hand quite wet.

"I am my own engineer, and my own carpenter, and my own plumber, and my own gardener, and my own Jack of all Trades," said Wemmick, in acknowledging my compliments. "Well, it's a good thing, you know. It brushes the Newgate cobwebs away, and pleases the Aged. You wouldn't mind being at once introduced to the Aged, would you? It wouldn't put you out?"

I expressed the readiness I felt, and we went into the Castle. There we found, sitting by a fire, a very old man in a flannel coat: clean, cheerful, comfortable, and well cared for, but intensely deaf.

"Well, aged parent," said Wemmick, shaking hands with him in a cordial and jocose way, "how are you?"

"All right, John; all right"; replied the old man.

"Here's Mr. Pip, aged parent," said Wemmick, "and I wish you could hear his name. Nod away at him, Mr. Pip; that's what he likes. Nod away at him, like winking!"

"This is a fine place of my son's, sir," piped the old man, while I nodded as hard as I possibly could. "This is a pretty pleasure-ground, sir. This spot and these beautiful works upon it ought to be kept together by the Nation after my son's time, for the people's enjoyment."

"You're as proud of it as Punch, ain't you, aged parent?" said Wemmick, contemplating the old man with his hard face really softened; "*there's* a nod for you," giving him a tremendous one, "*there's* another for you," giving him a still more tremendous one; "you like that, don't you? If you're not tired, Mr. Pip—though I know it's tiring to strangers—tip him one more. You can't think how it pleases him."

I tipped him several more, and he was in great spirits. We left him bestir-
ring himself to feed the fowls, and sat down to our punch in the arbor where
Wemmick told me as he smoked a pipe that it had taken him a good many
years to bring the property up to its present point of perfection.

"Is it your own, Mr. Wemmick?"

"Oh yes," said Wemmick; "I have got hold of it, a bit at a time. It's a free-
hold, by George!"

"Is it, indeed? I hope Mr. Jaggers admires it?"

"Never seen it," said Wemmick. "Never heard of it. Never seen the Aged.
Never heard of him. No; the office is one thing, and private life is another.
When I go into the office I leave the Castle behind me, and when I come into
the Castle I leave the office behind me. If it's not in any way disagreeable to
you, you'll oblige me by doing the same. I don't wish it professionally spoken
about."

Of course I felt my good faith to be involved in the observance of his
request. The punch being very nice, we sat there drinking it and talking until
it was almost nine o'clock. "Getting near gunfire," said Wemmick then, as he
laid down his pipe; "it's the Aged's treat."

Proceeding into the Castle again, we found the Aged heating the poker,
with expectant eyes, as a preliminary to the performance of this great nightly
ceremony. Wemmick stood with his watch in his hand, until the moment
was come for him to take the red-hot poker from the Aged, and repair to the
outworks. He took it and went out, and presently the Stinger went off with a
Bang that shook the crazy little box of a cottage as if it must fall to pieces, and
made every glass and teacup in it ring. Upon which the Aged—who I believe
would have been blown out of his armchair but for holding on by the
elbows—cried out, exultingly, "He's fired! I heerd him!" and I nodded at the
old gentleman until it is no figure of speech to declare that I absolutely could
not see him.

The interval between that time and supper Wemmick devoted to showing me his collection of curiosities. They were mostly of a felonious character; comprising the pen with which a celebrated forgery had been committed,
a distinguished razor or two, some locks of hair, and several manuscript con-
fessions written under condemnation—upon which Mr. Wemmick set a particular value as being, to use his own words, "every one of 'em lies, sir." These
were agreeably dispersed among small specimens of china and glass, various
neat trifles made by the proprietor of the museum, and some tobacco-
stoppers carved by the Aged. They were all displayed in that chamber of the
Castle into which I had been first inducted, and which served not only as the
general sitting-room but as the kitchen too, if I might judge from a saucepan
on the hob, and a brazen *bijou* over the fireplace designed for the suspension
of a roasting-jack.

There was a neat little girl in attendance, who looked after the Aged in
the day. When she had laid the supper cloth the bridge was lowered to give

her means of egress, and she withdrew for the night. The supper was excel-lent; and though the Castle was rather subject to dry-rot, insomuch that it tasted like a bad nut, and though the pig might have been farther off, I was heartily pleased with my whole entertainment. Nor was there any drawback on my little turret bedroom beyond there being such a thin ceiling between me and the flagstaff that when I lay down on my back in bed it seemed as if I had to balance that pole on my forehead all night.

Wemmick was up betimes in the morning, and I am afraid I heard him cleaning my boots. After that he fell to gardening, and I saw him from my Gothic window pretending to employ the Aged, and nodding at him in a most devoted manner. Our breakfast was as good as the supper, and at half past eight precisely we started for Little Britain. By degrees Wemmick got dryer and harder as we went along, and his mouth tightened into a post-office again. When we got to his place of business, and he pulled out his key from his coat-collar, he looked as unconscious of his Walworth property as if the Castle and the drawbridge and the arbor and the lake and the fountain and the Aged had all been blown into space together by the last discharge of the Stinger.

Twenty-six

IT FELL OUT, AS WEMMICK HAD TOLD ME IT WOULD, THAT I had an early opportunity of comparing my guardian's establishment with that of his cashier and clerk. My guardian was in his room washing his hands with his scented soap when I went into the office from Walworth, and he called me to him, and gave me the invitation for myself and friends which Wemmick had prepared me to receive. "No ceremony," he stipulated, "and no dinner dress, and say tomorrow." I asked him where we should come to (for I had no idea where he lived, and I believe it was in his general objec-tion to make anything like an objection), and he replied, "Come here, and I'll take you home with me." I embraced this opportunity of remarking that he washed his clients off as if he were a surgeon or a dentist. He had a closet in his room, fitted up for the purpose, which smelled of the scented soap like a perfumer's shop. It had an unusually large jack-towel on a roller inside the door, and he would wash his hands, and wipe them and dry them all over this towel, whenever he came in from a police-court or dismissed a client from his room. When I and my friends repaired to him at six o'clock next day, he seemed to have been engaged on a case of a darker complexion than

usual, for we found him with his head butted into this closet, not only washing his hands, but laving his face and gurgling his throat. And even when he
had done all that, and had gone all round the jack-towel, he took out his
penknife and scraped the case out of his nails before he put his coat on.

There were some people slinking about as usual when we passed out into
the street, who were evidently very anxious to speak with him; but there was
something so conclusive in the halo of scented soap that encircled his presence, and they gave it up for that day. As we walked along westward he was
recognized ever and again by some face in the crowd of the streets, and whenever that happened he talked louder; but he never otherwise recognized anybody, or took notice that anybody recognized him.

He conducted us to Gerrard Street, Soho, to a house on the south side
of that street. Rather a stately house of its kind, but doleful for want of
painting, and with dirty windows. He took out his key and opened the
door, and we all went into a stone hall, bare, gloomy, and little used. So, up
a dark brown staircase into a series of three dark brown rooms on the first
floor. There were carved garlands on the paneled walls, and as he stood
among them giving us welcome, I know what kind of loops I thought they
looked like.

Dinner was laid in the best of these rooms; the second was his dressing-
room; the third his bedroom. He told us that he held the whole house, but
rarely used more of it than we saw. The table was comfortably laid—no silver
in the service, of course—and at the side of his chair was a capacious dumbwaiter, with a variety of bottles on it, and four dishes of fruit for dessert. I
noticed then, and throughout, that he kept everything under his own hand,
distributed everything himself.

There was a bookcase in the room, and I saw, from the backs of the
books, that they were about evidence, criminal law, criminal biography, trials, acts of parliament, and such things. The furniture was all very solid and
good like his watch-chain. It had an official look, however, and there was
nothing merely ornamental to be seen. In a corner was a little table of papers
with a shaded lamp, so that he seemed to bring the office home with him in
that respect too, and to wheel it out of an evening and fall to work.

As he had scarcely seen my three companions until now—for he and I
had walked together—he stood on the hearth-rug, after ringing the bell, and
took a searching look at them. To my surprise, he seemed at once to be principally if not solely interested in Drummle.

"Pip," said he, putting his large hand on my shoulder and moving me to
the window, "I don't know one from the other. Who's the spider?"

"The spider?" said I.

"The blotchy, spanky, sulky fellow."

"That's Bentley Drummle," I replied; "the one with the delicate face is
Startop."

Not making the least account of "the one with the delicate face," he returned, "Bentley Drummle is his name, is it? Ah! I like the look of that fellow."

He immediately began to talk to Drummle; not at all deterred by his replying in his heavy reticent way, but apparently led on by it to screw discourse forcibly out of him. I was looking at the two when there came between me and them the housekeeper, with the first dish for the table.

She was a woman of about forty, I supposed—but I may have thought her older than she was, as it is the manner of youth to do. Rather tall, of a lithe nimble figure, extremely pale, with large blue eyes, and a quantity of streaming light hair. I cannot say whether any diseased affection of the heart caused her lips to be parted as if she were panting, and her face to bear a curious expression of suddenness and flutter; but I know that I had been to see Macbeth at the theater a night or two before, and that her face looked to me as if it were all disturbed by fiery air, like the faces I had seen rise out of the caldron.

She set the dish on, touched me quietly on the arm with a finger to notify that dinner was ready, and vanished. We took our seats at the round table, and my guardian kept Drummle on one side of him, while Startop sat on the other. It was a noble dish of fish that the housekeeper had put on the table, and we had a joint of equally choice mutton afterward, and then some equally choice birds. Sauces, wines, all the accessories we wanted, and all of the best, were given out by our host from his dumbwaiter, and when they had made the circuit of the table he always put them back again. Similarly, he dealt us clean plates, and knives and forks, for each course, and dropped those just disused into two baskets, on the ground, by his chair. No other attendant than the housekeeper appeared. She set on every dish, and I always saw in her face a face rising out of the caldron. Years afterward I made a dreadful likeness of that woman by causing a face that had no other natural resemblance to it than it derived from flowing light hair, to pass behind a bowl of flaming spirits in a dark room.

Induced to take particular notice of the housekeeper, both by her own striking appearance and by Wemmick's preparation, I observed that whenever she was in the room, she kept her eyes attentively on my guardian, and that she would quite remove her hands from any dish she put before him, watching as if she dreaded his calling her back, and wanted him to speak when she was nigh, as if he had anything to say. I fancied that I could detect in his manner a consciousness of this, and a purpose of holding her in suspense.

Dinner went off gaily, and although my guardian seemed to follow rather than originate subjects, I knew that he somehow wrenched the weakest part of our dispositions out of us. For myself, I found that I was expressing my tendency to lavish expenditure, and to patronize Herbert, and to boast of my great prospects, before I quite knew that I had opened my eyes. It was so with all of us, but with no one more than Drummle: the development of whose inclination to gird in a grudging and suspicious way at the rest, was screwed out of him before the fish was taken off.

It was not then, but when we had got to the cheese, that our conversation turned upon our rowing feats, and that Drummle was rallied for coming up behind of a night in that slow amphibious way of his. Drummle upon this informed our host that he much preferred our room to our company, and that as to skill he was more than our master, and that as to strength he could scatter us like chaff. By some invisible agency my guardian—it could have been no one else—wound him up to a pitch little short of ferocity about this trifle; and he fell to baring and spanning his arm to show how muscular it was, and we all fell to baring and spanning our arms in a ridiculous manner.

Now the housekeeper was at that time clearing the table, and my guardian, taking no heed of her, but with the side of his face turned from her, was leaning back in his chair biting the side of his forefinger, and showing an interest in Drummle that, to me, was quite inexplicable. Suddenly he clapped his large hand on the housekeeper's as she stretched it across the table, like a trap. So suddenly and smartly, that we all stopped in our foolish contention.

"If you talk of strength," said Mr. Jaggers, "I'll show you a wrist. Molly, let them see your wrist."

Her entrapped hand was on the table, but she had already put her other hand behind her waist. "Master," she said, in a low voice, with her eyes attentively and timidly fixed upon him. "Don't!"

"I'll show you a wrist," repeated Mr. Jaggers, with an immovable determination to show it. "Molly, let them see your wrist."

"Master," she again murmured. "Please!"

"Molly," said Mr. Jaggers, not looking at her, but obstinately compressing his lips, and looking at the opposite side of the room, "let them see *both* your wrists. Show them. Come!"

He roughly took his hands from hers, and turned that wrist up on the table. She brought her other hand from behind her, and held the two out side by side. The last wrist was much disfigured—deeply scarred, and scarred across and across. When she held her hands out she took her eyes from Mr. Jaggers, and turned them watchfully on every one of the rest of us in succession.

"There's power here," said Mr. Jaggers, tracing out the sinews with his forefinger without touching them. "Very few men have the power of wrist that this woman has. It's remarkable what mere force of grip there is in these hands. I have had occasion to notice many hands, but I never saw stronger in that respect, man's or woman's, than these."

While he said these words in a leisurely, critical way, she continued to look at every one of us in regular succession as we sat. The moment he ceased she looked at him again. "That'll do, Molly," said Mr. Jaggers, giving her a slight nod; "you have been admired, and can go." She withdrew her hands and went out of the room, and Mr. Jaggers, putting the decanters on from his dumbwaiter, filled his glass, and passed round the wine.

"At half past nine, gentlemen," said he, "we must break up. Pray make the best use of your time. I am glad to see you all. Mr. Drummle, I drink to you."

If his object in singling out Drummle were to bring him out still more, it perfectly succeeded. In a sulky triumph, Drummle showed his morose depreciation of the rest of us in a more and more offensive degree, until he became downright intolerable. Through all his stages Mr. Jaggers followed him with the same inexplicable interest. He actually seemed to serve as a zest to Mr. Jaggers's wine.

In our boyish want of discretion I dare say we took too much to drink, and I know we talked too much and too noisily. We became particularly hot upon some boorish sneer of Drummle's, to the effect that we were too free with our money. It led to my remarking, with more zeal than politeness, that it came with a bad grace from him, to whom Startop had lent money in my presence but a week or so before.

"Well," retorted Drummle, "he'll be paid."

"I don't mean to imply that he won't," said I; "but it might make you hold your tongue about us and our money, I should think."

"*You* should think!" retorted Drummle. "O Lord!"

"I dare say," I went on, meaning to be very severe, "that you wouldn't lend money to any of us if we wanted it."

"You do me justice," said Drummle. "I wouldn't lend one of you a sixpence. I wouldn't lend any body a sixpence."

"Rather mean to borrow under those circumstances, I should say."

"*You* should say," repeated Drummle. "O Lord!"

This was so very aggravating—the more especially as I found myself making no way against his surly obtuseness—that I said, disregarding Herbert's efforts to check me:

"Come, Mr. Drummle, since we are on the subject, I'll tell you what passed between Herbert here and me when you borrowed that money."

"*I* don't want to know what passed between Herbert there and you," growled Drummle. And I think he added, in a lower growl, that we might go to the Devil and shake ourselves.

"I'll tell you, however," said I, "whether you want to know or not. We said that as you put it in your pocket, you seemed to be immensely amused at his being such an ass as to lend it."

Drummle laughed outright, and sat laughing in our faces, with his hands in his pockets and his round shoulders raised, plainly signifying that it was quite true, and that he despised us as asses all.

Hereupon Startop took him in hand, though with a much better grace than I had shown, and exhorted him to be a little more agreeable. Startop being a lively, bright young fellow, and Drummle being the exact opposite, the latter was always disposed to resent him as a direct personal affront. He now retorted in a coarse, lumpish way, and Startop tried to turn the discussion aside with some small pleasantry that made us all laugh. Resenting this little success more than anything, Drummle, without any threat or warning, pulled his hands out of his pockets, dropped his round shoulders, swore an oath, took up a large glass, and would infallibly have flung it at his adversary's head, but for our entertainer's dexterously seizing it at the instant when it was raised for that purpose.

"Gentlemen," said Mr. Jaggers, very deliberately putting down the glass, and hauling out his gold repeater by its massive chain, "I am sorry to announce that it's half past nine."

On this hint we all rose to depart. Before we got to the street-door Startop was cheerily calling Drummle "old fellow," as if nothing had happened. But the old fellow was so far from responding that he would not even walk to Hammersmith on the same side of the way; so Herbert and I, who remained in town, saw them going down the street on opposite sides; Startop leading, and Drummle lagging behind in the shadow of the houses, much as he was wont to follow in his boat.

As the door was not yet shut I thought I would leave Herbert there for a moment and run up stairs again to say a word of apology to my guardian. I found him in his dressing-room, surrounded by his boots, already hard at it washing his hands of us.

I told him that I had come up again to say how sorry I was that anything disagreeable should have occurred, and that I hoped he would not blame me much.

"Pooh!" said he, sluicing his face, and speaking through the water-drops; "it's nothing, Pip. I like that Spider though."

He had turned toward me now, and was shaking his head, and blowing, and toweling himself.

"I am glad you like him, sir," said I; "but I don't."

"No, no," my guardian assented; "don't have too much to do with him. Keep as clear of him as may be. But I like the fellow, Pip; he is one of the true sort; I have not been disappointed in him. Why, if I were a fortuneteller—"

Looking out of the towel, he caught my eye.

"But I am not a fortuneteller," he said, letting his head drop into a festoon of towel, and toweling away at his two ears. "You know what I am. Good night, Pip."

"Good night, sir."

In about a month after that the Spider's time with Mr. Pocket was up for good, and, to the great relief of all the house but Mrs. Pocket, he went home to the family hole. He called me Blacksmith when he went away, qualified to be an indifferent hostler or a bad gamekeeper.

M Y DEAR MR. PIP—I WRITE THIS BY REQUEST OF MR. Gargery for to let you know that he is going to London in company with Mr. Wopsle, and would be glad if agreeable to be allowed to see you. He would call at Barnard's Hotel Tuesday morning 9 o'clock, when if not agreeable please leave word. Your poor sister is much the same as when you left. We talk of you in the kitchen every night, and wonder what you are saying and doing. If now considered in the light of a liberty, excuse it, for the love of poor old days. No more, dear Mr. Pip, from your ever obliged and affectionate Servant,

BIDDY

P.S.—He wishes me most particular to write *what larks*. He says you will understand I hope and do not doubt it will be agreeable to see him even though a gentleman, for you had ever a good heart and he is a worthy worthy man. I have read him all, excepting only the last little sentence, and he wishes me most particular to write again *what larks*.

I received this letter by the post on Monday morning, and therefore its appointment was for next day. Let me confess exactly with what feelings I looked forward to Joe's coming.

Not with pleasure, though I was bound to him by so many ties; no; with considerable disturbance, some mortification, and a keen sense of incongruity. If I could have kept him away by paying money, I certainly would have paid money. My greatest reassurance was that he was coming to Barnard's Inn, not to Hammersmith, and consequently would not fall in Bentley Drummle's way. I had little objection to his being seen by Herbert or his father, for both of whom I had respect; but I had the sharpest sensitiveness as to his being seen by Drummle, whom I held in contempt. So, throughout life, our worst weaknesses and meannesses are usually committed for the sake of the people whom we most despise.

I had begun to be always decorating the chambers in some quite unnecessary and inappropriate way or other, and very expensive those wrestles with Barnard proved to be. By this time the rooms were vastly different from what I had found them, and I enjoyed the honor of occupying a few prominent pages in the books of a neighboring upholsterer. I got on so fast of late that I had even started a boy in boots—top boots—in bondage and slavery to whom I might have been said to pass my days. For after I had made this monster (out of the refuse of my washerwoman's family), and had clothed him with a blue coat, canary waistcoat, white cravat, creamy breeches, and the boots already mentioned, I had to find him a little to do and a great deal to eat; and with both of those horrible requirements he haunted my existence.

This avenging phantom was ordered to be on duty at eight on Tuesday morning in the hall (it was two feet square, as charged for floor-cloth), and Herbert suggested certain things for breakfast that he thought Joe would like. While I felt sincerely obliged to him for being so interested and considerate, I had an odd, half-provoked sense of suspicion upon me that if Joe had been coming to see *him* he wouldn't have been quite so brisk.

However, I came into town on the Monday night to be ready for Joe, and I got up early in the morning, and caused the sitting-room and breakfast-table to assume their most splendid appearance. Unfortunately the morning was foggy, and an angel could not have concealed the fact that Barnard was shedding sooty tears outside the window, like some weak giant of a Sweep.

As the time approached I should have liked to run away, but the Avenger, pursuant to orders, was in the hall, and presently I heard Joe on the staircase. I knew it was Joe by his clumsy manner of coming upstairs—his state boots being always too big for him—and by the time it took him to read the names on the other floors in the course of his ascent. When at last he stopped outside our door, I could hear his finger tracing over the painted letters of my name, and I afterward heard him breathing in at the keyhole. Finally he gave a faint single rap, and Pepper—such was the name of the avenging boy—announced "Mr. Gargery!" I thought he never would have done wiping his feet, and that I must have gone out to lift him off the mat, but at last he came in.

"Joe, how are you, Joe?"

"Pip, how ARE you, Pip?"

With his good honest face all glowing and shining, and his hat put down on the floor between us, he caught both my hands and worked them straight up and down, as if I had been the last patented Pump.

"I am delighted to see you, Joe. Give me your hat."

But Joe, taking it up with both hands like a birdsnest with eggs in it, wouldn't hear of parting with that piece of property, and persisted in standing talking over it in a most uncomfortable way.

"Which you have that growed," said Joe, "and that swelled out, and that gentlefolked"; Joe considered a little before he discovered this word; "as to be sure you are a honor to your king and country."

"And you, Joe, look wonderfully well."

"Thank God," said Joe, "I'm ekerval to most. And your sister, she's no worse than she were. And Biddy, she's ever right and ready. And all friends is no backerder, if not no forarder. 'Ceptin' Wopsle; he's had a drop."

All this time (still with both hands taking great care of the birdsnest) Joe was rolling his eyes round and round the room, and round and round the flowered pattern of my dressing-gown.

"Had a drop, Joe?"

"Why, yes," said Joe, lowering his voice, "he's left the Church, and went into the playacting. Which the playacting have likeways brought him to London along with me. And his wish were," said Joe, getting the birdsnest under his left arm for the moment and groping in it for an egg with his right; "if no offense, as I would 'and you that."

I took what Joe gave me, and found it to be the crumpled playbill of a small metropolitan theater, announcing the first appearance on the ensuing Monday of "the celebrated Provincial Amateur of Roscian renown, whose unique performance in the highest tragic walk of our National Bard has lately occasioned so great a sensation in local dramatic circles."

"Were you at his performance, Joe?" I inquired.

"I *were*," said Joe, with solenmity.

"Was there a great sensation?"

"Why," said Joe. "yes, there certainly were a peck of orange-peel. Partickler, where he see the ghost. Though I put it to yourself, sir, whether it were calc'lated to keep a man up to his work with a good hart, to be continiwally cutting in betwixt him and the Ghost with 'Amen!' A man may have had a misfortun' and been in the Church," said Joe, lowering his voice to an argumentative and feeling tone, "but that is no reason why you should put him out at such a time. Which I meantersay, if the ghost of a man's own father can not be allowed to ockipy his attention, what can, sir? Still more, when his mourning 'at is unfortunately made so small as that the weight of the black feathers brings it off, try to keep it on how you may."

A ghost-seeing effect in Joe's own countenance informed me that Herbert had entered the room. So I presented Joe to Herbert, who held out his hand; but Joe backed from it, and held on by the birds-nest.

"Your servant, sir," said Joe, "which I hope as you and Pip"—here his eye fell on the Avenger, who was putting some eggs on the table, and so plainly denoted an intention to make that young gentleman one of the family, that I frowned it down and confused him—"I meantersay, you two gentlemen—which I hope as you get your elths in this close spot? For the present may be a werry good inn, according to London opinions," said Joe, persuasively, "and I believe its character do stand it; but I wouldn't keep a pig in it myself—not in the case that I wished him to fatten wholesome and to eat short with a meller flavor on him."

Having borne this flattering testimony to the merits of our dwelling-place, and having incidentally shown this tendency to call me "sir," Joe, being invited to sit down to table, looked all round the room for a suitable spot on which to deposit his hat—as if it were only on some very few rare substances in nature that it could find a resting-place—and ultimately stood it on an extreme corner of the chimney-piece, from which it ever afterward fell off at intervals.

"Do you take tea, or coffee, Mr. Gargery?" asked Herbert, who always presided of a morning.

"Thankee, sir," said Joe, stiff from head to foot, "I'll take whichever is most agreeable to yourself."

"What do you say to coffee?"

"Thankee, sir," returned Joe, evidently dispirited by the proposal, "since you *are* so kind as put that name to it, I will not run contrairy to your own opinions. But don't you never find it a little 'eating?"

"Say tea, then," said Herbert, pouring it out.

Here Joe's hat tumbled off the mantlepiece, and he started and picked it up, and fitted it to the same exact spot. As if it were an absolute point of good-breeding that it should tumble off again soon.

"When did you come to town, Mr. Gargery?"

"Were it yesterday afternoon?" said Joe, after coughing, as if he had caught the whooping-cough since he came. "No it were not. Yes it were. Yes. It were yesterday afternoon" (with an appearance of mingled wisdom, relief and strict impartiality).

"Have you seen anything of London yet?"

"Why, yes, sir," said Joe, "me and Wopsle went off to look at the Blacking Ware'us. But we didn't find that it come up to its likeness in the red picters at the shop-doors; which I meantersay," added Joe, in an explanatory manner, "as it's drawd too architectooralooral."

I really believe Joe would have prolonged this word (mightily expressive to my mind of some architecture that I know) into a perfect Chorus, but for his attention being providentially attracted by his hat, which was toppling. Indeed, it demanded from him a constant attention and a quickness of eye and hand very like that exacted by wicket-keeping. He made the most extraordinary play with it, and showed the greatest skill; now, rushing at it and catching it neatly as it dropped; now, merely stopping it midway, beating it up, and humoring it in various parts of the room and against a good deal of the pattern of the paper on the wall, before he felt it safe to close with it; finally splashing it into the slop-basin, where I took the liberty of laying hands upon it.

As to his shirt-collar and his coat-collar, they were perplexing to reflect upon—insoluble mysteries. Why should a man scrape himself to that extent before he could consider himself full dressed? Why should he suppose it necessary to be purified by suffering for his holiday clothes? Then he fell into such unaccountable fits of meditation, with his fork midway between his plate and his mouth; had his eyes attracted in such strange directions; was afflicted with such remarkable coughs; sat so far from the table, and dropped so much more than he ate, and pretended that he hadn't dropped it; that I was heartily glad when Herbert left us for the City.

I had neither the good sense nor the good feeling to know that this was all my fault, and that if I had been easier with Joe, Joe would have been easier with me. I felt impatient of him and out of temper with him; in which condition he heaped coals of fire on my head.

"Us two being now alone, sir"—began Joe.

"Joe," I interrupted, pettishly, "how can you call me sir?"

Joe looked at me for a single instant with something faintly like reproach. Utterly preposterous as his cravat was, and as his collars were, I was conscious of a sort of dignity in the look too.

"Us two being now alone," resumed Joe, "and me having the intentions and abilities to stay not many minutes more, I will now conclude—leastways begin—to mention what have led to my having had the present honor. For was it not," said Joe, with his old air of lucid exposition, "that my only wish were to be useful to you, I should not have had the honor of breaking wittles in the company and abode of gentlemen."

I was so unwilling to see the look again that I made no remonstrance against this tone.

"Well, sir," pursued Joe, "this is how it were. I were at the Bargemen t'other night, Pip"; whenever he subsided into affection, he called me Pip, and whenever he relapsed into politeness he called me sir, "when there come up in his shay-cart Pumblechook. Which that same identical," said Joe, going down a new track, "do comb my 'air the wrong way sometimes, by giving out up and down town as it were him which ever had your infant companiona-tion and were looked upon as a play-feller by yourself."

"Nonsense. It was you, Joe."

"Which I fully believed it were, Pip," said Joe, slightly tossing his head, "though it signify little now, sir. Well, Pip; this same identical, which his man-ners is given to blusterous, come to me at the Bargemen (wot a pipe and a pint of beer do give refreshment to the working man, sir, and do not overstimulate), and his word were, 'Joseph, Miss Havisham she wish to speak to you.' "

"Miss Havisham, Joe?"

" 'She wish,' were Pumblechook's word, 'to speak to you.' " Joe sat and rolled his eyes at the ceiling.

"Yes, Joe? Go on, please."

"Next day, sir," said Joe, looking at me as if I were a long way off, "hav-ing cleaned myself, I go and I see Miss A."

"Miss A., Joe? Miss Havisham?"

"Which I say, sir," replied Joe, Miss A., or Havisham. Her expression air then as follering: 'Mr. Gargery. You air in correspondence with Mr. Pip?' Having had a letter from you, I were able to say 'I am.' (When I married your sister, sir, I said 'I will'; and when I answered your friend, Pip, I said 'I am.') 'Would you tell him, then,' said she, 'that which Estella has come home and would be glad to see him?' "

I felt my face fire up as I looked at Joe. I hope one remote cause of its fir-ing may have been my consciousness that if I had known his errand I should have given him more encouragement.

"Biddy," pursued Joe, "when I got home and asked her fur to write the message to you, a little hung back. Biddy says, 'I know he will be very glad to have it by word of mouth, it is holiday-time, you want to see him, go!' I have now concluded, sir," said Joe, rising from his chair, "and, Pip, I wish you ever well and ever prospering to a greater and greater height."

"But you are not going now, Joe?"

"Yes, I am," said Joe.

"But you are coming back to dinner, Joe?"

"No, I am not," said Joe.

Our eyes met, and all the "sir" melted out of that honest open heart as he gave me his hand.

"Pip, dear old chap, life is made of ever so many partings welded together, as I may say, and one man's a blacksmith, and one's a whitesmith, and one's a goldsmith, and one's a coppersmith. Diwisions among such must come, and must be met as they come. If there's been any fault at all today, it's mine. You and me is not two figures to be together in London; nor yet anywheres else but what is private, and beknown, and understood among friends. It ain't that I am proud, but that I want to be right, as you shall never see me no more in these clothes. I'm wrong in these clothes. I'm wrong out of the forge, the kitchen, or off th' meshes. You won't find half so much fault in me if you think of me in my forge-dress, with my hammer in my hand, or even my pipe. You won't find half so much fault in me if, supposing as you should ever wish to see me, you come and put your head in at the forge-window and see Joe the blacksmith there at the old anvil, in the old burned apron, at the old work, as he used to be when he first carried you about. I'm awful dull, but I hope I've beat out something nigh the rights of this at last. And so GOD bless you, dear old Pip; old chap, GOD bless you!"

I had not been mistaken in my fancy that there was a simple dignity in him. The fashion of his dress could no more come in its way when he spoke these words than it could come in its way in Heaven. He touched me gently on the forehead and went out. As soon as I could recover myself sufficiently I ran out after him and looked for him in the neighboring streets; but he was gone.

Twenty-eight

IT WAS CLEAR THAT I MUST REPAIR TO OUR TOWN NEXT DAY, and in the first flow of my repentance it was equally clear that I must stay at Joe's. But when I had secured my box-place by tomorrow's coach and had been down to Mr. Pocket's and back, I was not by any means convinced on the last point, and began to invent reasons and make excuses for putting up at the Blue Boar. I should be an inconvenience at Joe's; I was not expected, and my bed would not be ready; I should be too far from Miss Havisham's, and she was exacting and mightn't like it. All other swindlers upon earth are nothing to the self-swindlers, and with such pretenses did I cheat myself. Surely a curious thing. That I should innocently take a bad half-crown of somebody else's manufacture is reasonable enough; but that I should knowingly reckon the spurious coin of my own make as good money! An obliging stranger, under pretense of compactly folding up my bank-notes for security's sake, abstracts the notes and gives me nutshells; but what is his sleight of hand to mine, when I fold up my own nutshells and pass them on myself as notes!

Having settled that I must go to the Blue Boar, my mind was much disturbed by indecision whether or no to take the Avenger. It was tempting to think of that expensive Mercenary publicly airing his boots in the archway of the Blue Boar's posting-yard; it was almost solemn to imagine him casually produced in the tailor's shop and confounding the disrespectful senses of Trabb's boy. On the other hand, Trabb's boy might worm himself into his intimacy and tell him things; or, reckless and desperate wretch as I knew he could be, might hoot him in the High Street. My patroness, too, might hear of him, and not approve. On the whole, I resolved to leave the Avenger behind.

It was the afternoon coach by which I had taken my place, and, as winter had now come round, I should not arrive at my destination until two or three hours after dark. Our time of starting from the Cross Keys was two o'clock. I arrived on the ground with a quarter of an hour to spare, attended by the Avenger—if I may connect that expression with one who never attended on me if he could possibly help it.

At that time it was customary to carry Convicts down to the dockyard by stagecoach. As I had often heard of them in the capacity of outside-passengers, and had more than once seen them on the high-road dangling their ironed legs over the coach roof, I had no cause to be surprised when Herbert, meeting me in the yard, came up and told me there were two convicts going down with me. But I had a reason that was an old reason now, for constitutionally faltering whenever I heard the word convict.

"You don't mind them, Handel?" said Herbert.

"Oh, no!"

"I thought you seemed as if you didn't like them?"

"I can't pretend that I do like them, and I suppose you don't particularly. But I don't mind them."

"See! There they are," said Herbert, "coming out of the Tap. What a degraded and vile sight it is!"

They had been treating their guard, I suppose, for they had a jailer with them, and all three came out wiping their mouths on their hands. The two convicts were handcuffed together, and had irons on their legs—irons of a pattern that I knew very well. They wore the dress that I likewise knew very well. Their keeper had a brace of pistols, and carried a thick-knobbed bludgeon under his arm; but he was on terms of good understanding with them, and stood, with them beside him, looking on at the putting-to of the horses, rather with an air as if they were an interesting Exhibition not formally open at the moment, and he the Curator. One was a taller and stouter man than the other, and appeared, as a matter of course, according to the mysterious ways of the world both convict and free, to have had allotted to him the smallest suit of clothes. His arms and legs were like great pincushions of those shapes, and his attire disguised him absurdly; but I knew his half-closed eye at one glance. There stood the man whom I had seen on the settle at the Three Jolly Bargemen on a Saturday night, and who had brought me down with his invisible gun!

It was easy to make sure that as yet he knew me no more than if he had never seen me in his life. He looked across at me, and his eye appraised my watch-chain, and then he incidentally spat and said something to the other convict, and they laughed, and slued themselves round with a clink of their coupling manacle, and looked at something else. The great numbers on their backs, as if they were street doors; their coarse, mangy, ungainly outer surface, as if they were lower animals; their ironed legs, apologetically garlanded with pocket-handkerchiefs; and the way in which all present looked at them and kept from them; made them (as Herbert had said) a most disagreeable and degraded spectacle.

But this was not the worst of it. It came out that the whole of the back of the coach had been taken by a family removing from London, and that there were no places for the two prisoners but on the seat in front behind the coachman. Hereupon a choleric gentleman, who had taken the fourth place on that seat, flew into a most violent passion, and said that it was a breach of contract, to mix him up with such villainous company, and that it was poisonous, and pernicious, and infamous, and shameful, and I don't know what else. At this time the coach was ready and the coachman impatient, and we were all preparing to get up, and the prisoners had come over with their keeper—bringing with them that curious flavor of bread-poultice, baize, rope-yarn, and hearthstone which attends the convict presence.

"Don't take it so much amiss, sir," said the keeper to the angry passenger; "I'll sit next to you myself. I'll put 'em on the outside of the row. They won't interfere with you, sir. You needn't know they're there."

"And don't blame *me*," growled the convict I had recognized. "*I* don't want to go. *I* am quite ready to stay behind. As far as I am concerned anyone's welcome to *my* place."

"Or mine," said the other gruffly. "*I* wouldn't have incommoded none of you, if I'd a had *my* way." Then they both laughed, and began cracking nuts, and spitting the shells about.—As I really think I should have liked to do myself, if I had been in their place and so despised.

At length it was voted that there was no help for the angry gentleman, and that he must either go in his chance company or remain behind. So he got into his place, still making complaints, and the keeper got into the place next to him, and the convicts hauled themselves up as well as they could, and the convict I had recognized sat behind me with his breath on the hair of my head.

"Good-bye, Handel!" Herbert called out, as we started. I thought what a blessed fortune it was that he had found another name for me than Pip.

It is impossible to express with what acuteness I felt the convict's breathing, not only on the back of my head, but all along my spine. The sensation was like being touched with some pungent and searching acid, and it set my very teeth on edge. He seemed to have more breathing to do than another man, and to make more noise in doing it; and I was conscious of growing high-shouldered on one side in my shrinking endeavors to fend him off.

The weather was miserably raw, and the two cursed the cold. It made us all lethargic before we had gone far, and when we had left the Halfway House behind, we habitually dozed and shivered and were silent. I dozed off myself in considering the question whether I ought to restore a couple of pounds to this creature before losing sight of him, and how it could best be done. In the act of dipping forward, as if I were going to bathe among the horses, I woke in a fright and took the question up again.

But I must have lost it longer than I had thought for, since, although I could recognize nothing in the darkness and the fitful lights and shadows of our lamps, I traced marsh country in the cold damp wind that blew at us. Cowering forward for warmth, and to make me a screen against the wind, the convicts were closer to me than before. The very first words I heard them interchange as I became conscious were the words of my own thoughts, "Two One-Pound notes."

"How did he get 'em?" said the convict I had never seen.

"How should I know?" returned the other. "He had 'em stowed away somehows. Giv him by friends, I expect."

"I wish," said the other, with a bitter curse upon the cold, "that I had 'em here."

"Two one-pound notes or friends?"

"Two one-pound notes. I'd sell all the friends I ever had for one. Well? So he says—?"

"So he says," resumed the convict I had recognized—"it was all said and done in half a minute behind the pile of timber in the yard—'you're going to be discharged?' Yes, I was. Would I find out that boy that had fed him and kep' his secret, and give him them two one-pound notes? Yes, I would. And I did."

"More fool you," growled the other. "I'd have spent 'em on a Man in wittles and drink. He must have been a green one. Mean to say he knowed nothing of you?"

"Not a ha'porth. Different gangs and different ships. He was tried again for prison breaking, and got made a Lifer. That's what he took by *his* motion, and that's all I know of him."

"And was that—Honor!—the only time you worked out in this part of the country?"

"The only time."

"What might have been your opinion of the place?"

"A most infernal place. Mudbank, mist, swamp, and work; work, swamp, mist, and mudbank."

They both execrated the place in very strong language, and gradually growled themselves out and had nothing left to say.

After overhearing this dialogue, I should assuredly have got down and been left in the solitude and darkness of the highway, but for feeling certain that the man had no suspicion of my identity. Indeed, I was not only so changed in the course of nature, but so differently dressed and so differently circumstanced, that it was not at all likely he could have known me without accidental help. Still, the coincidence of our being together on the coach was sufficiently strange to fill me with a dread that some other coincidence might at any moment connect me, in his hearing, with my name. For this reason I resolved to alight as soon as we touched the town, and put myself beyond his hearing. This device I executed successfully. My little portmanteau was in the boot under my feet; I had but to turn a hinge to get it out; I threw it down before me, got down after it, and was left at the first lamp on the first stones of the town pavement. As to the convicts, they went their way with the coach, and I knew at what point they would be spirited off to the river. In my fancy I saw the boat with its convict crew waiting for them at the slime-washed stairs—again heard the gruff "Give way, you!" like an order to dogs—again saw the wicked Noah's Ark lying out in the black water.

I could not have said what I was afraid of, for my fear was altogether undefined and vague, but there was fear upon me. As I walked on to the hotel, I felt that a dread, exceeding the mere apprehension of a painful or disagreeable recognition, made me tremble. I am confident that it took no distinctness of shape, and that it was the revival for a few minutes of the terror of childhood.

The coffee-room at the Blue Boar was empty, and I had not only ordered my dinner there, but had sat down to it, before the waiter knew me. As soon as ever he had apologized for the remissness of his memory, he asked me if he should send Boots for Mr. Pumblechook!

"No," said I, "certainly not."

The waiter (it was he who had brought up the Great Remonstrance from the Commercials on the day when I was bound) appeared surprised, and took the earliest opportunity of putting a dirty old copy of a local newspaper so directly in my way, that I took it up and read this paragraph:

"Our readers will learn, not altogether without interest, in reference to the recent romantic rise in fortune of a young artificer in iron of this neighborhood (what a theme, by-the-way, for the magic pen of our as yet not universally acknowledged townsman TOOBY, the poet of our columns!), that the youth's earliest patron, companion, and friend, was a highly-respected individual not entirely unconnected with the corn and seed trade, and whose eminently convenient and commodious business premises are situated within a hundred miles of the High Street. It is not wholly irrespective of our personal feelings that we record HIM as the Mentor of our young Telemachus, for it is good to know that our town produced the founder of the latter's fortunes. Does the thought-contracted brow of the local Sage or the lustrous eye of local Beauty inquire whose fortunes? We believe that Quentin Matsys was the BLACKSMITH of Antwerp. VERB. SAP."

I entertain a conviction, based upon large experience, that if in the days of my prosperity I had gone to the North Pole, I should have met somebody there, either wandering Eskimaux or civilized man, who would have told me that Pumblechook was my earliest patron and the founder of my fortunes.

T w e n t y - n i n e

BETIMES IN THE MORNING I WAS UP AND OUT. IT WAS TOO early yet to go to Miss Havisham's, so I loitered into the country on Miss Havisham's side of town—which was not Joe's side; I could go there tomorrow—thinking about my patroness, and painting brilliant pictures of her plans for me.

She had adopted Estella, she had as good as adopted me, and it could not fail to be her intention to bring us together. She reserved it for me to restore the desolate house, admit the sunshine into the dark rooms, set the clocks a going and the cold hearths a blazing, tear down the cobwebs, destroy the vermin—in short, do all the shining deeds of the young Knight of romance, and marry the Princess. I had stopped to look at the house as I passed; and its seared red brick walls, blocked windows, and strong green ivy clasping even the stacks of chimneys with its twigs and tendons, as if with sinewy old arms, had made up a rich attractive mystery, of which I was the hero. Estella was the inspiration of it, and the heart of it, of course. But though she had taken such strong possession of me, though my fancy and my hope were so set upon her, though her influence on my boyish life and character had been all-powerful, I did not, even that romantic morning, invest her with any attributes save those she possessed. I mention this in this place, of a fixed purpose, because it is the clew by which I am to be followed into my poor labyrinth, such as it is. According to my experience, the conventional notion of a lover cannot be always true. The unqualified truth is, that when I loved Estella with the love of a man, I loved her because I found her irresistible. Once for all; I knew to my sorrow, often and often, if not always, that I loved her against reason, against promise, against peace, against hope, against happiness, against all discouragement that could be. Once for all; I loved her none the less because I knew it, and it had no more influence in restraining me than if I had devoutly and conventionally believed her to be human perfection.

I so shaped out my walk as to arrive at the gate at my old time. When I had rung at the bell with an unsteady hand I turned my back upon the gate, while I tried to get my breath and keep the beating of my heart moderately quiet. I heard the side-door open and steps come across the courtyard; but I pretended not to hear, even when the gate swung on its rusty hinges.

Being at last touched on the shoulder, I started and turned. I started much more naturally then to find myself confronted by a man in a sober gray dress. The last man I should have expected to see in that place of porter at Miss Havisham's door.

"Orlick!"

"Ah, young master, there's more changes than yours. But come in, come in. It's opposed to my orders to hold the gate open."

I entered, and he swung it, and locked it, and took the key out. "Yes!" said he, facing round, after doggedly preceding me a few steps toward the house. "Here I am!"

"How did you come here?"

"I come here," he retorted, "on my legs. I had my box brought alongside me in a barrow."

"Are you here for good?"

"I ain't here for harm, young master, I suppose?"

I was not so sure of that. I had leisure to entertain the retort in my mind, while he slowly lifted his heavy glance from the pavement, up my legs and arms, to my face.

"Then you have left the forge?" I said.

"Do this look like a forge?" replied Orlick, sending his glance all around him with an air of injury. "Now, do it look like it?"

I asked him how long he had left Gargery's forge?

"One day is so like another here," he replied, "that I don't know without casting it up. However, I come here some time since you left."

"I could have told you that, Orlick."

"Ah!" said he, dryly. "But then you've got to be a scholar."

By this time we had come to the house, where I found his room to be one just within the side-door, with a little window in it looking on the courtyard. In its small proportions it was not unlike the kind of place usually assigned to a gate-porter in Paris. Certain keys were hanging on the wall, to which he now added the gate key, and his patchwork-covered bed was in a little inner division or recess. The whole had a slovenly, confined, and sleepy look, like a cage for a human dormouse: while he, looming dark and heavy in the shadow of a corner by the window, looked like the human dormouse for whom it was fitted up—as indeed he was.

"I never saw this room before," I remarked; "but there used to be no porter here."

"No," said he; "not till it got about that there was no protection on the premises, and it come to be considered dangerous, with convicts and Tag and Rag and Bobtail going up and down. And then I was recommended to the place as a man who could give another man as good as he brought, and I took it. It's easier than bellowsing and hammering.—That's loaded, that is."

My eye had been caught by a gun with a brass-bound stock over the chimney-piece, and his eye had followed mine.

"Well," said I, not desirous of more conversation, "shall I go up to Miss Havisham?"

"Burn me if I know!" he retorted, first stretching himself and then shaking himself; "my orders ends here, young master. I give this here bell a rap with this here hammer, and you go on along the passage till you meet somebody."

"I am expected, I believe?"

"Burn me twice over if I can say!" said he.

Upon that I turned down the long passage which I had first trodden in my thick boots, and he made his bell sound. At the end of the passage, while the bell was still reverberating, I found Sarah Pocket, who appeared to have now become constitutionally green and yellow by reason of me.

"Oh!" said she. "You, is it, Mr. Pip?"

"It is, Miss Pocket. I am glad to tell you that Mr. Pocket and family are all well."

"Are they any wiser?" said Sarah, with a dismal shake of the head; "they had better be wiser than well. Ah, Matthew, Matthew! You know your way, sir?"

Tolerably, for I had gone up the staircase in the dark many a time. I ascended it now, in lighter boots than of yore, and tapped in my old way at the door of Miss Havisham's room. "Pip's rap," I heard her say immediately; "come in, Pip."

She was in her chair near the old table, in the old dress, with her two hands crossed on her stick, her chin resting on them, and her eyes on the fire. Sitting near her, with the white shoe that had never been worn in her hand, and her head bent as she looked at it, was an elegant lady whom I had never seen.

"Come in, Pip," Miss Havisham continued to mutter, without looking round or up; "come in, Pip; how do you do, Pip? so you kiss my hand as if I were a queen, eh?—Well?"

She looked up at me suddenly, only moving her eyes, and repeated, in a grimly playful manner,

"Well?"

"I heard, Miss Havisham," said I, rather at a loss, "that you were so kind as to wish me to come and see you, and I came directly."

"Well?"

The lady whom I had never seen before lifted up her eyes and looked archly at me, and then I saw that the eyes were Estella's eyes. But she was so much changed, was so much more beautiful, so much more womanly, in all things winning admiration had made such wonderful advance that I seemed to have made none. I fancied, as I looked at her, that I slipped hopelessly back into the coarse and common boy again. Oh, the sense of distance and disparity that came upon me, and the inaccessibility that came about her!

She gave me her hand. I stammered something about the pleasure I felt in seeing her again, and my having looked forward to it for a long, long time.

"Do you find her much changed, Pip?" asked Miss Havisham with her greedy look, and striking her stick upon a chair that stood between them, as a sign to me to sit down there.

"When I came in, Miss Havisham, I thought there was nothing of Estella in the face or figure; but now it all settles down so curiously into the old—"

"What? You are not going to say, into the old Estella?" Miss Havisham interrupted. "She was proud and insulting, and you wanted to go away from her. Don't you remember?"

I said, confusedly, that that was long ago, and that I knew no better then, and the like. Estella smiled with perfect composure, and said she had no doubt of my having been quite right, and of her having been very disagreeable.

"Is he changed?" Miss Havisham asked her.

"Very much," said Estella, looking at me.

"Less coarse and common?" said Miss Havisham, playing with Estella's hair.

Estella laughed, and looked at the shoe in her hand, and laughed again, and looked at me, and put the shoe down. She treated me as a boy still, but she lured me on.

We sat in the dreamy room among the old strange influences which had so wrought upon me, and I learned that she had but just come home from France, and that she was going to London. Proud and willful as of old, she had brought those qualities into such subjection to her beauty that it was impossible and out of nature—or I thought so—to separate them from her beauty. Truly it was impossible to dissociate her presence from all those wretched hankerings after money and gentility that had disturbed my boyhood—from all those ill-regulated aspirations that had first made me ashamed of home and Joe—from all those visions that had raised her face in the glowing fire, struck it out of the iron on the anvil, extracted it from the darkness of night to look in at the wooden window of the forge and flit away. In a word, it was impossible for me to separate her, in the past or in the present, from the innermost life of my life.

It was settled that I should stay there all the rest of the day, and return to the hotel at night, and to London tomorrow. When we had conversed for a while, Miss Havisham sent us two out to walk in the neglected garden; on our coming in by-and-by, she said I should wheel her about a little as in times of yore.

So Estella and I went out into the garden by the gate through which I had strayed to my encounter with the pale young gentleman, now Herbert; I, trembling in spirit and worshiping the very hem of her dress; she, quite composed and most decidedly not worshiping the hem of mine. As we drew near to the place of encounter she stopped and said:

"I must have been a singular little creature to hide and see that fight that day; but I did, and I enjoyed it very much."

"You rewarded me very much."

"Did I?" she replied, in an incidental and forgetful way. "I remember I entertained a great objection to your adversary, because I took it ill that he should be brought here to pester me with his company."

"We are great friends now," said I.

"Are you? I think I recollect though, that you read with his father?"

"Yes."

I made the admission with reluctance, for it seemed to have a boyish look, and she already treated me more than enough like a boy.

"Since your change of fortune and prospects you have changed your companions," said Estella.

"Naturally," said I.

"And necessarily," she added, in a haughty tone; "what was fit company for you once would be quite unfit company for you now."

In my conscience, I doubt very much whether I had any lingering intention left of going to see Joe; but if I had, this observation put it to flight.

"You had no idea of your impending good fortune in those times?" said Estella, with a slight wave of her hand, signifying in the fighting times.

"Not the least."

The air of completeness and superiority with which she walked at my side, and the air of youthfulness and deference with which I walked at hers, made a contrast that I strongly felt. It would have rankled in me more than it did, if I had not regarded myself as eliciting it by being so set apart for her and assigned to her.

The garden was too overgrown and rank for walking in with ease, and after we had made the round of it twice or thrice we came out again into the brewery-yard. I showed her to a nicety where I had seen her walking on the casks, that first old day, and she said, with a cold and careless look in that direction, "Did I?" I reminded her where she had come out of the house, and given me my meat and drink, and she said, "I don't remember." "Not remember that you made me cry?" said I. "No," said she, and shook her head and looked about her. I verily believe that her not remembering, and not minding it in the least, made me cry again inwardly—and that is the sharpest crying of all.

"You must know," said Estella, condescending to me as a brilliant and beautiful woman might, "that I have no heart—if that has anything to do with my memory."

I got through some jargon to the effect that I took the liberty of doubting that. That I knew better. That there could be no such beauty without it.

"Oh! I have a heart to be stabbed in or shot in, I have no doubt," said Estella, "and, of course, if it ceased to beat I should cease to be. But you know what I mean. I have no softness there, no—sympathy—sentiment—nonsense."

What *was* it that was borne in upon my mind when she stood still and looked attentively at me? Anything that I had seen in Miss Havisham? No. In some of her looks and gestures there was that tinge of resemblance to Miss Havisham which may often be noticed to have been acquired by children from grown persons with whom they have been much associated and secluded, and which, when childhood is past, will produce a remarkable occasional likeness of expression between faces that are otherwise quite different. And yet I could not trace this to Miss Havisham. I looked again, and though she was still looking at me, the suggestion was gone.

What *was it?*

"I am serious," said Estella, not so much with a frown (for her brow was smooth) as with a darkening of her face; "if we are to be thrown much together, you had better believe it at once. No!" imperiously stopping me as I opened my lips. "I have not bestowed my tenderness anywhere. I have never had any such thing."

In another moment we were in the brewery so long disused, and she pointed to the high gallery where I had seen her going out on that same first day, and told me she remembered to have been up there, and to have seen me standing scared below. As my eyes followed her white hand, again the same dim suggestion that I could not possibly grasp crossed me. My involuntary start occasioned her to lay her hand upon my arm. Instantly the ghost passed once more, for the last time, and was gone.

What *was it?*

"What is the matter?" asked Estella; "are you scared again?"

"I should be, if I believed what you said just now," I replied, to turn it off.

"Then you don't? Very well. It is said, at any rate. Miss Havisham will soon be expecting you at your old post, though I think that might be laid aside now, with other old belongings. Let us make one more round of the garden, and then go in. Come! You shall not shed tears for my cruelty today; you shall be my Page, and give me your shoulder."

Her handsome dress had trailed upon the ground. She held it in one hand now, and with the other lightly touched my shoulder as we walked. We walked round the ruined garden twice or thrice more, and it was all in bloom for me. If the green and yellow growth of weed in the chinks of the old wall had been the most precious flowers that ever blew, it could not have been more cherished in my remembrance.

There was no discrepancy of years between us to remove her far from me; we were of nearly the same age, though of course the age told for more in her case than in mine; but the air of inaccessibility which her beauty and her manner gave her, tormented me in the midst of my delight, and at the height of the assurance I felt that our patroness had chosen us for one another. Wretched boy!

At last we went back into the house, and there I heard, with surprise, that my guardian had come down to see Miss Havisham on business and would come back to dinner. The old wintry branches of chandeliers in the room where the moldering table was spread, had been lighted while we were out, and Miss Havisham was in her chair waiting for me.

It was like pushing the chair itself back into the past, when we began the old slow circuit round about the ashes of the bridal feast. But in the funereal room, with that figure of the grave fallen back in the chair fixing its eyes upon her, Estella looked more bright and beautiful than before. I was under stronger enchantment.

The time so melted away that our early dinner-hour drew close at hand, and Estella left us to prepare herself. We had stopped near the center of the long table, and Miss Havisham, with one of her withered arms stretched out of the chair, rested that clenched hand upon the yellow cloth. As Estella looked back over her shoulder before going out at the door, Miss Havisham kissed that hand to her, with a ravenous intensity that was, of its kind, quite dreadful.

Then Estella being gone and we two left alone, she turned to me, and said, in a whisper,

"Is she beautiful, graceful, well-grown? Do you admire her?"

"Everybody must who sees her, Miss Havisham."

She drew an arm round my neck, and drew my head close down to hers as she sat in the chair. "Love her, love her, love her! How does she use you?"

Before I could answer (if I could have answered such a difficult question at all) she repeated, "Love her, love her, love her! If she favors you, love her. If she wounds you, love her. If she tears your heart to pieces—and as it gets older and stronger it will tear deeper—love her, love her, love her!"

Never had I seen such passionate eagerness as was joined to her utterance of these words. I could feel the muscles of the thin arm round my neck swell with the vehemence that possessed her.

"Hear me, Pip! I adopted her, to be loved. I bred her and educated her, to be loved. I developed her into what she is, that she might be loved. Love her!"

She said the word often enough, and there could be no doubt that she meant to say it; but if the often repeated word had been hate instead of love—despair—revenge—dire death—it could not have sounded from her lips more like a curse.

"I'll tell you," said she, in the same hurried passionate whisper, "what real love is. It is blind devotion, unquestioning self-humiliation, utter submission, trust and belief against yourself and against the world, giving up your whole heart and soul to the smiter—as I did!"

When she came to that, and to a desperate cry that followed that, I caught her round the waist. For she rose up in the chair, in her shroud of a dress, and wildly struck at the air as if she would as soon have struck herself against the wall and fallen dead.

All this passed in a few seconds. As I drew her down into her chair, I was conscious of a scent that I knew, and turning, saw my guardian in the room.

He always carried (I have not yet mentioned it, I think) a pocket-handkerchief of rich silk and of imposing proportions, which was of great value to him in his profession. I have seen him so terrify a client or a witness by ceremoniously unfolding his pocket-handkerchief as if he were immediately going to blow his nose, and then pausing, as if he knew he should not have time to do it before such client or witness committed himself, that the self-committal has followed directly, quite as a matter of course. When I saw him in the room, he had this expressive pocket-handkerchief in both hands, and was looking at us. On meeting my eye, he said plainly by a momentary and silent pause in that attitude, "Indeed? Singular!" and then put the handkerchief to its right use with wonderful effect.

Miss Havisham had seen him as soon as I, and was (like everybody else) afraid of him. She made a strong attempt to compose herself, and stammered that he was as punctual as ever.

"As punctual as ever," he repeated, coming up to us. "(How do you do, Pip? Shall I give you a ride, Miss Havisham? Once round?) And so you are here, Pip?"

I told him when I had arrived, and how Miss Havisham had wished me to come and see Estella. To which he replied, "Ah! Very fine young lady!" Then he pushed Miss Havisham in her chair before him with one of his large hands, and put the other in his trowsers-pocket as if the pocket were full of secrets.

"Well, Pip! How often have you seen Miss Estella before?" said he, when he came to a stop.

"How often?"

"Ah! How many times? Ten thousand times?"

"Oh! Certainly not so many."

"Twice?"

"Jaggers," interposed Miss Havisham, much to my relief; "leave my Pip alone, and go with him to your dinner."

He complied, and we groped our way down the dark stairs together. While we were still on our way to those detached apartments across the paved yard at the back, he asked me how often I had seen Miss Havisham eat and drink; offering me a breadth of choice, as usual, between a hundred times and once.

I considered, and said, "Never."

"And never will, Pip," he retorted, with a frowning smile. "She has never allowed herself to be seen doing either since she lived this present life of hers. She wanders about in the night, and lays hands on such food as she takes."

"Pray, sir," said I, "may I ask you a question?"

"You may," said he, "and I may decline to answer it. Put your question."

"Estella's name. Is it Havisham, or—?" I had nothing to add.

"Or what?" said he.

"Is it Havisham?"

"It is Havisham."

This brought us to the dinner-table, where she and Sarah Pocket awaited us. Mr. Jaggers presided, Estella sat opposite to him, I faced my green and yellow friend. We dined very well, and were waited on by a maid-servant whom I had never seen in all my comings and goings, but who, for anything I know, had been in that mysterious house the whole time. After dinner a bottle of choice old port was placed before my guardian (he was evidently well acquainted with the vintage), and the two ladies left us.

Anything to equal the determined reticence of Mr. Jaggers under that roof I never saw elsewhere, even in him. He kept his very looks to himself, and scarcely directed his eyes to Estella's face once during dinner. When she spoke to him, he listened, and in due course answered, but never looked at her that I could see. On the other hand, she often looked at him, with interest and curiosity, if not distrust, but his face never showed the least consciousness. Throughout dinner he took a dry delight in making Sarah Pocket greener and yellower, by often referring in conversation with me to my expectations; but here, again, he showed no consciousness, and even made it appear that he extorted—and even did extort, though I don't know how—those references out of my innocent self.

And when he and I were left alone together, he sat with an air upon him of general lying by in consequence of information he possessed, that really was too much for me. He cross-examined his very wine when he had nothing else in hand. He held it between himself and the candle, tasted the port, rolled it in his mouth, swallowed it, looked at the port again, smelled it, tried it, drank it, filled again, and cross-examined the glass again, until I was as nervous as if I had known the wine to be telling him something to my disadvantage. Three or four times I feebly thought I would start conversation; but whenever he saw me going to ask him anything he looked at me with his glass in his hand, and rolling his wine about in his mouth, as if requesting me to take notice that it was of no use, for he couldn't answer. I think Miss Pocket was conscious that the sight of me involved her in the danger of being goaded to madness, and perhaps tearing off her cap—which was a very hideous one, in the nature of a muslin mop—and strewing the ground with her hair—which assuredly had never grown on *her* head. She did not appear when we afterward went up to Miss Havisham's room, and we four played at whist. In the interval, Miss Havisham, in a wild way, had put some of the most beautiful jewels from her dressing-table into Estella's hair, and about her bosom and waist; and I saw even my guardian look at her from under his thick eyebrows, and raise them a little, when her loveliness was before him, with those rich flushes of glitter and color in it.

Of the manner and extent to which he took our trumps into custody, and came out with mean little cards at the ends of hands, before which the glory of our Kings and Queens was utterly abased, I say nothing; nor of the feeling that I had, respecting his looking upon us personally in the light of three very obvious and poor riddles that he had found out long ago. What I suffered from, was the incompatibility between his cold presence and my feelings toward Estella. It was not that I knew I could never bear to speak to him about her, that I knew I could never bear to hear him creak his boots at her, that I knew I could never bear to see him wash his hands of her; it was, that my admiration should be within a foot or two of him—it was, that my feelings should be in the same place with him—*that,* was the agonizing circumstance.

We played until nine o'clock, and then it was arranged that when Estella came to London I should be forewarned of her coming and should meet her at the coach; and then I took leave of her, and touched her and left her.

My guardian lay at the Boar, in the next room to mine. Far into the night, Miss Havisham's words, "Love her, love her, love her!" sounded in my ears. I adapted them for my own repetition, and said to my pillow, "I love her, I love her, I love her!" thousands of times. Then a burst of gratitude came upon me, that she should be destined for me, once the blacksmith's boy. Then, I thought, if she were, as I feared, by no means rapturously grateful for that destiny yet, when would she begin to be interested in me? When should I awaken the heart within her that was mute and sleeping now?

Ah me! I thought those were high and great emotions. But I never thought there was anything low and small in my keeping away from Joe, because I knew she would be contemptuous of him. It was but a day gone, and Joe had brought the tears into my eyes; they had soon dried, God forgive me! soon dried.

T h i r t y

AFTER WELL CONSIDERING THE MATTER WHILE I WAS dressing at the Blue Boar in the morning, I resolved to tell my guardian that I doubted Orlick's being the right sort of man to fill a post of trust at

Miss Havisham's. "Why, of course he is not the right sort of a man, Pip," said my guardian, comfortably satisfied beforehand on the general head, "because the man who fills the post of trust never is the right sort of man." It seemed quite to put him into spirits to find that this particular post was not accidentally and exceptionally held by the right sort of man, and he listened in a satisfied manner while I told him what knowledge I had of Orlick. "Very good, Pip," he observed, when I had concluded, "I'll go round presently, and pay our friend off." Rather alarmed by this summary action, I was for a little delay, and even hinted that our friend himself might be difficult to deal with. "Oh, no, he won't," said my guardian, making his pocket-handkerchief point, with perfect confidence; "I should like to see him argue the question with *me*."

As we were going back together to London by the midday coach, and as I breakfasted under such terrors of Pumblechook that I could scarcely hold my cup, this gave me an opportunity of saying that I wanted a walk, and that I would go on along the London Road while Mr. Jaggers was occupied, if he would let the coachman know that I would get into my place when overtaken. I was thus enabled to fly from the Blue Boar immediately after breakfast. By then making a loop of about a couple of miles into the open country at the back of Pumblechook's premises, I got round into the High Street again, a little beyond that pitfall, and felt myself in comparative security.

It was interesting to be in the quiet old town once more, and it was not disagreeable to be here and there suddenly recognized and stared after. One or two of the tradespeople even darted out of their shops and went a little way down the street before me, that they might turn, as if they had forgotten something, and pass me face to face—on which occasions I don't know whether they or I made the worse pretense; they of not doing it, or I of not seeing it. Still my position was a distinguished one, and I was not at all dissatisfied with it, until Fate threw me in the way of that unlimited miscreant, Trabb's boy.

Casting my eyes along the street at a certain point of my progress, I beheld Trabb's boy approaching, lashing himself with an empty blue bag. Deeming that a serene and unconscious contemplation of him would best beseem me, and would be most likely to quell his evil mind, I advanced with that expression of countenance, and was rather congratulating myself on my success, when suddenly the knees of Trabb's boy smote together, his hair uprose, his cap fell off, he trembled violently in every limb, staggered out in the road, and crying to the populace, "Hold me! I'm so frightened!" feigned to be in a paroxysm of terror and contrition, occasioned by the dignity of my appearance. As I passed him his teeth loudly chattered in his head, and, with every mark of extreme humiliation, he prostrated himself in the dust.

This was a hard thing to bear, but this was nothing. I had not advanced another two hundred yards, when, to my inexpressible terror, amazement, and indignation, I again beheld Trabb's boy approaching. He was coming round a narrow corner. His blue bag was slung over his shoulder, honest industry beamed in his eyes, a determination to proceed to Trabb's with cheerful briskness was indicated in his gait. With a shock he became aware of me, and was severely visited as before; but this time his motion was rotatory, and he staggered round and round me with knees more afflicted, and with uplifted hands as if beseeching for mercy. His sufferings were hailed with the greatest joy by a knot of spectators, and I felt utterly confounded.

I had not got as much further down the street as the post-office when I again beheld Trabb's boy shooting round by a back way. This time he was entirely changed. He wore the blue bag in the manner of my great-coat, and was strutting along the pavement toward me on the opposite side of the street, attended by a company of delighted young friends to whom he from time to time exclaimed, with a wave of his hand, "don't know yah!" Words cannot state the amount of aggravation and injury wreaked upon me by Trabb's boy, when, passing abreast of me, he pulled up his shirt-collar, twined his side hair, stuck an arm akimbo, and smirked extravagantly by, wriggling his elbows and body, and drawling to his attendants, "Don't know yah, don't know yah, 'pon my soul don't know yah!" The disgrace attendant on his immediately afterward taking to crowing and pursuing me across the bridge with crows as from an exceedingly dejected fowl who had known me when I was a blacksmith, culminated the disgrace with which I left the town, and was, so to speak, ejected by it into the open country.

But unless I had taken the life of Trabb's boy on that occasion, I really do not even now see what I could have done save endure. To have struggled with him in the street, or to have exacted any lower recompense from him than his heart's best blood would have been futile and degrading. Moreover, he was a boy whom no man could hurt; an invulnerable and dodging serpent who, when chased into a corner, flew out again between his captor's legs, scornfully yelping. I wrote, however, to Mr. Trabb by next day's post, to say that Mr. Pip must decline to deal further with one who could so far forget what he owed to the best interests of society, as to employ a boy who excited Loathing in every respectable mind.

The coach, with Mr. Jaggers inside, came up in due time, and I took my box-seat again, and arrived in London safe—but not sound, for my heart was gone. As soon as I arrived I sent a penitential codfish and barrel of oysters to Joe (as reparation for not having gone myself), and then went on to Barnard's Inn.

I found Herbert dining on cold meat, and delighted to welcome me back. Having dispatched the Avenger to the coffeehouse for an addition to the dinner, I felt that I must open my breast that very evening to my friend and chum. As confidence was out of the question with the Avenger in the hall, which could merely be regarded in the light of an antechamber to the keyhole, I sent him to the Play. A better proof of the severity of my bondage to that task-master could scarcely be afforded than the degrading shifts to which I was constantly driven to find him employment. So mean is extremity that I sometimes sent him to Hyde Park corner to see what o'clock it was.

Dinner done and we sitting with our feet upon the fender, I said to Herbert, "My dear Herbert, I have something very particular to tell you."

"My dear Handel," he returned, "I shall esteem and respect your confidence."

"It concerns myself, Herbert," said I, "and one other person."

Herbert crossed his feet, looked at the fire with his head on one side, and having looked at it in vain for some time, looked at me because I didn't go on.

"Herbert," said I, laying my hand upon his knee. "I love—I adore—Estella."

Instead of being transfixed, Herbert replied in an easy, matter-of-course way, "Exactly. Well?"

"Well, Herbert? Is that all you say? Well?"

"What next, I mean?" said Herbert. "Of course I know *that*."

"How do you know it?" said I.

"How do I know it, Handel? Why, from you."

"I never told you."

"Told me! You have never told me when you have got your hair cut, but I have had senses to perceive it. You have always adored her, ever since I have known you. You brought your adoration and portmanteau here together. Told me! Why you have always told me all day long. When you told me your own story, you told me plainly that you began adoring her the first time you saw her, when you were very young indeed."

"Very well, then," said I, to whom this was a new and not unwelcome light, "I have never left off adoring her. And she has come back a most beautiful and most elegant creature. And I saw her yesterday. And if I adored her before, I now doubly adore her."

"Lucky for you then, Handel," said Herbert, "that you are picked out for her and allotted to her. Without encroaching on forbidden ground, we may venture to say that there can be no doubt between ourselves of that fact. Have you any idea yet of Estella's views on the adoration question?"

I shook my head gloomily. "Oh! she is thousands of miles away from me," said I.

"Patience, my dear Handel: time enough, time enough. But you have something more to say?"

"I am ashamed to say it," I returned, "and yet it's no worse to say it than to think it. You call me a lucky fellow. Of course, I am. I was a blacksmith's boy but yesterday; I am—what shall I say I am—today?"

"Say a good fellow, if you want a phrase," returned Herbert, smiling, and clapping his hand on the back of mine, "a good fellow with impetuosity and hesitation, boldness and diffidence, action and dreaming, curiously mixed in him."

I stopped for a moment to consider whether there really was this mixture in my character. On the whole, I by no means recognized the analysis, but thought it not worth disputing.

"When I ask what I am to call myself today, Herbert," I went on, "I suggest what I have in my thoughts. You say I am lucky. I know I have done nothing to raise myself in life, and that Fortune alone has raised me; that is being very lucky. And yet, when I think of Estella—"

("And when don't you, you know?" Herbert threw in, with his eyes on the fire; which I thought kind and sympathetic of him.)

"—Then, my dear Herbert, I cannot tell you how dependent and uncertain I feel, and how exposed to hundreds of chances. Avoiding forbidden ground as you did just now, I may still say that on the constancy of one person (naming no person) all my expectations depend. And at the best, how indefinite and unsatisfactory only to know so vaguely what they are!" In saying this, I relieved my mind of what had always been there, more or less, though no doubt most since yesterday.

"Now, Handel," Herbert replied, in his gay, hopeful way, "it seems to me that in the despondency of the tender passion we are looking into our gift-horse's mouth with a magnifying glass. Likewise, it seems to me that concentrating our attention on that examination we altogether overlook one of the best points of the animal. Didn't you tell me that your guardian, Mr. Jaggers, told you in the beginning that you were not endowed with expectations only? And even if he had not told you so—though that is a very large If, I grant—could you believe that, of all men in London, Mr. Jaggers is the man to hold his present relations toward you unless he was sure of his ground?"

I said I could not deny that this was a strong point. I said it (people often do so in such cases) like a rather reluctant concession to truth and justice—as if I wanted to deny it!

"I should think it *was* a strong point," said Herbert, "and I should think you would be puzzled to imagine a stronger; as to the rest, you must bide your guardian's time, and he must bide his client's time. You'll be one-and-twenty before you know where you are, and then perhaps you'll get some further enlightenment. At all events you'll be nearer getting it, for it must come at last."

"What a hopeful disposition you have!" said I, gratefully admiring his cheery ways.

"I ought to have," said Herbert, "for I have not much else. I must acknowledge, by-the-by, that the good sense of what I have just said is not my own, but my father's. The only remark that I ever heard him make on your story was the final one: 'The thing is settled and done, or Mr. Jaggers would not be in it.' And now before I say anything more about my father, or my father's son, and repay confidence with confidence, I want to make myself seriously disagreeable to you for a moment—positively repulsive."

"You won't succeed," said I.

"Oh, yes I shall!" said he. "One, two, three, and now I am in for it. Handel, my good fellow"—though he spoke in this light tone he was much in earnest—"I have been thinking since we have been talking with our feet on this fender, that Estella surely cannot be a condition of your inheritance, if she was never referred to by your guardian. Am I right in so understanding what you have told me, as that he never referred to her, directly or indirectly, in any way? Never even hinted, for instance, that your patron might have views as to your marriage ultimately?"

"Never."

"Now, Handel, I am quite free from the flavor of sour grapes, upon my soul! Not being bound to her, can you not detach yourself from her?—I told you I should be disagreeable."

I turned my head aside, for, with a rush and a sweep, like the old marsh winds coming up from the sea, a feeling like that which had subdued me on the morning when I left the forge, when the mists were solemnly rising, and when I laid my hand upon the village finger-post, smote upon my heart again. There was silence between us for a little while.

"Yes, but my dear Handel," Herbert went on, as if we had been talking instead of silent, "its having been so strongly rooted in the breast of a boy whom nature and circumstances made so romantic renders it very serious. Think of her bringing-up, and think of Miss Havisham. Think of what she is herself (now I am repulsive, and you abominate me). This may lead to miserable things."

"I know it, Herbert," said I, with my head still turned away, "but I can't help it."

"You can't detach yourself?"

"No. Impossible!"

"You can't try, Handel?"

"No. Impossible!"

"Well!" said Herbert, getting up with a lively shake as if he had been asleep, and stirring the fire; "now I'll endeavor to make myself agreeable again!"

So he went round the room and shook the curtains out, put the chairs in their places, tidied the books and so forth that were lying about, looked into the hall, peeped into the letter-box, shut the door, and came back to his chair by the fire; where he sat down, nursing his left leg in both arms.

"I was going to say a word or two, Handel, concerning my father and my father's son. I am afraid it is scarcely necessary for my father's son to remark that my father's establishment is not particularly brilliant in its housekeeping."

"There is always plenty, Herbert," said I: to say something encouraging.

"Oh, yes! and so the dustman says, I believe, with the strongest approval, and so does the marine store-shop in the back street. Gravely, Handel, for the subject is grave enough; you know how it is as well as I do. I suppose there was a time once when my father had not given matters up; but if ever there was, the time is gone. May I ask you if you have ever had an opportunity of remarking down in your part of the country, that the children of not exactly suitable marriages are always most particularly anxious to be married?"

This was such a singular question that I asked him in return, "Is it so?"

"I don't know," said Herbert; "that's what I want to know. Because it is decidedly the case with us. My poor sister Charlotte, who was next me and died before she was fourteen, was a striking example. Little Jane is the same. In her desire to be matrimonially established, you might suppose her to have passed her short existence in the perpetual contemplation of domestic bliss. Little Alick, in a frock, has already made arrangements for his union with a suitable young person at Kew. And indeed, I think we are all engaged except the baby."

"Then you are?" said I.

"I am," said Herbert, "but it's a secret."

I assured him of my keeping the secret, and begged to be favored with further particulars. He had spoken so sensibly and feelingly of my weakness, that I wanted to know something about his strength.

"May I ask the name?" I said.

"Name of Clara," said Herbert.

"Live in London?"

"Yes. Perhaps I ought to mention," said Herbert, who had become curiously crestfallen and meek since we entered on the interesting theme, "that she is rather below my mother's nonsensical family notions. Her father had to do with the victualing of passenger-ships. I think he was a species of purser."

"What is he now?" said I.

"He's an invalid now," replied Herbert.

"Living on—?"

"On the first floor," said Herbert. Which was not at all what I meant, for I had intended my question to apply to his means. "I have never seen him, for he has always kept his room overhead since I have known Clara. But I have heard him constantly. He makes tremendous rows—roars, and pegs at the door with some frightful instrument." In looking at me, and then laughing heartily, Herbert for the time recovered his usual lively manner.

"Don't you expect to see him?" said I.

"Oh yes, I constantly expect to see him," returned Herbert, "because I never hear him without expecting him to come tumbling through the ceiling. But I don't know how long the rafters may hold."

When he had once more laughed heartily he became meek again, and told me that the moment he began to realize Capital it was his intention to marry this young lady. He added, as a self-evident proposition, engendering low spirits, "But you *can't* marry, you know, while you're looking about you."

As we contemplated the fire, and as I thought what a difficult vision to realize this same Capital sometimes was, I put my hands in my pockets. A folded piece of paper in one of them attracting my attention, I opened it, and found it to be the playbill I had received from Joe, relative to the celebrated provincial amateur of Roscian renown. "And bless my heart!" I involuntarily added aloud, "it's tonight!"

This changed the subject in an instant, and made us hurriedly resolve to go to the play. So, when I had pledged myself to comfort and abet Herbert in the affair of his heart by all practicable and impracticable means, and when Herbert had told me that his affianced already knew me by reputation, and that I should be presented to her, and when we had warmly shaken hands upon our mutual confidence, we blew out our candles, made up our fire, locked our door, and issued forth in quest of Mr. Wopsle and Denmark.

Thirty-one

ON OUR ARRIVAL IN DENMARK WE FOUND THE KING AND queen of that country elevated in two armchairs on a small kitchen table, holding a Court. The whole of the Danish nobility were in attendance; consisting of a noble boy in the wash leather boots of a gigantic ancestor, a venerable Peer with a dirty face, who seemed to have risen from the people late in life, and the Danish chivalry with a comb in its hair and a pair of white silk legs, and presenting on the whole a feminine appearance. My gifted townsman stood gloomily apart, with folded arms, and I could have wished that his curls and forehead had been more probable.

Several curious little circumstances transpired as the action proceeded. The late king of the country not only appeared to have been troubled with a cough at the time of his decease, but to have taken it with him to the tomb and to have brought it back. The royal phantom also carried a ghostly manuscript round its truncheon, to which it had the appearance of occasionally referring, and that, too, with an air of anxiety and a tendency to lose the place of reference which were suggestive of a state of mortality. It was this, I conceive, which led to the Shade's being advised by the gallery to "turn over!"—a recommendation which it took extremely ill. It was likewise to be noted of this majestic spirit that whereas it always appeared with an air of having been out a long time and walked an immense distance, it perceptibly came from a closely contiguous wall. This occasioned its terrors to be received derisively. The Queen of Denmark, a very buxom lady, though no doubt historically brazen, was considered by the public to have too much brass about her; her chin being attached to her diadem by a broad band of that metal (as if she had a gorgeous toothache), her waist being encircled by another, and each of her arms by another, so that she was openly mentioned as "the kettle drum." The noble boy in the ancestral boots was inconsistent, representing himself, as it were in one breath, as an able seaman, a strolling actor, a gravedigger, a clergyman, and a person of the utmost importance at a Court fencing-match, on the authority of whose practiced eye and nice discrimination the finest strokes were judged. This gradually led to a want of toleration for him, and even—on his being detected in holy orders, and declining to perform the funeral service—to the general indignation taking the form of nuts. Lastly, Ophelia was a prey to such slow musical madness, that when, in course of time, she had taken off her white muslin scarf, folded it up, and buried it, a sulky man who had been long cooling his impatient nose against an iron bar in the front row of the gallery, growled, "Now the baby's put to bed let's have supper!" which, to say the least of it, was out of keeping.

Upon my unfortunate townsman all these incidents accumulated with playful effect. Whenever that undecided Prince had to ask a question or state a doubt, the public helped him out with it. As for example: on the question whether 'twas nobler in the mind to suffer, some roared yes, and some no, and some inclining to both opinions said, "toss up for it"; and quite a Debating Society arose. When he asked what should such fellows as he do crawling between earth and heaven, he was encouraged with loud cries of "Hear, hear!" When he appeared with his stocking disordered (its disorder expressed, according to usage, by one very neat fold in the top, which I suppose to be always got up with a flatiron), a conversation took place in the gallery respecting the paleness of his leg, and whether it was occasioned by the turn the ghost had given him. On his taking the recorders—very like a little black flute that had just been played in the orchestra and handed out at the door— he was called upon unanimously for Rule Britannia. When he recommended the player not to saw the air thus, the sulky man said, "And don't *you* do it, neither; you're a deal worse than *him!*" And I grieve to add that peals of laughter greeted Mr. Wopsle on every one of these occasions.

But his greatest trials were in the churchyard, which had the appearance of a primeval forest, with a kind of small ecclesiastical wash-house on one side and a turnpike-gate on the other. Mr. Wopsle, in a comprehensive black cloak, being descried entering at the turnpike, the gravedigger was admonished in a friendly way, "Look out! Here's the undertaker a coming to see how you're a getting on with your work!" I believe it is well known in a constitutional country that Mr. Wopsle could not possibly have returned the skull, after moralizing over it, without dusting his fingers on a white napkin taken from his breast; but even that innocent and indispensable action did not pass without the comment "Wai-ter!" The arrival of the body for interment, in an empty black box, with the lid tumbling open, was the signal for a general joy, which was much enhanced by the discovery, among the bearers, of an individual obnoxious to identification. The joy attended Mr. Wopsle through his struggle with Laertes on the brink of the orchestra and the grave, and slackened no more until he had tumbled the king off the kitchen-table, and died by inches from the ankles upward.

We had made some pale efforts in the beginning to applaud Mr. Wopsle; but they were too hopeless to be persisted in. Therefore we had sat, feeling keenly for him, but laughing, nevertheless, from ear to ear. I laughed in spite of myself all the time, the whole thing was so droll; and yet I had a latent impression that there was something decidedly fine in Mr. Wopsle's elocution—not for old associations' sake, I am afraid, but because it was very slow, very dreary, very uphill and downhill, and very unlike any way in which any man in any natural circumstances of life or death ever expressed himself about anything. When the tragedy was over, and he had been called for and hooted, I said to Herbert, "Let us go at once, or perhaps we shall meet him."

We made all the haste we could downstairs, but we were not quick enough either. Standing at the door was a Jewish man with an unnaturally heavy smear of eyebrow, who caught my eye as we advanced, and said, when we came up with him:

"Mr. Pip and friend?"

Identity of Mr. Pip and friend confessed.

"Mr. Waldengarver," said the man, "would be glad to have the honor."

"Waldengarver?" I repeated—when Herbert murmured in my ear, "Probably Wopsle."

"Oh!" said I. "Yes. Shall we follow you?"

"A few steps, please." When we were in a side alley, he turned and asked, "How do you think he looked?—I dressed him."

I don't know what he had looked like, except a funeral; with the addition of a large Danish order hanging round his neck by a blue ribbon, that had given him the appearance of being insured in some extraordinary Fire Office. But I said he had looked very nice.

"When he come to the grave," said our conductor, "he showed his cloak beautiful. But, judging from the wing, it looked to me that when he see the ghost in the queen's apartment, he might have made more of his stockings."

I modestly assented, and we all fell through a little dirty swing-door, into a sort of hot packing-case immediately behind it. Here Mr. Wopsle was divesting himself of his Danish garments, and here there was just room for us to look at him over one another's shoulders, by keeping the packing-case door, or lid, wide open.

"Gentlemen," said Mr. Wopsle, "I am proud to see you. I hope, Mr. Pip, you will excuse my sending round. I had the happiness to know you in former times, and the Drama has ever had a claim which has ever been acknowledged, on the noble and the affluent."

Meanwhile, Mr. Waldengarver, in a frightful perspiration, was trying to get himself out of his princely sables.

"Skin the stockings off, Mr. Waldengarver," said the owner of that property, "or you'll bust 'em, and you'll bust five-and-thirty shillings. Shakespeare never was complimented with a finer pair. Keep quiet in your chair now, and leave 'em to me."

With that, he went upon his knees, and began to flay his victim; who, on the first stocking coming off, would certainly have fallen over backward with his chair, but for there being no room to fall anyhow.

I had been afraid until then to say a word about the play. But when Mr. Waldengarver looked up at us complacently, and said,

"Gentlemen, how did it seem to you to go, in front?"

Herbert said from behind (at the same time poking me), "capitally." So I said "capitally."

"How did you like my reading of the character, gentlemen?" said Mr. Waldengarver, almost, if not quite, with patronage.

Herbert said from behind (again poking me), "massive and excellent." So I said boldly, as if I had originated it, and must beg to insist upon it, "massive and excellent."

"I am glad to have your approbation, gentlemen," said Mr. Waldengarver, with an air of dignity, in spite of his being ground against the wall at the time, and holding on by the seat of the chair.

"But I'll tell you one thing, Mr. Waldengarver," said the man who was on his knees, "in which you're out in your reading. Now mind I don't care who says contrary; I tell you so. You're out in your reading of Hamlet when you get your legs in profile. The last Hamlet as I dressed, made the same mistakes in his reading at rehearsal, till I got him to put a large red wafer on each of his shins, and then at that rehearsal (which was the last) I went in front, sir, to the back of the pit, and whenever his reading brought him into profile, I called out 'I don't see no wafers!' And at night his reading was lovely."

Mr. Waldengarver smiled at me, as much as to say "A faithful dependent—I overlook his folly"; and then said aloud, "My view is a little classic and thoughtful for them here; but they will improve, they will improve."

Herbert and I said together, Oh, no doubt they would improve.

"Did you observe, gentlemen," said Mr. Waldengarver, "that there was a man in the gallery who endeavored to cast derision on the service—I mean, the representation?"

We basely replied that we rather thought we had noticed such a man. I added, "He was drunk, no doubt."

"Oh, dear no, sir," said Mr. Wopsle, "not drunk. His employer would see to that, sir. His employer would not allow him to be drunk."

"You know his employer?" said I.

Mr. Wopsle shut his eyes, and opened them again; performing both ceremonies very slowly. "You must have observed, gentlemen," said he, "an ignorant and a blatant ass, with a rasping throat, and a countenance expressive of low malignity, who went through—I will not say sustained—the rôle (if I may use a French expression) of Claudius King of Denmark. That is his employer, gentlemen. Such is the profession!"

Without distinctly knowing whether I should have been more sorry for Mr. Wopsle if he had been in despair, I was so sorry for him as it was, that I took the opportunity of his turning round to have his braces put on—which jostled us out at the doorway—to ask Herbert what he thought of having him home to supper? Herbert said he thought it would be kind to do so; therefore I invited him, and he went to Barnard's with us, wrapped up to the eyes, and we did our best for him, and he sat until two o'clock in the morning, reviewing his success and developing his plans. I forget in detail what they were, but I have a general recollection that he was to begin with reviving the Drama, and to end with crushing it; inasmuch as his decease would leave it utterly bereft and without a chance or hope.

Miserably I went to bed after all, and miserably thought of Estella, and miserably dreamed that my expectations were all canceled, and that I had to give my hand in marriage to Herbert's Clara, or play Hamlet to Miss Havisham's Ghost before twenty thousand people without knowing twenty words of it.

Thirty-two

ONE DAY WHEN I WAS BUSY WITH MY BOOKS AND MR. POCKET, I received a note by the post, the mere outside of which threw me into a great flutter; for, though I had never seen the handwriting in which it was addressed, I divined whose hand it was. It had no set beginning, as Dear Mr. Pip, or Dear Pip, or Dear Sir, or Dear Anything, but ran thus:

> I am to come to London the day after tomorrow by the midday coach. I believe it was settled you should meet me? at all events Miss Havisham has that impression, and I write in obedience to it. She sends you her regards.
>
> Yours,
> ESTELLA

If there had been time, I should probably have ordered several suits of clothes for this occasion; but as there was not, I was fain to be content with those I had. My appetite vanished instantly, and I knew no peace or rest until the day arrived. Not that its arrival brought me either, for then I was worse than ever, and began haunting the coach-office in Wood Street, Cheapside, before the coach had left the Blue Boar in our town. For all that I knew this perfectly well, I still felt as if it were not safe to let the coach-office be out of my sight longer than five minutes at a time; and in this condition of unreason I had performed the first half-hour of a watch of four or five hours, when Mr. Wemmick ran against me.

"Halloa, Mr. Pip," said he; "how do you do? I should hardly have thought this was *your* beat."

I explained that I was waiting to meet somebody who was coming up by coach, and I inquired after the Castle and the Aged.

"Both flourishing, thank ye," said Wemmick, "and particularly the Aged. He's in wonderful feather. He'll be eighty-two next birthday. I have a notion of firing eighty-two times, if the neighborhood shouldn't complain, and that cannon of mine should prove equal to the pressure. However, this is not London talk. Where do you think I am going to?"

"To the office?" said I, for he was tending in that direction.

"Next thing to it," returned Wemmick, "I am going to Newgate. We are in a banker's-parcel case just at present, and I have been down the road taking a squint at the scene of action, and thereupon must have a word or two with our client."

"Did your client commit the robbery?" I asked.

"Bless your soul and body, no," answered Wemmick, very drily. "But he is accused of it. So might you or I be. Either of us might be accused of it, you know."

"Only neither of us is," I remarked.

"Yah!" said Wemmick, touching me on the breast with his forefinger; "you're a deep one, Mr. Pip! Would you like to have a look at Newgate? Have you time to spare?"

I had so much time to spare that the proposal came as a relief, notwithstanding its unreconcilability with my latent desire to keep my eye on the coach-office. Muttering that I would make the inquiry whether I had time to walk with him, I went into the office, and ascertained from the clerk, with the nicest precision and much to the trying of his temper, the earliest moment at which the coach could be expected—which I knew beforehand quite as well as he. I then rejoined Mr. Wemmick, and affecting to consult my watch and to be surprised by the information I had received, accepted his offer.

We were at Newgate in a few minutes, and we passed through the lodge where some fetters were hanging up on the bare walls among the prison rules, into the interior of the jail. At that time jails were much neglected, and the period of exaggerated reaction consequent on all public wrongdoing—and which is always its heaviest and longest punishment—was still far off. So felons were not lodged and fed better than soldiers (to say nothing of paupers), and seldom set fire to their prisons with the excusable object of improving the flavor of their soup. It was visiting time when Wemmick took me in; and a potman was going his rounds with beer; and the prisoners behind bars in yards were buying beer and talking to friends; and a frowzy, ugly, disorderly, depressing scene it was.

It struck me that Wemmick walked among the prisoners much as a gardener might walk among his plants. This was first put into my head by his seeing a shoot that had come up in the night, and saying, "What, Captain

Tom? Are *you* there? Ah, indeed?" and also, "Is that Black Bill behind the cistern? Why, I didn't look for you these two months; how do you find yourself?" Equally in his stopping at the bars and attending to anxious whisperers—always singly—Wemmick, with his post-office in an immovable state, looked at them while in conference, as if he were taking particular notice of the advance they had made, since last observed, toward coming out in full blow at their trial.

He was highly popular, and I found that he took the familiar department of Mr. Jaggers's business: though something of the state of Mr. Jaggers hung about him too, forbidding approach beyond certain limits. His personal recognition of each successive client was comprised in a nod, and in his settling his hat a little easier on his head with both hands, and then tightening the post-office, and putting his hands in his pockets. In one or two instances, there was a difficulty respecting the raising of fees, and then Mr. Wemmick, backing as far as possible from the insufficient money produced, said, "It's no use, my boy. I'm only a subordinate. I can't take it. Don't go on in that way with a subordinate. If you are unable to make up your quantum, my boy, you had better address yourself to a principal; there are plenty of principals in the profession, you know, and what is not worth the while of one may be worth the while of another—that's my recommendation to you, speaking as a subordinate. Don't try on useless measures. Why should you! Now, who's next?"

Thus we walked through Wemmick's greenhouse until he turned to me and said, "Notice the man I shall shake hands with." I should have done so, without the preparation, as he had shaken hands with no one yet.

Almost as soon as he had spoken, a portly upright man (whom I can see now, as I write) in a well-worn, olive-colored frock-coat, with a peculiar pallor overspreading the red in his complexion, and eyes that went wandering about when he tried to fix them, came up to a corner of the bars, and put his hand to his hat—which had a greasy and fatty surface like cold broth—with a half serious and half jocose military salute.

"Colonel, to you!" said Wemmick; "how are you, Colonel?"

"All right, Mr. Wemmick."

"Everything was done that could be done, but the evidence was too strong for us, Colonel."

"Yes, it was too strong, sir—but *I* don't care."

"No, no," said Wemmick, coolly, "*you* don't care." Then, turning to me, "Served His Majesty this man. Was a soldier in the line and bought his discharge."

I said, "Indeed?" and the man's eyes looked over my head, and then looked all around me, and then he drew his hand across his lips and laughed.

"I think I shall be off on Monday, sir," he said to Wemmick.

"Perhaps," returned my friend, "but there's no knowing."

"I am glad to have the chance of bidding you good-bye, Mr. Wemmick," said the man, stretching out his hand between two bars.

"Thank ye," said Wemmick, shaking hands with him. "Same to you, Colonel."

"If what I had upon me when taken had been real, Mr. Wemmick," said the man, unwilling to let his hand go, "I should have asked the favor of your wearing another ring—in acknowledgment of your attention."

"I'll accept the will for the deed," said Wemmick. "By-the-by; you were quite a pigeon-fancier." The man looked up at the sky. "I am told you had a remarkable breed of tumblers. *Could* you commission any friend of yours to bring me a pair, if you've no further use for 'em?"

"It shall be done, sir."

"All right," said Wemmick, "they shall be taken care of. Good afternoon, Colonel. Good-bye!" They shook hands again, and as we walked away Wemmick said to me, "A Coiner, a very good workman. The Recorder's report is made today, and he is sure to be hanged on Monday. Still you see, as far as it goes, a pair of pigeons are portable property, all the same." With that he looked back, and nodded at this dead plant, and then cast his eyes about him in walking out of the yard, as if he were considering what other pot would go best in its place.

As we came out of the prison through the lodge, I found that the great importance of my guardian was appreciated by the turnkeys, no less than by those whom they held in charge. "Well, Mr. Wemmick," said the turnkey, who kept us between the two studded and spiked lodge gates, and carefully locked one before he unlocked the other, "what's Mr. Jaggers going to do with that waterside murder? Is he going to make it manslaughter, or what's he going to make of it?"

"Why don't you ask him?" returned Wemmick.

"Oh yes, I dare say!" said the turnkey.

"Now, that's the way with them here, Mr. Pip," remarked Wemmick, turning to me with the post-office elongated. "They don't mind what they ask of me, the subordinate; but you'll never catch 'em asking any questions of my principal."

"Is this young gentleman one of the 'prentices or articled ones of your office?" asked the turnkey, with a grin at Mr. Wemmick's humor.

"There he goes again, you see?" cried Wemmick, "I told you so! Asks another question of the subordinate before the first is dry! Well, supposing Mr. Pip is one of them?"

"Why then," said the turnkey, grinning again, "he knows what Mr. Jaggers is."

"Yah!" cried Wemmick, suddenly hitting out at the turnkey in a facetious way, "you're as dumb as one of your own keys when you have to do with my principal—you know you are. Let us out, you old fox, or I'll get him to bring an action of false imprisonment against you."

The turnkey laughed, and gave us good day, and stood laughing at us over the spikes of the wicket when we descended the steps into the street.

"Mind you, Mr. Pip," said Wemmick, gravely, in my ear, as he took my arm to be more confidential; "I don't know that Mr. Jaggers does a better thing than the way in which he keeps himself so high. He's always so high. His constant height is of a piece with his immense abilities. That Colonel durst no more take leave of *him,* than that turnkey durst ask him his intentions respecting a case. Then between his height and them he slips in his subordinate—don't you see?—and so he has 'em, soul and body."

I was very much impressed, and not for the first time, by my guardian's subtlety. To confess the truth, I very heartily wished, and not for the first time, that I had had some other guardian of minor abilities.

Mr. Wemmick and I parted at the office in Little Britain, where suppliants for Mr. Jaggers's notice were lingering about as usual, and I returned to my watch in the street of the coach-office, with some three hours on hand. I consumed the whole time in thinking how strange it was that I should be encompassed by all this taint of prison and crime; that in my childhood out on our lonely marshes on a winter evening I should have first encountered it; that it should have reappeared on two occasions, starting out like a stain that was faded but not gone; that it should in this new way pervade my fortune and advancement. I thought of the beautiful young Estella, proud and refined, coming toward me, while my mind was thus engaged, and thought with absolute abhorrence of the contrast between the jail and her. I wished that Wemmick had not met me, or that I had not yielded to him and gone with him, so that, of all days in the year, on this day I might not have had Newgate in my breath and on my clothes. I beat the prison dust off my feet as I sauntered to and fro, and I shook it out of my dress, and I exhaled its air from my lungs. So contaminated did I feel, remembering who was coming, that the coach came quickly after all, and I was not yet free from the soiling consciousness of Mr. Wemmick's conservatory, when I saw her face at the coach window and her hand waving to me.

What *was* the nameless shadow which again in that one instant had passed?

Thirty-three

IN HER FURRED TRAVELING-DRESS, ESTELLA SEEMED MORE delicately beautiful than she had ever seemed yet, even in my eyes. Her manner was more winning than she had cared to let it be to me before, and I thought I saw Miss Havisham's influence in the change.

We stood in the Inn Yard while she pointed out her luggage to me, and when it was all collected I remembered—having forgotten everything but herself in the meanwhile—that I knew nothing of her destination.

"I am going to Richmond," she told me. "Our lesson is, that there are two Richmonds, one in Surrey and one in Yorkshire, and that mine is Surrey Richmond. The distance is ten miles. I am to have a carriage, and you are to take me. This is my purse, and you are to pay my charges out of it. Oh, you must take the purse! We have no choice, you and I, but to obey our instructions. We are not free to follow our own devices, you and I."

As she looked at me in giving me the purse, I hoped there was an inner meaning in her words. She said them slightingly, but not with displeasure.

"A carriage will have to be sent for, Estella. Will you rest here a little?"

"Yes, I am to rest here a little, and I am to drink some tea and you are to take care of me the while."

She drew her arm through mine, as if it must be done, and I requested a waiter who had been staring at the coach like a man who had never seen such a thing in his life, to show us a private sitting-room. Upon that he pulled out a napkin, as if it were a magic clew without which he couldn't find the way upstairs, and led us to the black hole of the establishment; fitted up with a diminishing mirror (quite a superfluous article considering the hole's proportion), an anchovy sauce-cruet, and somebody's pattens. On my objecting to this retreat, he took us into another room with a dinner-table for thirty, and in the grate a scorched leaf of a copy-book under a bushel of coal-dust. Having looked at this extinct conflagration and shaken his head, he took my order: which, proving to be merely "Some tea for the lady," sent him out of the room in a very low state of mind.

I was, and I am, sensible that the air of this chamber, in its strong combination of stable with soup-stock, might have led one to infer that the coaching department was not doing well, and that the enterprising proprietor was boiling down the horses for the refreshment department. Yet the room was all in all to me, Estella being in it. I thought that with her I could have been happy there for life. (I was not at all happy there at the time, observe, and I knew it well.)

"Where are you going to, at Richmond?" I asked Estella.

"I am going to live," said she, "at a great expense, with a lady there, who has the power—or says she has—of taking me about and introducing me, and showing people to me and showing me to people."

"I suppose you will be glad of variety and admiration."

"Yes, I suppose so."

She answered so carelessly that I said, "You speak of yourself as if you were someone else."

"Where did you learn how I speak of others? Come, come," said Estella, smiling delightfully, "you must not expect me to go to school to *you;* I must talk in my own way. How do you thrive with Mr. Pocket?"

"I live quite pleasantly there; at least—" It appeared to me that I was losing a chance.

"At least?" repeated Estella.

"As pleasantly as I could anywhere, away from you."

"You silly boy," said Estella, quite composedly, "how can you talk such nonsense? Your friend Mr. Matthew, I believe, is superior to the rest of his family?"

"Very superior indeed. He is nobody's enemy—"

"Don't add 'but his own,' " interposed Estella, "for I hate that class of men. But he really is disinterested, and above small jealousy and spite, I have heard?"

"I am sure I have every reason to say so."

"You have not every reason to say so of the rest of his people," said Estella, nodding at me with an expression of face that was at once grave and rallying, "for they beset Miss Havisham with reports and insinuations to your disadvantage. They watch you, misrepresent you, write letters about you (anonymous sometimes), and you are the torment and the occupation of their lives. You can scarcely realize to yourself the hatred those people feel for you."

"They do me no harm, I hope?" said I.

Instead of answering, Estella burst out laughing. This was very singular to me, and I looked at her in considerable perplexity. When she let off—and she had not laughed languidly but with real enjoyment—I said, in my diffident way with her, "I hope I may suppose that you would not be amused if they did me any harm."

"No, no, you may be sure of that," said Estella. "You may be certain that I laugh because they fail. Oh, those people with Miss Havisham, and the tortures they undergo!" She laughed again, and even now when she had told me why, her laughter was very singular to me, for I could not doubt its being genuine, and yet it seemed too much for the occasion. I thought there must really be something more here than I knew; she saw the thought in my mind, and answered it.

"It is not easy for even you," said Estella, "to know what satisfaction it gives me to see those people thwarted, or what an enjoyable sense of the ridiculous I have when they are made ridiculous. For you were not brought up in that strange house from a mere baby. I was. You had not your little wits sharpened by their intriguing against you, suppressed and defenseless, under the mask of sympathy and pity and what not that is soft and soothing—I had. You did not gradually open your round childish eyes wider and wider to the discovery of that impostor of a woman who calculates her stores of peace of mind when she wakes up in the night.—I did."

It was no laughing matter with Estella now, nor was she summoning these remembrances from any shallow place. I would not have been the cause of that look of hers for all my expectations in a heap.

"Two things I can tell you," said Estella. "First, notwithstanding the proverb that constant dropping will wear away a stone, you may set your mind at rest that these people never will—never would, in a hundred years— impair your ground with Miss Havisham, in any particular, great or small. Second, I am beholden to you as the cause of their being so busy and so mean in vain, and there is my hand upon it."

As she gave it playfully—for her darker mood had been but momentary—I held it and put it to my lips. "You ridiculous boy," said Estella, "will you never take warning? Or do you kiss my hand in the spirit in which I once let you kiss my cheek?"

"What was it?" said I.

"I must think a moment. A spirit of contempt for the fawners and plotters."

"If I say yes, may I kiss the cheek again?"

"You should have asked before you touched the hand. But, yes, if you like."

I leaned down, and her calm face was like a statue's. "Now," said Estella, gliding away the instant I touched her cheek, "you are to take care that I have some tea, and you are to take me to Richmond."

Her reverting to this tone as if our association were forced upon us and we were mere puppets, gave me pain; but everything in our intercourse did give me pain. Whatever her tone with me happened to be, I could put no trust in it, and build no hope on it; and yet I went on against trust and against hope. Why repeat it a thousand times? So it always was.

I rang for the tea, and the waiter, reappearing with his magic clew, brought in by degrees some fifty adjuncts to that refreshment, but of tea not a glimpse. A tea-board, cups and saucers, plates, knives and forks (including carvers), spoons (various), salt-cellars, a meek little muffin confined with the utmost precaution under a large strong tin cover, Moses in the bulrushes typified by a soft bit of butter in a quantity of parsley, a pale loaf, with a powdered head, two proof impressions of the bars of the kitchen fireplace on triangular bits of bread, and ultimately a fat family urn, which the waiter staggered in with, expressing in his countenance burden and suffering. After a prolonged absence at this stage of the entertainment, he at length came back with a casket of precious appearance containing twigs. These I steeped in hot water, and so from the whole of these appliances extracted one cup of I don't know what, for Estella.

The bill paid, and the waiter remembered, and the hostler not forgotten, and the chambermaid taken into consideration—in a word, the whole house bribed into a state of contempt and animosity, and Estella's purse much lightened—we got into our post-coach and drove away. Turning into Cheapside and rattling up Newgate Street, we were soon under the walls of which I was so ashamed.

"What place is that?" Estella asked me.

I made a foolish pretense of not at first recognizing it, and then told her. As she looked at it, and drew in her head again, murmuring "Wretches!" I would not have confessed to my visit for any consideration.

"Mr. Jaggers," said I, by way of putting it neatly on somebody else, "has the reputation of being more in the secrets of that dismal place than any man in London."

"He is more in the secrets of everyplace I think," said Estella, in a low voice.

"You have been accustomed to see him often, I suppose?"

"I have been accustomed to see him at uncertain intervals ever since I can remember. But I know him no better now than I did before I could speak plainly. What is your own experience of him? Do you advance with him?"

"Once habituated to his distrustful manner," said I, "I have done very well."

"Are you intimate?"

"I have dined with him at his private house."

"I fancy," said Estella, shrinking, "that must be a curious place."

"It is a curious place."

I should have been chary of discussing my guardian too freely even with her; but I should have gone on with the subject so far as to describe the dinner in Gerrard Street, if we had not then come into a sudden glare of gas. It seemed, while it lasted, to be all alight and alive with that inexplicable feeling I had had before; and when we were out of it, I was as much dazed for a few moments as if I had been in lightning.

So we fell into other talk, and it was principally about the way by which we were traveling, and about what parts of London lay on this side of it, and what on that. The great city was almost new to her, she told me, for she had never left Miss Havisham's neighborhood until she had gone to France, and she had merely passed through London then in going and returning. I asked her if my guardian had any charge of her while she remained here? To that she emphatically said, "God forbid!" and no more.

It was impossible for me to avoid seeing that she cared to attract me; that she made herself winning; and would have won me even if the task had needed pains. Yet this made me none the happier, for, even if she had not taken that one of our being disposed of by others, I should have felt that she held my heart in her hand because she willfully chose to do it, and not because it would have wrung any tenderness in her to crush it and throw it away.

When we passed through Hammersmith I showed her where Mr. Matthew Pocket lived, and said it was no great way from Richmond, and that I hoped I should see her sometimes.

"Oh yes, you are to see me; you are to come when you think proper; you are to be mentioned to the family; indeed you are already mentioned."

I inquired was it a large household she was going to be a member of?

"No; there are only two—mother and daughter. The mother is a lady of some station, I believe, though not averse to increasing her income."

"I wonder Miss Havisham could part with you again so soon."

"It is a part of Miss Havisham's plans for me, Pip," said Estella, with a sigh, as if she were tired; "I am to write to her constantly and see her regularly, and report how I go on—I and the jewels—for they are nearly all mine now."

It was the first time she had ever called me by my name. Of course she did so purposely, and knew that I should treasure it up.

We came to Richmond all too soon, and our destination there was a house by the Green—a staid old house, where hoops and powder and patches, embroidered coats, rolled stockings, ruffles and swords had had their court day many a time. Some ancient trees before the house were still cut into fashions as formal and unnatural as the hoops and wigs and stiff skirts they had cast their shadows on; but their own allotted places in the great procession of the dead were not far off, and they would soon drop into them and go the silent way of the rest.

A bell with an old voice—which I dare say in its time had often said to the house, Here is the green farthingale, Here is the diamond-hilted sword, Here are the shoes with red heels and the blue solitaire—sounded gravely in the moonlight, and two cherry-colored maids came fluttering out to receive Estella. The doorway soon absorbed her boxes, and she gave me her hand and a smile, and said good night, and was absorbed likewise. And still I stood looking at the house, thinking how happy I should be if I lived there with her, and knowing that I never was happy with her, but always miserable.

I got into the carriage to be taken back to Hammersmith, and I got in with a bad heartache, and I got out with a worse heartache. At our own door I found little Jane Pocket coming home from a party escorted by her little lover; and I envied her little lover, in spite of his being subject to Flopson.

Mr. Pocket was out lecturing; for he was a most delightful lecturer on domestic economy, and his treatises on the management of children and servants were considered the very best textbooks on those themes. But Mrs. Pocket was at home, and was in a little difficulty, on account of the baby's having been accommodated with a needle-case to keep him quiet during the unaccountable absence (with a relative in the Foot Guards) of Millers, and of more needles being missing than it could be regarded as quite wholesome for a patient of such tender years either to apply externally or to take as a tonic.

As Mr. Pocket was also justly celebrated for giving most excellent practical advice, and for having a clear and sound perception of things and a highly judicious mind, I had some notion in my heartache of begging him to accept my confidence. But happening to look up at Mrs. Pocket as she sat reading her book of dignities after prescribing Bed as a sovereign remedy for baby, I thought, Well—No, I wouldn't.

Thirty-four

As I had grown accustomed to my expectations I had insensibly begun to notice their effect upon myself and those around me. Their influence on my own character I disguised from my recognition as much as possible; but I knew very well that it was not all good. I lived in a state of chronic uneasiness respecting my behavior to Joe. My conscience was not by any means comfortable about Biddy. When I woke up in the night—like Camilla—I used to think, with a weariness on my spirits, that I should have been happier and better if I had never seen Miss Havisham's face, and had risen to manhood content to be partners with Joe in the honest old forge. Many a time of an evening, when I sat alone, looking at the fire, I thought, after all there was no fire like the forge fire and the kitchen fire at home.

Yet Estella was so inseparable from all my restlessness and disquiet of mind; that I really fell into confusion as to the limits of my own part in its production. That is to say, supposing I had had no expectations, and yet had had Estella to think of, I could not make out to my satisfaction that I should have done much better. Now, concerning the influence of my position on others, I was in no such difficulty, and so I perceived—though dimly enough, perhaps—that it was not beneficial to anybody, and, above all, that it was not beneficial to Herbert. My lavish habits led his easy nature into expenses that he could not afford, corrupted the simplicity of his life, and disturbed his peace with anxieties and regrets. I was not at all remorseful for having unwittingly set those other branches of the Pocket family to the poor arts they practiced: because such littlenesses were their natural bent, and would have been evoked by anybody else, if I had left them slumbering. But Herbert's was a very different case, and it often caused me a twinge to think that I had done him evil service in crowding his sparely-furnished chambers with incongruous upholstery work, and placing the canary-breasted Avenger at his disposal.

So now, as an infallible way of making little ease great ease, I began to contract a quantity of debt. I could hardly begin but Herbert must begin too, so he soon followed. At Startop's suggestion, we put ourselves down for election into a club called The Finches of the Grove: the object of which institution I have never divined, if it were not that the members should dine expensively once a fortnight, to quarrel among themselves as much as possible after dinner, and to cause six waiters to get drunk on the stairs. I know that these gratifying social ends were so invariably accomplished that Herbert and I understood nothing else to be referred to in the first standing toast of the society, which ran: "Gentlemen, may the present promotion of good feeling ever reign predominant among the Finches of the Grove."

The Finches spent their money foolishly (the hotel we dined at was in Covent Garden), and the first Finch I saw, when I had the honor of joining the Grove, was Bentley Drummle: at that time floundering about town in a cab of his own, and doing a great deal of damage to the posts at the street corners. Occasionally he shot himself out of his equipage head-foremost over the apron; and I saw him, on one occasion, deliver himself at the door of the Grove in this unintentional way—like coals. But here I anticipate a little, for I was not a Finch, and could not be, according to the sacred laws of the society, until I came of age.

In my confidence in my own resources I would willingly have taken Herbert's expenses on myself; but Herbert was proud, and I could make no such proposal to him. So he got into difficulties in every direction, and continued to look about him. When we gradually fell into keeping late hours and late company, I noticed that he looked about him with a despondent eye at breakfast-time, that he began to look about him more hopelessly about midday; that he drooped when he came in to dinner; that he seemed to descry Capital in the distance rather clearly, after dinner; that he all but realized Capital and banked it toward midnight; and that at about two o'clock in the morning he became so deeply despondent again as to talk of buying a rifle and going to America, with a general purpose of compelling buffaloes to make his fortune.

I was usually at Hammersmith about half the week, and when I was at Hammersmith I haunted Richmond; whereof separately by-and-by. Herbert would often come to Hammersmith when I was there, and I think at those seasons his father would occasionally have some passing perception that the opening he was looking for had not appeared yet. But in the general tumbling up of the family, his tumbling out in life somewhere, was a thing to transact itself somehow. In the meantime Mr. Pocket grew graver, and tried oftener to lift himself out of his perplexities by the hair. While Mrs. Pocket tripped up the family with her footstool, read her book of dignities, lost her pocket-handkerchief, told us about her grandpapa, and taught the young idea how to shoot, by shooting it into bed whenever it attracted her notice.

As I am now generalizing a period of my life with the object of clearing the way before me, I can scarcely do so better than by at once completing the description of our usual manners and customs at Barnard's Inn.

We spent as much money as we could, and got as little for it as people could make up their minds to give us. We were always more or less miserable, and most of our acquaintance were in the same condition. There was a gay fiction among us that we were constantly enjoying ourselves, and a skeleton truth that we never did. To the best of my belief, our case was in the last aspect a rather common one.

Every morning, with an air ever new, Herbert went into the City to look about him. I often paid him a visit in the dark back-room in which he consorted with an ink-jar, a hat-peg, a coal-box, a string-box, an almanac, a desk and stool, and a ruler; and I do not remember that I ever saw him doing anything else but looking about him. If we all did what we undertake to do as faithfully as Herbert did, we might live in a Republic of the Virtues. He had nothing else to do, poor fellow, except at a certain hour of every afternoon to "go to Lloyd's"—in observance of a ceremony of seeing his principal, I think. He never did anything else in connection with Lloyd's that I could find out, except come back again. When he felt his case unusually serious, and that he positively must find an opening, he would go on 'Change at the busy time, and walk in and out, in a kind of gloomy country-dance figure, among the assembled magnates. "For," says Herbert to me, coming home to dinner on one of these special occasions, "I find the truth to be, Handel, that an opening won't come to one, but one must go to it—so I have been."

If we had been less attached to one another, I think we must have hated one another regularly every morning. I detested the chambers beyond expression at that period of repentance, and could not endure the sight of the Avenger's livery; which had a more expensive and a less remunerative appearance then than at any other time in the four-and-twenty hours. As we got more and more into debt, breakfast became a hollower and hollower form, and, being on one occasion at breakfast-time threatened (by letter) with legal proceedings, "not unwholly unconnected," as my local paper might put it, "with jewelry," I went so far as to seize the Avenger by his blue collar and shake him off his feet—so that he was actually in the air, like a booted Cupid—for presuming to suppose that we wanted a French roll.

At certain times—meaning at uncertain times, for they depended on our humor—I would say to Herbert, as if it were a remarkable discovery:

"My dear Herbert, we are getting on badly."

"My dear Handel," Herbert would say to me, in all sincerity, "if you will believe me, those very words were on my lips, by a strange coincidence."

"Then Herbert," I would respond, "let us look into our affairs."

We always derived profound satisfaction from making an appointment for this purpose. I always thought myself, this was business, this was the way to confront the thing, this was the way to take the foe by the throat. And I know Herbert thought so too.

We generally ordered something rather special for dinner, with a bottle of something similarly out of the common way, in order that our minds might be fortified for the occasion, and we might come well up to the mark. Dinner over, we produced a bundle of pens, a copious supply of ink, and a goodly show of writing and blotting paper. For there was something very comfortable in having plenty of stationery.

I would then take a sheet of paper, and write across the top of it, in a neat hand, the heading "Memorandum of Pip's debts"; with Barnard's Inn and the date very carefully added. Herbert would also take a sheet of paper, and write across it with similar formalities, "Memorandum of Herbert's debts."

Each of us would then refer to a confused heap of papers at his side, which had been thrown into drawers, worn into holes in pockets, half burned in lighting candles, stuck for weeks into the looking-glass, and otherwise damaged. The sound of our pens going refreshed us exceedingly, insomuch that I sometimes found it difficult to distinguish between this edifying business proceeding and actually paying the money. In point of meritorious character the two things seemed about equal.

When we had written a little while, I would ask Herbert how he got on? Herbert probably would have been scratching his head in a most rueful manner at the sight of his accumulating figures.

"They are mounting up, Handel," Herbert would say; "upon my life, they are mounting up."

"Be firm, Herbert," I would retort, plying my own pen with great assiduity. "Look the thing in the face. Look into your affairs. Stare them out of countenance."

"So I would, Handel, only they are staring *me* out of countenance."

However, my determined manner would have its effect, and Herbert would fall to work again. After a time, he would give up once more, on the plea that he had not got Cobbs's bill, or Lobbs's, or Nobbs's, as the case might be.

"Then, Herbert, estimate it; estimate it in round numbers, and put it down."

"What a fellow of resource you are!" my friend would reply, with admiration. "Really, your business powers are very remarkable."

I thought so too. I established with myself on these occasions the reputation of a first-rate man of business—prompt, decisive, energetic, clear, cool-headed. When I had got all my responsibilities down upon my list, I compared each with the bill, and ticked it off. My self-approval when I ticked an entry was almost a luxurious sensation. When I had no more ticks to make, I folded all my bills up uniformly, docketed each on the back, and tied the whole into a symmetrical bundle. Then I did the same for Herbert (who modestly said he had not my administrative genius), and felt that I had brought his affairs into a focus for him.

My business habits had one other bright feature, which I called, "leaving a margin." For example; supposing Herbert's debts to be one hundred and sixty-four pounds four-and-two pence, I would say, "leave a margin, and put them down at two hundred." Or supposing my own to be four times as much, I would leave a margin, and put them down at seven hundred. I had the highest opinion of the wisdom and prudence of this same margin; but I am bound to acknowledge that, on looking back, I deem it to have been an expensive device. For we always ran into new debt immediately, to the full extent of the margin, and sometimes, in the sense of freedom and solvency it imparted, got pretty far on into another margin.

But there was a calm, a rest, a virtuous hush, consequent on these examinations of our affairs, that gave me, for the time, an admirable opinion of myself. Soothed by my exertions, my method, and Herbert's compliments, I would sit with his symmetrical bundle and my own on the table before me among the stationery, and feel like a Bank of some sort, rather than a private individual.

We shut our outer door on these solemn occasions, in order that we might not be interrupted. I had fallen into my serene state one evening, when we heard a letter dropped through the slit in the said door, and fall on the ground. "It's for you, Handel," said Herbert, going out and coming back with it, "and I hope there is nothing the matter." This was in allusion to its heavy black seal and border.

The letter was signed TRABB & CO., and its contents were simply, that I was an honored Sir, and that they begged to inform me that Mrs. J. Gargery had departed this life on Monday last, at twenty minutes past six in the evening, and that my attendance was requested at the interment on Monday next at three o'clock in the afternoon.

Thirty-five

IT WAS THE FIRST TIME THAT A GRAVE HAD OPENED IN MY road of life, and the depth of the gap it made in the smooth ground was wonderful. The figure of my sister in her chair by the kitchen fire haunted me night and day. That the place could possibly be without her was something my mind seemed unable to compass; and whereas she had seldom or never been in my thoughts of late, I had now the strangest ideas that she was coming toward me in the street, or that she would presently knock at the door. In my rooms, too, with which she had never been at all associated, there was at once the blankness of death and a perpetual suggestion of the sound of her voice or the turn of her face or figure, as if she were still alive and had been often there.

Whatever my fortunes might have been, I could scarcely have recalled my sister with much tenderness. But I suppose there is a shock of regret which may exist without much tenderness. Under its influence (and perhaps to make up for the want of the softer feeling) I was seized with a violent indignation against the assailant from whom she had suffered so much; and I felt that, on sufficient proof, I could have revengefully pursued Orlick, or anyone else, to the last extremity.

Having written to Joe, to offer consolation, and to assure him that I should come to the funeral, I passed the intermediate days in the curious state of mind I have glanced at. I went down early in the morning, and alighted at the Blue Boar in good time to walk over to the forge.

It was fine summer weather again, and, as I walked along, the time when I was a little helpless creature, and my sister did not spare me, vividly returned. But they returned with a gentle tone upon them that softened even the edge of Tickler. For now the very breath of the beans and clover whispered to my heart that the day must come when it would be well for my memory that others walking in the sunshine should be softened as they thought of me.

At last I came within sight of the house, and then I immediately saw that Trabb & Co. had put in a funereal execution and taken possession. Two dismally absurd persons, each ostentatiously exhibiting a crutch done up in a black bandage—as if that instrument could possibly communicate any comfort to anybody—were posted at the front door; and in one of them I recognized a post-boy discharged from the Boar for turning a young couple into a saw-pit on their bridal morning, in consequence of intoxication rendering it necessary for him to ride his horse clasped round the neck with both arms. All the children of the village, and most of the women, were admiring these sable warders and the closed windows of the house and forge; and as I came up, one of the two warders (the post-boy) knocked at the door—implying that I was far too much exhausted by grief to have strength remaining to knock for myself.

Another sable warder (a carpenter, who had once eaten two geese for a wager) opened the door, and showed me into the best parlor. Here Mr. Trabb had taken unto himself the best table, and had got all the leaves up, and was holding a kind of black Bazaar, with the aid of a quantity of black pins. At the moment of my arrival he had just finished putting somebody's hat into black long-clothes, like an African baby; so he held out his hand for mine. But I, misled by the action, and confused by the occasion, shook hands with him with every testimony of warm affection.

Poor dear Joe, in a little black cloak tied in a large bow under his chin, was seated apart at the upper end of the room; where, as chief mourner, he had evidently been deposited by Trabb. When I bent down and said to him, "Dear Joe, how are you?" he said, "Pip, old chap, you knowd her when she were a fine figure of a—" and clasped my hand, and said no more.

Biddy, looking very neat and modest in her black dress, went quietly here and there, and was very helpful. When I had spoken to Biddy, as I thought it not a time for talking I went and sat down near Joe, and there began to wonder in what part of the house it—she—my sister—was. The air of the parlor being faint with the smell of sweet cake, I looked about for the table of refreshments; it was scarcely visible until one had got accustomed to the gloom, but there was a cut-up plum-cake upon it, and there were cut-up oranges, and sandwiches, and biscuits, and two decanters that I knew very well as ornaments, but had never seen used in all my life—one full of port and one of sherry. Standing at this table, I became conscious of the servile

Pumblechook, in a black cloak and several yards of hat-band, who was alternately stuffing himself, and making obsequious movements to catch my
attention. The moment he succeeded he came over to me (breathing sherry
and crumbs), and said, in a subdued voice, "May I, dear sir?" and did. I then
descried Mr. and Mrs. Hubble—the last-named in a decent speechless paroxysm in a corner. We were all going to "follow," and were all in course of being
tied up separately (by Trabb) into ridiculous bundles.

"Which I meantersay, Pip," Joe whispered me, as we were being what Mr.
Trabb called "formed" in the parlor, two and two—and it was dreadfully like
a preparation for some grim kind of dance—"which I meantersay, sir, as I
would in preference have carried her to the church myself, along with three
or four friendly ones wot come to it with willing harts and arms; but it were
considered wot the neighbors would look down on such, and would be of
opinions as it were wanting in respect."

"Pocket-handkerchiefs out, all!" cried Mr. Trabb at this point, in a
depressed businesslike voice. "Pocket-handkerchiefs out! We are ready!"

So we all put our pocket-handkerchiefs to our faces, as if our noses were
bleeding, and filed out two and two; Joe and I; Biddy and Pumblechook; Mr.
and Mrs. Hubble. The remains of my poor sister had been brought round by
the kitchen door; and, it being a point of Undertaking ceremony that the six
bearers must be stifled and blinded under a horrible black velvet housing
with a white border, the whole looked like a blind monster with twelve
human legs, shuffling and blundering along, under the guidance of two keepers—the post-boy and his comrade.

The neighborhood, however, highly approved of these arrangements,
and we were much admired as we went through the village; the more youthful and vigorous part of the community making dashes now and then to cut
us off, and lying in wait to intercept us at points of vantage. At such times the
more exuberant among them called out in an excited manner, on our emergence round some corner of expectancy, "*Here* they come! *Here* they are!" and
we were all but cheered. In this progress I was much annoyed by the abject
Pumblechook, who, being behind me, persisted all the way, as a delicate
attention, in arranging my streaming hat-band and smoothing my cloak. My
thoughts were further distracted by the excessive pride of Mr. and Mrs. Hubble, who were surpassingly conceited and vainglorious in being members of
so distinguished a procession.

At least the range of marshes lay clear before us, with the sails of the ships
on the river growing out of it; and we went into the churchyard close to the
graves of my unknown parents, Philip Pirrip, late of this parish, and Also
Georgiana, Wife of the Above. And there my sister was laid quietly in the
earth while the larks sang high above it, and the light wind strewed it with
beautiful shadows of clouds and trees.

Of the conduct of the worldly-minded Pumblechook while this was
doing I desire to say no more than it was all addressed to me; and that even

when those noble passages were read which remind humanity how it brought nothing into the world and can take nothing out, and how it fleeth like a shadow and never continueth long in one stay, I heard him cough a reservation of the case of a young gentleman who came unexpectedly into large property. When we got back, he had the hardihood to tell me that he wished my sister could have known I had done her so much honor, and to hint that she would have considered it purchased reasonably at the price of her death. After that he drank all the rest of the sherry, and Mr. Hubble drank the port; and the two talked (which I have since observed to be customary in such cases) as if they were of quite another race from the deceased, and were notoriously immortal. Finally, he went away with Mr. and Mrs. Hubble—to make an evening of it, I felt sure, and to tell the Jolly Bargemen that he was the founder of my fortunes and my earliest benefactor.

When they were all gone, and when Trabb and his men—but not his boy: I looked for him—had crammed their mummery into bags, and were gone too, the house felt wholesomer. Soon afterward Biddy, Joe, and I had a cold dinner together; but we dined in the best parlor, not in the old kitchen, and Joe was so exceedingly particular what he did with his knife and fork, and the saltcellar, and what not, that there was great restraint upon us. But after dinner, when I made him take his pipe, and when I had loitered with him about the forge, and when we sat down together on the great block of stone outside it, we got on better. I noticed that after the funeral Joe changed his clothes so far as to make a compromise between his Sunday dress and working dress; in which the dear fellow looked natural and like the Man he was.

He was very much pleased by my asking if I might sleep in my own little room, and I was pleased too; for I felt that I had done rather a great thing in making the request. When the shadows of evening were closing in, I took an opportunity of getting into the garden with Biddy for a little talk.

"Biddy," said I, "I think you might have written to me about these sad matters."

"Do you, Mr. Pip?" said Biddy. "I should have written if I had thought that."

"Don't suppose that I mean to be unkind, Biddy, when I say I consider that you ought to have thought that."

"Do you, Mr. Pip?"

She was so quiet, and had such an orderly, good, and pretty way with her, that I did not like the thought of making her cry again. After looking a little at her downcast eyes, as she walked beside me, I gave up that point.

"I suppose it will be difficult for you to remain here now, Biddy dear?"

"Oh! I can't do so, Mr. Pip," said Biddy, in a tone of regret, but still of quiet conviction. "I have been speaking to Mrs. Hubble, and I am going to her tomorrow. I hope we shall be able to take some care of Mr. Gargery, together, until he settles down."

"How are you going to live, Biddy? If you want any mo—"

"How am I going to live?" repeated Biddy, striking in, with a momentary flush upon her face. "I'll tell you, Mr. Pip. I am going to try to get the place of mistress in the new school nearly finished here. I can be well recommended by all the neighbors, and I hope I can be industrious and patient, and teach myself while I teach others. You know, Mr. Pip," pursued Biddy, with a smile, as she raised her eyes to my face, "the new schools are not like the old, but I learned a good deal from you after that time, and have had time since then to improve."

"I think you would always improve, Biddy, under any circumstances."

"Ah! Except in my bad side of human nature," murmured Biddy.

It was not so much a reproach as an irresistible thinking aloud. Well! I thought I would give up that point too. So I walked a little further with Biddy, looking silently at her downcast eyes.

"I have not heard the particulars of my sister's death, Biddy."

"They are very slight, poor thing! She had been in one of her bad states—though they had got better of late, rather than worse—for four days, when she came out of it in the evening, just at tea-time, and said, quite plainly, 'Joe.' As she had never said any word for a long while, I ran and fetched in Mr. Gargery from the forge. She made signs to me that she wanted him to sit down close to her, and wanted me to put her arms around his neck. So I put them round his neck, and she laid her head down on his shoulder quite content and satisfied. And so she presently said 'Joe' again, and once 'Pardon,' and once 'Pip.' And so she never lifted her head up anymore; and it was just an hour later when we laid it down on her own bed, because we found she was gone."

Biddy cried; the darkening garden, and the lane, and the stars that were coming out were blurred in my own sight.

"Nothing was ever discovered, Biddy?"

"Nothing."

"Do you know what is become of Orlick?"

"I should think, from the color of his clothes, that he is working in the quarries."

"Of course you have seen him then? Why are you looking at that dark tree in the lane?"

"I saw him there on the night she died."

"That was not the last time either, Biddy?"

"No; I have seen him there since we have been walking here. It's of no use," said Biddy, laying her hand upon my arm as I was for running out; "you know I would not deceive you; he was not there a minute, and he is gone."

It revived my utmost indignation to find that she was still pursued by this fellow, and I felt inveterate against him. I told her so, and told her that I would spend any money or take any pains to drive him out of that country. By degrees she led me into more temperate talk, and she told me how Joe loved me, and how Joe never complained of anything—she didn't say of me;

she had no need; I knew what she meant—but ever did his duty in his way of life with a strong hand, a quiet tongue, and a gentle heart.

"Indeed it would be hard to say too much for him," said I; "and Biddy, we must often speak of these things, for of course I shall be often down here now. I am not going to leave poor Joe alone."

Biddy said never a single word.

"Biddy, don't you hear me?"

"Yes, Mr. Pip."

"Not to mention your calling me Mr. Pip—which appears to me to be in bad taste, Biddy—what do you mean?"

"What do I mean?" asked Biddy, timidly.

"Biddy," said I, in a virtuously self-asserting manner, "I must request to know what you mean by this?"

"By this?" said Biddy.

"Now, don't echo," I retorted. "You used not to echo, Biddy."

"Used not!" said Biddy. "Oh, Mr. Pip! Used!"

Well! I rather thought I would give up that point too. After another silent turn in the garden I fell back on the main position.

"Biddy," said I, "I made a remark respecting my coming down here often to see Joe, which you received with a marked silence. Have the goodness, Biddy, to tell me why."

"Are you quite sure, then, that you WILL come to see him often?" asked Biddy, stopping in the narrow garden walk, and looking at me under the stars with a clear and honest eye.

"Oh, dear me!" said I, as I found myself compelled to give up Biddy in despair. "This really is a very bad side of human nature! Don't say any more, if you please, Biddy. This shocks me very much."

For which cogent reason I kept Biddy at a distance during supper, and when I went up to my own old little room took as stately a leave of her as I could, in my murmuring soul, deem reconcilable with the churchyard and the event of the day. As often as I was restless in the night, and that was every quarter of an hour, I reflected what an unkindness, what an injury, what an injustice Biddy had done me.

Early in the morning I was to go. Early in the morning I was out, and looking in, unseen, at one of the wooden windows of the forge. There I stood, for minutes, looking at Joe, already at work, with a glow of health and strength upon his face that made it show as if the bright sun of the life in store for him were shining on it.

"Good-bye, dear Joe!—No, don't wipe it off—for God's sake give me your blackened hand! I shall be down soon, and often!"

"Never too soon, sir," said Joe, "and never too often, Pip!"

Biddy was waiting for me at the kitchen door, with a mug of new milk and a crust of bread. "Biddy," said I, when I gave her my hand at parting, "I am not angry, but I am hurt!"

"No, don't be hurt," she pleaded, quite pathetically; "let only me be hurt, if I have been ungenerous."

Once more the mists were rising as I walked away. If they disclosed to me, as I suspect they did, that I should not come back, and that Biddy was quite right, all I can say is—they were quite right too.

T h i r t y - s i x

HERBERT AND I WENT ON FROM BAD TO WORSE, IN THE WAY of increasing our debts, looking into our affairs, leaving margins, and the like exemplary transactions; and Time went on, whether or no, as he has a way of doing; and I came of age—in fulfillment of Herbert's prediction that I should do so before I knew where I was.

Herbert himself had come of age eight months before me. As he had nothing else than his majority to come into, the event did not make a profound sensation in Barnard's Inn. But we had looked forward to my one-and-twentieth birthday with a crowd of speculations and anticipations, for we had both considered that my guardian could hardly help saying something definite on that occasion.

I had taken care to have it well understood in Little Britain when my birthday was. On the day before it I received an official note from Wemmick, informing me that Mr. Jaggers would be glad if I would call upon him at five in the afternoon of the auspicious day. This convinced us that something great was to happen, and threw me into an unusual flutter when I repaired to my guardian's office, a model of punctuality.

In the outer office Wemmick offered me his congratulations, and incidentally rubbed the side of his nose with a folded piece of tissue-paper that I liked the look of. But he said nothing respecting it, and motioned me with a nod into my guardian's room. It was November, and my guardian was standing before his fire leaning his back against the chimney-piece, with his hands under his coattails.

"Well, Pip," said he, "I must call you Mr. Pip today. Congratulations, Mr. Pip."

We shook hands—he was always a remarkably short shaker—and I thanked him.

"Take a chair, Mr. Pip," said my guardian.

As I sat down, and he preserved his attitude and bent his brows at his boots, I felt at a disadvantage, which reminded me of that old time when I had been put upon a tombstone. The two ghastly casts on the shelf were not far from him, and their expression was as if they were making a stupid apoplectic attempt to attend to the conversation.

"Now, my young friend," my guardian began, as if I were a witness in the box, "I am going to have a word or two with you."

"If you please, sir."

"What do you suppose," said Mr. Jaggers, bending forward to look at the ground, and then throwing his head back to look at the ceiling, "what do you suppose you are living at the rate of?"

"At the rate of, sir?"

"At," repeated Mr. Jaggers, still looking at the ceiling, "the—rate—of?" And then looked all round the room, and paused with his pocket-handkerchief in his hand, halfway to his nose.

I had looked into my affairs so often that I had thoroughly destroyed any slight notion I might ever have had of their bearings. Reluctantly, I confessed myself quite unable to answer the question. This reply seemed agreeable to Mr. Jaggers, who said, "I thought so!" and blew his nose with an air of satisfaction.

"Now, I have asked *you* a question, my friend," said Mr. Jaggers. "Have you anything to ask *me?*"

"Of course it would be a great relief to me to ask you several questions, sir; but I remember your prohibition."

"Ask one," said Mr. Jaggers.

"Is my benefactor to be made known to me today?"

"No. Ask another."

"Is that confidence to be imparted to me soon?"

"Waive that a moment," said Mr. Jaggers, "and ask another."

I looked about me, but there appeared to be now no possible escape from the inquiry, "Have—I—anything to receive, sir?" On that Mr. Jaggers said triumphantly, "I thought we should come to it!" and called to Wemmick to give him that piece of paper. Wemmick appeared, handed it in, and disappeared.

"Now, Mr. Pip," said Mr. Jaggers, "attend, if you please. You have been drawing pretty freely here; your name occurs pretty often in Wemmick's cash-book; but you are in debt, of course?"

"I am afraid I must say yes, sir."

"You know you must say yes, don't you?" said Mr. Jaggers.

"Yes, sir."

"I don't ask you what you owe, because you don't know; and if you did know, you wouldn't tell me—you would say less. Yes, yes, my friend," cried Mr. Jaggers, waving his forefinger to stop me, as I made a show of protesting, "it's likely enough that you think you wouldn't, but you would. You'll excuse me, but I know better than you. Now take this piece of paper in your hand. You have got it? Very good. Now unfold it and tell me what it is."

"This is a bank-note," said I, "for five hundred pounds."

"That is a bank-note," repeated Mr. Jaggers, "for five hundred pounds. And a very handsome sum of money, too, I think. You consider it so?"

"How could I do otherwise!"

"Ah! But answer the question," said Mr. Jaggers.

"Undoubtedly."

"You consider it, undoubtedly, a handsome sum of money. Now that handsome sum of money, Pip, is your own. It is a present to you on this day, in earnest of your expectations. And at the rate of that handsome sum of money per annum, and at no higher rate, you are to live until the donor of the whole appears. That is to say, you will now take your money affairs entirely into your own hands, and you will draw from Wemmick one hundred and twenty-five pounds per quarter, until you are in communication with the fountainhead, and no longer with the mere agent. As I have told you before, I am the mere agent. I execute my instructions, and I am paid for doing so. I think them injudicious, but I am not paid for giving any opinion on their merits."

I was beginning to express my gratitude to my benefactor for the great liberality with which I was treated, when Mr. Jaggers stopped me. "I am not paid, Pip," said he, coolly, "to carry your words to anyone"; and then gathered up his coattails, as he had gathered up the subject, and stood frowning at his boots as if he suspected them of designs against him.

After a pause, I hinted:

"There was a question just now, Mr. Jaggers, which you desired me to waive for a moment. I hope I am doing nothing wrong in asking it again?"

"What is it?" said he.

I might have known that he would never help me out; but it took me aback to have to shape the question afresh, as if it were quite new. "Is it likely," I said, after hesitating, "that my patron, the fountainhead you have spoken of, Mr. Jaggers, will soon—" There I delicately stopped.

"Will soon what?" asked Mr. Jaggers. "That's no question as it stands, you know."

"Will soon come to London," said I, after casting about for a precise form of words, "or summon me anywhere else?"

"Now here," replied Mr. Jaggers, fixing me for the first time with his dark deep-set eyes, "we must revert to the evening when we first encountered one another in your village. What did I tell you then, Pip?"

"You told me, Mr. Jaggers, that it might be years hence when that person appeared."

"Just so," said Mr. Jaggers; "that's my answer."

As we looked full at one another I felt my breath come quicker in my strong desire to get something out of him. And as I felt that it came quicker, and as I felt that he saw that it came quicker, I felt that I had less chance than ever of getting anything out of him.

"Do you suppose it will still be years hence, Mr. Jaggers?"

Mr. Jaggers shook his head—not in negativing the question, but in altogether negativing the notion that he could anyhow be got to answer it—and the two horrible casts of the twitched faces looked, when my eyes strayed up to them, as if they had come to a crisis in their suspended attention, and were going to sneeze.

"Come!" said Mr. Jaggers, warming the backs of his legs with his warmed hands, "I'll be plain with you, my friend, Pip. That's a question I must not be asked. You'll understand that better when I tell you it's a question that might compromise *me*. Come! I'll go a little further with you; I'll say something more."

He bent down so low to frown at his boots that he was able to rub the calves of his legs in the pause he made.

"When that person discloses," said Mr. Jaggers, straightening himself, "you and that person will settle your own affairs. When that person discloses, my part in this business will cease and determine. When that person discloses, it will not be necessary for me to know anything about it. And that's all I have got to say."

We looked at one another until I withdrew my eyes, and looked thoughtfully at the floor. From this last speech I derived the notion that Miss Havisham, for some reason or no reason, had not taken him into her confidence as to her designing me for Estella; that he resented this, and felt a jealousy about it; or that he really did object to that scheme, and would have nothing to do with it. When I raised my eyes again I found that he had been shrewdly looking at me all the time, and was doing so still.

"If that is all you have to say, sir," I remarked, "there can be nothing left for me to say."

He nodded assent, and pulled out his thief-dreaded watch, and asked me where I was going to dine? I replied at my own chambers, with Herbert. As a necessary sequence, I asked him if he would favor us with his company, and he promptly accepted the invitation. But he insisted on walking home with me, in order that I might make no extra preparation for him, and first he had a letter or two to write, and (of course) had his hands to wash. So I said I would go into the outer office and talk to Wemmick.

The fact was, that when the five hundred pounds had come into my pocket, a thought had come into my head which had been often there before; and it appeared to me that Wemmick was a good person to advise with concerning such thought.

He had already locked up his safe, and made preparations for going home. He had left his desk, brought out his two greasy office candlesticks and stood them in line with the snuffers on a slab near the door, ready to be extinguished; he had raked his fire low, put his hat and great-coat ready, and was beating himself all over the chest with his safe-key, as an athletic exercise after business.

"Mr. Wemmick," said I, "I want to ask your opinion. I am very desirous to serve a friend."

Wemmick tightened his post-office and shook his head, as if his opinion were dead against any fatal weakness of that sort.

"This friend," I pursued, "is trying to get on in commercial life, but has no money and finds it difficult and disheartening to make a beginning. Now, I want somehow to help him to a beginning."

"With money down?" said Wemmick, in a tone drier than any sawdust.

"With *some* money down," I replied, for an uneasy remembrance shot across me of that symmetrical bundle of papers at home; "with *some* money down, and perhaps some anticipation of my expectations."

"Mr. Pip," said Wemmick, "I should like just to run over with you on my fingers, if you please, the names of the various bridges up as high as Chelsea Reach. Let's see: there's London, one; Southwark, two; Blackfriars, three; Waterloo, four; Westminster, five; Vauxhall, six." He had checked off each bridge in its turn, with the handle of his safe-key on the palm of his hand. "There's as many as six, you see, to choose from."

"I don't understand you," said I.

"Choose your bridge, Mr. Pip," returned Wemmick, "and take a walk upon your bridge, and pitch your money into the Thames over the center arch of your bridge, and you know the end of it. Serve a friend with it, and you may know the end of it too—but it's a less pleasant and profitable end."

I could have posted a newspaper in his mouth, he made it so wide after saying this.

"This is very discouraging," said I.

"Meant to be," said Wemmick.

"Then is it your opinion," I inquired, with some little indignation, "that a man should never—"

"—Invest portable property in a friend?" said Wemmick. "Certainly he should not. Unless he wants to get rid of the friend—and then it becomes a question how much portable property it may be worth to get rid of him."

"And that," said I, "is your deliberate opinion, Mr. Wemmick?"

"That," he returned, "is my deliberate opinion in this office."

"Ah!" said I, pressing him, for I thought I saw him near a loophole here: "but would that be your opinion at Walworth?"

"Mr. Pip," he replied, with gravity, "Walworth is one place, and this office is another. Much as the Aged is one person, and Mr. Jaggers is another. They must not be confounded together. My Walworth sentiments must be taken at Walworth; none but my official sentiments can be taken in this office."

"Very well," said I, much relieved, "then I shall look you up at Walworth, you may depend upon it."

"Mr. Pip," he returned, "you will be welcome there in a private and personal capacity."

We had held this conversation in a low voice, well knowing my guardian's ears to be the sharpest of the sharp. As he now appeared in his doorway, toweling his hands, Wemmick got on his great-coat and stood by to snuff out the candles. We all three went into the street together, and from the doorstep Wemmick turned his way, and Mr. Jaggers and I turned ours.

I could not help wishing more than once that evening that Mr. Jaggers had had an Angel in Gerrard Street, or a Stinger, or a Something, or a Somebody, to unbend his brows a little. It was an uncomfortable consideration on a twenty-first birthday, that coming of age at all seemed hardly worthwhile in such a guarded and suspicious world as he made of it. He was a thousand times better informed and cleverer than Wemmick, and yet I would a thousand times rather have had Wemmick to dinner. And Mr. Jaggers made not me alone intensely melancholy, because, after he was gone, Herbert said of himself, with his eyes fixed on the fire, that he thought he must have committed a felony and forgotten it, he felt so dejected and guilty.

Thirty-seven

DEEMING SUNDAY THE BEST DAY FOR TAKING MR. Wemmick's Walworth sentiments, I devoted the next ensuing Sunday afternoon to a pilgrimage to the Castle. On arriving before the battlements I found the Union Jack flying and the drawbridge up; but undeterred by this show of defiance and resistance, I rang at the gate, and was admitted in a most pacific manner by the Aged.

"My son, sir," said the old man, after securing the drawbridge, "rather had it in his mind, that you might happen to drop in, and he left word that he would soon be home from his afternoon's walk. He is very regular in his walks, is my son. Very regular in everything, is my son."

I nodded at the old gentleman as Wemmick himself might have nodded, and we went in and sat down by the fireside.

"You made acquaintance with my son, sir," said the old man, in his chirping way, while he warmed his hands at the blaze, "at his office, I expect?" I nodded. "Hah! I have heerd that my son is a wonderful hand at his business, sir?" I nodded hard. "Yes; so they tell me. His business is the Law?" I nodded harder. "Which makes it more surprising in my son," said the old man, "for he was not brought up to the Law, but to the Wine-Coopering."

Curious to know how the old gentleman stood informed concerning the reputation of Mr. Jaggers, I roared that name at him. He threw me into the greatest confusion by laughing heartily, and replying, in a very sprightly manner, "No, to be sure; you're right." And to this hour I have not the faintest notion what he meant, or what joke he thought I had made.

As I could not sit there nodding at him perpetually, without making some other attempt to interest him, I shouted an inquiry whether his own calling in life had been "the Wine-Coopering." By dint of straining that term out of myself several times, and tapping the old gentleman on the chest to associate it with him, I at last succeeded in making my meaning understood.

"No," said the old gentleman; "the warehousing, the warehousing. First over yonder"; he appeared to mean up the chimney, but I believe he intended to refer me to Liverpool; "and then in the City of London here. However, having an infirmity—for I am hard of hearing, sir—"

I expressed in pantomime the greatest astonishment.

"—Yes, hard of hearing; having that infirmity coming upon me, my son he went into the Law, and he took charge of me, and he by little and little made out this elegant and beautiful property. But returning to what you said, you know," pursued the old man, again laughing heartily, "what I say is, No to be sure; you're right."

I was modestly wondering whether my utmost ingenuity would have enabled me to say anything that would have amused him half as much as this imaginary pleasantry, when I was startled by a sudden click in the wall on one side of the chimney, and the ghostly tumbling open of a little wooden flap with "JOHN" upon it. The old man, following my eyes, cried with great triumph, "My son's come home!" and we both went out to the drawbridge.

It was worth any money to see Wemmick waving a salute to me from the other side of the moat, when we might have shaken hands across it with the greatest ease. The Aged was so delighted to work the drawbridge that I made no offer to assist him, and stood quiet until Wemmick had come across, and had presented me to Miss Skiffins: a lady by whom he was accompanied.

Miss Skiffins was of wooden appearance, and was, like her escort, in the post-office branch of the service. She might have been some two or three years younger than Wemmick, and I judged her to stand possessed of portable property. The cut of her dress from the waist upward, both before and behind, made her figure very like a boy's kite; and I might have pronounced her gown a little too decidedly orange, and her gloves a little too intensely green. But she seemed to be a very good sort of fellow, and showed a high regard for the Aged. I was not long in discovering that she was a frequent visitor at the Castle; for, on our going in, and my complimenting Wemmick on his ingenious contrivance for announcing himself to the Aged, he begged me to give my attention for a moment to the other side of the chimney, and disappeared. Presently another click came, and another little door tumbled open with "Miss Skiffins" on it; then Miss Skiffins shut up, and John tumbled open; then Miss Skiffins and John both tumbled open together, and finally shut up together. On Wemmick's return from working these mechanical appliances I expressed the great admiration with which I regarded them, and he said, "Well, you know, they're both pleasant and useful to the Aged. And by George, sir, it's a thing worth mentioning, that of all the people who come to this gate, the secret of those pulls is only known to the Aged, Miss Skiffins, and me!"

"And Mr. Wemmick made them," added Miss Skiffins, "with his own hands out of his own head."

While Miss Skiffins was taking off her bonnet (she retained her green gloves during the evening, as an outward and visible sign that there was company), Wemmick invited me to take a walk with him round the property, and see how the island looked in wintertime. Thinking that he did this to give me an opportunity of taking his Walworth sentiments, I seized the opportunity as soon as we were out of the Castle.

Having thought of the matter with care, I approached my subject as if I had never hinted at it before. I informed Wemmick that I was anxious in behalf of Herbert Pocket, and I told him how we had first met, and how we had fought. I glanced at Herbert's home, and at his character, at his having no means but such as he was dependent on his father for: those, uncertain and unpunctual. I alluded to the advantages I had derived in my first rawness and ignorance from his society, and I confessed that I feared I had but ill repaid them, and that he might have done better without me and my expectations. Keeping Miss Havisham in the background at a great distance, I still hinted at the possibility of my having competed with him in his prospects, and at the certainty of his possessing a generous soul, and being far above any mean distrusts, retaliations, or designs. For all these reasons (I told Wemmick), and because he was my young companion and friend, and I had a great affection for him, I wished my own good fortune to reflect some rays upon him, and therefore I sought advice from Wemmick's experience and knowledge of men and affairs, how I could best try with my resources to help Herbert to some present income—say of a hundred a year, to keep him in good hope and heart—and gradually to buy him on to some small partnership. I begged Wemmick, in conclusion, to understand that my help must always be rendered without Herbert's knowledge or suspicion, and that there was no one else in the world with whom I could advise. I wound up by laying my hand upon his shoulder, and saying, "I can't help confiding in you, though I know it must be troublesome to you; but that is your fault, in having ever brought me here."

Wemmick was silent for a little while, and then said with a kind of start, "Well, you know, Mr. Pip, I must tell you one thing. This is devilish good of you."

"Say you'll help me to be good, then," said I.

"Ecod," replied Wemmick, shaking his head, "that's not my trade."

"Nor is this your trading-place," said I.

"You're right," he returned. "You hit the nail on the head. Mr. Pip, I'll put on my considering-cap, and I think all you want to do may be done by degrees. Skiffins (that's her brother) is an accountant and agent. I'll look him up and go to work for you."

"I thank you ten thousand times."

"On the contrary," said he, "I thank you, for though we are strictly in our private and personal capacity, still, there *are* Newgate cobwebs about, and it brushes them away."

After a little further conversation to the same effect we returned into the Castle, where we found Miss Skiffins preparing tea. The responsible duty of making the toast was delegated to the Aged, and that excellent old gentleman was so intent upon it that he seemed to me in some danger of melting his eyes. It was no nominal meal that we were going to make, but a vigorous reality. The Aged prepared such a haystack of buttered toast that I could scarcely see him over it as it simmered on an iron stand hooked onto the top-bar; while Miss Skiffins brewed such a jorum of tea that the pig in the back premises became strongly excited, and audibly expressed his desire to participate in the entertainment.

The flag had been struck and the gun had been fired at the right moment of time, and I felt as snugly cut off from the rest of Walworth as if the moat were thirty feet wide by as many deep. Nothing disturbed the tranquility of the Castle but the occasional tumbling open of John and Miss Skiffins; which little doors were a prey to some spasmodic infirmity that made me sympathetically uncomfortable until I got used to it. I inferred from the methodical nature of Miss Skiffins's arrangements that she made tea there every Sunday night; and I rather suspected that a classic brooch she wore, representing the profile of an undesirable female with a very straight nose and a very new moon, was a piece of portable property that had been given her by Wemmick.

We ate the whole of the toast and drank tea in proportion, and it was delightful to see how warm and greasy we all got after it. The Aged especially, might have passed for some clean old chief of a savage tribe, just oiled. After a short pause of repose, Miss Skiffins—in the absence of the little servant who, it seemed, retired to the bosom of her family on Sunday afternoons—washed up the tea-things in a trifling ladylike amateur manner that compromised none of us. Then she put on her gloves again, and we drew round the fire, and Wemmick said, "Now Aged Parent, tip us the paper."

Wemmick explained to me while the Aged got his spectacles out, that this was according to custom, and that it gave the old gentleman infinite satisfaction to read the news aloud. "I won't offer an apology," said Wemmick, "for he isn't capable of many pleasures—are you, Aged P.?"

"All right, John, all right," returned the old man, seeing himself spoken to.

"Only tip him a nod every now and then when he looks off his paper," said Wemmick, "and he'll be as happy as a king. We are all attention, Aged One."

"All right, John, all right!" returned the cheerful old man: so busy and so pleased that it really was quite charming.

The Aged's reading reminded me of the classes at Mr. Wopsle's great-aunt's with the pleasanter peculiarity that it seemed to come through a key-hole. As he wanted the candles close to him, and as he was always on the verge of putting either his head or the newspaper into them, he required as much watching as a powder-mill. But Wemmick was equally untiring and gentle in his vigilance, and the Aged read on, quite unconscious of his many rescues. Whenever he looked at us, we all expressed the greatest interest and amazement, and nodded until he resumed again.

As Wemmick and Miss Skiffins sat side by side, and as I sat in a shadowy corner, I observed a slow and gradual elongation of Mr. Wemmick's mouth, powerfully suggestive of his slowly and gradually stealing his arm round Miss Skiffins's waist. In course of time I saw his hand appear on the other side of Miss Skiffins; but at that moment Miss Skiffins neatly stopped him with the green glove, unwound his arm again as if it were an article of dress, and with the greatest deliberation laid it on the table before her. Miss Skiffins's composure while she did this was one of the most remarkable sights I have ever seen, and if I could have thought the act consistent with abstraction of mind, I should have deemed that Miss Skiffins performed it mechanically.

By-and-by I noticed Wemmick's arm beginning to disappear again, and gradually fading out of view. Shortly afterwards his mouth began to widen again. After an interval of suspense on my part that was quite enthralling and almost painful, I saw his hand appear on the other side of Miss Skiffins. Instantly Miss Skiffins stopped it with the neatness of a practiced boxer, took off that girdle or cestus as before, and laid it on the table. Taking the table to represent the path of virtue, I am justified in stating that during the whole time of the Aged's reading Wemmick's arm was straying from the path of virtue and being recalled to it by Miss Skiffins.

At last the Aged read himself into a light slumber. This was the time for Wemmick to produce a little kettle, a tray of glasses, and a black bottle with a porcelain-topped cork, representing some clerical dignitary of a rubicund and social aspect. With the aid of these appliances we all had something warm to drink: including the Aged, who was soon awake again. Miss Skiffins mixed, and I observed that she and Wemmick drank out of one glass. Of course I knew better than to offer to see Miss Skiffins home, and under the circumstances I thought I had best go first: which I did, taking a cordial leave of the Aged, and having passed a pleasant evening.

Before a week was out I received a note from Wemmick, dated Walworth, stating that he hoped he had made some advance in that matter appertaining to our private and personal capacities, and that he would be glad if I could come and see him again upon it. So I went out again, and yet again, and yet again, and I saw him by appointment in the City several times, but never held any communication with him on the subject in or near Little Britain. The upshot was that we found a worthy young merchant or shipping-broker, not long established in business, who wanted intelligent help, and who wanted capital, and who in due course of time and receipt would want a partner. Between him and me secret articles were signed of which Herbert was the subject, and I paid him half of my five hundred pounds down, and engaged for sundry other payments: some, to fall due at certain dates out of my income; some, contingent on my coming into my property. Miss Skiffins's brother conducted the negotiation; Wemmick pervaded it throughout, but never appeared in it.

The whole business was so cleverly managed that Herbert had not the least suspicion of my hand being in it. I never shall forget the radiant face with which he came home one afternoon, and told me, as a mighty piece of news, of his having fallen in with one Clarriker (the young merchant's name), and of Clarriker's having shown an extraordinary inclination toward him, and of his belief that the opening had come at last. Day by day as his hopes grew stronger and his face brighter, he must have thought me a more and more affectionate friend, for I had the greatest difficulty in restraining my tears of triumph when I saw him so happy. At length the thing being done, and he having that day entered Clarriker's House, and he having talked to me for a whole evening in a flush of pleasure and success, I did really cry in good earnest when I went to bed, to think that my expectations had done good to somebody.

A great event in my life, the turning point of my life, now opens on my view. But before I proceed to narrate it, and before I pass on to all the changes it involved, I must give a chapter to Estella. It is not much to give to the theme that so long filled my heart.

Thirty-eight

IF THAT STAID OLD HOUSE NEAR THE GREEN AT RICHMOND should ever come to be haunted when I am dead, it will be haunted, surely, by my ghost. Oh the many, many nights and days through which the unquiet spirit within me haunted that house when Estella lived there! Let my body be where it would, my spirit was always wandering, wandering, wandering about that house.

The lady with whom Estella was placed, Mrs. Brandley by name, was a widow, with one daughter several years older than Estella. The mother looked young, and the daughter looked old; the mother's complexion was pink, and the daughter's was yellow: the mother set up for frivolity, and the daughter for theology. They were in what is called a good position, and visited, and were visited by, numbers of people. Little if any community of feeling subsisted between them and Estella, but the understanding was established that they were necessary to her, and that she was necessary to them. Mrs. Brandley had been a friend of Miss Havisham's before the time of her seclusion.

In Mrs. Brandley's house, and out of Mrs. Brandley's house, I suffered every kind and degree of torture that Estella could cause me. The nature of my relations with her, which placed me on terms of familiarity without placing me on terms of favor, conduced to my distraction. She made use of me to tease other admirers, and she turned the very familiarity between herself and me to the account of putting a constant slight on my devotion to her. If I had been her secretary, steward, half brother, poor relation—if I had been a younger brother of her appointed husband—I could not have seemed to myself further from my hopes when I was nearest to her. The privilege of calling her by her name and hearing her call me by mine became, under the circumstances, an aggravation of my trials; and while I think it likely that it almost maddened her other lovers, I know too certainly that it almost maddened me.

She had admirers without end. No doubt my jealousy made an admirer of everyone who went near her, but there were more than enough of them without that.

I saw her often at Richmond, I heard of her often in town, and I used often to take her and the Brandleys on the water; there were picnics, fete days, plays, operas, concerts, parties—all sorts of pleasures, through which I pursued her—and they were all miseries to me. I never had one hour's happiness in her society, and yet my mind all round the four-and-twenty hours was harping on the happiness of having her with me unto death.

Throughout this part of our intercourse—and it lasted—as will presently be seen, for what I then thought a long time—she habitually reverted to that tone which expressed that our association was forced upon us. There were other times when she would come to a sudden check in this tone and in all her many tones, and would seem to pity me.

"Pip, Pip," she said, one evening, coming to such a check, when we sat apart at a darkening window of the house in Richmond, "will you never take warning?"

"Of what?"

"Of me."

"Warning not to be attracted by you, do you mean, Estella?"

"Do I mean! If you don't know what I mean you are blind."

I should have replied that Love was commonly reputed blind, but for the reason that I always was restrained—and this was not the least of my miseries—by a feeling that it was ungenerous to press myself upon her when she knew that she could not choose but obey Miss Havisham. My dread always was that this knowledge on her part laid me under a heavy disadvantage with her pride, and made me the subject of a rebellious struggle in her bosom.

"At any rate," said I, "I have no warning given me just now, for you wrote to me to come to you this time."

"That's true," said Estella, with a cold, careless smile, that always chilled me.

After looking at the twilight without for a little while, she went on to say:

"The time has come round when Miss Havisham wishes to have me for a day at Satis. You are to take me there, and bring me back, if you will. She would rather I did not travel alone, and objects to receiving my maid, for she has a sensitive horror of being talked of by such people. Can you take me?"

"Can I take you, Estella!"

"You can, then? The day after tomorrow, if you please. You are to pay all charges out of my purse. You hear the condition of your going?"

"And must obey," said I.

This was all the preparation I received for that visit, or for others like it; Miss Havisham never wrote to me, nor had I ever so much as seen her handwriting. We went down on the next day but one, and we found her in the room where I had first beheld her, and it is needless to add that there was no change in Satis House.

She was even more dreadfully fond of Estella than she had been when I last saw them together; I repeat the word advisedly, for there was something positively dreadful in the energy of her looks and embraces. She hung upon Estella's beauty, hung upon her words, hung upon her gestures, and sat mumbling her own trembling fingers while she looked at her as though she were devouring the beautiful creature she had reared.

From Estella she looked at me, with a searching glance that seemed to pry into my heart and probe its wounds. "How does she use you, Pip—how does she use you?" she asked me again, with her witchlike eagerness, even in Estella's hearing. But when we sat by her flickering fire at night she was most weird; for then, keeping Estella's hand drawn through her arm and clutched in her own hand, she extorted from her, by dint of referring back to what Estella had told her in her regular letters, the names and conditions of the men whom she had fascinated; and as Miss Havisham dwelt upon this roll, with the intensity of a mind mortally hurt and diseased, she sat with her other hand on her crutched stick, and her chin on that, and her wan bright eyes glaring at me, a very spectre.

I saw in this, wretched though it made me, and bitter the sense of dependence and even of degradation that it awakened—I saw in this, that Estella was set to wreak Miss Havisham's revenge on men, and that she was not to be given to me until she had gratified it for a term. I saw in this, a reason for her being beforehand assigned to me. Sending her out to attract and torment and do mischief, Miss Havisham sent her with the malicious assurance that she was beyond the reach of all admirers, and that all who staked upon that cast were secured to lose. I saw in this, that I, too, was tormented by a perversion of ingenuity, even while the prize was reserved for me. I saw in this, the reason for my being staved off so long, and the reason for my late guardian's declining to commit himself to the formal knowledge of such a scheme. In a word, I saw in this, Miss Havisham as I had her then and there before my eyes, and always had had her before my eyes; and I saw in this the distinct shadow of the darkened and unhealthy house in which her life was hidden from the sun.

The candles that lighted that room of hers were placed in sconces on the wall. They were high from the ground, and they burned with the steady dullness of artificial light in air that is seldom renewed. As I looked round at them, and the pale gloom they made, and at the stopped clock, and at the withered articles of bridal dress upon the table and the ground, and at her own awful figure with its ghostly reflection thrown large by the fire upon the ceiling and the wall, I saw in everything the construction that my mind had come to repeated and thrown back to me. My thoughts passed into the great room across the landing where the table was spread, and I saw it written, as it were, in the falls of the cobwebs from the centerpiece, in the crawlings of the spiders on the cloth, in the tracks of the mice as they betook their little quickened hearts behind the panels, and in the gropings and pausings of the beetles on the floor.

It happened on the occasion of this visit that some sharp words arose between Estella and Miss Havisham. It was the first time I had ever seen them opposed.

We were seated by the fire, as just now described, and Miss Havisham still had Estella's arm drawn through her own, and still clutched Estella's hand in hers, when Estella gradually began to detach herself. She had shown a proud impatience more than once before, and had rather endured that fierce affection than accepted or returned it.

"What!" said Miss Havisham, flashing her eyes upon her, "are you tired of me?"

"Only a little tired of myself," replied Estella, disengaging her arm, and moving to the great chimney-piece, where she stood looking down at the fire.

"Speak the truth, you ingrate!" cried Miss Havisham, passionately striking her stick upon the floor; "you are tired of me."

Estella looked at her with perfect composure, and again looked down at the fire. Her graceful figure and her beautiful face expressed a self-possessed indifference to the wild heat of the other that was almost cruel.

"You stock and stone!" exclaimed Miss Havisham. "You cold, cold heart!"

"What!" said Estella, preserving her attitude of indifference as she leaned against the great chimney-piece and only moving her eyes; "do you reproach me for being cold? You?"

"Are you not?" was the fierce retort.

"You should know," said Estella. "I am what you have made me. Take all the praise, take all the blame; take all the success, take all the failure: in short, take me."

"Oh, look at her, look at her!" cried Miss Havisham, bitterly. "Look at her, so hard and thankless, on the hearth where she was reared! Where I took her into this wretched breast when it was first bleeding from its stabs, and where I have lavished years of tenderness upon her!"

"At least I was no party to the compact," said Estella, "for if I could walk and speak when it was made it was as much as I could do. But what would you have? You have been very good to me, and I owe everything to you. What would you have?"

"Love," replied the other.

"You have it."

"I have not," said Miss Havisham.

"Mother by adoption," retorted Estella, never departing from the easy grace of her attitude, never raising her voice as the other did, never yielding either to anger or tenderness—"Mother by adoption, I have said that I owe everything to you. All I possess is freely yours. All that you have given me is at your command to have again. Beyond that I have nothing. And if you ask me to give you what you never gave me, my gratitude and duty cannot do impossibilities."

"Did I never give her love!" cried Miss Havisham, turning wildly to me. "Did I never give her a burning love, inseparable from jealousy at all times, and from sharp pain, while she speaks thus to me! Let her call me mad, let her call me mad!"

"Why should I call you mad," returned Estella, "I, of all people? Does anyone live who knows what set purposes you have, half as well as I do? Does anyone live who knows what a steady memory you have, half as well as I do? I, who have sat on this same hearth on the little stool that is even now beside you there, learning your lessons and looking up into your face, when your face was strange and frightened me?"

"Soon forgotten!" moaned Miss Havisham. "Times soon forgotten!"

"No, not forgotten," retorted Estella. "Not forgotten, but treasured up in my memory. When have you found me false to your teaching? When have you found me unmindful of your lessons? When have you found me giving admission here" she touched her bosom with her hand—"to anything that you excluded? Be just to me."

"So proud, so proud!" moaned Miss Havisham, pushing away her gray hair with both her hands.

"Who taught me to be proud?" returned Estella. "Who praised me when I learned my lesson?"

"So hard, so hard!" moaned Miss Havisham, with her former action.

"Who taught me to be hard?" returned Estella. "Who praised me when I learned my lesson?"

"But to be proud and hard to *me!*" Miss Havisham quite shrieked, as she stretched out her arms. "Estella, Estella, Estella, to be proud and hard to *me!*"

Estella looked at her for a moment with a kind of calm wonder, but was not otherwise disturbed; when the moment was passed she looked down at the fire again.

"I cannot think," said Estella, raising her eyes after a silence, "why you should be so unreasonable when I come to see you after a separation. I have never forgotten your wrongs and their causes. I have never been unfaithful to you or your schooling. I have never shown any weakness that I can charge myself with."

"Would it be weakness to return my love?" exclaimed Miss Havisham. "But yes, yes, she would call it so!"

"I begin to think," said Estella, in a musing way, after another moment of calm wonder, "that I almost understand how this comes about. If you had brought up your adopted daughter wholly in the dark confinement of these rooms, and had never let her know that there was such a thing as the daylight by which she has never once seen your face—if you had done that, and then, for a purpose had wanted her to understand the daylight, and know all about it, you would have been disappointed and angry?"

Miss Havisham with her head in her hands, sat making a low moaning, and swaying herself on her chair, but gave no answer.

"Or," said Estella—"which is a nearer case—if you had taught her, from the dawn of her intelligence, with your utmost energy and might, that there was such a thing as daylight, but that it was made to be her enemy and destroyer, and she must always turn against it, for it had blighted you and would else blight her; if you had done this, and then, for a purpose, had wanted her to take naturally to the daylight and she could not do it, you would have been disappointed and angry?"

Miss Havisham sat listening (or it seemed so, for I could not see her face), but still made no answer.

"So," said Estella, "I must be taken as I have been made. The success is not mine, the failure is not mine, but the two together are me."

Miss Havisham had settled down, I hardly knew how, upon the floor, among the faded bridal relics with which it was strewn. I took advantage of the moment—I had sought one from the first—to leave the room after beseeching Estella's attention to her, with a movement of my hand. When I left, Estella was yet standing by the great chimney-piece, just as she had stood throughout. Miss Havisham's gray hair was all adrift upon the ground, among the other bridal wrecks, and was a miserable sight to see.

It was with a depressed heart that I walked in the starlight for an hour and more, about the courtyard, and about the brewery, and about the ruined garden. When I at last took courage to return to the room, I found Estella sitting at Miss Havisham's knee, taking up some stitches in one of those old articles of dress that were dropping to pieces, and of which I have often been reminded since by the faded tatters of old banners that I have seen hanging up in cathedrals. Afterward, Estella and I played at cards, as of yore—only we were skillful now, and played French games—and so the evening wore away, and I went to bed.

I lay in that separate building across the courtyard. It was the first time I had ever lain down to rest in Satis House, and sleep refused to come near me. A million of Miss Havishams haunted me. She was on this side of my pillow, on that, at the head of the bed, at the foot, behind the half-opened door of the dressing-room, in the dressing-room, in the room overhead, in the room beneath—everywhere. At last, when the night was slow to creep on toward two o'clock, I felt that I absolutely could no longer bear the place as a place to lie down in, and that I must get up. I therefore got up and put on my clothes, and went out across the yard into the long stone passage, designing to gain the outer courtyard and walk there for the relief of my mind. But I was no sooner in the passage than I extinguished my candle; for I saw Miss Havisham going along it in a ghostly manner, making a low cry. I followed her at a distance, and saw her go up the staircase. She carried a bare candle in her hand, which she had probably taken from one of the sconces in her own room, and was a most unearthly object by its light. Standing at the bottom of the staircase, I felt the mildewed air of the feast-chamber, without seeing her open the door, and I heard her walking there, and so across into her own room, and so across again into that, never ceasing the low cry. After a time, I tried in the dark both to get out and to go back, but I could do neither until some streaks of day strayed in and showed me where to lay my hands. During the whole interval, whenever I went to the bottom of the staircase, I heard her footstep, saw her light pass above, and heard her ceaseless low cry.

Before we left next day, there was no revival of the difference between her and Estella, nor was it ever revived on any similar occasion; and there were four similar occasions, to the best of my remembrance. Nor did Miss Havisham's manner toward Estella in any wise change, except that I believed it to have something like fear infused among its former characteristics.

It is impossible to turn this leaf of my life without putting Bentley Drummle's name upon it; or I would, very gladly.

On a certain occasion when the Finches were assembled in force, and when good feeling was being promoted in the usual manner by nobody's agreeing with anybody else, the presiding Finch called the Grove to order, forasmuch as Mr. Drummle had not yet toasted a lady; which, according to the solemn constitution of the society, it was the brute's turn to do that day. I thought I saw him leer in an ugly way at me while the decanters were going round, but as there was no love lost between us, that might easily be. What was my indignant surprise when he called upon the company to pledge him to "Estella!"

"Estella who?" said I.

"Never you mind," retorted Drummle.

"Estella of where?" said I, "You are bound to say where." Which he was, as a Finch.

"Of Richmond, gentlemen," said Drummle, putting me out of the question, "and a peerless beauty."

Much he knew about peerless beauties, a mean miserable idiot! I whispered Herbert.

"I know that lady," said Herbert, across the table, when the toast had been honored.

"*Do* you?" said Drummle.

"And so do I," I added, with a scarlet face.

"*Do* you?" said Drummle. "*Oh,* Lord!"

This was the only retort—except glass or crockery—that the heavy creature was capable of making; but I became as highly incensed by it as if it had been barbed with wit, and I immediately rose in my place and said that I could not but regard it as being like the honorable Finch's impudence to come down to that Grove, as a neat Parliamentary turn of expression—down to that Grove, proposing a lady of whom he knew nothing. Mr. Drummle upon this, starting up, demanded what I meant by that? Whereupon, I made him the extreme reply that I believed he knew where I was to be found.

Whether it was possible in a Christian country to get on without blood, after this, was a question on which the Finches were divided. The debate upon it grew so lively indeed, that at least six more honorable members told six more, during the discussion, that they believed *they* knew where *they* were to be found. However, it was decided at last (the Grove being a Court of Honor), that if Mr. Drummle would bring never so slight a certificate from the lady, importing that he had the honor of her acquaintance, Mr. Pip must express his regret, as a gentleman and a Finch, for "having been betrayed into a warmth which." Next day was appointed for the production (lest our honor should take cold from delay), and next day Drummle appeared with a polite little avowal in Estella's hand, that she had had the honor of dancing with him several times. This left me no course but to regret that I had been "betrayed into a warmth which," and on the whole to repudiate, as untenable, the idea that I was to be found anywhere. Drummle and I then sat snorting at one another for an hour, while the Grove engaged in indiscriminate contradiction, and finally the promotion of good feeling was declared to have gone ahead at an amazing rate.

I tell this lightly, but it was no light thing to me. For I cannot adequately express what pain it gave me to think that Estella should show any favor to a contemptible, clumsy, sulky booby, so very far below the average. To the present moment, I believe it to have been referable to some pure fire of generosity and disinterestedness in my love for her that I could not endure the thought of her stooping to that hound. No doubt I should have been miserable whomsoever she had favored; but a worthier object would have caused me a different kind and degree of distress.

It was easy for me to find out, and I did soon find out, that Drummle had begun to follow her closely, and that she allowed him to do it. A little while, and he was always in pursuit of her, and he and I crossed one another every day. He held on, in a dull persistent way, and Estella held him on; now with encouragement, now with discouragement, now almost flattering him, now openly despising him, now knowing him very well, now scarcely remembering who he was.

The Spider, as Mr. Jaggers had called him, was used to lying in wait, however, and had the patience of his tribe. Added to that, he had a block-head confidence in his money and in his family greatness, which sometimes did him good service—almost taking the place of concentration and deter-mined purpose. So the Spider, doggedly watching Estella, outwatched many brighter insects, and would often uncoil himself and drop at the right nick of time.

At a certain Assembly Ball at Richmond (there used to be Assembly Balls at some places then), where Estella had outshone all other beauties, this blun-dering Drummle so hung about her, and with so much toleration on her part, that I resolved to speak to her concerning him. I took the next oppor-tunity: which was when she was waiting for Mrs. Brandley to take her home, and was sitting apart among some flowers, ready to go. I was with her, for I almost always accompanied them to and from such places.

"Are you tired, Estella?"

"Rather, Pip."

"You should be."

"Say, rather, I should not be; for I have my letter to Satis House to write before I go to sleep."

"Recounting tonight's triumph?" said I. "Surely a very poor one, Estella."

"What do you mean? I didn't know there had been any."

"Estella," said I, "do look at that fellow in the corner yonder, who is look-ing over here at us."

"Why should I look at him?" returned Estella, with her eyes on me instead. "What is there in that fellow in the corner yonder—to use your words—that I need look at?"

"Indeed, that is the very question I want to ask you," said I. "For he has been hovering about you all night."

"Moths, and all sorts of ugly creatures," replied Estella, with a glance toward him, "hover about a lighted candle. Can the candle help it?"

"No," I returned; "but cannot the Estella help it?"

"Well!" said she, laughing, after a moment, "perhaps. Yes. Anything you like."

"But, Estella, do hear me speak. It makes me wretched that you should encourage a man so generally despised. You know that he is despised."

"Well?" said she.

"You know he is as ungainly within as without. A deficient, ill-tempered, lowering, stupid fellow."

"Well?" said she.

"You know he has nothing to recommend him but money, and a ridiculous roll of addle-headed predecessors; now, don't you?"

"Well?" said she again; and each time she said it, she opened her lovely eyes the wider.

To overcome the difficulty of getting past that monosyllable, I took it from her, and said, repeating it with emphasis, "Well! Then, that is why it makes me wretched."

Now if I could have believed that she favored Drummle with any idea of making me—me—wretched, I should have been in better heart about it; but in that habitual way of hers, she put me so entirely out of the question that I could believe nothing of the kind.

"Pip," said Estella, casting her glance over the room, "don't be foolish about its effect on you. It may have its effect on others, and may be meant to have. It's not worth discussing."

"Yes it is," said I, "because I cannot bear that people should say, 'she throws away her graces and attractions on a mere boor, the lowest in the crowd.' "

"I can bear it," said Estella.

"Oh, don't be so proud, Estella, and so inflexible."

"Calls me proud and inflexible in this breath!" said Estella, opening her hands. "And in his last breath reproached me for stooping to a boor!"

"There is no doubt you do," said I, something hurriedly, "for I have seen you give him looks and smiles this very night such as you never give to—me."

"Do you want me, then," said Estella, turning suddenly with a fixed and serious, if not angry, look, "to deceive and entrap you?"

"Do you deceive and entrap him, Estella?"

"Yes, and many others—all of them but you. Here is Mrs. Brandley. I'll say no more."

And now that I have given the one chapter to the theme that so filled my heart, and so often made it ache and ache again, I pass on unhindered, to the event that had impended over me longer yet; the event that had begun to be prepared for, before I knew that the world held Estella, and in the days when her baby intelligence was receiving its first distortions from Miss Havisham's wasting hands.

In the Eastern story, the heavy slab that was to fall on the bed of state in the flush of conquest was slowly wrought out of the quarry, the tunnel for the rope to hold it in its place was slowly carried through the leagues of rock, the slab was slowly raised and fitted in the roof, the rope was rove to it and slowly taken through the miles of hollow to the great iron ring. All being made ready with much labor, and the hour come, the sultan was aroused in the dead of the night, and the sharpened axe that was to sever the rope from the great iron ring was put into his hand, and he struck with it, and the rope parted and rushed away, and the ceiling fell. So, in my case; all the work near and afar, that tended to the end, had been accomplished; and in an instant the blow was struck, and the roof of my stronghold dropped upon me.

Thirty-nine

I WAS THREE-AND-TWENTY YEARS OF AGE. NOT ANOTHER word had I heard to enlighten me on the subject of my expectations, and my twenty-third birthday was a week gone. We had left Barnard's Inn more than a year, and lived in the Temple. Our chambers were in Garden Court, down by the river.

Mr. Pocket and I had for some time parted company as to our original relations, though we continued on the best terms. Notwithstanding my inability to settle to anything—which I hope arose out of the restless and incomplete tenure on which I held my means—I had a taste for reading, and read regularly so many hours a day. That matter of Herbert's was still progressing, and everything with me was as I have brought it down to the close of the last chapter.

Business had taken Herbert on a journey to Marseilles. I was alone, and had a dull sense of being alone. Dispirited and anxious, long hoping that tomorrow or next week would clear my way, and long disappointed, I sadly missed the cheerful face and ready response of my friend.

It was wretched weather; stormy and wet, stormy and wet; and mud, mud, mud, deep in all the streets. Day after day, a vast heavy vail had been driving over London from the East, and it drove still, as if in the East there were an Eternity of cloud and wind. So furious had been the gusts that high buildings in town had had the lead stripped off their roofs; and in the country, trees had been torn up, and sails of windmills carried away; and gloomy accounts had come in from the coast of shipwreck and death. Violent blasts of rain had accompanied these rages of wind, and the day just closed as I sat down to read had been the worst of all.

Alterations have been made in that part of the Temple since that time, and it has not now so lonely a character as it had then, nor is it so exposed to the river. We lived at the top of the last house, and the wind rushing up the river shook the house that night like discharges of cannon or breaking of a sea. When the rain came with it and dashed against the windows, I thought, raising my eyes to them as they rocked, that I might have fancied myself in a storm-beaten lighthouse. Occasionally the smoke came rolling down the chimney as though it could not bear to go out into such a night; and when I set the doors open and looked down the staircase, the staircase lamps were blown out; and when I shaded my face with my hands and looked through the black windows (opening them ever so little was out of the question in the teeth of such wind and rain), I saw that the lamps in the court were blown out, and that the lamps on the bridges and the shore were shuddering, and that the coal fires in barges on the river were being carried away before the wind like red-hot splashes in the rain.

I read with my watch upon the table, purposing to close my book at eleven o'clock. As I shut it, Saint Paul's, and all the many church-clocks in the City—some leading, some accompanying, some following—struck that hour. The sound was curiously flawed by the wind; and I was listening, and thinking how the wind assailed it, and tore it, when I heard a footstep on the stair.

What nervous folly made me start, and awfully connect it with the footstep of my dead sister, matters not. It was past in a moment, and I listened again, and heard the footstep stumble in coming on. Remembering then that the staircase-lights were blown out, I took up my reading-lamp and went out to the stair-head. Whoever was below had stopped on seeing my lamp, for all was quiet.

"There is someone down there, is there not?" I called out, looking down.

"Yes," said a voice from the darkness beneath.

"What floor do you want?"

"The top. Mr. Pip."

"That is my name. There is nothing the matter?"

"Nothing the matter," returned the voice. And the man came on.

I stood with my lamp held out over the stair-rail, and he slowly came within its light. It was a shaded lamp, to shine upon a book, and its circle of light was very contracted; so that he was in it for a mere instant, and then out of it. In the instant I had seen a face that was strange to me, looking up with an incomprehensible air of being touched and pleased by the sight of me.

Moving the lamp as the man moved, I made out that he was substantially dressed, but roughly: like a voyager by sea. That he had long, iron-gray hair. That his age was about sixty. That he was a muscular man, strong on his legs, and that he was browned and hardened by exposure to weather. As he ascended the last stair or two, and the light of my lamp included us both, I saw, with a stupid kind of amazement, that he was holding both his hands to me.

"Pray what is your business?" I asked him.

"My business?" he repeated, pausing. "Ah! Yes. I will explain my business, by your leave."

"Do you wish to come in?"

"Yes," he replied, "I wish to come in, Master."

I had asked him the question inhospitably enough, for I resented the sort of bright and gratified recognition that still shone in his face. I resented it, because it seemed to imply that he expected me to respond to it. But I took him into the room I had just left, and, having set the lamp on the table, asked him as civilly as I could to explain himself.

He looked about him with the strangest air—an air of wondering pleasure, as if he had some part in the things he admired—and he pulled off a rough outer coat, and his hat. Then I saw that his head was furrowed and bald, and that the long, iron-gray hair grew only on its sides. But I saw nothing that in the least explained him. On the contrary, I saw him next moment once more holding out both his hands to me.

"What do you mean?" said I, half suspecting him to be mad.

He stopped in his looking at me, and slowly rubbed his right hand over his head. "It's disapinting to a man," he said, in a coarse, broken voice, "arter having looked for'ard so distant and come so fur; but you're not to blame for that—neither on us is to blame for that. I'll speak in half a minute. Give me half a minute, please."

He sat down on a chair that stood before the fire, and covered his forehead with his large brown veinous hands. I looked at him attentively then, and recoiled a little from him; but I did not know him.

"There's no one nigh," said he, looking over his shoulder; "is there?"

"Why do you, a stranger coming into my room at this time of the night, ask that question?" said I.

"You're a game one," he returned, shaking his head at me with a deliberate affection, at once most unintelligible and most exasperating; "I'm glad you've grow'd up, a game one! But don't catch hold of me. You'd be sorry arterward to have done it."

I relinquished the intention he had detected, for I knew him! Even yet, I could not recall a single feature, but I knew him! If the wind and the rain had driven away the intervening years, had scattered all the intervening objects, had swept us to the churchyard where we first stood face to face on such different levels, I could not have known my convict more distinctly than I knew him now, as he sat in the chair before the fire. No need to take a file from his pocket and show it to me; no need to take the handkerchief from his neck and twist it round his head; no need to hug himself with both his arms, and take a shivering turn across the room, looking back at me for recognition. I knew him before he gave me one of those aids, though, a moment before, I had not been conscious of remotely suspecting his identity.

He came back to where I stood, and again held out both his hands. Not knowing what to do—for in my astonishment I had lost my self-possession—I reluctantly gave him my hands. He grasped them heartily, raised them to his lips, kissed them, and still held them. "You acted noble, my boy," said he. "Noble, Pip! And I have never forgot it!"

At a change in his manner as if he were even going to embrace me, I laid a hand upon his breast and put him away.

"Stay!" said I. "Keep off! If you are grateful to me for what I did when I was a little child, I hope you have shown your gratitude by mending your way of life. If you have come here to thank me, it was not necessary. Still, however you have found me out, there must be something good in the feeling that has brought you here, and I will not repulse you; but surely you must understand that—I—"

My attention was so attracted by the singularity of his fixed look at me, that the words died away on my tongue.

"You was a saying," he observed, when we had confronted one another in silence, "that surely I must understand. What surely must I understand?"

"That I cannot wish to renew that chance intercourse with you of long ago, under these different circumstances. I am glad to believe you have repented and recovered yourself. I am glad to tell you so. I am glad that, thinking I deserve to be thanked, you have come to thank me. But our ways are different ways, none the less. You are wet, and you look weary. Will you drink something before you go?"

He had replaced his neckerchief loosely, and had stood, keenly observant of me, biting a long end of it. "I think," he answered, still with the end at his mouth and still observant of me, "that I *will* drink (I thank you) afore I go."

There was a tray ready on a side-table. I brought it to the table near the fire, and asked him what he would have? He touched one of the bottles without looking at it or speaking, and I made him some hot rum-and-water. I tried to keep my hand steady while I did so, but his look at me as he leaned back in his chair with the long draggled end of his neckerchief between his teeth—evidently forgotten—made my hand very difficult to master. When at last I put the glass to him, I saw with new amazement that his eyes were full of tears.

Up to this time I had remained standing, not to disguise that I wished him gone. But I was softened by the softened aspect of the man, and felt a touch of reproach. "I hope," said I, hurriedly putting something into a glass for myself, and drawing a chair to the table, "that you will not think I spoke harshly to you just now. I had no intention of doing it, and I am sorry for it if I did. I wish you well, and happy!"

As I put my glass to my lips he glanced with surprise at the end of his neckerchief, dropping from his mouth when he opened it, and stretched out his hand. I gave him mine, and then he drank, and drew his sleeve across his eyes and forehead.

"How are you living?" I asked him.

"I've been a sheep-farmer, stock-breeder, other trades besides away in the new world," said he; "many a thousand miles of stormy water off from this."

"I hope you have done well?"

"I've done wonderful well. There's others went out alonger me as has done well too, but no man has done nigh as well as me. I'm famous for it."

"I am glad to hear it."

"I hope to hear you say so, my dear boy."

Without stopping to try to understand those words or the tone in which they were spoken, I turned off to a point that had just come into my mind.

"Have you ever seen a messenger you once sent to me," I inquired, "since he undertook that trust?"

"Never set eyes upon him. I wasn't likely to it."

"He came faithfully, and he brought me the two one-pound notes. I was a poor boy then, as you know, and to a poor boy they were a little fortune. But, like you, I have done well since, and you must let me pay them back. You can put them to some other poor boy's use." I took out my purse.

He watched me as I laid my purse upon the table and opened it, and he watched me as I separated two one-pound notes from its contents. They were clean and new, and I spread them out and handed them over to him. Still watching me, he laid them one upon the other, folded them long-wise, gave them a twist, set fire to them at the lamp, and dropped the ashes into the tray.

"May I make so bold," he said then, with a smile that was like a frown, and with a frown that was like a smile, "as ask you *how* you have done well, since you and me was out on them lone shivering marshes?"

"How?"

"Ah!"

He emptied his glass, got up, and stood at the side of the fire, with his heavy brown hand on the mantle-shelf. He put a foot up to the bars, to dry and warm it, and the wet boot began to steam; but he neither looked at it, nor at the fire, but steadily looked at me. It was only now that I began to tremble.

When my lips had parted, and had shaped some words that were without sound, I forced myself to tell him (though I could not do it distinctly), that I had been chosen to succeed to some property.

"Might a mere warmint ask what property?" said he.

I faltered, "I don't know."

"Might a mere warmint ask whose property?" said he.

I faltered again, "I don't know."

"Could I make a guess, I wonder," said the Convict, "at your income since you come of age! As to the first figure now. Five?"

With my heart beating like a heavy hammer of discorded action, I rose out of my chair, and stood with my hand upon the back of it, looking wildly at him.

"Concerning a guardian," he went on. "There ought to have been some guardian or such-like, while you was a minor. Some lawyer, maybe. As to the first letter of that lawyer's name now. Would it be J?"

All the truth of my position came flashing on me; and its disappointments, dangers, disgraces, consequences of all kinds, rushed in in such a multitude that I was borne down by them, and had to struggle for every breath I drew.

"Put it," he resumed, "as the employer of that lawyer whose name begun with a J. and might be Jaggers—put it as he had come over sea to Portsmouth, and had landed there and had wanted to come on to you. 'However, you have found me out,' you says just now. Well! However did I find you out? Why, I wrote from Portsmouth to a person in London, for particulars of your address. That person's name? Why, Wemmick."

I could not have spoken one word though it had been to save my life. I stood, with a hand on the chair-back and a hand on my breast, where I seemed to be suffocating—I stood so, looking wildly at him, until I grasped at the chair, when the room began to surge and turn. He caught me, drew me to the sofa, put me up against the cushions, and bent on one knee before me, bringing the face that I now well remembered, and that I shuddered at, very near to mine.

"Yes, Pip, dear boy, I've made a gentleman on you! It's me wot has done it! I swore that time, sure as ever I earned a guinea, that guinea should go to you. I swore arterward, sure as ever I spec'lated and got rich, you should get rich. I lived rough, that you should live smooth; I worked hard that you should be above work. What odds, dear boy? Do I tell it fur you to feel a obligation! Not a bit. I tell it fur you to know as that there hunted dunghill dog what you kep life in got his head so high that he could make a gentleman—and Pip, you're him!"

The abhorrence in which I held the man, the dread I had of him, the repugnance with which I shrank from him, could not have been exceeded if he had been some terrible beast.

"Look'ee here, Pip. I'm your second father. You're my son—more to me nor any son. I've put away money, only for you to spend. When I was a hired-out shepherd in a solitary hut, not seeing no faces but faces of sheep till I half forgot wot men's and women's faces wos like, I see yourn. I drops my knife many a time in that hut when I was a eating my dinner or my supper, and says, 'Here's the boy again, a looking at me whiles I eats and drinks!' I see you there, a many times, as plain as ever I see you on them misty marshes. 'Lord strike me dead!' I says each time—and I goes out in the air to say it under the open heavens—'but wot, if I gets liberty and money, I'll make that boy a gentleman!' And I done it. Why, look at you, dear boy! Look at these here lodgings o' yourn, fit for a lord! A lord? Ah! You shall show money with lords for wagers, and beat 'em!"

In his heat and triumph, and in his knowledge that I had been nearly fainting, he did not remark on my reception of all this. It was the one grain of relief I had.

"Look'ee here!" he went on, taking out my watch, and turning toward him a ring on my finger, while I recoiled from his touch as if he had been a snake, "a gold 'un and a beauty; *that's* a gentleman's! A diamond, all set round with rubies; *that's* a gentleman's! Look at your linen; fine and beautiful. Look at your clothes; better ain't to be got! And your books too," turning his eyes round the room, "mounting up, on their shelves, by hundreds! And you read 'em; don't you? I see you'd been a reading of 'em when I come in. Ha, ha, ha! You shall read 'em to me, dear boy! And if they're in foreign languages wot I don't understand, I shall be just as proud as if I did."

Again he took both my hands and put them to his lips, while my blood ran cold within me.

"Don't you mind talking, Pip," said he, after again drawing his sleeve over his eyes and forehead, as the click came in his throat which I well remembered—and he was all the more horrible to me that he was so much in earnest; "you can't do better nor keep quiet, dear boy. You ain't looked slowly forward to this as I have; you wosn't prepared for this, as I wos. But didn't you never think it might be me?"

"Oh no, no, no," I returned. "Never, never!"

"Well, you see it *wos* me, and single-handed. Never a soul in it but my own self and Mr. Jaggers."

"Was there no one else?" I asked.

"No," said he, with a glance of surprise; "who else should there be? And, dear boy, how good-looking you have growed! There's bright eyes somewheres—eh? Isn't there bright eyes somewheres, wot you love the thoughts on?"

Oh Estella, Estella!

"They shall be yourn, dear boy, if money can buy 'em. Not that a gentleman like you, so well set up as you, can't win 'em off of his own game; but money shall back you! Let me finish wot I was a telling you, dear boy. From that there hut and that there hiring out, I got my liberty and went for myself. In every single thing I went for, I went for you. 'Lord strike a blight upon it,' I says, wotever it was I went for, 'if it ain't for him!' It all prospered wonderful. As I giv' you to understand just now, I'm famous for it. It was the gains of the first few year wot I sent home to Mr. Jaggers—all for you—when he first came arter you, agreeable to my letter."

Oh that he had never come! That he had left me at the forge—far from contented, yet, by comparison, happy!

"And then, dear boy, it was a recompense to me, look'ee here, to know in secret that I was making a gentleman. The blood-horses of them colonists might fling up the dust over me as I was walking; what do I say? I says to myself, 'I'm making a better gentleman nor ever *you*'ll be!' When one of 'em says to another, 'He was a convict, a few year ago, and is a ignorant common fellow now, for all he's lucky,' what do I say? I says to myself, 'If I ain't a gentleman, nor yet ain't got no learning, I'm the owner of such. All on you owns stock and land; which on you owns a brought-up London gentleman?' This way I kep' myself a going. And this way I held steady afore my mind that I would for certain come one day and see my boy, and make myself known to him, on his own ground."

He laid his hand on my shoulder. I shuddered at the thought that for anything I knew his hand might be stained with blood.

"It warn't easy, Pip, for me to leave them parts, not yet it warn't safe. But I held to it, and the harder it was the stronger I held, for I was determined, and my mind firm made up. At last I done it. Dear boy, I done it!"

I tried to collect my thoughts, but I was stunned. Throughout, I had seemed to myself to attend more to the wind and rain than to him; even now, I could not separate his voice from those voices, though those were loud and his was silent.

"Where will you put me?" he asked, presently. "I must be put some-wheres, dear boy."

"To sleep?" said I.

"Yes. And to sleep long and sound," he answered; "for I've been sea-tossed and sea-washed, weeks and months."

"My friend and companion," said I, rising from the sofa, "is absent, you must have his room."

"He won't come back tomorrow, will he?"

"No," said I, answering almost mechanically, in spite of my utmost efforts; "not tomorrow."

"Because, look'ee here, dear boy," he said, dropping his voice, and laying a long finger on my breast in an impressive manner, "caution is necessary."

"How do you mean? Caution?"

"By G—, it's Death!"

"What's death?"

"I was sent for life. It's death to come back. There's been overmuch coming back of late years, and I should of a certainty be hanged if took."

Nothing was needed but this; the wretched man, after loading wretched me with his gold and silver chains for years, had risked his life to come to me, and I held it there in my keeping! If I had loved him instead of abhorring him; if I had been attracted to him by the strongest admiration and affection, instead of shrinking from him with the strongest repugnance, it could have been no worse. On the contrary, it would have been better, for his preservation would then have naturally and tenderly addressed my heart.

My first care was to close the shutters, so that no light might be seen from without, and then to close and make fast the doors. While I did so, he stood at the table drinking rum and eating biscuit; and when I saw him thus engaged, I saw my convict on the marshes at his meal again. It almost seemed to me as if he must stoop down presently, to file at his leg.

When I had gone into Herbert's room, and had shut off any other communication between it and the staircase than through the room in which our conversation had been held, I asked him if he would go to bed? He said yes, but asked me for some of my "gentleman's linen" to put on in the morning. I brought it out, and laid it ready for him, and my blood again ran cold when he again took me by both hands to give me good night.

I got away from him, without knowing how I did it, and mended the fire in the room where we had been together, and sat down by it, afraid to go to bed. For an hour or more I remained too stunned to think, and it was not until I began to think that I began fully to know how wrecked I was, and how the ship in which I had sailed was gone to pieces.

Miss Havisham's intentions toward me all a mere dream; Estella not designed for me; I only suffered in Satis House as a convenience, a sting for the greedy relations, a model with a mechanical heart to practice on when no other practice was at hand; those were the first smarts I had. But, sharpest and deepest pain of all—it was for the convict, guilty of I know not what crimes, and liable to be taken out of those rooms where I sat thinking, and hanged at the Old Bailey door, that I had deserted Joe.

I would not have gone back to Joe now, I would not have gone back to Biddy now, for any consideration: simply, I suppose, because my sense of my own worthless conduct to them was greater than every consideration. No wisdom on earth could have given me the comfort that I should have derived from their simplicity and fidelity; but I could never, never, never undo what I had done.

In every rage of wind and rush of rain I heard pursuers. Twice I could have sworn there was a knocking and whispering at the outer door. With these fears upon me, I began either to imagine or recall that I had had mysterious warnings of this man's approach. That for weeks gone by I had passed faces in the streets which I had thought like his. That these likenesses had grown more numerous as he, coming over the sea, had drawn nearer. That his wicked spirit had somehow sent these messengers to mine, and that now on this stormy night he was as good as his word, and with me.

Crowding up with these reflections came the reflection that I had seen him with my childish eyes to be a desperately violent man; that I had heard that other convict reiterate that he had tried to murder him; that I had seen him down in the ditch tearing and fighting like a wild beast. Out of such remembrances I brought into the light of the fire a half-formed terror that it might not be safe to be shut up there with him in the dead of the wild, solitary night. This dilated until it filled the room, and impelled me to take a candle and go in and look at my dreadful burden.

There was still much of the old marsh character upon him, for he had rolled a handkerchief round his head, and his face was set and lowering in his sleep. But he was asleep, and quietly too, though he had a pistol lying on the pillow. Assured of this, I softly removed the key to the outside of his door and turned it on him before I again sat down by the fire. Gradually I slipped from the chair and lay on the floor. When I awoke, without having parted in my sleep with the perception of my wretchedness, the clocks of the Eastern churches were striking five, the candles were wasted out, the fire was dead, and the wind and rain intensified the thick black darkness.

THIS IS THE END OF THE SECOND STAGE OF PIP'S EXPECTATIONS.

Forty

IT WAS FORTUNATE FOR ME THAT I HAD TO TAKE PRECAU-
tions to insure (so far as I could) the safety of my dreaded visitor, for this
thought pressing on me when I awoke held other thoughts in a confused concourse at a distance.

The impossibility of keeping him concealed in the chambers was self-
evident. It could not be done, and the attempt to do it would inevitably
engender suspicion. True, I had no Avenger in my service now, but I was
looked after by an inflammatory old female, assisted by an animated rag-bag
whom she called her niece, and to keep a room secret from them would be
to invite curiosity and exaggeration. They both had weak eyes, which I had
long attributed to their chronically looking in at keyholes, and they were
always at hand when not wanted; indeed that was their only reliable quality
besides larceny. Not to get up a mystery with these people, I resolved to
announce in the morning that my uncle had unexpectedly come from the
country.

This course I decided on while I was yet groping about in the darkness
for the means of getting a light. Not stumbling on the means after all, I was
fain to go out to the Lodge and get the watchman there to come with his
lantern. Now, in groping my way down the black staircase I fell over something, and that something was a man crouching in a corner.

As the man made no answer when I asked him what he did there, but
eluded my touch in silence, I ran to the Lodge and urged the watchman to
come back quickly: telling him of the incident on the way back. The wind
being as fierce as ever, we did not care to endanger the light in the lantern by
rekindling the extinguished lamps on the staircase, but we examined the
staircase from the bottom to the top and found no one there. It then
occurred to me as possible that the man might have slipped into my rooms;
so, lighting my candle at the watchman's, and leaving him standing at the
door, I examined them carefully, including the room in which my dreaded
guest lay asleep. All was quiet, and assuredly no other man was in those
chambers.

It troubled me that there should have been a lurker on the stairs, on that
night of all nights in the year, and I asked the watchman as I handed him a
dram at the door, on the chance of eliciting some hopeful explanation,
whether he had admitted at his gate any gentleman who had perceptibly been
dining out? Yes, he said; at different times of the night, three. One lived in
Fountain Court, and the other two lived in the Lane, and he had seen them
all go home. Again, the only other man who dwelt in the house of which my

chambers formed a part had been in the country for some weeks; and he certainly had not returned in the night, because we had seen his door with his seal on it as we came up stairs.

"The night being so bad, sir," said the watchman, as he gave me back my glass, "uncommon few have come in at my gate. Besides them three gentlemen that I have named, I don't call to mind another since about eleven o'clock, when a stranger asked for you."

"My uncle," I muttered. "Yes."

"You saw him, sir?"

"Yes. Oh yes."

"Likewise the person with him?"

"Person with him!" I repeated.

"I judged the person to be with him," returned the watchman. "The person stopped when he stopped to make inquiry of me, and the person took this way when he took this way."

"What sort of person?"

The watchman had not particularly noticed; he should say a working person; to the best of his belief he had a dust-colored kind of clothes on, under a dark coat. The watchman made more light of the matter than I did, and naturally—not having my reason for attaching weight to it.

When I had got rid of him, which I thought it well to do without prolonging explanations, my mind was much troubled by these two circumstances taken together. Whereas they were easy of innocent solution apart— as, for instance, some diner-out or diner-at-home, who had not gone near this watchman's gate, might have strayed to my staircase and dropped asleep there—and my nameless visitor might have brought someone with him to show him the way—still, joined, they had an ugly look to one as prone to distrust and fear as the changes of a few hours had made me.

I lighted my fire, which burned with a raw pale look at that dead time of the morning, and fell into a doze before it. I seemed to have been dozing a whole night when the clocks struck six. As there was full an hour and a half between me and daylight, I dozed again; now, waking up uneasily, with prolix conversations about nothing in my ears; now, making thunder of the wind in the chimney: at length falling off into a profound sleep from which the daylight woke me with a start.

All this time I had never been able to consider my own situation, nor could I do so yet. I had not the power to attend to it. I was greatly dejected and distressed, but in an incoherent wholesale sort of way. As to forming any plan for the future, I could as soon have formed an elephant. When I opened the shutters and looked out at the wet wild morning, all of a leaden hue; when I walked from room to room; when I sat down again shivering, before the fire, waiting for my laundress to appear; I thought how miserable I was, but hardly knew why, or how long I had been so, or on what day of the week I made the reflection, or even who I was that made it.

At length the old woman and the niece came in—the latter with a head not easily distinguished from her broom—and testified surprise at sight of me and the fire. To whom I imparted how my uncle had come in the night and was then asleep, and how the breakfast preparations were to be modified accordingly. Then I washed and dressed while they knocked the furniture about and made a dust, and so, in a sort of dream or sleep-waking, found myself sitting by the fire again waiting for—Him—to come to breakfast.

By-and-by his door opened and he came out. I could not bring myself to bear the sight of him, and I thought he had a villainous look by daylight.

"I do not even know," said I, speaking low as he took his seat at the table, "by what name to call you. I have given out that you are my uncle."

"That's it, dear boy! Call me uncle."

"You assumed some name, I suppose, on board ship?"

"Yes, dear boy. I took the name of Provis."

"Do you mean to keep that name?"

"Why, yes, dear boy, it's as good as another—unless you'd like another."

"What is your own name?" I asked him in a whisper.

"Magwitch," he answered in the same tone; "chris'en'd Abel."

"What were you brought up to be?"

"A warmint, dear boy."

He answered quite seriously, and used the words as if it denoted some profession.

"When you came into the Temple last night—" said I, pausing to wonder whether that could really have been last night which seemed so long ago.

"Yes, dear boy?"

"When you came in at the gate and asked the watchman the way here, had you anyone with you?"

"With me? No, dear boy."

"But there was someone there?"

"I didn't take particular notice," he said, dubiously, "not knowing the ways of the place. But I think there *was* a person, too, come in alonger me."

"Are you known in London?"

"I hope not!" said he, giving his neck a jerk with his forefinger that made me turn hot and sick.

"Were you known in London, once?"

"Not over and above, dear boy. I was in the provinces mostly."

"Were you—tried—in London?"

"Which time?" said he, with a sharp look.

"The last time."

He nodded. "First knowed Mr. Jaggers that way. Jaggers was for me."

It was on my lips to ask him what he was tried for, but he took up a knife, gave it a flourish, and with the words, "And whatever I done is worked out and paid for!" fell to at his breakfast.

He ate in a ravenous way that was very disagreeable, and all his actions were uncouth, noisy and greedy. Some of his teeth had failed him since I saw him eat on the marshes, and as he turned his food in his mouth, and turned his head sideways to bring his strongest fangs to bear upon it, he looked terribly like a hungry old dog. If I had begun with any appetite he would have taken it away, and I should have sat much as I did—repelled from him by an insurmountable aversion, and gloomily looking at the cloth.

"I'm a heavy grubber, dear boy," he said, as a polite kind of apology when he had made an end of his meal, "but I always wos. If it had been in my constitution to be a lighter grubber, I might ha' got into lighter trouble. Similarly, I must have my smoke. When I was first hired out as shepherd t'other side the world, it's my belief I should ha' turned into a molloncolly-mad sheep myself, if I hadn't a had my smoke."

As he said so, he got up from table, and putting his hand into the breast of the peacoat he wore, brought out a short black pipe, and a handful of loose tobacco of the kind that is called Negro-head. Having filled his pipe, he put the surplus tobacco back again, as if his pocket were a drawer. Then he took a live coal from the fire with the tongs, and lighted his pipe at it, and then turned round on the hearth-rug with his back to the fire, and went through his favorite action of holding out both his hands for mine.

"And this," said he, dandling my hands up and down in his, as he puffed at his pipe—"and this is the gentleman wot I made! The real genuine One! It does me good fur to look at you, Pip. All I stip'late is to stand by and look at you, dear boy!"

I released my hands as soon as I could, and found that I was beginning slowly to settle down to the contemplation of my condition. What I was chained to, and how heavily, became intelligible to me, as I heard his hoarse voice, and sat looking up at his furrowed bald head with its iron-gray hair at the sides.

"I mustn't see my gentleman a footing it in the mire of the streets; there mustn't be no mud on *his* boots. My gentleman must have horses, Pip! Horses to ride, and horses to drive, and horses for his servant to ride and drive as well. Shall colonists have their horses (and blood 'uns, if you please, good Lord!) and not my London gentleman! No, no. We'll show 'em another pair of shoes than that, Pip; won't us?"

He took out of his pocket a great thick pocket-book, bursting with papers, and tossed it on the table.

"There's something worth spending in that there book, dear boy. It's yourn. All I've got ain't mine; it's yourn. Don't you be afraid on it. There's more where that come from. I've come to the old country fur to see my gentleman spend his money *like* a gentleman. That'll be *my* pleasure. *My* pleasure 'ull be fur to see him do it. And blast you all!" he wound up, looking round the cornice of the room and snapping his fingers once with a loud crack, "blast you every one, from the judge in his wig to the colonist a stirring up the dust, I'll show a better gentleman than the whole kit on you put together!"

"Stop!" said I, almost in a frenzy of fear and dislike, "I want to speak to you. I want to know what is to be done. I want to know how you are to be kept out of danger, how long you are going to stay, what projects you have."

"Look'ee here, Pip," said he, laying his hand on my arm in a suddenly altered and subdued manner; "first of all, look'ee here. I forgot myself half a minute ago. What I said was low; that's wot it was; low. Look'ee here, Pip. Look over it. I ain't a going to be low."

"First," I resumed, half groaning, "what precautions can be taken against your being recognized and seized?"

"No, dear boy," he said, in the same tone as before, "that don't go first. Lowness goes first. I ain't took so many year to make a gentleman not without knowing wot's due to him. Look'ee here, Pip. I was low; that's wot I was: low. Look over it, dear boy."

Some sense of the grimly-ludicrous moved me to a fretful laugh, as I replied, "I *have* looked over it. In Heaven's name, don't harp upon it!"

"Yes, but look'ee here," he persisted. "Dear boy, I ain't come so fur to be low. Now, go on, dear boy. You was saying—"

"How are you to be guarded from the danger you have incurred!"

"Well, dear boy, the danger ain't so great. Without I was informed against, the danger ain't so much to signify. There's Jaggers, and there's Wemmick, and there's you. Who else is there to inform?"

"Is there no chance person who might identify you in the street?" said I, bitterly.

"Well," he returned, "there ain't many. Nor yet I don't intend to advertise myself in the papers by the name A. M., come back from Botany Bay; and years have rolled away, and who's to gain by it? Still, look'ee here, Pip. If the danger had been fifty times as great, I should ha' come to see you, mind you, just the same."

"And how long do you remain?"

"How long!" said he, taking his black pipe from his mouth, and dropping his jaw as he stared at me. "I'm not a going back. I've come for good."

"Where are you to live?" said I. "What is to be done with you? Where will you be safe?"

"Dear boy," he returned, "there's disguising wigs can be bought for money, and there's hair powder, and spectacles, and black clothes—shorts, and wot not. Others has done it safe afore, and wot others has done afore others can do agen. As to the where and how of living, dear boy, give me your own opinions on it."

"You take it smoothly now," said I, "but you were very serious last night when you swore it was Death."

"And so I swear it is Death," said he, putting his pipe back in his mouth, "and Death by the rope, in the open street not fur from this, and it's serious that you should fully understand it to be so. Wot then, when that's once done? Here I am. To go back now 'ud be as bad as to stand ground—worse. Besides, Pip, I'm here, because I've meant it by you, years and years. As to wot I dare, I'm a old bird now, as has dared all manner of traps since first he was fledged, and I'm not afraid to perch upon a scarecrow. If there's Death hid inside of it, there is, and let him come out, and I'll face him, and then I'll believe in him and not afore. And now let me have a look at my gentleman agen."

Once more he took me by both hands and surveyed me with an air of admiring proprietorship; smoking with great complacency all the while.

It appeared to me that I could do no better than secure him some quiet lodging hard by, of which he might take possession when Herbert returned: whom I expected in two or three days. That the secret must be confided to Herbert as a matter of unavoidable necessity, even if I could have put the immense relief I should derive from sharing it with him out of the question, was plain to me. But it was by no means so plain to Mr. Provis (I resolved to call him by that name), who reserved his consent to Herbert's participation until he should have seen him and formed a favorable judgment of his physiognomy. "And even then, dear boy," said he, pulling a greasy little clasped black Testament out of his pocket, "we'll have him on his oath."

To state that my terrible patron carried this little black book about the world solely to swear people on in cases of emergency, would be to state what I never quite established—but this I can say, that I never knew him put it to any other use. The book itself had the appearance of having been stolen from some court of justice, and perhaps his knowledge of its antecedents combined with his own experience in that wise, gave him a reliance on its powers as a sort of legal spell or charm. On this first occasion of his produding it, I recalled how he had made me swear fidelity in the churchyard long ago, and how he had described himself last night as swearing to his resolution in his solitude.

As he was at present dressed in a seafaring slop suit, in which he looked as if he had some parrot or two and a few cigars to dispose of, I next discussed with him what dress he should wear. He cherished an extraordinary belief in the virtues of "shorts" as a disguise, and had in his own mind sketched a dress for himself that would have made him something between a dean and a dentist. It was with considerable difficulty that I won him over to the assumption of a dress more like a prosperous farmer's; and we arranged that he should cut his hair close and wear a little powder. Lastly, as he had not yet been seen by the laundress or her niece, he was to keep himself out of their view until his change of dress was made.

It would seem a simple matter to decide on these precautions; but in my dazed, not to say distracted, state, it took so long that I did not get out to further them until two or three in the afternoon. He was to remain shut up in the chambers while I was gone, and was on no account to open the door.

There being to my knowledge a respectable lodging-house in Essex Street, the back of which looked into the Temple, and was almost within hail of my windows, I first of all repaired to that house, and was so fortunate as to secure the second floor for Mr. Provis. I then went from shop to shop, making such purchases as were necessary to the change in his appearance. This business transacted, I turned my face on my own account, to Little Britain. Mr. Jaggers was at his desk, but, seeing me enter, got up immediately and stood before his fire.

"Now, Pip," said he, "be careful."

"I will, sir," I returned. For I had thought well of what I was going to say coming along.

"Don't commit yourself," said Mr. Jaggers, "and don't commit anyone. You understand—anyone. Don't tell me anything: I don't want to know anything; I am not curious."

Of course I saw that he knew the man was come.

"I merely want, Mr. Jaggers," said I, "to assure myself that what I have been told is true, I have no hope of its being untrue, but at least I may verify it."

Mr. Jaggers nodded. "But did you say 'told,' or 'informed?' " he asked me, with his head on one side, and not looking at me, but looking in a listening way at the floor. "Told would seem to imply verbal communication. You can't have verbal communication with a man in New South Wales."

"I will say informed, Mr. Jaggers."

"Good."

"I have been informed by a person named Abel Magwitch that he is the benefactor so long unknown to me."

"That is the man," said Mr. Jaggers, "—in New South Wales."

"And only he?" said I.

"And only he," said Mr. Jaggers.

"I am not so unreasonable, sir, as to think you at all responsible for my mistakes and wrong conclusions; but I always supposed it was Miss Havisham."

"As you say, Pip," returned Mr. Jaggers, turning his eyes upon me coolly, and taking a bite at his forefinger, "I am not at all responsible for that."

"And yet it looked so like it, sir," I pleaded, with a miserable heart.

"Not a particle of evidence, Pip," said Mr. Jaggers, shaking his head and gathering up his skirts. "Take nothing on its looks; take everything on evidence. There's no better rule."

"I have no more to say," said I, with a sigh, after standing downcast for a little while. "I have verified my information, and there an end."

"And Magwitch—in New South Wales—having at last disclosed himself," said Mr. Jaggers, "you will comprehend, Pip, how rigidly throughout my communication with you I have always adhered to the strict line of fact. There has never been the least departure from the strict line of fact. You are quite aware of that?"

"Quite, sir."

"I communicated to Magwitch—in New South Wales—when he first wrote to me—from New South Wales—the caution that he must not expect me ever to deviate from the strict line of fact. I also communicated to him another caution. He appeared to me to have obscurely hinted in his letter at some distant idea of seeing you in England here. I cautioned him that I must hear no more of that; that he was not likely to obtain a pardon; that he was expatriated for the term of his natural life; and that his presenting himself in this country would be an act of felony, rendering him liable to the extreme penalty of the law. I gave Magwitch that caution," said Mr. Jaggers, looking hard at me; "I wrote it to New South Wales. He guided himself by it, no doubt."

"No doubt," said I.

"I have been informed by Wemmick," pursued Mr. Jaggers, still looking hard at me, "that he has received a letter, under date Portsmouth, from a colonist of the name of Purvis, or—"

"Or Provis," I suggested.

"Or Provis—thank you, Pip. Perhaps it *is* Provis? Perhaps you know it's Provis?"

"Yes," said I.

"Just so. A letter, under date Portsmouth, from a colonist of the name of Provis, asking for the particulars of your address, on behalf of Magwitch. Wemmick sent him the particulars, I understand, by return of post. Probably it is through Provis that you have received the explanation of Magwitch—in New South Wales?"

"It came through Provis," I replied.

"Good day, Pip," said Mr. Jaggers, offering his hand; "glad to have seen you. In writing by post to Magwitch—in New South Wales—or in communicating with him through Provis, have the goodness to mention that the particulars and vouchers of our long account shall be sent to you, together with the balance; for there is still a balance remaining in my charge. Good day, Pip!"

We shook hands, and he looked hard at me as long as he could see me. I turned at the door, and he was still looking hard at me, while the two vile casts on the shelf seemed to be trying to get their eyelids open, and to force out of their swollen throats, "Oh, what a man he is!"

Wemmick was out, and though he had been at his desk he could have done nothing for me. I went straight back to the Temple, where I found the terrible Provis drinking rum-and-water and smoking Negro-head in safety.

Next day the clothes I had ordered all came home, and he put them on. Whatever he put on became him less (it dismally seemed to me) than what he had worn before. To my thinking, there was something in him that made it hopeless to attempt to disguise him. The more I dressed him, and the better I dressed him, the more he looked like the slouching fugitive on the marshes. This effect on my anxious fancy was partly referable, no doubt, to his old face and manner growing more familiar to me; but I believe, too, that he dragged one of his legs as if there were still a weight of iron on it, and that from head to foot there was Convict in the very grain of the man.

The influences of his solitary hut-life were upon him besides, and gave him a savage air that no dress could tame; added to these were the influences of his subsequent branded life among men, and crowning all, his consciousness that he was dodging and hiding now. In all his ways of sitting and standing, and eating and drinking—of brooding about in a high-shouldered reluctant style—of taking out his great horn-handled jackknife and wiping it on his legs and cutting his food—of lifting light glasses and cups to his lips as if they were great pannikins—of chopping a wedge off his bread, and soaking up with it the last fragments of gravy round and round his plate, as if to make the most of an allowance, and then drying his finger-ends on it, and then swallowing it—in these ways and a thousand other small nameless instances arising every minute in the day, there was Prisoner, Felon, Bondsman, plain as plain could be.

It had been his own idea to wear that touch of powder, and I had conceded the powder after overcoming the shorts. But I can compare the effect of it, when on, to nothing but the probable effect of rouge upon the dead; so awful was the manner in which everything in him that it was most desirable to repress started through that thin layer of pretense, and seemed to come blazing out at the crown of his head. It was abandoned as soon as tried, and he wore his grizzled hair cut short.

Words cannot tell what a sense I had, at the same time, of the dreadful mystery that he was to me. When he fell asleep of an evening, with his knotted hands clenching the sides of the easychair, and his bald head tattooed with deep wrinkles falling forward on his breast, I would sit and look at him, wondering what he had done, loading him with all the crimes in the Calendar, until the impulse was powerful on me to start up and fly from him. Every hour so increased my abhorrence of him that I even think I might have yielded to this impulse in the first agonies of being so haunted, notwithstanding all he had done for me, and the risk he ran, but for the knowledge that Herbert must soon come back. Once I actually did start out of bed in the night, and begin to dress myself in my worst clothes, hurriedly intending to leave him there with everything else I possessed, and enlist for India as a private soldier.

I doubt if a ghost could have been more terrible to me, up in those lonely rooms in the long evenings and long nights, with the wind and the rain always rushing by. A ghost could not have been taken and hanged on my account, and the consideration that he could be, and the dread that he would be, were no small addition to my horrors. When he was not asleep or playing a complicated kind of Patience with a ragged pack of cards of his own—a game that I never saw before or since, and in which he recorded his winnings by sticking his jackknife into the table—when he was not engaged in either of these pursuits he would ask me to read to him—"Some French, dear boy!" While I complied, he, not comprehending a single word, would stand before the fire surveying me with the air of an Exhibitor, and I would see him, between the fingers of the hand with which I shaded my face, appealing in dumb show to the furniture to take notice of my proficiency. The imaginary student pursued by the mis-shapen creature he had impiously made was not more wretched than I, pursued by the creature who had made me, and recoiling from him with a stronger repulsion the more he admired me and the fonder he was of me.

This is written of, I am sensible, as if it had lasted a year. It lasted about five days. Expecting Herbert all the time, I dared not go out, except when I took Provis for an airing after dark. At length, one evening when dinner was over and I had dropped into a slumber, quite worn out—for my nights had been agitated and my rest broken by fearful dreams—I was roused by the wel-come footstep on the staircase. Provis, who had been asleep too, staggered up at the noise I made, and in an instant I saw his jackknife shining in his hand.

"Steady! It's Herbert!" I said; and Herbert came bursting in, with the airy freshness of six hundred miles of France upon him.

"Handel, my dear fellow, how are you, and again how *are* you, and again how *are* you? I seem to have been gone a twelvemonth! Why, so I must have been, for you have grown quite thin and pale! Handel, my—Halloa! I beg your pardon."

He was stopped in his rattling on and in his shaking hands with me by seeing Provis. Provis, regarding him with a fixed attention, was slowly putting up his jackknife, and groping in another pocket for something else.

"Herbert, my dear friend," said I, shutting the double doors, while Her-bert stood staring and wondering, "something very strange has happened. This is—a visitor of mine."

"It's all right, dear boy!" said Provis, coming forward, with his little clasped black book, and then addressing himself to Herbert. "Take it in your right hand. Lord strike you dead on the spot if ever you split in any way sumever! Kiss it!"

"Do so, as he wishes it," I said to Herbert. So Herbert, looking with a friendly uneasiness at me, complied, and Provis immediately shaking hands with him, said, "Now you're on your oath, you know. And never believe me on mine if Pip don't make a gentleman on you!"

Forty-one

IN VAIN SHOULD I ATTEMPT TO DESCRIBE THE ASTONISHMENT and disquiet of Herbert when he and I and Provis sat down before the fire, and I recounted the whole of the secret. Enough that I saw my own feelings reflected in Herbert's face, and, not least among them, my repugnance toward the man who had done so much for me.

What would alone have set a division between that man and us, if there had been no other dividing circumstance, was his triumph in my story. Saving his troublesome sense of having been "low" on one occasion since his return—on which point he began to hold forth to Herbert the moment my revelation was finished—he had no perception of the possibility of my finding any fault with my good fortune. His boast that he had made me a gentleman, and that he had come to see me support the character on his ample resources, was made for me quite as much as for himself; and that it was a highly agreeable boast to both of us, and that we must both be very proud of it, was a conclusion quite established in his own mind.

"Though, look'ee here, Pip's comrade," he said to Herbert, after having discoursed for some time, "I know very well that once since I come back—for half a minute—I've been low. I said to Pip, I knowed as I had been low. But don't you fret yourself on that score. I ain't made Pip a gentleman, and Pip ain't a going to make you a gentleman, not fur me not to know what's due to ye both. Dear boy, and Pip's comrade, you two may count upon me always having a gen-teel muzzle on. Muzzled I have been since that half a minute when I was betrayed into lowness, muzzled I am at the present time, muzzled I ever will be."

Herbert said, "Certainly," but looked as if there were no specific consolation in this, and remained perplexed and dismayed. We were anxious for the time when he would go to his lodging and leave us together; but he was evidently jealous of leaving us together, and sat late. It was midnight before I took him round to Essex Street, and saw him safely in at his own dark door. When it closed upon him I experienced the first moment of relief I had known since the night of his arrival.

Never quite free from an uneasy remembrance of the man on the stairs, I had always looked about me in taking my guest out after dark, and in bringing him back; and I looked about me now. Difficult as it is in a large city to avoid the suspicion of being watched, when the mind is conscious of danger in that regard, I could not persuade myself that any of the people within sight cared about my movements. The few who were passing passed on their several ways, and the street was empty when I turned back into the Temple. Nobody had come out at the gate with us, nobody went in at the gate with me. As I crossed by the fountain, I saw his lighted back windows looking bright and quiet, and when I stood for a few moments in the doorway of the building where I lived, before going up the stairs, Garden Court was as still and lifeless as the staircase was when I ascended it.

Herbert received me with open arms, and I had never felt before, so blessedly, what it is to have a friend. When he had spoken some sound words of sympathy and encouragement, we sat down to consider the question, What was to be done?

The chair that Provis had occupied still remaining where it had stood—for he had a barrack way with him of hanging about one spot, in one unsettled manner, and going through one round of observances with his pipe and his Negro-head and his jackknife and his pack of cards, and what not, as if it were all put down for him on a slate—I say, his chair remaining where it had stood, Herbert unconsciously took it, but next moment started out of it, pushed it away, and took another. He had no occasion to say after that that he had conceived an aversion for my patron, neither had I occasion to confess my own. We interchanged that confidence without shaping a syllable.

"What," said I to Herbert, when he was safe in another chair, "what is to be done?"

"My poor dear Handel," he replied, holding his head, "I am too stunned to think."

"So was I, Herbert, when the blow first fell. Still, something must be done. He is intent upon various new expenses—horses, and carriages, and lavish appearances of all kinds. He must be stopped, somehow."

"You mean that you can't accept—?"

"How can I?" I interposed, as Herbert paused. "Think of him! Look at him!"

An involuntary shudder passed over both of us.

"Yet I am afraid the dreadful truth is, Herbert, that he is attached to me, strongly attached to me. Was there ever such a fate!"

"My poor dear Handel," Herbert repeated.

"Then," said I, "after all, stopping short here, never taking another penny from him, think what I owe him already! Then again: I am heavily in debt—very heavily for me, who have now no expectations at all—and I have been bred to no calling, and I am fit for nothing."

"Well, well, well!" Herbert remonstrated. "Don't say fit for nothing."

"What am I fit for? I know only one thing that I am fit for, and that is, to go for a soldier. And I might have gone, my dear Herbert, but for the prospect of taking counsel with your friendship and affection."

Of course I broke down there; and of course Herbert, beyond seizing a warm grip of my hand, pretended not to know it.

"Anyhow, my dear Handel," said he, presently, "soldiering won't do. If you were to renounce this patronage and these favors, I suppose you would do so with some faint hope of one day repaying what you have already had. Not very strong that hope if you went soldiering! Besides, it's absurd. You would be infinitely better in Clarriker's house, small as it is. I am working up toward a partnership, you know."

Poor fellow! He little suspected with whose money.

"But there is another question," said Herbert. "This is an ignorant, determined man, who has long had one fixed idea. More than that, he seems to me (I may misjudge him) to be a man of a desperate and fierce character."

"I know he is," I returned. "Let me tell you what evidence I have seen of it." And I told him what I had not mentioned in my narrative; of that encounter with the other convict.

"See, then!" said Herbert; "think of this! He comes here at the peril of his life for the realization of his fixed idea. In the moment of realization, after all his toil and waiting, you cut the ground from under his feet, destroy his idea, and make his gains worthless to him. Do you see nothing that he might do, under the disappointment?"

"I have seen it, Herbert, and dreamed of it ever since the fatal night of his arrival. Nothing has been in my thoughts so distinctly as his putting himself in the way of being taken."

"Then you may rely upon it," said Herbert, "that there would be great danger of his doing it. That is his power over you as long as he remains in England, and that would be his reckless course if you forsook him."

I was so struck by the horror of this idea, which had weighed upon me from the first, and the working out of which would make me regard myself, in some sort, as his murderer, that I could not rest in my chair but began pacing to and fro. I said to Herbert, meanwhile, that even if Provis were recognized and taken in spite of himself, I should be wretched as the cause, however innocently. Yes; even though I was so wretched in having him at large and near me, and even though I would far, far rather have worked at the forge all the days of my life than I would have ever come to this!

But there was no staving off the question, What was to be done?

"The first and the main thing to be done," said Herbert, "is to get him out of England. You will have to go with him, and then he may be induced to go."

"But get him where I will, could I prevent his coming back?"

"My good Handel, is it not obvious that, with Newgate in the next street, there must be far greater hazard in your breaking your mind to him and making him reckless here than elsewhere? If a pretext to get him away could be made out of that other convict, or out of anything else in his life now."

"There, again!" said I, stopping before Herbert, with my open hands held out as if they contained the desperation of the case. "I know nothing of his life. It has almost made me mad to sit here of a night and see him before me, so bound up with my fortunes and misfortunes, and yet so unknown to me, except as the miserable wretch who terrified me two days in my childhood!" Herbert got up, and linked his arm in mine, and we slowly walked to and fro together, studying the carpet.

"Handel," said Herbert, stopping, "you feel convinced that you can take no further benefits from him, do you?"

"Fully. Surely you would, too, if you were in my place?"

"And you feel convinced that you must break with him?"

"Herbert, can you ask me?"

"And you have, and are bound to have, that tenderness for the life he has risked on your account, that you must save him, if possible, from throwing it away. Then you must get him out of England before you stir a finger to extricate yourself. That done, extricate yourself, in Heaven's name, and we'll see it out together, dear old boy."

It was a comfort to shake hands upon it, and walk up and down again, with only that done.

"Now, Herbert," said I, "with reference to gaining some knowledge of his history. There is but one way that I know of. I must ask him point-blank."

"Yes. Ask him," said Herbert, "when we sit at breakfast in the morning." For he had said, on taking leave of Herbert, that he would come to breakfast with us.

With this project formed, we went to bed. I had the wildest dreams concerning him, and woke unrefreshed; I woke, too, to recover the fear which I had lost in the night, of his being found out as a returned transport. Waking, I never lost that fear.

He came round at the appointed time, took out his jackknife, and sat down to his meal. He was full of plans "for his gentleman's coming out strong, and like a gentleman," and urged me to begin speedily upon the pocket-book, which he had left in my possession. He considered the chambers and his own lodging as temporary residences, and advised me to look out at once for "a fashionable crib" in which he could have a "shake down," near Hyde Park. When he had made an end of his breakfast, and was wiping his knife on his leg, I said to him, without a word of preface:

"After you were gone last night I told my friend of the struggle that the soldiers found you engaged in on the marshes when we came up. You remember?"

"Remember!" said he. "I think so!"

"We want to know something about that man—and about you. It is strange to know no more about either, and particularly you, than I was able to tell last night. Is not this as good a time as another for our knowing more?"

"Well!" he said, after consideration. "You're on your oath, you know, Pip's comrade?"

"Assuredly," replied Herbert.

"As to anything I say, you know," he insisted. "The oath applies to all."

"I understand it to do so."

"And look'ee here! Whatever I done, is worked out and paid for," he insisted again.

"So be it."

He took out his black pipe and was going to fill it with Negro-head, when, looking at the tangle of tobacco in his hand, he seemed to think it might perplex the thread of his narrative. He put it back again, stuck his pipe in a buttonhole of his coat, spread a hand on each knee, and, after turning an angry eye on the fire for a few silent moments, looked round at us and said what follows.

"DEAR BOY, AND PIP'S COMRADE. I AM NOT A GOING FUR to tell you my life, like a song or a storybook. But to give it you short and handy, I'll put it at once into a mouthful of English. In jail and out of jail, in jail and out of jail, in jail and out of jail. There, you've got it. That's *my* life pretty much, down to such times as I got shipped off, arter Pip stood my friend.

"I've been done everything to, pretty well—except hanged. I've been locked up, as much as a silver teakettle. I've been carted here and carted there, and put out of this town and put out of that town, and stuck in the stocks, and whipped and worried and drove. I've no more notion where I was born than you have—if so much. I first became aware of myself, down in Essex, a thieving turnips for my living. Summun had run away from me—a man—a tinker—and he'd took the fire with him, and left me very cold.

"I know'd my name to be Magwitch, christen'd Abel. How did I know it? Much as I know'd the birds' names in the hedges to be chaffinch, sparrer, thrush. I might have thought it was all lies together, only as the birds' names come out true, I supposed mine did.

"So fur as I could find there warn't a soul that see young Abel Magwitch, with as little on him as in him, but what caught fright at him, and either drove him off or took him up. I was took up, took up, took up, to that extent that I reg'larly grow'd up took up.

"This is the way it was, that when I was a ragged little creetur as much to be pitied as ever I see (not that I looked in the glass, for there warn't many insides of houses known to me), I got the name of being hardened. 'This is a terrible hardened one,' they says to prison wisitors, picking out me. 'May be said to live in jails, this boy.' Then they looked at me, and I looked at them, and they measured my head, some on 'em—they had better a measured my stomach—and others on 'em giv me tracts what I couldn't read, and made me speeches what I couldn't unnerstand. They always went on agen me about the Devil. But what the Devil was I to do? I must put something into my stomach, mustn't I?—Howsomever, I'm a getting low, and I know what's due. Dear boy, and Pip's comrade, don't you be afeerd of me being low.

"Tramping, begging, thieving, working sometimes when I could—though that warn't as often as you may think, till you put the question whether you would ha' been over-ready to give me work yourselves—a bit of a poacher, a bit of a laborer, a bit of a wagoner, a bit of a haymaker, a bit of a hawker, a bit of most things that don't pay and lead to trouble, I got to be a man. A deserting soldier in a Traveler's Rest, what lay hid up to the chin under a lot of taturs, learnt me to read; and a traveling Dwarf what signed his name at a penny a time learnt me to write. I warn't locked up as often now as formerly, but I wore out my share of key metal still.

"At Epsom races, a matter of twenty years ago, I got acquainted wi' a man whose skull I'd crack wi' this poker, like the claw of a lobster, if I'd got it on this hob. His right name was Compey; and that's the man, dear boy, what you see me pounding in the ditch, according to wot you truly told your comrade arter I was gone last night.

"He set up fur a gentleman, this Compey, and he'd been to a public boarding-school and had learning. He was a smooth one to talk, and was a dab at the ways of gentlefolks. He was good-looking, too. It was the night afore the great race when I found him on the heath, in a booth that I know'd on. Him and some more were sitting among the tables when I went in, and the landlord (which had a knowledge of me, and was a sporting one) called him out, and said, 'I think this is a man that might suit you'—meaning I was.

"Compey, he looks at me very noticing, and I look at him. He has a watch and a chain and a ring and a breast-pin and a handsome suit of clothes.

"'To judge from appearances, you're out of luck,' says Compey to me.

"'Yes, master, and I've never been in it much.' (I come out of Kingston Jail last on a vagrancy committal. Not but what it might have been for something else; but it warn't.)

"'Luck changes,' says Compey; 'perhaps yours is going to change.'

"I says, 'I hope it may be so. There's room.'

"'What can you do?' says Compey.

"'Eat and drink,' I says, 'if you'll find the materials.'

"Compey laughed, looked at me again very noticing, giv me five shillings, and appointed me for next night. Same place.

"I went to Compey, next night, same place, and Compey took me on to be his man and pardner. And what was Compey's business in which we was to go pardners? Compey's business was the swindling, handwriting forging, stolen bank-note passing, and such like. All sorts of traps as Compey could set with his head, and keep his own legs out of and get the profits from and let another man in for, was Compey's business. He'd no more heart than a iron file, he was as cold as death, and had the head of the Devil afore mentioned.

"There was another in with Compey, as was called Arthur—not as being so chrisen'd, but as a surname. He was in a Decline, and was a shadow to look at. Him and Compey had been in a bad thing with a rich lady some years afore, and they'd made a pot of money by it; but Compey betted and gamed, and he'd have run through the king's taxes. So Arthur was a dying, and a dying poor and with the horrors on him, and Compey's wife (which Compey kicked mostly) was a having pity on him when she could, and Compey was a having pity on nothing and nobody.

"I might a took warning by Arthur, but I didn't; and I won't pretend I wos partic'ler—for where 'ud be the good on it, dear boy and comrade? So I begun wi' Compey, and a poor tool I was in his hands. Arthur lived at the top of Compey's house (over nigh Brentford it was), and Compey kept a careful account agen him for board and lodging, in case he should ever get better to work it out. But Arthur soon settled the account. The second or third time as ever I see him, he come a tearing down into Compey's parlor late at night, in only a flannel gown, with his hair all in a sweat, and he says to Compey's wife, Sally, she really is upstairs alonger me now, and I can't get rid of her. She's all in white,' he says, 'wi' white flowers in her hair, and she's awful mad, and she's got a white shroud hanging over her arm, and she says she'll put it on me at five in the morning.'

"Says Compey: 'Why, you fool, don't you know she's got a living body? And how should she be up there, without coming through the door, or in at the window, and up the stairs?'

"'I don't know how she's there,' says Arthur, shivering dreadful with the horrors, 'but she's standing in the corner at the foot of the bed, awful mad. And over where her heart's broke—*you* broke it—there's drops of blood.'

"Compey spoke hardy, but he was always a coward. 'Go up alonger this driveling sick man,' he says to his wife, 'and Magwitch, lend her a hand, will you?' But he never come nigh himself.

"Compey's wife and me took him up to bed agen, and he raved most dreadful. 'Why look at her!' he cries out, 'She a shaking the shroud at me! Don't you see her? Look at her eyes! Ain't it awful to see her so mad?' Next he cries, 'She'll put it on me, and then I'm done for! Take it away from her, take it away!' And then he catched hold of us, and kep on a talking to her, and answering of her, till I half believed I see her myself.

"Compey's wife, being used to him, giv him some liquor to get the horrors off, and by-and-by he quieted. 'Oh, she's gone! Has her keeper been for her?' he says. 'Yes,' says Compey's wife. 'Did you tell him to lock her and bar her in?' 'Yes.' 'And to take that ugly thing away from her?' 'Yes, yes, all right.' 'You're a good creetur'; he says, 'don't leave me, whatever you do, and thank you!'

"He rested pretty quiet till it might want a few minutes of five, and then he starts up with a scream, and screams out, 'Here she is! She's got the shroud again. She's unfolding it. She's coming out of the corner. She's coming to the bed. Hold me both on you—one of each side—don't let her touch me with it. Hah! She missed me that time. Don't let her throw it over my shoulders. Don't let her lift me up to get it round me. She's lifting me up. Keep me down!' Then he lifted himself up hard, and was dead.

"Compey took it easy enough as a good riddance for both sides. Him and me was soon busy, and first he swore me (being ever artful) on my own book—this here little black book, dear boy, what I swore your comrade on.

"Not to go into the things that Compey planned and I done—which 'ud take a week—I'll simply say to you, dear boy, and Pip's comrade, that that man got me into such nets as made me his black slave. I was always in debt to him, always under his thumb, always a working, always a getting into danger. He was younger than me, but he'd got craft, and he'd got learning, and he overmatched me five hundred times told and no mercy. My Missis as I had the hard time wi'—Stop though! I ain't brought *her* in—"

He looked about him in a confused way, as if he had lost his place in the book of his remembrance; and he turned his face to the fire, and spread his hands broader on his knees, and lifted them off and put them on again.

"There ain't no need to go into it," he said, looking round once more. "The time wi' Compey was a'most as hard a time as ever I had; that said, all's said. Did I tell you as I was tried, alone, for misdemeanor, while with Compey?"

I answered, No.

"Well!" he said, "I *was,* and got convicted. As to took up on suspicion, that was twice or three times in the four or five year that it lasted; but evidence was wanting. At last me and Compey was both committed for felony—on a charge of putting stolen notes in circulation—and there was other charges behind. Compey says to me, 'Separate defenses, no communication,' and that was all. And I was so miserable poor that I sold all the clothes I had, except what hung on my back, afore I could get Jaggers.

"When we was put in the dock, I noticed first of all what a gentleman Compey looked, wi' his curly hair and his black clothes and his white pocket-handkerchief, and what a common sort of wretch I looked. When the prosecution opened and the evidence was put short, aforehand, I noticed how heavy it all bore on me, and how light on him. When the evidence was giv in the box, I noticed how it was always me that had come for'ard, and could be swore to, how it was always me that the money had been paid to, how it was always me that had seemed to work the thing and get the profit. But, when the defense come on, then I see the plan plainer; for, says the counselor for Compey, 'My lord and gentlemen, here you have afore you, side by side, two persons as your eyes can separate wide; one, the younger, well brought up, who will be spoke to as such; one, the elder, ill brought up, who will be spoke to as a hardened offender; one, the younger, seldom if ever seen in these here transactions, and only suspected; t'other, the elder, always seen in 'em and always wi' his guilt brought home. Can you doubt, if there is but one in it, which is the one, and, if there is two in it, which is much the worst one?' And such like. And when it come to character, warn't it Compey as had been to school, and warn't it his school-fellows as was in this position and in that, and warn't it him as had been know'd by witnesses in such clubs and societies, and nowt to his disadvantage? And warn't it me as had been tried afore, and as had been know'd up hill and down dale in Bridewells and Lock-Ups? And when it come to speech-making, warn't it Compey as could speak to 'em wi' his face dropping every now and then into his white pocket-handkercher—ah! and wi' verses in his speech, too—and warn't it me as could only say, 'Gentlemen, this man at my side is a most precious rascal?' And when the verdict come, warn't it Compey as was recommended to mercy on account of good character and bad company, and giving up all the information he could agen me, and warn't it me as got never a word but Guilty? And when I says to Compey, 'Once out of this court, I'll smash that face of yourn!' ain't it Compey as prays the Judge to be protected, and gets two turnkeys stood betwixt us? And when we're sentenced, ain't it him as gets seven years and me fourteen, and ain't it him as the Judge is sorry for, because he might a done so well, and ain't it me as the Judge perceives to be a man of wiolent passion, likely to come to worse?"

He had worked himself into a state of great excitement, but he checked it, took two or three short breaths, swallowed as often, and stretching out his hand toward me said, in a reassuring manner, "I ain't a going to be low, dear boy!"

He had so heated himself that he took out his handkerchief and wiped his face and head and neck and hands, before he could go on.

"I had said to Compey that I'd smash that face of his, and I swore Lord smash mine! to do it. We was in the same prison-ship, but I couldn't get at him, for long, though I tried. At last I come behind him and hit him on the cheek to turn him round and get a smashing one at him, when I was seen and seized. The black-hole of that ship warn't a strong one, to a judge of black-holes that could swim and dive. I escaped to the shore, and I was a hiding among the graves there, envying them as was in 'em and all over, when I first see my boy!"

He regarded me with a look of affection that made him almost abhorrent to me again, though I had felt great pity for him.

"By my boy I was giv to understand as Compey was out on them marshes too. Upon my soul, I half believe he escaped in his terror to get quit of me, not knowing it was me as had got ashore. I hunted him down. I smashed his face. 'And now,' says I, 'as the worst thing I can do, caring nothing for myself, I'll drag you back.' And I'd have swum off, towing him by the hair, if it had come to that, and I'd a got him aboard without the soldiers.

"Of course he'd much the best of it to the last—his character was so good. He had escaped when he was made half wild by me and my murderous intentions; and his punishment was light. I was put in irons, brought to trial again, and sent for life. I didn't stop for life, dear boy and Pip's comrade, being here."

He wiped himself again, as he had done before, and then slowly took his tangle of tobacco from his pocket, and plucked his pipe from his buttonhole, and slowly filled it, and began to smoke.

"Is he dead?" I asked, after a silence.

"Is who dead, dear boy?"

"Compey."

"He hopes *I* am, if he's alive, you may be sure," with a fierce look. "I never heerd no more of him."

Herbert had been writing with his pencil in the cover of a book. He softly pushed the book over to me, as Provis stood smoking with his eyes on the fire, and I read in it:

"Young Havisham's name was Arthur. Compey is the man who professed to be Miss Havisham's lover."

I shut the book and nodded slightly to Herbert, and put the book by; but we neither of us said anything, and both looked at Provis as he stood smoking by the fire.

Forty-three

WHY SHOULD I PAUSE TO ASK HOW MUCH OF MY SHRINKING from Provis might be traced to Estella? Why should I loiter on my road, to compare the state of mind in which I had tried to rid myself of the stain of the prison before meeting her at the coach-office, with the state of mind in which I now reflected on the abyss between Estella in her pride and beauty, and the returned transport whom I harbored? The road would be none the smoother for it; the end would be none the better for it: he would not be helped, nor I extenuated.

A new fear had been engendered in my mind by his narrative; or, rather his narrative had given form and purpose to the fear that was already here. If Compey were alive and should discover his return, I could hardly doubt the consequence. That Compey stood in mortal fear of him, neither of the two could know much better than I; and that any such man as that man had been described to be would hesitate to release himself for good from a dreaded enemy, by the safe means of becoming an informer, was scarcely to be imagined.

Never had I breathed, and never would I breathe—or so I resolved—a word of Estella to Provis. But I said to Herbert that, before I could go abroad, I must see both Estella and Miss Havisham. This was when we were left alone on the night of the day when Provis told us his story. I resolved to go out to Richmond next day, and I went.

On my presenting myself at Mrs. Brandley's, Estella's maid was called to tell me that Estella had gone into the country. Where? To Satis House, as usual. Not as usual, I said, for she had never yet gone there without me; when was she coming back? There was an air of reservation in the answer which increased my perplexity, and the answer was that her maid believed she was only coming back at all for a little while. I could make nothing of this, except that it was meant that I should make nothing of it, and I went home again in complete discomfiture.

Another night consultation with Herbert after Provis was gone home (I always took him home, and always looked well about me), led us to the conclusion that nothing should be said about going abroad until I came back from Miss Havisham's. In the meantime, Herbert and I were to consider separately what it would be best to say—whether we should devise any pretense of being afraid that he was under suspicious observation; or whether I, who had never yet been abroad, should propose an expedition. We both knew that I had but to propose anything, and he would consent. We agreed that his remaining many days in his present hazard was not to be thought of.

Next day I had the meanness to feign that I was under a binding promise to go down to Joe; but I was capable of almost any meanness toward Joe or his name. Provis was to be strictly careful while I was gone, and Herbert was to take the charge of him that I had taken. I was to be absent only one night, and, on my return, the gratification of his impatience for my starting as a gentleman on a greater scale was to be begun. It occurred to me then; and as I afterward found to Herbert also, that he might be best got away across the water on that pretense—as, to make purchases, or the like.

Having thus cleared the way for my expedition to Miss Havisham's, I set off by the early morning coach before it was yet light, and was out on the open country-road when the day came creeping on, halting and whimpering and shivering, and wrapped in patches of cloud and rags of mist, like a beggar. When we drove up to the Blue Boar after a drizzly ride, whom should I see come out under the gateway, toothpick in hand, to look at the coach, but Bentley Drummle!

As he pretended not to see me, I pretended not to see him. It was a very lame pretense on both sides; the lamer, because we both went into the coffee-room, where he had just finished his breakfast and where I ordered mine. It was poisonous to me to see him in the town, for I very well knew why he had come there.

Pretending to read a smeary newspaper long out of date which had nothing half so legible in its local news as the foreign matter of coffee, pickles, fish sauces, gravy, melted butter, and wine, with which it was sprinkled all over, as if it had taken the measles in a highly irregular form, I sat at my table while he stood before the fire. By degrees it became an enormous injury to me that he stood before the fire, and I got up, determined to have my share of it. I had to put my hand behind his legs for the poker when I went up to the fireplace to stir the fire, but still pretended not to know him.

"Is this a cut?" said Mr. Drummle.

"Oh!" said I, poker in hand, "it's you, is it? How do you do? I was wondering who it was who kept the fire off."

With that I poked tremendously, and having done so, planted myself side by side with Mr. Drummle, my shoulders squared and my back to the fire.

"You have just come down?" said Mr. Drummle, edging me a little away with his shoulder.

"Yes," said I, edging *him* a little away with *my* shoulder.

"Beastly place," said Drummle. "Your part of the country, I think?"

"Yes," I assented. "I am told it's very like Shropshire."

"Not in the least like it," said Drummle.

Here Mr. Drummle looked at his boots, and I looked at mine; and then Mr. Drummle looked at my boots, and I looked at his.

"Have you been here long?" I asked, determined not to yield an inch of the fire.

"Long enough to be tired of it," returned Drummle, pretending to yawn, but equally determined.

"Do you stay here long?"

"Can't say," answered Mr. Drummle. "Do you?"

"Can't say," said I.

I felt here, through a tingling in my blood, that if Mr. Drummle's shoulder had claimed another hair's-breadth of room, I should have jerked him into the window; equally, that if my own shoulder had urged a similar claim, Mr. Drummle would have jerked me into the nearest box. He whistled a little. So did I.

"Large tract of marshes about here I believe?" said Drummle.

"Yes. What of that?" said I.

Mr. Drummle looked at me, and then at my boots, and then said, "Oh!" and laughed.

"Are you amused, Mr. Drummle?"

"No," said he, "not particularly. I am going out for a ride in the saddle. I mean to explore those marshes for amusement. Out-of-the-way villages there, they tell me. Curious little public houses—and smithies—and that. Waiter!"

"Yes, sir."

"Is that horse of mine ready?"

"Brought round to the door, sir."

"I say. Look here, you sir. The lady won't ride today; the weather won't do."

"Very good, sir."

"And I don't dine, because I am going to dine at the lady's."

"Very good, sir."

Then Drummle glanced at me, with an insolent triumph on his great-jowled face that cut me to the heart, dull as he was, and so exasperated me that I felt inclined to take him in my arms as the robber in the storybook is said to have taken the old lady, and seat him on the fire.

One thing was manifest to both of us, and that was, that until relief came neither of us could relinquish the fire. There we stood, well squared up before it, shoulder to shoulder, and foot to foot, with our hands behind us, not budging an inch. The horse was visible outside in the drizzle at the door, my breakfast was put on table, Drummle's was cleared away, the waiter invited me to begin, I nodded, we both stood our ground.

"Have you been to the Grove since?" said Drummle.

"No," said I, "I had quite enough of the Finches the last time I was there."

"Was that when we had a difference of opinion?"

"Yes," I replied very shortly.

"Come, come! They let you off easily enough," sneered Drummle. "You shouldn't have lost your temper."

"Mr. Drummle," said I, "you are not competent to give advice on that subject. When I lose my temper (not that I admit having done so on that occasion) I don't throw glasses."

"I do," said Drummle.

After glancing at him once or twice in an increased state of smoldering ferocity, I said:

"Mr. Drummle, I did not seek this conversation, and I don't think it an agreeable one."

"I am sure it's not," said he, superciliously, over his shoulder; "I don't think anything about it."

"And therefore," I went on, "with your leave, I will suggest that we hold no kind of conversation in future."

"Quite my opinion," said Drummle, "and what I should have suggested myself, or done—more likely—without suggesting. But don't lose your temper. Haven't you lost enough without that?"

"What do you mean, sir?"

"Wai-ter," said Drummle, by way of answering me.

The waiter reappeared.

"Look here, you sir. You quite understand that the young lady don't ride today, and that I dine at the young lady's?"

"Quite so, sir."

When the waiter had felt my fast-cooling teapot with the palm of his hand, and had looked imploringly at me, and had gone out, Drummle, careful not to move the shoulder next me, took a cigar from his pocket and bit the end off, but showed no sign of stirring. Choking and boiling as I was, I felt that we could not go a word further without introducing Estella's name, which I could not endure to hear him utter; and therefore I looked stonily at the opposite wall, as if there were no one present, and forced myself to silence. How long we might have remained in this ridiculous position it is impossible to say, but for the incursion of three thriving farmers—laid on by the waiter, I am inclined to think—who came into the coffee-room unbuttoning their great-coats and rubbing their hands, and before whom, as they charged at the fire, we were obliged to give way.

I saw him through the window, seizing his horse's mane, and mounting in his blundering brutal manner, and sidling and backing away. I thought he was gone when he came back, calling for a light for the cigar in his mouth, which he had forgotten. A man in a dust-colored dress appeared with what was wanted—I could not have said from where: whether from the inn-yard, or the street, or where not—and as Drummle leaned down from the saddle and lighted his cigar and laughed, with a jerk of his head toward the coffee-room windows, the slouching shoulders and ragged hair of this man, whose back was toward me, reminded me of Orlick.

Too heavily out of sorts to care much at the time whether it were he or not, or after all to touch the breakfast, I washed the weather and the journey from my face and hands, and went out to the memorable old house that it would have been so much the better for me never to have entered, never to have seen.

Forty-four

IN THE ROOM WHERE THE DRESSING-TABLE STOOD AND where the wax-candles burned on the wall, I found Miss Havisham and Estella; Miss Havisham seated on a settee near the fire, and Estella on a cushion at her feet. Estella was knitting, and Miss Havisham was looking on. They both raised their eyes as I went in, and both saw an alteration in me. I derived that from the look they interchanged.

"And what wind," said Miss Havisham, "blows you here, Pip?"

Though she looked steadily at me I saw that she was rather confused. Estella pausing for a moment in her knitting with her eyes upon me, and then going on, I fancied that I read in the action of her fingers, as plainly as if she had told me in the dumb alphabet, that she perceived I had discovered my real benefactor.

"Miss Havisham," said I, "I went to Richmond yesterday to speak to Estella, and finding that some wind had blown *her* here, I followed."

Miss Havisham motioning to me for the third or fourth time to sit down, I took the chair by the dressing-table which I had often seen her occupy. With all that ruin at my feet and about me, it seemed a natural place for me that day.

"What I had to say to Estella, Miss Havisham, I will say before you presently—in a few moments. It will not surprise you, it will not displease you. I am as unhappy as you can ever have meant me to be."

Miss Havisham continued to look steadily at me. I could see in the action of Estella's fingers as they worked that she attended to what I said, but she did not look up.

"I have found out who my patron is. It is not a fortunate discovery, and is not likely ever to enrich me in reputation, station, fortune, anything. There are reasons why I must say no more of that. It is not my secret, but another's."

As I was silent for a while, looking at Estella and considering how to go on, Miss Havisham repeated, "It is not your secret, but another's. Well?"

"When you first caused me to be brought here, Miss Havisham; when I belonged to the village over yonder that I wish I had never left; I suppose I did really come here as any other chance boy might have come—as a kind of servant, to gratify a want or a whim, and to be paid for it?"

"Ay, Pip," replied Miss Havisham, steadily nodding her head; "you did."

"And that Mr. Jaggers—"

"Mr. Jaggers," said Miss Havisham, taking me up in a firm tone, "had nothing to do with it, and knew nothing of it. His being my lawyer, and his being the lawyer of your patron, is a coincidence. He holds the same relation toward numbers of people, and it might easily arise. Be that as it may, it did arise, and was not brought about by anyone."

Anyone might have seen in her haggard face that there was no suppression or evasion so far.

"But when I fell into the mistake I have so long remained in, at least you led me on?" said I.

"Yes," she returned, again nodding steadily, "I let you go on."

"Was that kind?"

"Who am I," cried Miss Havisham, striking her stick upon the floor and flashing into wrath so suddenly that Estella glanced up at her in surprise, "who am I, for God's sake, that I should be kind!"

It was a weak complaint to have made, and I had not meant to make it. I told her so, as she sat brooding after this outburst.

"Well, well, well!" she said. "What else?"

"I was liberally paid for my old attendance here," said I, to soothe her, "in being apprenticed, and I have asked these questions only for my own information. What follows has another (and I hope more disinterested) purpose. In humoring my mistake, Miss Havisham, you punished—practiced on— perhaps you will supply whatever term expresses your intention, without offense—your self-seeking relations?"

"I did," said she. "Why, they would have it so! So would you. What has been my history, that I should be at the pains of entreating either them or you not to have it so? You made your own snares. *I* never made them."

Waiting until she was quiet again—for this, too, flashed out of her in a wild and sudden way—I went on.

"I have been thrown among one family of your relations, Miss Havisham, and have been constantly among them since I went to London. I know them to have been as honestly under my delusion as I myself. And I should be false and base if I did not tell you, whether it is acceptable to you or no, and whether you are inclined to give credence to it or no, that you deeply wrong both Mr. Matthew Pocket and his son Herbert if you suppose them to be otherwise than generous, upright, open, and incapable of anything designing or mean."

"They are your friends," said Miss Havisham.

"They made themselves my friends," said I, "when they supposed me to have superseded them; and when Sarah Pocket, Miss Georgiana, and Mistress Camilla were not my friends, I think."

This contrasting of them with the rest seemed, I was glad to see, to do them good with her. She looked at me keenly for a little while, and then said quietly,

"What do you want for them?"

"Only," said I, "that you would not confound them with the others. They may be of the same blood, but, believe me, they are not of the same nature."

Still looking at me keenly, Miss Havisham repeated:

"What do you want for them?"

"I am not so cunning, you see," I said, in answer, conscious that I reddened a little, "as that I could hide from you, even if I desired, that I do want something. Miss Havisham, if you would spare the money to do my friend Herbert a lasting service in life, but which from the nature of the case must be done without his knowledge, I could show you how."

"Why must it be done without his knowledge?" she asked, settling her hands upon her stick, and her chin upon them, that she might regard me the more attentively.

"Because," said I, "I began the service myself more than two years ago, without his knowledge, and I don't want to be betrayed. Why I fail in my ability to finish it I cannot explain. It is a part of the secret which is another person's and not mine."

She gradually withdrew her eyes from me, and turned them on the fire. After watching it for what appeared in the silence and by the light of the slowly wasting candles to be a long time, she was roused by the collapse of some of the red coals, and looked toward me again—at first vacantly and then with a gradually concentrating attention. All this time Estella knitted on. When Miss Havisham had fixed her attention on me, she said, speaking as if there had been no lapse in our dialogue:

"What else?"

"Estella," said I, turning to her now, and trying to command my trembling voice, "you know I love you. You know that I have loved you long and dearly."

She raised her eyes to my face on being thus addressed, and her fingers plied their work, and she looked at me with an unmoved countenance. I saw that Miss Havisham glanced from me to her, and from her to me.

"I should have said this sooner, but for my long mistake. It induced me to hope that Miss Havisham meant us for one another. While I thought you could not help yourself, as it were, I refrained from saying it. But I must say it now."

Preserving her unmoved countenance, and with her fingers still going, Estella shook her head.

"I know," said I, in answer to that action; "I know. I have no hope that I shall ever call you mine, Estella. I am ignorant what may become of me very soon, how poor I may be, or where I may go. Still, I love you; I have loved you ever since I first saw you in this house."

Looking at me perfectly unmoved and with her fingers busy, she shook her head again.

"It would have been cruel in Miss Havisham, very cruel, to practice on the affections of a poor boy, and to torture me through all these years with a vain hope and an idle pursuit, if she had reflected on the gravity of what she did. But I think she did not. I think that in the endurance of her own suffering she forgot mine, Estella."

I saw Miss Havisham put her hand to her heart and hold it there, as she sat looking by turns at Estella and at me.

"It seems," said Estella, very calmly, "that there are sentiments, fancies—I don't know how to call them—which I am not able to comprehend. When you say you love me, I know what you mean, as a form of words; but nothing more. You address nothing in my breast, you touch nothing there. I don't care for what you say at all. I have tried to warn you of this; now, have I not?"

I said in a miserable manner, "Yes."

"Yes. But you would not be warned, for you thought I didn't mean it. Now, did you not?"

"I thought and hoped you could not mean it. You, so young, untried, and beautiful, Estella! Surely it is not in Nature."

"It is in *my* nature," she returned. And then she added with a stress upon the words, "It is in the nature formed within me. I make a great difference between you and all other people when I say so much. I can do no more."

"Is it not true," said I, "that Bentley Drummle is in town here, and pursuing you?"

"It is quite true," she replied, referring to him with the indifference of utter contempt.

"That you encourage him, and ride out with him, and that he dines with you this very day?"

She seemed a little surprised that I should know it, but again replied, "Quite true."

"You cannot love him, Estella!"

Her fingers stopped for the first time, as she retorted rather angrily, "What have I told you? Do you still think, in spite of it, that I do not mean what I say?"

"You would never marry him, Estella?"

She looked toward Miss Havisham, and considered for a moment with her work in her hands. Then she said, "Why not tell you the truth? I am going to be married to him."

I dropped my face into my hands, but was able to control myself better than I could have expected, considering what agony it gave me to hear her say those words. When I raised my face again there was such a ghastly look upon Miss Havisham's that it impressed me, even in my passionate hurry and grief.

"Estella, dearest, dearest Estella, do not let Miss Havisham lead you into this fatal step. Put me aside forever—you have done so, I well know— but bestow yourself on some worthier person than Drummle. Miss Havisham gives you to him, as the greatest slight and injury that could be done to the many far better men who admire you, and to the few who truly love you. Among those few there may be one who loves you even as dearly, though he has not loved you as long, as I. Take him, and I can bear it better, for your sake!"

My earnestness awoke a wonder in her that seemed as if it would have been touched with compassion, if she could have rendered me at all intelligible to her mind.

"I am going," she said again, in a gentler voice, "to be married to him. The preparations for my marriage are making, and I shall be married soon. Why do you injuriously introduce the name of my mother by adoption? It is my own act."

"Your own act, Estella, to fling yourself away upon a brute?"

"On whom should I fling myself away?" she retorted with a smile. "Should I fling myself away upon the man who would the soonest feel (if people do feel such things) that I took nothing to him? There! It is done. I shall do well enough, and so will he. As to leading me into what you call this fatal step, Miss Havisham would have had me wait, and not marry yet; but I am tired of the life I have led, which has very few charms for me, and I am willing enough to change it. Say no more. We shall never understand each other."

"Such a mean brute, such a stupid brute!" I urged in despair.

"Don't be afraid of my being a blessing to him," said Estella; "I shall not be that. Come! Here is my hand. Do we part on this, you visionary boy— or man?"

"Oh, Estella!" I answered, as my bitter tears fell fast on her hand, do what I would to restrain them; "even if I remained in England and could hold my head up with the rest, how could I see you Drummle's wife!"

"Nonsense," she returned; "nonsense. This will pass in no time."

"Never, Estella!"

"You will get me out of your thoughts in a week."

"Out of my thoughts! You are part of my existence, part of myself. You have been in every line I have ever read since I first came here, the rough common boy whose poor heart you wounded even then. You have been in every prospect I have ever seen since—on the river, on the sails of the ships, on the marshes, in the clouds, in the light, in the darkness, in the wind, in the woods, in the sea, in the streets. You have been the embodiment of every graceful fancy that my mind has ever become acquainted with. The stones of which the strongest London buildings are made are not more real, or more impossible to be displaced by your hands, than your presence and influence have been to me, there and everywhere, and will be. Estella, to the last hour of my life you cannot choose but remain part of my character, part of the little good in me, part of the evil. But in this separation I associate you only with the good, and I will faithfully hold you to that always, for you must have done me far more good than harm, let me feel now what distress I may. God bless you, God forgive you!"

In what ecstasy of unhappiness I got these broken words out of myself I don't know. The rhapsody welled up within me, like blood from an inward wound, and gushed out. I held her hand to my lips some lingering moments, and so left her. But ever afterward I remembered—and soon afterward with stronger reason—that while Estella looked at me merely with incredulous wonder, the spectral figure of Miss Havisham, her hand still covering her heart, seemed all resolved into a ghastly stare of pity and remorse.

All done, all gone! So much was done and gone that when I went out at the gate the light of day seemed of a darker color than when I went in. For a while I hid myself among some lanes and by-paths, and then struck off to walk all the way to London. For I had by that time come to myself so far as to consider that I could not go back to the inn and see Drummle there; that I could not bear to sit upon the coach and be spoken to; that I could do nothing half so good for myself as tire myself out.

It was past midnight when I crossed London Bridge. Pursuing the narrow intricacies of the streets, which at that time tended westward near the Middlesex shore of the river, my readiest access to the Temple was close by the riverside, through Whitefriars. I was not expected till tomorrow, but I had my keys, and if Herbert were gone to bed I could get to bed myself without disturbing him.

As it seldom happened that I came in at that Whitefriars gate after the Temple was closed, and as I was very muddy and weary, I did not take it ill that the night-porter examined me with much attention as he held the gate a little way open for me to pass in. To help his memory I mentioned my name.

"I was not quite sure, sir, but I thought so. Here's a note, sir. The messenger that brought it said would you be so good as read it by my lantern."

Much surprised by the request, I took the note. It was directed to Philip Pip, Esquire, and on the top of the superscription were the words, "PLEASE READ THIS, HERE." I opened it, the watchman holding up his light, and read inside, in Wemmick's writing:

"DON'T GO HOME."

Forty-five

T URNING FROM THE TEMPLE GATE AS SOON AS I HAD READ
the warning, I made the best of my way to Fleet Street, and there got a
late hackney chariot and drove to the Hummums in Covent Garden. In those
times a bed was always to be got there at any hour of the night, and the chamberlain, letting me in at his ready wicket, lighted the candle next in order on
his shelf, and showed me straight into the bedroom next in order on his list.
It was a sort of vault on the ground-floor at the back, with a despotic old
monster of a four-post bedstead in it, straddling over the whole place, putting
one of his arbitrary legs into the fireplace and another into the doorway, and
squeezing the wretched little washing-stand in quite a Divinely Righteous
manner.

As I had asked for a nightlight, the chamberlain had brought me in,
before he left me, the good old constitutional rush-light of those virtuous
days—an object like the ghost of a walking-cane, which instantly broke its
back if it were touched, which nothing could ever be lighted at, and which
was placed in solitary confinement at the bottom of a high tin tower, perfo-
rated with round holes that made a staringly wide-awake pattern on the
walls. When I had got into bed, and lay there foot-sore, weary, and wretched,
I found that I could no more close my own eyes than I could close the eyes of
this foolish Argus. And thus, in the gloom and death of the night, we stared
at one another.

What a doleful night! How anxious, how dismal, how long! There was an
inhospitable smell in the room of cold soot and hot dust, and as I looked up
into the corners of the tester over my head, I thought what a number of blue-
bottle flies from the butchers, and earwigs from the market, and grubs from
the country, must be holding on up there, lying by for next summer. This led
me to speculate whether any of them ever tumbled down, and then I fancied
that I felt light falls on my face—a disagreeable turn of thought, suggesting
other and more objectionable approaches up my back. When I had lain
awake a little while, those extraordinary voices with which silence teems
began to make themselves audible. The closet whispered, the fireplace sighed,
the little washing-stand ticked, and one guitar-string played occasionally in
the chest of drawers. At about the same time the eyes on the wall acquired a
new expression, and in every one of those staring rounds I saw written,
DON'T GO HOME.

Whatever night-fancies and night-noises crowded on me, they never
warded off this DON'T GO HOME. It plaited itself into whatever I thought
of, as a bodily pain would have done. Not long before I had read in the

newspapers how a gentleman unknown had come to the Hummums in the night, and had gone to bed, and had destroyed himself, and had been found in the morning weltering in blood. It came into my head that he must have occupied this very vault of mine, and I got out of bed to assure myself that there were no red marks about; then opened the door to look out into the passages, and cheer myself with the companionship of a distant light, near which I knew the chamberlain to be dozing. But all this time, why I was not to go home, and what had happened at home, and when I should go home, and whether Provis was safe at home, were questions occupying my mind so busily that one might have supposed there could be no more room in it for any other theme. Even when I thought of Estella, and how we had parted that day forever, and recalled all the circumstances of our parting, and all her looks and tones, and the action of her fingers while she knitted—even then I was pursuing, here and there and everywhere, the caution, Don't go home. When at last I dozed, in sheer exhaustion of mind and body, it became a vast shadowy verb which I had to conjugate. Imperative mood, present tense: Do not thou go home, let him not go home, let us not go home, do not ye or you go home, let not them go home; then, potentially: I may not and I cannot go home; and I might not, could not, would not, and should not go home; until I felt that I was going distracted, and rolled over on the pillow, and looked at the staring rounds upon the wall again.

I had left directions that I was to be called at seven; for it was plain that I must see Wemmick before seeing anyone else, and equally plain that this was a case in which his Walworth sentiments only could be taken. It was a relief to get out of the room where the night had been so miserable, and I needed no second knocking at the door to startle me from my uneasy bed.

The Castle battlements arose upon my view at eight o'clock. The little servant happening to be entering the fortress with two hot rolls, I passed through the postern and crossed the drawbridge in her company, and so came without announcement into the presence of Wemmick as he was making tea for himself and the Aged. An open door afforded a perspective view of the Aged in bed.

"Halloa, Mr. Pip!" said Wemmick. "You did come home, then?"

"Yes," I returned; "but I didn't go home."

"That's all right," said he, rubbing his hands. "I left a note for you at each of the Temple gates, on the chance. Which gate did you come to?"

I told him.

"I'll go round to the others in the course of the day and destroy the notes," said Wemmick; "it's a good rule never to leave documentary evidence if you can help it, because you don't know when it may be put in. I'm going to take a liberty with you. *Would* you mind toasting this sausage for the Aged P.?"

I said I should be delighted to do it.

"Then you can go about your work, Mary Anne," said Wemmick to the little servant; "which leaves us to ourselves, don't you see, Mr. Pip?" he added, winking, as she disappeared.

I thanked him for his friendship and caution, and our discourse proceeded in a low tone, while I toasted the Aged's sausage and he buttered the crumb of the Aged's roll.

"Now, Mr. Pip, you know," said Wemmick, "you and I understand one another. We are in our private and personal capacities, and we have been engaged in a confidential transaction before today. Official sentiments are one thing. We are extra official."

I cordially assented. I was so very nervous that I had already lighted the Aged's sausage like a torch, and been obliged to blow it out.

"I accidentally heard yesterday morning," said Wemmick, "being in a certain place where I once took you—even between you and me, it's as well not to mention names when avoidable—"

"Much better not," said I. "I understand you."

"I heard there, by chance, yesterday morning," said Wemmick, "that a certain person not altogether of uncolonial pursuits, and not unpossessed of portable property—I don't know who it may really be—we won't name this person—"

"Not necessary," said I.

"—had made some little stir in a certain part of the world where a good many people go, not always in gratification of their own inclination, and not quite irrespective of the government expense—"

In watching his face I made quite a fire-work of the Aged's sausage, and greatly discomposed both my own attention and Wemmick's; for which I apologized.

"—by disappearing from such place, and being no more heard of thereabouts. From which," said Wemmick, "conjectures had been raised and theories formed. I also heard that you at your chambers in Garden Court, Temple, had been watched, and might be watched again."

"By whom?" said I.

"I wouldn't go into that," said Wemmick, evasively, "it might clash with official responsibilities. I heard it, as I have in my time heard other curious things in the same place. I don't tell it to you on information received. I heard it."

He took the toasting-fork and sausage from me as he spoke, and set forth the Aged's breakfast neatly on a little tray. Previous to placing it before him he went into the Aged's room with a clean white cloth, and tied the same under the old gentleman's chin, and propped him up, and put his night-cap on one side, and gave him quite a rakish air. Then he placed his breakfast before him with great care, and said, "All right, ain't you, Aged P.?" To which the cheerful Aged replied, "All right, John, my boy, all right." As there seemed to be a tacit understanding that the Aged was not in a presentable state, and was therefore to be considered invisible, I made a pretense of being in complete ignorance of these proceedings.

"This watching of me at my chambers (which I have once had reason to suspect)," I said to Wemmick when he came back, "is inseparable from the person to whom you have adverted; is it?"

Wemmick looked very grave. "I couldn't undertake to say that of my own knowledge. I mean, I couldn't undertake to say it was at first. But it either is, or it will be, or it's in great danger of being."

As I saw that he was restrained by fealty to Little Britain from saying as much as he could, and as I knew with thankfulness to him how far out of his way he went to say what he did, I could not press him. But I told him, after a little meditation over the fire, that I would like to ask him a question subject to his answering or not answering, as he deemed right, and sure that his course would be right. He paused in his breakfast, and crossing his arms, and pinching his shirtsleeves (his notion of indoor comfort was to sit without any coat), he nodded to me once, to put my question.

"You have heard of a man of bad character, whose true name is Compey?"

He answered with one other nod.

"Is he living?"

One other nod.

"Is he in London?"

He gave me one other nod, compressed the post-office exceedingly, gave me one last nod, and went on with his breakfast.

"Now," said Wemmick, "questioning being over"—which he emphasized and repeated for my guidance—"I come to what I did after hearing what I heard. I went to Garden Court to find you; not finding you, I went to Clarriker's to find Mr. Herbert."

"And him you found?" said I, with great anxiety.

"And him I found. Without mentioning any names or going into any details, I gave him to understand that if he was aware of anybody—Tom, Jack, or Richard—being about the chambers, or about the immediate neighborhood, he had better get Tom, Jack, or Richard out of the way while you were out of the way."

"He would be greatly puzzled what to do?"

"He *was* puzzled what to do; not the less because I gave him my opinion that it was not safe to try to get Tom, Jack, or Richard too far out of the way at present. Mr. Pip, I'll tell you something. Under existing circumstances there is no place like a great city when you are once in it. Don't break cover too soon. Lie close. Wait till things slacken before you try the open, even for foreign air."

I thanked him for his valuable advice, and asked him what Herbert had done.

"Mr. Herbert," said Wemmick, "after being all of a heap for half an hour, struck out a plan. He mentioned to me as a secret, that he is courting a young lady who has, as no doubt you are aware, a bedridden Pa. Which Pa having been in the Purser line of life, lies abed in a bow-window where he can see the ships sail up and down the river. You are acquainted with the young lady, most probably?"

"Not personally," said I.

The truth was, that she had objected to me as an expensive companion who did Herbert no good, and that when Herbert had first proposed to present me to her she had received the proposal with such very moderate warmth that Herbert had felt himself obliged to confide the state of the case to me, with a view to the passage of a little time before I made her acquaintance. When I had begun to advance Herbert's prospects by stealth, I had been able to bear this with cheerful philosophy; he and his affianced, for their part, had naturally not been very anxious to introduce a third person into their interviews; and thus, although I was assured that I had risen in Clara's esteem, and although the young lady and I had long regularly interchanged messages and remembrances by Herbert, I had never seen her. However, I did not trouble Wemmick with these particulars.

"The house with the bow-window," said Wemmick, "being by the riverside, down the Pool there between Limehouse and Greenwich, and being kept, it seems, by a very hospitable widow who has a furnished upper floor to let, Mr. Herbert put it to me, what did I think of that as a temporary tenement for Tom, Jack, or Richard? Now I thought very well of it, for three reasons I'll give you. That is to say *Firstly*, It's altogether out of all your beats, and is well away from the usual heap of streets great and small. *Secondly*, Without going near it yourself, you could always hear of the safety of Tom, Jack, or Richard, through Mr. Herbert. *Thirdly*, After a while, and when it might be prudent, if you should want to slip Tom, Jack, or Richard on board a foreign packet-boat, there he is—ready."

Much comforted by these considerations, I thanked Wemmick again and again, and begged him to proceed.

"Well, sir! Mr. Herbert threw himself into the business with a will, and by nine o'clock last night he housed Tom, Jack, or Richard—whichever it may be—you and I don't want to know—quite successfully. At the old lodgings it was understood that he was summoned to Dover, and, in fact, he was taken down the Dover road and cornered out of it. Now, another great advantage of all this is, that it was done without you, and when, if anyone was concerning himself about your movements, you must be known to be ever so many miles off and quite otherwise engaged. This diverts suspicion and confuses it; and for the same reason I recommended that even if you came back last night you should not go home. It brings in more confusion, and you want confusion."

Wemmick, having finished his breakfast, here looked at his watch, and began to get his coat on.

"And now, Mr. Pip," said he, with his hands still in the sleeves, "I have probably done the most I can do; but if I can ever do more—from a Walworth point of view, and in a strictly private and personal capacity—I shall be glad to do it. Here's the address. There can be no harm in your going here tonight and seeing for yourself that all is well with Tom, Jack, or Richard, before you go home—which is another reason for your not going home last night. But after you have gone home, don't go back here. You are very welcome, I am sure, Mr. Pip"; his hands were now out of his sleeves, and I was shaking them; "and let me finally impress one important point upon you." He laid his hands upon my shoulders, and added in a solemn whisper: "Avail yourself of this evening to lay hold of his portable property. You don't know what may happen to him. Don't let anything happen to the portable property."

Quite despairing of making my mind clear to Wemmick on this point, I forbore to try.

"Time's up," said Wemmick, "and I must be off. If you had nothing more pressing to do than to keep here till dark, that's what I should advise. You look very much worried, and it would do you good to have a perfectly quiet day with the Aged—he'll be up presently—and a little bit of—you remember the pig?"

"Of course," said I.

"Well; and a little bit of *him.* That sausage you toasted was his, and he was in all respects a first-rater. Do try him, if it is only for old acquaintance sake. Good-bye, Aged Parent!" in a cheery shout.

"All right, John; all right, my boy!" piped the old man from within.

I soon fell asleep before Wemmick's fire, and the Aged and I enjoyed one another's society by falling asleep before it more or less all day. We had loin of pork for dinner, and greens grown on the estate, and I nodded at the Aged with a good intention whenever I failed to do it accidentally. When it was quite dark, I left the Aged preparing the fire for toast; and I inferred from the number of teacups, as well as from his glances at the two little doors in the wall, that Miss Skiffins was expected.

Forty-six

EIGHT O'CLOCK HAD STRUCK BEFORE I GOT INTO THE AIR that was scented, not disagreeably, by the chips and shavings of the long-shore boat builders, and mast, oar, and block makers. All that waterside region of the upper and lower Pool below the bridge was unknown ground to me, and when I struck down by the river, I found that the spot I wanted was not where I had supposed it to be, and was anything but easy to find. It was called Mill Pond Bank, Chinks's Basin; and I had no other guide to Chinks's Basin than the Old Green Copper Rope-Walk.

It matters not what stranded ships repairing in dry docks I lost myself among, what old hulls of ships in course of being knocked to pieces, what ooze and slime and other dregs of tide, what yards of ship-builders and ship-breakers, what rusty anchors blindly biting into the ground though for years off duty, what mountainous country of accumulated casks and timber, how many rope-walks that were not the Old Green Copper. After several times falling short of my destination and as often over-shooting it, I came unexpectedly round a corner upon Mill Pond Bank. It was a fresh kind of place, all circumstances considered, where the wind from the river had room to turn itself round; and there were two or three trees in it, and there was the stump of a ruined windmill, and there was the Old Green Copper Rope-Walk—whose long and narrow vista I could trace in the moonlight, through a series of wooden frames set in the ground, that looked like infirm hay-making rakes which had grown old and lost most of their teeth.

Selecting from the few queer houses upon Mill Pond Bank a house with a wooden front and three stories of bow-windows (not bay-windows, which is another thing), I looked at the plate upon the door, and read there, Mrs. Whimple. That being the name I wanted, I knocked, and an elderly woman of a pleasant and thriving appearance responded. She was immediately deposed, however, by Herbert, with his finger on his lip, who led me into the parlor and shut the door. It was an odd sensation to see his very familiar face established quite at home in that very unfamiliar room and region; and I found myself looking at him, much as I looked at the corner cupboard with the glass and china, the shells upon the chimney-piece, and the colored engravings on the wall, representing the death of Captain Cook, a ship launch, and his Majesty King George the Third in a coachman's wig, leather-breeches, top boots, and profile, on the terrace at Windsor.

"All is well, Handel," said Herbert, "and he is quite satisfied, though eager to see you. My dear girl is with her father; if you'll wait till she comes down I'll make you known to her, and then we'll go upstairs. *That's* her father!"

I had become aware of an alarming growling overhead, and had probably expressed the fact in my countenance.

"I am afraid he is a sad old rascal," said Herbert, smiling, "but I have never seen him. Don't you smell rum? He is always at it."

"At rum?" said I.

"Yes," returned Herbert, "and you may suppose how mild it makes his gout. He persists, too, in keeping all the provisions upstairs in his room, and serving them out. He keeps them on shelves over his head, and *will* weigh them all. His room must be like a chandler's shop."

While he thus spoke, the growling noise became a prolonged roar, and then died away.

"What else can be the consequence," said Herbert, in explanation, "if he *will* cut the cheese? A man with the gout in his right hand—and everywhere else—can't expect to get through a Double Gloucester without hurting himself."

He seemed to have hurt himself very much, for he gave another furious roar.

"To have Provis for an upper lodger is quite a godsend to Mrs. Whimple," said Herbert, "for of course people in general won't stand that noise. A curious place, Handel; isn't it?"

It was a curious place, indeed; but remarkably well kept and clean.

"Mrs. Whimple," said Herbert, when I told him so, "is the best of housewives, and I really do not know what my Clara would do without her motherly help. For Clara has no mother of her own, Handel, and no relation in the world but old Gruffandgrim."

"Surely that's not his name, Herbert?"

"No, no," said Herbert, "that's my name for him. His name is Mr. Barley. But what a blessing it is for the son of my father and mother to love a girl who has no relations, and who can never bother herself, or anybody else, about her family!"

Herbert had told me on former occasions, and now reminded me, that he first knew Miss Clara Barley when she was completing her education at an establishment at Hammersmith, and that on her being recalled home to nurse her father, he and she had confided their affection to the motherly Mrs. Whimple, by whom it had been fostered and regulated with equal kindness and discretion, ever since. It was understood that nothing of a tender nature could possibly be confided to Old Barley, by reason of his being unequal to the consideration of any subject more psychological than Gout, Rum, and Purser's stores.

As we were thus conversing in a low tone while Old Barley's sustained growl vibrated in the beam that crossed the ceiling, the room door opened, and a very pretty slight dark-eyed girl of twenty or so came in with a basket in her hand: whom Herbert tenderly relieved of the basket, and presented, blushing, as "Clara." She really was a most charming girl, and might have passed for a captive fairy whom that truculent Ogre, Old Barley, had pressed into his service.

"Look here," said Herbert, showing me the basket with a smile after we had talked a little; "here's poor Clara's supper, served out every night. Here's her allowance of bread, and here's her slice of cheese, and here's her rum—which I drink. This is Mr. Barley's breakfast for tomorrow, served out to be cooked. Two mutton-chops, three potatoes, some split peas, a little flour, two ounces of butter, a pinch of salt, and all this black pepper. It's stewed up together and taken hot, and it's a nice thing for the gout, I should think!"

There was something so natural and winning in Clara's resigned way of looking at these stores in detail, as Herbert pointed them out, and something so confiding, loving, and innocent in her modest manner of yielding herself to Herbert's embracing arm—and something so gentle in her, so much needing protection on Mill Pond Bank, by Chinks's Basin and the Old Green Copper Rope-Walk, with Old Barley growling in the beam—that I would not have undone the engagement between her and Herbert for all the money in the pocket-book I had never opened.

I was looking at her with pleasure and admiration when suddenly the growl swelled into a roar again, and a frightful bumping noise was heard above, as if a giant with a wooden leg were trying to bore it through the ceiling to come at us. Upon this Clara said to Herbert, "Papa wants me, darling!" and ran away.

"There's an unconscionable old shark for you!" said Herbert. "What do you suppose he wants now, Handel?"

"I don't know," said I. "Something to drink?"

"That's it!" cried Herbert, as if I had made a guess of extraordinary merit. "He keeps his grog ready-mixed in a little tub on the table. Wait a moment, and you'll hear Clara lift him up to take some. There he goes!" Another roar, with a prolonged shake at the end. "Now," said Herbert, as it was succeeded by silence, "he's drinking. Now," said Herbert, as the growl resounded in the beam once more, "he's down again on his back!"

Clara returned soon afterward, Herbert accompanied me upstairs to see our charge. As we passed Mr. Barley's door he was heard hoarsely muttering within, in a strain that rose and fell like wind, the following Refrain; in which I substitute good wishes for something quite the reverse.

"Ahoy! Bless your eyes, here's old Bill Barley! Here's old Bill Barley, bless your eyes! Here's old Bill Barley on the flat of his back, by the Lord! Lying on the flat of his back, like a drifting old dead flounder, here's your old Bill Barley, bless your eyes! Ahoy! Bless you!"

In this strain of consolation, Herbert informed me the invisible Barley would commune with himself by the day and night together; often, while it was light, having at the same time one eye at a telescope which was fitted on his bed for the convenience of sweeping the river.

In his two cabin rooms at the top of the house, which were fresh and airy, and in which Mr. Barley was less audible than below, I found Provis comfortably settled. He expressed no alarm, and seemed to feel none that was worth mentioning; but it struck me that he was softened—indefinably, for I could not have said how, and could never afterward recall how, when I tried; but certainly.

The opportunity that the day's rest had given me for reflection had resulted in my fully determining to say nothing to him respecting Compey. For anything I knew, his animosity toward the man might otherwise lead to his seeking him out and rushing on his own destruction. Therefore, when Herbert and I sat down with him by his fire, I asked him first of all whether he relied on Wemmick's judgment and sources of information?

"Ay, ay, dear boy!" he answered, with a grave nod, "Jaggers's knows."

"Then I have talked with Wemmick," said I, "and have come to tell you what caution he gave me, and what advice."

This I did accurately, with the reservation just mentioned; and I told him how Wemmick had heard, in Newgate prison (whether from officers or prisoners I could not say), that he was under some suspicion, and that my chambers had been watched; how Wemmick had recommended his keeping close for a time, and my keeping away from him; and what Wemmick had said about getting him abroad. I added that, of course, when the time came, I should go with him, or should follow close upon him, as might be safest in Wemmick's judgment. What was to follow that I did not touch upon; neither indeed was I at all clear or comfortable about it in my own mind, now that I saw him in that softer condition, and in declared peril for my sake. As to altering my way of living, by enlarging my expenses, I put it to him whether, in our present unsettled and difficult circumstances it would not be simply ridiculous, if it were no worse?

He could not deny this, and indeed was very reasonable throughout. His coming back was a venture, he said, and he had always known it to be a venture. He would do nothing to make it a desperate venture, and he had very little fear of his safety with such good help.

Herbert, who had been looking at the fire and pondering, here said that something had come into his thoughts arising out of Wemmick's suggestion, which it might be worthwhile to pursue. "We are both good watermen, Handel, and could take him down the river ourselves when the right time comes. No boat would then be hired for the purpose, and no boatmen; that would save at least a chance of suspicion, and any chance is worth saving. Never mind the season; don't you think it might be a good thing if you began at once to keep a boat at the Temple stairs, and were in the habit of rowing up and down the river? You fall into that habit, and then who notices or minds? Do it twenty or fifty times, and there is nothing special in your doing it the twenty-first or fifty-first."

I liked this scheme, and Provis was quite elated by it. We agreed that it should be carried into execution, and that Provis should never recognize us if we came below bridge and rowed past Mill Pond Bank. But we further agreed that he should pull down the blind in that part of his window which gave upon the east, whenever he saw us and all was right.

Our conference being now ended, and everything arranged, I rose to go; remarking to Herbert that he and I had better not go home together, and that I would take half an hour's start of him. "I don't like to leave you here," I said to Provis, "though I cannot doubt your being safer here than near me. Good-bye!"

"Dear boy," he answered, clasping my hands, "I don't know when we may meet again, and I don't like Good-bye. Say Good night!"

"Good night! Herbert will go regularly between us, and when the time comes you may be certain I shall be ready. Good night, Good night!"

We thought it best that he should stay in his own rooms, and we left him on the landing outside his door, holding a light over the stair-rail to light us downstairs. Looking back at him, I thought of the first night of his return when our positions were reversed, and when I little supposed my heart could ever be as heavy and anxious at parting from him as it was now.

Old Barley was growling and swearing when we repassed his door, with no appearance of having ceased, or meaning to cease. When we got to the foot of the stairs, I asked Herbert whether he had preserved the name of Provis? He replied, certainly not, and that the lodger was Mr. Campbell. He also explained that the utmost known of Mr. Campbell there was, that he (Herbert) had Mr. Campbell consigned to him, and felt a strong personal interest in his being well cared for and living a secluded life. So when we went into the parlor where Mrs. Whimple and Clara were seated at work, I said nothing of my own interest in Mr. Campbell, but kept it to myself.

When I had taken leave of the pretty, gentle, dark-eyed girl, and the motherly woman who had not outlived her honest sympathy with a little affair of true love, I felt as if the Old Green Copper Rope-Walk had grown quite a different place. Old Barley might be as old as the hills, and might swear like a whole field of troopers, but there were redeeming youth and trust and hope enough in Chinks's Basin to fill it to overflowing. And then I thought of Estella, and of our parting, and went home very sadly.

All things were as quiet in the Temple as ever I had seen them. The windows of the rooms on that side, lately occupied by Provis, were dark and still, and there was no lounger in Garden Court. I walked past the fountain twice or thrice before I descended the steps that were between me and my rooms, but I was quite alone. Herbert coming to my bedside when he came in—for I went straight to bed, dispirited and fatigued—made the same report. Opening one of the windows after that, he looked out into the moonlight, and told me that the pavement was as solemnly empty as the pavement of any Cathedral at that same hour.

Next day I set myself to get the boat. It was soon done, and the boat was brought round to the Temple stairs, and lay where I could reach her within a minute or two. Then I began to go out, as for training and practice; sometimes alone, sometimes with Herbert. I was often out in cold, rain, and sleet, but nobody took much note of me after I had been out a few times. At first I kept above Blackfriars Bridge; but as the hours of the tides changed I took toward London Bridge. It was Old London Bridge in those days, and at certain states of the tide there was a race and fall of water there which gave it a bad reputation. But I knew well enough how to "shoot" the bridge after seeing it done, and so began to row about among the shipping in the Pool, and down to Erith. The first time I passed Mill Pond Bank, Herbert and I were pulling a pair of oars; and, both in going and returning, we saw the blind toward the east come down. Herbert was rarely there less frequently than three times in a week, and he never brought me a single word of intelligence that was at all alarming. Still I knew that there was cause for alarm, and I could not get rid of the notion of being watched. Once received, it is a haunting idea; how many undesigning persons I suspected of watching me it would be hard to calculate.

In short, I was always full of fears for the rash man who was in hiding. Herbert had sometimes said to me that he found it pleasant to stand at one of our windows after dark, when the tide was running down, and to think that it was flowing, with everything it bore, toward Clara. But I thought with dread that it was flowing toward Magwitch, and that any black mark on its surface might be his pursuers, going swiftly, silently, and surely to take him.

Forty-seven

SOME WEEKS PASSED WITHOUT BRINGING ANY CHANGE. WE waited for Wemmick, and he made no sign. If I had never known him out of Little Britain, and had never enjoyed the privilege of being on a familiar footing at the Castle, I might have doubted him; not so for a moment, knowing him as I did.

My worldly affairs began to wear a gloomy appearance, and I was pressed for money by more than one creditor. Even I myself began to know the want of money (I mean of ready money in my own pocket), and to relieve it by converting some easily spared articles of jewelry into cash. But I had quite determined that it would be a heartless fraud to take more money from my patron in the existing state of my uncertain thoughts and plans. Therefore, I had sent him the unopened pocketbook by Herbert, to hold in his own keeping, and I felt a kind of satisfaction—whether it was a false kind or a true, I hardly know—in not having profited by his generosity since his revelation of himself.

As the time wore on, an impression settled heavily upon me that Estella was married. Fearful of having it confirmed, though it was all but a conviction, I avoided the newspapers, and begged Herbert (to whom I had confided the circumstances of our last interview) never to speak of her to me. Why I hoarded up this last wretched little rag of the robe of hope that was rent and given to the winds, how do I know? Why did you who read this, commit that not dissimilar inconsistency of your own last year, last month, last week?

It was an unhappy life that I lived, and its one dominant anxiety, towering over all its other anxieties like a high mountain above a range of mountains, never disappeared from my view. Still, no new cause for fear arose. Let me start from my bed as I would, with the terror fresh upon me that he was discovered; let me sit listening as I would, with dread, for Herbert's returning step at night, lest it should be fleeter than ordinary, and winged with evil news; for all that, and much more to like purpose, the round of things went on. Condemned to inaction and a state of constant restlessness and suspense, I rowed about in my boat, and waited, waited, waited, as I best could.

There were states of the tide when, having been down the river, I could not get back through the eddy-chafed arches and starlings of Old London Bridge; then, I left my boat at a wharf near the Custom-house, to be brought up afterward to the Temple stairs. I was not averse to doing this, as it served to make me and my boat a commoner incident among the waterside people there. From this slight occasion sprang two meetings that I have now to tell of.

One afternoon, late in the month of February, I came ashore at the wharf at dusk. I had pulled down as far as Greenwich with the ebb tide, and had turned with the tide. It had been a fine bright day, but had become foggy as the sun dropped, and I had had to feel my way back among the shipping pretty carefully. Both in going and returning I had seen the signal in his window, All well.

As it was a raw evening and I was cold, I thought I would comfort myself with dinner at once; and as I had hours of dejection and solitude before me if I went home to the Temple, I thought I would afterward go to the play. The theater where Mr. Wopsle had achieved his questionable triumph was in that waterside neighborhood (it is nowhere now), and to that theater I resolved to go. I was aware that Mr. Wopsle had not succeeded in reviving the Drama, but, on the contrary, had rather partaken of its decline. He had been ominously heard of as a faithful Black, in connection with a little girl of noble birth, and a monkey. And Herbert had seen him as a predatory Tartar, of comic propensities, with a face like a red brick, and an outrageous hat all over bells.

I dined at what Herbert and I used to call a Geographical chop-house—where there were maps of the world in porter-pot rims on every half-yard of the tablecloths, and charts of gravy on every one of the knives—to this day there is scarcely a single chop-house in the Lord Mayor's dominions which is not Geographical—and wore out the time in dozing over crumbs, staring at gas, and baking in a hot blast of dinners. By-and-by I roused myself and went to the play.

There I found a virtuous boatswain in his Majesty's service—a most excellent man, though I could have wished his trowsers not quite so tight in some places and not quite so loose in others—who knocked all the little men's hats over their eyes, though he was very generous and brave, and who wouldn't hear of anybody's paying taxes on any account, though he was very patriotic. He had a bag of money in his pocket, like a pudding in the cloth, and on that property married a young person in bed-furniture with great rejoicings; the whole population of Portsmouth (nine in number at the last Census) turning out on the beach to rub their own hands and shake everybody else's, and sing, "Fill, fill!" A certain dark-complexioned Swab, however, who wouldn't fill, or do anything else that was proposed to him, and whose heart was openly stated (by the boatswain) to be as black as his figurehead, proposed to two other Swabs to get all mankind into difficulties; which was so effectually done (the Swab family having considerable political influence) that it took half the evening to set things right, and then it was only brought about through an honest little grocer with a white hat, black gaiters, and red nose, getting into a clock with a gridiron, and listening, and coming out, and knocking everybody down from behind with the gridiron whom he couldn't confute with what he had overheard. This led to Mr. Wopsle's (who had never been heard of before) coming in with a star and garter on, as a plenipotentiary of great power direct from the Admiralty, to say that the Swabs were all to go to prison on the spot, and that he had brought the boatswain down the Union Jack, as a slight acknowledgment of his public services. The boatswain, unmanned for the first time, respectfully dried his eyes on the Jack, and then cheering up and addressing Mr. Wopsle as Your Honor, solicited permission to take him by the fin. Mr. Wopsle conceding his fin with a gracious dignity, was immediately shoved into a dusty corner while everybody danced a hornpipe; and, from that corner, surveying the public with a discontented eye, became aware of me.

The second piece was the last new grand comic Christmas pantomime, in the first scene of which it pained me to suspect that I detected Mr. Wopsle, with red worsted legs under a highly magnified phosphoric countenance and a shock of red fringe for his hair, engaged in the manufacture of thunderbolts in a mine, and displaying great cowardice when his gigantic master came home, very hoarse, to dinner. But he presently presented himself under worthier circumstances; for, the Genius of Youthful Love being in want of assistance—on account of the parental brutality of an ignorant farmer who opposed the choice of his daughter's heart, by purposely falling upon the object in a flour sack, out of the first floor window—summoned a sententious Enchanter; and he, coming up from the antipodes rather unsteadily, after an apparently violent journey, proved to be Mr. Wopsle in a high-crowned hat, with a necromantic work in one volume under his arm. The business of this enchanter on earth being principally to be talked at, sung at, butted at, danced at, and flashed at with fires of various colors, he had a good deal of time on his hands. And I observed with great surprise that he devoted it to staring in my direction as if he were lost in amazement.

There was something so remarkable in the increasing glare of Mr. Wopsle's eye, and he seemed to be turning so many things over in his mind and to grow so confused, that I could not make it out. I sat thinking of it long after he had ascended to the clouds in a large watch-case, and still I could not make it out. I was still thinking of it when I came out of the theater an hour afterward, and found him waiting for me near the door.

"How do you do?" said I, shaking hands with him as we turned down the street together. "I saw that you saw me."

"Saw you, Mr. Pip!" he returned. "Yes, of course I saw you. But who else was there?"

"Who else?"

"It is the strangest thing," said Mr. Wopsle, drifting into his lost look again; "and yet I could swear to him."

Becoming alarmed, I entreated Mr. Wopsle to explain his meaning.

"Whether I should have noticed him at first but for your being there," said Mr. Wopsle, going on in the same lost way, "I can't be positive; yet I think I should."

Involuntarily I looked round me, as I was accustomed to look round me when I went home; for these mysterious words gave me a chill.

"Oh! he can't be in sight," said Mr. Wopsle. "He went out before I went off. I saw him go."

Having the reason that I had for being suspicious, I even suspected this poor actor. I mistrusted a design to entrap me into some admission. Therefore I glanced at him as we walked on together, but said nothing.

"I had a ridiculous fancy that he must be with you, Mr. Pip, till I saw that you were quite unconscious of him sitting behind you there, like a ghost."

My former chill crept over me again, but I was resolved not to speak yet, for it was quite consistent with his words that he might be set on to induce me to connect these references with Provis. Of course I was perfectly sure and safe that Provis had not been there.

"I dare say you wonder at me, Mr. Pip; indeed I see you do. But it is so very strange! You'll hardly believe what I am going to tell you. I could hardly believe it myself if you told me."

"Indeed?" said I.

"No, indeed. Mr. Pip, you remember in old times a certain Christmas-day, when you were quite a child, and I dined at Gargery's, and some soldiers came to the door to get a pair of handcuffs mended?"

"I remember it very well."

"And you remember that there was a chase after two convicts, and that we joined in it, and that Gargery took you on his back, and that I took the lead, and you kept up with me as well as you could?"

"I remember it all very well." Better than he thought—except the last clause.

"And you remember that we came up with the two in a ditch, and that there was a scuffle between them, and that one of them had been severely handled and much mauled about the face by the other?"

"I see it all before me."

"And that the soldiers lighted torches, and put the two in the center, and that we went on to see the last of them, over the black marshes, with the torchlight shining on their faces—I am particular about that; with the torchlight shining on their faces, when there was an outer ring of dark night all about us?"

"Yes," said I. "I remember all that."

"Then, Mr. Pip, one of those two prisoners sat behind you tonight. I saw him over your shoulder."

"Steady!" I thought. I asked him then, "Which of the two do you suppose you saw?"

"The one who had been mauled," he answered readily, "and I'll swear I saw him! The more I think of him the more certain I am of him."

"This is very curious!" said I, with the best assumption I could put on, of its being nothing more to me. "Very curious indeed!"

I cannot exaggerate the enhanced disquiet into which this conversation threw me, or the special and peculiar terror I felt at Compey's having been behind me "like a ghost." For, if he had ever been out of my thoughts for a few moments together since the hiding had begun, it was in those very moments when he was closest to me; and to think that I should be so unconscious and off my guard after all my care, was as if I had shut an avenue of a hundred doors to keep him out, and then had found him at my elbow. I could not doubt either that he was there, because I was there, and that however slight an appearance of danger there might be about us, danger was always near and active.

I put such questions to Mr. Wopsle as, When did the man come in? He could not tell me that; he saw me, and over my shoulder he saw the man. It was not until he had seen him for some time that he began to identify him; but he had from the first vaguely associated him with me, and known him as somehow belonging to me in the old village time. How was he dressed? Prosperously, but not noticeably otherwise; he thought in black. Was his face at all disfigured? No, he believed not. I believed not too, for, although in my brooding state I had taken no especial notice of the people behind me, I thought it likely that a face at all disfigured would have attracted my attention.

When Mr. Wopsle had imparted to me all that he could recall or I extract, and when I had treated him to a little appropriate refreshment after the fatigues of the evening, we parted. It was between twelve and one o'clock when I reached the Temple, and the gates were shut. No one was near me when I went in and went home.

Herbert had come in, and we held a very serious council by the fire. But there was nothing to be done, saving to communicate to Wemmick what I had that night found out, and to remind him that we waited for his hint. As I thought that I might compromise him if I went too often to the Castle, I made this communication by letter. I wrote it before I went to bed, and went out and posted it; and again no one was near me. Herbert and I agreed that we could do nothing else but be very cautious. And we were very cautious indeed—more cautious than before, if that were possible—and I, for my part, never went near Chink's Basin, except when I rowed by, and then I only looked at Mill Pond Bank as I looked at anything else.

Forty-eight

THE SECOND OF THE TWO MEETINGS REFERRED TO IN THE last chapter occurred about a week after the first. I had again left my boat at the wharf below bridge; the time was an hour earlier in the afternoon; and, undecided where to dine, I had strolled up into Cheapside, and was strolling along it, surely the most unsettled person in all the busy concourse, when a large hand was laid upon my shoulder by someone overtaking me. It was Mr. Jaggers's hand, and he passed it through my arm.

"As we are going in the same direction, Pip, we may walk together. Where are you bound for?"

"For the Temple, I think," said I.

"Don't you know?" said Mr. Jaggers.

"Well," I returned, glad for once to get the better of him in cross-examination, "I do *not* know, for I have not made up my mind."

"You are going to dine?" said Mr. Jaggers. "You don't mind admitting that, I suppose?"

"No," I returned, "I don't mind admitting that."

"And are not engaged?"

"I don't mind admitting also, that I am not engaged."

"Then," said Mr. Jaggers, "come and dine with me."

I was going to excuse myself, when he added, "Wemmick's coming." So I changed my excuse into an acceptance—the few words I had uttered serving for the beginning of either—and we went along Cheapside and slanted off to Little Britain, while the lights were springing up brilliantly in the shop windows, and the street lamplighters, scarcely finding ground enough to plant their ladders on in the midst of the afternoon's bustle, were skipping up and down and running in and out, opening more red eyes in the gathering fog than my rushlight tower at the Hummums had opened white eyes in the ghastly wall.

At the office in Little Britain there was the usual letter-writing, hand-washing, candle-snuffing, and safe-locking, that closed the business of the day. As I stood idle by Mr. Jagger's fire, its rising and falling flame made the two casts on the shelf look as if they were playing a diabolical game at bopeep with me; while the pair of coarse fat office-candles that dimly lighted Mr. Jaggers as he wrote in a corner, were decorated with dirty winding-sheets, as if in remembrance of a host of hanged clients.

We went to Gerrard Street, all three together, in a hackney-coach: and as soon as we got there dinner was served. Although I should not have thought of making, in that place, the most distant reference by so much as a look to Wemmick's Walworth sentiments, yet I should have had no objection to catching his eye now and then in a friendly way. But it was not to be done. He turned his eyes on Mr. Jaggers whenever he raised them from the table, and was as dry and distant to me as if there were twin Wemmicks, and this was the wrong one.

"Did you send that note of Miss Havisham's to Mr. Pip, Wemmick?" Mr. Jaggers asked, soon after we began dinner.

"No, sir," returned Wemmick: "it was going by post when you brought Mr. Pip into the office. Here it is." He handed it to his principal instead of to me.

"It's a note of two lines, Pip," said Mr. Jaggers, handing it on, "sent up to me by Miss Havisham on account of her not being sure of your address. She tells me that she wants to see you on a little matter of business you mentioned to her. You'll go down?"

"Yes," said I, casting my eyes over the note, which was exactly in those terms.

"When do you think of going down?"

"I have an impending engagement," said I, glancing at Wemmick, who was putting fish into the post-office, "that renders me rather uncertain of my time. At once, I think."

"If Mr. Pip has the intention of going at once," said Wemmick to Mr. Jaggers, "he needn't write an answer, you know."

Receiving this as an intimation that it was best not to delay, I settled that I would go tomorrow, and said so. Wemmick drank a glass of wine and looked with a grimly satisfied air at Mr. Jaggers, but not at me.

"So, Pip! our friend the Spider," said Mr. Jaggers, "has played his cards. He has won the pool."

It was as much as I could do to assent.

"Hah! He is a promising fellow—in his way—but he may not have it all his own way. The stronger will win in the end, but the stronger has to be found out first. If he should turn to, and beat her—"

"Surely," I interrupted, with a burning face and heart, "you do not seriously think that even he is scoundrel enough for that, Mr. Jaggers?"

"I didn't say so, Pip. I am putting a case. If he should turn to and beat her, he may possibly get the strength on his side; if it should be a question of intellect, he certainly will not. It would be chance work to give an opinion how a fellow of that sort will turn out in such circumstances, because it's a toss-up between two results."

"May I ask what they are?"

"A fellow like our friend the Spider," answered Mr. Jaggers, "either beats or cringes. He may cringe and growl, or cringe and not growl; but he either beats or cringes. Ask Wemmick *his* opinion."

"Either beats or cringes," said Wemmick, not at all addressing himself to me.

"So here's to Mrs. Bentley Drummle," said Mr. Jaggers, taking a decanter of choicer wine from his dumbwaiter, and filling for each of us and for himself, "and may the question of supremacy be settled to the lady's satisfaction! To the satisfaction of the lady *and* the gentleman it never will be. Now, Molly, Molly, Molly, Molly, how slow you are today!"

She was at his elbow when he addressed her, putting a dish upon the table. As she withdrew her hands from it she fell back a step or two, nervously muttering some excuse, and a certain action of her fingers as she spoke arrested my attention.

"What's the matter?" said Mr. Jaggers.

"Nothing. Only the subject we were speaking of," said I, "was rather painful to me."

The action of her fingers was like the action of knitting. She stood looking at her master, not understanding whether she was free to go, or whether he had more to say to her and would call her back if she did go. Her look was very intent. Surely, I had seen exactly such eyes and such hands on a memorable occasion very lately!

He dismissed her, and she glided out of the room. But she remained before me, as plainly as if she were still there. I looked at those hands, I looked at those eyes, I looked at that flowing hair; and I compared them with other hands, other eyes, other hair, that I knew of, and with what those might be after twenty years of a brutal husband and a stormy life. I looked again at those hands and eyes of the housekeeper, and thought of the inexplicable feeling that had come over me when I last walked—not alone—in the ruined garden and through the deserted brewery. I thought how the same feeling had come back when I saw a face looking at me, and a hand waving to me, from a stagecoach window; and how it had come back again and had flashed about me like Lightning, when I had passed in a carriage—not alone— through a sudden glare of light in a dark street. I thought how one link of association had helped that identification in the theater, and how such a link, wanting before, had been riveted for me now, when I had passed, by a chance, swift from Estella's name to the fingers with their knitting action, and the attentive eyes. And I felt absolutely certain that this woman was Estella's mother.

Mr. Jaggers had seen me with Estella, and was not likely to have missed the sentiment I had been at no pains to conceal. He nodded when I said the subject was painful to me, clapped me on the back, put round the wine again, and went on with his dinner.

Only twice more did the housekeeper reappear, and then her stay in the room was very short, and Mr. Jaggers was sharp with her. But her hands were Estella's hands, and her eyes were Estella's eyes, and if she had reappeared a hundred times I could have been neither more sure nor less sure that my conviction was the truth.

It was a dull evening, for Wemmick drew his wine when it came round quite as a matter of business—just as he might have drawn his salary when that came round—and with his eyes on his chief, sat in a state of perpetual readiness for cross-examination. As to the quantity of wine, his post-office was as indifferent and ready as any other post-office for its quantity of letters. From my point of view he was the wrong twin all the time and only externally like the Wemmick of Walworth.

We took our leave early, and left together. Even when we were groping among Mr. Jaggers's stock of boots for our hats, I felt that the right twin was on his way back; and we had not gone a half dozen yards down Gerrard Street in the Walworth direction before I found that I was walking arm in arm with the right twin, and that the wrong twin had evaporated into the evening air.

"Well!" said Wemmick, "that's over. He's a wonderful man, without his living likeness; but I feel that I have to screw myself up when I dine with him—and I dine more comfortably unscrewed."

I felt that this was a good statement of the case, and told him so.

"Wouldn't say it to anybody but yourself," he answered. "I know that what is said between you and me goes no further."

I asked him if he had ever seen Miss Havisham's adopted daughter, Mrs. Bentley Drummle? He said no. To avoid being too abrupt, I then spoke of the Aged, and of Miss Skiffins. He looked rather sly when I mentioned Miss Skiffins, and stopped in the street to blow his nose with a roll of the head and a flourish, not quite free from latent boastfulness.

"Wemmick," said I, "do you remember telling me before I first went to Mr. Jagger's private house, to notice that housekeeper?"

"Did I?" he replied. "Ah, I dare say I did. Deuce take me," he added, suddenly, "I know I did. I find I am not quite unscrewed yet."

"A wild beast tamed, you called her," said I.

"And what did *you* call her?" said he.

"The same. How did Mr. Jaggers tame her, Wemmick?"

"That's his secret. She has been with him many a long year."

"I wish you would tell me her story. I feel a particular interest in being acquainted with it. You know that what is said between you and me goes no further."

"Well!" Wemmick replied, "I don't know her story—that is, I don't know all of it. But what I do know, I'll tell you. We are in our private and personal capacities, of course."

"Of course."

"A score of years ago that woman was tried at the Old Bailey for murder, and was acquitted. She was a very handsome young woman, and I believe had some gipsy blood in her. Anyhow, it was hot enough when it was up, as you may suppose."

"But she was acquitted."

"Mr. Jaggers was for her," pursued Wemmick, with a look full of meaning, "and worked the case in a way quite astonishing. It was a desperate case, and it was comparatively early days with him then, and he worked it to general admiration; in fact, it may almost be said to have made him. He worked it himself at the police-office, day after day for many days, contending against even a committal; and at the trial, where he couldn't work it himself, sat under Counsel, and—everyone knew—put in all the salt and pepper. The murdered person was a woman—a woman a good ten years older, very much larger, and very much stronger. It was a case of jealousy. They both led tramping lives, and this woman in Gerrard Street here had been married very young, over the broomstick (as we say), to a tramping man, and was a perfect fury in point of jealousy. The murdered woman—more a match for the man, certainly, in point of years—was found dead in a barn near Hounslow Heath. There had been a violent struggle, perhaps a fight. She was bruised and scratched and torn all over, and had been held by the throat at last and choked. Now there was no reasonable evidence to implicate any person but this woman, and on the improbabilities of her having been able to do it, Mr. Jaggers principally rested his case. You may be sure," said Wemmick, touching me on the sleeve, "that he never dwelt upon the strength of her hands then, though he sometimes does now."

I had told Wemmick of his showing us her wrists that day of the dinner-party.

"Well, sir!" Wemmick went on; "it happened—happened, don't you see?—that this woman was so very artfully dressed from the time of her apprehension that she looked much slighter than she really was; in particular, her sleeves are always remembered to have been so skillfully contrived that her arms had quite a delicate look. She had only a bruise or two about her—nothing for a tramp—but the backs of her hands were lacerated, and the question was, was it with fingernails? Now, Mr. Jaggers showed that she had struggled through a great lot of brambles which were not as high as her face; but which she could not have got through and kept her hands out of; and bits of those brambles were actually found in her skin and put in evidence, as well as the fact that the brambles in question were found on examination to have been broken through, and to have little shreds of her dress and little spots of blood upon them here and there. But the boldest point he made was this. It was attempted to be set up in proof of her jealousy, that she was under strong suspicion of having, at about the time of the murder, frantically destroyed her child by this man—some three years old—to revenge herself upon him. Mr. Jaggers worked that in this way: 'We say these are not marks of fingernails but marks of brambles, and we show you the brambles. You say they are marks of fingernails, and you set up the hypothesis that she destroyed her child. You must accept all consequences of that hypothesis. For anything we know she may have destroyed her child, and the child in clinging to her may have scratched her hands. What then? You are not trying her for the murder of her child; why don't you? As to this case, if you *will* have scratches, we say that, for anything we know, you may have accounted for them, assuming for the sake of argument that you have not invented them?' To sum up, sir," said Wemmick, "Mr. Jaggers was altogether too many for the Jury, and they gave in."

"Has she been in his service ever since?"

"Yes; but not only that," said Wemmick. "She went into his service immediately after her acquittal tamed as she is now. She has since been taught one thing and another in the way of her duties, but she was tamed from the beginning."

"Do you remember the sex of the child?"

"Said to have been a girl."

"You have nothing more to say to me tonight?"

"Nothing. I got your letter and destroyed it. Nothing."

We exchanged a cordial Good night, and I went home, with new matter for my thoughts, yet with no relief from the old.

F o r t y - n i n e

PUTTING MISS HAVISHAM'S NOTE IN MY POCKET, THAT IT might serve as my credentials for so soon reappearing at Satis House, in case her waywardness should lead her to express any surprise at seeing me, I went down again by the coach next day. But I alighted at the Halfway House, and breakfasted there, and walked the rest of the distance; for I sought to get into the town quietly, by the unfrequented ways, and to leave it in the same manner.

The best light of the day was gone when I passed along the quiet echoing courts behind the High Street. The nooks of ruin where the old monks had once had their refectories and gardens, and where the strong walls were now pressed into the service of humble sheds and stables, were almost as silent as the old monks in their graves. The cathedral chimes had at once a sadder and a more remote sound to me, as I hurried on avoiding observation, than they had ever had before; so, the swell of the old organ was borne to my ears like funeral music; and the rooks, as they hovered about the gray tower and swung in the bare high trees of the priory-garden, seemed to call to me that the place was changed, and that Estella was gone out of it forever.

An elderly woman whom I had seen before as one of the servants who lived in the supplementary house across the back courtyard opened the gate. The lighted candle stood in the dark passage within, as of old, and I took it up and ascended the staircase alone. Miss Havisham was not in her own room, but was in the larger room across the landing. Looking in at the door, after knocking in vain, I saw her sitting on the hearth in a ragged chair, close before, and lost in the contemplation of the ashy fire.

Doing as I had often done, I went in, and stood, touching the old chimney-piece, where she could see me when she raised her eyes. There was an air of utter loneliness upon her that would have moved me to pity though she had willfully done me a deeper injury than I could charge her with. As I stood compassionating her, and thinking how in the progress of time I too had come to be a part of the wrecked fortunes of that house, her eyes rested on me. She stared, and said in a low voice, "Is it real!"

"It is I, Pip. Mr. Jaggers gave me your note yesterday, and I have lost no time."

"Thank you. Thank you."

As I brought another of the ragged chairs to the hearth and sat down I remarked a new expression on her face, as if she were afraid of me.

"I want," she said, "to pursue that subject you mentioned to me when you were last here, and to show you that I am not all stone. But perhaps you can never believe, now, that there is anything human in my heart?"

When I said some reassuring words, she stretched out her tremulous right hand, as though she was going to touch me; but she recalled it again before I understood the action, or knew how to receive it.

"You said, speaking for your friend, that you could tell me how to do something useful and good. Something that you would like done, is it not?"

"Something that I would like done, very, very much."

"What is it?"

I began explaining to her that secret history of the partnership. I had not got far into it when I judged from her look that she was thinking in a discursive way of me rather than of what I said. It seemed to be so, for when I stopped speaking many moments passed before she showed that she was conscious of the fact.

"Do you break off," she asked then, with her former air of being afraid of me, "because you hate me too much to bear to speak to me?"

"No, no," I answered, "how can you think so, Miss Havisham! I stopped because I thought you were not following what I said."

"Perhaps I was not," she answered, putting a hand to her head. "Begin again, and let me look at something else. Stay! Now tell me."

She set her hands upon her stick in the resolute way that sometimes was habitual to her, and looked at the fire with a strong expression of forcing herself to attend. I went on with my explanation, and told her how I had hoped to complete the transaction out of my means, but how in this I was disappointed. That part of the subject (I reminded her) involved matters which could form no part of my explanation, for they were the weighty secrets of another.

"So!" said she, assenting with her head, but not looking at me. "And how much money is wanting to complete the purchase?"

I was rather afraid of stating it, for it sounded a large sum. "Nine hundred pounds."

"If I give you the money for this purpose, will you keep my secret as you have kept your own?"

"Quite as faithfully."

"And your mind will be more at rest?"

"Much more at rest."

"Are you very unhappy now?"

She asked this question, still without looking at me, but in an unwonted tone of sympathy. I could not reply at the moment for my voice failed me. She put her left arm across the crutched head of her stick, and softly laid her forehead on it.

"I am far from happy, Miss Havisham; but I have other causes of disquiet than any you know of. They are the secrets I have mentioned."

After a little while she raised her head and looked at the fire again.

"It is noble in you to tell me that you have other causes of unhappiness. Is it true?"

"Too true."

"Can I only serve you, Pip, by serving your friend? Regarding that as done, is there nothing I can do for you yourself?"

"Nothing. I thank you for the question. I thank you even more for the tone of the question. But there is nothing."

She presently rose from her seat, and looked about the blighted room for the means of writing. There were none there, and she took from her pocket a yellow set of ivory tablets, mounted in tarnished gold, and wrote upon them with a pencil in a case of tarnished gold that hung from her neck.

"You are still on friendly terms with Mr. Jaggers?"

"Quite. I dined with him yesterday."

"This is an authority to him to pay you that money to lay out at your irresponsible discretion for your friend. I keep no money here, but if you would rather Mr. Jaggers knew nothing of the matter, I will send it to you."

"Thank you, Miss Havisham; I have not the least objection to receiving it from him."

She read me what she had written, and it was direct and clear, and evidently intended to absolve me from any suspicion of profiting by the receipt of the money. I took the tablets from her hand, and it trembled again, and it trembled more as she took off the chain to which the pencil was attached and put it in mine. All this she did without looking at me.

"My name is on the first leaf. If you can ever write under my name, 'I forgive her,' though ever so long after my broken heart is dust—pray do it!"

"Oh, Miss Havisham," said I, "I can do it now. There have been sore mistakes, and my life has been a blind and thankless one, and I want forgiveness and direction far too much to be bitter with you."

She turned her face to me for the first time since she had averted it, and, to my amazement, I may even add to my terror, dropped on her knees at my feet, with her folded hands raised to me in the manner in which, when her poor heart was young and fresh and whole, they must often have been raised to Heaven from her mother's side.

To see her with her white hair and her worn face kneeling at my feet, gave me a shock through all my frame. I entreated her to rise, and got my arms about her to help her up; but she only pressed that hand of mine which was nearest to her grasp, and hung her head over it and wept. I had never seen her shed a tear before, and, in the hope that the relief might do her good, I bent over her without speaking. She was not kneeling now, but was down upon the ground.

"Oh!" she cried, despairingly. "What have I done! What have I done!"

"If you mean, Miss Havisham, what have you done to injure me, let me answer. Very little. I should have loved her under any circumstances.—Is she married?"

"Yes."

It was a needless question, for a new desolation in the desolate house had told me so.

"What have I done! What have I done!" She wrung her hands, and crushed her white hair, and returned to this cry, over and over again. "What have I done! What have I done!"

I knew not how to answer, or how to comfort her. That she had done a grievous thing in taking an impressionable child to mold into the form that her wild resentment, spurned affection, and wounded pride found vengeance in, I knew full well. But that, in shutting out the light of day, she had shut out infinitely more than that; that, in seclusion, she had secluded herself from a thousand natural and healing influences; that her mind, brooding solitary, had grown diseased, as all minds do and must and will that reverse the appointed order of their Maker, I knew equally well. And could I look upon her without compassion, seeing her punishment in the ruin she was, in her profound unfitness for this earth on which she was placed, in the vanity of sorrow which had become a master mania, like the vanity of penitence, the vanity of remorse, the vanity of unworthiness, and other monstrous vanities that have been curses in this world?

"Until you spoke to her the other day, and until I saw in you a looking-glass that showed me what I once felt myself, I did not know what I had done. What have I done! what have I done!" And so again, twenty, fifty times over, What had she done!

"Miss Havisham," I said, when her cry had died away, "you may dismiss me from your mind and conscience. But Estella is a different case, and if you can ever undo any scrap of what you have done amiss in keeping a part of her right nature away from her, it will be better to do that than to bemoan the past through a hundred years."

"Yes, yes, I know it. But, Pip—my dear!" There was an earnest womanly compassion for me in her new affection. "My dear! Believe this: when she first came to me, I meant to save her from misery like my own. At first I meant no more."

"Well, well!" said I. "I hope so."

"But as she grew, and promised to be very beautiful, I gradually did worse, and with my praises, and with my jewels, and with my teachings, and with this figure of myself always before her a warning to back and point my lessons, I stole her heart away and put ice in its place."

"Better," I could not help saying, "to have left her a natural heart, even to be bruised or broken."

With that Miss Havisham looked distractedly at me for a while and then burst out again, What had she done!

"If you knew all my story," she pleaded, "you would have some compassion for me and a better understanding of me."

"Miss Havisham," I answered, as delicately as I could, "I believe I may say that I do know your story, and have known it ever since I first left this neighborhood. It has inspired me with great commiseration, and I hope I understand it and its influences. Does what has passed between us give me any excuse for asking you a question relative to Estella? Not as she is, but as she was when she first came here?"

She was seated on the ground, with her arms on the ragged chair, and her head leaning on them. She looked full at me when I said this, and replied, "Go on."

"Whose child was Estella?"

She shook her head.

"You don't know?"

She shook her head again.

"But Mr. Jaggers brought her here, or sent her here?"

"Brought her here."

"Will you tell me how that came about?"

She answered in a low whisper and with caution: "I had been shut up in these rooms a long time (I don't know how long; you know what time the clocks keep here), when I told him that I wanted a little girl to rear and save from my fate. I had first seen him when I sent for him to lay this place waste for me; having read of him in the newspapers, before I and the world parted.

He told me that he would look about him for such an orphan child. One night he brought her here asleep, and I called her Estella."

"Might I ask her age then?"

"About three. She herself knows nothing, but that she was left an orphan and I adopted her."

So convinced I was of that woman's being her mother, that I wanted no evidence to establish the fact in my own mind. But to any mind, I thought, the connection here was clear and straight.

What more could I hope to do by prolonging the interview? I had succeeded on behalf of Herbert, Miss Havisham had told me all she knew of Estella, I had said and done what I could to ease her mind. No matter with what other words we parted; we parted.

Twilight was closing in when I went downstairs into the natural air. I called to the woman who had opened the gate when I entered that I would not trouble her just yet, but would walk round the place before leaving. For I had a presentiment that I should never be there again, and I felt that the dying light was suited to my last view of it.

By the wilderness of casks that I had walked on long ago, and on which the rain of years had fallen since, rotting them in many places, and leaving miniature swamps and pools of water upon those that stood on end, I made my way to the ruined garden. I went all around it; round by the corner where Herbert and I had fought our battle; round by the paths where Estella and I had walked. So cold, so lonely, so dreary all!

Taking the brewery on my way back, I raised the rusty latch of a little door at the garden end of it, and walked through. I was going out at the opposite door—not easy to open now, for the damp wood had started and swelled, and the hinges were yielding, and the threshold was encumbered with a growth of fungus—when I turned my head to look back. A childish association revived with wonderful force in the moment of the slight action, and I fancied that I saw Miss Havisham hanging to the beam. So strong was the impression that I stood under the beam shuddering from head to foot before I knew it was a fancy—though to be sure I was there but an instant.

The mournfulness of the place and time, and the great terror of this illusion, though it was but momentary, caused me to feel an indescribable awe as I came out between the open wooden gates where I had once wrung my hair after Estella had wrung my heart. Passing on into the front courtyard, I hesitated whether to call the woman to let me out at the locked gate of which she had the key, or first go upstairs and assure myself that Miss Havisham was as safe and well as I had left her. I took the latter course and went up.

I looked in the room where I had left her, and I saw her seated in the ragged chair upon the hearth close to the fire, with her back toward me. In the moment when I was withdrawing my head to go quietly away I saw a great flaming light spring up. In the same moment I saw her running at me, shrieking, with a whirl of fire blazing all about her, and soaring at least as many feet above her head as she was high.

I had a double-caped great-coat on, and over my arm another thick coat. That I got them off, closed with her, threw her down, and got them over her; that I dragged the great cloth from the table for the same purpose, and with it dragged down the heap of rottenness in the midst, and all the ugly things that sheltered there; that we were on the ground struggling madly like desperate enemies, and that the closer I covered her, the more wildly she shrieked and tried to free herself; that this occurred I knew through the result, but not through anything I felt, or thought, or knew I did. I knew nothing until I knew that we were on the floor by the great table, and that patches of tinder yet alight were floating in the smoky air, which a moment ago, had been her faded bridal dress.

Then I looked round and saw the disturbed beetles and spiders running away over the floor, and the servants coming in with breathless cries at the door. I still held her forcibly down with all my strength, like a prisoner who might escape; and I doubt if I even knew who she was, or why we had struggled, or that she had been in flames, or that the flames were out, until I saw the patches of tinder that had been her garments no longer alight but falling in a black shower around us.

She was insensible, and I was afraid to have her moved or even touched. Assistance was sent for, and I held her until it came, as if I unreasonably fancied (I think I did) that if I let her go the fire would break out again and consume her. When I got up, on the surgeon's coming to her with other aid, I was astonished to see that both my hands were burned, for I had no knowledge of it through the sense of feeling.

On examination it was pronounced that she had received serious hurts, but that they of themselves were far from hopeless; the danger lay, however, mainly in the nervous shock. By the surgeon's directions her bed was carried into that room and laid upon the great table, which happened to be well suited to the dressing of her injuries. When I saw her again, an hour afterward, she lay indeed where I had seen her strike her stick, and heard her say she would lie one day.

Though every vestige of her dress was burned, as they told me, she still had something of her old ghastly bridal appearance; for they had covered her to the throat with white cotton-wool, and as she lay with a white sheet loosely overlying that, the phantom air of something that had been and was changed was still upon her.

I found, on questioning the servants, that Estella was in Paris, and I got a promise from the surgeon that he would write to her by the next post. Miss Havisham's family I took upon myself; intending to communicate with Mr. Matthew Pocket only, and leave him to do as he liked about informing the rest. This I did next day, through Herbert, as soon as I returned to town.

There was a stage that evening when she spoke collectedly of what had happened, though with a certain terrible vivacity. Toward midnight she began to wander in her speech, and after that it gradually set in that she said innumerable times in a low, solemn voice, "What have I done! What have I done!" And then, "When she first came, I meant to save her from misery like mine." And then, "Take the pencil and write under my name, 'I forgive her!'" She never changed the order of these three sentences, but she sometimes left out a word in one or other of them; never putting in another word, but always leaving a blank, and going on to the next word.

As I could do no service there, and as I had, nearer home, that pressing reason for anxiety and fear which even her wanderings could not drive out of my mind, I decided in the course of the night that I would return by the early morning coach; walking on a mile or so, and being taken up clear of the town. At about six o'clock of the morning, therefore, I leaned over her and touched her lips with mine, just as they said, not stopping for being touched, "Take the pencil and write under my name, 'I forgive her.'"

It was the first and the last time that I ever touched her in that way. And I never saw her more.

Fifty

MY HANDS HAD BEEN DRESSED TWICE OR THRICE IN THE night, and again in the morning. My left arm was a good deal burned to the elbow, and less severely as high as the shoulder; it was very painful, but the flames had set in that direction, and I felt thankful it was no worse. My right hand was not so badly burned but that I could move the fingers. It was bandaged, of course, but much less inconveniently than my left hand and arm; those I carried in a sling; and I could only wear my coat like a cloak, loose over my shoulders and fastened at the neck. My hair had been caught by the fire, but not my head or face.

When Herbert had been down to Hammersmith and seen his father, he came back to me at our chambers, and devoted the day to attending on me. He was the kindest of nurses, and at stated times took off the bandages, and steeped them in the cooling liquid that was kept ready, and put them on again with a patient tenderness that I was deeply grateful for.

At first, as I lay quiet on the sofa, I found it painfully difficult, I might say impossible, to get rid of the impression of the glare of the flames, their hurry and noise, and the fierce burning smell. If I dozed for a minute, I was

awakened by Miss Havisham's cries, and by her running at me with all that
height of fire above her head. This pain of the mind was much harder to
strive against than any bodily pain I suffered; and Herbert, seeing that, did
his utmost to hold my attention engaged.

Neither of us spoke of the boat, but we both thought of it. That was
made apparent by our avoidance of the subject, and by our agreeing—without agreement—to make my recovery of the use of my hands a question of so
many hours, not of so many weeks.

My first question when I saw Herbert had been, of course, whether all
was well down the river? As he replied in the affirmative, with perfect confidence and cheerfulness, we did not resume the subject until the day was
wearing away. But then, as Herbert changed the bandages, more by the light
of the fire than by the outer light, he went back to it spontaneously.

"I sat with Provis last night, Handel, two good hours."

"Where was Clara?"

"Dear little thing!" said Herbert. "She was up and down with Gruffandgrim all the evening. He was perpetually pegging at the floor the moment she
left his sight. I doubt if he can hold out long, though. What with rum and pepper—and pepper and rum—I should think his pegging must be nearly over."

"And then you will be married, Herbert?"

"How can I take care of the dear child otherwise? Lay your arm out upon
the back of the sofa, my dear boy, and I'll sit down here, and get the bandage
off so gradually that you shall not know when it comes. I was speaking of
Provis. Do you know, Handel, he improves?"

"I said to you I thought he was softened, when I last saw him."

"So you did. And so he is. He was very communicative last night, and
told me more of his life. You remember his breaking off here about some
woman that he had had great trouble with. Did I hurt you?"

I had started, but not under his touch. His words had given me a start.

"I had forgotten that, Herbert, but I remember it now you speak of it."

"Well! He went into that part of his life, and a dark, wild part it is. Shall
I tell you? Or would it worry you just now?"

"Tell me by all means. Every word!"

Herbert bent forward to look at me more nearly, as if my reply had been
rather more hurried or more eager than he could quite account for. "Your
head is cool?" he said, touching it.

"Quite," said I. "Tell me what Provis said, my dear Herbert."

"It seems," said Herbert, "—there's a bandage off most charmingly, and
now comes the cool one—makes you shrink at first, my poor dear fellow,
don't it? but it will be comfortable presently—it seems that the woman was a
young woman, and a jealous woman, and a revengeful woman; revengeful,
Handel, to the last degree."

"To what last degree?"

"Murder. Does it strike too cold on that sensitive place?"

"I don't feel it. How did she murder? Whom did she murder?"

"Why, the deed may not have merited quite so terrible a name," said Herbert, "but she was tried for it, and Jaggers defended her, and the reputation of that defense first made his name known to Provis. It was another and a stronger woman who was the victim, and there had been a struggle—in a barn. Who began it, or how fair it was, or how unfair, may be doubtful; but how it ended is certainly not doubtful, for the victim was found throttled."

"Was the woman brought in guilty?"

"No; she was acquitted. My poor Handel, I hurt you!"

"It is impossible to be gentler, Herbert. Yes? What else?"

"This acquitted young woman and Provis," said Herbert, "had a little child: a little child of whom Provis was exceedingly fond. On the evening of the very night when the object of her jealousy was strangled, as I tell you, the young woman presented herself before Provis for one moment, and swore that she would destroy the child (which was in her possession) and he should never see it again; then she vanished. There's the worst arm comfortably in the sling once more, and now there remains but the right hand, which is a far easier job. I can do it better by this light than by a stronger, for my hand is steadiest when I don't see the poor blistered patches too distinctly.—You don't think your breathing is affected, my dear boy? You seem to breathe quickly."

"Perhaps I do, Herbert. Did the woman keep her oath?"

"There comes the darkest part of Provis's life. She did."

"That is, he says she did."

"Why, of course, my dear boy," returned Herbert, in a tone of surprise, and again bending forward to get a nearer look at me. "He says it all. I have no other information."

"No, to be sure."

"Now, whether," pursued Herbert, "he had used the child's mother ill, or whether he had used the child's mother well, Provis doesn't say; but she had shared some four or five years of the wretched life he described to us at this fireside, and he seems to have felt pity for her, and forbearance toward her. Therefore, fearing he should be called upon to depose about this destroyed child, and so be the cause of her death, he hid himself (much as he grieved for the child), kept himself dark, as he says, out of the way and out of the trial, and was only vaguely talked of as a certain man called Abel, out of whom the jealousy arose. After the acquittal she disappeared, and thus he lost the child and the child's mother."

"I want to ask—"

"A moment, my dear boy," said Herbert, "and I have done. That evil Compey, the worst of scoundrels among many scoundrels, knowing of his keeping out of the way at that time, and of his reasons for doing so, of course afterward held the knowledge over his head as a means of keeping him poorer, and working him harder. It was clear last night that this barbed the point of Provis's hatred."

"I want to know," said I, "and particularly, Herbert, whether he told you when this happened?"

"Particularly? Let me remember, then, what he said as to that. His expression was, 'a round score o' year ago, and a'most directly after I took up wi' Compey.' How old were you when you came upon him in the little churchyard?"

"I think in my seventh year."

"Ay. It had happened about four years, then, he said, and you brought into his mind the little girl so tragically lost, who would have been your age."

"Herbert," said I, after a short silence, in a hurried way, "can you see me best by the light of the window, or the light of the fire?"

"By the firelight," answered Herbert, coming close again.

"Look at me."

"I do look at you, my dear boy."

"Touch me."

"I do touch you, my dear boy."

"You are not afraid that I am in any fever, or that my head is much disordered by the accident of last night?"

"N-no, my dear boy," said Herbert, after taking time to examine me. "You are rather excited, but you are quite yourself."

"I know I am quite myself. And the man we have in hiding down the river is Estella's Father."

Fifty-one

WHAT PURPOSE I HAD IN VIEW WHEN I WAS HOT ON TRACING out and proving Estella's parentage I cannot say. It will presently be seen that the question was not before me in a distinct shape until it was put before me by a wiser head than my own.

But when Herbert and I had held our momentous conversation, I was seized with a feverish conviction that I ought to hunt the matter down——that I ought not to let it rest, but that I ought to see Mr. Jaggers, and come at the bare truth. I really do not know whether I felt that I did this for Estella's sake, or whether I was glad to transfer to the man in whose preservation I was so much concerned some rays of the romantic interest that had so long surrounded her. Perhaps the latter possibility may be the nearer to the truth.

Anyway, I could scarcely be withheld from going out to Gerrard Street that night. Herbert's representations that, if I did, I should probably be laid up and stricken useless when our fugitive's safety would depend upon me, alone restrained my impatience. On the understanding, again and again reiterated, that come what would, I was to go to Mr. Jaggers tomorrow, I at length submitted to keep quiet, and to have my hurts looked after, and to stay at home. Early next morning we went out together, and at the corner of Gilt-spur Street by Smithfield, I left Herbert to go his way into the City, and took my way to Little Britain.

There were periodical occasions when Mr. Jaggers and Mr. Wemmick went over the office accounts, and checked off the vouchers, and put all things straight. On these occasions Wemmick took his books and papers into Mr. Jaggers's room, and one of the upstairs clerks came down into the outer office. Finding such clerk on Wemmick's post that morning, I knew what was going on; but I was not sorry to have Mr. Jaggers and Wemmick together, as Wemmick would then hear for himself that I said nothing to compromise him.

My appearance with my arm bandaged and my coat loose over my shoulders favored my object. Although I had sent Mr. Jaggers a brief account of the accident as soon as I had arrived in town, yet I had to give him all the details now; and the specialty of the occasion caused our talk to be less dry and hard, and less strictly regulated by the rules of evidence, than it had been before. While I described the disaster Mr. Jaggers stood, according to his wont, before the fire. Wemmick leaned back in his chair staring at me, with his hands in the pockets of his trowsers, and his pen put horizontally into the post. The two brutal casts, always inseparable in my mind from the official proceedings, seemed to be congestively considering whether they didn't smell fire at the present moment.

My narrative finished, and their questions exhausted, I then produced Miss Havisham's authority to receive the nine hundred pounds for Herbert. Mr. Jaggers's eyes retired a little deeper into his head when I handed him the tablets, but he presently handed them over to Wemmick, with instructions to draw the check for his signature. While that was in course of being done I looked on at Wemmick as he wrote, and Mr. Jaggers, poising and swaying himself on his well-polished boots, looked on at me. "I am sorry, Pip," said he, as I put the check in my pocket, when he had signed it, "that we do nothing for *you*."

"Miss Havisham was good enough to ask me," I returned, "whether she could do anything for me, and I told her No."

"Everybody should know his own business," said Mr. Jaggers. And I saw Wemmick's lips form the words "portable property."

"I should *not* have told her No, if I had been you," said Mr. Jaggers; "but every man ought to know his own business best."

"Every man's business," said Wemmick, rather reproachfully toward me, "is portable property."

As I thought the time was now come for pursuing the theme I had at heart, I said, turning on Mr. Jaggers:

"I did ask something of Miss Havisham, however, sir. I asked her to give me some information relative to her adopted daughter, and she gave me all she possessed."

"Did she?" said Mr. Jaggers, bending forward to look at his boots and then straightening himself. "Hah! I don't think I should have done so, if I had been Miss Havisham. But *she* ought to know her own business best."

"I know more of the history of Miss Havisham's adopted child than Miss Havisham herself does, sir. I know her mother."

Mr. Jaggers looked at me inquiringly, and repeated, "Mother?"

"I have seen her mother within these three days."

"Yes?" said Mr. Jaggers.

"And so have you, sir. And you have seen her still more recently."

"Yes?" said Mr. Jaggers.

"Perhaps I know more of Estella's history than even you do," said I. "I know her father too."

A certain stop that Mr. Jaggers came to in his manner—he was too self-possessed to change his manner, but he could not help its being brought to an indefinably attentive stop—assured me that he did not know who her father was. This I had strongly suspected from Provis's account (as Herbert had delivered it) of his having kept himself dark; which I pieced on to the fact that he himself was not Mr. Jaggers's client until some four years later, and when he could have no reason for claiming his identity. But I could not be sure of this unconsciousness on Mr. Jaggers's part before, though I was quite sure of it now.

"So! You know the young lady's father, Pip?" said Mr. Jaggers.

"Yes," I replied. "And his name is Provis—from New South Wales."

Even Mr. Jaggers started when I said those words. It was the slightest start that could escape a man, the most carefully repressed and the soonest checked, but he did start, though he made it a part of the action of taking out his pocket-handkerchief. How Wemmick received the announcement I am unable to say, for I was afraid to look at him just then, lest Mr. Jaggers's sharpness should detect that there had been some communication unknown to him between us.

"And on what evidence, Pip," asked Mr. Jaggers, very coolly, as he paused with his handkerchief halfway to his nose, "does Provis make this claim?"

"He does not make it," said I, "and has never made it, and has no knowledge or belief that his daughter is in existence."

For once the powerful pocket-handkerchief failed. My reply was so unexpected that Mr. Jaggers put the handkerchief back into his pocket without completing the usual performance, folded his arms, and looked with stern attention at me, though with an immovable face. Then I told him all I knew, and how I knew it; with the one reservation that I left him to infer that I knew from Miss Havisham what I in fact knew from Wemmick. I was very careful indeed as to that. Nor did I look toward Wemmick until I had finished all I had to tell, and had been for some time silently meeting Mr. Jaggers's look. When I did at last turn my eyes in Wemmick's direction, I found that he had unposted his pen, and was intent upon the table before him.

"Hah!" said Mr. Jaggers at last, as he moved toward the papers on the table. "—What item was it you were at, Wemmick, when Pip came in?"

But I could not submit to be thrown off in that way, and I made a passionate, almost an indignant, appeal to him to be more frank and manly with me. I reminded him of the false hopes into which I had lapsed, the length of time they had lasted, and the discovery I had made; and I hinted at the danger that weighed upon my spirits. I represented myself as being surely worthy of some little confidence from him, in return for the confidence I had just now imparted. I said that I did not blame him, or suspect him, or mistrust him, but I wanted assurance of the truth from him. And if he asked me why I wanted it, and why I thought I had any right to it, I would tell him, little as he cared for such poor dreams, that I had loved Estella dearly and long, and that, although I had lost her and must live a bereaved life, whatever concerned her was still nearer and dearer to me than anything else in the world. And seeing that Mr. Jaggers stood quite still and silent, and apparently quite obdurate, under this appeal, I turned to Wemmick, and said, "Wemmick, I know you to be a man with a gentle heart. I have seen your pleasant home, and your old father, and all the innocent, cheerful, playful ways with which you refresh your business life. And I entreat you to say a word for me to Mr. Jaggers, and to represent to him that, all circumstances considered, he ought to be more open with me!"

I have never seen two men look more oddly at one another than Mr. Jaggers and Wemmick did after this apostrophe. At first, a misgiving crossed me that Wemmick would be instantly dismissed from his employment; but it melted as I saw Mr. Jaggers relax into something like a smile, and Wemmick become bolder.

"What's all this?" said Mr. Jaggers. "You with an old father, and you with pleasant and playful ways?"

"Well!" returned Wemmick. "If I don't bring 'em here, what does it matter?"

"Pip," said Mr. Jaggers, laying his hand upon my arm, and smiling openly, "this man must be the most cunning impostor in all London."

"Not a bit of it," returned Wemmick, growing bolder and bolder. "I think you're another."

Again they exchanged their former odd looks, each apparently still distrustful that the other was taking him in.

"*You* with a pleasant home?" said Mr. Jaggers.

"Since it don't interfere with business," returned Wemmick, "let it be so. Now I look at you, sir, I shouldn't wonder if *you* might be planning and contriving to have a pleasant home of your own one of these days, when you're tired of all this work."

Mr. Jaggers nodded his head retrospectively two or three times, and actually drew a sigh. "Pip," said he, "we won't talk about 'poor dreams'; you know more about such things than I, having much fresher experience of that kind. But about this other matter. I'll put a case to you. Mind! I admit nothing."

He waited for me to declare that I quite understood that he expressly said that he admitted nothing.

"Now, Pip," said Mr. Jaggers, "put this case. Put the case that a woman, under such circumstances as you have mentioned, held her child concealed, and was obliged to communicate the fact to her legal adviser, on his representing to her that he must know, with an eye to the latitude of his defense, how the fact stood about that child. Put the case that at the same time he held a trust to find a child for an eccentric rich lady to adopt and bring up."

"I follow you, sir."

"Put the case that he lived in an atmosphere of evil, and that all he saw of children was their being generated in great numbers for certain destruction. Put the case that he often saw children solemnly tried at a criminal bar, where they were held up to be seen; put the case that he habitually knew of their being imprisoned, whipped, transported, neglected, cast out, qualified in all ways for the hangman, and growing up to be hanged. Put the case that pretty nigh all the children he saw in his daily business life he had reason to look upon as so much spawn, to develop into the fish that were to come to his net—to be prosecuted, defended, forsaken, made orphans, bedeviled somehow."

"I follow you, sir."

"Put the case, Pip, that here was one pretty little child out of the heap who could be saved; whom the father believed dead, and dare make no stir about; as to whom, over the mother, the legal adviser had this power: 'I know what you did, and how you did it. You came so and so, this was your manner of attack and this the manner of resistance, you went so and so, you did such and such things to divert suspicion. I have tracked you through it all, and I tell it you all. Part with the child, unless it should be necessary to produce it to clear you, and then it shall be produced. Give the child into my hands, and I will do my best to bring you off. If you are saved, your child will be saved too; if you are lost, your child is still saved.' Put the case that this was done, and that the woman was cleared."

"I understand you perfectly."

"But that I make no admissions?"

"That you make no admissions." And Wemmick repeated, "No admissions."

"Put the case, Pip, that passion and the terror of death had a little shaken the woman's intellects, and that when she was set at liberty she was scared out of the ways of the world, and went to him to be sheltered. Put the case that he took her in, and that he kept down the old wild violent nature whenever he saw an inkling of its breaking out, by asserting his power over her in the old way. Do you comprehend the imaginary case?"

"Quite."

"Put the case that the child grew up, and was married for money. That the mother was still living. That the father was still living. That the mother and father were known to one another, were dwelling within so many miles, furlongs, yards if you like, of one another. That the secret was still a secret, except that you had got wind of it. Put that last case to yourself very carefully."

"I do."

"I ask Wemmick to put it to *himself* very carefully."

And Wemmick said, "I do."

"For whose sake would you reveal the secret, Pip? For the father's? I think he would not be much the better for the mother. For the mother's? I think if she had done such a deed she would be safer where she was. For the daughter's? I think it would hardly serve her, to establish her parentage for the information of her husband, and to drag her back to disgrace after an escape of twenty years, pretty secure to last for life. But add the case that you had loved her, Pip, and had made her the subject of those 'poor dreams' which have, at one time or another, been in the heads of more men than you think likely, then I tell you that you had better—and would much sooner when you had thought well of it—chop off that bandaged left hand of yours with your bandaged right hand, and then pass the chopper on to Wemmick there, to cut *that* off, too."

I looked at Wemmick, whose face was very grave, and who gravely touched his lips with his forefinger. I did the same, and Mr. Jaggers did the same. "Now, Wemmick," said the latter then, resuming his usual manner, "what item was it you were at when Mr. Pip came in?"

Standing by for a little, while they were at work, I observed that the odd looks they had cast at one another were repeated several times: with this difference now, that each of them seemed suspicious, not to say conscious, of having shown himself in a weak and unprofessional light to the other. For this reason, I suppose, they were now inflexible with one another; Mr. Jaggers being highly dictatorial, and Wemmick obstinately justifying himself whenever there was the smallest point in abeyance for a moment. I had never seen them on such ill terms; for generally they got on very well indeed together.

But they were both happily relieved by the opportune appearance of Mike, the client with the fur cap and the habit of wiping his nose on his sleeve, whom I had seen on the very first day of my appearance within those walls. This individual, who, either in his own person or in that of some member of his family, seemed to be always in trouble (which in that place meant Newgate), called to announce that his eldest daughter was taken up on suspicion of shoplifting. As he imparted this melancholy circumstance to Wemmick, Mr. Jaggers standing magisterially before the fire, and taking no share in the proceedings, Mike's eye happened to twinkle with a tear.

"What are you about?" demanded Wemmick, with the utmost indignation. "What do you come sniveling here for?"

"I didn't go to do it, Mr. Wemmick."

"You did," said Wemmick. "How dare you? You're not in a fit state to come here, if you can't come here without spluttering like a bad pen. What do you mean by it?"

"A man can't help his feelings, Mr. Wemmick," pleaded Mike.

"His what?" demanded Wemmick, quite savagely. "Say that again!"

"Now, look here my man," said Mr. Jaggers, advancing a step, and pointing to the door. "Get out of this office. I'll have no feelings here. Get out."

"It serves you right," said Wemmick. "Get out."

So the unfortunate Mike very humbly withdrew, and Mr. Jaggers and Wemmick appeared to have reestablished their good understanding, and went to work again with a visible refreshment upon them, as if they had just had lunch.

Fifty-two

FROM LITTLE BRITAIN I WENT, WITH MY CHECK IN MY POCKET, to Miss Skiffins's brother, the accountant; and Miss Skiffins's brother, the accountant, going straight to Clarriker's and bringing Clarriker to me, I had the great satisfaction of completing that arrangement. It was the only good thing I had done, and the only completed thing I had done, since I was first apprised of my great expectations.

Clarriker informing me on that occasion that the affairs of the House were steadily progressing, that he would now be able to establish a small branch house in the East, which was much wanted for the extension of the business, and that Herbert in his new partnership capacity would go out and take charge of it, I found that I must have prepared for a separation from my friend, even though my own affairs had been more settled. And now indeed I felt as if my last anchor were loosening its hold, and I should soon be driving with the winds and waves.

But there was recompense in the joy with which Herbert came home of a night and told me of these changes, little imagining that he told me no news, and sketched airy pictures of himself conducting Clara Barley to the land of the Arabian Nights, and of me going out to join them (with a caravan of camels, I believe), and of our going up the Nile and seeing wonders. Without being sanguine as to my own part in these bright plans, I felt that

Herbert's way was clearing fast, and that old Bill Barley had but to stick to his pepper and rum, and his daughter would soon be happily provided for.

We had now got into the month of March. My left arm, though it presented no bad symptoms, took in the natural course so long to heal that I was still unable to get a coat on. My right hand was tolerably restored—disfigured, but fairly serviceable.

On a Monday morning, when Herbert and I were at breakfast, I received the following letter from Wemmick by the post:

"Walworth. Burn this as soon as read. Early in the week, or say Wednesday, you might do what you know of if you felt disposed to try it. Now burn."

When I had shown this to Herbert, and had put it in the fire—but not before we had both got it by heart—we considered what to do. For, of course, my being disabled could now be no longer kept out of view.

"I have thought it over, again and again," said Herbert, "and I think I know a better course than taking a Thames waterman. Take Startop. A good fellow, a skilled hand, fond of us, and enthusiastic and honorable."

I had thought of him more than once.

"But how much would you tell him, Herbert?"

"It is necessary to tell him very little. Let him suppose it a mere freak, but a secret one, until the morning comes; then let him know that there is urgent reason for your getting Provis aboard and away. You go with him?"

"No doubt."

"Where?"

It had seemed to me, in the many anxious considerations I had given the point, almost indifferent what port we made for—Hamburg, Rotterdam, or Antwerp. The place signified little, so that he was got out of England. Any foreign steamer that fell in our way, and would take us up, would do. I had always proposed to myself to get him well down the river in the boat, certainly well beyond Gravesend, which was a critical place for search or inquiry if suspicion were afoot. As foreign steamers would leave London at about the time of high-water, our plan would be to get down the river by a previous ebbtide, and lie by in some quiet spot until we could pull off to one.

The time when one would be due where we lay, wherever that might be, could be calculated pretty nearly, if we made inquiries beforehand.

Herbert assented to all this, and we went out immediately after breakfast to pursue our investigations. We found that a steamer for Hamburg was likely to suit our purpose best, and we directed our thoughts chiefly to that vessel. But we noted down what other foreign steamers would leave London with the same tide, and we satisfied ourselves that we knew the build and color of each. We then separated for a few hours; I to get at once such passports as were necessary, Herbert to see Startop at his lodgings. We both did what we had to do without any hindrance, and when we met again at one o'clock reported it done. I, for my part, was prepared with passports; Herbert had seen Startop, and he was more than ready to join.

Those two should pull a pair of oars, we settled, and I could steer; our charge would be sitter, and keep quiet; as speed was not our object, we should make way enough. We arranged that Herbert should not come home to dinner before going to Mill Pond Bank that evening; that we should not go there at all tomorrow evening, Tuesday; that he should prepare Provis to come down to some Stairs hard by the house, on Wednesday, when he saw us approach, and not sooner; that all the arrangements with him should be concluded that Monday night; and that he should be communicated with no more in any way until we took him on board.

These precautions well understood by both of us, I went home.

On opening the outer door of our chambers with my key, I found a letter in the box, directed to me—a very dirty letter, although not ill-written. It had been delivered by hand (of course since I left home), and its contents were these:

"If you are not afraid to come to the old marshes tonight or tomorrow night at Nine, and to come to the little sluice-house by the lime-kiln, you had better come. If you want information regarding *your uncle Provis,* you had much better come and tell no one and lose no time. *You must come alone.* Bring this with you."

I had had load enough upon my mind before the receipt of this strange letter. What to do now I could not tell. And the worst was, that I must decide quickly, or I should miss the afternoon coach, which would take me down in time for tonight. Tomorrow night I could not think of going, for it would be too close upon the time of the flight. And again, for anything I knew, the proffered information might have some important bearing on the flight itself.

If I had had ample time for consideration I believe I should still have gone. Having hardly any time for consideration—my watch showing me that the coach started within half an hour—I resolved to go. I should certainly not have gone but for the reference to my Uncle Provis; that, coming on Wemmick's letter and the morning's busy preparation, turned the scale.

It is so difficult to become clearly possessed of the contents of almost any letter, in a violent hurry, that I had to read this mysterious epistle again, twice, before its injunction to me to be secret got mechanically into my mind. Yielding to it in the same mechanical kind of way, I left a note in pencil for Herbert, telling him that as I should be so soon going away, I knew not for how long, I had decided to hurry down and back, to ascertain for myself how Miss Havisham was faring. I had then barely time to get my great-coat, lock up the chambers, and make for the coach-office by the short by-ways. If I had taken a hackney-chariot and gone by the streets, I should have missed my aim; going as I did, I caught the coach just as it came out of the yard. I was the only inside passenger, jolting away knee-deep in straw, when I came to myself.

For I really had not been myself since the receipt of the letter; it had so bewildered me, ensuing on the hurry of the morning. The morning hurry and flutter had been great, for, long and anxiously as I had waited for Wemmick, his hint had come like a surprise at last. And now I began to wonder at myself for being in the coach, and to doubt whether I had sufficient reason for being there, and to consider whether I should get out presently and go back, and to argue against ever heeding an anonymous communication, and, in short, to pass through all those phases of contradiction and indecision to which I suppose very few hurried people are strangers. Still, the reference to Provis by name mastered everything. I reasoned as I had reasoned already without knowing it—if that be reasoning—in case any harm should befall him through my not going, how could I ever forgive myself!

It was dark before we got down, and the journey seemed long and dreary to me who could see little of it inside, and who could not go outside in my disabled state. Avoiding the Blue Boar, I put up at an inn of minor reputation down the town, and ordered some dinner. While it was preparing, I went to Satis House and inquired for Miss Havisham; she was still very ill, though considered something better.

My inn had once been a part of an ancient ecclesiastical house, and I dined in a little octagonal common-room, like a font. As I was not able to cut my dinner, the old landlord with a shining bald head did it for me. This bringing us into conversation, he was so good as to entertain me with my own story—of course with the popular feature that Pumblechook was my earliest benefactor and the founder of my fortunes.

"Do you know the young man?" said I.

"Know him!" repeated the landlord. "Ever since he was no height at all."

"Does he ever come back to this neighborhood?"

"Ay, he comes back," said the landlord, "to his great friends now and again, and gives the cold shoulder to the man that made him."

"What man is that?"

"Him that I speak of," said the landlord. "Mr. Pumblechook."

"Is he ungrateful to no one else?"

"No doubt he would be if he could," returned the landlord; "but he can't. And why? Because Pumblechook done everything for him."

"Does Pumblechook say so?"

"Say so!" replied the landlord. "He han't no call to say so."

"But does he say so?"

"It would turn a man's blood to white winegar to hear him tell of it, sir," said the landlord.

I thought, "Yet Joe, dear Joe, *you* never tell of it! Long-suffering and loving Joe, *you* never complain! Nor you, sweet-tempered Biddy!"

"Your appetite's been touched like by your accident," said the landlord, glancing at the bandaged arm under my coat. "Try a tenderer bit."

"No, thank you," I replied, turning from the table to brood over the fire. "I can eat no more. Please take it away."

I had never been struck at so keenly for my thanklessness to Joe as through the brazen impostor Pumblechook. The falser he, the truer Joe; the meaner he, the nobler Joe.

My heart was deeply and most deservedly humbled as I mused over the fire for an hour or more. The striking of the clock aroused me, but not from my dejection or remorse, and I got up and had my coat fastened around my neck, and went out. I had previously sought in my pockets for the letter that I might refer to it again, but I could not find it, and was uneasy to think that it must have been dropped in the straw of the coach. I knew very well, however, that the appointed place was the little sluice-house by the lime-kiln on the marshes, and the hour nine. Toward the marshes I now went straight, having no time to spare.

Fifty-three

IT WAS A DARK NIGHT, THOUGH THE FULL MOON ROSE AS I left the inclosed lands, and passed out upon the marshes. Beyond their dark line there was a ribbon of clear sky, hardly broad enough to hold the red large moon. In a few minutes she had ascended out of that clear field, in among the piled mountains of cloud.

There was a melancholy wind, and the marshes were very dismal. A stranger would have found them insupportable, and even to me they were so oppressive that I hesitated, half inclined to go back. But I knew them well, and could have found my way on a far darker night, and had no excuse for returning, being there. So, having come there against my inclination, I went on against it.

The direction that I took was not that in which my old home lay, nor that in which we had pursued the convicts. My back was turned toward the distant Hulks as I walked on, and though I could see the old lights away on the spits of sand, I saw them over my shoulder. I knew the lime-kiln as well as I knew the old Battery, but they were miles apart; so that if a light had been burning at each point that night there would have been a long strip of the blank horizon between the two bright specks.

At first I had to shut some gates after me, and now and then to stand still while the cattle that were lying in the banked-up pathway arose and blundered down among the grass and reeds. But after a little while I seemed to have the whole flats to myself.

It was another half hour before I drew near to the kiln. The lime was burning with a sluggish, stifling smell, but the fires were made up and left, and no workmen were visible. Hard by was a small stone quarry. It lay directly in my way, and had been worked that day, as I saw by the tools and barrows that were lying about.

Coming up again to the marsh level out of this excavation—for the rude path lay through it—I saw a light in the old sluice-house. I quickened my pace, and knocked at the door with my hand. Waiting for some reply, I looked about me, noticing how the sluice was abandoned and broken, and how the house—of wood with a tiled roof—would not be proof against the weather much longer, if it were so even now, and how the mud and ooze were coated with lime, and how the choking vapor of the kiln crept in a ghostly way toward me. Still there was no answer, and I knocked again. No answer still, and I tried the latch.

It rose under my hand, and the door yielded. Looking in, I saw a lighted candle on a table, a bench, and a mattress on a truckle bedstead. As there was a loft above, I called, "Is there anyone here?" but no voice answered. Then I looked at my watch, and finding that it was past nine, called again, "Is there anyone here?" There being still no answer, I went out at the door, irresolute what to do.

It was beginning to rain fast. Seeing nothing save what I had seen already, I turned back into the house and stood just within the shelter of the door, looking out into the night. While I was considering that someone must have been there lately and must soon be coming back, or the candle would not be burning, it came into my head to look if the wick were long. I turned round to do so, and had taken up the candle in my hand, when it was extinguished by some violent shock, and the next thing I comprehended was, that I had been caught in a strong running noose, thrown over my head from behind.

"Now," said a suppressed voice with an oath, "I've got you?"

"What is this?" I cried, struggling. "Who is it? Help, help, help!"

Not only were my arms pulled close to my sides, but the pressure on my bad arm caused me exquisite pain. Sometimes a strong man's hand, sometimes a strong man's breast was set against my mouth to deaden my cries, and with a hot breath always close to me, I struggled ineffectually in the dark, while I was fastened tight to the wall. "And now," said the suppressed voice, with another oath, "call out again, and I'll make short work of finishing you!"

Faint and sick with the pain of my injured arm, bewildered by the surprise, and yet conscious how easily this threat could be put in execution, I desisted, and tried to ease my arm were it ever so little. But it was bound too tight for that. I felt as if, having been burned before, it were now being boiled.

The sudden exclusion of the night and the substitution of black darkness in its place, warned me that the man had closed a shutter. After groping about for a little, he found the flint and steel he wanted, and began to strike a light. I strained my sight upon the sparks that fell among the tinder, and upon which he breathed and breathed, match in hand, but I could only see his lips, and the blue point of the match; even those but fitfully. The tinder was damp—no wonder there—and one after another the sparks died out.

The man was in no hurry, and struck again with the flint and steel. As the sparks fell thick and bright about him I could see his hands, and touches of his face, and could make out that he was seated and bending over the table; but nothing more. Presently I saw his blue lips again breathing on the tinder, and then a flare of light flashed up, and showed me Orlick.

Whom I had looked for I don't know. I had not looked for him. Seeing him, I felt that I was in a dangerous strait indeed, and I kept my eyes upon him.

He lighted the candle from the flaring match with great deliberation, and dropped the match and trod it out. Then he put the candle away from him on the table, so that he could see me, and sat with his arms folded on the table and looked at me. I made out that I was fastened to a stout perpendicular ladder a few inches from the wall—a fixture there—the means of ascent to the loft above.

"Now," said he, when we had surveyed one another for some time, "I've got you."

"Unbind me. Let me go!"

"Ah!" he returned. "*I'll* let you go. I'll let you go to the moon, I'll let you go to the stars. All in good time."

"Why have you lured me here?"

"Don't you know," said he, with a deadly look.

"Why have you set upon me in the dark?"

"Because I mean to do it all myself. One keeps a secret better than two. Oh you enemy, you enemy!"

His enjoyment of the spectacle I furnished, as he sat with his arms folded on the table, shaking his head at me and hugging himself, had a malignity in it that made me tremble. As I watched him in silence he put his hand into the corner at his side and took up a gun with a brass-bound stock.

"Do you know this?" said he, making as if he would take aim at me. "Do you know where you saw it afore? Speak, wolf!"

"Yes," I answered.

"You cost me that place. You did. Speak!"

"What else could I do?"

"You did that, and that would be enough, without more. How dared you come betwixt me and a young woman I liked?"

"When did I?"

"When didn't you? It was you as always gave Old Orlick a bad name to her."

"You gave it to yourself: you gained it for yourself. I could have done you no harm if you had done yourself none."

"You're a liar. And you'll take any pains, and spend any money, to drive me out of this country, will you?" said he, repeating my words to Biddy in the last interview I had with her. "Now, I'll tell you a piece of information. It was never so well worth your while to get me out of this country as it is tonight. Ah! If it was all your money twenty times told, to the last brass farden!" As he shook his heavy hand at me, with his mouth snarling like a tiger's, I felt that it was true.

"What are you going to do to me?"

"I'm a going," said he, bringing his fist down upon the table with a heavy blow, and rising as the blow fell, to give it greater force, "I'm a going to have your life!" He leaned forward staring at me, slowly unclenched his hand and drew it across his mouth as if his mouth watered for me, and sat down again.

"You was always in Old Orlick's way since ever you was a child. You goes out of his way this present night. He'll have no more on you. You're as good as dead."

I felt that I had come to the brink of my grave. For a moment I looked wildly round my trap for any chance of escape; but there was none.

"More than that," said he, folding his arms on the table again, "I won't have a rag of you, I won't have a bone of you, left on earth. I'll put your body in the kiln—I'd carry two such to it, on my shoulders—and, let people suppose what they may of you, they shall never know nothing."

My mind, with inconceivable rapidity, followed out all the consequences of such a death. Estella's father would believe I had deserted him, would be taken, would die accusing me; even Herbert would doubt me, when he compared the letter I had left for him, with the fact that I had called at Miss Havisham's gate for only a moment; Joe and Biddy would never know how sorry I had been that night; none would ever know what I had suffered, how true I had meant to be, what an agony I had passed through. The death close before me was terrible, but far more terrible than death was the dread of being misremembered after death. And so quick were my thoughts, that I saw myself despised by unborn generations—Estella's children and their children—while the wretch's words were yet on his lips.

"Now, wolf," said he, "afore I kill you like any other beast—which is wot I mean to do and wot I have tied you up for—I'll have a good look at you and a good goad at you. Oh, you enemy!"

It had passed through my thoughts to cry out for help again; though few could know better than I the solitary nature of the spot and the hopelessness of aid. But as he sat gloating over me, I was supported by a scornful detestation of him that sealed my lips. Above all things, I resolved that I would not entreat him, and that I would die making some last poor resistance to him. Softened as my thoughts of all the rest of men were in that dire extremity; humbly beseeching pardon, as I did, of Heaven; melted at heart, as I was, by the thought that I had taken no farewell, and never never now could take farewell of those who were dear to me, or could explain myself to them, or ask for their compassion on my miserable errors; still, if I could have killed him, even in dying, I would have done it.

He had been drinking, and his eyes were red and bloodshot. Around his neck was slung a tin bottle, as I had often seen his meat and drink slung about him in other days. He brought the bottle to his lips, and took a fiery drink from it; and I smelled the strong spirits that I saw flare into his face.

"Wolf!" said he, folding his arms again, "Old Orlick's a going to tell you somethink. It was you as did for your shrew sister."

Again my mind, with its former inconceivable rapidity, had exhausted the whole subject of the attack upon my sister, her illness, and her death, before his slow and hesitating speech had formed those words.

"It was you, villain!" said I.

"I tell you it was your doing—I tell you it was done through you," he retorted, catching up the gun, and making a blow with the stock at the vacant air between us. "I come upon her from behind, as I come upon you tonight. I giv' it her! I left her for dead, and if there had been a lime-kiln as nigh her as there is now nigh you, she shouldn't have come to life again. But it wasn't Old Orlick as did it; it was you. You was favored, and he was bullied and beat. Old Orlick bullied and beat, eh? Now you pays for it. You done it; now you pays for it."

He drank again and became more ferocious. I saw by his tilting of the bottle that there was no great quantity left in it. I distinctly understood that he was working himself up with its contents to make an end of me. I knew that every drop it held was a drop of my life. I knew that when I was changed into a part of the vapor that had crept toward me but a little while before, like my own warning ghost, he would do as he had done in my sister's case—make all haste to the town, and be seen slouching about there, drinking at the ale-houses. My rapid mind pursued him to the town, made a picture of the street with him in it, and contrasted its lights and life with the lonely marsh and the white vapor creeping over it, into which I should have dissolved.

It was not only that I could have summed up years and years and years while he said a dozen words, but that what he did say presented pictures to me, and not mere words. In the excited and exalted state of my brain I could not think of a place without seeing it, or of persons without seeing them. It is impossible to overstate the vividness of these images, and yet I was so intent, all the time, upon him himself—who would not be intent on the tiger crouching to spring!—that I knew of the slightest action of his fingers.

When he had drunk this second time he rose from the bench on which he sat and pushed the table aside. Then he took up the candle, and shading it with his murderous hand so as to throw its light on me, stood before me, looking at me and enjoying the sight.

"Wolf, I'll tell you something more. It was Old Orlick as you tumbled over on your stairs that night."

I saw the staircase with its extinguished lamps. I saw the shadows of the heavy stair-rails, thrown by the watchman's lantern on the wall. I saw the rooms that I was never to see again; here, a door half open; there, a door closed; all the articles of furniture around.

"And why was Old Orlick there? I'll tell you something more, wolf. You and her *have* pretty well hunted me out of this country, so far as getting a easy living in it goes, and I've took up with new companions. Some of 'em writes my letters when I wants 'em wrote—do you mind?—writes my letters, wolf! They writes fifty hands; they're not like sneaking you, as writes but one. I've had a firm mind and a firm will to have your life since you was down here at your sister's burying. I han't seen a way to get you safe, and I've looked arter you to know your ins and outs. For, says Old Orlick to himself, 'Somehow or another I'll have him!' What! When I looks for you, I finds your uncle Provis, eh?"

Mill Pond Bank, and Chink's Basin, and the Old Green Copper Rope-Walk, all so clear and plain! Provis in his rooms, and the signal whose use was over, pretty Clara, the good motherly woman, old Bill Barley on his back, all drifting by, as on the swift stream of my life fast running out to sea!

"*You* with a uncle, too! Why, I know'd you at Gargery's when you was so small a wolf that I could have took your weazen betwixt this finger and thumb and chucked you away dead (as I'd thoughts o' doing, odd times, when I see you loitering among the pollards on a Sunday), and you hadn't found no uncles then. No, not you! But when Old Orlick come for to hear that your uncle Provis had most like wore the leg-iron what Old Orlick had picked up, filed asunder on these meshes ever so many year ago, and wot he kep by him till he dropped your sister with it like a bullock, as he means to drop you—hey?—when he come for to hear that—hey?"

In his savage taunting he flared the candle so close at me that I turned my face aside to save it from the flame.

"Ah!" he cried, laughing, after doing it again, "the burnt child dreads the fire! Old Orlick knowed you was burnt, Old Orlick knowed you was smuggling your uncle Provis away, Old Orlick's a match for you, and knowed you'd come tonight! Now I'll tell you something more, wolf, and this ends it. There's them that's as good a match for your uncle Provis as Old Orlick has been for you. Let him 'ware them, when he's lost his nevvy! Let him 'ware them, when no man can't find a rag of his dear relation's clothes, nor yet a bone of his body? There's them that can't and that won't have Magwitch—yes, *I* know the name!—alive in the same land with them, and that's had such sure information of him when he was alive in another land, as that he couldn't and shouldn't leave it unbeknown, and put them in danger. P'raps it's them that writes fifty hands, and that's not like sneaking you as writes but one. 'Ware Compey, Magwitch, and the gallows!"

He flared the candle at me again, smoking my face and hair, and for an instant blinding me, and turned his powerful back as he replaced the light on the table. I had thought a prayer and had been with Joe and Biddy and Herbert, before he turned toward me again.

There was a clear space of a few feet between the table and the opposite wall. Within this space he now slouched backward and forward. His great strength seemed to sit stronger upon him than ever before, as he did this with his hands hanging loose and heavy at his sides, and with his eyes scowling at me. I had no grain of hope left. Wild as my inward hurry was, and wonderful the force of the pictures that rushed by me instead of thoughts, I could clearly understand that unless he had resolved that I was within a few moments of surely perishing out of all human knowledge, he would never have told me what he had told.

Of a sudden he stopped, took the cork out of his bottle, and tossed it away. Light as it was, I heard it fall like a plummet. He swallowed slowly, tilting up the bottle by little and little, and now he looked at me no more. The last few drops of liquor he poured into the palm of his left hand, and licked up. Then with a sudden hurry of violence and swearing horribly, he threw the bottle from him, and stooped, and I saw in his hand a stone hammer with a long heavy handle.

The resolution I had made did not desert me, for, without uttering one vain word of appeal to him, I shouted out with all my might, and struggled with all my might. It was only my head and my legs that I could move, but to that extent I struggled with all the force, until then unknown, that was within me. In the same instant I heard responsive shouts, saw figures and a gleam of light dash in at the door, heard voices and tumult, and saw Orlick emerge from a struggle of men as if it were tumbling water, clear the table at a leap, and fly out into the night.

After a blank I found that I was lying unbound on the floor, in the same place, with my head on someone's knee. My eyes were fixed on the ladder against the wall when I came to myself—had opened on them long before my mind saw it—and thus, as I recovered consciousness, I knew that I was in the place where I had lost it.

Too indifferent at first even to look round and ascertain who supported me, I was lying looking at the ladder, when there came between me and it a face. The face of Trabb's boy!

"I think he's all right!" said Trabb's boy, in a sober voice; "but ain't he just pale though!"

At these words the face of him who supported me looked over into mine; and I saw my supporter to be—

"Herbert! Good Heaven!"

"Softly," said Herbert. "Gently, Handel. Don't be too eager."

"And our old comrade, Startop," I cried, as he too bent over me.

"Remember what he is going to assist us in," said Herbert, "and be calm."

The allusion made me spring up, though I dropped again from the pain in my arm. "The time has not gone by, Herbert, has it? What night is to-night? How long have I been here?" For I had a strange and strong misgiving that I had been lying there a long time—a day and a night—two days and nights—more.

"The time has not gone by. It is still Monday night."

"Thank God."

"And you have all tomorrow, Tuesday, to rest in," said Herbert. "But you can't help groaning, my dear Handel. What hurt have you got? Can you stand?"

"Yes, yes," said I, "I can walk. I have no hurt but in this throbbing arm."

They laid it bare, and did what they could. It was violently swollen and inflamed, and I could scarcely endure to have it touched. But they tore up their handkerchiefs to make fresh bandages, and carefully replaced it in the sling, until we could get to the town and obtain some cooling lotion to put upon it. In a little while we had shut the door of the dark and empty sluice-house, and were passing through the quarry on our way back. Trabb's boy—Trabb's overgrown young man now—went before us with a lantern, which was the light I had seen come in at the door. But the moon was a good two hours higher than when I had last seen the sky, and the night, though rainy, was much lighter. The white vapor of the kiln was passing from us as we went by, and, as I had thought a prayer before, I thought a thanksgiving now.

Entreating Herbert to tell me how he had come to my rescue—which at first he had flatly refused to do, but had insisted on my remaining quiet—I learned that I had in my hurry dropped the letter, open, in our chambers, where he, coming home to bring with him Startop, whom he had met in the street on his way to me, found it very soon after I was gone. Its tone made him uneasy; and the more so because of the inconsistency between it and the hasty letter I had left for him. His uneasiness increasing instead of subsiding after a quarter of an hour's consideration, he set off for the coach-office with Startop, who volunteered his company, to make inquiry when the next coach went down. Finding that the afternoon coach was gone, and finding that his uneasiness grew into positive alarm as obstacles came in his way, he resolved to follow in a post-chaise. So he and Startop arrived at the Blue Boar, fully expecting there to find me, or tidings of me; but finding neither, went on to Miss Havisham's, where they lost me. Hereupon they went back to the hotel (doubtless at about the time when I was hearing the popular local version of my own story) to refresh themselves, and to get someone to guide them out upon the marshes. Among the loungers under the Boar's archway happened to be Trabb's boy—true to his ancient habit of happening to be everywhere where he had no business—and Trabb's boy had seen me passing from Miss Havisham's in the direction of my dining-place. Thus Trabb's boy became their guide, and with him they went out to the sluice-house: though by the town way to the marshes, which I had avoided. Now as they went along Herbert reflected that I might, after all, have been brought there on some genuine and serviceable errand tending to Provis's safety, and bethinking himself that in that case interruption might be mischievous, left his guide and Startop on the edge of the quarry, and went on by himself, and stole round the house two or three times, endeavoring to ascertain whether all was right within. As he could hear nothing but indistinct sounds of one deep rough voice (this was while my mind was so busy), he even at last began to doubt whether I was there, when suddenly I cried out loudly, and he answered the cries, and rushed in, closely followed by the other two.

When I told Herbert what had passed within the house, he was for our immediately going before a magistrate in the town, late at night as it was, and getting out a warrant. But I had already considered that such a course, by detaining us there or binding us to come back, might be fatal to Provis. There was no gainsaying this difficulty, and we relinquished all thoughts of pursuing Orlick at that time. For the present, under the circumstances, we deemed it prudent to make rather light of the matter to Trabb's boy; who I am convinced would have been much affected by disappointment if he had known that his intervention saved me from the lime-kiln. Not that Trabb's boy was of a malignant nature, but that he had too much vivacity to spare, and that it was in his constitution to want variety and excitement, at anybody's expense. When we parted I presented him with two guineas (which seemed to meet his views), and told him that I was sorry ever to have had an ill opinion of him (which made no impression on him at all).

Wednesday being so close upon us, we determined to go back to London that night, three in the post-chaise; the rather as we should then be clear away before the night's adventure began to be talked of. Herbert got a large bottle of stuff for my arm, and by dint of having this stuff dropped over it all the night through, I was just able to bear its pain on the journey. It was daylight when we reached the Temple, and I went at once to bed, and lay in bed all day.

My terror, as I lay there, of falling ill and being unfitted for tomorrow was so besetting, that I wonder it did not disable me of itself. It would have done so, pretty surely, in conjunction with the mental wear and tear I had suffered, but for the unnatural strain upon me that tomorrow was. So anxiously looked forward to, charged with such consequences, its results so impenetrably hidden though so near.

No precaution could have been more obvious than our refraining from communication with him that day; yet this again increased my restlessness. I started at every footstep and every sound, believing that he was discovered and taken, and this was the messenger to tell me so. I persuaded myself that I knew he was taken; that there was something more upon my mind than a fear or a presentiment; that the fact had occurred, and I had a mysterious knowledge of it. As the day wore on and no ill news came, as the day closed in and darkness fell, my overshadowing dread of being disabled by illness before tomorrow morning altogether mastered me. My burning arm throbbed, and my burning head throbbed, and I fancied I was beginning to wander. I counted up to high numbers, to make sure that I was steady, and repeated passages that I knew, in prose and verse. It happened sometimes that, in the mere escape of a fatigued mind, I dozed for some moments, or forgot; then I would say to myself with a start, "Now it has come, and I am turning delirious!"

They kept me very quiet all day, and kept my arm constantly dressed, and gave me cooling drinks. Whenever I fell asleep I awoke with the notion I had had in the sluice-house, that a long time had elapsed and the opportunity to save him was gone. About midnight I got out of bed and went to Herbert with the conviction that I had been asleep for four-and-twenty hours, and that Wednesday was past. It was the last self-exhausting effort of my fretfulness, for after that I slept soundly.

And the Wednesday morning was dawning when I looked out of window. The winking lights upon the bridges were already pale; the coming sun was like a marsh of fire in the horizon. The river, still dark and mysterious, was spanned by bridges that were turning coldly gray, with here and there, at top, a warm touch from the burning in the sky. As I looked along the clustered confusion of roofs, with church-towers and spires shooting into the unusually clear air, the sun rose up, and a vail seemed to be drawn from the river, and millions of sparkles burst upon its waters. From me, too, a vail seemed to be drawn, and I felt strong and well.

Herbert lay asleep in his bed, and our old fellow-student lay asleep on the sofa. I could not dress myself without help, but I made up the fire, which was still burning, and got some coffee ready for them. In good time they too started up strong and well, and we admitted the sharp morning air at the windows, and looked at the tide that was still flowing toward us.

"When it turns, at nine o'clock," said Herbert, cheerfully, "look out for us, and stand ready, you over there at Mill Pond Bank!"

Fifty-four

IT WAS ONE OF THOSE MARCH DAYS WHEN THE SUN SHINES hot and the wind blows cold: when it is summer in the light, and winter in the shade. We had our peacoats with us, and I took a bag. Of all my worldly possessions I took no more than the few necessaries that filled the bag. Where I might go, what I might do, or when I might return, were questions utterly unknown to me; nor did I vex my mind with them, for it was wholly set on Provis's safety. I only wondered for the passing moment, as I stopped at the door and looked back, under what altered circumstances I should next see those rooms, if ever.

We loitered down to the Temple stairs, and stood loitering there as if we were not quite decided to go upon the water at all. Of course I had taken care that the boat should be ready and everything in order. After a little show of indecision, which there were none to see but the two or three amphibious creatures belonging to our Temple stairs, we went on board and cast off; Herbert in the bow, I steering. It was then about high-water—half past eight.

Our plan was this: The tide, beginning to run down at nine, and being with us until three, we intended still to creep on after it had turned, and row against it until dark. We should then be well in those long reaches below Gravesend, between Kent and Essex, where the river is broad and solitary, where the waterside inhabitants are very few, and where lone public houses are scattered here and there, of which we could choose one for a resting-place. There we meant to lay by all night. The steamer for Hamburg and the steamer for Rotterdam would start from London at about nine on Thursday morning, and would be in our part of the river at about noon. We should know at what time to expect them according to where we were and would hail the first; so that if by any accident we were not taken aboard, we should have another chance. We had a pocket-glass with us, and knew the distinguishing marks of each vessel.

The relief of being at last engaged in the execution of the purpose was so great to me that I felt it difficult to realize the condition in which I had been a few hours before. The crisp air, the sunlight, the movement on the river, and the moving river itself—the road that ran with us, seeming to sympathize with us, animate us, and encourage us on—freshened me with new hope. I felt mortified to be of so little use in the boat; but there were few better oarsmen than my two friends, and they rowed with a steady stroke that was to last all day.

At that time the steam traffic on the Thames was far below its present extent, and watermen's boats were far more numerous. Of barges, sailing colliers, and coasting-traders, there were perhaps as many as now; but of steamships, great and small, not a tithe or a twentieth part so many. Early as it was, there were plenty of scullers going here and there that morning, and plenty of barges dropping down with the tide; the navigation of the river between bridges, in an open boat, was a much easier and commoner matter in those days than it is in these; and we went ahead among many skiffs and wherries briskly.

Old London Bridge was soon passed, and old Billingsgate Market, with its oyster-boats and Dutchmen, and the White Tower and Traitors' Gate, and we were in among the tiers of shipping. Here were the Leith, Aberdeen, and Glasgow steamers loading and unloading goods, and looking immensely high out of the water as we passed alongside; here were colliers by the score and score, with the coal-whippers, plunging off stages on deck, as counterweights to measures of coal swinging up, which were then rattled over the side into barges; here, at her moorings, was tomorrow's steamer for Rotterdam, of which we took good notice; and here tomorrow's for Hamburg, under whose bowsprit we crossed. And now I, sitting in the stern, could see with a faster beating heart, Mill Pond Bank and Mill Pond stairs.

"Is he there?" said Herbert.

"Not yet."

"Right! He was not to come down till he saw us. Can you see his signal?"

"Not well from here; but I think I see it. Now, I see him! Pull both. Easy, Herbert. Oars!"

We touched the stairs lightly for a single moment, and he was on board and we were off again. He had a boat-cloak with him, and a black canvas bag, and he looked as like a river pilot as my heart could have wished.

"Dear boy!" he said, putting his arm on my shoulder as he took his seat. "Faithful dear boy, well done. Thankye, thankye!"

Again among the tiers of shipping, in and out, avoiding rusty chain-cables, frayed hempen hawsers, and bobbing buoys, sinking for the moment floating baskets, scattering floating chips of wood and shaving, cleaving floating scum of coal, in and out, under the figurehead of the John of Sunderland making a speech to the winds (as is done by many Johns), and the Betsy of Yarmouth with a firm formality of bosom and her knobby eyes starting two inches out of her head, in and out, hammers going in shipbuilders' yards, saws going at timber, clashing engines going at things unknown, pumps going in leaky ships, capstans going, ships going out to sea, and unintelligible sea-monsters roaring curses over the bulwarks at respondent lightermen, in and out—out at last upon the clearer river, where the ships' boys might take their fenders in, no longer fishing in troubled waters with them over the side, and where the festooned sails might fly out to the wind.

At the stairs where we had taken him aboard, and ever since, I had looked warily for any token of our being suspected. I had seen none. We certainly had not been, and at that time as certainly we were not, either attended or followed by any boat. If we had been waited on by any boat, I should have run in to shore, and have obliged her to go on, or to make her purpose evident. But we held our own, without any appearance of molestation.

He had his boat-cloak on him, and looked, as I have said, a natural part of the scene. It was remarkable (but perhaps the wretched life he had led accounted for it), that he was the least anxious of any of us. He was not indifferent, for he told me that he hoped to see his gentleman one of the best of gentlemen in a foreign country; he was not disposed to be passive or resigned, as I understood it; but he had no notion of meeting danger halfway. When it came upon him he confronted it, but it must come before he troubled himself.

"If you knowed, dear boy," he said to me, "what it is to sit here alonger my dear boy and have my smoke, arter having been day by day betwixt four walls, you'd envy me. But you don't know what it is."

"I think I know the delights of freedom," I answered.

"Ah," said he, shaking his head gravely. "But you don't know it equal to me. You must have been under lock and key, dear boy, to know it equal to me—but I ain't a going to be low."

It occurred to me as inconsistent that for any mastering idea he should have endangered his freedom and even his life. But I reflected that perhaps freedom without danger was too much apart from all the habit of his existence to be to him what it would be to another man. I was not far out, since he said, after smoking a little:

"You see, dear boy, when I was over yonder, t'other side of the world, I was always a looking to this side; and it come flat to be there, for all I was a growing rich. Everybody knowed Magwitch, and Magwitch could come, and Magwitch could go, and nobody's head would be troubled about him. They ain't so easy concerning me here, dear boy—wouldn't be, leastwise, if they knowed where I was."

"If all goes well," said I, "you will be perfectly free and safe again within a few hours."

"Well," he returned, drawing a long breath, "I hope so."

"And think so?"

He dipped his hand in the water over the boat's gunwale, and said, smiling with that softened air upon him which was not new to me,

"Aye, I s'pose I think so, dear boy. We'd be puzzled to be more quiet and easygoing than we are at present. But—it's a flowing so soft and pleasant through the water, p'raps, as makes me think it—I was a thinking through my smoke just then, that we can no more see to the bottom of the next few hours than we can see to the bottom of this river what I catches hold of. Nor yet we can't no more hold their tide than I can hold this. And it's run through my fingers and gone, you see!" holding up his dripping hand.

"But for your face, I should think you were a little despondent," said I.

"Not a bit on it, dear boy! It comes of flowing on so quiet, and of that there rippling at the boat's head making a sort of a Sunday tune. Maybe I'm a growing a trifle old besides."

He put his pipe back in his mouth with an undisturbed expression of face, and sat as composed and contented as if we were already out of England. Yet he was as submissive to a word of advice as if he had been in constant terror, for when we ran ashore to get some bottles of beer into the boat, and he was stepping out, I hinted that I thought he would be safest where he was, and he said, "Do you, dear boy," and quietly sat down again.

The air felt cold upon the river, but it was a bright day, and the sun was very cheering. The tide ran strong, I took care to lose none of it, and our steady stroke carried us on thoroughly well. By imperceptible degrees, as the tide run out, we lost more and more of the nearer woods and hills, and dropped lower and lower between the muddy banks, but the tide was yet with us when we were off Gravesend. As our charge was wrapped in his cloak,

I purposely passed within a boat or two's length of the floating Custom House, and so out to catch the stream, alongside of two emigrant ships, and under the bows of a large transport with soldiers on the forecastle looking down at us. And soon the tide began to slacken, and the craft lying at anchor to swing, and presently they had all swung round, and the ships that were taking advantage of the new tide to get up to the Pool, began to crowd upon us in a fleet, and we kept under the shore, as much out of the strength of the tide now as we could, standing carefully off from low shallows and mud-banks.

Our oarsmen were so fresh, by dint of having occasionally let her drive with the tide for a minute or two, that a quarter of an hour's rest proved full as much as they wanted. We got ashore among some slippery stones while we ate and drank what we had with us, and looked about. It was like my own marsh country, flat and monotonous, and with a dim horizon while the winding river turned and turned, and the great floating buoys upon it turned and turned, and everything else seemed stranded and still. For now the last of the fleet of ships was round the last low point we had headed; and the last green barge, straw-laden, with a brown sail, had followed; and some ballast-lighters, shaped like a child's first rude imitation of a boat, lay low in the mud; and a little squat shoal lighthouse on open piles, stood crippled in the mud on stilts and crutches; and slimy stakes stuck out of the mud, and slimy stones stuck out of the mud, and red landmarks and tidemarks stuck out of the mud, and an old landing-stage and an old roofless building slipped into the mud, and all about us was stagnation and mud.

We pushed off again, and made what way we could. It was much harder work now, but Herbert and Startop persevered, and rowed, and rowed, and rowed, until the sun went down. By that time the river had lifted us a little, so that we could see above the bank. There was the red sun, on the low level of the shore, in a purple haze, fast deepening into black; and there was the solitary flat marsh; and far away there were the rising grounds, between which and us there seemed to be no life, save here and there in the fore-ground a melancholy gull.

As the night was fast falling, and as the moon, being past the full, would not rise early, we held a little council: a short one, for clearly our course was to lie by at the first lonely tavern we could find. So they plied their oars once more, and I looked out for anything like a house. Thus we held on, speaking little, for four or five dull miles. It was very cold, and a collier coming by us with her galley-fire smoking and flaring, looked quite a comfortable home. The night was dark by this time as it would be until morning, and what light we had seemed to come more from the river than the sky, as the oars in their dipping struck at a few reflected stars.

At this dismal time we were evidently all possessed by the idea that we were followed. As the tide made, it flapped heavily at irregular intervals against the shore; and whenever such a sound came, one or other of us was sure to start and look in that direction. Here and there, the set of the current had worn down the bank into a little creek and we were all suspicious of such places, and eyed them nervously. Sometimes, "What was that ripple?" one of us would say in a low voice. Or another. "Is that a boat yonder?" And afterward we would fall into a dead silence, and I would sit impatiently thinking with what an unusual amount of noise the oars worked in the thowels.

At length we descried a light and a roof, and presently afterward ran alongside a little causeway made of stones that had been picked up hard by. Leaving the rest in the boat, I stepped ashore, and found the light to be in the window of a public house. It was a dirty place enough, and I dare say not unknown to smuggling adventurers; but there was a good fire in the kitchen, and there were eggs and bacon to eat, and various liquors to drink. Also, there were two double-bedded rooms—"such as they were," the landlord said. No other company was in the house than the landlord, his wife, and a grizzled male creature, the "Jack" of the little causeway, who was as slimy and smeary as if he had been low-water mark, too.

With this assistant I went down to the boat again, and we all came ashore, and brought out the oars, and rudder, and boat-hook, and all else, and hauled her up for the night. We made a very good meal by the kitchen fire, and then apportioned the bedrooms. Herbert and Startop were to occupy one; I and our charge the other. We found the air as carefully excluded from both as if air were fatal to life; and there were more dirty clothes and bandboxes under the beds than I should have thought the family possessed. But we considered ourselves well off, notwithstanding, for a more solitary place we could not have found.

While we were comforting ourselves by the fire after our meal, the Jack—who was sitting in a corner, and who had a bloated pair of shoes on, which he had exhibited while we were eating our eggs and bacon, as interesting relics that he had taken a few days ago from the feet of a drowned seaman washed ashore—asked me if we had seen a four-oared galley going up with the tide? When I told him No, he said she must have gone down, then, and yet she "took up too," when she left there.

"They must ha' thought better on't for some reason or another," said the Jack, "and gone down."

"A four-oared galley, eh?" said I.

"A four," said the Jack, "and two sitters."

"Did they come ashore here?"

"They put in with a stone two-gallon jar for some beer. I'd ha' been glad to pison the beer myself," said the Jack, "or put some rattling physic in it at least."

"Why?"

"_I_ knows why," said the Jack. He spoke in a slushy voice, as if much mud had washed into his throat.

"He thinks," said the landlord—a weakly meditative man with a pale eye, who seemed to rely greatly on his Jack—"he thinks they was what they wasn't."

"*I* knows what I thinks," observed the Jack.

"*You* thinks Custom 'Us, Jack?" said the landlord.

"I do," said the Jack.

"Then you're wrong, Jack."

"AM I?"

In the infinite meaning of his reply, and his boundless confidence in his views, the Jack took one of his bloated shoes off, looked into it, knocked a few stones out of it on the kitchen floor, and put it on again. He did this with the air of a Jack who was so right that he could afford to do anything.

"Why, what do you make out that they done with their buttons, then, Jack?" asked the landlord, vacillating weakly.

"Done with their buttons?" returned the Jack. "Chucked 'em overboard. Swallered 'em. Sowed 'em to come up small salad. Done with their buttons!"

"Don't be cheeky, Jack," remonstrated the landlord, in a melancholy and pathetic way.

"A Custom 'Us officer knows what to do with his Buttons," said the Jack, repeating the obnoxious word with the greatest contempt, "when they comes betwixt him and his own light. A Four and two sitters don't go hanging and hovering, up with one tide and down with another, and both with and against another, without there being Custom 'Us at the bottom of it." Saying which, he went out disgusted; and the landlord having no one to rely upon, found it impracticable to pursue the subject.

This dialogue made us all uneasy, and me very uneasy. The dismal wind was muttering round the house, the tide was flapping at the shore, and I had a feeling that we were caged and threatened. A four-oared galley hovering about in so unusual a way as to attract this notice, was an ugly circumstance that I could not get rid of. When I had induced Provis to go up to bed, I went outside with my two companions (Startop by this time knew the state of the case), and held another council. Whether we should remain at the house until near the steamer's time, which would be about one in the afternoon; or whether we should put off early in the morning, was the question we discussed. On the whole we deemed it the better course to lie where we were until within an hour or so of the steamer's time, and then to get out in her track, and drift easily with the tide. Having settled to do this, we returned into the house and went to bed.

I lay down with the greater part of my clothes on, and slept for a few hours well. When I awoke, the wind had risen, and the sign of the house (the Ship) was creaking and banging about, with noises that startled me. Rising softly, for my charge lay fast asleep, I looked out of the window. It commanded the causeway where we had hauled up our boat, and, as my eyes adapted themselves to the light of the clouded moon, I saw two men looking into her. They passed by under the window, looking at nothing else, and did not go down to the landing-place, which I could discern to be empty, but struck across the marsh in the direction of the sea.

My first impulse was to call up Herbert, and show him the two men going away. But reflecting before I got into his room, which was at the back of the house and adjoined mine, that he and Startop had had a harder day than I, and were fatigued, I forbore. Going back to my window, I could see the two men moving over the marsh. In that light, however, I soon lost them, and feeling very cold, lay down to think of the matter, and fell asleep again.

We were up early. As we walked to and fro, all four together, before breakfast, I deemed it right to recount what I had seen. Again our charge was the least anxious of the party. It was very likely that the men belonged to the Custom-house, he said, quietly, and that they had no thought of us. I tried to persuade myself that it was so: as, indeed, it might easily be. However, I proposed that he and I should walk away together to a distant point we could see, and that the boat should take us aboard there, or as near there as might prove feasible, at about noon. This being considered a good precaution, soon after breakfast he and I set forth, without saying anything at the tavern.

He smoked his pipe as we went along, and sometimes stopped to clap me on the shoulder or take me by the hand. One would have supposed that it was I who was in danger, not he, and that he was reassuring me. We spoke very little. As we approached the point, I begged him to remain in a sheltered place while I went on to reconnoiter, for it was toward it that the men had passed in the night. He complied, and I went on alone. There was no boat off the point, nor drawn up anywhere near it, nor were there any signs of the men having embarked there. But to be sure the tide was high, and there might have been some footprints underwater.

When he looked out from his shelter in the distance, and saw that I waved my hat to him to come up, he rejoined me, and there we waited—sometimes lying on the bank wrapped in our coats, and sometimes moving about to warm ourselves—until we saw our boat coming round. We got aboard easily, and rowed out into the track of the steamer. By that time it wanted but ten minutes of one o'clock, and we began to look out for her smoke.

But it was half past one before we saw her smoke, and soon afterward we saw behind it the smoke of the other steamer. As they were coming on at full speed, we got the two bags ready, and took that opportunity of saying good-bye to Herbert and Startop. We had all shaken hands cordially, and neither Herbert's eyes nor mine were quite dry when I saw a four-oared galley shoot out from under the bank but a little way ahead of us, and row out into the same track.

A stretch of shore had been as yet between us and the steamer's smoke, by reason of the bend and wind of the river; but now she was visible, coming head-on. I called to Herbert and Startop to keep before the tide, that she might see us lying by for her, and adjured Provis to sit still, wrapped in his cloak. He answered cheerily, "Trust to me, dear boy," and sat like a statue. Meantime the galley, which was very skillfully handled, had borne down upon us, crossed us, and come alongside. Leaving just enough room for the play of the oars, she kept alongside, drifting when we drifted, and pulling a stroke or two when we pulled. Of the two sitters, one held the rudder lines, and looked at us attentively—as did all the rowers; the other sitter was wrapped up, much as Provis was, and seemed to shrink, and whisper some instruction to the stranger as he looked at us. Not a word was spoken in either boat.

Startop could make out, after a few minutes, which steamer was first, and gave me the word "Hamburg," in a low voice as we sat face to face. She was nearing us very fast, and the beating of her paddles grew louder and louder. I felt as if her shadow were absolutely upon us when the galley hailed us. I answered.

"You have a returned Transport there," said the man who held the lines. "That's the man wrapped in the cloak. His name is Abel Magwitch, otherwise Provis. I apprehend that man, and call upon him to surrender, and you to assist."

At the same moment, without giving any audible direction to his crew, he ran the galley aboard of us. They had pulled one sudden stroke ahead, had got their oars in, had run athwart us, and were holding on to our gunwale before we knew what they were doing. This caused great confusion on board the steamer, and I heard them calling to us, and heard the order given to stop the paddles, and heard them stop, but felt her driving down upon us irresistibly. In the same moment, I saw the steersman of the galley lay his hand on his prisoner's shoulder, and saw that both boats were swinging round with the force of the tide, and saw that all hands on board the steamer were running forward quite frantically. Still in the same moment, I saw the prisoner start up, lean across his captor, and pull the cloak from the neck of the shrinking sitter in the galley. Still in the same moment, I saw that the face disclosed was the face of the other convict of long ago. Still in the same moment, I saw the face tilt backward with a white terror on it that I shall never forget, and heard a great cry on board the steamer and a loud splash in the water, and felt the boat sink from under me.

It was but for an instant that I seemed to struggle with a thousand mill-weirs and a thousand flashes of light; that instant past, I was taken on board the galley. Herbert was there, and Startop was there; but our boat was gone, and the two convicts were gone.

What with the cries aboard the steamer, and the furious blowing-off of her steam, and her driving on, and our driving on, I could not at first distinguish sky from water or shore from shore; but the crew of the galley righted her with great speed, and, pulling certain swift strong strokes ahead, lay upon their oars, every man looking silently and eagerly at the water astern. Presently a dark object was seen in it, bearing toward us on the tide. No man spoke, but the steersman held up his hand, and all softly backed water, and kept the boat straight and true before it. As it came nearer, I saw it to be Magwitch, swimming. He was taken on board, and instantly manacled at the wrists and ankles.

The galley was kept steady, and the silent, eager lookout at the water was resumed. But the Rotterdam steamer now came up, and apparently not understanding what had happened, came on at speed. By the time she had been hailed and stopped both steamers were drifting away from us, and we were rising and falling in a troubled wake of water. The lookout was kept long after all was still again and the two steamers were gone; but everybody knew that it was hopeless now.

At length we gave it up, and pulled under the shore toward the tavern we had lately left, where we were received with no little surprise. Here I was able to get some comforts for Magwitch—Provis no longer—who had received some very severe injury in the chest and a deep cut in the head.

He told me that he believed himself to have gone under the keel of the steamer, and to have been struck on the head in rising. The injury to his chest (which rendered his breathing extremely painful) he thought he had received against the side of the galley. He added that he did not pretend to say what he might or might not have done to Compey, but that in the moment of his laying his hand on his cloak to identify him that villain had staggered up and staggered back, and they had both gone overboard together; when the sudden wrenching of him (Magwitch) out of our boat, and the endeavor of his captor to keep him in it, had capsized us. He told me in a whisper that they had gone down fiercely locked in each other's arms, and that there had been a struggle underwater, and that he had disengaged himself, struck out, and swum away.

I never had any reason to doubt the exact truth of what he thus told me. The officer who steered the galley gave the same account of their going overboard.

When I asked this officer's permission to change the prisoner's wet clothes by purchasing any spare garments I could get at the public house, he gave it readily, merely observing that he must take charge of everything his prisoner had about him. So the pocket-book which had once been in my hands passed into the officer's. He further gave me leave to accompany the prisoner to London; but declined to accord that grace to my two friends.

The Jack at the Ship was instructed where the drowned man had gone down, and undertook to search for the body in the places where it was likeliest to come ashore. His interest in its recovery seemed to me to be much heightened when he heard that it had stockings on. Probably, it took about a dozen drowned men to fit him out completely; and that may have been the reason why the different articles of his dress were in various stages of decay.

We remained at the public house until the tide turned, and then Magwitch was carried down to the galley and put on board. Herbert and Startop were to get to London by land, as soon as they could. We had a doleful parting, and when I took my place by Magwitch's side I felt that that was my place henceforth while he lived.

For now my repugnance to him had all melted away, and in the hunted, wounded, ironed creature who held my hand in his, I only saw a man who had meant to be my benefactor, and who had felt affectionately, gratefully, and generously toward me with great constancy through a series of years. I only saw in him a much better man than I had been to Joe.

His breathing became more difficult and painful as the night drew on, and often he could not repress a groan. I tried to rest him on the arm I could use, in any easy position; but it was dreadful to think that I could not be sorry at heart for his being badly hurt, since it was unquestionably best that he should die. That there were, still living, people enough who were able and willing to identify him, I could not doubt. That he would be mercifully treated, I could not hope. He who had been presented in the worst light at his trial, who had since broken prison and been tried again, who had returned from transportation under a life sentence, and who had occasioned the death of the man who was the cause of his arrest.

As we returned toward the setting sun we had yesterday left behind us, and as the stream of our hopes seemed all running back, I told him how grieved I was to think he had come home for my sake.

"Dear boy," he answered, "I'm quite content to take my chance. I've seen my boy, and he'll be a gentleman without me."

I had thought about that, while we had been there side by side. No. Apart from any inclinations of my own I understood Wemmick's hint now. I foresaw that, being convicted, his possessions would be forfeited to the Crown.

"Lookee here, dear boy," said he. "It's best as a gentleman should not be knowed to belong to me now. Only come to see me as if you come by chance alonger Wemmick. Sit where I can see you when I am swore to, for the last o' many times, and I don't ask no more."

"I will never stir from your side," said I, "when I am suffered to be near you. Please God, I will be as true to you as you have been to me!"

I felt his hand shake as it held mine, and he turned his face away as he lay in the bottom of the boat, and I heard that old sound in his throat—softened now, like all the rest of him. It was a good thing that he had touched this point, for it put into my mind what I might not otherwise have thought of until too late: That he need never know how his hopes of enriching me had perished.

H E WAS TAKEN TO THE POLICE COURT NEXT DAY, AND WOULD
have been immediately committed for trial, but that it was necessary to
send down for an old officer of the prison-ship from which he had once
escaped to speak to his identity. Nobody doubted it; but Compey, who had
meant to depose to it, was tumbling on the tides, dead, and it happened that
there was not at that time any prison officer in London who could give the
required evidence. I had gone direct to Mr. Jaggers at his private house, on
my arrival overnight, to retain his assistance, and Mr. Jaggers on the prisoner's behalf would admit nothing. It was the sole resource, for he told me
that the case must be over in five minutes when the witness was there, and
that no power on earth could prevent its going against us.

I imparted to Mr. Jaggers my design of keeping him in ignorance of the
fate of his wealth. Mr. Jaggers was querulous and angry with me for having "let
it slip through my fingers," and said we must memorialize by-and-by, and try
at all events for some of it. But he did not conceal from me that although there
might be many cases in which the forfeiture would not be exacted, there were
no circumstances in this case to make it one of them. I understood that very
well. I was not related to the outlaw, or connected with him by any recognizable tie; he had put his hand to no writing or settlement in my favor before his
apprehension, and to do so now would be idle. I had no claim, and I finally
resolved, and ever afterward abided by the resolution, that my heart should
never be sickened with the hopeless task of attempting to establish one.

There appeared to be reason for supposing that the drowned informer had
hoped for a reward out of this forfeiture, and had obtained some accurate
knowledge of Magwitch's affairs. When his body was found, many miles from
the scene of his death, and so horribly disfigured that he was only recognizable
by the contents of his pockets, notes were still legible, folded in the outer case
of the watch he wore. Among these, were the name of a banking-house in
New South Wales where a sum of money was, and the designation of certain
lands of considerable value. Both these heads of information were in a list that
Magwitch, while in prison, gave to Mr. Jaggers, of the possessions he supposed
I should inherit. His ignorance, poor fellow, at last served him; he never mistrusted but that my inheritance was quite safe, with Mr. Jaggers's aid.

After three days' delay, during which the crown prosecution stood over
for the production of the witness from the prison-ship, the witness came, and
completed the easy case. He was committed to take his trial at the next Ses-
sion's, which would come on in a month.

It was at this dark time of my life that Herbert returned home one evening, a good deal cast down, and said:

"My dear Handel, I fear I shall soon have to leave you."

His partner having prepared me for that, I was less surprised than he thought.

"We shall lose a fine opportunity if I put off going to Cairo, and I am very much afraid I must go, Handel, when you most need me."

"Herbert, I shall always need you, because I shall always love you; but my need is no greater now than at another time."

"You will be so lonely."

"I have not leisure to think of that," said I. "You know that I am always with him to the full extent of the time allowed, and that I should be with him all day long, if I could. And when I come away from him, you know that my thoughts are with him."

The dreadful condition to which he was brought was so appalling to both of us that we could not refer to it in plainer words.

"My dear fellow," said Herbert, "let the near prospect of our separation—for it is very near—be my justification for troubling you about yourself. Have you thought of your future?"

"No, for I have been afraid to think of any future."

"But yours cannot be dismissed; indeed my dear, dear Handel, it must not be dismissed. I wish you would enter on it now, as far as a few friendly words go, with me."

"I will," said I.

"In this branch house of ours, Handel, we must have a—"

I saw that his delicacy was avoiding the right word, so I said, "A clerk."

"A clerk. And I hope it is not at all unlikely that he may expand (as a clerk of your acquaintance has expanded) into a partner. Now, Handel—in short, my dear boy, will you come to me?"

There was something charmingly cordial and engaging in the manner in which after saying "Now, Handel," as if it were the grave beginning of a portentous business exordium, he had suddenly given up that tone, stretched out his honest hand, and spoken like a schoolboy.

"Clara and I have talked about it again and again," Herbert pursued, "and the dear little thing begged me only this evening, with tears in her eyes, to say to you that if you will live with us when we come together, she will do her best to make you happy, and to convince her husband's friend that he is her friend too. We should get on so well, Handel!"

I thanked her heartily, and I thanked him heartily, but said I could not yet make sure of joining him as he so kindly offered. Firstly, my mind was too preoccupied to be able to take in the subject clearly. Secondly—Yes! Secondly, there was a vague something lingering in my thoughts that will come out very near the end of this slight narrative.

"But if you thought, Herbert, that you could, without doing any injury to your business, leave the question open for a little while—"

"For any while," cried Herbert. "Six months, a year!"

"Not so long as that," said I. "Two or three months at most."

Herbert was highly delighted when we shook hands on this arrangement, and said he could now take courage to tell me that he believed he must go away at the end of the week.

"And Clara?" said I.

"The dear little thing," returned Herbert, "holds dutifully to her father as long as he lasts; but he won't last long. Mrs. Whimple confides to me that he is certainly going."

"Not to say an unfeeling thing," said I, "he cannot do better than go."

"I am afraid that must be admitted," said Herbert: "and then I shall come back for the dear little thing, and the dear little thing and I will walk quietly into the nearest church. Remember! The blessed darling comes of no family, my dear Handel, and never looked into the red book, and hasn't a notion about her grandpapa. What a fortune for the son of my mother!"

On the Saturday in that same week I took my leave of Herbert—full of bright hope, but sad and sorry to leave me—as he sat on one of the seaport mail-coaches. I went into a coffeehouse to write a little note to Clara, telling her he had gone off sending his love to her over and over again, and then went to my lonely home—if it deserved the name, for it was now no home to me, and I had no home anywhere.

On the stairs I encountered Wemmick, who was coming down, after an unsuccessful application of his knuckles to my door. I had not seen him alone since the disastrous issue of the attempted flight; and he had come, in his private and personal capacity, to say a few words of explanation in reference to that failure.

"The late Compey," said Wemmick, "had by little and little got at the bottom of half of the regular business now transacted, and it was from the talk of some of his people in trouble (some of his people being always in trouble) that I heard what I did. I kept my ears open, seeming to have them shut, until I heard that he was absent, and I thought that would be the best time for making the attempt. I can only suppose now that it was a part of his policy, as a very clever man, habitually to deceive his own instruments. You don't blame me, I hope, Mr. Pip? I am sure I tried to serve you with all my heart."

"I am as sure of that, Wemmick, as you can be, and I thank you most earnestly for all your interest and friendship."

"Thank you, thank you very much. It's a bad job," said Wemmick, scratching his head, "and I assure you I haven't been so cut up for a long time. What I look at is the sacrifice of so much portable property. Dear me!"

"What *I* think of, Wemmick, is the poor owner of the property."

"Yes, to be sure," said Wemmick. "Of course there can be no objection to your being sorry for him, and I'd put down a five-pound note myself to get him out of it. But what I look at is this. The late Compey having been before-hand with him in intelligence of his return, and being so determined to bring him to book, I don't think he could have been saved. Whereas the portable property certainly could have been saved. That's the difference between the property and the owner, don't you see?"

I invited Wemmick to come upstairs and refresh himself with a glass of grog before walking to Walworth. He accepted the invitation, and while he was drinking his moderate allowance said, with nothing to lead up to it, and after having appeared rather fidgety:

"What do you think of my meaning to take a holiday on Monday, Mr. Pip?"

"Why, I suppose you have not done such a thing these twelve months."

"These twelve years, more likely," said Wemmick. "Yes, I'm going to take a holiday. More than that; I'm going to take a walk. More than that; I'm going to ask you to take a walk with me."

I was about to excuse myself, as being but a bad companion just then, when Wemmick anticipated me.

"I know your engagements," said he, "and I know you are out of sorts, Mr. Pip. But if you *could* oblige me, I should take it as a kindness. It ain't a long walk, and it's an early one. Say it might occupy you (including breakfast on the walk) from eight to twelve. Couldn't you stretch a point and manage it?"

He had done so much for me at various times that this was very little to do for him. I said I could manage it—would manage it—and he was so very much pleased by my acquiescence that I was pleased too. At his particular request I appointed to call for him at the Castle at half past eight on Monday morning, and so we parted for the time.

Punctual to my appointment, I rang at the Castle gate on the Monday morning, and was received by Wemmick himself; who struck me as looking tighter than usual, and having a sleeker hat on. Within, there were two glasses of rum-and-milk prepared, and two biscuits. The Aged must have been stir-ring with the lark, for, glancing into the perspective of his bedroom, I observed that his bed was empty.

When we had fortified ourselves with the rum-and-milk and biscuits, and were going out for the walk with that training preparation on us, I was considerably surprised to see Wemmick take up a fishing-rod, and put it over his shoulder. "Why, we are not going fishing!" said I. "No," returned Wem-mick, "but I like to walk with one."

I thought this odd; however, I said nothing, and we set off. We went toward Camberwell Green, and when we were thereabouts Wemmick said, suddenly,

"Halloa! Here's a church!"

There was nothing very surprising in that; but again, I was rather sur-prised, when he said, as if he were animated by a brilliant idea,

"Let's go in!"

We went in, Wemmick leaving his fishing-rod in the porch, and looked all round. In the meantime Wemmick was diving into his coat-pockets, and getting something out of paper there.

"Halloa!" said he. "Here's a couple of pair of gloves! Let's put 'em on!"

As the gloves were white kid gloves, and as the post-office was widened to its utmost extent, I now began to have my strong suspicions. They were strengthened into certainty when I beheld the Aged enter at a side door, escorting a lady.

"Halloa!" said Wemmick. "Here's Miss Skiffins! Let's have a wedding."

That discreet damsel was attired as usual, except that she was now engaged in substituting for her green kid gloves a pair of white. The Aged was likewise occupied in preparing a similar sacrifice for the altar of Hymen. The old gentleman, however, experienced so much difficulty in getting his gloves on, that Wemmick found it necessary to put him with his back against a pillar, and then to get behind the pillar himself and pull away at them, while I for my part held the old gentleman round the waist, that he might present an equal and safe resistance. By dint of this ingenious scheme his gloves were got on to perfection.

The clerk and clergyman then appearing, we were ranged in order at those fatal rails. True to his notion of seeming to do it all without preparation, I heard Wemmick say to himself as he took something out of his waistcoat pocket before the service began, "Halloa! Here's a ring!"

I acted in the capacity of backer, or best-man, to the bridegroom; while a little limp pew opener, in a soft bonnet like a baby's, made a feint of being the bosom friend of Miss Skiffins. The responsibility of giving the lady away devolved upon the Aged, which led to the clergyman's being unintentionally scandalized, and it happened thus: When he said, "Who giveth this woman to be married to this man?" the old gentleman, not in the least knowing what point of the ceremony we had arrived at, stood most amiably beaming at the ten commandments. Upon which the clergyman said again, "Who giveth this woman to be married to this man?" The old gentleman being still in a state of most estimable unconsciousness, the bridegroom cried out in his accustomed voice, "Now Aged P. you know; who giveth?" To which the Aged replied with great briskness, before saying that *he* gave, "All right, John, all right, my boy!" And the clergyman came to so gloomy a pause upon it, that I had doubts for the moment whether we should get completely married that day.

It was completely done, however, and when we were going out of church Wemmick took the cover off the font and put his white gloves in it, and put the cover on again. Mrs. Wemmick, more heedful of the future, put her white gloves in her pocket and assumed her green. "*Now*, Mr. Pip," said Wemmick, triumphantly shouldering the fishing-rod as we came out, "let me ask you whether anybody would suppose this to be a wedding party?"

Breakfast had been ordered at a pleasant little tavern a mile or so away upon the rising ground beyond the Green; and there was a bagatelle board in the room in case we should desire to unbend our minds after the solemnity. It was pleasant to observe that Mrs. Wemmick no longer unwound Wemmick's arm when it adapted itself to her figure, but sat in a high-backed chair against the wall, like a violoncello in its case, and submitted to be embraced as that melodious instrument might have done.

We had an excellent breakfast, and when anyone declined anything on table, Wemmick said, "Provided by contract, you know; don't be afraid of it!" I drank to the new couple, drank to the Aged, drank to the Castle, saluted the bride at parting, and made myself as agreeable as I could.

Wemmick came down to the door with me, and I again shook hands with him, and wished him joy.

"Thankee!" said Wemmick, rubbing his hands. "She's such a manager of fowls you have no idea. You shall have some eggs, and judge for yourself. I say, Mr. Pip!" calling me back, and speaking low. "This is altogether a Walworth sentiment, please."

"I understand. Not to be mentioned in Little Britain," said I.

Wemmick nodded. "After what you let out the other day, Mr. Jaggers may as well not know of it. He might think my brain was softening, or something of the kind."

Fifty-six

HE LAY IN PRISON VERY ILL, DURING THE WHOLE INTERVAL between his committal for trial and the coming round of the Sessions. He had broken two ribs, they had wounded one of his lungs, and he breathed with great pain and difficulty, which increased daily. It was a consequence of his hurt that he spoke so low as to be scarcely audible; therefore he spoke very little. But he was ever ready to listen to me, and it became the first duty of my life to say to him, and read to him what I knew he ought to hear.

Being far too ill to remain in the common prison he was removed, after the first day or so, into the Infirmary. This gave me opportunities of being with him that I could not otherwise have had. And but for his illness he would have been put in irons, for he was regarded as a determined prison-breaker, and I know not what else.

Although I saw him every day, it was for only a short time; hence the regularly recurring spaces of our separation were long enough to record on his face any slight changes that occurred in his physical state. I do not recollect that I once saw any change in it for the better; he wasted, and became slowly weaker and worse, day by day, from the day when the prison door closed upon him.

The kind of submission or resignation that he showed was that of a man who was tired out. I sometimes derived an impression, from his manner, or from a whispered word or two which escaped him, that he pondered over the question whether he might have been a better man under better circumstances. But he never justified himself by a hint tending that way, or tried to bend the past out of its eternal shape.

It happened on two or three occasions in my presence that his desperate reputation was alluded to by one or other of the people in attendance on him. A smile crossed his face then, and he turned his eyes on me with a trustful look, as if he were confident that I had seen some small redeeming touch in him, even so long ago as when I was a little child. As to all the rest, he was humble and contrite, and I never knew him to complain.

When the Sessions came round Mr. Jaggers caused an application to be made for the postponement of his trial until the following Sessions. It was obviously made with the assurance that he could not live so long, and was refused. The trial came on at once, and when he was put to the bar he was seated in a chair. No objection was made to my getting close to the dock, on the outside of it, and holding the hand that he stretched forth to me.

The trial was very short and very clear. Such things as could be said for him were said—how he had taken to industrious habits, and had thriven lawfully and reputably. But nothing could unsay the fact that he had returned, and was there in presence of the Judge and Jury. It was impossible to try him for that, and do otherwise than find him Guilty.

At that time it was the custom (as I learned from my terrible experience of that Sessions) to devote a concluding day to the passing of Sentences, and to make a finishing effect with the Sentence of Death. But for the indelible picture that my remembrance now holds before me, I could scarcely believe, even as I write these words, that I saw two-and-thirty men and women put before the Judge to receive that sentence together. Foremost among the two-and-thirty was he; seated, that he might get breath enough to keep life in him.

The whole scene starts out again in the vivid colors of the moment, down to the drops of April rain on the windows of the court, glittering in the rays of April sun. Penned in the dock, as I again stood outside it at the corner with his hand in mine, were the two-and-thirty men and women; some defiant, some stricken with terror, some sobbing and weeping, some covering their faces, some staring gloomily about. There had been shrieks from among the women convicts, but they had been stilled, and a hush had succeeded. The sheriffs with their great chains and nosegays, other civic gewgaws and monsters, criers, ushers, a great gallery full of people—a large theatrical audience—looked on, as the two-and-thirty and the Judge were solemnly confronted. Then the Judge addressed them. Among the wretched creatures before him whom he must single out for special address was one who almost from his infancy had been an offender against the laws; who, after repeated imprisonments and punishments, had been at length sentenced to exile for a term of years; and who, under circumstances of great violence and daring had made his escape, and been resentenced to exile for life. That miserable man would seem for a time to have become convinced of his errors when far removed from the scenes of his old offenses, and to have lived a peaceable and honest life. But in a fatal moment yielding to those propensities and passions, the indulgence of which had so long rendered him a scourge to society, he had quitted his haven of rest and repentance, and had come back to the country where he was proscribed. Being here presently denounced, he had for a time succeeded in evading the officers of Justice, but being at length seized while in the act of flight, he had resisted them, and had—he best knew whether by express design, or in the blindness of his hardihood—caused the death of his denouncer, to whom his whole career was known. The appointed punishment for his return to the land that had cast him out being Death, and his case being this aggravated case, he must prepare himself to Die.

The sun was striking in at the great windows of the court through the glittering drops of rain upon the glass, and it made a broad shaft of light between the two-and-thirty and the Judge, linking both together, and perhaps reminding some among the audience how both were passing on, with absolute equality, to the greater Judgment that knoweth all things and never errs. Rising for a moment, a distinct speck of face in this way of light, the prisoner said, "My Lord, I have received my sentence of Death from the Almighty, but I bow to yours," and sat down again. There was some hushing, and the Judge went on with what he had to say to the rest. Then they were all formally doomed, and some of them were supported out, and some of them sauntered out with a haggard look of bravery, and a few nodded to the gallery, and two or three shook hands, and others went out chewing the fragments of herb they had taken from the sweet herbs lying about. He went last of all, because of having to be helped from his chair and to go very slowly; and he held my hand while all the others were removed, and while the audience got up (putting their dresses right, as they might at church or elsewhere) and pointed down at this criminal or at that, and most of all at him and me.

I earnestly hoped and prayed that he might die before the Recorder's Report was made, but, in the dread of his lingering on, I began that night to write out a petition to the Home Secretary of State, setting forth my knowledge of him, and how it was that he had come back for my sake. I wrote it as fervently and pathetically as I could, and when I had finished it and sent it in, I wrote out other petitions to such men in authority as I hoped were the most merciful, and drew up one to the Crown itself. For several days and nights after he was sentenced I took no rest except when I fell asleep in my chair, but was wholly absorbed in these appeals. And after I had sent them in, I could not keep away from the places where they were, but felt as if they were more hopeful and less desperate when I was near them. In this unreasonable restlessness and pain of mind I would roam the streets of an evening, wandering by those offices and houses where I had left the petitions. To the present hour the weary western streets of London on a cold dusty spring night, with their ranges of stern shut-up mansions, and their long rows of lamps, are melancholy to me from this association.

The daily visits I could make him were shortened now, and he was more strictly kept. Seeing, or fancying, that I was suspected of an intention of carrying poison to him, I asked to be searched before I sat down at his bedside, and told the officer who was always there, that I was willing to do anything that would assure him of the singleness of my designs. Nobody was hard with him or with me. There was duty to be done, and it was done, but not harshly. The officer always gave me the assurance that he was worse, and some other sick prisoners in the room, and some other prisoners who attended on them as sick nurses (malefactors but not incapable of kindness, GOD be thanked!) always joined in the same report.

As the days went on, I noticed more and more that he would lie, placidly looking at the white ceiling with an absence of light in his face, until some word of mine brightened it for an instant, and then it would subside again. Sometimes he was almost, or quite, unable to speak; then he would answer me with slight pressures on my hand, and I grew to understand his meaning very well.

The number of the days had mounted up to ten, when I saw a greater change in him than I had seen yet. His eyes were turned toward the door, and lighted up as I entered.

"Dear boy," he said, as I sat down by his bed: "I thought you was late. But I knowed you couldn't be that."

"It is just the time," said I. "I waited for it at the gate."

"You always waits at the gate; don't you, dear boy?"

"Yes. Not to lose a moment of the time."

"Thankee, dear boy, thankee. God bless you! You've never deserted me, dear boy."

I pressed his hand in silence, for I could not forget that I had once meant to desert him.

"And what's the best of all," he said, "you've been more cornfortable alonger me, since I was under a dark cloud, than when the sun shone. That's best of all."

He lay on his back breathing with great difficulty. Do what he would, and love me though he did, the light left his face ever and again, and a film came over the placid look at the white ceiling.

"Are you in much pain today?"

"I don't complain of none, dear boy."

"You never do complain, dear Magwitch."

He had spoken his last words. He smiled, and I understood his touch to mean that he wished to lift my hand, and lay it on his breast. I laid it there, and he smiled again, and put both his hands upon it.

The allotted time ran out while we were thus; but looking round, I found the governor of the prison standing by me, and he whispered, "You needn't go yet." I thanked him gratefully, and asked, "Might I speak to him if he can hear me?"

The governor stepped aside, and beckoned the officer away. The change, though it was made without noise, drew back the film from the placid look at the white ceiling, and he looked most affectionately at me.

"Dear Magwitch, I must tell you, now at last. You understand what I say?"

A gentle pressure on my hand.

"You had a child once whom you loved and lost."

A stronger pressure on my hand.

"She lived and found powerful friends. She is living now. She is a lady and very beautiful. And I love her!"

With a last faint effort, which would have been powerless but for my yielding to it and assisting it, he raised my hand to his lips. Then he gently let it sink upon his breast again, with his own hands lying on it. The placid look at the white ceiling came back, and passed away, and his head dropped quietly on his breast.

Mindful, then, of what we had read together, I thought of the two men who went up into the Temple to pray, and knew that there were no better words that I could say beside his bed than "O Lord, be merciful to him, a sinner!"

Fifty-seven

NOW THAT I WAS LEFT WHOLLY TO MYSELF, I GAVE NOTICE of my intention to quit the chambers in the Temple as soon as my tenancy could legally determine, and in the meanwhile to underlet them. At once I put bills up in the windows; for I was in debt, and had scarcely any money, and began to be seriously alarmed by the state of my affairs. I ought rather to write that I should have been alarmed if I had had energy and concentration enough to help me to the clear perception of any truth beyond the fact that I was falling very ill. The late stress upon me had enabled me to put off illness, but not to put it away; I knew that it was coming on me now, and I knew very little else, and was even careless as to that.

For a day or two, I lay on the sofa, or on the floor—anywhere according as I happened to sink down—with a heavy head and aching limbs, and no purpose, and no power. Then there came one night, which appeared of great duration, and which teemed with anxiety and horror; and when, in the morning, I tried to sit up in my bed and think of it, I found I could not do so.

Whether I really had been down in the Court in the dead of the night, groping about for the boat that I supposed to be there; whether I had two or three times come to myself on the staircase with great terror, not knowing how I had got out of bed; whether I had found myself lighting the lamp, possessed by the idea that he was coming up the stairs, and that the lights were blown out; whether I had been inexpressibly harassed by the distracted talking, laughing, and groaning, of someone, and had half suspected those sounds to be of my own making; whether there had been a closed iron furnace in a dark corner of the room, and a voice had called out over and over again that Miss Havisham was consuming within it; these were things that I tried to settle with myself and get into some order, as I lay that morning on my bed. But the vapor of a lime-kiln would come between me and them, disordering them all, and it was through the vapor at last that I saw two men looking at me.

"What do you want?" I asked, starting; "I don't know you."

"Well, sir," returned one of them, bending down and touching me on the shoulder, "this is a matter that you'll soon arrange, I dare say, but you're arrested."

"What is the debt?"

"Hundred and twenty-three pound, fifteen, six. Jeweler's account, I think."

"What is to be done?"

"You had better come to my house," said the man. "I keep a very nice house."

I made some attempt to get up and dress myself. When I next attended to them, they were standing a little off from the bed, looking at me. I still lay there.

"You see my state," said I. "I would come with you if I could; but indeed I am quite unable. If you take me from here, I think I shall die by the way."

Perhaps they replied, or argued the point, or tried to encourage me to believe that I was better than I thought. Forasmuch as they hang in my memory by only this one slender thread, I don't know what they did, except that they forbore to remove me.

That I had a fever and was avoided, that I suffered greatly, that I often lost my reason, that the time seemed interminable, that I confounded impossible existences with my own identity; that I was a brick in the house wall, and yet entreating to be released from the giddy place where the builders had set me; that I was a steel beam of a vast engine, clashing and whirling over a gulf, and yet that I implored in my own person to have the engine stopped, and my part in it hammered off; that I passed through these phases of disease, I know of my own remembrance, and did in some sort know at the time. That I sometimes struggled with real people, in the belief that they were murderers, and that I would all at once comprehend that they meant to do me good, and would then sink exhausted in their arms, and suffer them to lay me down, I also knew at the time. But, above all, I knew that there was a constant tendency in all these people—who, when I was very ill, would present all kinds of extraordinary transformations of the human face, and would be much dilated in size—above all, I say, I knew that there was an extraordinary tendency in all these people, sooner or later to settle down into the likeness of Joe.

After I had turned the worst point of my illness, I began to notice that while all its other features changed, this one consistent feature did not change. Whoever came about me, still settled down into Joe. I opened my eyes in the night, and I saw in the great chair at the bedside, Joe. I opened my eyes in the day, and, sitting on the window-seat, smoking his pipe in the shaded open window, still I saw Joe. I asked for cooling drink, and the dear hand that gave it me was Joe's. I sank back on my pillow after drinking, and the face that looked so hopefully and tenderly upon me was the face of Joe.

At last, one day, I took courage, and said, "*Is* it Joe?"

And the dear old home-voice answered, "Which it air, old chap."

"O Joe, you break my heart! Look angry at me, Joe. Strike me, Joe. Tell me of my ingratitude. Don't be so good to me!"

For, Joe had actually laid his head down on the pillow at my side, and put his arm round my neck, in his joy that I knew him.

"Which dear old Pip, old chap," said Joe, "you and me was ever friends. And when you're well enough to go out for a ride—what larks!"

After which, Joe withdrew to the window, and stood with his back towards me, wiping his eyes. And as my extreme weakness prevented me from getting up and going to him, I lay there, penitently whispering, "O God bless him! O God bless this gentle Christian man!"

Joe's eyes were red when I next found him beside me; but I was holding his hand, and we both felt happy.

"How long, dear Joe?"

"Which you meantersay, Pip, how long have your illness lasted, dear old chap?"

"Yes, Joe."

"It's the end of May, Pip. Tomorrow is the first of June."

"And have you been here all the time, dear Joe?"

"Pretty nigh, old chap. For, as I says to Biddy when the news of your being ill were brought by letter, which it were brought by the post and being formerly single he is now married though underpaid for a deal of walking and shoe-leather, but wealth were not a object on his part, and marriage were the great wish of his hart—"

"It is so delightful to hear you, Joe! But I interrupt you in what you said to Biddy."

"Which it were," said Joe, "that how you might be amongst strangers, and that how you and me having been ever friends, a wisit at such a moment might not prove unacceptabobble. And Biddy, her word were, 'Go to him, without loss of time.' That," said Joe, summing up with his judicial air, "were the word of Biddy. 'Go to him,' Biddy say, 'without loss of time.' In short, I shouldn't greatly deceive you," Joe added, after a little grave reflection, "if I represented to you that the word of that young woman were, 'without a minute's loss of time.'"

There Joe cut himself short, and informed me that I was to be talked to in great moderation, and that I was to take a little nourishment at stated frequent times, whether I felt inclined for it or not, and that I was to submit myself to all his orders. So, I kissed his hand, and lay quiet, while he proceeded to indite a note to Biddy, with my love in it.

Evidently, Biddy had taught Joe to write. As I lay in bed looking at him, it made me, in my weak state, cry again with pleasure to see the pride with which he set about his letter. My bedstead, divested of its curtains, had been removed with me upon it, into the sitting room, as the airiest and largest, and the carpet had been taken away, and the room kept always fresh and wholesome night and day. At my own writing-table, pushed into a corner and cumbered with little bottles, Joe now sat down to his great work, first choosing a pen from the pen-tray as if it were a chest of large tools, and tucking up his sleeves as if he were going to wield a crowbar or sledgehammer. It was necessary for Joe to hold on heavily to the table with his left elbow, and to get his right leg well out behind him, before he could begin, and when he did begin, he made every downstroke so slowly that it might have been six feet long, while at every upstroke I could hear his pen spluttering extensively. He had a curious idea that the inkstand was on the side of him where it was not, and constantly dipped his pen into space, and seemed quite satisfied with the result. Occasionally he was tripped up by some orthographical stumbling-block, but on the whole he got on very well indeed, and when he had signed his name, and had removed a finishing blot from the paper to the crown of his head with his two forefingers, he got up and hovered about the table, trying the effect of his performance from various points of view as it lay there, with unbounded satisfaction.

Not to make Joe uneasy by talking too much, even if I had been able to talk much, I deferred asking him about Miss Havisham until next day. He shook his head when I then asked him if she had recovered.

"Is she dead, Joe?"

"Why you see, old chap," said Joe, in a tone of remonstrance, and by way of getting at it by degrees, "I wouldn't go so far as to say that, for that's a deal to say; but she ain't—"

"Living, Joe?"

"That's nigher where it is," said Joe; "she ain't living."

"Did she linger long, Joe?"

"Arter you was took ill, pretty much about what you might call (if you was put to it) a week," said Joe; still determined on my account, to come at everything by degrees.

"Dear Joe, have you heard what becomes of her property?"

"Well, old chap," said Joe, "it do appear that she had settled the most of it, which I meantersay tied it up, on Miss Estella. But she had wrote out a little coddleshell in her own hand a day or two afore the accident, leaving a cool four thousand to Mr. Matthew Pocket. And why, do you suppose, above all things, Pip, she left that cool four thousand unto him? 'Because of Pip's account of him the said Matthew.' I am told by Biddy, that air the writing," said Joe, repeating the legal turn as if it did him infinite good, " 'account of him the said Matthew.' And a cool four thousand, Pip!"

I never discovered from whom Joe derived the conventional temperature of the four thousand pounds, but it appeared to make the sum of money more to him, and he had a manifest relish in insisting on its being cool.

This account gave me great joy, as it perfected the only good thing I had done since I left the forge. I asked Joe whether he had heard if any of the other relations had any legacies?

"Miss Sarah," said Joe, "she have twenty-five pound perannium fur to buy pills, on account of being bilious. Miss Georgiana, she have twenty pound down. Mrs.—what's the name of them wild beasts with humps, old chap?"

"Camels?" said I, wondering why he could possibly want to know.

Joe nodded. "Mrs. Camels," by which I presently understood he meant Camilla, "she have five pound fur to buy rush-lights to put her in spirits when she wake up in the night."

The accuracy of these recitals was sufficiently obvious to me, to give me great confidence in Joe's information. "And now," said Joe, "you ain't that strong yet, old chap, that you can take in more nor one additional shovelfull today. Old Orlick he's been a bustin' open a dwelling-ouse."

"Whose?" said I.

"Well! Not but what his manners is given to blusterous," said Joe, apologetically; "still a Englishman's ouse is his Castle, and castles must not be busted 'cept when done in wartime. And wotsume'er the failings on his part, he were a corn and seedsman in his hart."

"Is it Pumblechook's house that has been broken into, then?"

"That's it, Pip," said Joe; "and they took his till, and they took his cashbox, and they drinked his wine, and they partook of his wittles, and they slapped his face, and they pulled his nose, and they tied him up to his bedpust, and they giv' him a dozen, and they stuffed his mouth full of flowering annuals to prewent his crying out. But he knowed Orlick, and Orlick's in the county jail."

By these approaches, we arrived at unrestricted conversation. I was slow to gain strength, but I did slowly and surely become less weak, and Joe stayed with me, and I fancied I was little Pip again.

For the tenderness of Joe was so beautifully proportioned to my need, that I was like a child in his hands. He would sit and talk to me in the old confidence, and with the old simplicity, and in the old unassertive protecting way, so that I would half believe that all my life since the days of the old kitchen was one of the mental troubles of the fever that was gone. He did everything for me except the household work, for which he had engaged a very decent woman, after paying off the laundress on his first arrival. "Which I do assure you, Pip," he would often say, in way of explanation of that liberty; "I found her a tapping the spare bed, like a cask of beer, and drawing off the feathers in a bucket, for sale. Which she would have tapped yourn next and draw'd it off with you a laying on it, and was then a carrying away the coals gradivally in the soup-tureen and wegetable dishes, and the wine and spirits in your Wellington boots."

We looked forward to the day when I should go out for a ride, as we had once looked forward to the day of my apprenticeship. And when the day came, and an open carriage was got into the lane, Joe wrapped me up, took me in his arms, carried me down to it, and put me in, as if I were still the small helpless creature to whom he had so abundantly given of the wealth of his great nature.

And Joe got in beside me, and we drove away together into the country, where the rich summer growth was already on the trees and on the grass, and sweet summer scents filled all the air. The day happened to be Sunday, and when I looked on the loveliness around me, and thought how it had grown and changed, and how the little wildflowers had been forming, and the voices of the birds had been strengthening, by day and by night, under the sun and under the stars, while poor I lay burning and tossing on my bed, the mere remembrance of having burned and tossed there, came like a check upon my peace. But when I heard the Sunday bells, and looked round a little more upon the outspread beauty, I felt that I was not nearly thankful enough—that I was too weak yet, to be even that—and I laid my head on Joe's shoulder, as I had laid it long ago when he had taken me to the Fair or where not, and it was too much for my young senses.

More composure came to me after a while, and we talked as we used to talk, lying on the grass at the old Battery. There was no change whatever in Joe. Exactly what he had been in my eyes then, he was in my eyes still; just as simply faithful and as simply right.

When we got back again and he lifted me out, and carried me, so easily, across the court and up the stairs, I thought of that eventful Christmas Day when he had carried me over the marshes. We had not yet made any allusion to my change of fortune, nor did I know how much of my late history he was acquainted with. I was so doubtful of myself now, and put so much trust in him, that I could not satisfy myself whether I ought to refer to it when he did not.

"Have you heard, Joe," I asked him that evening, upon further consideration, as he smoked his pipe at the window, "who my patron was?"

"I heerd," returned Joe, "as it were not Miss Havisham, old chap."

"Did you hear who it was, Joe?"

"Well! I heerd as it were a person what sent the person what giv' you the bank-notes at the Jolly Bargemen, Pip."

"So it was."

"Astonishing!" said Joe, in the placidest way.

"Did you hear that he was dead, Joe?" I presently asked, with increasing diffidence.

"Which? Him as sent the bank-notes, Pip?"

"Yes."

"I think," said Joe, after meditating a long time, and looking rather evasively at the window-seat, "as I *did* hear tell that how he were something or another in a general way in that direction."

"Did you hear anything of his circumstances, Joe?"

"Not partickler, Pip."

"If you would like to hear, Joe—" I was beginning, when Joe got up and came to my sofa.

"Lookee here, old chap," said Joe, bending over me. "Ever the best of friends; ain't us, Pip?"

I was ashamed to answer him.

"Wery good, then," said Joe, as if I *had* answered; "that's all right; that's agreed upon. Then why go into subjects, old chap, which as betwixt two sech must be forever onnecessary? There's subjects enough as betwixt two sech, without onnecessary ones. Lord! To think of your poor sister and her Rampages! And don't you remember Tickler?"

"I do indeed, Joe."

"Lookee here, old chap," said Joe. "I done what I could to keep you and Tickler in sunders, but my power were not always fully equal to my inclinations. For when your poor sister had a mind to drop into you, it were not so much," said Joe, in his favorite argumentative way, "that she dropped into me too, if I put myself in opposition to her, but that she dropped into you always heavier for it. I noticed that. It ain't a grab at a man's whisker, nor yet a shake or two of a man (to which your sister was quite welcome) that 'ud put a man off from getting a little child out of punishment. But when that little child is dropped into, heavier, for that grab of whisker or shaking, then that man naterally up and says to himself, 'Where is the good as you are a doing? I grant you I see the 'arm,' says the man, 'but I don't see the good. I call upon you, sir, theerfore, to pint out the good.'"

"The man says," I observed, as Joe waited for me to speak.

"The man says," Joe assented. "Is he right, that man?"

"Dear Joe, he is always right."

"Well, old chap," said Joe, "then abide by your words. If he's always right (which in general he's more likely wrong) he's right when he says this:—Supposing ever you kep' any little matter to yourself when you was a little child, you kep' it mostly because you know'd as J. Gargery's power to part you and Tickler in sunders, were not fully equal to his inclinations. Theerfore, think no more of it as betwixt two sech, and do not let us pass remarks upon onnecessary subjects. Biddy giv' herself a deal o' trouble with me afore I left (for I am most awful dull), as I should view it in this light, and viewing it in this light, as I should so put it. Both of which," said Joe, quite charmed with his logical arrangement, "being done, now this to you a true friend, say. Namely. You mustn't go a overdoing on it, but you must have your supper and your wine and water, and you must be put betwixt the sheets."

The delicacy with which Joe dismissed this theme, and the sweet tact and kindness with which Biddy—who with her woman's wit had found me out so soon—had prepared him for it, made a deep impression on my mind. But whether Joe knew how poor I was, and how my great expectations had all dissolved, like our own marsh mists before the sun, I could not understand.

Another thing in Joe that I could not understand when it first began to develop itself, but which I soon arrived at a sorrowful comprehension of, was this: As I became stronger and better, Joe became a little less easy with me. In my weakness and entire dependence on him, the dear fellow had fallen into the old tone, and called me by the old names, the dear "old Pip, old chap," that now were music in my ears. I too had fallen into the old ways, only happy and thankful that he let me. But, imperceptibly, though I held by them fast, Joe's hold upon them began to slacken; and whereas I wondered at this at first I soon began to understand that the cause of it was in me, and that the fault of it was all mine.

Alas! Had I given Joe no reason to doubt my constancy, and to think that in prosperity I should grow cold to him and cast him off? Had I given Joe's innocent heart no cause to feel instinctively that as I got stronger, his hold upon me would be weaker, and that he had better loosen it in time and let me go, before I plucked myself away?

It was on the third or fourth occasion of my going out walking in the Temple Gardens leaning on Joe's arm, that I saw this change in him very plainly. We had been sitting in the bright warm sunlight, looking at the river, and I chanced to say as we got up:

"See, Joe! I can walk quite strongly. Now, you shall see me walk back by myself."

"Which do not overdo it, Pip," said Joe; "but I shall be happy for to see you able, sir."

The last word grated on me; but how could I remonstrate! I walked no further than the gate of the gardens, and then pretended to be weaker than I was, and asked Joe for his arm. Joe gave it me, but was thoughtful.

I, for my part, was thoughtful, too; for how best to check this growing change in Joe, was a great perplexity to my remorseful thoughts. That I was ashamed to tell him exactly how I was placed, and what I had come down to, I do not seek to conceal; but I hope my reluctance was not quite an unworthy one. He would want to help me out of his little savings, I knew, and I knew that he ought not to help me, and that I must not suffer him to do it.

It was a thoughtful evening with both of us. But before we went to bed, I had resolved that I would wait over tomorrow, tomorrow being Sunday, and would begin my new course with the new week. On Monday morning I would speak to Joe about this change, I would lay aside this last vestige of reserve, I would tell him what I had in my thoughts (that Secondly, not yet arrived at), and why I had not decided to go out to Herbert, and then the change would be conquered forever. As I cleared, Joe cleared, and it seemed as though he had sympathetically arrived at a resolution too.

We had a quiet day on the Sunday, and we rode out into the country, and then walked in the fields.

"I feel thankful that I have been ill, Joe," I said.

"Dear old Pip, old chap, you're a'most come round, sir."

"It has been a memorable time for me, Joe."

"Likeways for myself, sir," Joe returned.

"We have had a time together, Joe, that I can never forget. There were days once, I know, that I did for a while forget; but I never shall forget these."

"Pip," said Joe, appearing a little hurried and troubled, "there has been larks. And, dear sir, what has been betwixt us—have been."

At night, when I had gone to bed, Joe came into my room, as he had done all through my recovery. He asked me if I felt sure that I was as well as in the morning.

"Yes, dear Joe, quite."

"And are always a getting stronger, old chap?"

"Yes, dear Joe, steadily."

Joe patted the coverlet on my shoulder with his great good hand, and said, in what I thought a husky voice, "Good night!"

When I got up in the morning, refreshed and stronger yet, I was full of my resolution to tell Joe all, without delay. I would tell him before breakfast. I would dress at once and go to his room and surprise him; for it was the first day I had been up early. I went to his room, and he was not there. Not only was he not there, but his box was gone.

I hurried then to the breakfast-table, and on it found a letter. These were its brief contents:

"Not wishful to intrude I have departed fur you are well again dear Pip and will do better without

"P.S. Ever the best of friends."

Enclosed in the letter, was a receipt for the debt and costs on which I had been arrested. Down to that moment I had vainly supposed that my creditor had withdrawn or suspended proceedings until I should be quite recovered. I had never dreamed of Joe's having paid the money; but Joe had paid it, and the receipt was in his name.

What remained for me now, but to follow him to the dear old forge, and there to have out my disclosure to him, and my penitent remonstrance with him, and there to relieve my mind and heart of that reserved Secondly, which had begun as a vague something lingering in my thoughts, and had formed into a settled purpose?

The purpose was, that I would go to Biddy, that I would show her how humbled and repentant I came back, that I would tell her how I had lost all I once hoped for, that I would remind her of our old confidences in my first unhappy time. Then I would say to her, "Biddy, I think you once liked me very well, when my errant heart, even while it strayed away from you, was quieter and better with you than it ever has been since. If you can like me only half as well once more, if you can take me with all my faults and disappointments on my head, if you can receive me like a forgiven child (and indeed I am as sorry, Biddy, and have as much need of a hushing voice and a soothing hand), I hope I am a little worthier of you than I was—not much, but a little. And, Biddy, it shall rest with you to say whether I shall work at the forge with Joe, or whether I shall try for any different occupation down in this country, or whether we shall go away to a distant place where an opportunity awaits me, which I set aside, when it was offered, until I knew your answer. And now, dear Biddy, if you can tell me that you will go through the world with me, you will surely make it a better world for me, and me a better man for it, and I will try hard to make it a better world for you."

Such was my purpose. After three days more of recovery, I went down to the old place, to put it in execution; and how I sped in it, is all I have left to tell.

Fifty-eight

THE TIDINGS OF MY HIGH FORTUNES HAVING HAD A HEAVY fall had got down to my native place and its neighborhood before I got there. I found the Blue Boar in possession of the intelligence, and I found that it made a great change in the Boar's demeanor. Whereas the Boar had cultivated my good opinion with warm assiduity when I was coming into property, the Boar was exceedingly cool on the subject now that I was going out of property.

It was evening when I arrived, much fatigued by the journey I had so often made so easily. The Boar could not put me into my usual bedroom, which was engaged (probably by someone who had expectations), and could only assign me a very indifferent chamber among the pigeons and post-chaises up the yard. But I had as sound a sleep in that lodging as in the most superior accommodation the Boar could have given me, and the quality of my dreams was about the same as in the best bedroom.

Early in the morning, while my breakfast was getting ready, I strolled round by Satis House. There were printed bills on the gate, and on bits of carpet hanging out of the windows, announcing a sale by auction of the Household Furniture and Effects next week. The house itself was to be sold as old building materials and pulled down. LOT 1 was marked in whitewashed knock-knee letters on the brew-house; LOT 2 on that part of the main building which had been so long shut up. Other lots were marked off on other parts of the structure, and the ivy had been torn down to make room for the inscriptions, and much of it trailed low in the dust and was withered already. Stepping in for a moment at the open gate, and looking around me with the uncomfortable air of a stranger who had no business there, I saw the auctioneer's clerk walking on the casks and telling them off for the information of a catalogue-compiler, pen in hand, who made a temporary desk of the wheeled chair I had so often pushed along to the tune of Old Clem.

When I got back to my breakfast in the Boar's coffee-room, I found Mr. Pumblechook conversing with the landlord. Mr. Pumblechook (not improved in appearance by his late nocturnal adventure), was waiting for me, and addressed me in the following terms:

"Young man, I am sorry to see you brought low. But what else could be expected! What else could be expected!"

As he extended his hand with a magnificently forgiving air, and as I was broken by illness and unfit to quarrel, I took it.

"William," said Mr. Pumblechook to the waiter, "put a muffin on table. And has it come to this! Has it come to this!"

I frowningly sat down to my breakfast. Mr. Pumblechook stood over me and poured out my tea—before I could touch the teapot—with the air of a benefactor who was resolved to be true to the last.

"William," said Mr. Pumblechook, mournfully, "put the salt on. In happier times," addressing me, "I think you took sugar? And did you take milk? You did. Sugar and milk. William, bring a watercress."

"Thank you," said I, shortly, "but I don't eat watercresses."

"You don't eat 'em," returned Mr. Pumblechook, sighing and nodding his head several times, as if he might have expected that, and as if abstinence from watercresses were consistent with my downfall. "True. The simple fruits of the earth. No. You needn't bring any, William."

I went on with my breakfast, and Mr. Pumblechook continued to stand over me, staring fishily, and breathing noisily, as he always did.

"Little more than skin and bone!" mused Mr. Pumblechook, aloud. "And yet when he went away from here (I may say with my blessing), and I spread afore him my humble store, like the Bee, he was as plump as a Peach!"

This reminded me of the wonderful difference between the servile manner in which he had offered his hand in my new prosperity, saying, "May I?" and the ostentatious clemency with which he had just now exhibited the same fat five fingers.

"Hah!" he went on, handing me the bread-and-butter. "And air you a going to Joseph?"

"In Heaven's name," said I, firing in spite of myself, "what does it matter to you where I am going? Leave that teapot alone."

It was the worst course I could have taken, because it gave Pumblechook the opportunity he wanted.

"Yes, young man," said he, releasing the handle of the article in question, retiring a step or two from my table, and speaking for the behoof of the landlord and waiter at the door, "I *will* leave that teapot alone. You are right, young man. For once you are right. I forgit myself when I take such an interest in your breakfast as to wish your frame, exhausted by the debilitating effects of prodigygality, to be stimilated by the 'olesome nourishment of your forefathers. And yet," said Pumblechook, turning to the landlord and waiter, and pointing me out at arm's length, "this is him as I ever sported with in his days of happy infancy. Tell me not it cannot be; I tell you this is him!"

A low murmur from the two replied. The waiter appeared to be particularly affected.

"This is him," said Pumblechook, "as I have rode in my shay-cart. This is him as I have seen brought up by hand. This is him untoe the sister of which I was uncle by marriage, as her name was Georgiana M'ria, from her own mother. Let him deny it if he can!"

The waiter seemed convinced that I could not deny it, and that it gave the case a black look.

"Young man," said Pumblechook, screwing his head at me in the old fashion, "you air a going to Joseph. What does it matter to me, you ask me, where you air a going? I say to you, sir, you air a going to Joseph."

The waiter coughed, as if he modestly invited me to get over that.

"Now," said Pumblechook, and all this with a most exasperating air of saying in the cause of virtue what was perfectly convincing and conclusive, "I will tell you what to say to Joseph. Here is Squires of the Boar present, known and respected in this town, and here is William, which his father's name was Potkins if I do not deceive myself."

"You do not, sir," said William.

"In their presence," pursued Pumblechook, "I will tell you, young man, what to say to Joseph. Says you, 'Joseph, I have this day seen my earliest benefactor and the founder of my fortun's. I will name no names, Joseph, but so they are pleased to call him uptown, and I have seen that man.' "

"I swear I don't see him here," said I.

"Say that likewise," retorted Pumblechook. "Say you said that, and even Joseph will probably betray surprise."

"There you quite mistake him," said I. "I know better."

"Says you," Pumblechook went on, " 'Joseph, I have seen that man, and that man bears you no malice and bears me no malice. He knows your character, Joseph, and is well acquainted with your pig-headedness and ignorance; and he knows my character, Joseph, and he knows my want of gratitoode. Yes, Joseph,' says you"—here Pumblechook shook his head and hand at me—" 'he knows my total deficiency of common human gratitoode. *He* knows it, Joseph, as none can. *You* do not know it, Joseph, having no call to know it, but that man do.' "

Windy donkey as he was, it really amazed me that he could have the face to talk thus to mine.

"Says you, 'Joseph, he gave me a little message, which I will now repeat. It was, that in my being brought low, he saw the finger of Providence. He knowed that finger when he saw it, Joseph, and he saw it plain. It pinted out this writing, Joseph. *Reward of ingratitoode to his earliest benefactor, and founder of fortun's.* But that man said that he did not repent of what he had done, Joseph. Not at all. It was right to do it, it was kind to do it, it was benevolent to do it, and he would do it again.' "

"It's a pity," said I, scornfully, as I finished my interrupted breakfast, "that the man did not say what he had done and would do again."

"Squires of the Boar!" Pumblechook was now addressing the landlord, "and William! I have no objections to your mentioning, either uptown or downtown, if such should be your wishes, that it was right to do it, kind to do it, benevolent to do it, and that I would do it again."

With those words the impostor shook them both by the hand, with an air, and left the house; leaving me much more astonished than delighted by the virtues of that same indefinite "it." I was not long after him in leaving the house too, and when I went down the High Street I saw him holding forth (no doubt to the same effect) at his shop door, to a select group, who honored me with very unfavorable glances as I passed on the opposite side of the way.

But it was only the pleasanter to turn to Biddy and to Joe, whose great forbearance shone more brightly than before, if that could be, contrasted with this brazen pretender. I went toward them slowly, for my limbs were weak, but with a sense of increasing relief as I drew nearer to them, and a sense of leaving arrogance and untruthfulness further and further behind.

The June weather was delicious. The sky was blue, the larks were soaring high over the green corn, I thought all that countryside more beautiful and peaceful by far than I had ever known it to be yet. Many pleasant pictures of the life that I would lead there, and of the change for the better that would come over my character when I had a guiding spirit at my side whose simple faith and clear home-wisdom I had proved, beguiled my way. They awakened a tender emotion in me, for my heart was softened by my return, and such a change had come to pass, that I felt like one who was toiling home barefoot from distant travel and whose wanderings had lasted many years.

The schoolhouse where Biddy was mistress I had never seen, but the little roundabout lane by which I entered the village for quietness' sake took me past it. I was disappointed to find that the day was a holiday; no children were there, and Biddy's house was closed. Some hopeful notion of seeing her busily engaged in her daily duties, before she saw me, had been in my mind and was defeated.

But the forge was a very short distance off, and I went toward it under the sweet green limes, listening for the clink of Joe's hammer. Long after I ought to have heard it, and long after I had fancied I heard it and found it but a fancy, all was still. The limes were there, and the white thorns were there, and the chestnut-trees were there, and their leaves rustled harmoniously when I stopped to listen; but the clink of Joe's hammer was not in the midsummer wind.

Almost fearing, without knowing why, to come in view of the forge, I saw it at last, and saw that it was closed. No gleam of fire, no glittering shower of sparks, no roar of bellows; all shut up and still.

But the house was not deserted, and the best parlor seemed to be in use, for there were white curtains fluttering in its window, and the window was open and gay with flowers. I went softly toward it, meaning to peep over the flowers, when Joe and Biddy stood before me, arm in arm.

At first Biddy gave a cry, as if she thought it was my apparition, but in another moment she was in my embrace. I wept to see her, and she wept to see me; I, because she looked so fresh and pleasant; she, because I looked so worn and white.

"But dear Biddy, how smart you are!"

"Yes, dear Pip."

"And Joe, how smart *you* are!"

"Yes, dear old Pip, old chap."

I looked at both of them, from one to the other, and then—

"It's my wedding-day," cried Biddy, in a burst of happiness, "and I am married to Joe!"

They had taken me into the kitchen, and I had laid my head down on the old deal table, Biddy held one of my hands to her lips, and Joe's restoring touch was on my shoulder. "Which he warn't strong enough, my dear, fur to be surprised," said Joe. And Biddy said, "I ought to have thought of it, dear Joe, but I was too happy." They were both so overjoyed to see me, so proud to see me, so touched by my coming to them, so delighted that I should have come by accident to make their day complete!

My first thought was one of great thankfulness that I had never breathed this last baffled hope to Joe. How often, while he was with me in my illness, had it risen to my lips. How irrevocable would have been his knowledge of it, if he had remained with me but another hour!

"Dear Biddy," said I, "you have the best husband in the whole world, and if you could have seen him by my bed you would have— But no, you couldn't love him better than you do."

"No, I couldn't, indeed," said Biddy.

"And, dear Joe, you have the best wife in the whole world, and she will make you as happy as ever you deserve to be, you dear, good, noble Joe!"

Joe looked at me with a quivering lip, and fairly put his sleeve before his eyes.

"And Joe and Biddy both, as you have been in church today, and are in charity and love with all mankind, receive my humble thanks for all you have done for me, and all I have so ill repaid! And when I say that I am going away within the hour, for I am soon going abroad, and that I shall never rest until I have worked for the money with which you have kept me out of prison, and have sent it to you, don't think, dear Joe and Biddy, that if I could repay it a thousand times over I suppose I could cancel a farthing of the debt I owe you, or that I would do so if I could!"

They were both melted by these words, and both entreated me to say no more.

"But I must say more. Dear Joe, I hope you will have children to love, and that some little fellow will sit in this chimney-corner, of a winter's night, who may remind you of another little fellow gone out of it forever. Don't tell him, Joe, that I was thankless; don't tell him, Biddy, that I was ungenerous and unjust; only tell him that I honored you both, because you were both so good and and true, and that, as your child, I said it would be natural to him to grow up a much better man than I did."

"I ain't a going," said Joe, from behind his sleeve, "to tell him nothink o' that natur, Pip. Nor Biddy ain't. Nor yet no one ain't."

"And now, though I know you have already done it in your own kind hearts, pray tell me both that you forgive me! Pray let me hear you say the words, that I may carry the sound of them away with me, and then I shall be able to believe that you can trust me, and think better of me, in the time to come!"

"Oh dear old Pip, old chap," said Joe. "God knows as I forgive you, if I have anything to forgive!"

"Amen! And God knows I do!" echoed Biddy.

"Now let me go up and look at my old little room, and rest there a few minutes by myself, and then when I have eaten and drunk with you, go with me as far as the finger-post, dear Joe and Biddy, before we say good-bye!"

I sold all I had, and put aside as much as I could, for a composition with my creditors—who gave me ample time to pay them in full—and I went out and joined Herbert. Within a month I had quitted England, and within two months I was clerk to Clarriker and Co., and within four months I assumed my first undivided responsibility. For the beam across the parlor-ceiling at Mill Pond Bank had then ceased to tremble under old Bill Barley's growls, and was at peace, and Herbert had gone away to marry Clara, and I was left in sole charge of the Eastern Branch until he brought her back.

Many a year went round before I was a partner in the House; but I lived happily with Herbert and his wife, and lived frugally, and paid my debts, and maintained a constant correspondence with Biddy and Joe. It was not until I became third in the Firm that Clarriker betrayed me to Herbert; but he then declared that the secret of Herbert's partnership had been long enough upon his conscience, and he must tell it. So he told it, and Herbert was as much moved as amazed, and the dear fellow and I were not the worse friends for the long concealment. I must not leave it to be supposed that we were ever a great House, or that we made mints of money. We were not in a grand way of business; but we had a good name, and worked for our profits, and did very well. We owed so much to Herbert's ever-cheerful industry and readiness, that I often wondered how I had conceived the old idea of his inaptitude, until I was one day enlightened by the reflection that, perhaps, the inaptitude had never been in him at all, but had been in me.

Fifty-nine

FOR ELEVEN YEARS I HAD NOT SEEN JOE NOR BIDDY WITH my bodily eyes—though they had both been often before my fancy in the East—when upon an evening in December, an hour or two after dark, I laid my hand softly on the latch of the old kitchen door. I touched it so softly that I was not heard and looked in unseen. There, smoking his pipe in the old place by the kitchen firelight—as hale and as strong as ever, though a little gray—sat Joe; and there, fenced into the corner with Joe's leg, and sitting on my own little stool, looking at the fire, was—I again.

"We giv' him the name of Pip for your sake, dear old chap," said Joe, delighted when I took another stool by the child's side (but I did *not* rumple his hair), "and we hoped he might grow a little bit like you, and we think he do."

I thought so too, and I took him out for a walk next morning, and we talked immensely, understanding one another to perfection. And I took him down to the churchyard, and set him on a certain tombstone there, and he showed me from that elevation which stone was sacred to the memory of Philip Pirrip, late of this Parish, and also Georgiana, Wife of the Above.

"Biddy," said I, when I talked with her after dinner, as her little girl lay sleeping in her lap, "you must give Pip to me, one of these days; or lend him, at all events."

"No, no," said Biddy gently. "You must marry."

"So Herbert and Clara say, but I don't think I shall, Biddy. I have so settled down in their home, that it's not at all likely. I am already quite an old bachelor."

Biddy looked down at her child, and put its little hand to her lips, and then put the good matronly hand with which she had touched it into mine. There was something in the action and in the light pressure of Biddy's wedding-ring that had a very pretty eloquence in it.

"Dear Pip," said Biddy, "you are sure you don't fret for her?"

"Oh, no—I think not, Biddy."

"Tell me, as an old, old friend. Have you quite forgotten her?"

"My dear Biddy, I have forgotten nothing in my life that ever had a foremost place there, and little that ever had any place there. But that poor dream, as I once used to call it, has all gone by, Biddy, all gone by!"

Nevertheless I knew while I said those words that I secretly intended to revisit the site of the old house that evening alone for her sake. Yes, even so. For Estella's sake.

I had heard of her as leading a most unhappy life, and as being separated from her husband, who had used her with great cruelty, and who had become quite renowned as a compound of pride, avarice, brutality, and meanness. And I had heard of the death of her husband, from an accident consequent on his ill-treatment of a horse. This release had befallen her some two years before; for anything I knew she was married again.

The early dinner-hour at Joe's left me abundance of time, without hurrying my talk with Biddy, to walk over to the old spot before dark. But what with loitering on the way, to look at old objects and to think of old times, the day had quite declined when I came to the place.

There was no house now, no brewery, no building whatever left, but the wall of the old garden. The cleared space had been enclosed with a rough fence, and, looking over it, I saw that some of the old ivy had struck root anew, and was growing green on low, quiet mounds of ruin. A gate in the fence standing ajar, I pushed it open and went in.

A cold, silvery mist had vailed the afternoon, and the moon was not yet up to scatter it; but the stars were shining beyond the mist, and the moon was coming, and the evening was not dark. I could trace out where every part of the old house had been, and where the brewery had been, and where the gates, and where the casks. I had done so, and was looking along the desolate garden-walk, when I beheld a solitary figure in it.

The figure showed itself aware of me as I advanced. It had been moving toward me, but it stood still. As I drew nearer I saw it to be the figure of a woman. As I drew nearer yet, it was about to turn away, when it stopped, and let me come up with it. Then it faltered, as if much surprised, and uttered my name, and I cried out, "Estella!"

"I am greatly changed. I wonder you know me."

The freshness of her beauty was indeed gone, but its indescribable majesty and its indescribable charm remained. Those attractions in it I had seen before; what I had never seen before was the saddened, softened light of the once proud eyes; what I had never felt before was the friendly touch of the once insensible hand.

We sat down on a bench that was near, and I said, "After so many years, it is strange that we should thus meet again, Estella, here where our first meeting was! Do you often come back?"

"I have never been here since."

"Nor I."

The moon began to rise, and I thought of the placid look at the white ceiling, which had passed away. The moon began to rise, and I thought of the pressure on my hand when I had spoken the last words he had heard on earth.

Estella was the next to break the silence that ensued between us.

"I have very often hoped and intended to come back, and have been prevented by many circumstances. Poor, poor old place!"

The silvery mist was touched with the first rays of the moonlight, and the same rays touched the tears that dropped from her eyes. Not knowing that I saw them, and setting herself to get the better of them, she said, quietly,

"Were you wondering, as you walked along, how it came to be left in this condition?"

"Yes, Estella."

"The ground belongs to me. It is the only possession I have not relinquished. Everything else has gone from me, little by little, but I have kept this. It was the subject of the only determined resistance I could make in all the wretched years."

"Is it to be built on?"

"At last it is. I came here to take leave of it before its change. And you," she said, in a voice of touching interest to a wanderer, "you live abroad still?"

"Still."

"And do well, I am sure?"

"I work pretty hard for a sufficient living, and therefore—Yes, I do well."

"I have often thought of you," said Estella.

"Have you?"

"Of late, very often. There was a long hard time when I kept far from me the remembrance of what I had thrown away when I was quite ignorant of its worth. But since my duty has not been incompatible with the admission of that remembrance, I have given it a place in my heart."

"You have always held your place in my heart," I answered.

And we were silent again, until she spoke.

"I little thought," said Estella, "that I should take leave of you in taking leave of this spot. I am very glad to do so."

"Glad to part again, Estella? To me, parting is a painful thing. To me, the remembrance of our last parting has been ever mournful and painful."

"But you said to me," returned Estella, very earnestly, " 'God bless you, God forgive you!' And if you could say that to me then, you will not hesitate to say that to me now—now, when suffering has been stronger than all other teaching, and has taught me to understand what your heart used to be. I have been bent and broken, but—I hope—into a better shape. Be as considerate and good to me as you were, and tell me we are friends."

"We are friends," said I, rising and bending over her, as she rose from the bench.

"And will continue friends apart," said Estella.

I took her hand in mine, and we went out of the ruined place; and as the morning mists had risen long ago when I first left the forge, so the evening mists were rising now, and in all the broad expanse of tranquil light they showed to me, I saw the shadow of no parting from her.

MASTER
HUMPHREY'S
CLOCK

One

Master Humphrey from His Clock-Side in the Chimney-Corner

THE READER MUST NOT EXPECT TO KNOW WHERE I LIVE. AT present, it is true, my abode may be a question of little or no import to anybody; but if I should carry my readers with me, as I hope to do, and there should spring up, between them and me, feelings of homely affection and regard attaching something of interest to matters ever so slightly connected with my fortunes or my speculations, even my place of residence might one day have a kind of charm for them. Bearing this possible contingency in mind, I wish them to understand in the outset, that they must never expect to know it.

I am not a churlish old man. Friendless I can never be, for all mankind are my kindred, and I am on ill terms with no one member of my great family. But for many years I have led a lonely, solitary life;—what wound I sought to heal, what sorrow to forget, originally, matters not now; it is sufficient that retirement has become a habit with me, and that I am unwilling to break the spell which for so long a time has shed its quiet influence upon my home and heart.

I live in a venerable suburb of London, in an old house which in bygone days was a famous resort for merry roysterers and peerless ladies, long since departed. It is a silent shady place, with a paved courtyard so full of echoes, that sometimes I am tempted to believe that faint responses to the noises of old times linger there yet, and that these ghosts of sound haunt my footsteps as I pace it up and down. I am the more confirmed in this belief, because, of late years, the echoes that attend my walks have been less loud and marked than they were wont to be; and it is pleasanter to imagine in them the rustling of silk brocade, and the light step of some lovely girl, than to recognize in their altered note the failing tread of an old man.

Those who like to read of brilliant rooms and gorgeous furniture would derive but little pleasure from a minute description of my simple dwelling. It is dear to me for the same reason that they would hold it in slight regard. Its worm-eaten doors, and low ceilings crossed by clumsy beams; its walls of wainscot, dark stairs, and gaping closets; its small chambers, communicating with each other by winding passages or narrow steps; its many nooks, scarce larger than its corner-cupboards; its very dust and dullness, are all dear to me. The moth and spider are my constant tenants; for in my house the one basks in his long sleep, and the other plies his busy loom secure and undisturbed. I have a pleasure in thinking on a summer's day how many butterflies have sprung for the first time into light and sunshine from some dark corner of these old walls.

When I first came to live here, which was many years ago, the neighbors were curious to know who I was, and whence I came, and why I lived so much alone. As time went on, and they still remained unsatisfied on these points, I became the center of a popular ferment, extending for half a mile round, and in one direction for a full mile. Various rumors were circulated to my prejudice. I was a spy, an infidel, a conjurer, a kidnapper of children, a refugee, a priest, a monster. Mothers caught up their infants and ran into their houses as I passed; men eyed me spitefully, and muttered threats and curses. I was the object of suspicion and distrust—ay, of downright hatred too.

But when in course of time they found I did no harm, but, on the contrary, inclined towards them despite their unjust usage, they began to relent. I found my footsteps no longer dogged, as they had often been before, and observed that the women and children no longer retreated, but would stand and gaze at me as I passed their doors. I took this for a good omen, and waited patiently for better times. By degrees I began to make friends among these humble folks; and though they were yet shy of speaking, would give them "good day," and so pass on. In a little time, those whom I had thus accosted would make a point of coming to their doors and windows at the usual hour, and nod or curtsey to me; children, too, came timidly within my reach, and ran away quite scared when I patted their heads and bade them be good at school. These little people soon grew more familiar. From exchanging mere words of course with my older neighbors, I gradually became their friend and adviser, the depositary of their cares and sorrows, and sometimes, it may be, the reliever, in my small way, of their distresses. And now I never walk abroad but pleasant recognitions and smiling faces wait on Master Humphrey.

It was a whim of mine, perhaps as a whet to the curiosity of my neighbors, and a kind of retaliation upon them for their suspicions—it was, I say, a whim of mine, when I first took up my abode in this place, to acknowledge no other name than Humphrey. With my detractors, I was Ugly Humphrey. When I began to convert them into friends, I was Mr. Humphrey and Old Mr. Humphrey. At length I settled down into plain Master Humphrey, which was understood to be the title most pleasant to my ear; and so completely a matter of course has it become, that sometimes when I am taking my morning walk in my little courtyard, I overhear my barber—who has a profound respect for me, and would not, I am sure, abridge my honors for the world—holding forth on the other side of the wall, touching the state of "Master Humphrey's" health, and communicating to some friend the substance of the conversation that he and Master Humphrey have had together in the course of the shaving which he has just concluded.

That I may not make acquaintance with my readers under false pretenses, or give them cause to complain hereafter that I have withheld any matter which it was essential for them to have learnt at first, I wish them to know—and I smile sorrowfully to think that the time has been when the confession would have given me pain—that I am a misshapen, deformed old man.

I have never been made a misanthrope by this cause. I have never been stung by any insult, nor wounded by any jest upon my crooked figure. As a child I was melancholy and timid, but that was because the gentle consideration paid to my misfortune sank deep into my spirit and made me sad, even in those early days. I was but a very young creature when my poor mother died, and yet I remember that often when I hung around her neck, and oftener still when I played about the room before her, she would catch me to her bosom, and bursting into tears, soothe me with every term of fondness and affection. God knows I was a happy child at those times—happy to nestle in her breast—happy to weep when she did—happy in not knowing why.

These occasions are so strongly impressed upon my memory, that they seem to have occupied whole years. I had numbered very, very few when they ceased forever, but before then their meaning had been revealed to me.

I do not know whether all children are imbued with a quick perception of childish grace and beauty, and a strong love for it, but I was. I had no thought that I remember, either that I possessed it myself or that I lacked it, but I admired it with an intensity I cannot describe. A little knot of playmates—they must have been beautiful, for I see them now—were clustered one day round my mother's knee in eager admiration of some picture representing a group of infant angels, which she held in her hand. Whose the picture was, whether it was familiar to me or otherwise, or how all the children came to be there, I forget; I have some dim thought it was my birthday, but the beginning of my recollection is that we were all together in a garden, and it was summer weather—I am sure of that, for one of the little girls had roses in her sash. There were many lovely angels in this picture, and I remember the fancy coming upon me to point out which of them represented each child there, and that when I had gone through all my companions, I stopped and hesitated, wondering which was most like me. I remember the children looking at each other, and my turning red and hot, and their crowding round to kiss me, saying that they loved me all the same; and then, and when the old sorrow came into my dear mother's mild and tender look, the truth broke upon me for the first time, and I knew, while watching my awkward and ungainly sports, how keenly she had felt for her poor crippled boy.

I used frequently to dream of it afterwards, and now my heart aches for that child as if I had never been he, when I think how often he awoke from some fairy change to his own old form, and sobbed himself to sleep again.

Well, well—all these sorrows are past. My glancing at them may not be without its use, for it may help in some measure to explain why I have all my life been attached to the inanimate objects that people my chamber, and how I have come to look upon them rather in the light of old and constant friends, than as mere chairs and tables which a little money could replace at will.

Chief and first among all these is my Clock—my old, cheerful, companionable Clock. How can I ever convey to others an idea of the comfort and consolation that this old Clock has been for years to me!

It is associated with my earliest recollections. It stood upon the staircase at home (I call it home still, mechanically), nigh sixty years ago. I like it for that; but it is not on that account, nor because it is a quaint old thing in a huge oaken case curiously and richly carved, that I prize it as I do. I incline to it as if it were alive, and could understand and give me back the love I bear it.

And what other thing that has not life could cheer me as it does; what other thing that has not life (I will not say how few things that have) could have proved the same patient, true, untiring friend? How often have I sat in the long winter evenings feeling such society in its cricket-voice, that raising my eyes from my book and looking gratefully towards it, the face reddened by the glow of the shining fire has seemed to relax from its staid expression and to regard me kindly; how often in the summer twilight, when my thoughts have wandered back to a melancholy past, have its regular whisperings recalled them to the calm and peaceful present; how often in the dead tranquility of night has its bell broken the oppressive silence, and seemed to give me assurance that the old clock was still a faithful watcher at my chamber-door! My easychair, my desk, my ancient furniture, my very books, I can scarcely bring myself to love even these last like my old Clock!

It stands in a snug corner, midway between the fireside and a low arched door leading to my bedroom. Its fame is diffused so extensively throughout the neighborhood, that I have often the satisfaction of hearing the publican or the baker, and sometimes even the parish-clerk, petitioning my house-keeper (of whom I shall have much to say by-and-by) to inform him the exact time by Master Humphrey's Clock. My barber, to whom I have referred, would sooner believe it than the sun. Nor are these its only distinctions. It has acquired, I am happy to say, another, inseparably connecting it not only with my enjoyments and reflections, but with those of other men; as I shall now relate.

I lived alone here for a long time without any friend or acquaintance. In the course of my wanderings by night and day, at all hours and seasons, in city streets and quiet country parts, I came to be familiar with certain faces, and to take it to heart as quite a heavy disappointment if they failed to present themselves each at its accustomed spot. But these were the only friends I knew, and beyond them I had none.

It happened, however, when I had gone on thus for a long time, that I formed an acquaintance with a deaf gentleman, which ripened into inti-macy and close companionship. To this hour, I am ignorant of his name. It is his humor to conceal it, or he has a reason and purpose for so doing. In either case, I feel that he has a right to require a return of the trust he has reposed; and as he has never sought to discover my secret, I have never sought to penetrate his. There may have been something in this tacit confi-dence in each other flattering and pleasant to us both, and it may have imparted in the beginning an additional zest, perhaps, to our friendship. Be this as it may, we have grown to be like brothers, and still I only know him as the deaf gentleman.

I have said that retirement has become a habit with me. When I add that the deaf gentleman and I have two friends, I communicate nothing which is inconsistent with that declaration. I spend many hours of every day in soli-tude and study, have no friends or change of friends but these, only see them at stated periods, and am supposed to be of a retired spirit by the very nature and object of our association.

We are men of secluded habits, with something of a cloud upon our early fortunes, whose enthusiasm nevertheless has not cooled with age, whose spirit of romance is not yet quenched, who are content to ramble through the world in a pleasant dream, rather than ever waken again to its harsh realities. We are alchemists who would extract the essence of perpetual youth from dust and ashes, tempt coy Truth in many light and airy forms from the bot-tom of her well, and discover one crumb of comfort or one grain of good in the commonest and least-regarded matter that passes through our crucible. Spirits of past times, creatures of imagination, and people of today are alike the objects of our seeking, and, unlike the objects of search with most philosophers, we can ensure their coming at our command.

The deaf gentleman and I first began to beguile our days with these fan-cies, and our nights in communicating them to each other. We are now four. But in my room there are six old chairs, and we have decided that the two empty seats shall always be placed at our table when we meet, to remind us that we may yet increase our company by that number, if we should find two men to our mind. When one among us dies, his chair will always be set in its usual place, but never occupied again; and I have caused my will to be so drawn out, that when we are all dead the house shall be shut up, and the vacant chairs still left in their accustomed places. It is pleasant to think that even then our shades may, perhaps, assemble together as of yore we did, and join in ghostly converse.

One night in every week, as the Clock strikes ten, we meet. At the second stroke of two, I am alone.

And now shall I tell how that my old servant, besides giving us note of time, and ticking cheerful encouragement of our proceedings, lends its name to our society, which for its punctuality and my love is christened "Master Humphrey's Clock"? Now shall I tell how that in the bottom of the old dark closet, where the steady pendulum throbs and beats with healthy action, though the pulse of him who made it stood still long ago and never moved again, there are piles of dusty papers constantly placed there by our hands, that we may link our enjoyments with my old friend, and draw means to beguile time from the heart of time itself? Shall I, or can I, tell with what a secret pride I open this repository when we meet at night, and still find new store of pleasure in my dear old Clock?

Friend and companion of my solitude! mine is not a selfish love; I would not keep your merits to myself, but disperse something of pleasant association with your image through the whole wide world; I would have men couple with your name cheerful and healthy thoughts; I would have them believe that you keep true and honest time; and how it would gladden me to know that they recognized some hearty English work in Master Humphrey's Clock!

THE CLOCK-CASE

It is my intention constantly to address my readers from the chimney-corner, and I would fain hope that such accounts as I shall give them of our histories and proceedings, our quiet speculations or more busy adventures, will never be unwelcome. Lest, however, I should grow prolix in the outset by lingering too long upon our little association, confounding the enthusiasm with which I regard this chief happiness of my life with that minor degree of interest which those to whom I address myself may be supposed to feel for it, I have deemed it expedient to break off as they have seen.

But, still clinging to my old friend and naturally desirous that all its merits should be known, I am tempted to open (somewhat irregularly and against our laws, I must admit) the Clock-case. The first roll of paper on which I lay my hand is in the writing of the deaf gentleman. I shall have to speak of him in my next paper; and how can I better approach that welcome task than by prefacing it with a production of his own pen, consigned to the safekeeping of my honest Clock by his own hands?

The manuscript runs thus:

INTRODUCTION TO THE GIANT CHRONICLES

Once upon a time, that is to say, in this our time—the exact year, month, and day are of no matter—there dwelt in the city of London a substantial citizen, who united in his single person the dignities of wholesale fruiterer, Alderman, Common-Councilman, and member of the Worshipful Company of Patten-makers; who had superadded to these extraordinary distinctions the important post and title of Sheriff, and who at length, and to crown all, stood next in rotation for the high and honorable office of Lord Mayor.

He was a very substantial citizen indeed. His face was like the full moon in a fog, with two little holes punched out for his eyes, a very ripe pear stuck on for his nose, and a wide gash to serve for a mouth. The girth of his waistcoat was hung up and lettered in his tailor's shop as an extraordinary curiosity. He breathed like a heavy snorer, and his voice in speaking came thickly forth, as if it were oppressed and stifled by feather-beds. He trod the ground like an elephant, and eat and drank like—like nothing but an Alderman, as he was.

This worthy citizen had risen to his great eminence from small beginnings. He had once been a very lean, weazen little boy, never dreaming of carrying such a weight of flesh upon his bones or of money in his pockets, and glad enough to take his dinner at a baker's door, and his tea at a pump. But he had long ago forgotten all this, as it was proper that a wholesale fruiterer, Alderman, Common-Councilman, member of the Worshipful Company of Patten-makers, past Sheriff, and, above all, a Lord Mayor that was to be, should; and he never forgot it more completely in all his life than on the eighth of November in the year of his election to the great golden civic chair, which was the day before his grand dinner at Guildhall.

It happened that as he sat that evening all alone in his counting-house, looking over the bill of fare for next day, and checking off the fat capons in fifties, and the turtle-soup by the hundred quarts, for his private amusement—it happened that as he sat alone occupied in these pleasant calculations, a strange man came in and asked him how he did, adding, "If I am half as much changed as you, sir, you have no recollection of me, I am sure."

The strange man was not over and above well-dressed, and was very far from being fat or rich-looking in any sense of the word, yet he spoke with a kind of modest confidence, and assumed an easy, gentlemanly sort of air, to which nobody but a rich man can lawfully presume. Besides this, he interrupted the good citizen just as he had reckoned three hundred and seventy-two fat capons, and was carrying them over to the next column; and as if that were not aggravation enough, the learned Recorder for the City of London had only ten minutes previously gone out at that very same door, and had turned round and said, "Good night, my lord." Yes, he had said, "my lord";—he, a man of birth and education, of the Honorable Society of the Middle Temple, Barrister-at-Law—he who had an uncle in the House of Commons, and an aunt almost but not quite in the House of Lords (for she had married a feeble peer, and made him vote as she liked)—he, this man, this learned Recorder had said, "my lord." "I'll not wait till tomorrow to give you your title, my Lord Mayor," says he, with a bow and a smile; "you are Lord Mayor *de facto,* if not *de jure.* Good night, my lord!"

The Lord Mayor elect thought of this, and turning to the stranger, and sternly bidding him "go out of his private counting-house," brought forward the three hundred and seventy-two fat capons, and went on with his account.

"Do you remember," said the other, stepping forward—"*do* you remember little Joe Toddyhigh?"

The port wine fled for a moment from the fruiterer's nose as he muttered, "Joe Toddyhigh! What about Joe Toddyhigh?"

"*I* am Joe Toddyhigh," cried the visitor. "Look at me, look hard at me—harder, harder. You know me now? You know little Joe again? What a happiness to us both, to meet the very night before your grandeur! Oh! give me your hand, Jack—both hands—both, for the sake of old times."

"You pinch me, sir. You're a-hurting of me," said the Lord Mayor elect pettishly: "don't—suppose anybody should come—Mr. Toddyhigh, sir."

"Mr. Toddyhigh!" repeated the other ruefully.

"Oh! don't bother," said the Lord Mayor elect, scratching his head. "Dear me! Why, I thought you was dead. What a fellow you are!"

Indeed, it was a pretty state of things, and worthy the tone of vexation and disappointment in which the Lord Mayor spoke. Joe Toddyhigh had been a poor boy with him at Hull, and had oftentimes divided his last penny and parted his last crust to relieve his wants; for though Joe was a destitute child in those times, he was as faithful and affectionate in his friendship as ever man of might could be. They parted one day to seek their fortunes in different directions. Joe went to sea, and the now wealthy citizen begged his way to London. They separated with many tears, like foolish fellows as they were, and agreed to remain fast friends, and if they lived, soon to communicate again.

When he was an errand-boy, and even in the early days of his apprenticeship, the citizen had many a time trudged to the post-office to ask if there were any letter from poor little Joe, and had gone home again with tears in his eyes, when he found no news of his only friend. The world is a wide place, and it was a long time before the letter came; when it did, the writer was forgotten. It turned from white to yellow from lying in the post-office with nobody to claim it, and in course of time was torn up with five hundred others, and sold for waste-paper. And now at last, and when it might least have been expected, here was this Joe Toddyhigh turning up and claiming acquaintance with a great public character, who on the morrow would be cracking jokes with the Prime Minister of England, and who had only, at any time during the next twelve months, to say the word, and he could shut up Temple Bar, and make it no thoroughfare for the King himself!

"I am sure I don't know what to say, Mr. Toddyhigh," said the Lord Mayor elect; "I really don't. It's very inconvenient. I'd sooner have given twenty pound—it's very inconvenient, really."

A thought had struggled into his mind, that perhaps his old friend might say something passionate which would give him an excuse for being angry himself. No such thing. Joe looked at him steadily, but very mildly, and did not open his lips.

"Of course I shall pay you what I owe you," said the Lord Mayor elect, fidgeting in his chair. "You lent me—I think it was a shilling or some small coin—when we parted company, and that of course I shall pay, with good interest. I can pay my way with any man, and always have done. If you look into the Mansion House the day after tomorrow—sometime after dusk— and ask for my private clerk, you'll find he has a draft for you. I haven't got time to say anything more just now, unless"—he hesitated, for, coupled with a strong desire to glitter for once in all his glory in the eyes of his former companion, was a distrust of his appearance which might be more shabby than he could tell by that feeble light—"unless you'd like to come to the dinner tomorrow. I don't mind your having this ticket, if you like to take it. A great many people would give their ears for it, I can tell you."

His old friend took the card without speaking a word, and instantly departed. His sunburnt face and grey hair were present to the citizen's mind for a moment; but by the time he reached three hundred and eighty-one fat capons, he had quite forgotten him.

Joe Toddyhigh had never been in the capital of Europe before, and he wandered up and down the streets that night, amazed at the number of churches and other public buildings, the splendor of the shops, the riches that were heaped up on every side, the glare of light in which they were displayed, and the concourse of people who hurried to and fro, indifferent apparently to all the wonders that surrounded them. But in all the long streets and broad squares, there were none but strangers; it was quite a relief to turn down a byway and hear his own footsteps on the pavement. He went home to his inn, thought that London was a dreary, desolate place, and felt disposed to doubt the existence of one true-hearted man in the whole Worshipful Company of Patten-makers. Finally, he went to bed, and dreamed that he and the Lord Mayor elect were boys again.

He went next day to the dinner; and when, in a burst of light and music, and in the midst of splendid decorations and surrounded by brilliant company, his former friend appeared at the head of the Hall, and was hailed with shouts and cheering, he cheered and shouted with the best, and for the moment could have cried. The next moment he cursed his weakness in behalf of a man so changed and selfish, and quite hated a jolly-looking old gentleman opposite for declaring himself in the pride of his heart a Patten-maker.

As the banquet proceeded, he took more and more to heart the rich citizen's unkindness; and that, not from any envy, but because he felt that a man of his state and fortune could all the better afford to recognize an old friend, even if he were poor and obscure. The more he thought of this, the more lonely and sad he felt. When the company dispersed and adjourned to the ballroom, he paced the hall and passages alone, ruminating in a very melancholy condition upon the disappointment he had experienced.

It chanced, while he was lounging about in this moody state, that he stumbled upon a flight of stairs, dark, steep, and narrow, which he ascended without any thought about the matter, and so came into a little music-gallery, empty and deserted. From this elevated post, which commanded the whole hall, he amused himself in looking down upon the attendants who were clearing away the fragments of the feast very lazily, and drinking out of all the bottles and glasses with most commendable perseverance.

His attention gradually relaxed, and he fell fast asleep.

When he awoke, he thought there must be something the matter with his eyes; but, rubbing them a little, he soon found that the moonlight was really streaming through the east window, that the lamps were all extinguished, and that he was alone. He listened, but no distant murmur in the echoing passages, not even the shutting of a door broke the deep silence; he groped his way down the stairs, and found that the door at the bottom was locked on the other side. He began now to comprehend that he must have slept a long time, that he had been overlooked, and was shut up there for the night.

His first sensation, perhaps, was not altogether a comfortable one, for it was a dark, chilly, earthy-smelling place, and something too large, for a man so situated, to feel at home in. However, when the momentary consternation of his surprise was over, he made light of the accident, and resolved to feel his way up the stairs again, and make himself as comfortable as he could in the gallery until morning. As he turned to execute this purpose, he heard the clocks strike three.

Any such invasion of a dead stillness as the striking of distant clocks, causes it to appear the more intense and insupportable when the sound has ceased. He listened with strained attention in the hope that some clock, lagging behind its fellows, had yet to strike—looking all the time into the profound darkness before him until it seemed to weave itself into a black tissue, patterned with a hundred reflections of his own eyes. But the bells had all pealed out their warning for that once, and the gust of wind that moaned through the place seemed cold and heavy with their iron breath.

The time and circumstances were favorable to reflection. He tried to keep his thoughts to the current, unpleasant though it was, in which they had moved all day, and to think with what a romantic feeling he had looked forward to shaking his old friend by the hand before he died, and what a wide and cruel difference there was between the meeting they had had, and that which he had so often and so long anticipated. Still he was disordered by waking to such sudden loneliness, and could not prevent his mind from running upon odd tales of people of undoubted courage, who, being shut up by night in vaults or churches, or other dismal places, had scaled great heights to get out, and fled from silence as they had never done from danger. This brought to his mind the moonlight through the window, and bethinking himself of it, he groped his way back up the crooked stairs—but very stealthily, as though he were fearful of being overheard.

He was very much astonished when he approached the gallery again, to see a light in the building: still more so, on advancing hastily and looking round, to observe no visible source from which it could proceed. But how much greater yet was his astonishment at the spectacle which this light revealed!

The statues of the two giants, Gog and Magog, each above fourteen feet in height, those which succeeded to still older and more barbarous figures after the Great Fire of London, and which stand in the Guildhall to this day, were endowed with life and motion. These guardian genii of the City had quitted their pedestals, and reclined in easy attitudes in the great stained-glass window. Between them was an ancient cask, which seemed to be full of wine; for the younger Giant, clapping his huge hand upon it, and throwing up his mighty leg, burst into an exulting laugh, which reverberated through the hall like thunder.

Joe Toddyhigh instinctively stooped down, and, more dead than alive, felt his hair stand on end, his knees knock together, and a cold damp break out upon his forehead. But even at that minute curiosity prevailed over every other feeling, and somewhat reassured by the good-humor of the Giants and their apparent unconsciousness of his presence, he crouched in a corner of the gallery, in as small a space as he could, and, peeping between the rails, observed them closely.

It was then that the elder Giant, who had a flowing grey beard, raised his thoughtful eyes to his companion's face, and in a grave and solemn voice addressed him thus:

First Night of the Giant Chronicles

Turning towards his companion, the elder Giant uttered these words in a grave, majestic tone:—

"Magog, does boisterous mirth beseem the Giant Warder of this ancient city? Is this becoming demeanor for a watchful spirit over whose bodiless head so many years have rolled, so many changes swept like empty air—in whose impalpable nostrils the scent of blood and crime, pestilence, cruelty, and horror, has been familiar as breath to mortals—in whose sight Time has gathered in the harvest of centuries, and garnered so many crops of human pride, affections, hopes, and sorrows? Bethink you of our compact. The night wanes; feasting, revelry, and music have encroached upon our usual hours of solitude, and morning will be here apace. Ere we are stricken mute again, bethink you of our compact."

Pronouncing these latter words with more of impatience than quite accorded with his apparent age and gravity, the Giant raised a long pole (which he still bears in his hand) and tapped his brother Giant rather smartly on the head; indeed the blow was so smartly administered, that the latter quickly withdrew his lips from the cask to which they had been applied, and catching up his shield and halberd assumed an attitude of defense. His irritation was but momentary, for he laid these weapons aside as hastily as he had assumed them, and said as he did so:—

"You know, Gog, old friend, that when we animate these shapes which the Londoners of old assigned (and not unworthily) to the guardian genii of their city, we are susceptible of some of the sensations which belong to humankind. Thus when I taste wine, I feel blows; when I relish the one, I disrelish the other. Therefore, Gog, the more especially as your arm is none of the lightest, keep your good staff by your side, else we may chance to differ. Peace be between us!"

"Amen!" said the other, leaning his staff in the window-corner. "Why did you laugh just now?"

"To think," replied the Giant Magog, laying his hand upon the cask, "of him who owned this wine, and kept it in a cellar hoarded from the light of day, for thirty years—'till it should be fit to drink,' quoth he. He was two-score and ten years old when he buried it beneath his house, and yet never thought that he might be scarcely 'fit to drink' when the wine became so. I wonder it never occurred to him to make himself unfit to be eaten. There is very little of him left by this time."

"The night is waning," said Gog mournfully.

"I know it," replied his companion, "and I see you are impatient. But look. Through the eastern window—placed opposite to us, that the first beams of the rising sun may every morning gild our giant faces—the moon-rays fall upon the pavement in a stream of light that to my fancy sinks through the cold stone and gushes into the old crypt below. The night is scarcely past its noon, and our great charge is sleeping heavily."

They ceased to speak, and looked upward at the moon. The sight of their large, black, rolling eyes filled Joe Toddyhigh with such horror that he could scarcely draw his breath. Still they took no note of him, and appeared to believe themselves quite alone.

"Our compact," said Magog after a pause, "is, if I understand it, that, instead of watching here in silence through the dreary nights, we entertain each other with stories of our past experience; with tales of the past, the present, and the future; with legends of London and her sturdy citizens from the old simple times. That every night at midnight, when St. Paul's bell tolls out one, and we may move and speak, we thus discourse, nor leave such themes till the first grey gleam of day shall strike us dumb. Is that our bargain, brother?"

"Yes," said the Giant Gog, "that is the league between us who guard this city, by day in spirit, and by night in body also; and never on ancient holidays have its conduits run wine more merrily than we will pour forth our legendary lore. We are old chroniclers from this time hence. The crumbled walls encircle us once more, the postern-gates are closed, the drawbridge is up, and pent in its narrow den beneath, the water foams and struggles with the sunken starlings. Jerkins and quarter-staves are in the streets again, the nightly watch is set, the rebel, sad and lonely in his Tower dungeon, tries to sleep and weeps for home and children. Aloft upon the gates and walls are noble heads glaring fiercely down upon the dreaming city, and vexing the hungry dogs that scent them in the air and tear the ground beneath with dismal howlings. The axe, the block, the rack, in their dark chambers give signs of recent use. The Thames, floating past long lines of cheerful windows whence come a burst of music and a stream of light, bears sullenly to the Palace wall the last red stain brought on the tide from Traitor's Gate. But your pardon, brother. The night wears, and I am talking idly."

The other Giant appeared to be entirely of this opinion, for during the foregoing rhapsody of his fellow-sentinel he had been scratching his head with an air of comical uneasiness, or rather with an air that would have been very comical if he had been a dwarf or an ordinary-sized man. He winked too, and though it could not be doubted for a moment that he winked to himself, still he certainly cocked his enormous eye towards the gallery where the listener was concealed. Nor was this all, for he gaped; and when he gaped, Joe was horribly reminded of the popular prejudice on the subject of Giants, and of their fabled power of smelling out Englishmen, however closely concealed.

His alarm was such that he nearly swooned, and it was some little time before his power of sight or hearing was restored. When he recovered he found that the elder Giant was pressing the younger to commence the Chronicles, and that the latter was endeavoring to excuse himself, on the ground that the night was far spent, and it would be better to wait until the next. Well assured by this that he was certainly about to begin directly, the listener collected his faculties by a great effort, and distinctly heard Magog express himself to the following effect:—

In the sixteenth century and in the reign of Queen Elizabeth of glorious memory (albeit her golden days are sadly rusted with blood), there lived in the city of London a bold young 'prentice who loved his master's daughter. There were no doubt within the walls a great many young 'prentices in this condition, but I speak of only one, and his name was Hugh Graham.

This Hugh was apprenticed to an honest Bowyer who dwelt in the ward of Cheype, and was rumored to possess great wealth. Rumor was quite as infallible in those days as at the present time, but it happened then as now to be sometimes right by accident. It stumbled upon the truth when it gave the old Bowyer a mint of money. His trade had been a profitable one in the time of King Henry the Eighth, who encouraged English archery to the utmost, and he had been prudent and discreet. Thus it came to pass that Mistress Alice, his only daughter, was the richest heiress in all his wealthy ward. Young Hugh had often maintained with staff and cudgel that she was the handsomest. To do him justice, I believe she was.

If he could have gained the heart of pretty Mistress Alice by knocking this conviction into stubborn people's heads, Hugh would have had no cause to fear. But though the Bowyer's daughter smiled in secret to hear of his doughty deeds for her sake, and though her little waiting-woman reported all her smiles (and many more) to Hugh, and though he was at a vast expense in kisses and small coin to recompense her fidelity, he made no progress in his love. He durst not whisper it to Mistress Alice save on sure encouragement, and that she never gave him. A glance of her dark eye as she sat at the door on a summer's evening after prayer-time, while he and the neighboring 'prentices exercised themselves in the street with blunted sword and buckler, would fire Hugh's blood so that none could stand before him; but then she glanced at others quite as kindly as on him, and where was the use of cracking crowns if Mistress Alice smiled upon the cracked as well as on the cracker?

Still Hugh went on, and loved her more and more. He thought of her all day, and dreamed of her all night long. He treasured up her every word and gesture, and had a palpitation of the heart whenever he heard her footstep on the stairs or her voice in an adjoining room. To him, the old Bowyer's house was haunted by an angel; there was enchantment in the air and space in which she moved. It would have been no miracle to Hugh if flowers had sprung from the rush-strewn floors beneath the tread of lovely Mistress Alice.

Never did 'prentice long to distinguish himself in the eyes of his lady-love so ardently as Hugh. Sometimes he pictured to himself the house taking fire by night, and he, when all drew back in fear, rushing through flame and smoke, and bearing her from the ruins in his arms. At other times he thought of a rising of fierce rebels, an attack upon the city, a strong assault upon the Bowyer's house in particular, and he falling on the threshold pierced with numberless wounds in defense of Mistress Alice. If he could only enact some prodigy of valor, do some wonderful deed, and let her know that she had inspired it, he thought he could die contented.

Sometimes the Bowyer and his daughter would go out to supper with a worthy citizen at the fashionable hour of six o'clock, and on such occasions Hugh, wearing his blue 'prentice-cloak as gallantly as 'prentice might, would attend with a lantern and his trusty club to escort them home. These were the brightest moments of his life. To hold the light while Mistress Alice picked her steps, to touch her hand as he helped her over broken ways, to have her leaning on his arm—it sometimes even came to that—this was happiness indeed!

When the nights were fair, Hugh followed in the rear, his eyes riveted on the graceful figure of the Bowyer's daughter as she and the old man moved on before him. So they threaded the narrow winding streets of the city, now passing beneath the overhanging gables of old wooden houses whence creaking signs projected into the street, and now emerging from some dark and frowning gateway into the clear moonlight. At such times, or when the shouts of straggling brawlers met her ear, the Bowyer's daughter would look timidly back at Hugh, beseeching him to draw nearer; and then how he grasped his club and longed to do battle with a dozen rufflers, for the love of Mistress Alice!

The old Bowyer was in the habit of lending money on interest to the gallants of the Court, and thus it happened that many a richly-dressed gentleman dismounted at his door. More waving plumes and gallant steeds, indeed, were seen at the Bowyer's house, and more embroidered silks and velvets sparkled in his dark shop and darker private closet than at any merchant's in the city. In those times no less than in the present it would seem that the richest-looking cavaliers often wanted money the most.

Of these glittering clients there was one who always came alone. He was always nobly mounted, and having no attendant gave his horse in charge to Hugh while he and the Bowyer were closeted within. Once as he sprang into the saddle Mistress Alice was seated at an upper window, and before she could withdraw he had doffed his jeweled cap and kissed his hand. Hugh watched him caracoling down the street, and burned with indignation. But how much deeper was the glow that reddened in his cheeks when raising his eyes to the casement he saw that Alice watched the stranger too!

He came again and often, each time arrayed more gaily than before, and still the little casement showed him Mistress Alice. At length one heavy day, she fled from home. It had cost her a hard struggle, for all her old father's gifts were strewn about her chamber as if she had parted from them one by one, and knew that the time must come when these tokens of his love would wring her heart—yet she was gone.

She left a letter commending her poor father to the care of Hugh, and wishing he might be happier than he could ever have been with her, for he deserved the love of a better and a purer heart than she had to bestow. The old man's forgiveness (she said) she had no power to ask, but she prayed God to bless him—and so ended with a blot upon the paper where her tears had fallen.

At first the old man's wrath was kindled, and he carried his wrong to the Queen's throne itself; but there was no redress he learnt at Court, for his daughter had been conveyed abroad. This afterwards appeared to be the truth, as there came from France, after an interval of several years, a letter in her hand. It was written in trembling characters, and almost illegible. Little could be made out save that she often thought of home and her old dear pleasant room—and that she had dreamt her father was dead and had not blessed her—and that her heart was breaking.

The poor old Bowyer lingered on, never suffering Hugh to quit his sight, for he knew now that he had loved his daughter, and that was the only link that bound him to earth. It broke at length and he died, bequeathing his old 'prentice his trade and all his wealth, and solemnly charging him with his last breath to revenge his child if ever he who had worked her misery crossed his path in life again.

From the time of Alice's flight, the tilting-ground, the fields, the fencing-school, the summer-evening sports, knew Hugh no more. His spirit was dead within him. He rose to great eminence and repute among the citizens, but was seldom seen to smile, and never mingled in their revelries or rejoicings. Brave, humane, and generous, he was beloved by all. He was pitied too by those who knew his story, and these were so many that when he walked along the streets alone at dusk, even the rude common people doffed their caps and mingled a rough air of sympathy with their respect.

One night in May—it was her birthnight, and twenty years since she had left her home—Hugh Graham sat in the room she had hallowed in his boyish days. He was now a grey-haired man, though still in the prime of life. Old thoughts had borne him company for many hours and the chamber had gradually grown quite dark, when he was roused by a low knocking at the outer door.

He hastened down, and opening it, saw by the light of a lamp which he had seized upon the way, a female figure crouching in the portal. It hurried swiftly past him and glided up the stairs. He looked out for pursuers. There were none in sight. No, not one.

He was inclined to think it a vision of his own brain, when suddenly a vague suspicion of the truth flashed upon his mind. He barred the door, and hastened wildly back. Yes, there she was—there, in the chamber he had quitted—there in her old innocent happy home, so changed that none but he could trace one gleam of what she had been—there upon her knees—with her hands clasped in agony and shame before her burning face.

"My God, my God!" she cried, "now strike me dead! Though I have brought death and shame and sorrow on this roof, Oh, let me die at home in mercy!"

There was no tear upon her face then, but she trembled and glanced round the chamber. Everything was in its old place. Her bed looked as if she had risen from it but that morning. The sight of these familiar objects, marking the dear remembrance in which she had been held, and the blight she had brought upon herself, was more than the woman's better nature that had carried her there could bear. She wept and fell upon the ground.

A rumor was spread about, in a few days' time, that the Bowyer's cruel daughter had come home, and that Master Graham had given her lodging in his house. It was rumored too that he had resigned her fortune, in order that she might bestow it in acts of charity, and that he had vowed to guard her in her solitude, but that they were never to see each other more. These rumors greatly incensed all virtuous wives and daughters in the ward, especially when they appeared to receive some corroboration from the circumstance of Master Graham taking up his abode in another tenement hard by. The estimation in which he was held, however, forbade any questioning on the subject; and as the Bowyer's house was close shut up, and nobody came forth when public shows and festivities were in progress, or to flaunt in the public walks, or to buy new fashions at the mercers' booths, all the well-conducted females agreed among themselves that there could be no woman there.

These reports had scarcely died away when the wonder of every good citizen, male and female, was utterly absorbed and swallowed up by a Royal Proclamation, in which her Majesty, strongly censuring the practice of wearing long Spanish rapiers of preposterous length (as being a bullying and swaggering custom, tending to bloodshed and public disorder), commanded that on a particular day therein named, certain grave citizens should repair to the city gates, and there, in public, break all rapiers worn or carried by persons claiming admission, that exceeded, though it were only by a quarter of an inch, three standard feet in length.

Royal Proclamations usually take their course, let the public wonder never so much. On the appointed day two citizens of high repute took up their stations at each of the gates, attended by a party of the city guard, the main body to enforce the Queen's will, and take custody of all such rebels (if any) as might have the temerity to dispute it: and a few to bear the standard measures and instruments for reducing all unlawful sword-blades to the prescribed dimensions. In pursuance of these arrangements, Master Graham and another were posted at Lud Gate, on the hill before St. Paul's.

A pretty numerous company were gathered together at this spot; for, besides the officers in attendance to enforce the proclamation, there was a motley crowd of lookers-on of various degrees, who raised from time to time such shouts and cries as the circumstances called forth. A spruce young courtier was the first who approached: he unsheathed a weapon of burnished steel that shone and glistened in the sun, and handed it with the newest air to the officer, who, finding it exactly three feet long, returned it with a bow. Thereupon the gallant raised his hat and crying, "God save the Queen!" passed on amidst the plaudits of the mob. Then came another—a better courtier still—who wore a blade but two feet long, whereat the people laughed, much to the disparagement of his honor's dignity. Then came a third, a sturdy old officer of the army, girded with a rapier at least a foot and a half beyond her Majesty's pleasure; at him they raised a great shout, and most of the spectators (but especially those who were armorers or cutlers) laughed very heartily at the breakage which would ensue. But they were disappointed; for the old campaigner, coolly unbuckling his sword and bidding his servant carry it home again, passed through unarmed, to the great indignation of all the beholders. They relieved themselves in some degree by hooting a tall blustering fellow with a prodigious weapon, who stopped short on coming in sight of the preparations, and after a little consideration turned back again: but all this time no rapier had been broken, although it was high noon, and all cavaliers of any quality or appearance were taking their way towards Saint Paul's churchyard.

During these proceedings Master Graham had stood apart, strictly confining himself to the duty imposed upon him, and taking little heed of anything beyond. He stepped forward now as a richly-dressed gentleman on foot, followed by a single attendant, was seen advancing up the hill.

As this person drew nearer, the crowd stopped their clamor and bent forward with eager looks. Master Graham standing alone in the gateway, and the stranger coming slowly towards him, they seemed, as it were, set face to face. The nobleman (for he looked one) had a haughty and disdainful air, which bespoke the slight estimation in which he held the citizen. The citizen on the other hand preserved the resolute bearing of one who was not to be frowned down or daunted, and who cared very little for any nobility but that of worth and manhood. It was perhaps some consciousness on the part of each, of these feelings in the other, that infused a more stern expression into their regards as they came closer together.

"Your rapier, worthy sir!"

At the instant that he pronounced these words Graham started, and falling back some paces, laid his hand upon the dagger in his belt.

"You are the man whose horse I used to hold before the Bowyer's door? You are that man? Speak!"

"Out, you 'prentice hound!" said the other.

"You are he! I know you well now!" cried Graham. "Let no man step between us two, or I shall be his murderer." With that he drew his dagger and rushed in upon him.

The stranger had drawn his weapon from the scabbard ready for the scrutiny, before a word was spoken. He made a thrust at his assailant, but the dagger which Graham clutched in his left hand being the dirk in use at that time for parrying such blows promptly turned the point aside. They closed. The dagger fell rattling upon the ground, and Graham, wresting his adversary's sword from his grasp, plunged it through his heart. As he drew it out it snapped in two, leaving a fragment in the dead man's body.

All this passed so swiftly that the bystanders looked on without an effort to interfere; but the man was no sooner down than an uproar broke forth which rent the air. The attendant rushing through the gate proclaimed that his master, a nobleman, had been set upon and slain by a citizen; the word quickly spread from mouth to mouth; Saint Paul's Cathedral, and every bookshop, ordinary, and smoking-house in the churchyard poured out its stream of cavaliers and their followers, who, mingling together in a dense tumultuous body, struggled, sword in hand, towards the spot.

With equal impetuosity, and stimulating each other by loud cries and shouts, the citizens and common people took up the quarrel on their side, and encircling Master Graham a hundred deep, forced him from the gate. In vain he waved the broken sword above his head, crying that he would die on London's threshold for their sacred homes. They bore him on, and ever keeping him in the midst, so that no man could attack him, fought their way into the city.

The clash of swords and roar of voices, the dust and heat and pressure, the trampling underfoot of men, the distracted looks and shrieks of women at the windows above as they recognized their relatives or lovers in the crowd, the rapid tolling of alarm-bells, the furious rage and passion of the scene, were fearful. Those who, being on the outskirts of each crowd, could use their weapons with effect fought desperately, while those behind, maddened with baffled rage, struck at each other over the heads of those before them, and crushed their own fellows. Wherever the broken sword was seen above the people's heads, towards that spot the cavaliers made a new rush. Every one of these charges was marked by sudden gaps in the throng where men were trodden down, but as fast as they were made, the tide swept over them and still the multitude pressed on again, a confused mass of swords, clubs, staves, broken plumes, fragments of rich cloaks and doublets, and angry bleeding faces, all mixed up together in inextricable disorder.

The design of the people was to force Master Graham to take refuge in his dwelling, and to defend it until the authorities could interfere, or they could gain time for parley. But either from ignorance or in the confusion of the moment they stopped at his old house, which was closely shut. Some time was lost in beating the doors open and passing him to the front. About a score of the boldest of the other party threw themselves into the torrent while this was being done, and reaching the door at same moment with himself cut him off from his defenders.

"I never will turn in such a righteous cause, so help me Heaven!" cried Graham in a voice that at last made itself heard, and confronting them as he spoke. "Least of all will I turn upon this threshold which owes its desolation to such men as ye. I give no quarter, and I will have none! Strike!"

For a moment they stood at bay. At that moment a shot from an unseen hand, apparently fired by some person who had gained access to one of the opposite houses, struck Graham in the brain and he fell dead. A low wail was heard in the air—many people in the concourse cried that they had seen a spirit glide across the little casement-window of the Bowyer's house——

A dead silence succeeded. After a short time some of the flushed and heated throng laid down their arms and softly carried the body within doors. Others fell off or slunk away in knots of two or three, others whispered together in groups, and before a numerous guard which then rode up could muster in the street, it was nearly empty.

Those who carried Master Graham to the bed upstairs were shocked to see a woman lying beneath the window with her hands clasped together. After trying to recover her in vain, they laid her near the citizen, who still retained, tightly grasped in his right hand, the first and last sword that was broken that day at Lud Gate.

The Giant uttered these concluding words with sudden precipitation, and on the instant the strange light which had filled the hall faded away. Joe Toddyhigh glanced involuntarily at the eastern window and saw the first pale gleam of morning. He turned his head again towards the other window in which the Giants had been seated. It was empty. The cask of wine was gone, and he could dimly make out that the two great figures stood mute and motionless upon their pedestals.

After rubbing his eyes and wondering for full half an hour, during which time he observed morning come creeping on apace, he yielded to the drowsiness which overpowered him and fell into a refreshing slumber. When he awoke it was broad day; the building was open, and workmen were busily engaged in removing the vestiges of last night's feast.

Stealing gently down the little stairs and assuming the air of some early lounger who had dropped in from the street, he walked up to the foot of each pedestal in turn, and attentively examined the figure it supported. There could be no doubt about the features of either; he recollected the exact expression they had worn at different passages of their conversation, and recognized in every line and lineament the Giants of the night. Assured that it was no vision, but that he had heard and seen with his own proper senses, he walked forth, determining at all hazards to conceal himself in the Guildhall again that evening. He further resolved to sleep all day, so that he might be very wakeful and vigilant, and above all that he might take notice of the figures at the precise moment of their becoming animated and subsiding into their old state, which he greatly reproached himself for not having done already.

CORRESPONDENCE

TO MASTER HUMPHREY

SIR,

Before you proceed any further in your account of your friends and what you say and do when you meet together, excuse me if I proffer my claim to be elected to one of the vacant chairs in that old room of yours. Don't reject me without full consideration; for if you do you'll be sorry for it afterwards—you will, upon my life.

I inclose my card, sir, in this letter. I never was ashamed of my name, and I never shall be. I am considered a devilish gentlemanly fellow, and I act up to the character. If you want a reference, ask any of the men at our club. Ask any fellow who goes there to write his letters, what sort of conversation mine is. Ask him if he thinks I have the sort of voice that will suit your deaf friend and make him hear, if he can hear anything at all. Ask the servants what they think of me. There's not a rascal among 'em, sir, but will tremble to hear my name. That reminds me—don't you say too much about that housekeeper of yours; it's a low subject, damned low.

I'll tell you what, sir. If you vote me into one of those empty chairs, you'll have among you a man with a fund of gentlemanly information that'll rather astonish you. I can let you into a few anecdotes about some fine women of title, that are quite high life, sir—the tiptop sort of thing. I know the name of every man who has been out on an affair of honor within the last five-and-twenty years; I know the private particulars of every cross and squabble that has taken place upon the turf, at the gaming-table, or elsewhere, during the whole of that time. I have been called the gentlemanly chronicle. You may consider yourself a lucky dog; upon my soul, you may congratulate yourself, though I say so.

It's an uncommon good notion that of yours, not letting anybody know where you live. I have tried it, but there has always been an anxiety respecting me, which has found me out. Your deaf friend is a cunning fellow to keep his name so close. I have tried that too, but have always failed. I shall be proud to make his acquaintance—tell him so, with my compliments.

You must have been a queer fellow when you were a child, confounded queer. It's odd, all that about the picture in your first paper—prosy, but told in a devilish gentlemanly sort of way. In places like that I could come in with great effect with a touch of life—don't you feel that?

I am anxiously waiting for your next paper to know whether your friends live upon the premises, and at your expense, which I take it for granted is the case. If I am right in this impression, I know a charming fellow (an excellent companion and most delightful company) who will be proud to join you. Some years ago he seconded a great many prize-fighters, and once fought an amateur match himself; since then he has driven several mails, broken at different periods all the lamps on the right-hand side of Oxford Street, and six times carried away every bell-handle in Bloomsbury Square, besides turning off the gas in various thoroughfares. In point of gentlemanliness he is unrivaled, and I should say that next to myself he is of all men the best suited to your purpose.

Expecting your reply,
I am,
&C. &C.

Master Humphrey informs this gentleman that his application, both as it concerns himself and his friend, is rejected.

Two

MASTER HUMPHREY FROM HIS CLOCK-SIDE IN THE CHIMNEY-CORNER

My OLD COMPANION TELLS ME IT IS MIDNIGHT. THE FIRE glows brightly, crackling with a sharp and cheerful sound as if it loved to burn. The merry cricket on the hearth (my constant visitor), this ruddy blaze, my Clock, and I, seem to share the world among us, and to be the only things awake. The wind, high and boisterous but now, has died away and hoarsely mutters in its sleep. I love all times and seasons each in its turn, and am apt perhaps to think the present one the best; but past or coming I always love this peaceful time of night, when long-buried thoughts favored by the gloom and silence steal from their graves and haunt the scenes of faded happiness and hope.

The popular faith in ghosts has a remarkable affinity with the whole current of our thoughts at such an hour as this, and seems to be their necessary and natural consequence. For who can wonder that man should feel a vague belief in tales of disembodied spirits wandering through those places which they once dearly affected, when he himself, scarcely less separated from his old world than they, is forever lingering upon past emotions and bygone times, and hovering, the ghost of his former self, about the places and people that warmed his heart of old? It is thus that at this quiet hour I haunt the house where I was born, the rooms I used to tread, the scenes of my infancy, my boyhood, and my youth; it is thus that I prowl around my buried treasure (though not of gold or silver) and mourn my loss; it is thus that I revisit the ashes of extinguished fires, and take my silent stand at old bedsides. If my spirit should ever glide back to this chamber when my body is mingled with the dust, it will but follow the course it often took in the old man's lifetime and add but one more change to the subjects of its contemplation.

In all my idle speculations I am greatly assisted by various legends connected with my venerable house, which are current in the neighborhood, and are so numerous that there is scarce a cupboard or corner that has not some dismal story of its own. When I first entertained thoughts of becoming its tenant I was assured that it was haunted from roof to cellar, and I believe that the bad opinion in which my neighbors once held me had its rise in my not being torn to pieces or at least distracted with terror on the night I took possession; in either of which cases I should doubtless have arrived by a shortcut at the very summit of popularity.

But traditions and rumors all taken into account, who so abets me in every fancy and chimes with my every thought, as my dear deaf friend; and how often have I cause to bless the day that brought us two together! Of all days in the year I rejoice to think that it should have been Christmas Day, with which from childhood we associate something friendly, hearty, and sincere.

I had walked out to cheer myself with the happiness of others, and in the little tokens of festivity and rejoicing of which the streets and houses present so many upon that day had lost some hours. Now I stopped to look at a merry party hurrying through the snow on foot to their place of meeting, and now turned back to see a whole coachful of children safely deposited at the welcome house. At one time, I admired how carefully the working-man carried the baby in its gaudy hat and feathers, and how his wife, trudging patiently on behind, forgot even her care of her gay clothes, in exchanging greetings with the child as it crowed and laughed over the father's shoulder; at another, I pleased myself with some passing scene of gallantry or courtship, and was glad to believe that for a season half the world of poverty was gay.

As the day closed in, I still rambled through the streets, feeling a companionship in the bright fires that cast their warm reflection on the windows as I passed, and losing all sense of my own loneliness in imagining the sociality and kind-fellowship that everywhere prevailed. At length I happened to stop before a Tavern and encountering a Bill of Fare in the window, it all at once brought it into my head to wonder what kind of people dined alone in Taverns upon Christmas Day.

Solitary men are accustomed, I suppose, unconsciously to look upon solitude as their own peculiar property. I had sat alone in my room on many, many anniversaries of this great holiday, and had never regarded it but as one of universal assemblage and rejoicing. I had excepted, and with an aching heart, a crowd of prisoners and beggars; but *these* were not the men for whom the Tavern doors were open. Had they any customers, or was it a mere form?—a form, no doubt.

Trying to feel quite sure of this I walked away; but before I had gone many paces, I stopped and looked back. There was a provoking air of business in the lamp above the door which I could not overcome. I began to be afraid there might be many customers—young men perhaps struggling with the world, utter strangers in this great place, whose friends lived at a long distance off, and whose means were too slender to enable them to make the journey. The supposition gave rise to so many distressing little pictures that in preference to carrying them home with me, I determined to encounter the realities. So I turned and walked in.

I was at once glad and sorry to find that there was only one person in the dining-room; glad to know that there were not more, and sorry to think that he should be there by himself. He did not look so old as I, but like me he was advanced in life, and his hair was nearly white. Though I made more noise in entering and seating myself than was quite necessary, with the view of attracting his attention and saluting him in the good old form of that time of year, he did not raise his head but sat with it resting on his hand, musing over his half-finished meal.

I called for something which would give me an excuse for remaining in the room (I had dined early, as my housekeeper was engaged at night to partake of some friend's good cheer) and sat where I could observe without intruding on him. After a time he looked up. He was aware that somebody had entered, but could see very little of me as I sat in the shade and he in the light. He was sad and thoughtful, and I forbore to trouble him by speaking.

Let me believe that it was something better than curiosity which riveted my attention and impelled me strongly towards this gentleman. I never saw so patient and kind a face. He should have been surrounded by friends, and yet here he sat dejected and alone when all men had their friends about them. As often as he roused himself from his reverie he would fall into it again, and it was plain that whatever were the subject of his thoughts they were of a melancholy kind, and would not be controlled.

He was not used to solitude. I was sure of that; for I know by myself that if he had been, his manner would have been different, and he would have taken some slight interest in the arrival of another. I could not fail to mark that he had no appetite—that he tried to eat in vain—that time after time the plate was pushed away, and he relapsed into his former posture.

His mind was wandering among old Christmas Days, I thought. Many of them sprang up together, not with a long gap between each, but in unbroken succession like days of the week. It was a great change to find himself for the first time (I quite settled that it *was* the first) in an empty silent room with no soul to care for. I could not help following him in imagination through crowds of pleasant faces, and then coming back to that dull place with its bough of mistletoe sickening in the gas, and sprigs of holly parched up already by a simoom of roast and boiled. The very waiter had gone home; and his representative, a poor lean hungry man, was keeping Christmas in his jacket.

I grew still more interested in my friend. His dinner done, a decanter of wine was placed before him. It remained untouched for a long time, but at length with a quivering hand he filled a glass and raised it to his lips. Some tender wish to which he had been accustomed to give utterance on that day, or some beloved name that he had been used to pledge, trembled upon them at the moment. He put it down very hastily—took it up once more—again put it down—pressed his hand upon his face—yes—and tears stole down his cheeks, I am certain.

Without pausing to consider whether I did right or wrong, I stepped across the room, and sitting down beside him laid my hand gently on his arm.

"My friend," I said, "forgive me if I beseech you to take comfort and consolation from the lips of an old man. I will not preach to you what I have not practiced, indeed. Whatever be your grief, be of a good heart—be of a good heart, pray!"

"I see that you speak earnestly," he replied, "and kindly I am very sure, but——"

I nodded my head to show that I understood what he would say; for I had already gathered, from a certain fixed expression in his face and from the attention with which he watched me while I spoke, that his sense of hearing was destroyed. "There should be a freemasonry between us," said I, pointing from himself to me to explain my meaning—"if not in our grey hairs, at least in our misfortunes. You see that I am but a poor cripple."

I never felt so happy under my affliction since the trying moment of my first becoming conscious of it, as when he took my hand in his with a smile that has lighted my path in life from that day, and we sat down side by side.

This was the beginning of my friendship with the deaf gentleman; and when was ever the slight and easy service of a kind word in season repaid by such attachment and devotion as he has shown to me!

He produced a little set of tablets and a pencil to facilitate our conversation, on that our first acquaintance; and I well remember how awkward and constrained I was in writing down my share of the dialogue, and how easily he guessed my meaning before I had written half of what I had to say. He told me in a faltering voice that he had not been accustomed to be alone on that day—that it had always been a little festival with him—and seeing that I glanced at his dress in the expectation that he wore mourning, he added hastily that it was not that; if it had been he thought he could have borne it better. From that time to the present we have never touched upon this theme. Upon every return of the same day we have been together; and although we make it our annual custom to drink to each other hand in hand after dinner, and to recall with affectionate garrulity every circumstance of our first meeting, we always avoid this one as if by mutual consent.

Meantime we have gone on strengthening in our friendship and regard and forming an attachment which, I trust and believe, will only be interrupted by death, to be renewed in another existence. I scarcely know how we communicate as we do, but he has long since ceased to be deaf to me. He is frequently the companion of my walks, and even in crowded streets replies to my slightest look or gesture as though he could read my thoughts. From the vast number of objects which pass in rapid succession before our eyes, we frequently select the same for some particular notice or remark; and when one of these little coincidences occurs I cannot describe the pleasure that animates my friend, or the beaming countenance he will preserve for half an hour afterwards at least.

He is a great thinker from living so much within himself, and having a lively imagination has a facility of conceiving and enlarging upon odd ideas, which renders him invaluable to our little body, and greatly astonishes our two friends. His powers in this respect are much assisted by a large pipe, which he assures us once belonged to a German Student. Be this as it may, it has undoubtedly a very ancient and mysterious appearance, and is of such capacity that it takes three hours and a half to smoke it out. I have reason to believe that my barber who is the chief authority of a knot of gossips, who congregate every evening at a small tobacconist's hard by, has related anecdotes of this pipe and the grim figures that are carved upon its bowl at which all the smokers in the neighborhood have stood aghast; and I know that my housekeeper, while she holds it in high veneration, has a superstitious feeling connected with it which would render her exceedingly unwilling to be left alone in its company after dark.

Whatever sorrow my deaf friend has known, and whatever grief may linger in some secret corner of his heart, he is now a cheerful, placid, happy creature. Misfortune can never have fallen upon such a man but for some good purpose; and when I see its traces in his gentle nature and his earnest feeling, I am the less disposed to murmur at such trials as I may have undergone myself. With regard to the pipe, I have a theory of my own; I cannot help thinking that it is in some manner connected with the event that brought us together; for I remember that it was a long time before he even talked about it; that when he did, he grew reserved and melancholy; and that it was a long time yet before he brought it forth. I have no curiosity, however, upon this subject; for I know that it promotes his tranquility and comfort, and I need no other inducement to regard it with my utmost favor.

Such is the deaf gentleman. I can call up his figure now, clad in sober grey, and seated in the chimney-corner. As he puffs out the smoke from his favorite pipe, he casts a look on me brimful of cordiality and friendship, and says all manner of kind and genial things in a cheerful smile; then he raises his eyes to my Clock, which is just about to strike, and, glancing from it to me and back again, seems to divide his heart between us. For myself, it is not too much to say that I would gladly part with one of my poor limbs, could he but hear the old Clock's voice.

Of our two friends, the first has been all his life one of that easy wayward truant class whom the world is accustomed to designate as nobody's enemies but their own. Bred to a profession for which he never qualified himself, and reared in the expectation of a fortune he has never inherited, he has undergone every vicissitude of which such an existence is capable. He and his younger brother, both orphans from their childhood, were educated by a wealthy relative who taught them to expect an equal division of his property; but too indolent to court, and too honest to flatter, the elder gradually lost ground in the affections of a capricious old man, and the younger, who did not fail to improve his opportunity, now triumphs in the possession of enormous wealth. His triumph is to hoard it in solitary wretchedness, and probably to feel with the expenditure of every shilling a greater pang than the loss of his whole inheritance ever cost his brother.

Jack Redburn—he was Jack Redburn at the first little school he went to, where every other child was mastered and surnamed, and he has been Jack Redburn all his life or he would perhaps have been a richer man by this time—has been an inmate of my house these eight years past. He is my librarian, secretary, steward, and first minister; director of all my affairs and inspector-general of my household. He is something of a musician, something of an author, something of an actor, something of a painter, very much of a carpenter, and an extraordinary gardener, having had all his life a wonderful aptitude for learning everything that was of no use to him. He is remarkably fond of children, and is the best and kindest nurse in sickness that ever drew the breath of life. He has mixed with every grade of society, and known the utmost distress; but there never was a less selfish, a more tenderhearted, a more enthusiastic, or a more guileless man; and I dare say, if few have done less good, fewer still have done less harm in the world than he. By what chance Nature forms such whimsical jumbles I don't know; but I do know that she sends them among us very often, and that the king of the whole race is Jack Redburn.

I should be puzzled to say how old he is. His health is none of the best, and he wears a quantity of iron-grey hair, which shades his face and gives it rather a worn appearance; but we consider him quite a young fellow notwithstanding; and if a youthful spirit, surviving the roughest contact with the world, confers upon its possessor any title to be considered young, then he is a mere child. The only interruptions to his careless cheerfulness are on a wet Sunday, when he is apt to be unusually religious and solemn, and sometimes of an evening, when he has been blowing a very slow tune on the flute. On these last-named occasions he is apt to incline towards the mysterious or the terrible. As a specimen of his powers in this mood, I refer my readers to the extract from the Clock-case which follows this paper: he brought it to me not long ago at midnight, and informed me that the main incident had been suggested by a dream of the night before.

His apartments are two cheerful rooms looking towards the garden, and one of his great delights is to arrange and rearrange the furniture in these chambers, and put it in every possible variety of position. During the whole time he has been here, I do not think he has slept for two nights running with the head of his bed in the same place; and everytime he moves it, is to be the last. My housekeeper was at first well nigh distracted by these frequent changes; but she has become quite reconciled to them by degrees and has so fallen in with his humor, that they often consult together with great gravity upon the next final alteration. Whatever his arrangements are, however, they are always a pattern of neatness; and every one of the manifold articles connected with his manifold occupations is to be found in its own particular place. Until within the last two or three years he was subject to an occasional fit (which usually came upon him in very fine weather) under the influence of which he would dress himself with peculiar care, and going out under pretense of taking a walk, disappear for several days together. At length, after the interval between each outbreak of this disorder had gradually grown longer and longer, it wholly disappeared; and now he seldom stirs abroad, except to stroll out a little way on a summer's evening. Whether he yet mistrusts his own constancy in this respect, and is therefore afraid to wear a coat, I know not; but we seldom see him in any other upper garment than an old spectral-looking dressing-gown, with very disproportionate pockets, full of a miscellaneous collection of odd matters which he picks up wherever he can lay his hands upon them.

Everything that is a favorite with our friend is a favorite with us; and thus it happens that the fourth among us is Mr. Owen Miles, a most worthy gentleman, who had treated Jack with great kindness before my deaf friend and I encountered him by an accident, to which I may refer on some future occasion. Mr. Miles was once a very rich merchant; but receiving a severe shock in the death of his wife, he retired from business and devoted himself to a quiet unostentatious life. He is an excellent man, of thoroughly sterling character: not of quick apprehension, and not without some amusing prejudices, which I shall leave to their own development. He holds us all in profound veneration; but Jack Redburn he esteems as a kind of pleasant wonder, that he may venture to approach familiarly. He believes, not only that no man ever lived who could do so many things as Jack, but that no man ever lived who could do anything so well; and he never calls my attention to any of his ingenious proceedings but he whispers in my ear, nudging me at the same time with his elbow—"If he had only made it his trade, sir—if he had only made it his trade!"

They are inseparable companions; one would almost suppose that, although Mr. Miles never by any chance does anything in the way of assistance, Jack could do nothing without him. Whether he is reading, writing, painting, carpentering, gardening, flute-playing, or what not, there is Mr. Miles beside him, buttoned up to the chin in his blue coat, and looking on with a face of incredulous delight as though he could not credit the testimony of his own senses and had a misgiving that no man could be so clever but in a dream.

These are my friends; I have now introduced myself and them.

THE CLOCK-CASE

A CONFESSION FOUND IN A PRISON
IN THE TIME OF CHARLES THE SECOND

I held a lieutenant's commission in His Majesty's army and served abroad in the campaigns of 1677 and 1678. The Treaty of Nimeguen being concluded, I returned home, and retiring from the service withdrew to a small estate lying a few miles east of London, which I had recently acquired in right of my wife.

This is the last night I have to live, and I will set down the naked truth without disguise. I was never a brave man, and had always been from my childhood of a secret, sullen, distrustful nature. I speak of myself as if I had passed from the world; for while I write this, my grave is digging, and my name is written in the black book of death.

Soon after my return to England, my only brother was seized with mortal illness. This circumstance gave me slight or no pain, for since we had been men we had associated but very little together. He was openhearted and generous, handsomer than I, more accomplished, and generally beloved. Those who sought my acquaintance abroad or at home because they were friends of his, seldom attached themselves to me long, and would usually say in our first conversation that they were surprised to find two brothers so unlike in their manners and appearance. It was my habit to lead them on to this avowal; for I knew what comparisons they must draw between us; and having a rankling envy in my heart, I sought to justify it to myself.

We had married two sisters. This additional tie between us, as it may appear to some, only estranged us the more. His wife knew me well. I never struggled with any secret jealousy or gall when she was present but that woman knew it as well as I did. I never raised my eyes at such times but I found hers fixed upon me; I never bent them on the ground or looked another way but I felt that she overlooked me always. It was an inexpressible relief to me when we quarreled, and a greater relief still when I heard abroad that she was dead. It seems to me now as if some strange and terrible foreshadowing of what has happened since must have hung over us then. I was afraid of her; she haunted me; her fixed and steady look comes back upon me now like the memory of a dark dream, and makes my blood run cold.

She died shortly after giving birth to a child—a boy. When my brother knew that all hope of his own recovery was past, he called my wife to his bedside and confided this orphan, a child of four years old, to her protection. He bequeathed to him all the property he had, and willed that in case of his child's death it should pass to my wife, as the only acknowledgment he could make her for her care and love. He exchanged a few brotherly words with me, deploring our long separation; and being exhausted, fell into a slumber from which he never awoke.

We had no children; and as there had been a strong affection between the sisters, and my wife had almost supplied the place of a mother to this boy, she loved him as if he had been her own. The child was ardently attached to her; but he was his mother's image in face and spirit and always mistrusted me.

I can scarcely fix the date when the feeling first came upon me, but I soon began to be uneasy when this child was by. I never roused myself from some moody train of thought but I marked him looking at me: not with mere childish wonder, but with something of the purpose and meaning that I had so often noted in his mother. It was no effort of my fancy, founded on close resemblance of feature and expression. I never could look the boy down. He feared me, but seemed by some instinct to despise me while he did so; and even when he drew back beneath my gaze—as he would when we were alone, to get nearer to the door—he would keep his bright eyes upon me still.

Perhaps I hide the truth from myself, but I do not think that when this began, I meditated to do him any wrong. I may have thought how serviceable his inheritance would be to us, and may have wished him dead; but I believe I had no thought of compassing his death. Neither did the idea come upon me at once, but by very slow degrees, presenting itself at first in dim shapes at a very great distance, as men may think of an earthquake or the Last Day; then drawing nearer and nearer, and losing something of its horror and improbability; then coming to be part and parcel—nay, nearly the whole sum and substance—of my daily thoughts, and resolving itself into a question of means and safety; not of doing or abstaining from the deed.

While this was going on within me, I never could bear that the child should see me looking at him, and yet I was under a fascination which made it a kind of business with me to contemplate his slight and fragile figure and think how easily it might be done. Sometimes I would steal upstairs and watch him as he slept; but usually I hovered in the garden near the window of the room in which he learnt his little tasks; and there, as he sat upon a low seat beside my wife, I would peer at him for hours together from behind a tree; starting like the guilty wretch I was at every rustling of a leaf, and still gliding back to look and start again.

Hard by our cottage, but quite out of sight, and (if there were any wind astir) of hearing too, was a deep sheet of water. I spent days in shaping with my pocketknife a rough model of a boat, which I finished at last and dropped in the child's way. Then I withdrew to a secret place which he must pass if he stole away alone to swim this bauble, and lurked there for his coming. He came neither that day nor the next, though I waited from noon till nightfall. I was sure that I had him in my net, for I had heard him prattling of the toy, and knew that in his infant pleasure he kept it by his side in bed. I felt no weariness or fatigue, but waited patiently, and on the third day he passed me, running joyously along, with his silken hair streaming in the wind, and he singing—God have mercy upon me!—singing a merry ballad—who could hardly lisp the words.

I stole down after him, creeping under certain shrubs which grow in that place, and none but devils know with what terror I, a strong full-grown man, tracked the footsteps of that baby as he approached the water's brink. I was close upon him, had sunk upon my knee and raised my hand to thrust him in, when he saw my shadow in the stream and turned him round.

His mother's ghost was looking from his eyes. The sun burst forth from behind a cloud; it shone in the bright sky, the glistening earth, the clear water, the sparkling drops of rain upon the leaves. There were eyes in everything. The whole great universe of light was there to see the murder done. I know not what he said; he came of bold and manly blood, and, child as he was, he did not crouch or fawn upon me. I heard him cry that he would try to love me—not that he did—and then I saw him running back towards the house. The next I saw was my own sword naked in my hand, and he lying at my feet stark dead—dabbled here and there with blood, but otherwise no different from what I had seen him in his sleep—in the same attitude too, with his cheek resting upon his little hand.

I took him in my arms and laid him—very gently now that he was dead—in a thicket. My wife was from home that day, and would not return until the next. Our bedroom window, the only sleeping-room on that side of the house, was but a few feet from the ground, and I resolved to descend from it at night and bury him in the garden. I had no thought that I had failed in my design, no thought that the water would be dragged and nothing found, that the money must now lie waste since I must encourage the idea that the child was lost or stolen. All my thoughts were bound up and knotted together in the one absorbing necessity of hiding what I had done.

How I felt when they came to tell me that the child was missing, when I ordered scouts in all directions, when I gasped and trembled at everyone's approach, no tongue can tell or mind of man conceive. I buried him that night. When I parted the boughs and looked into the dark thicket, there was a glowworm shining like the visible spirit of God upon the murdered child. I glanced down into his grave when I had placed him there and still it gleamed upon his breast: an eye of fire looking up to Heaven in supplication to the stars that watched me at my work.

I had to meet my wife, and break the news, and give her hope that the child would soon be found. All this I did—with some appearance, I suppose, of being sincere, for I was the object of no suspicion. This done, I sat at the bedroom window all day long and watched the spot where the dreadful secret lay.

It was in a piece of ground which had been dug up to be newly turfed, and which I had chosen on that account as the traces of my spade were less likely to attract attention. The men who laid down the grass must have thought me mad. I called to them continually to expedite their work, ran out and worked beside them, trod down the turf with my feet, and hurried them with frantic eagerness. They had finished their task before night, and then I thought myself comparatively safe.

I slept—not as men do who wake refreshed and cheerful, but I did sleep, passing from vague and shadowy dreams of being hunted down, to visions of the plot of grass, through which now a hand, and now a foot, and now the head itself was starting out. At this point I always woke and stole to the window to make sure that it was not really so. That done, I crept to bed again; and thus I spent the night in fits and starts, getting up and lying down full twenty times, and dreaming the same dream over and over again—which was far worse than lying awake, for every dream had a whole night's suffering of its own. Once I thought the child was alive and that I had never tried to kill him. To wake from that dream was the most dreadful agony of all.

The next day I sat at the window again, never once taking my eyes from the place, which, although it was covered by the grass, was as plain to me— its shape, its size, its depth, its jagged sides, and all—as if it had been open to the light of day. When a servant walked across it, I felt as if he must sink in; when he had passed, I looked to see that his feet had not worn the edges. If a bird lighted there, I was in terror lest by some tremendous interposition it should be instrumental in the discovery; if a breath of air sighed across it, to me it whispered murder. There was not a sight or a sound—how ordinary, mean, or unimportant soever—but was fraught with fear. And in this state of ceaseless watching I spent three days.

On the fourth there came to the gate one who had served with me abroad, accompanied by a brother officer of his whom I had never seen. I felt that I could not bear to be out of sight of the place. It was a summer evening, and I bade my people take a table and a flask of wine into the garden. Then I sat down *with my chair upon the grave,* and being assured that nobody could disturb it now without my knowledge, tried to drink and talk.

They hoped that my wife was well—that she was not obliged to keep her chamber—that they had not frightened her away. What could I do but tell them with a faltering tongue about the child? The officer whom I did not know was a down-looking man, and kept his eyes upon the ground while I was speaking. Even that terrified me! I could not divest myself of the idea that he saw something there which caused him to suspect the truth. I asked him hurriedly if he supposed that—and stopped. "That the child has been murdered?" said he, looking mildly at me: "Oh no! what could a man gain by murdering a poor child?" *I* could have told him what a man gained by such a deed, no one better: but I held my peace and shivered as with an ague.

Mistaking my emotion, they were endeavoring to cheer me with the hope that the boy would certainly be found—great cheer that was for me!— when we heard a low deep howl, and presently there sprang over the wall two great dogs, who bounding into the garden repeated the baying sound we had heard before.

"Bloodhounds!" cried my visitors.

What need to tell me that! I had never seen one of that kind in all my life, but I knew what they were and for what purpose they had come. I grasped the elbows of my chair, and neither spoke nor moved.

"They are of the genuine breed," said the man whom I had known abroad, "and being out for exercise have no doubt escaped from their keeper."

Both he and his friend turned to look at the dogs, who with their noses to the ground moved restlessly about, running to and fro, and up and down, and across, and round in circles, careering about like wild things, and all this time taking no notice of us, but ever and again lifting their heads and repeating the yell we had heard already, then dropping their noses to the ground again and tracking earnestly here and there. They now began to snuff the earth more eagerly than they had done yet, and although they were still very restless, no longer beat about in such wide circuits, but kept near to one spot, and constantly diminished the distance between themselves and me.

At last they came up close to the great chair on which I sat, and raising their frightful howl once more, tried to tear away the wooden rails that kept them from the ground beneath. I saw how I looked, in the faces of the two who were with me.

"They scent some prey," said they, both together.

"They scent no prey!" cried I.

"In Heaven's name, move!" said the one I knew, very earnestly, "or you will be torn to pieces."

"Let them tear me limb from limb, I'll never leave this place!" cried I. "Are dogs to hurry men to shameful deaths? Hew them down, cut them in pieces."

"There is some foul mystery here!" said the officer whom I did not know, drawing his sword. "In King Charles's name, assist me to secure this man."

They both set upon me and forced me away, though I fought and bit and caught at them like a madman. After a struggle, they got me quietly between them; and then, my God! I saw the angry dogs tearing at the earth and throwing it up into the air like water.

What more have I to tell? That I fell upon my knees, and with chattering teeth confessed the truth, and prayed to be forgiven. That I have since denied, and now confess to it again. That I have been tried for the crime, found guilty, and sentenced. That I have not the courage to anticipate my doom or to bear up manfully against it. That I have no compassion, no consolation, no hope, no friend. That my wife has happily lost for the time those faculties which would enable her to know my misery or hers. That I am alone in this stone dungeon with my evil spirit, and that I die tomorrow!

CORRESPONDENCE

Master Humphrey has been favored with the following letter written on strongly-scented paper, and sealed in light-blue wax with the representation of two very plump doves interchanging beaks. It does not commence with any of the usual forms of address, but begins as is here set forth.

Bath, Wednesday night

Heavens! into what an indiscretion do I suffer myself to be betrayed! To address these faltering lines to a total stranger, and that stranger one of a conflicting sex!—and yet I am precipitated into the abyss, and have no power of self-snatchation (forgive me if I coin that phrase) from the yawning gulf before me.

Yes, I am writing to a man; but let me not think of that, for madness is in the thought. You will understand my feelings? Oh yes! I am sure you will! and you will respect them too, and not despise them—will you?

Let me be calm. That portrait—smiling as once he smiled on me; that cane—dangling as I have seen it dangle from his hand I know not how oft; those legs that have glided through my nightly dreams and never stopped to speak; the perfectly gentlemanly, though false origi-nal—can I be mistaken? Oh no, no.

Let me be calmer yet; I would be calm as coffins. You have published a letter from one whose likeness is engraved, but whose name (and wherefore?) is suppressed. Shall *I* breathe that name! Is it—but why ask when my heart tells me too truly that it is!

I would not upbraid him with his treachery; I would not remind him of those times when he plighted the most eloquent of vows, and pro-cured from me a small pecuniary accommodation; and yet I would see him—see him did I say—*him*—alas! such is woman's nature. For as the poet beautifully says—but you will already have anticipated the senti-ment. Is it not sweet? Oh yes!

It was in this city (hallowed by the recollection) that I met him first; and assuredly if mortal happiness be recorded anywhere, then those rub-bers with their three-and-six-penny points are scored on tablets of celes-tial brass. He always held an honor—generally two. On that eventful night we stood at eight. He raised his eyes (luminous in their seductive sweetness) to my agitated face. "*Can* you?" said he, with peculiar mean-ing. I felt the gentle pressure of his foot on mine; our corns throbbed in unison. "*Can* you?" he said again; and every lineament of his expressive countenance added the words "resist me?" I murmured "No," and fainted.

They said, when I recovered, it was the weather. *I* said it was the nut-meg in the negus. How little did they suspect the truth! How little did they guess the deep mysterious meaning of that inquiry! He called next morning on his knees; I do not mean to say that he actually came in that position to the house-door, but that he went down upon those joints directly the servant had retired. He brought some verses in his hat, which he said were original, but which I have since found were Milton's. Like-wise a little bottle labelled laudanum; also a pistol and a sword-stick. He drew the latter, uncorked the former, and clicked the trigger of the pocket firearm. He had come, he said, to conquer or to die. He did not die. He wrested from me an avowal of my love, and let off the pistol out of a back window previous to partaking of a slight repast.

Faithless, inconstant man! How many ages seem to have elapsed since his unaccountable and perfidious disappearance! Could I still forgive him both that and the borrowed lucre that he promised to pay next week! Could I spurn him from my feet if he approached in penitence, and with a matrimonial object! Would the blandishing enchanter still weave his spells around me, or should I burst them all and turn away in coldness! I dare not trust my weakness with the thought.

My brain is in a whirl again. You know his address, his occupations, his mode of life—are acquainted perhaps with his inmost thoughts. You are a humane and philanthropic character; reveal all you know—all; but especially the street and number of his lodgings. The post is departing, the bellman rings—pray Heaven it be not the knell of love and hope to

BELINDA

P.S. Pardon the wanderings of a bad pen and a distracted mind. Address to the post-office. The bellman rendered impatient by delay is ringing dreadfully in the passage.

P.P.S. I open this to say that the bellman is gone and that you must not expect it till the next post, so don't be surprised when you don't get it.

Master Humphrey does not feel himself at liberty to furnish his fair correspondent with the address of the gentleman in question, but he publishes her letter as a public appeal to his faith and gallantry.

Three

MASTER HUMPHREY'S VISITOR

WHEN I AM IN A THOUGHTFUL MOOD, I OFTEN SUCCEED IN diverting the current of some mournful reflections, by conjuring up a number of fanciful associations with the objects that surround me, and dwelling upon the scenes and characters they suggest.

I have been led by this habit to assign to every room in my house and every old staring portrait on its walls a separate interest of its own. Thus, I am persuaded that a stately dame, terrible to behold in her rigid modesty, who hangs above the chimney-piece of my bedroom, is the former lady of the mansion. In the courtyard below is a stone face of surpassing ugliness, which I have somehow—in a kind of jealousy, I am afraid—associated with her husband. Above my study is a little room with ivy peeping through the lattice, from which I bring their daughter, a lovely girl of eighteen or nineteen years of age, and dutiful in all respects save one, that one being her devoted attachment to a young gentleman on the stairs, whose grandmother (degraded to a disused laundry in the garden) piques herself upon an old family quarrel and is the implacable enemy of their love. With such materials as these I work out many a little drama, whose chief merit is that I can bring it to a happy end at will; I have so many of them on hand, that if on my return home one of these evenings I were to find some bluff old wight of two centuries ago comfortably seated in my easychair, and a lovelorn damsel vainly appealing to his obdurate heart and leaning her white arm upon my Clock itself, I verily believe I should only express my surprise that they had kept me waiting so long, and never honored me with a call before.

I was, in such a mood as this, sitting in my garden yesterday morning under the shade of a favorite tree, reveling in all the bloom and brightness about me, and feeling every sense of hope and enjoyment quickened by this most beautiful season of Spring, when my meditations were interrupted by the unexpected appearance of my barber at the end of the walk, who I immediately saw was coming towards me with a hasty step that betokened something remarkable.

My barber is at all times a very brisk, bustling, active little man—for he is, as it were, chubby all over, without being stout or unwieldy—but yesterday his alacrity was so very uncommon that it quite took me by surprise. Nor could I fail to observe when he came up to me that his grey eyes were twinkling in a most extraordinary manner, that his little red nose was in an unusual glow, that every line in his round bright face was twisted and curved into an expression of pleased surprise, and that his whole countenance was radiant with glee. I was still more surprised to see my housekeeper, who usually preserves a very staid air and stands somewhat upon her dignity, peeping round the hedge at the bottom of the walk, and exchanging nods and smiles with the barber, who twice or thrice looked over his shoulder for that purpose. I could conceive no announcement to which these appearances could be the prelude, unless it were that they had married each other that morning.

I was, consequently, a little disappointed when it only came out that there was a gentleman in the house who wished to speak with me.

"And who is it?" said I.

The barber, with his face screwed up still tighter than before, replied that the gentleman would not send his name, but wished to see me. I pondered for a moment, wondering who this visitor might be, and I remarked that he embraced the opportunity of exchanging another nod with the housekeeper, who still lingered in the distance.

"Well!" said I, "bid the gentleman come here."

This seemed to be the consummation of the barber's hopes, for he turned sharp round, and actually ran away.

Now, my sight is not very good at a distance, and therefore when the gentleman first appeared in the walk, I was not quite clear whether he was a stranger to me or otherwise. He was an elderly gentleman, but came tripping along in the pleasantest manner conceivable, avoiding the garden-roller and the borders of the beds with inimitable dexterity, picking his way among the flowerpots, and smiling with unspeakable good-humor. Before he was half-way up the walk he began to salute me; then I thought I knew him; but when he came towards me with his hat in his hand, the sun shining on his bald head, his bland face, his bright spectacles, his fawn-colored tights, and his black gaiters—then my heart warmed towards him, and I felt quite certain that it was Mr. Pickwick.

"My dear sir," said that gentleman as I rose to receive him, "pray be seated. Pray sit down. Now, do not stand on my account. I must insist upon it, really." With these words Mr. Pickwick gently pressed me down into my seat, and taking my hand in his, shook it again and again with a warmth of manner perfectly irresistible. I endeavored to express in my welcome something of that heartiness and pleasure which the sight of him awakened and made him sit down beside me. All this time he kept alternately releasing my hand and grasping it again, and surveying me through his spectacles with such a beaming countenance as I never beheld.

"You knew me directly!" said Mr. Pickwick. "What a pleasure it is to think that you knew me directly!"

I remarked that I had read his adventures very often, and that his features were quite familiar to me from the published portraits. As I thought it a good opportunity of adverting to the circumstance, I condoled with him upon the various libels on his character which had found their way into print. Mr. Pickwick shook his head and for a moment looked very indignant, but smiling again directly, added that no doubt I was acquainted with Cervantes' introduction to the second part of *Don Quixote,* and that it fully expressed his sentiments on the subject.

"But now," said Mr. Pickwick, "don't you wonder how I found you out?"

"I will never wonder, and with your good leave, never know," said I, smiling in my turn. "It is enough for me that you give me this gratification. I have not the least desire that you should tell me by what means I have obtained it."

"You are very kind," returned Mr. Pickwick, shaking me by the hand again, "you are so exactly what I expected! But for what particular purpose do you think I have sought you out, my dear sir? Now, what *do* you think I have come for?"

Mr. Pickwick put this question as though he were persuaded that it was morally impossible that I could by any means divine the deep purpose of his visit, and that it must be hidden from all human ken. Therefore, although I was rejoiced to think that I anticipated his drift, I feigned to be quite ignorant of it, and after a brief consideration shook my head despairingly.

"What should you say," said Mr. Pickwick, laying the forefinger of his left hand upon my coat-sleeve, and looking at me with his head thrown back, and a little on one side, "what should you say if I confessed that after reading your account of yourself and your little society, I had come here, a humble candidate for one of those empty chairs?"

"I should say," I returned, "that I know of only one circumstance which could still further endear that little society to me, and that would be the associating with it my old friend—for you must let me call you so—my old friend, Mr. Pickwick."

As I made him this answer, every feature of Mr. Pickwick's face fused itself into one all-pervading expression of delight. After shaking me heartily by both hands at once, he patted me gently on the back, and then—I well understood why—colored up to the eyes, and hoped with great earnestness of manner that he had not hurt me.

If he had, I would have been content that he should have repeated the offense a hundred times rather than suppose so; but as he had not, I had no difficulty in changing the subject by making an inquiry which had been upon my lips twenty times already.

"You have not told me," said I, "anything about Sam Weller."

"Oh! Sam," replied Mr. Pickwick, "is the same as ever. The same true, faithful fellow that he ever was. What should I tell you about Sam, my dear sir, except that he is more indispensable to my happiness and comfort every day of my life?"

"And Mr. Weller senior?" said I.

"Old Mr. Weller," returned Mr. Pickwick, "is in no respect more altered than Sam, unless it be that he is a little more opinionated than he was formerly, and perhaps at times more talkative. He spends a good deal of his time now in our neighborhood, and has so constituted himself a part of my bodyguard, that when I ask permission for Sam to have a seat in your kitchen on Clock nights (supposing your three friends think me worthy to fill one of the chairs) I am afraid I must often include Mr. Weller too."

I very readily pledged myself to give both Sam and his father a free admission to my house at all hours and seasons, and this point settled, we fell into a lengthy conversation which was carried on with as little reserve on both sides as if we had been intimate friends from our youth, and which conveyed to me the comfortable assurance that Mr. Pickwick's buoyancy of spirit, and indeed all his old cheerful characteristics, were wholly unimpaired. As he had spoken of the consent of my friends as being yet in abeyance, I repeatedly assured him that his proposal was certain to receive their most joy-

ful sanction, and several times entreated that he would give me leave to introduce him to Jack Redburn and Mr. Miles (who were near at hand) without
further ceremony.

To this proposal, however, Mr. Pickwick's delicacy would by no means
allow him to accede, for he urged that his eligibility must be formally discussed, and that, until this had been done, he could not think of obtruding
himself further. The utmost I could obtain from him was a promise that he
would attend upon our next night of meeting, that I might have the pleasure
of presenting him immediately on his election.

Mr. Pickwick, having with many blushes placed in my hands a small roll
of paper, which he termed his "qualification," put a great many questions to
me touching my friends and particularly Jack Redburn, whom he repeatedly
termed "a fine fellow," and in whose favor I could see he was strongly predis-
posed. When I had satisfied him on these points, I took him up into my
room that he might make acquaintance with the old chamber which is our
place of meeting.

"And this," said Mr. Pickwick, stopping short, "is the Clock! Dear me!
And this is really the old Clock!"

I thought he would never have come away from it. After advancing
towards it softly, and laying his hand upon it with as much respect and as
many smiling looks as if it were alive, he set himself to consider it in every
possible direction, now mounting on a chair to look at the top, now going
down upon his knees to examine the bottom, now surveying the sides with
his spectacles almost touching the case, and now trying to peep between it
and the wall to get a slight view of the back. Then he would retire a pace or
two and look up at the dial to see it go, and then draw near again and stand
with his head on one side to hear it tick: never failing to glance towards me
at intervals of a few seconds each, and nod his head with such complacent
gratification as I am quite unable to describe. His admiration was not confined to the clock either, but extended itself to every article in the room; and
really, when he had gone through them every one, and at last sat himself
down in all the six chairs, one after another, to try how they felt, I never saw
such a picture of good-humor and happiness as he presented, from the top of
his shining head down to the very last button of his gaiters.

I should have been well pleased, and should have had the utmost enjoyment of his company, if he had remained with me all day, but my favorite,
striking the hour, reminded him that he must take his leave. I could not forbear telling him once more how glad he had made me, and we shook hands
all the way downstairs.

We had no sooner arrived in the hall than my housekeeper, gliding out of
her little room (she had changed her gown and cap, I observed) greeted Mr.
Pickwick with her best smile and curtsey; and the barber, feigning to be accidentally passing on his way out, made him a vast number of bows. When the
housekeeper curtseyed, Mr. Pickwick bowed with the utmost politeness, and

when he bowed, the housekeeper curtseyed again; between the housekeeper and the barber, I should say that Mr. Pickwick faced about and bowed with undiminished affability fifty times at least.

I saw him to the door; an omnibus was at the moment passing the corner of the lane, which Mr. Pickwick hailed and ran after with extraordinary nimbleness. When he had got about halfway he turned his head, and seeing that I was still looking after him and that I waved my hand, stopped, evidently irresolute whether to come back and shake hands again, or to go on. The man behind the omnibus shouted, and Mr. Pickwick ran a little way towards him: then he looked round at me, and ran a little way back again. Then there was another shout, and he turned round once more and ran the other way. After several of these vibrations, the man settled the question by taking Mr. Pickwick by the arm and putting him into the carriage; but his last action was to let down the window and wave his hat to me as it drove off.

I lost no time in opening the parcel he had left with me. The following were its contents:—

MR. PICKWICK'S TALE

A good many years have passed away since old John Podgers lived in the town of Windsor, where he was born, and where in course of time he came to be comfortably and snugly buried. You may be sure that in the time of King James the First, Windsor was a very quaint queer old town, and you may take it upon my authority that John Podgers was a very quaint queer old fellow; consequently he and Windsor fitted each other to a nicety, and seldom parted company even for half a day.

John Podgers was broad, sturdy, Dutch-built, short, and a very hard eater, as men of his figure often are. Being a hard sleeper likewise, he divided his time pretty equally between these two recreations, always falling asleep when he had done eating, and always taking another turn at the trencher when he had done sleeping, by which means he grew more corpulent and more drowsy every day of his life. Indeed it used to be currently reported that when he sauntered up and down the sunny side of the street before dinner (as he never failed to do in fair weather) he enjoyed his soundest nap; but many people held this to be a fiction, as he had several times been seen to look after fat oxen on market-days, and had even been heard by persons of good credit and reputation to chuckle at the sight, and say to himself with great glee, "Live beef, live beef!" It was upon this evidence that the wisest people in Windsor (beginning with the local authorities of course) held that John Podgers was a man of strong sound sense—not what is called smart, perhaps, and it might be of a rather lazy and apoplectic turn, but still a man of solid parts, and one who meant much more than he cared to show. This impression was confirmed by a very dignified way he had of shaking his head and imparting at the same time a pendulous motion to his double chin; in short he passed for one of those people who being plunged into the Thames would make no vain efforts to set it afire, but would straightway flop down to the bottom with a deal of gravity and be highly respected in consequence by all good men.

Being well to do in the world, and a peaceful widower—having a great appetite, which, as he could afford to gratify it, was a luxury and no inconvenience, and a power of going to sleep, which, as he had no occasion to keep awake, was a most enviable faculty—you will readily suppose that John Podgers was a happy man. But appearances are often deceptive when they least seem so, and the truth is that, notwithstanding his extreme sleekness, he was rendered uneasy in his mind and exceedingly uncomfortable by a constant apprehension that beset him night and day.

You know very well that in those times there flourished divers evil old women who under the name of Witches spread great disorder through the land, and inflicted various dismal tortures upon Christian men: sticking pins and needles into them when they least expected it, and causing them to walk in the air with their feet upwards, to the great terror of their wives and families, who were naturally very much disconcerted when the master of the house unexpectedly came home, knocking at the door with his heels and combing his hair on the scraper. These were their commonest pranks, but they every day played others, of which none were less objectionable and many were much more so, being improper besides; the result was that vengeance was denounced against all old women, with whom even the King himself had no sympathy (as he certainly ought to have had), for with his own most Gracious hand he penned a most Gracious consignment of them to everlasting wrath, and devised most Gracious means for their confusion and slaughter, in virtue whereof scarcely a day passed but one witch at the least was most graciously hanged, drowned, or roasted in some part of his dominions. Still the press teemed with strange and terrible news from the North or the South or the East or the West, relative to witches and their unhappy victims in some corner of the country, and the Public's hair stood on end to that degree that it lifted its hat off its head, and made its face pale with terror.

You may believe that the little town of Windsor did not escape the general contagion. The inhabitants boiled a witch on the King's birthday and sent a bottle of the broth to court, with a dutiful address expressive of their loyalty. The King, being rather frightened by the present, piously bestowed it upon the Archbishop of Canterbury, and returned an answer to the address, wherein he gave them golden rules for discovering witches and laid great stress upon certain protecting charms, and especially horseshoes. Immediately the townspeople went to work nailing up horseshoes over every door, and so many anxious parents apprenticed their children to farriers, to keep them out of harm's way, that it became quite a genteel trade and flourished exceedingly.

In the midst of all this bustle John Podgers ate and slept as usual, but shook his head a great deal oftener than was his custom, and was observed to look at the oxen less, and at the old women more. He had a little shelf put up in his sitting-room, whereon was displayed in a row which grew longer every week all the witchcraft literature of the time; he grew learned in charms and exorcisms, hinted at certain questionable females on broomsticks whom he had seen from his chamber window, riding in the air at night, and was in constant terror of being bewitched. At length, from perpetually dwelling upon this one idea which being alone in his head had it all its own way, the fear of witches became the single passion of his life. He, who up to that time had never known what it was to dream, began to have visions of witches whenever he fell asleep; waking, they were incessantly present to his imagination likewise; and, sleeping or waking, he had not a moment's peace. He began to set witch-traps in the highway, and was often seen lying in wait round the corner for hours together, to watch their effect. These engines were of simple construction, usually consisting of two straws disposed in the form of a cross, or a piece of a Bible-cover with a pinch of salt upon it; but they were infallible, and if an old woman chanced to stumble over them (as not unfrequently happened, the chosen spot being a broken and stony place), John started from a doze, pounced out upon her, and hung round her neck till assistance arrived, when she was immediately carried away and drowned. By dint of constantly inveigling old ladies and disposing of them in this summary manner, he acquired the reputation of a great public character; and as he received no harm in these pursuits beyond a scratched face or so, he came in the course of time to be considered witch-proof.

There was but one person who entertained the least doubt of John Podgers's gifts, and that person was his own nephew, a wild roving young fellow of twenty who had been brought up in his uncle's house and lived there still—that is to say, when he was at home, which was not as often as it might have been. As he was an apt scholar, it was he who read aloud every fresh piece of strange and terrible intelligence that John Podgers bought; and this he always did of an evening in the little porch in front of the house, round which the neighbors would flock in crowds to hear the direful news—for people like to be frightened, and when they can be frightened for nothing and at another man's expense, they like it all the better.

One fine midsummer evening, a group of persons were gathered in this place listening intently to Will Marks (that was the nephew's name), as with his cap very much on one side, his arm coiled slyly round the waist of a pretty girl who sat beside him, and his face screwed into a comical expression intended to represent extreme gravity, he read—with Heaven knows how many embellishments of his own—a dismal account of a gentleman down in Northamptonshire under the influence of witchcraft and taken forcible possession of by the Devil, who was playing his very self with him. John Podgers, in a high sugar-loaf hat and short cloak, filled the opposite seat, and surveyed the auditory with a look of mingled pride and horror very edifying to see; while the hearers, with their heads thrust forward and their mouths open, listened and trembled, and hoped there was a great deal more to come. Sometimes Will stopped for an instant to look round upon his eager audience, and then, with a more comical expression of face than before and a settling of himself comfortably, which included a squeeze of the young lady before mentioned, he launched into some new wonder surpassing all the others.

The setting sun shed his last golden rays upon this little party, who, absorbed in their present occupation, took no heed of the approach of night or the glory in which the day went down, when the sound of a horse approaching at a good round trot, invading the silence of the hour, caused the reader to make a sudden stop and the listeners to raise their heads in wonder. Nor was their wonder diminished when a horseman dashed up to the porch, and abruptly checking his steed, inquired where one John Podgers dwelt.

"Here!" cried a dozen voices, while a dozen hands pointed out sturdy John, still basking in the terrors of the pamphlet.

The rider, giving his bridle to one of those who surrounded him, dismounted and approached John, hat in hand, but with great haste.

"Whence come ye?" said John.

"From Kingston, Master."

"And wherefore?"

"On most pressing business."

"Of what nature?"

"Witchcraft."

Witchcraft! Everybody looked aghast at the breathless messenger, and the breathless messenger looked equally aghast at everybody—except Will Marks who, finding himself unobserved, not only squeezed the young lady again, but kissed her twice. Surely he must have been bewitched himself, or he never could have done it—and the young lady too, or she never would have let him.

"Witchcraft?" cried Will, drowning the sound of his last kiss, which was rather a loud one.

The messenger turned towards him, and with a frown repeated the word more solemnly than before; then told his errand, which was, in brief, that the people of Kingston had been greatly terrified for some nights past by hideous revels, held by witches beneath the gibbet within a mile of the town, and related and deposed to by chance wayfarers who had passed within earshot of the spot—that the sound of their voices in their wild orgies had been plainly heard by many persons—that three old women labored under strong suspicion, and that precedents had been consulted and solemn council had, and it was found that to identify the hags some single person must watch upon the spot alone—that no single person had the courage to perform the task—and that he had been despatched express to solicit John Podgers to undertake it that very night, as being a man of great renown, who bore a charmed life, and was proof against unholy spells.

John received this communication with much composure, and said in a
few words, that it would have afforded him inexpressible pleasure to do the
Kingston people so slight a service, if it were not for his unfortunate propensity to fall asleep, which no man regretted more than himself upon the present
occasion, but which quite settled the question. Nevertheless, he said, there *was*
a gentleman present (and here he looked very hard at a tall farrier) who, having been engaged all his life in the manufacture of horseshoes, must be quite
invulnerable to the power of witches, and who, he had no doubt, from his
known reputation for bravery and good-nature, would readily accept the commission. The farrier politely thanked him for his good opinion, which it
would always be his study to deserve, but added that with regard to the present
little matter he couldn't think of it on any account, as his departing on such an
errand would certainly occasion the instant death of his wife, to whom, as they
all knew, he was tenderly attached. Now, so far from this circumstance being
notorious, everybody had suspected the reverse, as the farrier was in the habit
of beating his lady rather more than tender husbands usually do; all the married men present, however, applauded his resolution with great vehemence,
and one and all declared that they would stop at home and die if needful
(which happily it was not) in defense of their lawful partners.

This burst of enthusiasm over, they began to look as by one consent
toward Will Marks, who with his cap more on one side than ever, sat watching the proceedings with extraordinary unconcern. He had never been heard
openly to express his disbelief in witches, but had often cut such jokes at their
expense as left it to be inferred; publicly stating on several occasions that he
considered a broomstick an inconvenient charger and one especially unsuited
to the dignity of the female character, and indulging in other free remarks of
the same tendency, to the great amusement of his wild companions.

As they looked at Will they began to whisper and murmur among themselves, and at length one man cried, "Why don't you ask Will Marks?"

As this was what everybody had been thinking of, they all took up the
word, and cried in concert, "Ah! why don't you ask Will?"

"*He* don't care," said the farrier.

"Not he," added another voice in the crowd.

"He don't believe in it, you know," sneered a little man with a yellow face
and a taunting nose and chin, which he thrust out from under the arm of a
long man before him.

"Besides," said a red-faced gentleman with a gruff voice, "he's a single
man."

"That's the point!" said the farrier; and all the married men murmured,
ah! that was it, and they only wished they were single themselves; they would
show him what spirit was, very soon.

The messenger looked towards Will Marks beseechingly.

"It will be a wet night, friend, and my grey nag is tired after yesterday's
work—"

Here there was a general titter.

"But," resumed Will, looking about him with a smile, "if nobody else puts in a better claim to go for the credit of the town, I am your man, and I would be if I had to go afoot. In five minutes I shall be in the saddle, unless I am depriving any worthy gentleman here of the honor of the adventure, which I wouldn't do for the world."

But here arose a double difficulty, for not only did John Podgers combat the resolution with all the words he had, which were not many, but the young lady combated it too with all the tears she had, which were very many indeed. Will, however, being inflexible, parried his uncle's objections with a joke, and coaxed the young lady into a smile in three short whispers. As it was plain that he would go and set his mind upon it, John Podgers offered him a few first-rate charms out of his own pocket, which he dutifully declined to accept; and the young lady gave him a kiss, which he also returned.

"You see what a rare thing it is to be married," said Will, "and how careful and considerate all these husbands are. There's not a man among them but his heart is leaping to forestall me in this adventure, and yet a strong sense of duty keeps him back. The husbands in this one little town are a pattern to the world, and so must the wives be too, for that matter, or they could never boast half the influence they have!"

Waiting for no reply to this sarcasm, he snapped his fingers and withdrew into the house, and thence into the stable, while some busied themselves in refreshing the messenger, and others in baiting his steed. In less than the specified time he returned by another way, with a good cloak hanging over his arm, a good sword girded by his side, and leading his good horse caparisoned for the journey.

"Now," said Will, leaping into the saddle at a bound, "up and away. Upon your mettle, friend, and push on. Good night!"

He kissed his hand to the girl, nodded to his drowsy uncle, waved his cap to the rest—and off they flew pellmell, as if all the witches in England were in their horses' legs. They were out of sight in a minute.

The men who were left behind shook their heads doubtfully, stroked their chins, and shook their heads again. The farrier said that certainly Will Marks was a good horseman, nobody should ever say he denied that: but he was rash, very rash, and there was no telling what the end of it might be; what did he go for, that was what he wanted to know? He wished the young fellow no harm, but why did he go? Everybody echoed these words, and shook their heads again, having done which they wished John Podgers good night, and straggled home to bed.

The Kingston people were in their first sleep when Will Marks and his conductor rode through the town and up to the door of a house where sundry grave functionaries were assembled, anxiously expecting the arrival of the renowned Podgers. They were a little disappointed to find a gay young man in his place; but they put the best face upon the matter, and gave him full instructions how he was to conceal himself behind the gibbet, and watch and listen to the witches, and how at a certain time he was to burst forth and cut and slash among them vigorously, so that the suspected parties might be found bleeding in their beds next day, and thoroughly confounded. They gave him a great quantity of wholesome advice besides, and—which was more to the purpose with Will—a good supper. All these things being done, and midnight nearly come, they sallied forth to show him the spot where he was to keep his dreary vigil.

The night was by this time dark and threatening. There was a rumbling of distant thunder, and a low sighing of wind among the trees, which was very dismal. The potentates of the town kept so uncommonly close to Will that they trod upon his toes, or stumbled against his ankles, or nearly tripped up his heels at every step he took, and besides these annoyances their teeth chattered so with fear, that he seemed to be accompanied by a dirge of castanets.

At last they made a halt at the opening of a lonely desolate space, and, pointing to a black object at some distance, asked Will if he saw that, yonder.

"Yes," he replied. "What then?"

Informing him abruptly that it was the gibbet where he was to watch, they wished him good night in an extremely friendly manner, and ran back as fast as their feet would carry them.

Will walked boldly to the gibbet and, glancing upward when he came under it, saw—certainly with satisfaction—that it was empty, and that nothing dangled from the top but some iron chains, which swung mournfully to and fro as they were moved by the breeze. After a careful survey of every quarter, he determined to take his station with his face towards the town; both because that would place him with his back to the wind, and because, if any trick or surprise were attempted, it would probably come from that direction in the first instance. Having taken these precautions, he wrapped his cloak about him so that it left the handle of his sword free, and ready to his hand, and leaning against the gallows-tree with his cap not quite so much on one side as it had been before, took up his position for the night.

SECOND CHAPTER OF MR. PICKWICK'S TALE

We left Will Marks leaning under the gibbet with his face towards the town, scanning the distance with a keen eye which sought to pierce the darkness and catch the earliest glimpse of any person or persons that might approach towards him. But all was quiet, and, save the howling of the wind as it swept across the heath in gusts, and the creaking of the chains that dangled above his head, there was no sound to break the sullen stillness of the night. After half an hour or so this monotony became more disconcerting to Will than the most furious uproar would have been, and he heartily wished for someone antagonist with whom he might have a fair stand-up fight, if it were only to warm himself.

Truth to tell, it was a bitter wind and seemed to blow to the very heart of a man whose blood, heated but now with rapid riding, was the more sensitive to the chilling blast. Will was a daring fellow and cared not a jot for hard knocks or sharp blades; but he could not persuade himself to move or walk about, having just that vague expectation of a sudden assault which made it a comfortable thing to have something at his back, even though that something were a gallows-tree. He had no great faith in the superstitions of the age; still such of them as occurred to him did not serve to lighten the time or to render his situation the more endurable. He remembered how witches were said to repair at that ghostly hour to churchyards and gibbets and such-like dismal spots, to pluck the bleeding mandrake or scrape the flesh from dead men's bones as choice ingredients for their spells; how, stealing by night to lonely places, they dug graves with their fingernails or anointed themselves before riding in the air, with a delicate pomatum made of the fat of infants newly boiled. These, and many other fabled practices of a no less agreeable nature, and all having some reference to the circumstances in which he was placed, passed and repassed in quick succession through the mind of Will Marks, and adding a shadowy dread to that distrust and watchfulness which his situation inspired, rendered it upon the whole sufficiently uncomfortable. As he had foreseen too, the rain began to descend heavily, and driving before the wind in a thick mist obscured even those few objects which the darkness of the night had before imperfectly revealed.

"Look!" shrieked a voice. "Great Heaven, it has fallen down and stands erect as if it lived!"

The speaker was close behind him—the voice was almost at his ear. Will threw off his cloak, drew his sword, and darting swiftly round, seized a woman by the wrist, who, recoiling from him with a dreadful shriek, fell struggling upon her knees. Another woman clad like her whom he had grasped, in mourning garments, stood rooted to the spot on which they were, gazing upon his face with wild and glaring eyes that quite appalled him.

"Say," cried Will, when they had confronted each other thus for some time, "what are ye?"

"Say what are *you*," returned the woman, "who trouble even this obscene resting-place of the dead, and strip the gibbet of its honored burden? Where is the body?"

He looked in wonder and affright from the woman who questioned him to the other whose arm he clutched.

"Where is the body?" repeated his questioner more firmly than before. "You wear no livery which marks you for the hireling of the Government. You are no friend to us, or I should recognize you, for the friends of such as we are few in number. What are you then, and wherefore are you here?"

"I am no foe to the distressed and helpless," said Will. "Are ye among that number? ye should be by your looks."

"We are!" was the answer.

"It is ye who have been wailing and weeping here under cover of the night?" said Will.

"It is," replied the woman sternly; and pointing, as she spoke, towards her companion, "she mourns a husband, and I a brother. Even the bloody law that wreaks its vengeance on the dead does not make that a crime, and if it did 'twould be alike to us who are past its fear or favor."

Will glanced at the two females, and could barely discern that the one whom he addressed was much the elder, and that the other was young and of a slight figure. Both were deadly pale, their garments wet and worn, their hair disheveled and streaming in the wind, themselves bowed down with grief and misery; their whole appearance most dejected, wretched, and forlorn. A sight so different from any he had expected to encounter touched him to the quick, and all idea of anything but their pitiable condition vanished before it.

"I am a rough, blunt yeoman," said Will. "Why I came here is told in a word; you have been overheard at a distance in the silence of the night, and I have undertaken a watch for hags or spirits. I came here expecting an adventure and prepared to go through with any. If there be aught that I can do to help or aid you, name it, and on the faith of a man who can be secret and trusty I will stand by you to the death."

"How comes this gibbet to be empty?" asked the elder female.

"I swear to you," replied Will, "that I know as little as yourself. But this I know, that when I came here an hour ago or so, it was as it is now; and if, as I gather from your question, it was not so last night, sure I am that it has been secretly disturbed without the knowledge of the folks in yonder town. Bethink you, therefore, whether you have no friends in league with you or with him on whom the law has done its worst, by whom these sad remains have been removed for burial."

The women spoke together, and Will retired a pace or two while they conversed apart. He could hear them sob and moan, and saw that they wrung their hands in fruitless agony. He could make out little that they said, but between whiles he gathered enough to assure him that his suggestion was not very wide of the mark, and that they not only suspected by whom the body had been removed, but also whither it had been conveyed. When they had been in conversation a long time, they turned towards him once more. This time the younger female spoke.

"You have offered us your help?"

"I have."

"And given a pledge that you are still willing to redeem?"

"Yes. So far as I may, keeping all plots and conspiracies at arm's length."

"Follow us, friend."

Will, whose self-possession was now quite restored, needed no second bidding, but with his drawn sword in his hand, and his cloak so muffled over his left arm as to serve for a kind of shield without offering any impediment to its free action, suffered them to lead the way. Through mud and mire and

wind and rain, they walked in silence a full mile. At length they turned into
a dark lane, where, suddenly starting out from beneath some trees where he
had taken shelter, a man appeared, having in his charge three saddled horses.
One of these (his own apparently), in obedience to a whisper from the
women, he consigned to Will, who seeing that they mounted, mounted also.
Then without a word spoken they rode on together, leaving the attendant
behind.

They made no halt nor slackened their pace until they arrived near Put-
ney. At a large wooden house which stood apart from any other they alighted,
and giving their horses to one who was already waiting, passed in by a side
door, and so up some narrow creaking stairs into a small paneled chamber,
where Will was left alone. He had not been here very long, when the door
was softly opened, and there entered to him a cavalier whose face was concealed beneath a black mask.

Will stood upon his guard, and scrutinized this figure from head to foot.
The form was that of a man pretty far advanced in life, but of a firm and
stately carriage. His dress was of a rich and costly kind, but so soiled and disordered that it was scarcely to be recognized for one of those gorgeous suits
which the expensive taste and fashion of the time prescribed for men of any
rank or station. He was booted and spurred, and bore about him even as
many tokens of the state of the roads as Will himself. All this he noted, while
the eyes behind the mask regarded him with equal attention. The survey over,
the cavalier broke silence.

"Thou'rt young and bold, and wouldst be richer than thou art?"

"The two first I am," returned Will. "The last I have scarcely thought of.
But be it so. Say that I would be richer than I am; what then?"

"The way lies before thee now," replied the Mask.

"Show it me."

"First let me inform thee, that thou wert brought here tonight lest thou
shouldst too soon have told thy tale to those who placed thee on the watch."

"I thought as much when I followed," said Will. "But I am no blab, not I."

"Good," returned the Mask. "Now listen. He who was to have executed
the enterprise of burying that body which as thou hast suspected was taken
down tonight, has left us in our need."

Will nodded, and thought within himself that if the Mask were to
attempt to play any tricks, the first eyelet-hole on the lefthand side of his
doublet, counting from the buttons up the front, would be a very good place
in which to pink him neatly.

"Thou art here, and the emergency is desperate. I propose his task to
thee. Convey the body (now coffined in this house) by means that I shall
show, to the church of St. Dunstan in London tomorrow night, and thy service shall be richly paid. Thou'rt about to ask whose corpse it is. Seek not to
know. I warn thee, seek not to know. Felons hang in chains on every moor
and heath. Believe, as others do, that this was one, and ask no further. The

murders of state policy, its victims or avengers, had best remain unknown to such as thee."

"The mystery of this service," said Will, "bespeaks its danger. What is the reward?"

"One hundred golden unities," replied the cavalier. "The danger to one who cannot be recognized as the friend of a fallen cause is not great, but there is some hazard to be run. Decide between that and the reward."

"What if I refuse?" said Will.

"Depart in peace, in God's name," returned the Mask in a melancholy tone, "and keep our secret, remembering that those who brought thee here were crushed and stricken women, and that those who bade thee go free could have had thy life with one word, and no man the wiser."

Men were readier to undertake desperate adventures in those times than they are now. In this case the temptation was great and the punishment even in case of detection was not likely to be very severe, as Will came of a loyal stock, and his uncle was in good repute, and a passable tale to account for his possession of the body and his ignorance of the identity might be easily devised. The cavalier explained that a covered cart had been prepared for the purpose; that the time of departure could be arranged so that he should reach London Bridge at dusk and proceed through the City after the day had closed in; that people should be ready at his journey's end to place the coffin in a vault without a minute's delay; that officious inquirers in the streets would be easily repelled by the tale that he was carrying for interment the corpse of one who had died of the plague; and in short showed him every reason why he should succeed and none why he should fail. After a time they were joined by another gentleman, masked like the first, who added new arguments to those which had been already urged; the wretched wife too added her tears and prayers to their calmer representations; and in the end Will, moved by compassion and good-nature, by a love of the marvelous, by a mischievous anticipation of the terrors of the Kingston people when he should be missing next day, and finally by the prospect of gain, took upon himself the task, and devoted all his energies to its successful execution.

The following night when it was quite dark, the hollow echoes of old London Bridge responded to the rumbling of the cart which contained the ghastly load, the object of Will Marks's care. Sufficiently disguised to attract no attention by his garb, Will walked at the horse's head, as unconcerned as a man could be who was sensible that he had now arrived at the most dangerous part of his undertaking, but full of boldness and confidence.

It was now eight o'clock. After nine, none could walk the streets without danger of their lives, and even at this hour, robberies and murder were of no uncommon occurrence. The shops upon the bridge were all closed; the low wooden arches thrown across the way were like so many black pits, in every one of which ill-favored fellows lurked in knots of three or four; some standing upright against the wall, lying in wait; others skulking in gateways, and thrusting out their uncombed heads and scowling eyes; others crossing and recrossing, and constantly jostling both horse and man to provoke a quarrel; others stealing away and summoning their companions in a low whistle. Once, even in that short passage, there was the noise of scuffling and the clash of swords behind him, but Will, who knew the City and its ways, kept straight on and scarcely turned his head.

The streets being unpaved, the rain of the night before had converted them into a perfect quagmire, which the splashing waterspouts from the gables, and the filth and offal cast from the different houses, swelled in no small degree. These odious matters being left to putrefy in the close and heavy air, emitted an insupportable stench, to which every court and passage poured forth a contribution of its own. Many parts, even of the main streets, with their projecting stories tottering overhead and nearly shutting out the sky, were more like huge chimneys than open ways. At the corners of some of these, great bonfires were burning to prevent infection from the plague, of which it was rumored that some citizens had lately died; and few, who availing themselves of the light thus afforded paused for a moment to look around them, would have been disposed to doubt the existence of the disease or wonder at its dreadful visitations.

But it was not in such scenes as these, or even in the deep and miry road, that Will Marks found the chief obstacles to his progress. There were kites and ravens feeding in the streets (the only scavengers the City kept) who scenting what he carried, followed the cart or fluttered on its top and croaked their knowledge of its burden and their ravenous appetite for prey. There were distant fires where the poor wood and plaster tenements wasted fiercely, and whither crowds made their way clamoring eagerly for plunder, beating down all who came within their reach, and yelling like devils let loose. There were single-handed men flying from bands of ruffians, who pursued them with naked weapons, and hunted them savagely; there were drunken desperate robbers issuing from their dens and staggering through the open streets where no man dare molest them; there were vagabond servitors returning from the Bear Garden, where had been good sport that day, dragging after them their torn and bleeding dogs or leaving them to die and rot upon the road. Nothing was abroad but cruelty, violence, and disorder.

Many were the interruptions which Will Marks encountered from these stragglers, and many the narrow escapes he made. Now some stout bully would take his seat upon the cart insisting to be driven to his own home, and now two or three men would come down upon him together and demand that on peril of his life he showed them what he had inside. Then a party of the City Watch upon their rounds would draw across the road, and not satisfied with his tale, question him closely and revenge themselves by a little cuffing and hustling for maltreatment sustained at other hands that night. All these assailants had to be rebutted, some by fair words, some by foul, and some by blows. But Will Marks was not the man to be stopped or turned back now he had penetrated so far, and though he got on slowly, still he made his way down Fleet Street and reached the church at last.

As he had been forewarned, all was in readiness. Directly he stopped, the coffin was removed by four men who appeared so suddenly that they seemed to have started from the earth. A fifth mounted the cart, and scarcely allowing Will time to snatch from it a little bundle containing such of his own clothes as he had thrown off on assuming his disguise, drove briskly away. Will never saw cart or man again.

He followed the body into the church, and it was well he lost no time in doing so, for the door was immediately closed. There was no light in the building save that which came from a couple of torches borne by two men in cloaks who stood upon the brink of a vault. Each supported a female figure, and all observed a profound silence.

By this dim and solemn glare, which made Will feel as though light itself were dead, and its tomb the dreary arches that frowned above, they placed the coffin in the vault, with uncovered heads, and closed it up. One of the torch-bearers then turned to Will and stretched forth his hand, in which was a purse of gold. Something told him directly that those were the same eyes which he had seen beneath the mask.

"Take it," said the cavalier in a low voice, "and be happy. Though these have been hasty obsequies, and no priest has blessed the work, there will not be the less peace with thee hereafter, for having laid his bones beside those of his little children. Keep thy own counsel, for thy sake no less than ours, and God be with thee!"

"The blessing of a widowed mother on thy head, good friend!" cried the younger lady through her tears; "the blessing of one who has now no hope or rest but in this grave!"

Will stood with the purse in his hand, and involuntarily made a gesture as though he would return it, for though a thoughtless fellow he was of a frank and generous nature. But the two gentlemen extinguishing their torches cautioned him to be gone, as their common safety would be endangered by a longer delay; and at the same time their retreating footsteps sounded through the church. He turned, therefore, towards the point at which he had entered, and seeing by a faint gleam in the distance that the door was again partially open, groped his way towards it and so passed into the street.

Meantime the local authorities of Kingston had kept watch and ward all the previous night, fancying every now and then that dismal shrieks were borne towards them on the wind, and frequently winking to each other and drawing closer to the fire as they drank the health of the lonely sentinel, upon whom a clerical gentleman present was especially severe by reason of his levity and youthful folly. Two or three of the gravest in company, who were of a theological turn, propounded to him the question whether such a character was not but poorly armed for single combat with the Devil, and whether he himself would not have been a stronger opponent; but the clerical gentleman, sharply reproving them for their presumption in discussing such questions, clearly showed that a fitter champion than Will could scarcely have been selected, not only for that being a child of Satan he was the less likely to be alarmed by the appearance of his own father, but because Satan himself would be at his ease in such company, and would not scruple to kick up his heels to an extent which it was quite certain he would never venture before clerical eyes, under whose influence (as was notorious) he became quite a tame and milk-and-water character.

But when next morning arrived and with it no Will Marks, and when a strong party repairing to the spot, as a strong party ventured to do in broad day, found Will gone and the gibbet empty, matters grew serious indeed. The day passing away and no news arriving, and the night going on also without any intelligence, the thing grew more tremendous still; in short the neighborhood worked itself up to such a comfortable pitch of mystery and horror, that it is a great question whether the general feeling was not one of excessive disappointment when, on the second morning, Will Marks returned.

However this may be, back Will came in a very cool and collected state, and appearing not to trouble himself much about anybody except old John Podgers, who, having been sent for, was sitting in the Town Hall crying slowly and dozing between whiles. Having embraced his uncle and assured him of his safety, Will mounted on a table and told his story to the crowd.

And surely they would have been the most unreasonable crowd that ever assembled together, if they had been in the least respect disappointed with the tale he told them; for besides describing the Witches' Dance to the minutest motion of their legs, and performing it in character on the table, with the assistance of a broomstick, he related how they had carried off the body in a copper caldron, and so bewitched him that he lost his senses until he found himself lying under a hedge at least ten miles off whence he had straightway returned as they then beheld. The story gained such universal applause that it soon afterwards brought down express from London the great witch-finder of the age, the Heaven-born Hopkins, who having examined Will closely on several points, pronounced it the most extraordinary and the best accredited witch story ever known, under which title it was published at the Three Bibles on London Bridge, in small quarto, with a view of the caldron from an original drawing, and a portrait of the clerical gentleman as he sat by the fire.

On one point Will was particularly careful: and that was to describe for the witches he had seen, three impossible old females whose likenesses never were or will be. Thus he saved the lives of the suspected parties, and of all other old women who were dragged before him to be identified.

This circumstance occasioned John Podgers much grief and sorrow, until happening one day to cast his eyes upon his housekeeper, and observing her to be plainly afflicted with rheumatism, he procured her to be burnt as an undoubted witch. For this service to the state he was immediately knighted, and became from that time Sir John Podgers.

Will Marks never gained any clue to the mystery in which he had been an actor, nor did any inscription in the church which he often visited afterwards, nor any of the limited inquiries that he dared to make, yield him the least assistance. As he kept his own secret, he was compelled to spend the gold discreetly and sparingly. In course of time he married the young lady of whom I have already told you, whose maiden name is not recorded, with whom he led a prosperous and happy life. Years and years after this adventure, it was his wont to tell her upon a stormy night that it was a great comfort to him to think that those bones, to whomsoever they might have once belonged, were not bleaching in the troubled air, but were moldering away with the dust of their own kith and kindred in a quiet grave.

FURTHER PARTICULARS OF MASTER HUMPHREY'S VISITOR

Being very full of Mr. Pickwick's application and highly pleased with the compliment he had paid me, it will be readily supposed that long before our next night of meeting I communicated it to my three friends, who unanimously voted his admission into our body. We all looked forward with some impatience to the occasion which would enroll him among us, but I am greatly mistaken if Jack Redburn and myself were not by many degrees the most impatient of the party.

At length the night came, and a few minutes after ten Mr. Pickwick's knock was heard at the street-door. He was shown into a lower room, and I directly took my crooked stick and went to accompany him upstairs, in order that he might be presented with all honor and formality.

"Mr. Pickwick," said I, on entering the room, "I am rejoiced to see you—rejoiced to believe that this is but the opening of a long series of visits to this house, and but the beginning of a close and lasting friendship."

That gentleman made a suitable reply with a cordiality and frankness peculiarly his own, and glanced with a smile towards two persons behind the door, whom I had not at first observed, and whom I immediately recognized as Mr. Samuel Weller and his father.

It was a warm evening, but the elder Mr. Weller was attired notwithstanding in a most capacious great-coat, and had his chin enveloped in a large speckled shawl, such as is usually worn by stage coachmen on active service. He looked very rosy and very stout, especially about the legs, which appeared to have been compressed into his top-boots with some difficulty. His broad-brimmed hat he held under his left arm, and with the forefinger of his right hand he touched his forehead a great many times, in acknowledgment of my presence.

"I am very glad to see you in such good health, Mr. Weller," said I.

"Why, thankee sir," returned Mr. Weller, "the axle an't broke yet. We keeps up a steady pace—not too sewere, but vith a moderate degree o' friction—and the consekens is that ve're still a runnin' and comes in to the time, reg'lar.—My son Samivel, sir, as you may have read on in history," added Mr. Weller, introducing his firstborn.

I received Sam very graciously, but before he could say a word his father struck in again.

"Samivel Veller, sir," said the old gentleman, "has con-ferred upon me the ancient title o' grandfather vich had long laid dormouse, and wos s'posed to be nearly hextinct in our family. Sammy, relate a anecdote o' vun o' them boys—that 'ere little anecdote about young Tony sayin' as he *vould* smoke a pipe unbeknown to his mother."

"Be quiet, can't you?" said Sam, "I never see such a old magpie—never!"

"That 'ere Tony is the blessedest boy—" said Mr. Weller, heedless of this rebuff, "the blessedest boy as ever *I* see in *my* days! of all the charmin'est infants as ever I heerd tell on, includin' them as was kivered over by the robin-redbreasts arter they'd committed sooicide with blackberries, there never wos any like that 'ere little Tony. He's alvays a playin' vith a quart pot, that boy is! To see him a settin' down on the doorstep pretending to drink out of it, and fetching a long breath artervards, and smoking a bit of firevood and sayin', 'Now I'm grandfather'—to see him a doin' that at two year old is better than any play as wos ever wrote. 'Now I'm grandfather!' He wouldn't take a pint pot if you wos to make him a present on it, but he gets his quart and then he says, 'Now I'm grandfather!' "

Mr. Weller was so overpowered by this picture that he straightway fell into a most alarming fit of coughing, which must certainly have been attended with some fatal result but for the dexterity and promptitude of Sam, who taking a firm grasp of the shawl just under his father's chin shook him to and fro with great violence, at the same time administering some smart blows between his shoulders. By this curious mode of treatment Mr. Weller was finally recovered, but with a very crimson face and in a state of great exhaustion.

"He'll do now, Sam," said Mr. Pickwick, who had been in some alarm himself.

"He'll do, sir!" cried Sam, looking reproachfully at his parent. "Yes, he *will* do one o' these days—he'll do for his-self and then he'll wish he hadn't. Did anybody ever see sich a inconsiderate old file—laughing into conwulsions afore company, and stamping on the floor as if he'd brought his own carpet vith him and wos under a wager to punch the pattern out in a given time? He'll begin again in a minute. There—he's a-goin' off—I said he would!"

In fact, Mr. Weller, whose mind was still running upon his precocious grandson, was seen to shake his head from side to side, while a laugh, working like an earthquake, below the surface, produced various extraordinary appearances in his face, chest, and shoulders—the more alarming because unaccompanied by any noise whatever. These emotions, however, gradually subsided, and after three or four short relapses he wiped his eyes with the cuff of his coat, and looked about him with tolerable composure.

"Afore the governor vith-draws," said Mr. Weller, "there is a pint, respecting vich Sammy has a qvestion to ask. Vile that qvestion is a perwadin this here conwersation, p'raps the genl'men vill permit me to re-tire."

"Wot are you goin' away for?" demanded Sam, seizing his father by the coattail.

"I never see such a undootiful boy as you, Samivel," returned Mr. Weller. "Didn't you make a solemn promise, amountin' almost to a speeches o' wow, that you'd put that 'ere qvestion on my account?"

"Well, I'm agreeable to do it," said Sam, "but not if you go cuttin' away like that, as the bull turned round and mildly observed to the drover ven they wos a goadin' him into the butcher's door. The fact is, sir," said Sam, addressing me, "that he wants to know somethin' respectin' that 'ere lady as is housekeeper here."

"Ay. What is that?"

"Vy, sir," said Sam, grinning still more, "he wishes to know vether she—"

"In short," interposed old Mr. Weller decisively, a perspiration breaking out upon his forehead, "vether that 'ere old creetur is or is not a widder."

Mr. Pickwick laughed heartily and so did I, as I replied decisively that "my housekeeper was a spinster."

"There!" cried Sam, "now you're satisfied. You hear she's a spinster."

"A wot?" said his father, with deep scorn.

"A spinster," replied Sam.

Mr. Weller looked very hard at his son for a minute or two, and then said,

"Never mind vether she makes jokes or not, that's no matter. Wot I say is, is that 'ere female a widder, or is she not?"

"Wot do you mean by her making jokes?" demanded Sam, quite aghast at the obscurity of his parent's speech.

"Never you mind, Samivel," returned Mr. Weller gravely; "puns may be wery good things or they may be wery bad 'uns, and a female may be none the better or she may be none the vurse for making of 'em; that's got nothing to do vith widders."

"Wy now," said Sam, looking round, "would anybody believe as a man at his time o' life could be running his head agin spinsters and punsters being the same thing?"

"There an't a straw's difference between 'em," said Mr. Weller. "Your father didn't drive a coach for so many years, not to be ekal to his own langvidge as far as *that* goes, Sammy."

Avoiding the question of etymology, upon which the old gentleman's mind was quite made up, he was several times assured that the housekeeper had never been married. He expressed great satisfaction on hearing this, and apologized for the question, remarking that he had been greatly terrified by a widow not long before and that his natural timidity was increased in consequence.

"It wos on the rail," said Mr. Weller, with strong emphasis; "I wos a goin' down to Birmingham by the rail, and I wos locked up in a close carriage vith a living widder. Alone we wos; the widder and me wos alone; and I believe it wos only because we *wos* alone and there wos no clergyman in the conwayance, that that 'ere widder didn't marry me afore ve reached the halfway station. Ven I think how she began a screaming as we wos a goin' under them tunnels in the dark—how she kept on a faintin' and ketchin' hold o' me—and how I tried to bust open the door as was tight-locked and perwented all escape—Ah! It was a awful thing, most awful!"

Mr. Weller was so very much overcome by this retrospect that he was unable, until he had wiped his brow several times, to return any reply to the question whether he approved of railway communication, notwithstanding that it would appear from the answer which he ultimately gave, that he entertained strong opinions on the subject.

"I con-sider," said Mr. Weller, "that the rail is unconstitootional and an inwaser o' priwileges, and I should wery much like to know what that 'ere old Carter as once stood up for our liberties and wun 'em too—I should like to know wot he vould say if he wos alive now, to Englishmen being locked up with widders, or with anybody, again their wills. Wot a old Carter would have said, a old Coachman may say, and I as-sert that in that pint o' view alone, the rail is an inwaser. As to the comfort, vere's the comfort o' sittin' in a harm-cheer lookin' at brick walls or heaps o' mud, never comin' to a public-house, never seein' a glass o' ale, never goin' through a pike, never meetin' a change o' no kind (horses or othervise), but alvays comin' to a place, ven you come to one at all, the wery picter o' the last, vith the same p'leesemen standing about, the same blessed old bell a ringin', the same unfort'nate people standing behind the bars, a waitin' to be let in; and everythin' the same except the name, vich is wrote up in the same sized letters as the last name and vith the same colors. As to the honor and dignity o' travelin', vere can that be vithout a coachman; and wot's the rail to sich coachmen and guards as is sometimes forced to go by it, but a outrage and a insult? As to the pace, wot sort o' pace do you think I, Tony Veller, could have kept a coach goin' at, for five hundred thousand pound a mile, paid in adwance afore the coach was on the road? And as to the ingein—a nasty, wheezin', creakin', gaspin', puffin', bustin' monster, alvays out o' breath, with a shiny green-and-gold back, like a unpleasant beetle in that 'ere gas magnifier—as to the ingein as is alvays a pourin' out red-hot coals at night, and black smoke in the day, the sensiblest thing it does in my opinion, is, ven there's somethin' in the vay and it sets up that 'ere frightful scream vich seems to say, 'Now here's two hundred and forty passengers in the wery greatest extremity o' danger, and here's their two hundred and forty screams in vun!' "

By this time I began to fear that my friends would be rendered impatient by my protracted absence. I therefore begged Mr. Pickwick to accompany me upstairs, and left the two Mr. Wellers in the care of the housekeeper, laying strict injunctions upon her to treat them with all possible hospitality.

F o u r

THE CLOCK

A S WE WERE GOING UPSTAIRS, MR. PICKWICK PUT ON HIS spectacles which he had held in his hand hitherto; arranged his neckerchief, smoothed down his waistcoat, and made many other little preparations of that kind which men are accustomed to be mindful of, when they are going among strangers for the first time and are anxious to impress them pleasantly. Seeing that I smiled, he smiled too, and said that if it had occurred to him before he left home, he would certainly have presented himself in pumps and silk stockings.

"I would indeed, my dear sir," he said very seriously; "I would have shown my respect for the society, by laying aside my gaiters."

"You may rest assured," said I, "that they would have regretted your doing so, very much, for they are quite attached to them."

"No, really!" cried Mr. Pickwick, with manifest pleasure. "Do you think they care about my gaiters? Do you seriously think that they identify me at all with my gaiters?"

"I am sure they do," I replied.

"Well now," said Mr. Pickwick, "that is one of the most charming and agreeable circumstances that could possibly have occurred to me!"

I should not have written down this short conversation, but that it developed a slight point in Mr. Pickwick's character, with which I was not previously acquainted. He has a secret pride in his legs. The manner in which he spoke, and the accompanying glance he bestowed upon his tights, convince me that Mr. Pickwick regards his legs with much innocent vanity.

"But here are our friends," said I, opening the door and taking his arm in mine; "let them speak for themselves.—Gentlemen, I present to you Mr. Pickwick."

Mr. Pickwick and I must have been a good contrast just then. I, leaning quietly on my crutch-stick with something of a careworn, patient air; he, having hold of my arm, and bowing in every direction with the most elastic politeness, and an expression of face whose sprightly cheerfulness and good-humor knew no bounds. The difference between us must have been more striking yet as we advanced towards the table, and the amiable gentleman, adapting his jocund step to my poor tread, had his attention divided between treating my infirmities with the utmost consideration, and affecting to be wholly unconscious that I required any.

I made him personally known to each of my friends in turn. First, to the deaf gentleman, whom he regarded with much interest, and accosted with great frankness and cordiality. He had evidently some vague idea, at the moment, that my friend being deaf must be dumb also; for when the latter opened his lips to express the pleasure it afforded him to know a gentleman of whom he had heard so much, Mr. Pickwick was so extremely disconcerted, that I was obliged to step in to his relief.

His meeting with Jack Redburn was quite a treat to see. Mr. Pickwick smiled, and shook hands, and looked at him through his spectacles, and under them, and over them, and nodded his head approvingly, and then nodded to me, as much as to say, "This is just the man; you were quite right," and then turned to Jack and said a few hearty words, and then did and said everything over again with unimpaired vivacity. As to Jack himself, he was quite as much delighted with Mr. Pickwick as Mr. Pickwick could possibly be with him. Two people never can have met together since the world began, who exchanged a warmer or more enthusiastic greeting.

It was amusing to observe the difference between this encounter and that which succeeded, between Mr. Pickwick and Mr. Miles. It was clear that the latter gentleman viewed our new member as a kind of rival in the affections of Jack Redburn, and besides this, he had more than once hinted to me, in secret, that although he had no doubt Mr. Pickwick was a very worthy man, still he did consider that some of his exploits were unbecoming a gentleman of his years and gravity. Over and above these grounds of distrust, it is one of his fixed opinions that the law never can by possibility do anything wrong; he therefore looks upon Mr. Pickwick as one who has justly suffered in purse and peace for a breach of his plighted faith to an unprotected female, and holds that he is called upon to regard him with some suspicion on that account. These causes led to a rather cold and formal reception; which Mr. Pickwick acknowledged with the same stateliness and intense politeness as was displayed on the other side. Indeed he assumed an air of such majestic defiance that I was fearful he might break out into some solemn protest or declaration, and therefore inducted him into his chair without a moment's delay.

This piece of generalship was perfectly successful. The instant he took his seat, Mr. Pickwick surveyed us all with a most benevolent aspect, and was taken with a fit of smiling full five minutes long. His interest in our ceremonies was immense. They are not very numerous or complicated, and a description of them may be comprised in very few words. As our transactions have already been, and must necessarily continue to be, more or less anticipated by being presented in these pages at different times, and under various forms, they do not require a detailed account.

Our first proceeding when we are assembled is to shake hands all round, and greet each other with cheerful and pleasant looks. Remembering that we assemble, not only for the promotion of our own happiness, but with the view of adding something to the common stock, an air of languor or indifference in any member of our body would be regarded by the others as a kind of treason. We have never had an offender in this respect; but if we had, there is no doubt that he would be taken to task pretty severely.

Our salutation over, the venerable piece of antiquity from which we take our name is wound up in silence. This ceremony is always performed by Master Humphrey himself (in treating of the club, I may be permitted to assume the historical style, and speak of myself in the third person), who mounts upon a chair for the purpose, armed with a large key. While it is in progress, Jack Redburn is required to keep at the further end of the room under the guardianship of Mr. Miles, for he is known to entertain certain aspiring and unhallowed thoughts connected with the Clock, and has even gone so far as to state that if he might take the works out for a day or two, he thinks he could improve them. We pardon him his presumption in consideration of his good intentions, and his keeping this respectful distance, which last penalty is insisted on, lest by secretly wounding the object of our regard in some tender part, in the ardor of his zeal for its improvement, he should fill us all with dismay and consternation.

This regulation afforded Mr. Pickwick the highest delight, and seemed, if possible, to exalt Jack in his good opinion.

The next ceremony is the opening of the Clock-case (of which Master Humphrey has likewise the key), the taking from it as many papers as will furnish forth our evening's entertainment, and arranging in the recess such new contributions as have been provided since our last meeting. This is always done with peculiar solemnity. The deaf gentleman then fills and lights his pipe, and we once more take our seats round the table before mentioned, Master Humphrey acting as president—if we can be said to have any president, where all are on the same social footing—and our friend Jack as secretary. Our preliminaries being now concluded, we fall into any train of conversation that happens to suggest itself, or proceed immediately to one of our readings. In the latter case, the paper selected is consigned to Master Humphrey, who flattens it carefully on the table and makes dog's ears in the corner of every page, ready for turning over easily; Jack Redburn trims the lamp with a small machine of his own invention, which usually puts it out; Mr. Miles looks on with great approval notwithstanding; the deaf gentleman draws in his chair, so that he can follow the words on the paper or on Master Humphrey's lips, as he pleases; and Master Humphrey himself, looking round with mighty gratification and glancing up at his old Clock, begins to read aloud.

Mr. Pickwick's face while his tale was being read would have attracted the attention of the dullest man alive. The complacent motion of his head and forefinger as he gently beat time and corrected the air with imaginary punctuation, the smile that mantled on his features at every jocose passage and the sly look he stole around to observe its effect, the calm manner in which he shut his eyes and listened when there was some little piece of description, the changing expression with which he acted the dialogue to himself, his agony that the deaf gentleman should know what it was all about, and his extraordinary anxiety to correct the reader when he hesitated at a word in the manuscript or substituted a wrong one, were alike worthy of remark. And when at last, after endeavoring to communicate with the deaf gentleman by means of the finger alphabet, with which he constructed such words as are unknown in any civilized or savage language, he took up a slate and wrote in large text, one word in a line, the question, "How—do—you—like—it?"—when he did this, and handing it over the table awaited the reply, with a countenance only brightened and improved by his great excitement, even Mr. Miles relaxed, and could not forbear looking at him for the moment with interest and favor.

"It has occurred to me," said the deaf gentleman, who had watched Mr. Pickwick and everybody else with silent satisfaction, "it has occurred to me," said the deaf gentleman, taking his pipe from his lips, "that now is our time for filling our only empty chair."

As our conversation had naturally turned upon the vacant seat, we lent a willing ear to this remark, and looked at our friend inquiringly.

"I feel sure," said he, "that Mr. Pickwick must be acquainted with somebody who would be an acquisition to us; that he must know the man we want. Pray let us not lose any time, but set this question at rest. Is it so, Mr. Pickwick?"

The gentleman addressed was about to return a verbal reply, but remembering our friend's infirmity he substituted for this kind of answer some fifty nods. Then taking up the slate and printing on it a gigantic "Yes," he handed it across the table, and rubbing his hands as he looked round upon our faces, protested that he and the deaf gentleman quite understood each other, already.

"The person I have in my mind," said Mr. Pickwick, "and whom I should not have presumed to mention to you until sometime hence, but for the opportunity you have given me, is a very strange old man. His name is Bamber."

"Bamber!" said Jack, "I have certainly heard the name before."

"I have no doubt then," returned Mr. Pickwick, "that you remember him in those adventures of mine (the Posthumous Papers of our old club, I mean) although he is only incidentally mentioned; and, if I remember right, appears but once."

"That's it," said Jack. "Let me see. He is the person who has a grave interest in old moldy chambers and the Inns of Court, and who relates some anecdotes having reference to his favorite theme—and an odd ghost story—is that the man?"

"The very same. Now," said Mr. Pickwick, lowering his voice to a mysterious and confidential tone, "he is a very extraordinary and remarkable person; living, and talking, and looking, like some strange spirit, whose delight is to haunt old buildings; and absorbed in that one subject which you have just mentioned, to an extent which is quite wonderful. When I retired into private life, I sought him out, and I do assure you that the more I see of him, the more strongly I am impressed with the strange and dreamy character of his mind."

"Where does he live?" I inquired.

"He lives," said Mr. Pickwick, "in one of those dull, lonely old places with which his thoughts and stories are all connected; quite alone, and often shut up close for several weeks together. In this dusty solitude he broods upon the fancies he has so long indulged, and when he goes into the world, or anybody from the world without goes to see him, they are still present to his mind and still his favorite topic. I may say, I believe, that he has brought himself to entertain a regard for me, and an interest in my visit; feelings which I am certain he would extend to Master Humphrey's Clock if he were once tempted to join us. All I wish you to understand is, that he is a strange secluded visionary, in the world but not of it; and as unlike anybody here as he is unlike anybody elsewhere that ever I have met or known."

Mr. Miles received this account of our proposed companion with rather a wry face, and after murmuring that perhaps he was a little mad, inquired if he were rich.

"I never asked him," said Mr. Pickwick.

"You might know, sir, for all that," retorted Mr. Miles, sharply.

"Perhaps so, sir," said Mr. Pickwick, no less sharply than the other, "but I do not. Indeed," he added, relapsing into his usual mildness, "I have no means of judging. He lives poorly, but that would seem to be in keeping with his character. I never heard him allude to his circumstances, and never fell into the society of any man who had the slightest acquaintance with them. I really have told you all I know about him, and it rests with you to say whether you wish to know more, or know quite enough already."

We were unanimously of opinion that we would seek to know more; and as a sort of compromise with Mr. Miles (who, although he said "Yes—Oh certainly—he should like to know more about the gentleman—he had no right to put himself in opposition to the general wish—" and so forth, shook his head doubtfully and hemmed several times with peculiar gravity), it was arranged that Mr. Pickwick should carry me with him on an evening visit to the subject of our discussion, for which purpose an early appointment between that gentleman and myself was immediately agreed upon; it being understood that I was to act upon my own responsibility, and invite him to join us, or not, as I might think proper. This solemn question determined, we returned to the Clock-case (where we have been forestalled by the reader), and between its contents, and the conversation they occasioned, the remainder of our time passed very quickly.

When we broke up, Mr. Pickwick took me aside to tell me that he had spent a most charming and delightful evening. Having made this communication with an air of the strictest secrecy, he took Jack Redburn into another corner to tell him the same, and then retired into another corner with the deaf gentleman and the slate, to repeat the assurance. It was amusing to observe the contest in his mind whether he should extend his confidence to Mr. Miles, or treat him with dignified reserve. Half a dozen times he stepped up behind him with a friendly air, and as often stepped back again without saying a world; at last, when he was close at that gentleman's ear and upon the very point of whispering something conciliating and agreeable, Mr. Miles happened suddenly to turn his head, upon which Mr. Pickwick skipped away, and said with some fierceness, "Good night, sir—I was about to say good night, sir—nothing more"; and so made a bow and left him.

"Now, Sam," said Mr. Pickwick, when he got down stairs.

"All right, sir," replied Mr. Weller. "Hold hard, sir. Right arm fust—now the left—now one strong conwulsion, and the great-coat's on, sir."

Mr. Pickwick acted upon these directions, and being further assisted by Sam who pulled at one side of the collar, and the elder Mr. Weller who pulled hard at the other, was speedily enrobed. Mr. Weller senior then produced a full-sized stable lantern, which he had carefully deposited in a remote corner on his arrival, and inquired whether Mr. Pickwick would have "the lamps alight."

"I think not tonight," said Mr. Pickwick.

"Then if this here lady vill per-mit," rejoined Mr. Weller, "we'll leave it here, ready for next journey. This here lantern, mum," said Mr. Weller, handing it to the housekeeper, "vunce belonged to the celebrated Bill Blinder as is now at grass, as all on us vill be in our turns. Bill, mum, wos the hostler as had charge o' them two vell-known piebald leaders that run in the Bristol fast coach, and vould never go to no other tune but a sutherly vind and a cloudy sky, which wos consekvently played incessant, by the guard, wenever they wos on duty. He wos took wery bad one arternoon, arter having been off his feed, and wery shaky on his legs for some veeks; and he says to his mate, 'Matey,' he says, 'I think I'm a-goin' the wrong side o' the post, and that my foot's wery near the bucket. Don't say I an't,' he says, 'for I know I am, and don't let me be interrupted,' he says, 'for I've saved a little money, and I'm a-goin' into the stable to make my last vill and testymint.' 'I'll take care as nobody interrupts,' says this mate, 'but you on'y hold up your head, and shake your ears a bit, and you're good for twenty year to come.' Bill Blinder makes him no answer, but he goes away into the stable, and there he soon artervards lays himself down a'tween the two piebalds, and dies—previously a-writin' outside the corn-chest, 'This is the last vill and testymint of Villiam Blinder.' They wos nat'rally wery much amazed at this, and arter looking among the litter, and up in the loft, and vere not, they opens the corn-chest, and finds that he'd been and chalked his vill inside the lid; so the lid wos obligated to be took off the hinges, and sent up to Doctor Commons to be proved, and under that 'ere wery instrument this here lantern was passed to Tony Veller; vich circumstarnce, mum, gives it a wally in my eyes, and makes me rek-vest, if you vill be so kind, as to take partickler care on it."

The housekeeper graciously promised to keep the object of Mr. Weller's regard in the safest possible custody, and Mr. Pickwick, with a laughing face, took his leave. The bodyguard followed, side by side: old Mr. Weller buttoned and wrapped up from his boots to his chin; and Sam with his hands in his pockets and his hat half off his head, remonstrating with his father as he went, on his extreme loquacity.

I was not a little surprised, on turning to go upstairs, to encounter the barber in the passage at that late hour; for his attendance is usually confined to some half-hour in the morning. But Jack Redburn, who finds out (by instinct, I think) everything that happens in the house, informed me with great glee, that a society in imitation of our own had been that night formed in the kitchen, under the title of "Mr. Weller's Watch," of which the barber was a member; and that he could pledge himself to find means of making me acquainted with the whole of its future proceedings, which I begged him, both on my own account and that of my readers, by no means to neglect doing.

F i v e

MR. WELLER'S WATCH

IT SEEMS THAT THE HOUSEKEEPER AND THE TWO MR. Wellers were no sooner left together on the occasion of their first becoming acquainted, than the housekeeper called to her assistance Mr. Slithers the barber, who had been lurking in the kitchen in expectation of her summons; and with many smiles and much sweetness introduced him as one who would assist her in the responsible office of entertaining her distinguished visitors.

"Indeed," said she, "without Mr. Slithers I should have been placed in quite an awkward situation."

"There is no call for any hock-erdness, mum," said Mr. Weller with the utmost politeness; "no call wotsumever. A lady," added the old gentleman, looking about him with the air of one who establishes an incontrovertible position, "a lady can't be hock'erd. Natur has otherwise purwided."

The housekeeper inclined her head and smiled yet more sweetly. The barber, who had been fluttering about Mr. Weller and Sam in a state of great anxiety to improve their acquaintance, rubbed his hands and cried, "Hear! hear! Very true, sir"; whereupon Sam turned about and steadily regarded him for some seconds in silence.

"I never knew," said Sam, fixing his eyes in a ruminative manner upon the blushing barber, "I never knew but vun o' your trade, but *he* wos worth a dozen and wos indeed dewoted to his callin'!"

"Was he in the easy shaving way, sir," inquired Mr. Slithers; "or in the cutting and curling line?"

"Both," replied Sam; "easy shavin' was his natur; and cuttin' and curlin' was his pride and glory. His whole delight wos in his trade. He spent all his money in bears and run in debt for 'em besides, and there they wos a growling avay down in the front cellar all day long, and ineffectooally gnashing their teeth, vile the grease o' their relations and friends wos being retailed in gallipots in the shop above, and the first-floor winder wos ornamented vith their heads; not to speak o' the dreadful aggrawation it must have been to 'em to see a man alvays a walkin' up and down the pavement outside, vith the portrait of a bear in his last agonies, and underneath in large letters, 'Another fine animal wos slaughtered yesterday at Jinkinson's!' Hows'ever, there they wos, and there Jinkinson wos, till he wos took wery ill with some inn'ard disorder, lost the use of his legs, and wos confined to his bed vere he laid a wery long time, but sich wos his pride in his profession even then, that wenever he wos worse than usual the doctor used to go downstairs and say, 'Jinkinson's wery low this mornin'; we must give the bears a stir'; and as sure as ever they stirred 'em up a bit and made 'em roar, Jinkinson opens his eyes if he wos ever so bad, calls out, 'There's the bears!' and rewives agin."

"Astonishing!" cried the barber.

"Not a bit," said Sam, "human natur' neat as imported. Vun day the doctor happenin' to say, 'I shall look in as usual tomorrow mornin',' Jinkinson catches hold of his hand and says, 'Doctor,' he says, 'will you grant me one favor?' 'I will, Jinkinson,' says the doctor; 'Then, doctor,' says Jinkinson, 'vill you come unshaved, and let me shave you?' 'I will,' says the doctor. 'God bless you,' says Jinkinson. Next day the doctor came, and arter he'd been shaved all skillful and reg'lar, he says, 'Jinkinson,' he says, 'it's wery plain this does you good. Now,' he says, 'I've got a coachman as has got a beard that it 'ud warm your heart to work on, and though the footman,' he says, 'hasn't got much of a beard, still he's a trying it on vith a pair o' viskers to that extent that razors is Christian charity. If they take it in turns to mind the carriage when it's a waitin' below,' he says, 'wot's to hinder you from operatin' on both of 'em ev'ry day as well as upon me? you've got six children,' he says, 'wot's to hinder you from shavin' all their heads and keepin' 'em shaved? you've got two assistants in the shop downstairs, wot's to hinder you from cuttin' and curlin' them as often as you like? Do this,' he says, 'and you're a man agin.' Jinkinson squeedged the doctor's hand and begun that wery day; he kept his tools upon the bed, and wenever he felt his-self gettin' worse, he turned to at vun o' the children who wos a runnin' about the house vith heads like clean Dutch cheeses, and shaved him agin. Vun day the lawyer come to make his vill; all the time he wos a takin' it down, Jinkinson was secretly a clippin' avay at his hair vith a large pair of scissors. 'Wot's that 'ere snippin' noise?' says the lawyer every now and then, 'it's like a man havin' his hair cut.' 'It *is* wery like a man havin' his hair cut,' says poor Jinkinson, hidin' the scissors and lookin' quite innocent. By the time the lawyer found it out, he was wery nearly bald. Jinkinson wos kept alive in this vay for a long time, but at last vun day he has in all the children vun arter another, shaves each on 'em wery clean, and gives him vun kiss on the crown o' his head; then he has in the two assistants, and arter cuttin' and curlin' of 'em in the first style of elegance, says he should like to hear the woice o' the greasiest bear, vich rekvest is immedetly complied with; then he says that he feels wery happy in his mind and vishes to be left alone; and then he dies, prevously cuttin' his own hair and makin' one flat curl in the wery middle of his forehead."

This anecdote produced an extraordinary effect, not only upon Mr. Slithers, but upon the housekeeper also, who evinced so much anxiety to please and to be pleased, that Mr. Weller, with a manner betokening some alarm, conveyed a whispered inquiry to his son whether he had gone "too fur."

"Wot do you mean by too fur?" demanded Sam.

"In that 'ere little compliment respectin' the want of hock'erdness in ladies, Sammy," replied his father.

"You don't think she's fallen in love with you in consekens o' that, do you?" said Sam.

"More unlikelier things have come to pass, my boy," replied Mr. Weller in a hoarse whisper; "I'm always afeerd of inadwertent captiwation, Sammy. If I know'd how to make myself ugly or unpleasant, I'd do it, Samivel, rayther than live in this here state of perpetival terror!"

Mr. Weller had, at that time, no further opportunity of dwelling upon the apprehensions which beset his mind, for the immediate occasion of his fears proceeded to lead the way downstairs, apologizing as they went for conducting him into the kitchen, which apartment, however, she was induced to proffer for his accommodation in preference to her own little room, the rather as it afforded greater facilities for smoking, and was immediately adjoining the ale-cellar. The preparations which were already made sufficiently proved that these were not mere words of course, for on the deal table were a sturdy ale-jug and glasses, flanked with clean pipes and a plentiful supply of tobacco for the old gentleman and his son, while on a dresser hard by was goodly store of cold meat and other eatables. At sight of these arrangements Mr. Weller was at first distracted between his love of joviality and his doubts whether they were not to be considered as so many evidences of captivation having already taken place; but he soon yielded to his natural impulse, and took his seat at the table with a very jolly countenance.

"As to imbibin' any o' this here flagrant veed, mum, in the presence of a lady," said Mr. Weller, taking up a pipe and laying it down again, "it couldn't be. Samivel, total abstinence, if *you* please."

"But I like it of all things," said the housekeeper.

"No," rejoined Mr. Weller, shaking his head. "No."

"Upon my word I do," said the housekeeper. "Mr. Slithers knows I do."

Mr. Weller coughed, and notwithstanding the barber's confirmation of the statement, said "No" again, but more feebly than before. The housekeeper lighted a piece of paper and insisted on applying it to the bowl of the pipe with her own fair hands; Mr. Weller resisted; the housekeeper cried that her fingers would be burnt; Mr. Weller gave way. The pipe was ignited, Mr. Weller drew a long puff of smoke, and detecting himself in the very act of smiling on the housekeeper, put a sudden constraint upon his countenance and looked sternly at the candle, with a determination not to captivate, himself, or encourage thoughts of captivation in others. From this iron frame of mind he was roused by the voice of his son.

"I don't think," said Sam, who was smoking with great composure and enjoyment, "that if the lady wos agreeable, it 'ud be wery far out o' the vay for us four to make up a club of our own like the governors does upstairs, and let him," Sam pointed with the stem of his pipe towards his parent, "be the president."

The housekeeper affably declared that it was the very thing she had been thinking of. The barber said the same. Mr. Weller said nothing, but he laid down his pipe as if in a fit of inspiration, and performed the following manœuvres.

Unbuttoning the three lower buttons of his waistcoat, and pausing for a moment to enjoy the easy flow of breath consequent upon this process, he laid violent hands upon his watch-chain, and slowly and with extreme difficulty drew from his fob an immense double-cased silver watch, which brought the lining of the pocket with it and was not to be disentangled but by great exertions and an amazing redness of face. Having fairly got it out at last, he detached the outer case and wound it up with a key of corresponding magnitude; then put the case on again, and having applied the watch to his ear to ascertain that it was still going, gave it some half-dozen hard knocks on the table to improve its performance.

"That," said Mr. Weller, laying it on the table with its face upwards, "is the title and emblem o' this here society. Sammy, reach them two stools this vay for the wacant cheers. Ladies and gen'lmen, Mr. Weller's Watch is vound up and now a goin'. Order!"

By way of enforcing this proclamation, Mr. Weller, using the watch after the manner of a president's hammer, and remarking with great pride that nothing hurt it, and that falls and concussions of all kinds materially enhanced the excellence of the works and assisted the regulator, knocked the table a great many times and declared the association formally constituted.

"And don't let's have no grinnin' at the cheer, Samivel," said Mr. Weller to his son, "or I shall be committin' you to the cellar, and then p'r'aps we may get into what the 'Merrikins call a fix, and the English a qvestion o' privileges."

Having uttered this friendly caution, the president settled himself in his chair with great dignity, and requested that Mr. Samuel would relate an anecdote.

"I've told one," said Sam.

"Wery good, sir; tell another," returned the chair.

"We wos a talking jist now, sir," said Sam, turning to Slithers, "about barbers. Pursuing that 'ere fruitful theme, sir, I'll tell you in a wery few words a romantic little story about another barber, as p'r'aps you may never have heerd."

"Samivel!" said Mr. Weller, again bringing his watch and the table into smart collision, "address your obserwations to the cheer, sir, and not to priwate indiwiduals!"

"And if I might rise to order," said the barber in a soft voice, and looking round him with a conciliatory smile as he leant over the table with the knuckles of his left hand resting upon it, "if I *might* rise to order, I would suggest that 'barbers' is not exactly the kind of language which is agreeable and soothing to our feelings. You, sir, will correct me if I'm wrong, but I believe there *is* such a word in the dictionary as hairdressers."

"Well, but suppose he wasn't a hairdresser," suggested Sam.

"Wy then, sir, be parliamentary, and call him vun all the more," returned his father. "In the same vay as ev'ry gen'lman in another place is a *h*onorable, ev'ry barber in this place is a hairdresser. Ven you read the speeches in the papers, and see as vun gen'lman says of another, 'the *h*onorable member, if he vill allow me to call him so,' you vill understand, sir, that that means, 'if he vill allow me to keep up that 'ere pleasant and uniwersal fiction.' "

It is a common remark, confirmed by history and experience, that great men rise with the circumstances in which they are placed. Mr. Weller came out so strong in his capacity of chairman, that Sam was for some time prevented from speaking by a grin of surprise, which held his faculties enchained, and at last subsided in a long whistle of a single note. Nay, the old gentleman appeared even to have astonished himself, and that to no small extent, as was demonstrated by the vast amount of chuckling in which he indulged after the utterance of these lucid remarks.

"Here's the story," said Sam. "Vunce upon a time there wos a young hairdresser as opened a wery smart little shop vith four wax dummies in the winder, two gen'lmen and two ladies—the gen'lmen vith blue dots for their beards, wery large viskers, oudacious heads of hair, uncommon clear eyes, and nostrils of amazin' pinkness—the ladies with their heads o' one side, their right forefingers on their lips, and their forms deweloped beautiful, in vich last respect they had the adwantage over the gen'lmen, as wasn't allowed but wery little shoulder and terminated rayther abrupt in fancy drapery. He had also a many hairbrushes and toothbrushes bottled up in the winder, neat glass-cases on the counter, a floor-clothed cuttin'-room upstairs, and a weighin'-macheen in the shop, right opposite the door; but the great attraction and ornament wos the dummies, which this here young hairdresser wos constantly a runnin' out in the road to look at, and constantly a runnin' in agin to touch up and polish; in short he wos so proud on 'em that ven Sunday come, he wos always wretched and mis'rable to think they wos behind the shutters, and looked anxiously for Monday on that account. Vun o' these dummies wos a fav'rite vith him beyond the others; and ven any of his acquaintance asked him wy he didn't get married—as the young ladies he know'd, in partickler, often did—he used to say, 'Never! I never vill enter into the bonds of vedlock,' he says, 'until I meet with a young 'ooman as realizes my idea o' that 'ere fairest dummy with the light hair. Then and not till then,' he says, 'I vill approach the altar!' All the young ladies he know'd as had got dark hair told him this was wery sinful, and that he wos wurshippin' a idle; but them as wos at all near the same shade as the dummy colored up wery much, and wos observed to think him a wery nice young man."

"Samivel," said Mr. Weller, gravely; "a member of this associashun bein' one o' that 'ere tender sex which is now immedetly referred to, I have to rekvest that you vill make no reflexions."

"I ain't a makin' any, am I?" inquired Sam.

"Order, sir!" rejoined Mr. Weller, with severe dignity; then sinking the chairman in the father, he added in his usual tone of voice, "Samivel, drive on!"

Sam interchanged a smile with the housekeeper, and proceeded:

"The young hairdresser hadn't been in the habit o' makin' this avowal above six months, ven he en-countered a young lady as wos the wery picter o' the fairest dummy. 'Now,' he says, 'it's all up. I am a slave!' The young lady wos not only the picter o' the fairest dummy, but she was very romantic, as the young hairdresser wos too, and he says, 'Oh!' he says, 'here's a community o' feelin', here's a flow o' soul!' he says, 'here's a interchange o' sentiment!' The young lady didn't say much, o' course, but she expressed herself agreeable, and shortly artervards vent to see him with a mutual friend. The hairdresser rushes out to meet her, but d'rectly she sees the dummies she changes color and falls a tremblin' wiolently. 'Look up, my love,' says the hairdresser, 'behold your imige in my winder, but not correcter than in my art!' 'My imige!' she says. 'Yourn!' replies the hairdresser. 'But whose imige is *that?*' she says, a pinting at vun o' the gen'lmen. 'No vun's, my love,' he says, 'it is but a idea.' 'A idea!' she cries, 'it is a portrait, I feel it is a portrait, and that 'ere noble face must be in the milingtary!' 'Wot do I hear!' says he, a crumplin' his curls. 'Villiam Gibbs,' she says, quite firm, 'never renoo the subject. I respect you as a friend,' she says, 'but my affections is set upon that manly brow.' 'This,' says the hairdresser, 'is a reg'lar blight, and in it I perceive the hand of Fate. Farevell!' Vith these vords he rushes into the shop, breaks the dummy's nose vith a blow of his curlin'-irons, melts him down at the parlor fire, and never smiles artervards."

"The young lady, Mr. Weller?" said the housekeeper.

"Why, ma'am," said Sam, "finding that Fate had a spite agin her and everybody she come into contact vith, she never smiled neither, but read a deal o' poetry and pined avay—by rayther slow degrees, for she an't dead yet. It took a deal o' poetry to kill the hairdresser, and some people say arter all that it was more the gin and water as caused him to be run over; p'r'aps it was a little o' both, and came o' mixing the two."

The barber declared that Mr. Weller had related one of the most interesting stories that had ever come within his knowledge, in which opinion the housekeeper entirely concurred.

"Are you a married man, sir?" inquired Sam.

The barber replied that he had not that honor.

"I s'pose you mean to be?" said Sam.

"Well," replied the barber, rubbing his hands smirkingly, "I don't know, I don't think it's very likely."

"That's a bad sign," said Sam; "if you'd said you meant to be vun o' these days, I should ha' looked upon you as bein' safe. You're in a wery precarious state."

"I am not conscious of any danger, at all events," returned the barber.

"No more wos I, sir," said the elder Mr. Weller, interposing, "those vere my symptoms exactly. I've been took that vay twice. Keep your vether eye open, my friend, or you're gone."

There was something so very solemn about this admonition, both in its matter and manner, and also in the way in which Mr. Weller still kept his eye fixed upon the unsuspecting victim, that nobody cared to speak for some little time, and might not have cared to do so for some time longer, if the housekeeper had not happened to sigh, which called off the old gentleman's attention and gave rise to a gallant inquiry whether "there wos anythin' wery piercin' in that 'ere little heart?"

"Dear me, Mr. Weller!" said the housekeeper, laughing.

"No, but is there anythin' as agitates it?" pursued the old gentleman. "Has it always been obderrate, always opposed to the happiness o' human creeturs? Eh? Has it?"

At this critical juncture for her blushes and confusion, the housekeeper discovered that more ale was wanted, and hastily withdrew into the cellar to draw the same, followed by the barber, who insisted on carrying the candle. Having looked after her with a very complacent expression of face, and after him with some disdain, Mr. Weller caused his glance to travel slowly round the kitchen until at length it rested on his son.

"Sammy," said Mr. Weller, "I mistrust that barber."

"Wot for?" returned Sam; "wot's he got to do with you? You're a nice man, you are, arter pretendin' all kinds o' terror, to go a payin' compliments and talkin' about hearts and piercers."

The imputation of gallantry appeared to afford Mr. Weller the utmost delight, for he replied in a voice choked by suppressed laughter and with the tears in his eyes,

"Wos I a talkin' about hearts and piercers—wos I though, Sammy, eh?"

"Wos you? of course you wos."

"She don't know no better, Sammy, there an't no harm in it—no danger, Sammy; she's only a punster. She seemed pleased though, didn't she? O' course she wos pleased, it's nat'ral she should be, wery nat'ral."

"He's wain of it!" exclaimed Sam, joining in his father's mirth. "He's actually wain!"

"Hush!" replied Mr. Weller, composing his features, "they're a comin' back, the little heart's a comin' back. But mark these wurds o' mine once more, and remember 'em ven your father says he said 'em. Samivel, I mistrust that 'ere deceitful barber."

Six

MASTER HUMPHREY FROM HIS CLOCK-SIDE IN THE CHIMNEY-CORNER

Two or three evenings after the institution of Mr. Weller's Watch, I thought I heard as I walked in the garden the voice of Mr. Weller himself at no great distance; and stopping once or twice to listen more attentively, I found that the sounds proceeded from my housekeeper's little sitting-room, which is at the back of the house. I took no further notice of the circumstance at that time, but it formed the subject of a conversation between me and my friend Jack Redburn next morning, when I found that I had not been deceived in my impression. Jack furnished me with the following particulars; and as he appeared to take extraordinary pleasure in relating them, I have begged him in future to jot down any such domestic scenes or occurrences that may please his humor, in order that they may be told in his own way. I must confess that, as Mr. Pickwick and he are constantly together, I have been influenced, in making this request, by a secret desire to know something of their proceedings.

On the evening in question, the housekeeper's room was arranged with particular care, and the housekeeper herself was very smartly dressed. The preparations, however, were not confined to mere showy demonstrations, as tea was prepared for three persons, with a small display of preserves and jams and sweet cakes, which heralded some uncommon occasion. Miss Benton (my housekeeper bears that name) was in a state of great expectation too, frequently going to the front door and looking anxiously down the lane, and more than once observing to the servant-girl that she expected company and hoped no accident had happened to delay them.

A modest ring at the bell at length allayed her fears, and Miss Benton, hurrying into her own room and shutting herself up, in order that she might preserve that appearance of being taken by surprise which is so essential to the polite reception of visitors, awaited their coming with a smiling countenance.

"Good ev'nin', mum," said the older Mr. Weller, looking in at the door after a prefatory tap, "I'm afeerd we've come in rayther arter the time, mum, but the young colt being full o' wice has been a boltin' and shyin' and gettin' his leg over the traces to sich a ex-tent that if he an't wery soon broke in, he'll wex me into a broken heart, and then he'll never be brought out no more except to learn his letters from the writin' on his grandfather's tombstone."

With these pathetic words, which were addressed to something outside the door about two feet six from the ground, Mr. Weller introduced a very small boy firmly set upon a couple of very sturdy legs, who looked as if nothing could ever knock him down. Besides having a very round face strongly resembling Mr. Weller's, and a stout little body of exactly his build, this young gentleman, standing with his little legs very wide apart as if the top-boots were familiar to them, actually winked upon the housekeeper with his infant eye, in imitation of his grandfather.

"There's a naughty boy, mum," said Mr. Weller, bursting with delight, "there's a immoral Tony. Wos there ever a little chap o' four year and eight months old as vinked his eye at a strange lady afore?"

As little affected by this observation as by the former appeal to his feelings, Master Weller elevated in the air a small model of a coach whip which he carried in his hand, and addressing the housekeeper with a shrill "ya—hip!" inquired if she was "going down the road"; at which happy adaptation of a lesson he had been taught from infancy, Mr. Weller could restrain his feelings no longer, but gave him twopence on the spot.

"It's in wain to deny it, mum," said Mr. Weller, "this here is a boy arter his grandfather's own heart, and beats out all the boys as ever wos or will be. Though at the same time, mum," added Mr. Weller, trying to look gravely down upon his favorite, "it was wery wrong on him to want to over all the posts as we come along, and wery cruel on him to force poor grandfather to lift him cross-legged over every vun of 'em. He wouldn't pass vun single blessed post, mum, and at the top o' the lane there's seven-and-forty on 'em all in a row and wery close together."

Here Mr. Weller, whose feelings were in a perpetual conflict between pride in his grandson's achievements and a sense of his own responsibility, and the importance of impressing him with moral truths, burst into a fit of laughter, and suddenly checking himself, remarked in a severe tone that little boys as made their grandfathers put 'em over posts never went to heaven at any price.

By this time the housekeeper had made tea, and little Tony placed on a chair beside her, with his eyes nearly on a level with the top of the table, was provided with various delicacies which yielded him extreme contentment. The housekeeper (who seemed rather afraid of the child, notwithstanding her caresses) then patted him on the head and declared that he was the finest boy she had ever seen.

"Wy, mum," said Mr. Weller, "I don't think you'll see a many sich, and that's the truth. But if my son Samivel vould give me my vay, mum, and only dis-pense vith his—*might* I wenter to say the vurd?"

"What word, Mr. Weller?" said the housekeeper, blushing slightly.

"Petticuts, mum," returned that gentleman, laying his hand upon the garments of his grandson. "If my son Samivel, mum, vould only dis-pense vith these here, you'd see such a alteration in his appearance, as the imagination can't depicter."

"But what would you have the child wear instead, Mr. Weller?" said the housekeeper.

"I've offered my son Samivel, mum, agen and agen," returned the old gentleman, "to purwide him at my own cost vith a suit o' clothes as 'ud be the makin' on him, and form his mind in infancy for those pursuits as I hope the family o' the Vellers vill always dewote themselves to. Tony, my boy, tell the lady wot them clothes are, as grandfather says father ought to let you vear."

"A little white hat and a little sprig weskut and little knee cords and little top-boots and a little green coat with little bright buttons and a little welwet collar," replied Tony, with great readiness and no stops.

"That's the cos-toom, mum," said Mr. Weller, looking proudly at the housekeeper. "Once make sich a model on him as that, and you'd say he *was* a angel!"

Perhaps the housekeeper thought that in such a guise young Tony would look more like the angel at Islington than anything else of that name, or perhaps she was disconcerted to find her previously-conceived ideas disturbed, as angels are not commonly represented in top-boots and sprig waistcoats. She coughed doubtfully, but said nothing.

"How many brothers and sisters have you, my dear?" she asked, after a short silence.

"One brother and no sister at all," replied Tony. "Sam his name is, and so's my father's. Do you know my father?"

"Oh yes, I know him," said the housekeeper, graciously.

"Is my father fond of you?" pursued Tony.

"I hope so," rejoined the smiling housekeeper.

Tony considered a moment, and then said, "Is my grandfather fond of you?"

This would seem a very easy question to answer, but instead of replying to it, the housekeeper smiled in great confusion, and said that really children did ask such extraordinary questions that it was the most difficult thing in the world to talk to them. Mr. Weller took upon himself to reply that he was very fond of the lady; but the housekeeper entreating that he would not put such things into the child's head, Mr. Weller shook his own while she looked another way, and seemed to be troubled with a misgiving that captivation was in progress. It was perhaps on this account that he changed the subject precipitately.

"It's wery wrong in little boys to make game o' their grandfathers, an't it, mum?" said Mr. Weller, shaking his head waggishly, until Tony looked at him, when he counterfeited the deepest dejection and sorrow.

"Oh very sad!" assented the housekeeper. "But I hope no little boys do that?"

"There is vun young Turk, mum," said Mr. Weller, "as havin' seen his grandfather a little overcome with drink on the occasion of a friend's birthday, goes a reelin' and staggerin' about the house, and makin' believe that he's the old gen'lm'n."

"Oh quite shocking!" cried the housekeeper.

"Yes, mum," said Mr. Weller; "and prevously to so doin', this here young traitor that I'm a speakin' of, pinches his little nose to make it red, and then he gives a hiccup and says, 'I'm all right,' he says, 'give us another song!' Ha ha! 'Give us another song,' he says. Ha ha ha!"

In his excessive delight, Mr. Weller was quite unmindful of his moral responsibility, until little Tony kicked up his legs, and laughing immoderately cried, "That was me, that was"; whereupon the grandfather by a great effort became extremely solemn.

"No, Tony, not you," said Mr. Weller. "I hope it warn't you, Tony. It must ha' been that 'ere naughty little chap as comes sometimes out o' the empty watch-box round the corner—that same little chap as wos found standing on the table afore the looking-glass, pretending to shave himself vith a oyster-knife."

"He didn't hurt himself, I hope?" observed the housekeeper.

"Not he, mum," said Mr. Weller proudly; "bless your heart, you might trust that 'ere boy vith a steam-engine a'most, he's such a knowin' young"— but suddenly recollecting himself and observing that Tony perfectly understood and appreciated the compliment, the old gentleman groaned and observed that "it wos all wery shockin'—wery.

"Oh he's a bad 'un," said Mr. Weller, "is that 'ere watch-box boy, makin' such a noise and litter in the backyard, he does, waterin' wooden horses and feedin' of 'em vith grass, and perpetivally spillin' his little brother out of a veelbarrow and frightenin' his mother out of her wits, at the wery moment wen she's expectin' to increase his stock of happiness vith another play-feller—oh he's a bad 'un! He's even gone so far as to put on a pair o' paper spectacles as he got his father to make for him, and walk up and down the garden vith his hands behind him in imitation of Mr. Pickwick—but Tony don't do sich things, Oh no!"

"Oh no!" echoed Tony.

"He knows better, he does," said Mr. Weller, "he knows that if he wos to come sich games as these nobody wouldn't love him, and that his grandfather in partickler couldn't abear the sight on him; for vich reasons Tony's always good."

"Always good," echoed Tony; and his grandfather immediately took him on his knee and kissed him, at the same time with many nods and winks slyly pointing at the child's head with his thumb, in order that the housekeeper, otherwise deceived by the admirable manner in which he (Mr. Weller) had sustained his character, might not suppose that any other young gentleman was referred to, and might clearly understand that the boy of the watch-box was but an imaginary creation, and a fetch of Tony himself, invented for his improvement and reformation.

Not confining himself to a mere verbal description of his grandson's abilities, Mr. Weller, when tea was finished, incited him by various gifts of pence and halfpence to smoke imaginary pipes, drink visionary beer from real pots, imitate his grandfather without reserve, and in particular to go through the drunken scene, which threw the old gentleman into ecstasies and filled the housekeeper with wonder. Nor was Mr. Weller's pride satisfied with even this display, for when he took his leave he carried the child, like some rare and astonishing curiosity, first to the barber's house and afterwards to the tobacconist's, at each of which places he repeated his performances with the utmost effect to applauding and delighted audiences. It was half-past nine o'clock when Mr. Weller was last seen carrying him home upon his shoulder, and it has been whispered abroad that at that time the infant Tony was rather intoxicated.

MASTER HUMPHREY FROM HIS CLOCK-SIDE IN THE CHIMNEY-CORNER

I WAS MUSING THE OTHER EVENING UPON THE CHARACTERS and incidents with which I had been so long engaged; wondering how I could ever have looked forward with pleasure to the completion of my tale, and reproaching myself for having done so, as if it were a kind of cruelty to those companions of my solitude whom I had now dismissed, and could never again recall; when my clock struck ten. Punctual to the hour, my friends appeared.

On our last night of meeting, we had finished the story which the reader has just concluded. Our conversation took the same current as the meditations which the entrance of my friends had interrupted, and the Old Curiosity Shop was the staple of our discourse.

I may confide to the reader now, that in connection with this little history I had something upon my mind—something to communicate which I had all along with difficulty repressed—something I had deemed it, during the progress of the story, necessary to its interest to disguise, and which, now that it was over, I wished, and was yet reluctant to disclose.

To conceal anything from those to whom I am attached, is not in my nature. I can never close my lips where I have opened my heart. This temper and the consciousness of having done some violence to it in my narrative, laid me under a restraint which I should have had great difficulty in overcoming, but for a timely remark from Mr. Miles, who, as I hinted in a former paper, is a gentleman of business habits, and of great exactness and propriety in all his transactions.

"I could have wished," my friend objected, "that we had been made acquainted with the single gentleman's name. I don't like his withholding his name. It made me look upon him at first with suspicion, and caused me to doubt his moral character, I assure you. I am fully satisfied by this time of his being a worthy creature, but in this respect he certainly would not appear to have acted at all like a man of business."

"My friends," said I, drawing to the table at which they were by this time seated in their usual chairs, "do you remember that this story bore another title besides that one we have so often heard of late?"

Mr. Miles had his pocket-book out in an instant, and referring to an entry therein, rejoined, "Certainly. Personal Adventures of Master Humphrey. Here it is. I made a note of it at the time."

I was about to resume what I had to tell them, when the same Mr. Miles again interrupted me, observing that the narrative originated in a personal adventure of my own, and that was no doubt the reason for its being thus designated.

This led me to the point at once.

"You will one and all forgive me," I returned, "if, for the greater convenience of the story, and for its better introduction, that adventure was fictitious. I had my share indeed—no light or trivial one—in the pages we have read but it was not the share I feigned to have at first. The younger brother, the single gentleman, the nameless actor in this little drama, stands before you now."

It was easy to see they had not expected this disclosure.

"Yes," I pursued. "I can look back upon my part in it with a calm, half-smiling pity for myself as for some other man. But I am he indeed; and now the chief sorrows of my life are yours."

I need not say what true gratification I derived from the sympathy and kindness with which this acknowledgment was received; nor how often it had risen to my lips before; nor how difficult I had found it—how impossible, when I came to those passages which touched me most, and most nearly concerned me—to sustain the character I had assumed. It is enough to say that I replaced in the Clock-case the record of so many trials—sorrowfully, it is true, but with a softened sorrow which was almost pleasure; and felt that in living through the past again, and communicating to others the lesson it had helped to teach me, I had been a happier man.

We lingered so long over the leaves from which I had read, that as I consigned them to their former resting-place, the hand of my trusty Clock pointed to twelve, and there came towards us upon the wind the voice of the deep and distant bell of St. Paul's as it struck the hour of midnight.

"This," said I, returning with a manuscript I had taken at the moment, from the same repository, "to be opened to such music, should be a tale where London's face by night is darkly seen, and where some deed of such a time as this is dimly shadowed out. Which of us here has seen the working of that great machine whose voice has just now ceased?"

Mr. Pickwick had, of course, and so had Mr. Miles. Jack and my deaf friend were in the minority.

I had seen it but a few days before, and could not help telling them of the fancy I had had about it.

I paid my fee of twopence upon entering, to one of the money-changers who sit within the Temple; and falling, after a few turns up and down, into the quiet train of thought which such a place awakens, paced the echoing stones like some old monk whose present world lay all within its walls. As I looked afar up into the lofty dome, I could not help wondering what were his reflections whose genius reared that mighty pile, when, the last small wedge of timber fixed, the last nail driven into its home for many centuries, the clang of hammers, and the hum of busy voices gone, and the Great Silence whole years of noise had helped to make, reigning undisturbed around, he mused as I did now, upon his work, and lost himself amid its vast extent. I could not quite determine whether the contemplation of it would impress him with a sense of greatness or of insignificance; but when I remembered how long a time it had taken to erect, in how short a space it might be traversed even to its remotest parts, for how brief a term he, or any of those who cared to bear his name, would live to see it, or know of its existence, I imagined him far more melancholy than proud, and looking with regret upon his labor done. With these thoughts in my mind, I began to ascend, almost unconsciously, the flight of steps leading to the several wonders of the building, and found myself before a barrier where another money-taker sat, who demanded which among them I would choose to see. There were the stone gallery, he said, and the whispering gallery, the geometrical staircase, the room of models, the Clock—the Clock being quite in my way, I stopped him there, and chose that sight from all the rest.

I groped my way into the Turret which it occupies, and saw before me, in a kind of loft, what seemed to be a great, old oaken press with folding doors. These being thrown back by the attendant (who was sleeping when I came upon him, and looked a drowsy fellow, as though his close companionship with Time had made him quite indifferent to it) disclosed a complicated crowd of wheels and chains in iron and brass—great, sturdy, rattling engines—suggestive of breaking a finger put in here or there, and grinding the bone to powder—and these were the Clock! Its very pulse, if I may use the word, was like no other clock. It did not mark the flight of every moment with a gentle second stroke as though it would check old Time, and have him stay his pace in pity, but measured it with one sledgehammer beat, as if its business were to crush the seconds as they came trooping on, and remorselessly to clear a path before the Day of Judgment.

I sat down opposite to it, and hearing its regular and never-changing voice, that one deep constant note, uppermost amongst all the noise and clatter in the streets below—marking that, let that tumult rise or fall, go on or stop—let it be night or noon, tomorrow or today, this year or next—it still performed its functions with the same dull constancy, and regulated the progress of the life around, the fancy came upon me that this was London's Heart, and that when it should cease to beat, the City would be no more.

It is night. Calm and unmoved amidst the scenes that darkness favors, the great heart of London throbs in its Giant breast. Wealth and beggary, vice and virtue, guilt and innocence, repletion and the direst hunger, all treading on each other and crowding together, are gathered round it. Draw but a little circle above the clustering housetops, and you shall have within its space everything, with its opposite extreme and contradiction, close beside. Where yonder feeble light is shining, a man is but this moment dead. The taper at a few yards' distance is seen by eyes that have this instant opened on the world. There are two houses separated by but an inch or two of wall. In one, there are quiet minds at rest; in the other, a waking conscience that one might think would trouble the very air. In that close corner where the roofs shrink down and cower together as if to hide their secrets from the handsome street hard by, there are such dark crimes, such miseries and horrors, as could be hardly told in whispers. In the handsome street, there are folks asleep who have dwelt there all their lives, and have no more knowledge of these things than if they had never been, or were transacted at the remotest limits of the world—who, if they were hinted at, would shake their heads, look wise, and frown, and say they were impossible, and out of Nature—as if all great towns were not. Does not this Heart of London, that nothing moves, nor stops, nor quickens—that goes on the same, let what will be done—does it not express the City's character well?

The day begins to break, and soon there is the hum and noise of life. Those who have spent the night on doorsteps and cold stones crawl off to beg; they who have slept in beds come forth to their occupation too, and business is astir. The fog of sleep rolls slowly off, and London shines awake. The streets are filled with carriages, and people gaily clad. The jails are full, too, to the throat, nor have the workhouses or hospitals much room to spare. The courts of law are crowded. Taverns have their regular frequenters by this time, and every mart of traffic has its throng. Each of these places is a world, and has its own inhabitants; each is distinct from, and almost unconscious of the existence of any other. There are some few people well to do, who remember to have heard it said, that numbers of men and women—thousands, they think it was—get up in London every day, unknowing where to lay their heads at night; and that there are quarters of the town where misery and famine always are. They don't believe it quite—there may be some truth in it, but it is exaggerated of course. So, each of these thousand worlds goes on intent upon itself, until night comes again—first with its lights and pleasures, and its cheerful streets; then with its guilt and darkness.

Heart of London, there is a moral in thy every stroke! as I look on at thy indomitable working, which neither death, nor press of life, nor grief, nor gladness out of doors will influence one jot, I seem to hear a voice within thee which sinks into my heart, bidding me, as I elbow my way among the crowd, have some thought for the meanest wretch that passes, and, being a man, to turn away with scorn and pride from none that bear the human shape.

I am by no means sure that I might not have been tempted to enlarge upon this subject, had not the papers that lay before me on the table been a silent reproach for even this digression. I took them up again when I had got thus far, and seriously prepared to read.

The handwriting was strange to me, for the manuscript had been fairly copied. As it is against our rules in such a case to inquire into the authorship until the reading is concluded, I could only glance at the different faces round me, in search of some expression which should betray the writer. Whoever he might be, he was prepared for this, and gave no sign for my enlightenment.

I had the papers in my hand, when my deaf friend interposed with a suggestion.

"It has occurred to me," he said, "bearing in mind your sequel to the tale we have finished, that if such of us as have anything to relate of our own lives could interweave it with our contribution to the Clock, it would be well to do so. This need be no restraint upon us, either as to time, or place, or incident, since any real passage of this kind may be surrounded by fictitious circumstances, and represented by fictitious characters. What if we made this an article of agreement among ourselves?"

The proposition was cordially received, but the difficulty appeared to be that here was a long story written before we had thought of it.

"Unless," said I, "it should have happened that the writer of this tale— which is not impossible, for men are apt to do so when they write—has actually mingled with it something of his own endurance and experience."

Nobody spoke, but I thought I detected in one quarter that this was really the case.

"If I have no assurance to the contrary," I added therefore, "I shall take it for granted that he has done so, and that even these papers come within our new agreement. Everybody being mute, we hold that understanding if you please."

And here I was about to begin again, when Jack informed us softly, that during the progress of our last narrative, Mr. Weller's watch had adjourned its sittings from the kitchen, and regularly met outside our door, where he had no doubt that august body would be found at the present moment. As this was for the convenience of listening to our stories, he submitted that they might be suffered to come in, and hear them more pleasantly.

To this we one and all yielded a ready assent, and the party being discovered as Jack had supposed, and invited to walk in, entered (though not without great confusion at having been detected) and were accommodated with chairs at a little distance.

Then, the lamp being trimmed, the fire well stirred and burning brightly, the hearth clean swept, the curtains closely drawn, the Clock wound up, we entered on our new story—BARBABY RUDGE.

Eight

MASTER HUMPHREY FROM HIS CLOCK-SIDE IN THE CHIMNEY-CORNER

IT IS AGAIN MIDNIGHT. MY FIRE BURNS CHEERFULLY; THE room is filled with my old friend's sober voice; and I am left to muse upon the story we have just now finished.

It makes me smile, at such a time as this, to think if there were anyone to see me sitting in my easychair, my grey head hanging down, my eyes bent thoughtfully upon the glowing embers, and my crutch—emblem of my helplessness—lying upon the hearth at my feet, how solitary I should seem. Yet though I am the sole tenant of this chimney-corner, though I am childless and old, I have no sense of loneliness at this hour; but am the center of a silent group whose company I love.

Thus, even age and weakness have their consolations. If I were a younger man; if I were more active, more strongly bound and tied to life; these visionary friends would shun me, or I should desire to fly from them. Being what I am, I can court their society, and delight in it; and pass whole hours in picturing to myself the shadows that perchance flock every night into this chamber, and in imagining with pleasure what kind of interest they have in the frail, feeble mortal who is its sole inhabitant.

All the friends I have ever lost I find again among these visitors. I love to fancy their spirits hovering about me, feeling still some earthly kindness for their old companion, and watching his decay. "He is weaker, he declines apace, he draws nearer and nearer to us, and will soon be conscious of our existence." What is there to alarm me in this? It is encouragement and hope.

These thoughts have never crowded on me half so fast as they have done tonight. Faces I had long forgotten have become familiar to me once again; traits I had endeavored to recall for years have come before me in an instant; nothing is changed but me: and even I can be my former self at will.

Raising my eyes but now to the face of my old Clock, I remember, quite involuntarily, the veneration, not unmixed with a sort of childish awe, with which I used to sit and watch it, as it ticked unheeded in a dark staircase corner. I recollect looking more grave and steady when I met its dusty face, as if, having that strange kind of life within it, and being free from all excess of vulgar appetite, and warning all the house by night and day, it were a sage. How often have I listened to it as it told the beads of time, and wondered at its constancy! How often watched it slowly pointing round the dial, and, while I panted for the eagerly-expected hour to come, admired, despite myself, its steadiness of purpose and lofty freedom from all human strife, impatience, and desire!

I thought it cruel once. It was very hard of heart, to my mind, I remember. It was an old servant, even then; and I felt as though it ought to show some sorrow; as though it wanted sympathy with us in our distress, and were a dull, heartless, mercenary creature. Ah! how soon I learnt to know that in its ceaseless going on, and in its being checked or stayed by nothing, lay its greatest kindness, and the only balm for grief and wounded peace of mind!

Tonight, tonight, when this tranquility and calm are on my spirits, and memory presents so many shifting scenes before me, I take my quiet stand, at will, by many a fire that has been long extinguished, and mingle with the cheerful group that cluster round it. If I could be sorrowful in such a mood, I should grow sad to think what a poor blot I was upon their youth and beauty once, and now how few remain to put me to the blush; I should grow sad to think that such among them as I sometimes meet with in my daily walks are scarcely less infirm than I; that time has brought us to a level; and that all distinctions fade and vanish as we take our trembling steps towards the grave.

But memory was given us for better purposes than this: and mine is not a torment, but a source of pleasure. To muse upon the gaiety and youth I have known suggests to me glad scenes of harmless mirth that may be passing now. From contemplating them apart, I soon become an actor in these little dramas, and humoring my fancy, lose myself among the beings it invokes.

When my fire is bright and high, and a warm blush mantles in the walls and ceiling of this ancient room; when my Clock makes cheerful music, like one of those chirping insects who delight in the warm hearth, and are sometimes, by a good superstition, looked upon as the harbingers of fortune and plenty to that household in whose mercies they put their humble trust; when everything is in a ruddy genial glow, and there are voices in the crackling flame, and smiles in its flashing light; other smiles and other voices congregate around me, invading with their pleasant harmony the silence of the time.

For then a knot of youthful creatures gather round my fireside, and the room reechoes to their merry voices. My solitary chair no longer holds its ample place before the fire, but is wheeled into a smaller corner, to leave more room for the broad circle formed about the cheerful hearth. I have sons and daughters, and grandchildren; and we are assembled on some occasion of rejoicing common to us all. It is a birthday, perhaps, or perhaps it may be Christmastime; but be it what it may, there is rare holiday among us: we are full of glee.

In the chimney-corner, opposite myself, sits one who has grown old beside me. She is changed, of course; much changed; and yet I recognize the girl, even in that grey hair and wrinkled brow. Glancing from the laughing child who half hides in her ample skirts, and half peeps out—and from her to the little matron of twelve years old, who sits so womanly and so demure at no great distance from me—and from her again to a fair girl in the full bloom of early womanhood, the center of the group, who has glanced more than once towards the opening door, and by whom the children, whispering and tittering among themselves, *will* leave a vacant chair, although she bids them not—I see her image thrice repeated, and feel how long it is before one form and set of features wholly pass away, if ever, from among the living. While I am dwelling upon this, and tracing out the gradual change from infancy to youth; from youth to perfect growth; from that to age; and thinking, with an old man's pride, that she is comely yet; I feel a slight thin hand upon my arm, and, looking down, see seated at my feet a crippled boy—a gentle, patient child—whose aspect I know well. He rests upon a little crutch—I know it, too—and leaning on it as he climbs my footstool, whispers in my ear, "I am hardly one of these, dear grandfather, although I love them dearly. They are very kind to me, but you will be kinder still, I know."

I have my hand upon his neck, and stoop to kiss him, when my Clock strikes, my chair is in its old spot, and I am alone.

What if I be? What if this fireside be tenantless, save for the presence of one weak old man? From my housetop I can look upon a hundred homes, in every one of which these social companies are matters of reality. In my daily walks I pass a thousand men whose cares are all forgotten, whose labors are made light, whose dull routine of work from day to day is cheered and brightened by their glimpses of domestic joy at home. Amid the struggles of this struggling town what cheerful sacrifices are made; what toil endured with readiness; what patience shown and fortitude displayed for the mere sake of home and its affections! Let me thank Heaven that I can people my fireside with shadows such as these: with shadows of bright objects that exist in crowds about me: and let me say, "I am alone no more."

I never was less so—I write it with a grateful heart—than I am tonight. Recollections of the past and visions of the present come to bear me company; the meanest man to whom I have ever given alms appears, to add his mite of peace and comfort to my stock; and whenever the fire within me shall grow cold, to light my path upon this earth no more, I pray that it may be at such an hour as this, and when I love the world as well as I do now.

N i n e

THE DEAF GENTLEMAN FROM HIS OWN APARTMENT

OUR DEAR FRIEND LAID DOWN HIS PEN AT THE END OF THE foregoing paragraph, to take it up no more. I little thought ever to employ mine upon so sorrowful a task as that which he has left me, and to which I now devote it.

As he did not appear among us at his usual hour next morning, we knocked gently at his door. No answer being given, it was softly opened; and then, to our surprise, we saw him seated before the ashes of his fire, with a little table I was accustomed to set at his elbow when I left him for the night, at a short distance from him, as though he had pushed it away with the idea of rising and retiring to his bed. His crutch and footstool lay at his feet as usual, and he was dressed in his chamber-gown, which he had put on before I left him. He was reclining in his chair, in his accustomed posture, with his face towards the fire, and seemed absorbed in meditation—indeed, at first, we almost hoped he was.

Going up to him, we found him dead. I have often, very often, seen him sleeping, and always peacefully; but I never saw him look so calm and tranquil. His face wore a serene, benign expression, which had impressed me very strongly when we last shook hands: not that he had ever any other look, God knows: but there was something in this so very spiritual, so strangely and indefinably allied to youth, although his head was grey and venerable, that it was new even in him. It came upon me all at once, when on some slight pretense he called me back upon the previous night to take me by the hand again, and once more say, "God bless you."

A bell-rope hung within his reach, but he had not moved towards it; nor had he stirred, we all agreed, except, as I have said, to push away his table, which he could have done, and no doubt did, with a very slight motion of his hand. He had relapsed for a moment into his late train of meditation, and, with a thoughtful smile upon his face, had died.

I had long known it to be his wish that, whenever this event should come to pass, we might be all assembled in the house. I therefore lost no time in sending for Mr. Pickwick and for Mr. Miles, both of whom arrived before the messenger's return.

It is not my purpose to dilate upon the sorrow and affectionate emotions of which I was at once the witness and the sharer. But I may say, of the humbler mourners, that his faithful housekeeper was fairly heartbroken; that the poor barber would not be comforted; and that I shall respect the homely truth and warmth of heart of Mr. Weller and his son to the last moment of my life.

"And the sweet old creetur, sir," said the elder Mr. Weller to me in the afternoon, "has bolted. Him as had no wice, and was so free from temper that a infant might ha' drove him, has been took at last with that 'ere unawoidable fit o' staggers as we all must come to, and gone off his feed forever! I see him," said the old gentleman, with a moisture in his eye which could not be mistaken, "I see him gettin', every journey, more and more groggy; I says to Samivel, 'My boy! the Grey's a goin' at the knees'; and now my predilictions is fatally werified, and him as I could never do enough to serve or show my likin' for, is up the great uniwersal spout o' natur."

I was not the less sensible of the old man's attachment because he expressed it in his peculiar manner. Indeed, I can truly assert of both him and his son, that notwithstanding the extraordinary dialogues they held together, and the strange commentaries and corrections with which each of them illustrated the other's speech, I do not think it possible to exceed the sincerity of their regret; and that I am sure their thoughtfulness and anxiety, in anticipating the discharge of many little offices of sympathy, would have done honor to the most delicate-minded persons.

Our friend had frequently told us that his will would be found in a box in the Clock-case, the key of which was in his writing-desk. As he had told us also that he desired it to be opened immediately after his death, whenever that should happen, we met together that night for the fulfillment of his request.

We found it where he had told us, wrapped in a sealed paper, and with it a codicil of recent date, in which he named Mr. Miles and Mr. Pickwick his executors—as having no need of any greater benefit from his estate than a generous token (which he bequeathed to them) of his friendship and remembrance.

After pointing out the spot in which he wished his ashes to repose, he gave to "his dear old friends," Jack Redburn and myself, his house, his books, his furniture—in short, all that his house contained; and with this legacy more ample means of maintaining it in its present state than we, with our habits and at our terms of life, can ever exhaust. Besides these gifts, he left to us, in trust, an annual sum of no insignificant amount, to be distributed in charity among his accustomed pensioners—they are a long list—and such other claimants on his bounty as might, from time to time, present themselves. And as true charity not only covers a multitude of sins, but includes a multitude of virtues, such as forgiveness, liberal construction, gentleness and mercy to the faults of others, and the remembrance of our own imperfections and advantages, he bade us not inquire too closely into the venial errors of the poor, but finding that they *were* poor, first to relieve and then endeavor—at an advantage—to reclaim them.

To the housekeeper he left an annuity, sufficient for her comfortable maintenance and support through life. For the barber, who had attended him many years, he made a similar provision. And I may make two remarks in this place: first, that I think this pair are very likely to club their means together and make a match of it; and secondly, that I think my friend had this result in his mind; for I have heard him say, more than once, that he could not concur with the generality of mankind in censuring equal marriages made in later life, since there were many cases in which such unions could not fail to be a wise and rational source of happiness to both parties.

The elder Mr. Weller is so far from viewing this prospect with any feelings of jealousy, that he appears to be very much relieved by its contemplation; and his son, if I am not mistaken, participates in this feeling. We are all of opinion, however, that the old gentleman's danger, even at its crisis, was very slight; and that he merely labored under one of those transitory weaknesses to which persons of his temperament are now and then liable, and which become less and less alarming at every return, until they wholly subside. I have no doubt he will remain a jolly old widower for the rest of his life, as he has already inquired of me, with much gravity, whether a writ of habeas corpus would enable him to settle his property upon Tony beyond the possibility of recall; and has, in my presence, conjured his son, with tears in his eyes, that in the event of his ever becoming amorous again, he will put him in a strait-waistcoat until the fit is past, and distinctly inform the lady that his property is "made over."

Although I have very little doubt that Sam would dutifully comply with these injunctions in a case of extreme necessity, and that he would do so with perfect composure and coolness, I do not apprehend things will ever come to that pass: as the old gentleman seems perfectly happy in the society of his son, his pretty daughter-in-law, and his grandchildren, and has solemnly announced his determination to "take arter the old 'un in all respects"; from which I infer that it is his intention to regulate his conduct by the model of Mr. Pickwick, who will certainly set him the example of a single life.

I have diverged for a moment from the subject with which I set out, for I know that my friend was interested in these little matters, and I have a natural tendency to linger upon any topic that occupied his thoughts or gave him pleasure and amusement. His remaining wishes are very briefly told. He desired that we would make him the frequent subject of our conversation; at the same time, that we would never speak of him with an air of gloom or restraint, but frankly, and as one whom we still loved and hoped to meet again. He trusted that the old house would wear no aspect of mourning, but that it would be lively and cheerful; and that we would not remove or cover up his picture, which hangs in our dining-room, but make it our companion as he had been. His own room, our place of meeting, remains, at his desire, in its accustomed state: our seats are placed about the table, as of old; his easychair, his desk, his crutch, his footstool, hold their accustomed places; and the Clock stands in its familiar corner. We go into the chamber at stated times to see that all is as it should be, and to take care that the light and air are not shut out, for on that point he expressed a strong solicitude. But it was his fancy that the apartment should not be inhabited; that it should be religiously preserved in this condition; and that the voice of his old companion should be heard no more.

My own history may be summed up in very few words; and even those I should have spared the reader but for my friend's allusion to me some time since. I have no deeper sorrow than the loss of a child—an only daughter, who is living, and who fled from her father's house but a few weeks before our friend and I first met. I had never spoken of this, even to him; because I have always loved her, and I could not bear to tell him of her error, until I could tell him also of her sorrow and regret. Happily I was enabled to do so some time ago. And it will not be long, with Heaven's leave, before she is restored to me—before I find in her and her husband the support of my declining years.

For my pipe—it is an old relic of home, a thing of no great worth, a poor trifle, but sacred to me for her sake.

Thus, since the death of our venerable friend, Jack Redburn and I have been the sole tenants of the old home; and day by day, have lounged together in his favorite walks. Mindful of his injunctions, we have long been able to speak of him with ease and cheerfulness, and to remember him as he would be remembered. From certain allusions which Jack has dropped, to his having been deserted and cast off in early life, I am inclined to believe that some passages of his youth may possibly be shadowed out in the history of Mr. Chester and his son: but seeing that he avoids the subject, I have not pursued it.

My task is done. The chamber in which we have whiled away so many happy hours, not I hope without some pleasure and some profit, is deserted; our happy hour of meeting strikes no more; the chimney-corner has grown cold; and MASTER HUMPHREY'S CLOCK has stopped forever.